KATHERINE ASHE

D1248934

# Montfort

# The Angel with the Sword

Wake Robin Press
160 King Hill Road, Starrucca, PA 18462, U.S.A.

ISBN:  1452844232
ISBN-13:  9781452844237

Library of Congress Control Number:  2010916283

visit simon-de-montfort.com
    katherineashe.com
    Simon de Montfort Facebook
    Katherine Ashe Facebook

## Summary of Volumes I, II and III

### Montfort, Vol. I, The Early Years

Arriving at the court of Henry III of England, Simon becomes the king's favorite and secretly marries the king's sister, who is a nun. He retrieves her vows through a timely gift to the Vatican, but will be in debt for life. Returning to England, his attraction to the queen results in the throne's needed heir, but when Henry realizes Edward's birth is no miracle, Simon flees to Palestine. There he triumphs, but refuses the Crown of Jerusalem. Returning from the East, he becomes Henry's vassal again, and commander of England's armies.

### Montfort Vol. II, The Viceroy

When invaders from Persia overrun and desecrate the Holy Land, the Christian lords of Palestine, once united by Simon, fail to join forces. Guilty for having left, Simon's goal is to return to the East. But Henry has work for him in England's dukedom of Gascony, work that will entangle him and permit the king to accuse him of treason.

### Montfort Vol. III The Revolutionary

Unable to destroy Simon, Henry sends him away to Paris as ambassador. But Simon returns unbidden when Prince Edward commits an atrocity and the king, as punishment, has ordered him to very unequal battle against the Welsh. Rescuing Edward and his young followers, Simon becomes entangled in the English lords' revolt against Henry's abuses. A program for elective government is created, the Provisions of Oxford, but when the lords abandon their project, it is Simon who seizes England and makes newborn democracy a reality – at risk of torture and trial again for treason.

# Montfort

## The Founder of Parliament
## The Angel with the Sword
## 1 2 6 0 - 1 2 6 5

## VOLUME IV

## BOOK 5: THE ANGEL WITH THE SWORD

# Acknowledgments

Among the many to whom I am indebted are Dr. Henry Pachter, who urged me to pursue this adventure and whose lectures on the Philosophy of History and the History of Revolution no doubt inspired me; Dr. Madeleine Cosman, founder of the Institute of Medieval and Renaissance Studies at The City University of New York, who encouraged and guided me; Sr. Donald Corcoran, O.S.B. Cam., PhD. Theology, for her advice and friendship; Dr. Karen Edis-Barzman and the Center for Medieval and Renaissance Studies at Binghamton University for their generosity in granting me access to their research facilities and lecture series; Mark Peel of the New York Society Library for his considerate long-term lending of books; Valentina Baciu for sharing with me her genealogical investigations; Gordon Jackson for his insights into and translations of Robert Grosseteste's works; Prof. G. K. Martin of the University of Leicester for his assistance; Virginia Gale for her steady helpfulness in seeing Montfort into print; Emile Capouya, Jonathan Segal and James Clark for their editorial advice; Lucia Woods Lindley for her friendship, which has sustained me; and my husband, for his patience and helpfulness during the many years it has taken to write Montfort.

# Contents

# Volume IV Book 5

## THE ANGEL
## WITH
## THE SWORD

Per convalles nota
Laicos exleges,
Notos turpi nora
Principes et reges
Quos pari iudico
Luxus et ambito
Quasi nox obscurat
Quos celestis ultio
Bisacuto gladio
Perdere maturat.

Gualtier de Chatillon (1135 – 1184)

Those who should stand
Upon Virtue's bright heights,
Wallow in the shadows
Of the valley of corruption:
Princes and Kings,
Condemned by greed,
Infected with ambition.
Yet, at the Last,
They shall fall, struck down by
Heaven's two-edged sword.

# Chapter One

## KING HENRY VICTORIOUS
### 1260 - 1261

Consciousness came slowly and at first was only of pain. A pain too familiar, that brought a longing to return to the void. But the void was receding out of reach and the pain was growing more insistent, more engulfing till at last he opened his eyes with the thought there might be help.

His squire Peter's face filled his view, its tense expression easing then softening to a slight smile. "Master, your fever has broken. What can I do for you?"

"Otton's armagnac."

"He's coming, I hope with a cask. At present the good wine of Normandy, or a strong apple wine…"

"Whatever's strongest," Simon whispered, the pain of his shattered legs was threatening to take complete hold of his mind. A hand pressed his hand gently, he looked to see whose hand it was.

The Countess Eleanor sat by him, tears rimming her eyelids. "Thank God," she murmured. "We didn't know if you would live."

"Where am I?"

"In France. At one of Louis' fiefs in Normandy. Archbishop Rigaud and our son Guy brought you here from London, after my vile royal brother Henry had done… nearly his worst."

The squire Peter brought the apple liquor and Simon drank until the void's relief enfolded him again.

When next he woke, Peter was unwrapping his bandaged legs and dousing the wounds with the apple brandy. Seeing that his master was alert again, Peter said calmly, "You're fortunate, my lord, the vices didn't much displace the bones, though they're severely broken." The squire was a barber and surgeon as well and had tended his master's wounds after many battles. But never before had he seen injuries such as these.

A doctor, come from Paris, had studied the breaks the King of England's machine of torture inflicted, and pronounced his opinion that the shattering of knees, ankles and shins would heal — if the fever broke and the earl lived. But he would never walk again.

For days Simon and his squire fought the pain with apple brandy and valerian. Arnaud Otton arrived from Bigorre with a cask of armagnac, and Simon admitted that the apple distillate of Normandy was very near as good as the best the south offered.

In a week the pain receded enough for Simon to sit up and be carried outside on pleasant days to let the sweet, fresh air play across his legs and face; his cheeks and chin now hid in a rich growth of black beard.

"I'll shave you tomorrow," Peter announced brightly.

"No. Leave it. Let me look solemn as a prophet, the better to shout imprecations at the English." Simon met his squire's look with a slight twinkle in his dark, nearsighted eyes. The squire pondered this hint of odd humor and wondered what other surprising changes torture might have worked upon his master's spirit.

The manse's open courtyard gave view of a green pasture where Louis' stud horses grazed, dots of brown and gray and white upon the emerald lawn of Normandy's late summer. The sky arched, an infinite haze of cloudless blue breathing a gentle breeze that, caressing lawns and distant orchards, bore the soothing scent of Nature in her cleanliness.

For some time Simon watched the horses' slow and passive drifting as they grazed, vague dots of contrast upon flat green to his weak eyes. Turning his head toward his wife, sitting by him, he said in a voice softened with pain and armagnac's lassitude, "When I was a boy at Montfort l'Amaury I never watched the horses. That was a pastime for peasants and old men... I've grown old..."

"You turned forty-seven last week. And you've hardly a gray hair." Eleanor tenderly brushed a straying black lock from his brow. She lied. His hair, black entirely four months ago, was visibly graying in streaks at the roots.

He grasped her wrist, holding it firmly but not hurtfully. His eyes sought hers, more steady and intent than she had seen at any time before during his recovery. "A doctor has seen my wounds? What did he say? Will I be able to walk?" he demanded.

It was the question that all who heard the doctor dreaded. She glanced away, but he held her wrist and drew her closer to him.

"The doctor doesn't know you." She met his questioning dark eyes and saw her own worried reflection in them. "Peter thinks he may be wrong. But it will be many weeks before you can so much as try to walk."

He sighed and released her wrist. For a long time he said nothing. Then, "What of King Henry?"

"Henry has agreed to have your trial heard here in France."

"The trial... again? It isn't over?"

"No." She whispered the word, unable to conceal her despair. "All that could be bargained for your release from London Tower was a new trial."

The trial for treason, and all it would entail of preparation and of peril, was far beyond his strength to contemplate. He shut his eyes, feeling the sun on his skin and thinking of another time and place when the sun's glare, red under his shut eyelids, had filled him with a sense of peace. "The sun is pleasant here, but not as warm as in Palestine. Pray God, I shall not die until I'm there again," he murmured as he feebly sank back into sleep.

At Louis' obscure rural manse the days passed tranquilly. Simon was tended by his wife the Countess Eleanor, their daughter Eleanor and his squire. His son Guy was at King Louis's Court, befriended by Louis' brother Charles, but came from time to time to tell his father how the family's interests fared there.

In England the eldest Montfort sons, Henry and Simon, had stayed with Prince Edward after helping in their father's rescue. They were doing all they could to protect their father's Leicester earldom from punitive confiscation before the final judgment of the coming trial.

---

John Harcourt, Simon's friend since childhood, came from Paris frequently to keep Louis informed of the state of Simon's slow recovery. Sight of the devastation King Henry had wrought revolted his senses and set him to a rage that he kept barely in control in his reports.

Arnaud Otton, Simon's seneschal for his purchased, and temporary, little Pyrenees land of Bigorre, returned home with the notion that his master might be following him soon for sanctuary. And he took with him negotiation for extension of the Montfort lordship of Bigorre.

In late September a royal writ reached Louis' guest. Simon's title Steward of England, the paired honor with his title Earl of Leicester, had been stripped from him. It would be granted to King Henry's nephew, Henry of Alemaine, at the October Feast of Saint Edward. The Earl Montfort's presence would not be required. And he was excused from attending the convening of Parliament afterward.

"If all goes well at my coming trial, I shall be well rid of England," Simon remarked to his wife, his lips turning in a caustic smile bracketed by his new beard. "Our sons may have to make their fortunes in the East."

As the weeks sank deeper into autumn, Simon began to test his powers of walking with a cane, leaning heavily upon Peter. But his fractures would not yet hold any weight.

In mid-October Simon was carried in a litter and the family returned to their own rented house in Paris, on the Greve. There, old and scrawny but far from frail Lady Mary, the countess's waiting woman, presided over servants and the youngest child, Richard. The Montfort's next youngest son, Amaury, was already a scholar living in the student quarter on the Left Bank.

In a deeply cushioned chair by the oriel window of his paneled room overlooking the Seine, Simon sat inhaling a pungent smoke of healing herbs that Peter burned in a brazier.

Guy made regular reports of the doings at King Louis' Court. The sun-burnished buff walls and turrets of the palace on the Isle de la Cite, lapped by the Seine's narrow channel, stood in full view of Simon's window. Tantalizingly, on occasion the invalid could watch the King of France and courtiers strolling in the rose garden that opened from the doors of Louis's private chambers.

Much of Simon's childhood had been spent in that same garden. Like the palace, it was filled with memories: of Louis' mother, Queen Blanche, who had been a mother to him also when he was orphaned at the age of eight. And memories of his own service as Regent of France, only ten years past — of his serving Louis' little son who was now dead. Had Louis remained in Palestine, would he be Regent still? And if so, for whom? Louis then had no other son, and the lords of France, when he was Regent, were murmuring that Simon would be the better king. That, above all else, had brought Louis home.

The invalid dismissed the thought with some repugnance. Kings were born, were God's appointed. He was born to serve his king, not to presume to replace him. A knowing frown flickered across his brow. Who, with a good view of kingship, would wish it upon himself? He recalled King Henry saying once, "No one remembers my brother's errors. Everyone remembers mine."

The hours of his convalescence passed with the slowness of a seed germinating, growing, blossoming and bearing fruit with such slight motion it was imperceptible regardless of how fixedly the senses were intent on it.

To pass the time, young Eleanor practiced her playing of the lute and singing of old songs, and the countess read the latest writings of Aquinas, which Simon thought detestable, pandering to lordly pride. Eventually the countess laid aside the treatise that the Vatican was embracing, and picked up lighter matter to sooth his nerves: *Aucassin and Nicollette,* then Wace's tales of Arthur.

Unused to being convalescent for an extended time, as his energies were restlessly returning, Simon found the dragging hours maddeningly tedious, the view from his window a new variety of torture, as he watched autumn turn to brown the roses in the now abandoned royal garden and he came to know the daily business of each river barge.

Then a letter arrived from his eldest son, Henry, in England: *At the Feast of Saint Edward we and some thirty of Prince Edward's companions received full knighthood at the prince's hands. I've received the title* knight banneret. *I am to bear my own banner in the prince's service, an honor granted very few, and those all sons of earls. Our entire company will come to France soon, as King Henry has given us leave to attend the tournaments.*

Simon smiled to the countess, pleased by the unexpected news. "Our sons are doing well. They've not been penalized for me. It seems possible Henry will be able to retain the honour of the Leicester earldom."

But Eleanor was looking at their son Guy whose face was twisted with an effort to control his emotions. Consumed with envy, he got up from his seat by the window and strode to leave the room.

"Guy!" his father stopped him.

His third son turned and looked at him. Flaring in his eyes was the frustration of years of having been the one too young for the advantages his older brothers had. "I am not doing well, father!"

Simon's dark gaze softened. "I didn't mean to slight you, Guy. Come." He put out his hand to the one he believed the best of his sons. There was little he could do for him. Any hope of Montfort lands for him in France was gone, Louis had made that clear despite his brother's fondness for the boy. Simon did what he could to comfort him. Guy knelt beside his father's chair and let his father rest his arm across his broad shoulders.

"You've not yet been knighted," Simon met his eyes with the love he felt for this most knightly of his son, "but the strength and skill of your right arm surpasses your brothers. The world is fickle in its offerings of honor. True honor lies within, where horns don't blare it. In hard battle in Wales you won my respect, and the respect of many others. You are mighty, skillful and you have great courage. You'll make your own way far better than any of your brothers could. But, if you'll feel happier for it, go and prove your worth again. Attend the tournaments. I ask only one pledge. You will not fight your brothers or Prince Edward."

"I promise, father." Guy's glower spread to a wide grin, his heart rising with the battle joy that he had learned at Ewloe.

"We must have you properly armed to tilt against France's lordlings." Simon's own mood brightened and he sent for a commended armorer.

Measuring the youth, the craftsman asked, "With the coif also? The hood from head to shoulders? It protects the neck." He gestured with the point of his fingers at his own throat as if plunging a blade at the vulnerable place where helm and hauberk, neck and shoulder meet.

Simon needed no further persuading, he bore a scar from just such a stroke. "Of course," he nodded approvingly.

"My lord, may I venture... might I measure you also? There will be no charge. To say that I am armorer to the great Earl of Leicester would be recompense enough."

"If I live, I go to Palestine..."

"Then you will have good use of it."

In a few days the armorer was back, trailing assistants bearing the new, hooded hauberks, sleeves and leggings. Simon, pleased, tried on the neatly fitted chain mail, his beard catching and tugging in the steel links that framed his face.

The armorer shrugged apologetically. "Beards..."

"I'll trim it, or remove it if I must, in Palestine."

His son, wading in the unfamiliar weight, swung his right arm in combat sweeps and found the fit snug yet not in the least hampering. The links, softly rustling like rain, moved freely, following his body's changing curves. He grinned to his father, and his father grinned back.

Elated, Guy de Montfort went to the tourneys, incognito in his new chain mail, with a plain black surcoat and shield, riding a deceptively shambling, foundered-looking roan that he himself had trained as a superb destrier.

Unlike the clandestine English country tourneys of Simon's youth, a grand tournament in France drew challengers and spectators from all of Europe. Such an event could be held only on extensive level acres, their crops sacrificed for the high rents paid by contenders and spectators for tent and horse-line space, and by merchants for booth space in the aisles of a grand ad hoc bazaar.

Fabrics of the finest damask, gold-shot samite, delicate blue silks dark as the sea or pale as the sky, brocades in gem hues of ruby and verdant chrysoprase, yellows and purples richer than topaz or amethyst were brought from the East by Italian merchants, and hung in sumptuous swags along the drapers' aisles. Dense winter furs: heavy, rich martin skins, white-and-brown patterned vair, and snowy coney pelts to line ladies cloaks, or, for lords, wolf and bear for cloaks warm in the bitterest storms, were heaped in careless abundance in the strange, domed tents of traders from the far North.

Hammers rang on anvils. Furnaces, assembled out of stones, made a blaze like a lane of Hades in the armorers' aisle, where metal was beaten to fine blades, smoothed to sheets then bent and curved and riveted for helms, or extruded into wire and curled to links for mail. At the eastern perimeter of the bazaar was the horse fair with long lines of animals: massive prick-eared, nervous destriers; mild broad-backed palfreys; smooth-gaited white mules from Spain – the height of fashion for clerics and ladies; and all manner of pack horses and jennets for servants.

Between the bazaar and the tilt-ground with its flat oval of lawn, its barriers, its high, stepped seating and taller, satin-roofed pavilions, was a virtual town of tents that the contestants and spectators made their temporary homes. Here were tents more elegant in draperies, silk cording and tassels than would be seen in any other place, as their owners vied to impress with their wealth if not their jousting prowess. For here daughters and sons were brought with hopes of making a rich match.

Set like *bright lady in bower,* demoiselles blushing with shy embarrassment, or brazenly coy toward every likely passerby, made of the tourney a marriage fair to which youths, many who had no notion of raising a lance, were drawn. Some had honest hopes; most sought only a brief joy. Mothers kept close watch upon their daughters, but no guard was sufficient, in the hurly burly of the fair, to forestall clandestine trysts. The perfumes of mating hung in the air as if Venus herself breathed into the nostrils of young France.

Up and down these aisles, shouldering among the idling youths, came a parade of peddlers. Bent under tall frames hung with swinging brass bells, bead necklaces and tassels in every color to match milady's heraldry, hawkers cried their pretty goods. Piemen, trays strapped to their shoulders and projecting like shelves from their chests, cried their pastries stuffed with pork or goose or finely minced beef flavored with pepper. Their sausages were wrapped in luridly dyed crusts. Dainty foods for dainty ladies' fingers. With small casks hitched heavily to their thin breasts, innkeepers' boys offered wine, opening the spigot protruding at one side to fill a customer's own cup. A band of ragged gypsies, presumed pickpockets, gained general tolerance by offering the rare treat of oranges they had smuggled from Arab Spain.

Guy, solitary without squire or servant, and well muffled in a woolen hood, set up his plain, military tent on the rim of the contestants' allotted land, choosing a spot surrounded by the tents of foreigners who could not know him. On one side was a wealthy Italian lad, full of eagerness at his first joust. On the other was a massive, haughty young German.

Quiet of demeanor, Guy quickly attracted the German's private challenge. It came in the form of a remark that a man who wore a hood and was ashamed to show his face ought not to be allowed to pitch his tent there. The German made his point by pulling the hood from Guy's head and tossing it away. Guy went to fetch it, but as he bent to pick it up, the German pinned it to the ground with his sword point. Guy kicked the blade aside and in an instant had the German gripped about the neck, his dagger pressed to the pale, muscular throat. Thus they became fast friends. The Italian, who watched the contretemps with dismay, became Guy's adoring acolyte.

When their preparations were completed, their tents furnished with their modest cots and bundles and their horses fed and watered for the night, the German grossly winked, "Let's have a look at the bride market. One needn't buy, to sample." The German's earthiness was not to Guy's taste, but he was nothing averse to viewing the demoiselles. The Italian demurred. "I'm betrothed." He flushed as if the very words evoked sweet, overwhelming desire. The German stared, then laughed, and he and Guy, who had resumed his engulfing hood, went on their way.

It was well Guy's hood concealed him. Among the aisles of spectators' tents, draped open on their tasseled cording and glowing with candlelight, Prince Edward and his friends were roaming, pausing to exchange gallantries, moving almost methodically from tent to tent. Where the girls were lovely enough and friendly, they paused, but if a parent joined their bantering they moved on.

Gorgeous Edward, golden, tall, dressed in a crimson velvet riding robe heavy with gold thread, and cut tantalizingly short to display a near full-length of the well-turned, crimson-stockinged legs that earned him the name *Longshanks*, was recognized by everyone. He was far above the aim of any parent here, and well known to be married. Nonetheless he left a wake of gazing eyes and cheeks with heightened blush. Already he had secretly arranged for his night's pleasures, but he continued browsing.

Most of his young English followers were unmarried, and might have been prime targets for parents' hopes. But those who came to fairs seeking bridegrooms for their daughters were nobles in decline, or knights with aspirations, not suitable alliances for young lords in the royal entourage. Like their leader, the prince's friends were only in pursuit of brief delight.

Guy saw his brown-haired, amiable brother Henry mildly chatting with a damsel and her mother, and observed his brother Simon walking stealthily with an unguarded servant to a shadowed gap behind the tents.

His hood drawn low over his brow, Guy went unrecognized.

Morning brought the first matches of the tournament. The long oval field was fenced, and the fence boards were draped so that no bare, crude wood was visible to mar the grandeur of the festival. Behind the barricade the crowd of common spectators was herded: cloak pressed to dirty shift, brewer next to beggar, housewife squeezed by villein. The tall pavilions, held aloft by satin-wrapped masts, were stroked by a rising breeze till their bellying awnings of blue satin rippled and shook like spilling sails over the wimpled and capped heads of the wealthier, more noble onlookers. Flags in every tincture of heraldry fluttered beside the mantled horses and the mail-clad, surcoated knights waiting their turns at the far ends of the field.

Though this was combat, it was not war and every rider used what costly means he could to draw attention to himself. Plumes flounced at horses' headstalls, and garnished the gilded helms that nestled in mailed elbow-crooks until the signal of summoning to joust. Scalloped, gilded, painted bridles and reins were commonplace, and there were a few high saddles fancifully shaped, embossed with wings or lion heads. Mantels, draping to the destriers' hocks, boldly displayed each knight's colors and devices in white, red, yellow, blue, green and black.

Guy had not imagined what such an event would be. Among the waiting challengers he sat upon his undistinguished, mantel-less and naked-seeming roan. He was in black from head to foot, his long, slit riding surcoat of black wool over his new chain mail meticulously rubbed with oily blacking to protect it from the damp. A precaution he had learnt from his father. Though no one else wore a helmet until his turn to enter the lists, Guy sat helmeted, stewing in the morning sun and peering at this gay and gaudy world through his narrow eye-slit.

His anonymous and austere black so differed from the bright array of every other rider that he drew everyone's attention. He was an instant mystery among the knights of the first day's trials. Parsifal on his nag. Ribald bets were placed on him. When at last he cantered onto the field, he faced a knight who had already downed four men. The unknown black contestant struck the morning's champion from his mount with a clean aim of his lance that brought merry roaring from the spectators.

What Guy's victory earned was another, and another joust throughout the remainder of the morning. The crowd demanded that the unknown knight ought not to leave the field until he met a rider who was his equal. Each newcomer moved from his waiting group, and plummeted to the ground as the black knight passed with his shield at perfect angle for deflection, his lance irresistible. No one could defeat him, though a few held their seats for a second or third pass.

Edward, drinking with his friends in a pavilion — the prince and noblest knights would not ride till the next day — shouted drunkenly, "Let him face me tomorrow!"

The tourney of young contestants went on, each riding against the tantalizingly invincible black challenger.

His ungainly-looking roan finally weakening, trampling over the flattened grass at gallop, too far spent to reach the swift and powerful volant, Guy still faultlessly found the angle of leverage on each incoming shield and pitched his opponents down. Yet he too was tiring.

Opposing him at last was his young, merry neighbor from Italy. Guy recognized the gentle lad's unlikely device of a roaring bear. For honor's sake he had to unseat him, though he would rather not. The boy came toward him at the full, surging volant. Guy couched his lance to touch the bear shield's rim. Lance points and shields met. The youth, at impact of his own lance square on Guy's shield, forced the black knight nearly to topple. Spectators shrieked with astonishment, and hardly saw the black lance slide skidding under the bear shield, through mail and padded pourpoint deep into the bear knight's side.

Guy felt the tipping force on his lance at once as the Italian was still carried forward by his horse and leaned away, pierced on the point. He let go his hold on the lance, reining in and turning his mount as quickly as he could. The boy lay with the long shaft jutting from his side across the trampled grass. Guy dismounted, horror-struck. "Oh God," he muttered, kneeling in the angle of the boy's bleeding body and the lance. The Italian raised a hand as if to remove his helm, but then lost consciousness.

Attendants from behind the barricades were on the field now running toward them. A surgeon arrived and knelt, holding the point steady while the boy's own valet gently drew the long lance away. Quickly the surgeon applied a thick pad of cloth as blood flooded from the wound. With the pad gripped in place, the boy was lifted, placed on a litter and borne to his tent. There would be no more jousting for Guy today.

Guy would have followed at once, but it was with some difficulty that he managed to shed a crowd of admirers eagerly urging that the accident was no fault of his. His brother Henry was among them, sent by Edward.

Confounded and embarrassed, Guy, still in his black helm, listened to his eldest brother, who had never complimented him before, praising his skill and urging him to accept the prince's invitation to join them in the royal pavilion. Pitching his voice low, and mimicking the German's rough accent, politely he declined the offer.

When at last he could return to the obscurity of his own tent, taking off his helm, surcoat, armor and pourpoint, he drew on his long black robe and hood and went to the Italian's tent.

A priest with his vessels for the Last Sacrament was leaving. The boy lay conscious now but very quiet on his cot, his valet tending him. The valet's look was bleak, cringing with guilt. The young Italian's face was livid, purplish and flushed with sweat. He looked up at Guy and smiled, his eyes awash with tears of pain. "I nearly downed you didn't I? Look what I won," he said mildly, without accusation, turning back his coverlet. The gash was a long pool of blood and pus, the flesh ripped wide as he had fallen, the lance deep in him torqueing as it fell. The surgeon had drenched it with strong wine and tried to pack it with lint and unguent, but the flow of the wound was too great. The boy's life was draining from his side.

"I'm going to disappoint… my lady. My father doesn't know…" A surge of pain gripped him. When it passed, his face was white, his limbs already cold. 'Tell my lord Aldobrandesca…" he murmured as his eyes clouded. He said a few words more, not in French. Guy's Latin was of no use, he looked to the servant for translation. But the old valet had helped the boy to come despite his father's command to the contrary. Seeing his young master could not live, he had fled.

Guy and the German carried the slight, young body to the nearest church and paid the priest for a Mass and burial in consecrated ground.

After writing a letter describing how the youth had honorably died, Guy searched the fair for anyone who knew the name Aldobrandesca. He gave the note into the hand of an elderly Italian knight, not knowing if the name was of the dead boy's family, or his betrothed, or his liege lord.

The next day the noblest contestants met to joust. Guy had been challenged by Prince Edward. He had promised not to fight his brothers or the prince and, with the Italian's death, he no longer found the tourney enticing. He went home.

Guy was already at the house on the Greve when the first news of the tournament reached Paris. Most thrilling was the tale of an unknown knight, broad-shouldered, riding an ungainly mount and dressed entirely in black, who unhorsed all comers on the first day of the tourneys, but accidentally killed a man, then vanished. Debate raged over who the dark paladin could be.

Simon observed his sullen son who spoke not a word of where he had been for the past week. "You've had enough of tourneys?" he asked with arch perceptiveness. Guy nodded his head.

The Parliament at Westminster had opened on October the eighteenth. Gregory de Boscellis, the former tutor of the Montfort sons, attended with the Bishop of Worcester, Walter Cantaloup, Simon's old friend. Three weeks afterward the scholar monk arrived in Paris to give the earl a full report of the results.

King Henry, as if championing the Ordinances, had taken up the complaints of the shire knights, the common people's representatives. Astonishingly, he even lodged his own complaint before the Parliament – against England's earls. By the Provisions made at Oxford in 1258, the king had granted his lords rights that would curb many of the Crown's powers, but the lords refused to extend those same rights to the men in liege beneath them. It was those rights for commoners, for townsmen and the knightly class, that the Ordinances would grant. King Henry accused his earls of gross hypocrisy, self-seeking, and being forsworn of their own principals.

Further, Henry accused the Justiciar, the chief justice of the king's law courts, of ignorance of his office. And he denounced the Council that the Provisions had set over him. He claimed it was the tool of a few earls seizing power for themselves.

He was not wrong. The high-minded Provisions, created just two years before to halt the king's abuses, already was corrupted. The sovereign power that the Provisions redirected to the people had been seized by several of the highest ranking lords, determined not to share the rights they'd won.

Henry masqueraded as the Parliament and people's friend. The popularly elected shire representatives clamored their approval of the king's attacks against the earls.

Hugh Bigod the Justiciar, an honest man, resigned. But the Council held on. Exercising its rights by the Provisions, it chose Hugh Despensar to be the new Justiciar, and sent Bigod as castellan of the fortress of Dover. But still the earls of the Council refused to permit a vote on the Ordinances that would grant the people's rights.

"They're falling into Henry's trap," Simon ruminated, as Boscellis finished his report. "This meanness of the lords toward their own people will undo them."

"That may be so," the monk nodded dejectedly.

Simon gave a curt, bitter laugh. "No doubt Henry, as soon as he feels safe enough, will renounce the Council and rule by his own whim again, wringing all he can in taxes 'til the lords gnash their teeth. The king's half-brothers of Lusignan will return, ever more devoted brigands, and law again will be whatever strength and guile provide."

He sighed and shifted his position as his healing knee took his awareness with a sharp spike of pain. Then, meeting Boscellis' sad gray eyes as they peered from under his Franciscan cowl, he added in a softer tone, "The lords will reap what they've sown. But I pity the common folk. They had such hope."

"They remember you, my lord, as the one who gave them that hope," Boscellis said quietly.

Simon gestured toward his legs, propped on a chair. "What can a cripple do? If I regain my strength, it shall not be for England's sake but for the Holy Land's."

The Countess Eleanor, sitting across the room, sorting her embroidery threads, looked up. "I would be happier if England sank into the sea like Lyoness, and we had no more word of Henry or his Council."

She was seeing a gradual change in her husband, which she both welcomed and feared. Slowly healing, he sat in his chair by the window in the steamy, invalid-warm chamber. Peter kept the pot on the brazier at a constant boil with mists of pungent smelling stuffs suggested by the pharmacopias he found in the Latin Quarter. Almost more strong than his master's will to heal was his servant's will for him to heal. And the master's will was rising as his strength increased.

For hours now Simon's attention was absorbed in reading the books that Boscellis had brought: Saint Augustine's *The City of God*, and Joachim del Flor's banned *Here Begins the Eternal Gospel* and *Exposito en Apocalypsin*, volumes with outer pages scorched by the burning of the theologian's condemned works. Numerous Joachite Franciscans and Dominicans found their way to the Montfort house – the countess had no notion why — to talk with the earl of the coming New Age.

Friends of Boscellis, William and Robert of Leicester came from England. Famous for their preaching of Joachim's Millennium, they spent days with the earl in conference heard by no one else.

When they returned to England it was with encouraging word of the Earl of Leicester's gradual recovery. Simon's name, inserted in their preaching, became linked firmly with the rising New Age. Montfort, the Ordinances' champion, who had nearly suffered death for the cause of the common folk, surely would return. Then the Thousand Years of the Holy Spirit would begin to unfold: a world at one in faith and peace, with neither Church nor kings, but each man in direct communion with the Lord, choosing wisely his own governance, led by divine inspiration.

Friars in every part of England took up and spread the prayer. The call for the return of Simon de Montfort.

In Paris, insulated from such English prayers, Simon's whole focus was to regain his mobility. He forced himself to walk, learning just how much he safely could ignore his pain. Eating sparingly, he made his body gaunt to ease the weight upon his healing knees, ankles and shins. Thigh and calf muscles, from lack of use, withered, leaving his legs shockingly like spindles. He forced his ligaments and muscles to learn anew their function as partners of joints shattered and regrown distorted, fused and crusted with new bone. From a few steps across his room, aided by Peter, then unaided except by canes, Simon advanced to climbing his house's stairs, slowly, so the muscles would not overtax the fresh-knit shins and joints. Agony brought him near to fainting, but his will overrode the pain as if it were an enemy he trod down.

King Louis never came to visit his recuperating friend. Simon understood. It would have been a gesture highly impolitic, as Simon was indicted for treason against England's king. Any public show of favor might even imperil his retrial in France. But as soon as he was confident that he could walk the distance from the palace gate to Louis' chambers, he hired a litter with four bearers, and had himself conveyed to the palace on the Isle de la Cite.

It was evening, a time when he knew Louis was retired from the Court, receiving visitors in private. Walking with his two canes, slowly and painfully, Simon followed the page who went ahead to announce him. The distance between him and the brisk young page grew to such length that Louis and his guests stood waiting for some time, with Louis' own high, gable-backed chair vacated and supplied with a thick cushion. At last Simon arrived, his face bleached white with the effort, the canes trembling in his hands.

The King of France and his guests were stunned by the sight of the lord Montfort, Louis' childhood companion who bore the English title Earl of Leicester, yet who, but a few years ago, had served so honorably as Regent of France.

The page guided Simon to the pillowed chair and he sat with an audible sigh despite the sternness of his self-control. Unshaven, with a full black beard streaked gray, and so gaunt that his familiar, plain black robe hung upon him as if draping a skeleton, Simon presented a harrowing picture of ruin.

Louis sat on the stool nearest the chair and placed his hand on Simon's thin, still trembling hand. "I'll send a chaise for you to visit me when you are better. You understand why I couldn't come…"

"Of course. You mustn't show regard for one accused of treason against England's Crown. Henry might add it to his list of excuses to make war on France." Simon smiled benignly, forcing his body to calm its humiliating trembling.

King Louis saw to it his friend drank a goblet of wine, unwatered and strong. Then he sent for the chair and bearers that Queen Blanche had used in her last illness. And he sent Simon home.

In a week, the chair arrived again at the house on the Greve, and Simon attended the king's private supper. There were no servants present, and two guests only: Louis' favorite, the young Steward of France, Jean de Joinville, and Guy Folques, the priest who was Louis' confessor. Folques had a stern and pinched, pale face, a bitter and high-handed manner. The gentle king chose a harsh confessor as counterbalance to his own mildness. As for Joinville, Simon noted he looked somewhat like himself when he was young, with similar black hair, dark eyes and white skin, but he was smaller, more delicate of build and, where in temperament Simon was serious, Joinville was irrepressible with sly humor.

After seeing Simon seated in a chair plump with cushions, and pouring wine for everyone, a diluted goblet only for himself, Louis, to spare the invalid a lengthy visit that could tax his meager strength, at once opened the issue on his mind.

"We rescued you from England because we know the treaty funds we granted to King Henry, for troops to fight Manfred's moors in Sicily, were spent instead to raise armed force against his own subjects and their parliament in England."

"Of course," Joinville cocked his head to one side and smiled, "we're glad we stopped King Henry from reducing you to paste."

Simon glanced at the young Steward warily.

Louis, ignoring the remark, leaned against the hearth's stone mantel, his broad, blond-fringed brow gathered to a frown. "What your reasons were for taking to England, on your own initiative, those first troops raised for Henry, will be matter to be heard at your trial."

Joinville tittered explosively. Then covered his mouth and tried to appear serious.

"I advise you," Louis drew Simon's distracted attention back from the Steward, "write an account of your services to England. And, if you haven't done so, put your will in writing. I must warn you, the trial may go against you."

Simon had not taken the prospect of retrial lightly, but this was a harsh cautioning he had not expected. He took a deep drink of his wine. "I've committed no treason. I only kept my vows, given to the provisions made at Oxford for the stability of King Henry's sovereignty."

"You stole his army," Joinville snickered.

"*Imperium in imperio,*" Folques' rasping voice hissed. "You created a government within the government, and one especially obnoxious in the eyes of our Lord!"

"How is that?" Simon asked the priest, somewhat surprised. "Would you deny a means that thrice yearly brings to the Crown fresh word of the condition of the realm, down to the smallest hamlet?"

"It sounds reasonable to me." Joinville struck a pose of contemplation until Louis glared at him. The King of France was regretting he had allowed the Steward to be present, though he kept him by his side much of the time.

Glad for any ally, Simon nodded to Joinville. "Louis is a wise and able king, with honest, learned counselors." He tossed a sugared compliment in Folques' direction without lifting his gaze from the Steward. "King Henry is surrounded by greedy kin, and lacks a stable temperament."

He held his cup for Louis to refill, then turned to Folques. "Do understand, it was for the king's support that I committed myself to the Parliament devised by the Provisions. In keeping with my pledge to serve Henry, as best as I'm able."

"If that is not an outright lie, you delude yourself!" Folques retorted, his words more brash than any man of honor would tolerate.

Joinville stared. Simon's hand upon his metal goblet strained white at the knuckles. Louis tensed and his expression warned his confessor to temporize.

"For what purpose I would not now judge," Folques said in a milder tone, yet added, "but the principals to which you swore are opposed to the very nature of Our Lord's Creation."

"Oooo..." Joinville hooted as if a fatal blow in the argument was stuck. He looked on Folques intently.

"Does a team of mice trammel a lion? Does the sparrow, brought to feed the eagle's young, dictate to the eagle and her clutch?" Folques asked with a malicious smile.

"Ought a king to feed upon his people, as the eagle upon hapless birds?" Simon responded with an iron calm imposed in respect of Folques' clerical robes. "Is not the king the first servant of his people, as I was taught in this very chamber by a wise and able queen?"

Joinville flapped his slender, white hands in delight.

Simon saw the favorite, though perhaps quite drunk, was on his side. Or maybe he was merely happy to see anyone contend with Folques. As for himself, he had been taking strong drink and valerian all day for his pain. Louis' wine had soothed him to a state of greater calm than usual, and rather reckless insouciance.

"Thomas has shown..." Folques' stern voice intoned, as if the name itself should annihilate all opposition.

"Ah, yes, the revered Aquinas," Simon broke in on the priest. "He would deny souls' equal value before God, and have every creature chained in endless file like slaves, each bracketed by his immediate superior and inferior. In Heaven, we usefully might be known just by a number."

"It's so comforting to be sure that those below me are inferior to me in every way, by the will of God." Joinville raised his dark, arching brows and looked to Louis.

Simon was wondering if Louis kept this cheery and perceptive puppy by him in the place of a fool, to reduce to absurdity the ponderous convictions of his confessor. In any case the Steward clearly was no fool. Simon had disliked him when they first met, but was beginning to see him as the very balance of piquant good sense that Louis needed.

Gladdened by his wine and this unexpected sport, Simon challenged Folques again. "Where does Jesus ever speak of such a Divine Order? Does He not urge us all to call the Lord 'father,' even 'Abba,' as a child says, 'Papah?'"

"Does He?" the Steward asked, his tone thrilled.

Folques crossed himself hastily. "You speak blasphemy! To so reduce the King of Heaven and Earth, the Creator of all that is, to a child's lispings!"

Louis was standing by the hearth, his face turned from the firelight, his expression lost in shadow. There was a long, silent pause in which Folques looked to the king, expecting him to eject the outrageous blasphemer from their midst, or better, imprison him for heresy. But Louis did nothing.

Simon stretched, cat-like, in the cushioned chair, thoroughly enjoying pricking the royal confessor. He took another swallow of strong wine, and at his leisure launched into the tense silence. "Father Folques, I speak the words our Holy Book tells us Christ spoke. What our Lord Himself uttered can be no blasphemy. So it must be that Aquinas, and those who embrace him…" he took another long sip of his wine, and smiled genially on the livid priest, "…contradict our Lord's lessons with heresies."

"The Bible, in the hands of ignorance, is a dangerous tool! See where it's brought you!" Folques blustered like a bursting pod, scattering a white fluff of saliva.

"The Earl Montfort is not yet judged." Louis spoke at last into the contretemps.

Simon looked to Louis and said in an earnest, sober tone, "I'll prove my innocence. If it *can* be proved to you against the doctrines of this priest."

Louis shook his head. "I won't be the judge of your trial, it would offend King Henry. Queen Margaret is to be your judge."

Simon nodded. Louis was being very politic. And his tactic might be kind, depending upon how great an influence Folques had with Louis' gentle wife. "Your priest holds views quite different from those your noble mother held," he ventured.

But Louis at last defended his confessor. "Scholarly studies advance. It's ever been my effort to advance with them." It was his warning that Folques was firmly in his trust.

The King of France was now convinced that the Pope was solely and directly under Heaven, the first of all Creation upon earth. Then came emperors and kings, the aristocracy, and then all else, from shopkeeper down to the ant and worm. There was an immutable, Divine Order that was God's Will, and dictated through Nature all ethics and politics. In Louis' Court, Aquinas, not the mild, egalitarian Saint Francis, had become supreme.

Simon, with paining joints, rose from his pillowed seat and bowed, then asked if the chair with bearers might be brought for him to return home.

As his bearers pattered over the bridge and along the Greve, Simon, in the cushioned, pole-borne chaise, gently rocking with the rhythm of their tread, pondered the meeting. He felt an unexpected fondness for the witty, pretty Steward Joinville. But loathing in him rose for Folques and the self-serving theology he promoted. The Franciscans and Dominicans, with their concern for the humble and the poor, were in eclipse.

Simon sensed impending threat to all that he held dear: noble obligation and restraint, all that checked lordly pride, that argued the good of the people was God's Will, the highest good, and kings but held their thrones as servants of that good. Were Aquinas to prevail for long, what Christian land would escape tyranny backed by the full powers of the Church? He began to question if the Lord's most pressing work was indeed in Palestine, or here?

Gradually, resting in his heated, herb-reeking chamber and laboriously exercising by limping up and down his stairs, Simon was recovering. At last one day late in February he ordered that his horse be saddled and brought to his door. Mounting for the first time in seven months, with much help from Guy and the squire Peter, he went for a short ride along the Greve. Then every day he rode further, the balance, the pressure of his legs upon the saddle bringing acute pains that Peter treated later with salves rich with mint. Beyond all expectations, beyond hope, he was riding, and walking. The knees, the shins, the ankles, shattered by the headsman in London Tower, reknit, though joints protested at a shrieking pitch. But pain Simon could master.

His beard was full and trimmed now, like the saints who ringed King Louis' Sainte Chapelle. Simon's nearsighted, richly dark-lashed eyes, tutored to conceal his pain, had gained a yet more piercing gaze. Since he shunned the vanity of mirrors, it was by his devoted squire-barber's hands that this image of a patriarch deliberately was shaped. Simon, uncaring but for cleanliness and decency, was ignorant of how imposing the sight of him had become. His wife, his sons noticed and took heart, considering his metamorphosis a cheering sign of recovery. Always daunting in his dark and grave beauty, Simon now seemed the image of God the Father on His Judgment Seat. Or the Lord's avenging angel.

Uneasy at the rising influence of Aquinas, Simon was increasingly drawn to word of doings in England. There, in the Provisions and Ordinances, might be a trailing last hope against the ruthless theology of hierarchy. He gathered whatever news the friars could bring.

It seemed, at every chance, Henry attacked the Councilors, challenging them to pass the Ordinances. As if to prove his accusations of corruption right, they still refused. In London's streets the Council's lords were jeered.

Simon listened to reports from a steady flow of visitors, and said to Eleanor, "There will be war."

"If so, it's none of our concern," the countess retorted. But his interest in the matter filled her with dread. The impending trial terrified her, and she feared the visits of the English friars must be compromising.

In spring the news that Simon was expecting came. King Henry, with the mercenaries he had brought from France the year before, and still kept by him, had marched on Dover. He expelled Hugh Bigod from the fortress and opened the port.

Waiting to land was a fleet of ships bringing the king's half-brothers of Lusignan, and all the pandering highborn criminals and avaricious sheriffs and bailiffs who had been banished from England by the Parliament. As these leeches had not been idle in their years abroad, even more of their kind came with them. Enough to fill every function of the royal government with men loyal not to England but, presumably, to King Henry, and undoubtedly to their own personal gain.

The reliefs the Provisions had won, from local injustices to murderous abuse by the royal kin, were cancelled by this surging arrival.

Returning to London triumphant, King Henry issued writs dismissing all the well-known and honest sheriffs and bailiffs appointed by the Parliament. Officials who had been cast out by the elected government returned to their shires, intent on punishing those who had expelled them. The people's Parliamentary representatives were their first targets, then the people themselves.

Throughout the country, the people's sheriffs and the elected knights of the shires fled. Many went into hiding, striking at the king's men by stealth, then vanishing into the forests of Lincoln, Sussex and the Weald.

Sheltering in those same woods and wastelands were bands of a shunned folk who lived outside the law and Church since ancient times, who practiced old rites and survived by poaching and by thievery They were led by men called Weyland or Robin, and they welcomed the newcomers, joining in their disruptive fight. Songs of the woodland rebels' exploits spread, and were wedded to the songs of Simon de Montfort.

Across England prayers rose louder for the return of the people's champion who lingered in France.

# Chapter Two

## THE TRIAL BEFORE QUEEN MARGARET
### 1261 - 1262

In Paris, Simon's trial was postponed. King Henry had more pressing business.

Accused, but neither convicted nor exonerated, Simon lived excluded from the Court. Communication with him was a political risk, and a threat to the integrity of his trial. Even private suppers with Louis were rare and strained. The summer and autumn of 1261 passed quietly at the house on the Greve.

Simon had written his will some years before, but now composed a record of his relationship with King Henry since his going to England as a youth in 1229. He would submit the document to Queen Margaret before his trial. In it he described a king erratic and hostile despite his liegeman's valuable services. It was a damning work, and deliberately told only half the truth. But any gratitude that Simon owed Henry had been crushed out in London Tower.

As he grew stronger, on fine days Simon rode out to the Forest of Boulogne with Guy, or walked long distances through Paris's streets, despite a lurching limp that use of his cane but partially relieved. Intent upon regaining the strength he always had taken for granted, he bore suffering with a determined, seething spirit that was akin to rage. Slowly the spindly legs grew muscular again, in pace with the coarsely mending bones. With Guy he practiced his sword strokes and parries, forcing his crippled feet to move swiftly.

More friars visited, holding long, intense discussions with the earl in his oak-paneled room. Events in England confirmed Simon's worst speculations. Joachim's predictions of warlike upheavals seemed to be fulfilled. Nor was it surprising, given the friars' urging of the commons to take up arms for the New Age.

In bursts like scattered flames erupting from suppressed wildfire, the folk rose up in places least expected. Villeins invaded the king's sheriffs' courts, armed with pitchforks and axes against the bailiffs' swords. The rural counties were turning into battlefields.

Everywhere, friars preached the rising of the common man to bring in the New Era. The Old Order must be destroyed. The time of the Apocalypse was now: *Thy Kingdom come, Thy Will be done on earth as it is in Heaven.* The *Paternoster* itself cried out for the New Order. The Lord's Kingdom was aborning. Kings, lords, every holder of power in the era that was passing must be overthrown. From time immemorial this Redemption was God's plan. Englishmen, from knight to villein to burgher and apprentice, looked for the coming of the Angel with the Sword, *he whom the common man bid reap*, for it was he who would lead them.

No one doubted who the Angel was. They prayed for his return from France, and spoke of it like the return of Arthur. Or even the Risen Christ.

One visiting priest, bolder than the rest, broached the subject with Simon. "You're meant to return to England, for you are the Lord's Chosen!"

Simon only smiled sardonically. "Chosen to serve as the king's prime sufferer? I thank you. No. Understand this, Father, I'm only a repentant sinner. That Our Lord in His mercy has spared my life thus far I must assume is because, in His judgment, I've not yet repented enough on this earth. My one hope is that, by His grace, I may be spared the fires of hell that I deserve."

"We've cast your chart," the priest persisted, undaunted by what he took to be the earl's meticulous and saintly conscience.

"How did you obtain my date and place of birth?"

"I'm not at liberty to say."

Simon thought a moment. "Ah... Walter." The Franciscan Bishop Cantaloup of Worcester was his close friend since schoolboy days in Paris. He knew the bishop was eager to have him back, even beyond the limits of friendship's trust. "Walter shall hear of my displeasure, if I see him again."

"My lord, your chart shouts from the heavens. You are the Angel of the predictions. It is blazed in the stars."

Simon laughed shortly. "My chart says that? No doubt, when Michael Scott drew my chart for the Holy Roman Emperor, to whom I could not well deny my facts, if it said that, it lost for me the viceroyship of Palestine. Frederic would ill countenance an angel in his Jerusalem. I say this to you, Father," Simon bent his magisterial dark gaze on the audacious priest, "I know you speak from an earnest desire to have me return, but I hold astrology as fool's work, and findings such as you describe are blasphemy. Do not mention this to me again."

After that the Joachites who met with Simon kept their beliefs to themselves.

Simon's sons Henry and Simon too were well aware of the cult the peasantry were fastening upon their father. They dismissed it as the madness of the lowly and did not trouble him about it. His trial, they felt, gave him concerns enough.

So Simon, deluged with prayer, worshipped as an angel sent from God, if he was not indeed the Risen Christ himself, felt none of this tide of spirit engulfing him. His own prayers for his future were for health, liberty after his trial, and a speedy crossing to Palestine.

The more the commons rose up in rebellion, the longer Henry was delayed in England, and Simon's trial was postponed. The winter of 1262 had yielded to spring, and still King Henry could not come to France for the trial.

But word of the cult woven upon Simon's fame sang loudly in the King of England's ears. He began to think these uprisings might be better met in Paris after all. An angel sent from God, who was convicted, hanged, drawn and quartered publicly, would be seen as no angel, but merely the ugly remains of anguish, blood and severed guts no different from any other man of mortal flesh.

Henry, leaving off pursuing common outlaws through the greenwood, arrived in France in July of 1262. King Louis gave him and his entourage accommodations at Vincennes. While delayed in England, Henry's legal counsels had continued to earn their salaries preparing their case. Now Gaston de Bearne and Arnaud de Gramont were summoned from Gascony to bear witness.

In August, within the great double-gabled hall of Louis' palace, under its soaring ceilings painted blue and spangled with gold stars, two daises were set up opposite each other. Behind an ornately carved chair at the center of one dais hung the red and gold flag with three lions *passant guardant* of Plantagenet. At that dais' base was set a long bench for the King of England's counselors. Above the facing dais, an awning of blue silk embroidered with gold *fleurs des lis* canopied the central chair, flanked on each side by velvet-cushioned benches.

On the morning of the trial the Peers of France took their places on the cushioned benches beneath the blue awning. Chiefly the lords were young, come into their titles no more than twelve years earlier, when the debacle in Egypt destroyed their fathers' crusade and ended forty thousand French lives. The lawyers for King Henry filed in, clutching the bulging pages of their briefs, and found seats on their hard bench. At one end of the oblong space between the daises were benches for the witnesses. At the other was the bench for the accused.

The witnesses: the Gascons; Peter of Savoy, the Queen of England's uncle and King Henry's most favored courtier; the king's half-brothers of Lusignan: Guy, William and Aimery, the Bishop-elect of Winchester; and numerous of Henry's clerks, took their places. Several of the Queen of France's ladies entered and found seats among the Peers.

Then all waited. The accused was not yet present.

At the hall's rear a steward cried at last, "The Earl of Leicester, Simon de Montfort." Simon, dressed in his plain robe of black wool, walked forward leaning on a walking stick. Following him was one clerk, a white-robed Dominican well schooled in the laws of France.

Few at Court had seen the earl since his return from England. The ladies, the Peers stared at the changed man with the head of a prophet and a body so clearly wracked with the destruction wrought by his accuser.

Simon was known to them as France's excellent Regent in King Louis' absence, after the ruinous crusade, and the monarch's vow in shame that he would stay and die in the Holy Land. Many still thought the sovereign power had been better wielded in Montfort's hands. It was the rumor that the Crown might pass from Valois to Montfort that brought Louis back. Simon had no such ambition. He merely had done his best, trusting that, if the king returned, he was to be rewarded with the post of Steward of France. But Louis denied him the honor, or any sinecure at all, forcing him to return to England's service.

The Peers had not broached Simon's isolation, protecting the integrity of his trial. Seeing, for the first time, this evidence that he had suffered tortures unfit to inflict on any person of high birth, chilled some, brought uncontrolled tears to the eyes of the queen's ladies, and filled the Peer-judges with a rage their practiced courtiers' faces well concealed.

Simon held in one hand a wax tablet and stylus, with the other he leaned heavily on his cane. As he passed the benches of witness, he let his weak eyes play over his accusers in their opportune nearness. His expression remained calm, almost disinterested. He gave a brief glance toward the bench of lawyers before taking his seat beside his clerk on the bench for the accused.

A herald blew a fanfare when all were in their places. From opposite ends of the hall the King of England and the Queen of France entered accompanied by pages and courtiers, and walked to their regal chairs. Henry was splendid in silk crimson robes of state garlanded with gold chains and an impressive jeweled cross. Upon his head was a trefoil crown crusted with cabochon gems, rimmed with satin and lined with silk, airy fabrics chosen for the summertime. But no finery could ennoble the palsied face that sagged on the left side, flaccidly drawing down his eye and the corner of his mouth to a half-mask of pity, while his right eye peered with a sharp wariness equally unbecoming.

Queen Margaret, in a pale blue gown, her veil dotted with the lily of France embroidered in gold, wore Queen Blanche's stately Spanish crown surmounted with a cross and massive ruby. Her face, once a plain version of her sister, England's queen, had matured sweetly, while Queen Eleanor's had puffed with dissipation. Margaret's blue-gray eyes gained sparkle with the years. Her mouth had a set of humor and assurance. Her years in Palestine with Louis, negotiating his release from captivity while she was in the very act of giving birth, had given her a calm and confidence, a knowledge that nothing in her life would ever be so difficult again. Graciously she nodded to King Henry, and to her Peers of France.

Trial opened with a prayer. Then a tall, gaunt member of the king's battery of lawyers rose and read King Henry's charges against Simon de Montfort.

Simon's white-robed advocate stood and read his client's claims of innocence and counterclaims against King Henry. The monk spoke in the bland, scholarly Latin of the university and made no strong impression on the English. The counselors on the long bench exchanged nudges and complacent smiles.

The hearing of witnesses commenced. The same tall clerk who had read out the charges, unfolded himself from the bench and stepped into the open, oblong space. He spoke of Gascony, where Simon served as viceroy for King Henry, commissioned to end the revolt of Gascon barons seeking to be free of England's rule. The rebels, manipulating Henry, had moved the king to bring Simon to trial on charges of treason a full ten years ago. Now those barons, witnesses once more, poured forth their claims of the viceroy's abuses, his misuse of power, his avarice and cruelty.

Simon sat unmoved, his eyes upon his writing tablet, and offered no rebuttal. From time to time he sketched idly upon the wax tablet: ground plans of defensive towers or dispositions of besieging troops. But he said nothing and did not even look up.

When the Gascon witnesses were finished, Queen Margaret turned to the accused and asked, "Lord Earl of Leicester, have you nothing to reply to these charges?"

Setting down the tablet, Simon stood and faced her and the Peers of France. "Your Majesty... good lords of France, I have been tried before King Henry and the lords of England on these very accusations. King Henry, when the memories of these witnesses were fresher, declared me innocent. I've nothing more to say."

The trial turned to the issue of the recent treaty between England and France.

"Is it not so that you were King Henry's ambassador to treat for peace with King Louis?" a rotund, stern-eyed attorney stood glaring, directly before the earl, his French richly suffused with a London accent redolent of the shambles.

Simon stood up from his bench, taller than the lawyer by head and shoulders, his hands clasped comfortably in front of him. "I was his representative, together with others."

The lawyer, at close quarters, had to tip his head far back, straining to be threatening, while Simon stood entirely at ease, mildly gazing over his head. "Is it not so that, before this peace between two great kingdoms could be embraced, it was required that the Countess of Leicester, your wife, make quitclaim, renouncing her lands in France, and that King Henry was required to make recompense to her of valuable lands in England?"

"The King of France wished it. She is the King of England's sister. The lands in France were hers by inheritance. No king is glad to see the daughter of kings stripped of all she owns."

"Yet the King of France did not require quitclaims from the King of England's brother Richard or King Henry's own heirs? A strange anomaly, and much to your advantage." The lawyer turned, eyes glittering with his own cleverness, scanning his fellow counselors for smiles of approval.

"It was by the will of the King of France." Simon gazed calmly down upon the little man. "It was not by my *purchase*."

Queen Margaret blinked at the last word as if she had been stung.

The clerk drew his chubby hand across his brow where drops of perspiration suddenly emerged. He tried again. "Did you not use your position to *recommend...*" he turned and made a slight bow to the queen, to clear himself of any implication that the Most Christian King of France might have stooped to graft. "Did you not *recommend* to King Louis that the quitclaim be asked of the countess?"

"I did not obtain, or procure, or *recommend*, or have it recommended," Simon said in smiling imitation of the lawyer's low accent, causing a momentary upturn to the corners of Queen Margaret's lips. Then he dropped his playful tone and bowed to the queen. "I wish to put this on record. I call the King France to witness to the truth of what I say. The quitclaim required for the peace was in no way to my benefit. My wife's claims in France, and rights of mine to lands in France as well, which were quite clear before, are now obstructed."

"Did you not grant," the attorney stepped back several paces from the earl to hurl his bolt, "did you not grant, by letter to King Louis, that the countess would give her quitclaim in exchange for certain monies owed her? And if certain wrongs done her were righted?" Sweating profusely now, he caught himself just as his colleagues on the bench began to rise and gesticulate. "...That is, if King Henry had ever done her any wrongs."

Simon raised his eyebrows in broad, comical astonishment. "Of the funds long owed to the countess, I thought King Henry acted voluntarily, fulfilling his duties to his sister as a brother should. Surely not because his peace with France required it."

It was a deft blow at Henry's honor.

Queen Margaret drew her veil across her mouth, concealing a broad smile. The Peers of France looked to one another with smirks.

The lawyer's jowls shook, scattering beads of perspiration. King Henry, frowning, ordered him replaced.

A lean, nervous young clerk stood forth from the king's bench. This man, the foremost student of the law at Oxford only recently, had been an ardent partisan of the Provisions, and a passionate admirer of the earl who had made their liberal principles into a functioning government. But he was cruelly disillusioned by the Council, and by Simon's conduct of the treaty, and the rebellious cult that claimed him as a more than mortal agent of the Lord. He was yearning to trample his besmirched hero.

"Is it not true, Sire," the youth began, with inadequate title and in a disrespectful tone, "you, with others, swore at Oxford that the holdings of the royal demesne ought not to be divided? Especially that men of foreign birth ought not to receive gifts of land from that which belongs properly to the Crown?"

"I did so swear," Simon admitted with the first trace of discomfort. He paused, then said carefully, "But I was not in England at the time the quitclaim was asked, nor when lands were allotted from the English Crown's demesne, as compensation for the lands in France the quitclaim forced my wife to relinquish. Nor is she foreign born. As King Henry was under oath to act on the advice of his Council, I assumed the allotments had their approval, that they considered the king's own sister's disinheritance was an exception. If Henry was not acting on his Council's advice, as his oath required, that is no fault of mine."

Henry's face turned crimson under the Peers' stares. He ordered the bright young clerk replaced.

"Is it not true..." a hitherto unheard lawyer rose from the bench with the grace of writhing smoke. He drew the thin line of his eyebrows to a pathetic gable. His voice was resonant and threatening. "Is it not true that you tried to interfere with the marriage of the King's daughter Beatrice to the son of the Duke of Brittany, by telling the duke that the King of England had not the power to grant his daughter so much as a foot of land?"

Simon looked up from his writing tablet, hearing this absurd raindrop hurled at him with the gravity of a thunderclap. With his most open gaze of surprise he turned to Queen Margaret. "I did everything I could to advance the marriage, not to hinder it. I merely told the Count that the King had sworn that nothing should be granted from the royal demesne without the Council's knowledge." He looked innocently to Henry, "My lord, was that not right, and quite as your own lawyer has just argued?"

Before he could be dismissed, the lawyer with the linear eyebrows threw another dart. "Is it not true that you drove the King's own half-brothers to take flight from the country?"

"They were banished by decision of the Council, who at that time were prudent men," Simon said smoothly.

There were none among the Peers of France who did not smile at this. The Lusignan brothers were famous for their malice, greed, brigandry and worse. During the campaign between England and France in Poitou in 1242, they had infected the King of France and his entire army with dysentery, by deliberately fouling wells with slops from latrines. None who drank the tainted waters of Frontenay ever fully recovered. The deaths of most of the Peers' own fathers with Louis on crusade was not in battle, but from the chronic sickness that the Lusignan had wrought. To rid one's country of this spawn of Melusine was a wise act.

Queen Margaret looked down, avoiding Henry's eyes across the room. She too had cast his Lusignan half-brothers from her Court.

Seeing his target go unscathed, the clerk took aim once more. He came at last to the main issue. He was the senior and most skilled member of the king's battery of counsels, not to be briskly dismissed. "Is it not true that you brought armed men and horses to the Candlemas meeting of the Parliament two years ago?"

"I've done nothing to harm anyone. I have acted always in good faith, and for the security of the Crown of England's sovereignty," Simon said quietly.

The eyebrows from their gable-slant bent downward like an arrow. "Is it not true that when King Henry was in France for the treaty signing, you left for England before he did?"

"It is true he was delayed," Simon, meeting the clerk's eyes, said simply.

"And you left secretly, without taking leave of him."

"I took leave of the King of France. I saw no need to take leave of the King of England, as I was going where he ought to have been going."

Stunned by the riposte, the Court burst into open laughter. They knew that King Henry, to undermine the people's Parliament that he had sworn to uphold, had lingered long in France – past time for his Parliament to meet – with the intent to bring an army back with him to force the disbanding of the elected government. Among the Peers there were knowing nods as the laughter subsided. It was just as well known that the Earl Montfort, discovering Henry's intent, had stolen all his mercenaries so far gathered, and taken them to England to defend the Parliament. This audacity was at the very core of his supposed treason.

Trying to ignore the laughter, the English clerk demanded, "Did you not, once you arrived in London with armed men, tell the Justiciar to withhold funds that the King had ordered sent to France?"

"That may be as you say," Simon admitted.

The thin brows arched with happy achievement. "And did not the Justiciar instruct you, and others, not to hold the Parliament until the King's return?"

"That is what the Justiciar said. By King Henry's own order, that same Justiciar has since been cast out from his post for incompetence."

Laughter again.

"We are not judging *the Justiciar* here," the lean clerk retorted. "Did you not, despite the Justiciar's warning, go to London and hold Parliament *in the king's absence?*"

"By King Henry's own sworn oath, a Parliament, including every shire's elected representatives, is to meet three times a year at a fixed time and place. I went, with others, to the appointed place at the appointed time. At our first meeting, the Justiciar asked us to wait until the King's return, which he believed would be in no more than three weeks. The Parliament was suspended for those three weeks, despite great inconvenience to the knights who had come long distances from the shires."

*"Is it not true that you went with horses and men?"* The clerk brought the full power of his high, resounding voice to bear. The stone walls rang.

Simon looked at him blandly and smiled. "I seldom go without horses and men. It is the way I usually travel."

Buffeted by fresh laughter, the king's prime counselor shouted, throwing his most deadly bolt. "Have you not drawn men to yourself? Forming new alliances?" His words were charged with the implication that the people's chaotic rise in England was Simon's work.

Simon sat with his calm fingers interlaced and resting on his writing tablet, and directed his open gaze past the clerk to King Henry. "I swear by my faith that I have never attempted to draw anyone from his allegiance to the King of England, and to the common enterprise to which we all have sworn."

The lawyer, displaying utmost disgust, turned to Queen Margaret. "King Henry, while in France to sign the treaty, was informed that the Earl of Leicester did not obey his orders and the commands of the Justiciar, but held a Parliament, and made alliances that to this very day cause peril to the Crown, destroying England's peace! The whole of England is disturbed because of this man's Parliament and his alliances..."

"I did not hold a Parliament by myself alone, or seek any alliances!" Simon's voice rose loud and clear.

"...which was the sole reason," the clerk continued at a shriek, "why the King was forced to return to England with hired men-at-arms from France! And those men cost him much!"

"I did not cause the king to bring an army into England. I'm sorry that he did. He had no need of it."

"Is it not true you said that you would give the men the King brought such a welcome that they would not come again!"

Simon looked at the clerk, then laughed outright and turned to the Peers of France. "I may have said as much on behalf of King Henry's honor. I knew their coming did him no good service. It seemed he only trusted Frenchmen, and thought his own people nothing but faithless cowards."

The Peers buckled, doubled, held their sides convulsed with laughter. In France the favorite slur for Englishmen was *faithless cowards.*

King Henry sat as rigid and composed as a statue carved of stone. Years of fronting contempt and protest from his lords had inured him to insult. But then he had been asking taxes. His opponents could be thought of coolly in the abstract as his vassals, and dealt with through each one's vulnerabilities which he knew well how to wrench. Here he had one adversary, a man for whom he once felt love that had long since turned to hate. His nurtured, cultivated hatred flared with every insolent smirk and laugh of France's Peers.

Henry looked to Queen Margaret, but she did not return his glance.

Simon was disarming the king's case with deft mockery. He had calculated his defense, knowing both Queen Margaret and his jury well. In Paris Simon lost what little Englishness he had acquired and became thoroughly French. He used his native speech with delicacy to turn, parry and counter-thrust in ways that Louis' courtiers loved, and the English with their Anglo-Norman French and blunt address, had no means to combat. At each sally he pricked and skewered the king's clerks with panache. In England, such a defense would be suicide. But in France gallantry could win.

Henry, unable to capture Queen Margaret's attention and seeing he was losing his case, stood, demanding a recess. Beckoning to a page, he sent word to the queen that he wished to speak with her and with King Louis.

In a private chamber with Queen Margaret by his side, Louis spoke to his fellow monarch gravely. "Henry I must tell you, I'm aware that before the Earl of Leicester left France with those armed men, the monies I had granted you for use in Sicily had gone instead to hire forces to embark for England. That was a severe breach of our treaty. And a move no king should make against his own subjects. That the earl appeared to confiscate your troops, taking them to England to protect your Parliament, saved your honor before God. If Montfort requires me as witness, I must speak the truth, although it may impair the peace between our lands."

Henry, astounded at the unexpected rebuff, scowled so sourly that the right side of his face matched the sagging left. He had sought out Louis for assurance he would win his case. He was exposed instead, and in a way so damning that he had no words for answer. His clerks had pressed the point that the only reason he brought soldiers into England was to oppose the earl. To be given the lie, and by King Louis himself, not only guaranteed loss of his case, but could cancel the treaty and bring on renewed war. The issue now was far more weighty than the earl's guilt or innocence.

Brother," reassuringly Louis rested his hand on the stricken King of England's arm, "permit us to drop this matter. Before it can cause harm that neither of us wants."

Grudgingly, Henry nodded his consent. There would be no judgment, no decision. The case against Simon de Montfort would be closed as if the charges of treason never had been brought.

# Chapter Three

## THE HERO OF THE GREENWOOD
### 1262

It was October the sixth when the trial came to a subdued close. When Simon was informed the accusations had been dropped, Queen Margaret would make no decision, he remarked acidly to Louis, "You've deprived me of the happiness of winning publicly."

"It is the queen who would have borne the cost," Louis frowned. "And perhaps France. But you're safe and free, don't let vindictiveness deprive you of your peace."

As the King and Queen of France dined with the morose King of England, Countess Eleanor held a discreet celebration *en famille* at the house on the Greve.

Guy stood and offered as toast, "To father, whose tongue is as deft as his sword."

"And to the fools the English schools of law produce," Simon, laughing, drank the toast.

When the meal was near its end the countess asked her two eldest sons, "Do you mean to return to Prince Edward?"

They glanced at their father. He nodded. Henry answered readily for himself and young Simon, "We do." Edward was believed to be in Gascony, his duchy in southwestern France, or he might already have returned to England. There was no thought to include Guy in the prince's company.

Simon looked at his sullen third son. "Guy will come with us to Palestine, where I don't doubt he'll win an Outremerine heiress," he predicted cheerfully. The Christian lords of Palestine were rich from trade; their kohl-eyed daughters as festooned as sultanas with jewels and silk gauze. Guy, with his martial skills, and cousin to the leading lord Philip de Montfort, could be a prime target for betrothal. Philip's son Philip was among his friends in Charles of Anjou's household.

Such was the countess's happy plan for Guy. Eyes gleaming, she recalled the sumptuous bazaars of Jerusalem and Acre, and her camel-borne excursions with Philip's pearl-laden wife, the Princess of Armenia.

Guy looked up and tried to smile. For him the East had no reality. His brother Henry's unwitting offer that he join the prince rang in his memory, both tempting and hopeless. The offer was not made to him, but to a fiction.

Squire Peter entered briskly and went to the earl. "There's a friar at the door asking to see you at once, my lord. He says it's urgent."

"Bring him to my chamber." Simon, touching his napkin to his mouth, got up from the table. "Pardon, but I must speak with someone."

"Now?" the countess protested.

"Apparently now," and Simon left the room.

In the privacy of the paneled chamber, without word of introduction, the Dominican drew from his black, hooded cloak a rolled parchment. In a low voice like a conspirator afraid of being overheard even in the isolated room, he murmured, "Good Earl, I've been sent to put a letter in your own hands from my superior in Rome."

There were in fact two documents, one rolled within the other. As the earl took them, the inner one fell out. It was a small sheet but its gilded wax Papal seal fell with a ring like coin upon the floor. The friar bent and picked it up, handing it back to the earl.

Simon unrolled the first parchment, asking with curiosity, "Who is your superior?"

In a whisper the monk replied from beneath his lowered hood, "His Eminence, Cardinal Hugh, the Bishop of Messina." He named the highest prelate of his Order. It was said that the cardinal had saved the Dominicans from extinction when he ordered the burning of Joachim's books. But whether he had done so from necessity, for the survival of the Order, or out of real offense at Joachim's theology, no one seemed to know.

The letter, in a beautiful scholarly hand that must have been the cardinal's own, began: *Cardinal Hugh, Bishop of Messina, Almoner to His Late Holiness Pope Alexander IV, to Simon de Montfort, Earl of Leicester, greetings,*

*Questions regarding certain oaths given in England were brought before His Holiness, and he gave answer to those questions. He has passed from us now. But, shortly before he died, he pondered those issues again and dictated to myself the epistle here enclosed. Between the hour it was transcribed and sealed, and the hour it was to have been given to the legate for England, Pope Alexander died. The document has remained in my hands since. I send it to you for I trust you will know what to do with it.*

*Your brother in conscience, Hugh*

Quickly Simon unrolled the smaller parchment with the gold seal. It revoked the absolution of the oaths to the Provisions, placing those oaths, taken to protect the rights of Englishmen against the powers of their king, into full force again.

Simon read the scroll a second time, hardly daring to believe what he read. He inspected the seal carefully by candlelight. He knew well the look of documents from the papal chancery. It seemed authentic.

Turning to the friar, Simon said earnestly, "Tell your master that I do know what to do with it."

The Dominican left and Simon, with the two scrolls in his hand, returned to his family still at table. He was smiling, his patriarchal face as radiant as Moses on the Mount.

Eleanor was alarmed at once. "What did the friar want?"

"To give me a fine strike at Aquinas and King Henry." His white teeth showed in the frame of his bearded smile. "I must go to England."

"What!" the countess cried. "What devil was it at the door who suggested such madness!"

"No devil, but a messenger from Christ's own voice on earth."

"This surely is a trick to get you back to England where Henry can arrest you!" She tried to snatch the letters from his hand.

He easily held them beyond her reach. "Henry hasn't wit enough to contrive such a trap. I'll be safe if I go quickly."

Simon knew that Parliament was to meet on its regular, appointed day, the thirteenth of October. When Henry saw the trial in France would hamper his timely return, he had sent word the meeting, under his trusted Justiciar and Chancellor, should be held nonetheless in his absence. The gesture, he thought, would add strength to his case against the earl.

Henry had little to fear now from the lords. Richard de Clare, the driving force behind the oath to the Provisions, and the first to refuse its rights to his own villeins, was dead. Simon was in France. With their two leaders gone, and with the common folk irate against them, the lords' strength to resist the royal power seemed well enough impaired.

Simon meant to read Pope Alexander's letter to this Parliament. Though walking still was agony, he could ride now with ease. He would make the trip and cast back in the faces of the lords their vows to Provisions: their vows to uphold the elected government that he, virtually alone, had made a functioning reality.

Guy he ordered to remain and help the countess to prepare for Palestine. Henry he dispatched to Edward, retaining his son Simon to go with him.

Riding fast, with changes of horses at inns, the Earl of Leicester and his son arrived at Westminster the morning of October the thirteenth, in time for the opening of Parliament. The walls of the royal hall, in fading and now peeling paint, still displayed the great mural of the battle of Antioch, mute remnant from the time when Simon was the king's best friend, advising him on matters no more serious than his palace's adornment. The crowd of faces in the hall could not have shown more astonishment had Simon risen from the dead.

In his full black beard, with his black riding robe coated with dust and his spurs leaving flecks of horse blood on the floor, he strode with a marked limp up to the dais and elbowed the surprised

Chancellor Richard Merton to one side. No one in England had yet heard the outcome of his trial.

"I bring you a letter from Pope Alexander!" Simon's voice rang out, resounding from the painted walls and gabled ceiling. He drew the small scroll with the golden seal from his sleeve and read it clearly and loudly.

As he read, the looks upon his hearers' faces turned from wonder to rage. The barons had no desire to renew their oaths. Oaths that had brought them strife.

"You have no business here!" Merton shrilly piped. He tried to push the earl aside.

Simon, unmoved as stone against Merton's puny shoving, looked and listened for the response to his reading. He could see no faces clearly beyond the first two rows below him. In the sullen silence his expression darkened. He let his eyes scan the room, then spat, "Faithless cowards! All of you!"

"How did you get that letter! How do we know it's genuine!" Ralph Basset the Justiciar challenged.

But the earl already was leaving. The clink of his spurs was the only answer that he gave.

At the rear door Simon's cousin Peter de Montfort caught his arm. "There are many who are strongly with you! But they're afraid to speak out here. Don't judge us all by them," he nodded toward the forepart of the room.

"If you can neither act nor speak, what use are you?" Simon retorted. He pulled his arm from Peter's grasp, and left.

In the courtyard the earl remounted his tired horse and, with his son, rode to the nearest inn. There, with fresh horses, they turned again toward the coast. They had come by way of Winchelsea and they galloped south. Though changing to better horses at Camberwell, by the time they reached the edge of the New Forest, those mounts were far spent and could only be walked.

As the earl and his son passed at a winded plod through a dense thicket-bordered stretch of road, suddenly a band of men carrying long staves and bows appeared in the way in front of them.

"My lords you'd best dismount and let us have those horses before they perish under you," the foremost of the archers said with a polite bow. "And offer us all your money, before you spend it just as badly as you've spent your mounts."

Young Simon moved as if to draw his sword, but his father put out his hand and stopped him.

"We're in a hurry! We must pass!" Simon Fils shouted.

"Oh, must you? That's what everybody claims." The insouciant outlaw smiled broadly.

The earl had dismounted. Two of the woodsmen shouldered their bows and began searching him. Reluctantly, young Simon dismounted and submitted to the search. A drawstring bag of coins and the two scrolls were drawn from the blousing of the earl's riding coat.

The find was taken to the leader of the band who eyed the small gold seal suspiciously but did not unroll the letter. He dropped the bag of coins down the front of his leather jerkin, saying, "You don't look much like a legate. If you did, I'd run you through straight off." He moved close to Simon. Not as tall as the earl, he looked up into his bearded face, "What does the letter say?"

"It says Pope Alexander, before he died, had a change of heart. The letter revokes the absolution of the lords' vows to the Provisions. And places the Provisions in full force again."

The archer made a long, low whistle of mock wonder. "You don't say! And who might you be to be carrying such news?"

"I am the Earl of Leicester."

"Come now Sire Grimvisage, do better than that. The Earl of Leicester is in France standing trial, the worse for England."

"Would you know his seal?" Simon asked. His small seal was in the bag with the coins, now warm under the archer's leather jerkin.

The archer cocked his head to one side but said only, "Come along, Grimsby, I'd best bring you to my master. For, just in case you did turn out to be the man you say, I'd catch the very hell for having let you pass ungreeted. And if you're a legate, I'd catch hell again."

Young Simon was in a fit of fury, sure the archers meant to turn them over to a sheriff, pocketing a ransom in addition to their booty for their work. But his father calmly walked into the woods, with the aid of a thoughtful outlaw's shoulder when the man saw how he limped. Simon Fils, surrounded by the archers, could do nothing but follow after him.

Beyond the dense undergrowth bordering the road, the forest opened, broad well-tended and shaded by tall, spreading oaks.

"Who is your master?" Simon asked of the brazen archer who, leading the way ahead of him, strode with a jaunty gait over the parti-colored fallen leaves that damply wadded on the forest floor.

"Ah, Grimsby, that is for thee to find out." It was clear from his bantering tone and use of the familiar "*thee*" that he did not at all believe the lame and nearly unattended traveler riding a galled, common hack could be the Earl of Leicester.

After walking for some time through the autumn-ruddy, sunlit woods, a walk slowed by Simon's painful limp, they reached a dell completely cleared, in the middle of which stood a large, decaying wattle and daub cottage. The earl's spent horses, on a tether line with perhaps twenty others, were grazing on the coarse grass of the clearing. Chickens scurried, clucking in retreat around the feet of the arriving men. A flock of geese honked, reliable as watchdogs; their gander beat soft thunder with his plucked and flightless wings. From behind the hunch of the thatched roof a column of roast-meat-scented smoke rose up, drifting like fog among the treetops.

As Simon and his son emerged onto the open ground, the door of the house was flung back and a tall youth of some twenty years came out. He was dressed as a lordling in a good, short riding robe of blue velvet, but the fine cloth was badly worn and soiled. His face was narrow, pale, with large eyes of ice blue, framed by long, unwashed strands of blond hair. He studied his two prisoners for several moments in silence. They returned his gaze with equal, vague recognition. Then suddenly the youth's expression cleared and he knelt down on one knee.

"My lord, forgive us. We didn't recognize you with the beard."

Simon breathed relief. He had assumed when he saw the archers, they were the sort of men the friars described, men made outlaws by the king's reversals of policy. Strong partisans of the

Provisions. But the lengthy, strained walk through the forest had given him time to consider that they might be nothing more than ordinary brigands after all. He put his hand out to the youth who knelt before him, raising him up.

"My friend, beard or no beard, you have the better of me. I don't recall who you are."

"Roger Leybourne, my lord. My father's a lord in Kent. I was with Prince Edward at Ewloe, when you rescued us and led us out against the Welsh."

"I do remember you!" Simon Fils exclaimed, recalling one of the youngest boys in Edward's following. He cast his glance about the thatched house and the clearing with a quizzical and disapproving look.

Leybourne's delicate, translucent skin took on a flush of chagrin. "Forgive the modest hospitality I offer. I was declared outlaw, my lands, such as they were, have been seized. My father dares not have anything to do with me. I've been here with these men since spring." He gave no further excuse for his outcast state. "My lord," he bowed low to Simon, "your money, letters and horses will be returned to you at once. That is, if you won't accept fresh mounts from me, and a good dinner, which I beg you to consider. Your own horses won't last many more miles and," he tossed his greasy yellow locks haughtily, "we can offer you the king's best venison."

Simon grinned genially in his beard. "We accept. The flavor of illegal royal venison will be particularly pleasing." Young Simon scowled at the delay, but his father was curious about these woodland partisans of whom he'd heard the friars speak.

They entered the house, a very dusty building with a broad, oak-beamed room ideal for the headquarters of a clandestine crew. An incongruously ornate, carved table stood near the center of the rustic, tree-trunk-columned space. Around the walls were heaped and stacked every variety of hapless freight diverted from the forest road: barrels and chests, casks of wine and beer, woolsacks and flour sacks, and furniture: tied sheaves of bed boards and their bundled curtains, assorted stools, and one elaborately painted chair blazoned with the arms of Aumale.

There also were supplies of a more useful sort: saddles and other horse equipment, boughs of elm for bows; light, straight sticks for arrow shafts and heavy ones for cudgels; and a miscellaneous collection of swords, knives, helmets and chain armor.

A few men, dressed in odd bits of much abused clothes from their victims' traveling sacks, sat in a group fletching new-cut arrows with goose quills. They were chatting animatedly but went silent when the visitors came in. Other men lay sleeping soundly on the commandeered woolsacks.

Leybourne dragged the painted chair to the table for the earl. The rest seated themselves on stools.

"Lord Earl, praise God you've returned to England!" Leybourne's eyes rested on his guest with a look approaching adoration.

Simon met the worshipful blue stare sadly, then looked down. A bitter smile turned his lips. "The lords of England aren't so welcoming."

"They're dogs! Old men afraid of their own shadows," Leybourne tossed out spitefully. "Here are your loyal soldiers, lord Earl." He made a sweeping gesture that took in not only the cozy fletchers and his several night-sentinels sleeping curled like puppies on the big woolsacks, their longbows unstrung by their hands, but whomever else might be out in the forest he claimed as his own.

The earl gave a doubtful smile.

"There are many of us, my lord," the youth insisted. "And all are ready to fight for you."

"How many?" Simon asked, more to humor the naive, feisty lad than out of any serious interest.

"Three hundred at least in the New Forest. And many more are in the Weald and Sherwood."

A mawkish, toothless man, his hair and beard stiff with filth and matted in thick cords, came through the bright doorway, bobbing several bows in Simon's and the youth's direction. He wore a patched wool jerkin, with strips of cloth bound round his legs and tied with ragged strings of leather for cross-gartering. His dirty hand, garnished with long, broken nails, tidily brushed off the table.

Leybourne watched young Simon's look of revulsion. "See what the honorable sheriff of Kent, beaten to injury of the brain and cast out by the king's men, has been reduced to," he said low.

As the sheriff departed, two husky fellows carrying the flayed, spitted, smoking carcass of a deer entered and flung the carcass on the table with a resounding thud. Leybourne gave a pettish glance in their direction. He would accept any crudity from the sheriff, but from these men he expected a trifle more finesse. The men, seeing the blue eyes not smiling on them, cowered and bowed in hasty departure.

Leybourne touched the earl's wrist lightly for his attention. "My lord, it happens opportunely that we meet here tomorrow with woodsmen of Sherwood. Your questions will find better answers then. Pray, be my guest until tomorrow, and let us prove what worthy followers you have."

The cord-haired sheriff took up his place as steward at the door, shouting and ringing a hand bell as other men brought in skinned, gutted and roasted hares, squirrels and partridges skewered on scorched branches. More of the outlaws came tumbling into their hall. They wiped their hunting knifes upon their shirts, and cut off for themselves whatever meat they wanted. With their dinners pinioned on their knife points, they settled themselves on stools, woolsacks and the floor. The night-sentinels roused and staggered to the table, hacking out portions of the meat for what would be their breakfast.

Leybourne's henchmen used their stomachs and laps for tables, their jerkins as both tablecloth and napkin. They were bereft of manners, and unkempt to a degree only the human animal seems able to achieve. Their uncombed hair dangled about their beards and the odor of their bodies was rank. New grease stains only blended with the old on their clothing as they slobbered.

Young Simon looked at them, revolted, nauseated. Never, not among the lowliest villeins, had he ever seen such accomplished slovenliness. He wanted to be gone. Every moment wasted here was dangerous as well as vile.

The sheriff, his hands now moderately washed in honor of the guests, served the earl, his son and Leybourne with meticulously carved slices from the haunch of the deer.

Simon smiled and nodded his thanks, then asked Leybourne, "I see your booty here... Do you have men trained in using those swords?" He asked more to make conversation than from any thought of strategy.

"Many of these men were swordsmen. And my lord, our longbows too can win battles."

"Archers have their use, but they can serve only briefly against a charge of armored cavalry." The earl's tone was patient, his intention was to bring a light of reality into the outcast youth's pathetic, grandiose notions.

"It may not be a soldier's weapon, but have you seen a longbow shot, my lord?" Leybourne asked carefully. The bow of war was a crossbow with a ratchet to draw back the string, cumbersome to carry and slow to operate. Simon had employed mercenary archers many times, but had not seen bows like the long, clean, simple arcs the poachers in the king's forests employed.

"The longbow can pierce chain mail and pourpoint at a distance better than a sword at arm's reach," Leybourne boasted implausibly. "I don't doubt these crude men's arrows can stop a charge of knights."

Simon recoiled. While he championed the rights of common men, the assertion that these coarse ruffians with their whittled branches could defeat the finest armament yet known to man was military heresy.

Young Simon concluded Leybourne had gone out of his mind from his misfortunes. Never before had he seen anyone whose state in life and puffed-up claims were so far out of joint. He sat covering his mouth with his venison-greased fingers, trying not to laugh outright in the youth's face. Desperate to be going on to Winchelsea, every moment spent was deepening his pique.

But his father seemed to be listening seriously. "I'd like to see what your archers can do."

"You'll stay then for tomorrow's meeting with the men of Sherwood?" Leybourne worked hard to conceal his joy, to appear the leader that he actually was, not just an eager boy.

"I'll stay," Simon replied.

His son looked at him, bursting with frustration. "Father, we must be going! We've been here already too long."

Simon cast a glance at him that stifled his protest. "We shall stay. I'll see what these bowmen can do."

Wrapped in their traveling cloaks, which were little protection from the fleas and lice inhabiting the woolsacks, father and son slept fitfully through the night amid the unclean odors and cataracts of mucous-laden snores.

Just before dawn the blare of a hunting horn was heard sounding from deep in the forest. The flock of watch-geese gave alarm in full-throated voice.

Leybourne rose from where he had been sleeping near the door. Taking a horn that hung by a lanyard strung over a peg, he stepped from the doorway and blew an answering blast. If the first notes had not wakened all the sleepers, the geese and Leybourne's reply jolted them alert.

Scratching, the outlaws got up and went outside to void their bladders, then to prepare a huge porridge of barley with diced meat from last night's feast for their new guests. Soon another horn trill was heard, this time much nearer. Leybourne answered promptly, giving his visitors the sound to find their way.

Simon and his son washed as best they could in a stone trough behind the house, where water burbled frigid from a spring nearby the cook-fire with its copious iron cauldron and its gluey barley lake. Then they joined Leybourne, who waited at the center of the clearing, his horn in his hand.

There was another horn blast from the trees, and answer. In a few moments a final trill sounded, this time so near it seemed to come from the very edge of the cleared ground, yet still no one of the arriving party could be seen.

As if taking shape out of the mottled leaves and shadows, thirteen men appeared, standing in the dell. They walked easily, gladly forward, led by a dark, curly-headed youth with impish black eyes. All wore the green jerkins and hooded cowls of true woodland folk, and across the back of each was the long, slender arc of a bow such as was seen only in England's forests. They were no better off than Leybourne's outlaws, but they weren't particularly disheveled, accustomed as they were to their sylvan way of life. The youth at the fore smiled freely with a flash of beautiful white teeth. Loose-limbed of movement, self-assured, he had the air of noble children, pampered from birth and ignorant of fear or punishment. A spoilt boy, a cosset who could do no wrong.

Young Simon watched him uneasily and felt an itch to knock him down. He had seen sons of earls like him, but never before so impudent a commoner.

Simon too observed the youth with an odd feeling of discomfort. He studied him from head to foot. His green-dyed clothes were no finer than those of his companions. The long bow, the quiver of stout arrows, the large hunting knife thrust in his belt, were much like theirs. But, unlike them, he had a sheathed, double-edged sword hung from the belt. The earl's glaze traveled downward and stopped. Over the cross-gartering of his left calf, just below his knee, the youth wore a curiously knotted leather thong.

The curly haired lad saw where the earl was looking and shifted his stance, the gartered knee gracefully bent forward, and he made a little bow. "I'm known as Robin," he said, unperturbed.

Young Simon looked to his father, chilled.

Simon frowned and glanced to Leybourne, his distaste clear in his expression.

The youth, not insensitive, pursed his lips and looked directly at the earl. "I didn't think that you, my lord of Leicester who are so friendly with the Welsh, would despise our equally ancient race."

"Llewellyn is a decent Christian," Simon replied tartly.

The youth's nostrils flared and his look grew hard. With a swift grace he took his bow from his shoulder, placed one end at the instep of his foot and bent the tall arc, briskly looping its string to the other end, which was above his head. Drawing an arrow from his quiver, he nocked it, held the bow at full arm's length, drew the taut string back to his ear and took aim. Across the clearing the degenerate sheriff was trudging, carrying an old iron cook-pot by its bail handle. The arrow's shaft flew from the longbow with speed faster than the eye could see. The pot lurched from the codger's grip and landed several feet away, the arrow piercing one side through, the point deep buried in the other.

The archer turned back to the earl and asked lightly, yet challenging, "And do you still despise me?"

The sheriff, in wonder, came running with the pot pierced by the arrow.

Simon frowned but said nothing. His son looked at the pot in astonishment, then at Robin with fresh interest.

"My lord," Leybourne pressed, "as I said, these woodsmen could be helpful to your cause."

"What would you have of me and of my folk, good Earl? What can we do to show our oneness with your cause?" the archer asked, his tone both sweet and teasing.

"Remove that thing." Simon pointed at the knotted cord below the youth's knee.

"If it puts your mind at rest." Robin smiled, bent down and untied the thong, rolling its strangely knotted length into a ball and palming it.

Young Simon watched this youth whose ease and natural elegance entranced him. They were walking to the house. It seemed his father was willing to talk to these unhallowed men.

"How many of you are there in Sherwood? And how many can shoot an arrow as you did?" Simon asked.

The day was spent around the great table in the shadowy, malodorous house as Simon talked, apparently with some seriousness, eliciting information of what the outlaws and the forest folk could, or would do, if war came. But he gave them no assurance of his help.

The afternoon light, beaming, shimmering with dust-specks through the room's open door and small casements, grew dimmer. Another supper of fresh-killed game was served, and the earl still talked with Leybourne and with Robin. It was clear he would not leave for Winchelsea till the next morning's light.

That night young Simon lay awake, unable to sleep, his eyes wide, staring at the rafters lit with a full moon's glow through the unshuttered little windows. Cobwebs hung below the thatch like a laundry of diaphanous rags in the pale light.

He sat up, leaning on his elbow, and peered across the room to where the youth called Robin lay. Silently he got up and crept across the floor, then knelt, uncertain what it was he wanted – except to get a closer look at the knotted cord. But of course it was no longer tied to the cross-gartered leg.

Robin opened his eyes, his hand already raising his dagger. He could tell by the silhouette of the well-cut riding robe who was crouching beside him. Slowly, to cause no further alarm, he sat up.

Young Simon nonetheless was startled. Abashed, he muttered, "I'm sorry that I woke you…"

Robin tucked the dagger back into his belt. As Simon Fils said nothing more, he softly asked with a sardonic smile, "What is it that you want to know?"

Embarrassed, Simon shrugged. "I just wanted to see the cord."

Robin stood up, reached into the blousing of his jerkin and drew out the knotted leather lace. Young Simon stood up also.

"If you want to see it," Robin spoke low not to wake the others, "come outside where there's more light.

Outside, the moon, a blurred white dot pinned high above the trees, erased the starlight with bright mist and filled the clearing with a soft illumination.

Robin unwound the cord, letting Simon look at, but not touch, it.

"Each knot is for a different thing?" Simon's peasant nurse, when he was very young, had told him of such mysteries, before the outraged countess had hastily dismissed her.

Robin nodded. From a straight length of the cord he deftly fashioned a knot, curiously entwined. "This binds the wind. But we wouldn't want to do that just now, would we?" He quickly untied the knot.

"I've heard of love knots…?" Simon asked leadingly.

"Have you?" Robin replied as if humoring an infant.

"Show me," Simon begged, licking his lips nervously.

The curly-headed lad showed him a handsome interlacing of the cord.

"That... will bring a lady's love?" Simon asked. He was fascinated. "You use it... it truly works?"

With a twinkle in his eye, Robin shrugged. "It may keep a lover faithful. To attract... I've never needed it."

"You can have anyone you want?" Simon's curiosity was past control. All night he had been ruminating on his nurse's wicked tales of the lecherous freedoms enjoyed by the leaders of such folk as this.

"What are you asking?" the lad replied with some reserve.

"Several at a time, I've heard. How do you do it?" His information from his nurse suggested orgies, preferably held in churchyards late on Saturday nights. Had he learned what his proper tutors taught half so well as he recalled his nurse's lubricious tales of the Old Faith, he would have been a scholar.

Robin said nothing, but wrapped the cord around his hand and dropped it down his jerkin's neck again.

"It would almost be worth it." Young Simon was beginning to perspire from his own imaginings. "I've heard what you do on your sabbaths."

"What we do at our sabbaths is no concern of yours," Robin said curtly. Then he added with a sly smile, "Unless you'd like to wear the lace yourself? I could give it to you. Take it," he drew out the thong and held it out to the Christian youth. "You'll learn the answers to our secrets, and satisfy your every itch. Or does our weird daunt you?"

Tempted, entranced, Simon looked at the dark eyes and at the hand dangling the knotted cord, as if weighing the offer. But he shook his head.

"You're frightened?" Robin's tone was sneering.

Simon asked breathlessly, "Aren't you?"

The youth shrugged off the question.

"When's your time? How much longer do you have?" Simon pressed.

Robin watched him narrowly, but did not speak.

"They'll tie you up and cut you, and they'll drain your blood," Simon whispered tauntingly, remembering the lurid endings of the nurse's tales. "And when you're nearly dead, they'll strangle you with that cord you wear. It's your bond to them, so that you're reminded..." He stopped, struck hard across his face.

"I don't mock your god, suffering on his cross. Don't you mock me!" Robin turned and strode back to the house.

"Pagan! Blasphemer!" young Simon called after him, his voice sounding hollow and strange in the settling fog of the glade.

Robin turned in the white haze and bowed with his elegant flourish. "Call me what you please. But when your father dies, then you'll see hallowed bleeding! The folk will be sated with his blood."

The earl and his son left at dawn the next morning, riding swiftly on toward Winchelsea. Young Simon, his cheek purple with a large bruise, was silent, sullen all the way. To his father's question as to how he came to be so marked, he lied. "I went outside for a piss and fell down in the dark."

When they reached the port, found the captain of the little ship that had brought them, and were safely out to sea, the earl at last asked his son directly, "What's troubling you, Simon? Were you fighting with someone?"

The youth shook his head. Then suddenly he blurted, "Father, you must have nothing to do with those men of the forest!"

The earl sighed. "I much doubt I'll ever go to England again. But if war comes, they could be of some service."

"Truly, you won't go back?"

"Judging from what I saw at the Parliament, no."

Still young Simon was so distressed he spoke again. "Father, if a man, a Christian, should suffer a pagan death, would his soul go to Hell?"

Simon was astonished by the question but, recalling his son's interest in Robin, he guessed he and the forest youth must have had a fight. He gave the question careful thought, sifting his penitential late-night readings of theology through the years, before he answered. "If the death were forced upon the Christian, I think not. The Lord judges our intentions. Augustine wrote that women who are truly chaste, though they suffer rape, remain chaste in the eyes of our Lord. A man overpowered probably commits no sin." He studied his son. "The lad called Robin troubles you?"

Gripping the ship's railing with both his hands, Simon Fils stared into the water. Robin's last words rang in his ears.

Simon rested his arm across his son's shoulder. "Those men dwell in the horror from which Christ's sacrifice redeems us," he said quietly.

Simon Fils still gazed at the water. His shoulder, beneath his father's hand, trembled.

After a time his father asked plainly, "You had a fight with Robin?"

Simon Fils nodded, then blurted, "He thinks he's a god!"

Simon laughed outright. "He can shoot an arrow through a rusted pot, but can he raise the dead?"

Young Simon turned his head and tried to smile. "I know your soul is good, father. So good that I'm not worthy to be your son. I believe no harm of the spirit can touch you. Yet I still beg... have nothing to do with those men."

Simon moved his hand to press the hand clutching the railing. Never before had his second son spoken to him with such love and concern. He could not meet his eyes. "I wish I were... truly as you say. And that I'd shown more love for you. You'll yet make me glad you are my son." Leaning his elbows on the railing, he took a deep breath of sea air and watched the coast of England growing narrow, no more than a dark line to his sight. "No, I won't go back. I'm not the man to do the work the Lord requires there," he said at last. Meeting his son's troubled eyes, he smiled with sunny ease, "We'll go to the East and, God willing, we'll reclaim Jerusalem."

# Chapter four

## THE YOUNG BARONS
### 1263

Simon prepared to leave for Palestine. If he had any lingering thought of England and her plight, his visit had convinced him that the English lords were worthless. Though Leybourne and his pathetic outcast villeins moved his pity, outlaws could not be the foundation for a new order.

On his return to Paris, King Louis summoned him and they met in the garden off the royal chambers: that garden where the child-king and Simon his child-page had played at Arthur and Sir Kaye, where Simon had broken his betrothal to the Princess of Flanders and where not so long ago, as Regent of France he had pondered an empty future and decided to take service with King Henry again. The garden was saturated with memories for him, but today it was only a convenient place of privacy, its herbs withered, its last roses too chilled by the autumn air to yield their perfume. Today all memories were set into a coffer and the lid closed tight. It was the promise of the future that held Simon's mind.

"Come to Palestine," he urged Louis, his eyes sparkling with clear happiness. He had planned a crusade with Louis before, but had been detained by King Henry. Then, in Egypt, Louis lost nearly all the forty-thousand men he led.

For Louis, the recapture of Jerusalem might wipe away his grief. For Simon, return to the East at last might undo the cardinal error of his life – having left the Christian kingdom in Palestine when apparently only he could keep its warring factions unified.

At the time he had thought the credit given him preposterous. But events had proved the worth of his carefully groomed friendships with all factions, his absence a catastrophe. As acting viceroy, appointed by Prince Richard, he had contrived, through constant and impartial care, to keep the lords and knightly Orders unified. A task that no one else seemed able to achieve. But the Emperor Frederic had not ratified his commission. Leaving, with the purpose of persuading Frederic, he never had been able to return. In disarray the quarrelsome Christian factions had been overrun, their Kingdom of Jerusalem, protector of pilgrims and Christ's holy shrines for more than a hundred years, had been all but destroyed.

At the core of their souls' healing, for both Simon and Louis, was the return to the East.

"You're free, you have treaties to secure the peace of France. Has this not been your goal since you returned from Acre?" Simon urged.

"It's not my freedom that concerns me now, Simon. It's yours."

"This is the best of times for me! There's nothing in the world to hold me anywhere." His spirit had a lightness; his tone of voice, his dark-bearded face glowed with a peace and hopefulness that Louis never had seen before.

"I fear there is. King Henry has asked me to reopen your trial."

The earl's eyebrows rose in disbelief. "But you told him what you knew. You've agreed to have the case argued again?"

"I cannot refuse him.'

"By Christ's blood, is there no justice!" His rare, bright demeanor darkened as in eclipse.

"Do not swear in my presence, Simon! I'll not have it! I cannot openly deny King Henry what he asks. But delay may serve as well. I give you my word, so far as I am able, you won't need to defend yourself before a court in France on this matter again. But stay at least a year so it may seem to Henry that I'm acting in earnest."

Furious, Simon stared down at the river heaving its slow brown swells below the garden wall. Louis offered his hand in pledge, but Simon ignored it. Without asking leave, he strode out of the garden through the palace door.

"Don't embarrass me by leaving France, Simon!" Louis called after him in a stern tone.

"You needn't worry!" Simon threw back over his shoulder. "I've seen outlaws lately and I've no wish to live like one!"

He left the palace and crossed the Petit Pont, not wanting to go home, not wanting to face Eleanor, who had most of their belongings packed for Palestine.

The air was crisp with autumn's chill. A gust of wind blew along the quay, ruffling his black robe around his black-stockinged legs. Leaning on his cane, he wandered aimlessly along the Rue Saint Jacques then turned away from it, sunk in thought, unmindful of the traffic of students, merchants, housewives and servants going about their day. A hawker of fresh fruit, her apple-laden booth set up between the spider-legs of Saint Severin's wide, crouching buttresses, called out to him, but he heard nothing and saw nothing.

Then someone said close to his ear, "Good Earl you look more troubled than I ever saw you at your trial." The voice issued from under a black hood. The monk threw back his cowl. "May I be of some help?"

"Brother Ambrose," Simon nodded, recognizing the gray-bearded Dominican he knew from Louis' scholarly suppers. The friar was a devoted follower of Joachim, whose teachings had been banned. Simon gave a bitter laugh. "Yes, father, perhaps you can explain to me the workings of Our Lord's justice."

"This is not yet Our Lord's kingdom. Expect no justice here. Ah," the old man sighed, "but such answers don't satisfy. My cell isn't far. Come, let us talk."

Simon went with the Dominican and entered the shadowy, vaulted hall of the friary on the Rue Jacob. Down a corridor was Ambrose's narrow cell, littered with unbound texts and scrolls. They sat at a small table and shared a beaker of cheap, sour wine.

Simon told of the threatened renewal of his trial, and of Louis' injunction against his leaving for the East.

"Good Earl, the righteous, holy war for the Kingdom of the Lord is no longer in Palestine. I thought you understood this." Ambrose's steely gray gaze peered into Simon's eyes. "It is here, in Paris. And above all in England."

"Perhaps. But I no longer have any part in that war," Simon replied in polite withdrawal from the subject.

The theologian was not about to be denied so easily. "Do you imagine that your service to Our Lord is left for you to choose?" he smiled wryly. "There are many signs. Signs from the heavens. ... I have word, just received, that the palace at Westminster has been struck by lightening and burned to the ground."

"This is a sign no doubt," Simon smiled patiently at the credulous old man, "that Henry will extract new taxes and spend much time with his drawing tablets. And, I predict, Peter of Savoy will arrange his percentage from the drapers' guild."

Seeing the earl was not disposed to listen to his counsel, Ambrose changed his approach. "You obtained a letter, and you took it to England and read it..."

"You know of that..."

"What concerns us we know quickly."

"Then you know, too, how coldly I was received."

"Be that as it may, our newly chosen Father in Rome is surely aware of the letter's contents. Give the letter to us. It will strengthen our cause."

"Gladly. There's no more that I can do with it."

They left the friary and Ambrose accompanied Simon to his house. Taking the letter of Pope Alexander and tucking it within his black cloak, the Dominican said at parting, "It doesn't surprise me that you find your way to the East obstructed. Don't be of angry mind, good Earl. What our Father in Heaven will have, will be done. When you see such unexpected walls rise up before you, or doors opening where there seemed walls before, you should perceive the Hand of God."

As Christmastide ended, King Henry, seeing that any retrial would not open soon, left France at last and returned to view the cinders at Westminster.

The eldest of the Montfort sons, Simon and Henry, were now with Edward in Gascony, but they came to Paris. The prince was planning to renew his campaign in Wales.

"Father, we've come to ask your leave to follow Edward," Henry said with hesitation.

"You don't need my leave. You're fully knighted and you've pledged your liege to him," Simon told them, somewhat surprised.

"Truly father, in serving England we feel that we're serving your enemies."

"England is not my enemy, Henry. For that matter, it is to England's Crown that I still owe my liege."

Guy, sitting on the window seat, listening, spoke up. "If I may say so plain, father, I believe King Henry is your mortal enemy, and hence ours."

Simon looked to him with a frown. "Guy, do you recall an occasion when we heard Archbishop Boniface celebrate the Mass?"

Guy let out a short, derisive laugh. "The sacristan had to prompt him through nearly every word."

"Boniface is an evil man, an extortioner, a brute and an untutored priest. Yet you took communion from his hand."

Guy shrugged and grudgingly admitted, "He is a priest. Consecrated."

"You don't judge the office by the man who is administering it at the moment."

Forced, Guy shook his head.

"Your brothers have bound themselves to serve England in the person of Prince Edward. What they feel for King Henry is of no consequence. Even for myself, as my oath of liege binds me to serve the Crown, though I may despise the man who holds it, I may not condemn him."

"It looks, father, as if he might no longer be God's *chosen temporal arm.*" Henry's tone was arch but his expression serious. "The messenger who brought us news of Wales said there are signs and wonders now in England."

"You'll tell me next that the palace's burning surely is a sign of the fall of the Plantagenets? Let other men put faith in such auguries. King Henry is England's king. Henry, you asked my permission to continue serving Edward, and you have it. Both you and Simon owe your liege to the prince and should go."

"You may resist it, father," Henry said with quiet earnestness, "but I believe you'll be in England again before you go to Palestine."

Simon looked at his eldest son sharply. "You're being impertinent. You know my intentions."

In England, King Henry was not so sanguine as the earl about the signs and wonders. He was terrified. The friars in their preaching declared the lightning bolt that destroyed the palace was a stroke from the Almighty. A judgment against Henry for breaking his oaths to the Provisions. And for his cruelty to the Earl of Leicester.

Henry called a meeting of the lords, announcing that the Council, which had all but ceased to function, would be restored. Solemnly he again renewed his oath to the Provisions. But he filled his new Council not with the Parliament's choices, but with his own clerks and his half-brothers of Lusignan.

Signs of Divine Wrath continued. What had been tried by fire was tried by ice. The Thames at Westminster froze solidly from bank to bank, a thing unknown in living memory. Friars promptly claimed the English Channel itself would freeze to make a bridge for the Great Earl's return.

King Henry wrote to King Louis, begging him to intercede for him to offer Simon peace.

Louis summoned Simon to his chamber.

"If Henry truly means me peace," Simon replied, his eyes narrowed in distrust, "let him first show that he has learned to keep his oaths by casting out the Lusignan from his new Council, and observing the Provisions' stipulation that the Council be chosen by the Parliament of lords and elected commoners."

The earl's answer was sent to Henry. The King of England kept the Lusignan and went on suffering from the freeze.

But Henry's offer released Simon from further threat of trial. As he prepared to close his Paris household, gathering his finances and equipment for Palestine, a steady traffic of petitioners from England came to his door: friars, displaced sheriffs, guildsmen, even the masters and captains of the Cinque Ports. Simon's response to all was cold and skeptical.

Then one afternoon, as he was arranging with a clerk a transfer of funds from the Knights Hospitalers' banking house in Paris to the Order's office at Acre, four young lords arrived, begging to speak with him. First among them was elegant young Gilbert de Clare whose deceased father, Richard the Earl of Gloucester, had done the most at Oxford to devise the Provisions, and later had betrayed their very essence. Next was John de Warenne, Earl of Surrey and Sussex, whose father too had died in the sweep of Lusignan poisonings that eventually killed Clare. After him in rank was the sixteen-year-old Robert Ferrers, heir to the earldom of Derby, and John Giffard, an able-looking young knight from the Welsh borderlands.

The four were shown into the paneled room. They found the earl no longer dressed in his accustomed black but in the red-crossed white woolen robe of a crusader.

De Clare, just twenty-two, was as delicate and beautiful as his father had been, with flowing auburn curls and a lavish way of dressing to display his charm. A long scar creased his cheek, gained at the battle of Ewloe when Simon, with a force of mercenaries of his own, had come from his post as ambassador to France to rescue Edward and his friends from Llewellyn.

Gilbert bowed low to the earl and crossed himself at sight of the red crusader's cross. Warenne, a year older than Clare and a cousin of King Henry, went down on one knee, as did Giffard and Ferrers, then Clare as well.

"My Lord of Leicester we've not met since that day when you were taken to the Tower, yet I have hope you remember me not too shamefully," the scarred, exquisite youth asked.

"Of course. There was no shame to you then. I asked no one to take my part," Simon said earnestly. He gestured for them to rise, and smiled benignly, "I remember, Gilbert, how you got that mark bringing down a Welshman thrice your size." The youth also jostled thought of the father, the young Richard de Clare whom he had allowed into his small circle of friends, but who had become his bitter enemy. "You're now Earl of Gloucester and Hereford..."

Clare, proud that the earl remembered his boyhood feat in battle, winced nonetheless. "No, my lord, I'm not yet an earl. The king claims I'm in wardship still, though I'm past the age of twenty-one. My mother-in-law controls my holdings for the

Crown." When Gilbert was fourteen his father had been forced to make him marry Henry's niece, a hated Lusignan. It was that insult above all that spurred his father's rage, and the onset of the lords' revolt that produced the Provisions.

Ferrers, small, and nervous as a sparrow, blurted, "Lord Earl, my estates are suffering as well."

"You have my pity," Simon replied coolly, determined to be unmoved.

"Good Earl, as you were my father's friend, I beg you, hear the whole of it!" Clare pled.

A pained look darted across Simon's face. But the youth was insistent and he felt some sadness for him. He dismissed the banking clerk and motioned for the youths to sit on the broad, cushioned window-seat as he sat in his chair.

"I held a meeting of my neighbors in Gloucestershire," Clare began. "We chose a sheriff of our own, as the Provisions grant. Your cousin, the lord Peter de Montfort, has been much with us in this. When our sheriff first went to meet the Wittenmote of folk on one of my estates, we went in arms to guard him. But it was not the expected royal sheriff and bailiffs who met us. The king pitched against us two hundred of his mercenary knights. They dragged our man away and trampled him to death beneath their horses' feet, then hung his corpse from a tree as warning for us all."

"These were the knights given to Henry by his treaty with France to fight the Saracens in Sicily!" Warrenne cried. "See how they're used!"

"As I knew they would be," Simon remarked calmly. He had warned the lords when the army first was raised, but they had not believed him.

"My lord, come back and lead us!" Ferrers begged.

His expression severe, Simon studied the four. "I took the first of those mercenaries to England for the Parliament's defense, and warned the lords of Henry's intentions. I was called a liar and abandoned to punishment. Nonetheless, I returned recently, at peril of my life, to read to the Parliament Pope Alexander's affirmation of the Provisions. What I got for my effort was cold stares. Now I can do nothing for England, I am signed with the Cross."

John Giffard spoke for the first time. "Lord Earl, the whole of Gloucestershire has risen against King Henry's men. Your cousin Peter leads them, even as we speak. We've come at his bidding to beg you to return."

"King Henry cowed the great barons," Gilbert de Clare pressed, "and he duped us into leaving for the tournaments in France. He kept us out of the land for as long as he could, knowing we wouldn't stand for what he's doing."

Giffard urged, "We're true soldiers. We've taken up arms. Lord Earl, we pray, be our commander!"

"What forces do you have?" Simon asked skeptically.

Warenne brought from his robe a petition and handed it to him.

The earl unrolled it and read it carefully while the four watched intent for any sign their plea was gaining ground. Dangling from the scroll's lower edge like coined fringe were the wax seals of the Earls of Oxford and Lincoln and the Bishops of London, Worcester, Chichester and Lincoln. But its muster of several hundred names was chiefly not the senior barony. Instead it gave a lengthy count of sons of noble families, and clerics. Nearly all of Edward's young companions, called the Bachelory, had signed. Prince Edward's friends, rescued at Ewloe, had long been Simon's partisans, though the prince himself had defected to the king's side when, in 1260, war seemed imminent.

With exaggerated claim Gilbert pointed out, "Those who are with us have been tried in more fierce battling than their fathers ever saw. We've matched lances with the best schooled knights at tourney and swords with Llewellyn's savages."

"We've made ourselves a fitting force for you to lead." Warenne's eyes sought the earl's. "All England, excepting a few old forsworn cowards, is ready to rise. Everything is changed! We're meeting at Oxford to plan our campaign. We beg you to come as our leader!"

Simon studied the faces of the four desperate young men, then he said in a low voice, reluctantly, "I will go. But to do no more than see the nature of this change you claim."

"The Lord's guidance be with you," Warenne rose from the window seat and knelt, kissing the hem of Simon's red-crossed robe. The others knelt and did the same.

Embarrassed, Simon raised them up. "Make ready for me as you will. I'll judge for myself what can and what cannot be done."

That night he told the countess of his decision to return to England one more time.

Eleanor's face was hard with anger. "It is a madman who, being burnt, puts his hand into the fire again and again."

"I've hoped to do something of true worth," he said gently. "The future of Christian rule is balancing between mercy and pride, with Aquinas' weight heavy on the side of pride. If a parliament of common men can yet prevail, pride may be subdued for a time."

Two months later, at the end of April the town of Oxford was alive with preparations for what seemed a very large convening of Dominicans. But the inns' stable yards were not filled with the mules and jennets of clerics. In the stalls stood destriers.

Black-cloaked, hooded, faceless figures were in the streets in multitude, gathering in groups, talking animatedly, moving with the self-conscious stealth of conspirators. Students and shopkeepers welcomed the strange monks. There was an air of excitement, of a welling tide brimming a seawall about to burst.

Southward, on the coast, beneath the castle of the honour of Warenne at Pevensey harbor, a ship came in at nightfall and was met by a small band of heavily armed, black-hooded men.

The Earl of Leicester stepped ashore. Wrapped in an enveloping black, hooded cloak, with little sign of his limp he strode across the quay to where the armed guard held a powerful and swift horse for him. His son Guy followed, also hooded in black.

"Heaven keep you, father," the man holding the horse murmured as he offered the stirrup.

The earl pressed his son Simon's hand. "May the Lord guide us all," he said low. He mounted and looked among the other cowled figures waiting in the dark. "Is my son Henry here?"

"Yes, father," the familiar, gentle voice of his eldest son answered from beneath a hood. "And John de Warenne, John Giffard and Roger Clifford."

Simon acknowledged his escort, then they all turned their mounts and took the road north, spurring the fresh coursers to a gallop.

The night was spellbound. Word of Leicester's coming had been whispered across the land. Everywhere along his route faces peered from cottage windows. Field gates barring short-cut paths were opened by hurrying, dim figures. A ferry barge lay ready. Changes of mounts were made quickly and several times. Lights burned in the churches. Prayers were whispered. The songs of the great Earl were sung. During the long passage from the coast, the faith the common folk had spun round the name of Simon de Montfort enwrapped the man himself. The leader who would vanquish the oppressor had returned at last. He was moving through the country and the country rose to new, heightened, dangerous spirit as he passed. The Angel of the New Era, bidden by the common man to reap, was now amongst his people.

When dawn broke, the riders rested, hidden from daylight at a farm near Guildford. They went on as darkness closed, black-cloaked figures hurtling through the night.

Just after dawn of the second day of travel, the earl and his guard reached the Dominican refectory at Oxford. It was here, in this selfsame hall that the Provisions had been born. Here that Simon had rescued the fruit of the lords' and clerics' work, inscribed only on erasable wax tablets. Led by Clare, all the lords, with the single exception of Simon, had abandoned everything for unwise pursuit of the Lusignan, and had found poisoning and death as they besieged the king's half-brothers at Winchester.

It was here, working alone but for a few clerics, in the devastating absence of the lords, that Simon had the Provisions transcribed, published and sent to every shire. The Provisions required representatives to be elected by the common folk, and sent to meet with the lords and newly chosen Councilors in a Parliament with powers to control the king.

It was the first time such a government was seen on earth, and it was Simon, Earl of Leicester, who made it a reality.

And he protected the infant government, seizing and provisioning the king's castles and England's ports to resist the foreign armies Henry tried to bring. Repeatedly armies were raised to defeat the Provisions and, facing the Earl's precautions, were forced to disband. Only when Simon resigned and left England, disgusted at the refusal of the barons to extend their new won rights to commoners, did King Henry find the means to destroy the new government, and then only by diverting the army Louis gave him to fight Saracens in Sicily. Even that last time, Simon did what he could to divert the threat and warn the Parliament, at mortal risk.

For Simon, Oxford and the cause of the Provisions reeked of past achievements betrayed and abandoned. Yet still had hooks embedded in his soul.

On this early morning the Dominican refectory was filled with black-cloaked men who had been waiting through the night. They spoke to one another in hushed, expectant tones, the tension far too palpable for any to have slept.

In the tall rafters, where the lords' flags, in those momentous days of 1258, had hung in vivid close-packed files, the first pale yellow sunbeams were stretching through an emptiness dotted with bright motes of dust, as if this morning were no different from any other but for the mass of murmuring black hoods below.

There was a clattering of hooves on the paving outside. All speaking in the refectory ceased. The air itself seemed held in a long, tense pause. The spell began to spin.

Black-hooded men entered, making their way among the black figures who parted to let them pass then closed again, engulfing them, black hoods among black, indistinguishable save by the dust of their travel.

As the new arrivals moved through, several in their path pulled back their hoods and bared their faces: Richard de Gray, the Provisions' castellan of Dover; Gilbert de Clare; Hugh Despensar; the Earls Robert de Vere of Oxford and John de Lacey of Lincoln;

Nicholas Seagrave Simon's own steward-general with his son and liege knights of Leicester, men Simon had led to Palestine so many years ago.

No one spoke a word.

As the travelers entered, a door at the front of the room, leading to the abbot's chambers, opened. Through it poured a stream of mitered bishops in their sacred robes. Ten bishops: of Worcester, London, Lincoln, Bath, Coventry, Chichester, Salisbury, Chester, Exeter and Durham. They ranged in a half circle at the fore. The dusty figures made their way to them and the foremost knelt.

The Bishop of London, drawing the kneeling man's hood back, placed his hand upon the head of tousled black, gray-streaked hair.

"May the Grace of God be upon you, Simon Montfort, Earl of Leicester. And may He who has shaped the heavens and the earth fill you with strength." The bishop made the sign of the Cross in blessing.

Simon arose, then turned and faced the assembly. Letting his black cloak fall from his shoulders, he stood before them in the white robe of a crusader, the red cross blazoned on his chest. "I come to you," his voice resounded down the utter silence of the hall, "as you see... signed with the Holy Cross."

There was a sound, a tumult in the hall, cries erupted like a cataract breaking its impounding and shaking the earth as it gushed. On and on the shouting rose, higher and louder, the walls and the arched ceiling ringing till the noise was deafening. And it did not subside.

At the force he saw before him, Simon stood astounded. He shut his eyes and the rushing din flooded over him. He breathed it. It raised him like a roaring incoming tide, buoying him in its swell. He brought his hands up.

Miraculously, the room fell quiet at his gesture, a vast, living force, calmed or roused at his voice and touch. He scanned the mass of black dotted with faces turned toward him, faces featureless to his nearsighted eyes, yet whose very breath was held and stilled, waiting for him to speak.

His voice caught in his throat, hardly above a whisper at first. "I've seen the bad faith of the English, and I've turned my back on it to fight and die in the Holy Land."

Had he been audible there would have been bellowing protest. But only now his voice grew, filled the room, as if fed on the straining, listening expectation of the multitude.

"But I'll as willingly die fighting bad Christians here! For the freedom of the Holy Church… and England!"

He spread out his hands as before him the black sea flecked with faces sent forth a roar, a cheer, sustained, heightening like the blast of a joyful chord from a massive pipe organ played by his touch and magnified.

He raised his hands for silence again, and received it. "Let us swear to the Provisions! And swear, as we did here five years ago, to count all those who will not keep them, as our mortal enemies!"

The words resounded in that room where they first were offered by the Earl de Clare. They were met by a ringing, echo-doubling cheer. The text was known to all, the response only was needed. Simon raised his right hand high in pledge. "Upon the head of God I do so swear!"

At his leading gesture, the single massive voice of the crowd replied, reverberating downward through the floor into the very earth, and upward through the rafters and high gables to the sky. "Upon the Head of God we do so swear!"

In his grip Simon felt a force, a power such as he had never known. Had Ambrose and the friars spoken truly? Was this indeed what the Lord meant him to do? Here was a tool stronger than any he had ever thought to touch. He had no notion of how far it reached beyond the refectory's walls, beyond Oxford, to England's very borders and shores. But he did not doubt that he knew how to use it.

# Chapter Five

## THE COMMON UPRISING
### 1263

In the private chamber of Oxford's Provost Thomas Cantaloup, the Bishop Walter's brother, the leaders of the burgeoning revolt met: the bishops and the earls, the young lords Warenne, Clare, Ferrers and many more, even Henry of Alemaine, Prince Richard's son, and Roger Leybourne from the forest of the Weald. Still wrapped in black, their hoods thrown back, they waited for the Earl of Leicester's orders.

Looking among their familiar faces, Simon asked, "Where is Peter de Montfort, my cousin?"

"He's in Herefordshire, good Earl," Warenne answered. "He holds the king's sheriff and the Bishop Aigueblanche at siege."

"There are few I'd rather see discomfited than the king's bad counselor Aigueblanche." The Earl's lips curved in a broad smile. It was Aigueblanche who urged Henry to reach for the Sicilian Crown. That ambition pitched the land to dire debt, requiring the king's nastiest proceedings to raise taxes. And that, in turn, caused the revolt that created the Provisions.

Simon turned to Gilbert de Clare. "How are matters in Gloucester?"

"King Henry's mercenaries hold the city," Gilbert confessed.

Simon looked toward his own sons. "Henry, Simon, take with you our knights of Leicester. Go and reclaim Kenilworth. Supply and garrison the castle in the name of the Provisions, should our partisans need a safe retreat."

He turned to Ferrers, heir to the earldom of Derby. "Robert, go to those lands that are rightly yours and raise as many men as you can to beset the royal sheriff. Do all you can to have King Henry's remaining mercenaries drawn to Derbyshire. We want no reinforcements free to send to Gloucester and the other points we strike."

Simon was settling into his command, the rationale of his strategy unfolding to his trained mind.

"Richard," he turned to Gray, "take the men you have with you and visit each of the Cinque Ports. Reclaim Dover and the other ports. Replace the castellans on grounds you act for the Provisions, which the king himself just lately reconfirmed."

He turned to the others. "With the ports held, we have good chance that Henry will receive no help from abroad. Gilbert," he rested his hand on Clare's shoulder, "take your knights to the southeast also. Block the road from London to the ports. Leybourne, go with Clare and set your archers to harass the Dover Road."

He looked among them all. "I'll march west to Hereford and Gloucester. Once the cities on the Severn River are secure, I'll complete England's pending treaty with Llewellyn and his Welsh."

Clare and Giffard's expressions hardened at such a plan for their longtime enemy. They were near enough that Simon saw the aggrieved looks. He regarded them sharply. "We and Llewellyn, suffer from a common wrong – King Henry's abuses. We cannot afford to ignore any ally, or risk the diverting of our strength to counter raids in the west. Warenne, Clifford, Giffard, Seagrave, my son Guy, and the rest will come with me."

He turned then to the bishops. "We must send a delegation to King Henry to state our cause. We seek full reinstatement of the elected Parliament, a true Council, and an honest Chancellor and Justiciar to guarantee justice. We must have honest sheriffs, recommended by the people, to replace his marauders. And faithful native-born castellans, not the foreigners he's appointed as if no Englishman was to be trusted."

"Simon, I'd go with you," Bishop Walter, the earl's oldest and closest friend apart from Louis, insisted. "I've had my fill of words.

My vows as priest forbid my handling a sword, but there's nothing to prevent me from wielding a battle axe."

Simon placed his hand on the bishop's burly shoulder. "Then come with me," he grinned, "I'll be glad for your prayers by my side, even more than for your axe."

He turned to the Bishops of Chichester and London, Stephen Berkstead and Henry of Sandwich. "Carry our words to King Henry," he said earnestly.

Then, looking from one face to another in the room, his gaze rested on Henry of Alemaine. He studied the thoughtful, intelligent young man. Prince Richard's son had balked at swearing to the Provisions five years ago, asking to consult his father first. Despite his hesitancy, he had been made to swear. Simon was amazed but glad to see him. "Henry," he said after some consideration, "I'll not have you come west with us. You can best serve with the bishops representing our cause. Your presence itself will be a loud testament at Court."

Having completed his instructions, Simon looked about the room, then raised his hands. "At ringing of the matins bell tomorrow, we march to bring back England's avowed government!"

At matins the next morning, bells all over Oxford rang in wild clangor, a jubilation like the merrymaking of a hundred weddings. The somber convocation of friars was transformed. The streets of the town were a whirl of brilliant colors: ruffling mantles draping high-spirited destriers, flags snapping their heraldry in the gusty breeze, surcoats and liveries everywhere sifting through throngs of well-wishing students. Horses pranced, ears pricked with excitement at the familiar hiss and jingle of their riders' chain mail. Sunlight glinted from steel helms hooked at saddlebows and from the points of pikes.

In the field beyond the River Cherwell, riders gathered around the banners of their appointed leaders: the unicorn of Clare, the lion-dappled flag of Henry de Montfort, the black, horseshoe-spangled flag of Robert Ferrers, and the white flag with the fork-tailed red lion rampant of the Earl Montfort.

Seagrave had brought from Leicester's stud the most noble and finest trained of the earl's destriers, and the earl's old, sturdy helm and shield and suit of mail. Simon, bearded as a prophet, dressed in mail beneath his red-crossed robe and mounted on his magnificent white horse, appeared truly the arm of the Lord's vengeance.

Stories of the Oxford meeting, embellished at each telling, spread quickly through the shire, then eddied out across the land a day ahead of Simon. "The Earl commands that the king's sheriffs be overthrown!" "We must drive out the foreign leeches!" The wave of rousing words rushed on as fast as swift horses could spread it. Every hope was changed to a command. Commands with the speed of wings and the sharp edge of knives and swords.

Before the armies moved from Oxford's meadow, the first fully concerted villein uprisings broke out. Where there had been riots and disorder, now there was deliberate, fierce slaughter. Attack was made upon a manor of Peter of Savoy. Then houses belonging to William de Valence and his brother Aimery de Lusignan, Bishop-elect of Winchester, were sacked and their defenders killed with pitchforks and knives. Holdings of Savoy's brother Boniface, the Archbishop of Canterbury, and of Giles Argentine, the king's longtime Poitouvin aide, were burnt to the ground. Everywhere, servants and agents of the king were dragged into the streets and murdered. Houses were emptied by loot-seeking mobs. Like a caged, tormented bear let loose, the common folk rampaged, ravaging, burning and murdering.

In public squares Franciscan monks inveighed against King Henry and bestowed the Sacrament upon the frenzied mobs. "The time is here! Is now!" the friars preached. "Power is given unto Him who Reaps! He shall take peace from the earth! There shall be great death and tribulation! The Way shall be made clear for Our Lord's Kingdom on Earth!"

There had been scattered and sporadic fighting before Simon arrived, but now the uprising swelled into engulfing chaos, mad, ecstatic, a holiday of blood.

Simon led his portion of the army west. His lion flag and Bishop Walter's cross on a staff went at the head of the cavalcade, brilliant in the morning sun. Friars and students crowded the roadside, strewing spring flowers in the Earl's path and singing songs in his praise.

The march encountered the first smoking ruin at Whitney. Frightened faces, refugees fleeing eastward to the coast, peeped from a tented wagon drawn over to the shoulder of the road to let the long double-column of knights and their foot soldiers pass.

John de Warenne, riding near Simon, remarked with a hard smile and a jerk of his head toward the wagon, "I'd as soon be an infidel in Rome as a Poitouvin in England today."

Simon didn't answer. He was not pleased with what he saw.

At each village the army passed the devastation grew worse. Crazed bands of villeins followed the march cheering, tossing their grim trophies in the air: a silver tray, a velvet hat, a severed hand. Great houses were in flames or smoldering.

"Henry has abused his people for too long." Walter Cantaloup pitched his voice low, answering Simon's look of disgust. "He reaps the whirlwind he's sown."

At Hereford the army found no besiegers camped at the city's walls. The gate was open, the earl's men rode in. At the castle they found Peter de Montfort and several knights emerging from the tower door. Peter was dragging out the sheriff, disarmed and bound. Behind him, his knights had the bailiffs firmly tied, lying like tossed bundles in the carpeting of reeds on the keep's floor. As he caught sight of the earl and bishop at the head of knights arriving at the bailey gate, Peter went down on one knee, forcing the sheriff down to his knees also.

Simon dismounted, went to his cousin and raised him up, embracing him and grinning broadly. "We've come in time to see your victory. God's blessing may indeed be upon us."

Peter concealed as best he could his flood of emotion. He had not believed that Simon ever would come back. When he could speak, he gestured toward the tower and said simply, "I've set a garrison. I thought to hold the sheriff and his bailiffs in a stronger place. We took the keep at Eardisley. It's more secure."

"Good. Do as you see fit. You command here." Simon answered in the same, practical manner. He knew his cousin well, that when his feelings were engaged he had no words for them. "Where's the Archbishop Aigueblanche? We were told he was here."

"He's in the cathedral, saying an interminable Mass. He thinks we've come to martyr him like Becket." With a curt laugh Peter nodded toward the tall, ornate edifice of stone nearby.

"We won't give him that happiness," Simon replied, his strong hand fondly pressing Peter's hand. He motioned to Roger Clifford, Seagrave, his son Guy and several knights to follow him.

Before the cathedral's gilded high altar the gaunt Provençal priest, King Henry's advisor for more than twenty years, stood in his jeweled and gold-embroidered cope, with all the black-cowled monks of Hereford attending his Mass. The painted vaulting and stone-tracery windows rang with their sonorous *Kyrie*. "Lord have mercy, Christ have mercy." The jingling sound of knights' chain mail and crunch of steel riding-slippers approached down the long nave. Bishop Aigueblanche stood with his back turned, the heavy gold thread-work of his cope shimmering as he trembled, murmuring the chant with his monks.

The Earl and knights strode down the nave.

The monks went on with their singing, their pitch rising with each cadence. *Kyrie eleison*, "Lord have mercy." No one moved from his place. The armed men walked through the choir. The incantation spiraled higher, *Kyrie eleison! Christe eleison!*

The Earl reached the altar. Putting out his hand, he gripped the bishop's shoulder. And the monks burst from their bleak *Kyrie* into the joyful *Sanctus* and the *Benedictus*, "Holy, holy, holy. Blessed is He who comes in the Name of the Lord!"

The quaking Provençal was led from the cathedral. His monks came streaming after the Earl and knights, through the stone porch's wide door with their cowls thrown back, their faces beaming with triumph.

Simon handed Aigueblanche to Peter. "Here, cousin. Send the bishop with the sheriff to Eardisley, before his own monks grant the martyrdom he fears."

Leaving Peter in command, the next morning Simon's army marched from Hereford, doubling east to Gloucester and the Severn River. As they neared the city, word reached them the king's mercenaries had been withdrawn to protect London.

The gate of the city of Gloucester's wooden palisade stood open. The earl's army entered without challenge, as at Hereford. But at the castle in the center of the town the portcullis was down. As the column of knights passed through narrow Castle Street toward the tower's gate, arrows suddenly flew from the loop windows of the barbican. Simon's horse shied as a shaft ricocheted from the cobbles near its feet. Simon held his mount steady, then backed against the advance of his men, forcing the compressed vanguard to buckle to the shelter of a side street.

Townspeople leaned from the windows of houses and waved from their shop doors shouting, "Long live the Provisions!" "Death to the sheriffs!" and "Blessed is the Avenging Angel of the Lord!"

Simon scanned the blur of the cheering crowd. He called to them, "If you're with us, then bring picks and shovels! And strong men to wield them! We'll tear out Gloucester Castle by its root!"

In moments the street was filling with men bringing tools. At Simon's command a makeshift barricade of carts and planks was built across Castle Street as shield from the castle's archers. Behind it diggers set to work, prying out cobbles, then shoveling a great gap in the roadbed beneath. By evening a tunnel had been dug under the street, burrowing toward the foundation of the barbican.

All the next day, by the light of clay rush lamps the tunnel was extended and enlarged. A line of men sent pots, buckets and baskets full of earth up to the surface where carts with teams of oxen waited to carry the debris away. By the same line, sturdy wooden beams went down into the tunnel. The sappers dug deep and wide beneath the castle gate, bracing the heavy masonry above with the beams until a bridge of wood spanned and supported the gate's foundation. Beneath the span a pit was dug. Then tinder was passed down the tunnel and cast into the pit. The massive wooden frame on which the barbican now rested was thickly daubed with pitch.

By evening on the second day the tunnel was completed and the tinder in the pit was heaped up to the tarry beams. The sappers left, playing out behind them a long twist of fat-soaked rope. When the last men emerged to the street, Simon called out cheerfully, "Shall we light our oven, lads?" and touched the flame of the torch he held to the end of the greasy rope.

The long wick lit at once. Its orange flame went gaily flickering and spitting down the tunnel. Many minutes passed, then smoke began rising from the tunnel's mouth. At first only a thin stream turning in the air, then more, until a dense gray plume billowed into the street. The tinder in the pit was blazing, its flames lapping the pitch-daubed beams. Smoke began sifting from between the street's cobbles in front of the gate.

Behind the barricade, torches were held high to illuminate the street and the barbican. Simon, his knights and the people of Gloucester watched the orange-lit space intently. Muffled sounds of cracking came from underground.

Towering above the smoke-filled street, glowing in the warm light of the torches, the stone blocks of the barbican very slowly shifted. A long seam drew itself across the building's face, then gaped. As if in a graceful gesture of a dance, the keystone of the gate turned, twisted and leaned down onto the iron portcullis, bending, bulging the iron grill with its ill-balanced weight. Shouts were heard from within as the defense work's archers fled down the loosening, parting steps.

With no more danger from the gate's rooftop, Simon sent several of his knights with torches to the wall, well sheltered far to each side of the sagging gate. They drew their swords.

In the flare-lit smoke billowing up from hot cracks in the street, the blank face of the barbican stood bowing, its parapet leaning far out from its tipped and sunk keystone. Then deep in the earth there was a concussion, a breaking and the roar of rushing flame. The blazing span of timbers had collapsed. The building bowed further and further, and slowly tumbled in a cataract of stones and powdery dust.

As the smoke and haze settled enough to show the crumbled heap of blocks and twisted iron of the vanquished gate, the Earl's knights, with torches and drawn swords, climbed over the rubble and into the castle yard.

Lit by the torch-illumined smoke and dust, the yard appeared vacant. The castle tower was tight shut. Simon ordered his men to withdraw, and set a strong guard by the ruined gate for the remainder of the night.

At the first light of morning Simon ranged his men within the castle's defeated wall. "Will you surrender?" he called to the tower.

"Not to you, traitor! " a voice called from a loop window. "We're loyal to the king!"

Another voice from the roof cried out, "It's you who'll surrender when the king's knights come back!"

"Let them come!" Simon called. "They'll be cast out of England with you!"

He turned to Seagrave, "Bring the ram."

The Earl had ordered a massive log fashioned into a ram and fitted with a wicker arrow screen like a long hood. Twenty men of the town had volunteered to heft the ram. In double file, their free hands bracing the wicker screen over their heads, the men crept like a stiff snake over the tumbled blocks of the gate.

Arrows hissed from the tower's roof, lodging in the screen like quills on a hedgehog. Carefully the ram was borne over the rubble heap and reached the level cobbles of the yard. The arrows came faster as the men maneuvered clumsily to face the door. One arrow, arching below the screen, lodged in a man's leg and he fell away. Unprotected, he at once was struck with another, fatal shaft. Not accustomed to warfare, the ram's bearers faltered at the sight. Simon bellowed from the gate, "Keep moving forward! You cannot help him now and only risk yourselves!" The ram swung into position with its blunt head to the door.

"Now!" Simon cried, and the cumbersome double-file of men broke to a run. The ram struck the ironbound oak door with a dull thud. Its bearers drew back and ran again. Arrows from above pelted the screen and pricked another man, who fell shrieking. Bristling with arrow shafts, the ram was drawn back and hit the door a third time. Oak splintered under the blow. Again and again the ram struck despite the archers' assault. By the eighth blow, the door was staved. The Earl and his knights drew their shields from their backs and angled them toward the tower, unsheathed their swords then dashed across the yard and tore away the splintered wood as the ram-bearers retreated.

Within, three bailiffs armed with halberds showed themselves an instant, then fled up a dark, spiraling staircase. The first of Simon's men inside, swords at ready, started up after them. In the blind darkness of the stairwell there was fighting. Swords rang against metal and stone like high-pitched bells reverberating and echoing. The defenders gave ground, leaving a void of quiet blackness.

The Earl's knights moved up the stairs warily. Daylight seeped into the well way around a curve. An arrow struck against the wall as the knight in the lead neared the roof.

"Be fast onto the parapet!" Simon shouted, his voice overlaid with echoes in the stone stair-shaft.

The first men, low behind their shields, swords poised, rushed up the steps and out. The rest poured after them. Running across the roof, they fanned out from the stairs. An arrow at pointblank drove through shield and chain hauberk and a knight fell. But most of the archers in their panic shot wildly. Before they could nock their arrows for a second shot, the knights' blades reached them. In moments the assault was done, the sheriff's men surrendered.

More of Simon's men were still arriving from the stairs. Two of them held the Poitouvin sheriff between them. They had found a door within a turning of the stair, and behind it a chamber with the sheriff cowering with his three halberdiers. The Poitouvin went on his knees before the Earl. "I beg mercy!" he pled.

Gloucester was taken.

# Chapter Six

## BRIDGENORTH
### 1263

The Sheriff of Gloucester and his men were sent to join the other prisoners penned at Eardisley, and a garrison was set in Gloucester's tower with Roger Clifford left in charge. The castle was held in King Henry's name, under the Provisions.

Simon ordered Clifford to confiscate all that was found in the sheriff's possession, and he called upon the free men of Gloucestershire to nominate their choice for a new sheriff.

The next day the Earl and his army marched on, following the Severn River north. Simon had sent couriers ahead to find the Welsh leader Llewellyn for parley. Simon well knew the prince of northern Wales and looked forward to meeting him at Bridgenorth, midway between Gloucester and Chester.

Devastation from the common uprising was everywhere. Abandoned, vandalized and burnt houses. Caravans of refugees. And there were signs of celebration everywhere as well. Crowds followed the Earl Montfort's march. Inns and houses hung out painted wooden replicas of the Earl's red lion flag to declare their support of the people's champion, or perhaps merely to spare themselves from ransacking. The ubiquitous sign of the red lion rampant made it appear Simon was resident in every village, and on each town's major street.

At Worcester the monks of the cathedral led out the whole population to greet their Bishop Walter and the Earl. It was nightfall when they came, in candlelit procession singing Hallelujahs, twinkling in the blue twilight like a brook of evening stars.

Walter, in a shirt of mail, his broad, rosy face beaming, his blond head with its circled tonsure bare, led the march of soldiers up the street to his cathedral's door. Still proudly dressed in armor, at his own altar he said Mass, blessing Simon de Montfort, his knights and all his army.

A feast was given for the conquerors of Hereford and Gloucester. The next day they moved on.

It was the day after that when the march was met at Kidderminster, at a river ford, by a group of riders led by the lord of Ludlow, Roger Mortimer. He cantered to Simon, surveying the army as he came. Wind blew his dark hair about his angry face.

"Lord Earl, we of the Marches don't need the help we hear you mean to bring us," he said with an arrogant tilt of his head. "Llewellyn and the Welsh are our concern. We deal with them ourselves."

The bitter hatred of the March lords for the Welsh had stymied treaties before, including a treaty Simon himself had negotiated between King Henry and Llewellyn. The earl's own daughter Eleanor's betrothal once had been the Welsh leader's required bond of peace. That was before Simon's arrest and trials, and the treaty never had been ratified. Renewing its negotiation was the earl's intent.

"Treaty with Wales is necessary for England's security," Simon answered Mortimer with curt firmness.

"We don't want your treaty!" Mortimer retorted. His horse recoiled, sidestepping at his harsh, thundering tone.

"England needs peace. Those who tangle her in warfare are as much her enemies as the foreign leeches who bleed off her wealth," Simon answered in plain truth.

"Peace!" Mortimer scoffed. "You, of all men, speak of peace! Do you mean to frighten me with threats from God on high? It seems you're His Right Arm," and he spat.

"I mean for you to know," Simon said steadily, "that those who break the treaties of this land will be punished. Be they Welsh or English."

"Who gave you the right to impose treaties?"

"Under the Provisions, I was so appointed. I've served the king in that capacity often, as you well know."

Mortimer gave a twisted smile. "You speak as someone who dwells in the past. King Henry may swear to the Provisions, but he's never wanted them. In this bizarre uprising there is no substance. When the madness settles, the Crown will prevail. And you'll be hunted as the worst traitor that ever lived!"

Simon flushed with anger. But the Marcher lord had set spurs to his horse before his last words were out. Guy de Montfort, his sword out from its sheath, made a move to go after him, but Simon reached over and grasped his rein. "Let him go. We must deal with Llewellyn. Then, if the Marchers break the peace, we'll bring them before the Parliament for trial."

The advance along the Severn resumed.

At Bridgenorth, unlike the other towns they passed since Gloucester, the city gates were shut. As the Earl's column of knights neared the bridge, beyond which the city stood high on the far bank of the river, a volley of stones came from the bridge-gate's tower as a warning.

Simon made camp just beyond a suburb of modest half-timbered houses and thatch cottages on the east bank of the river, and sent Seagrave to find who was in command of the town.

Seagrave returned, reporting that an alderman, as spokesman for Bridgenorth, said they had no complaint against the king. They looked upon the disorders in the Earl of Leicester's name as insurrection.

"They haven't suffered here, so they care nothing for their neighbors' pains," the knight John Giffard sneered. "Do we attack?"

"No. We'll wait here for our meeting with Llewellyn." Simon made his comfortable headquarters at an inn by the bridge road. The strain of so much travel was costing him much pain in his new-mended limbs. He posted sentinels, and let himself and his army rest.

Late that night he was awakened by his squire Peter. The sentinels were reporting strange lights in the city.

Simon opened the wood shutters of his window and squinted in the direction of the city on the hill. From a bracket on the windowsill his lion flag, the genuine among so many imitations, hung lazily unfurling in the night's soft air.

Across the river, within the dark mass of the cliff-perched city silhouetted against the starlit lesser darkness of the sky, even Simon's weak eyes could see a rosy flickering of lights.

"Raise our men in arms!" Simon called down to one of his sentinels who was standing in the street below and peering toward burning Bridgenorth. "Have them bring torches and ladders from our wagons of supply!" Since Gloucester, he had kept with his march a goodly number of implements for sapping and besieging.

In minutes Simon, fully armed, with his son Guy carrying his flag, was in the street and his destrier was being brought up. All down the way between the suburb's house-fronts, lit by moving torches now, his army was rapidly assembling. Curious heads clustered in every window.

The Earl led his armed column to the towered gate at the bridgehead. No missiles were discharged. He called out. There was no response from the gatehouse.

"Seagrave," Simon ordered, "have a ladder brought."

A long ladder was placed to the gatehouse parapet without challenge. Seagrave climbed the ladder with a flare in hand. The bridge defense was vacant. The steward found the winch and raised the bridge's gate.

Simon and his army crossed over the Severn and entered Bridgenorth.

A broad stone horse-stairs led from the riverfront, ascending to the upper city's wall. But before Simon had mounted half of its wide, sloping steps, the gate above was flung open. Torchlight filled the entrance, washing a few dim figures with its warm light.

Simon drew his sword.

A shout came from above. "Peace, lord Earl of Leicester! We beg peace!"

"If you speak truly, we are of like mind," Simon bellowed back.

"Peace! In truth! By God's head!" The city's aldermen hurriedly came down the steps. Their leader, the mayor, knelt by Simon's horse's feet. "The Welsh are besieging our west gate. The city is on fire! We beg your aid, good Earl!"

"You hold our cause as insurrection yet you ask our help?" Simon asked coldly.

"We'll swear to the Provisions!" the mayor pled.

"And swear to look on those who'll not defend them, as your enemies, as we have sworn before?" Simon insisted.

The mayor drew out a cross from where it hung on a chain under his cloak, and placed it between his two hands clasped as in prayer. "By the Lord's Truth, upon Holy Cross, I swear to uphold the Provisions!" He turned to his aldermen, who also were kneeling now, and they intoned, "We swear!"

"Very well," Simon nodded, though he knew the small value of a pledge extracted under such duress. But he could ask no more.

The mayor clambered to his feet and, with the aldermen, led Simon and his knights into the city.

The first steep streets were dark and quiet, but as the earl and his men neared the city's summit, the smell of smoke grew strong. Bursts of confused voices could be heard. Then, turning a corner, the mayor led the way toward a vacated market square in the city's flaming western quarter. All around the paved square, buildings with thatched roofs were ablaze, lighting the sky. Through the brilliant glow of smoke, arrows tied with burning rags fell like a rain of comets.

In the streets bordering the square crowds were fighting fires with hand-over-hand lines of buckets, clumsily splashing water across the cobbles and soaking the men's nightshifts.

Simon took his flag from his son Guy, commanding him and his men to help staunch the flames.

Dismounting, holding his shield in one hand before him, his flag in the other, he ran alone across the vacated marketplace where arrows were falling thick as fiery hail. Rag-bound shafts lay scattered all about, flames guttering on the cobbles. Running swiftly despite sharp pain that cost him a lurching limp, Simon held his shield over him, turning it deftly, deflecting darts that came hissing at random, pelting lethally from the west. He crossed the square, dancing like a crippled jongleur around the fires underfoot. His fluttering flag, its white reflecting vivid orange in the blaze, was pierced by a bright streaking arrow, then another, leaving smoldering holes in their wake.

The crowd behind the Earl paused in their work to watch him. When he reached the shelter of the city wall at the square's far side, a shout went up, a cheer with cries of "Long live Leicester! Montfort! Montfort!"

Simon made his way along the wall until he found a stairway to the roof of a gate. His damaged joints were throbbing now, but he climbed the stairs, forcing himself to go on moving at a run. From the shelter of a merlon on the parapet, he held his flaming, gaping flag out high, its fork-tailed lion rampant lit by its own fire.

In moments there was a horn blast from beyond the wall. The flight of arrows ceased. Then a voice called loudly, "Earl Montfort, Llewellyn comes to parley!"

Simon leaned through the opening of the crenel. Below, the Welsh leader, holding his own flag, stood just outside the gate. Head bare, his demeanor shed of any trace of his former restraint, Llewellyn was grinning like a triumphant cat. "I see I owe you a new flag."

"For what reason are you besieging this city, my friend?" Simon called down, not quite able to match the Welshman's cheerful tone so soon after dodging his fiery arrows.

"Are not *all who won't support the Provisions our mortal enemies?*" Llewellyn shouted back, the merriment of his grin audible in his tone.

"They are," Simon admitted.

"We asked you to meet us here so we could put down your enemies for you. We'd have you know our worth as allies!"

"My friend, no one who has met Welsh forces in the field, as I have, needs any such proof. Once we've doused these flames and had a night of rest, I'll meet you at your camp."

With that, Simon dropped the smoldering remnant of his flag, left the parapet, climbed down the stairs and recrossed the square.

The fires were coming under control. But the townspeople, overhearing the Earl's exchange with the Welshman who, with all his ancestors, had been their foe for time beyond memory, were not cheered by an alliance of their conquerors.

Throughout the next day the Earl met with Llewellyn at his camp, and a new treaty was made.

"I'd far rather fight with words in fair meeting, than with swords in our own hills and fens," Llewellyn said. "But fair parley has never been offered by King Henry's Marcher barons. Secure your Parliament and we'll keep to our treaty. Your cause may bring peace."

"No more can I ask." Simon gripped the hand of the Prince of Northern Wales, with whom he'd hunted boar, and whom he held in high respect.

Llewellyn spoke again. "There is still the matter of your promise to me."

Simon looked perplexed.

"I speak of your daughter."

"She is in France... planning to leave for the Holy Land..."

"When all is orderly, under the governance of the Provisions, she will be sent to me? It has been my understanding."

There could be no reneging. "She will," Simon nodded, trying not to let his reluctance show, lest it prick Llewellyn's pride and set at naught all he had been working to achieve. He remembered that little Eleanor appeared fond of the Welshman who had sent his child-betrothed love letters written in verse. Nor had her mother objected, remarking that her own sister – sister to King Henry – had been wedded to Llewellyn's grandfather.

"We look to Eleanor's coming," Llewellyn said in a voice softened with anticipation. Her girlish letters to him had touched his heart as well. And he looked forward to sons descended from Montfort.

Simon marched from Bridgenorth eastward.

Kenilworth, the great castle in the Midlands, had been given to him by King Henry as a wedding present, to be his and the Countess Eleanor's home. They had ruined themselves financially in making the decaying fortress habitable. But Simon, of necessity, had relinquished it when his own party, at the framing of the Provisions, required that all lands bestowed out of the royal demesne be returned, with the intent that the king henceforth should live on his own rents. Eleanor's fury at the loss had been tempered only by her wish to be rid of England entirely. Now Simon's sons Henry and Simon had claimed it for their forces' headquarters.

Simon sent Guy ahead to announce his arrival.

When the Earl and his knights, with the resounding tread and clatter of an army, passed through Kenilworth's small village, the villeins gathered from the fields and stood along the road that passed their cottages, the abbey church, the bathhouse, inn and smithy. They cheered and wept to see their lord returned at last. Their lord whom they knew now was God's own Chosen.

Simon remembered most of his folk by name and expected to be welcomed. But the welcome he received, many of these people he had known for years crossed themselves and knelt as he passed by, shocked him and was far from his liking. He addressed them by their names and spoke to them in English to dispel this unseemly awe that had come over them. But it was with relief he left the last of them behind and, at the head of his cavalcade, entered Kenilworth's wood, then reached the grassy slope that spread down to the Mere.

The lake was bright blue, a motionless reflection of the April sky. The red sandstone block of the castle, with its foursquare corner towers, rose high as its twin lay across the water's smooth mirror. A flag waved from a corner battlement. Henry Montfort's lion-dotted flag. The castle bell rang out in a clangor of welcome.

Tears started to the rims of Simon's eyelids, his dark lashes blinked them away. Kenilworth was the home of his happiest days. Kenilworth was his truest home. At this distance the great tower was no more than ruddy color without detail, yet he knew every stone.

Billeting his army in the broad triangle of the outer yard, bounded by the Mere, the cut of the channel and the inner bailey's wall, Simon made close observation of the castle. The old walls were in good repair. Within them, the inner yard still embraced its chapel, its service sheds and Eleanor's garden. The sheds showed evidence of recent mending, but the garden suffered badly from neglect. Tussocks of weeds were smothering the young stalks of asparagus. But the roses bravely were in bloom. There was a sturdy new roof over the foyer that gave entrance to the tower.

Nicholas Seagrave, nudging his horse forward, dismounted and, taking up his accustomed office of steward, held Simon's stirrup as he swung down from his horse. Together they went up the foyer steps, as they had done every day so many years before.

In the hall, the red lion rampant painted on the wall behind the dais was peeled away almost entirely. The draperies that Henry, at an earlier reclaiming of his castle, had hung across the sets of three great arches in the north and south walls, were still there but looked moldy.

Seagrave opened the tower door to the right of the entrance and peered down into its dark depths. The manacles the king supplied in his past renovation were still stapled to the oozing wall, but the casks of Bordeaux wine the Earl had stored in the cool pit were still there too. The castle had been left untouched since Countess Eleanor last lived in it.

"Prepare what feast you can for our knights," Simon told Seagrave, then turned to Guy. "Come. Let's enjoy the reward of a bath."

Though the tower never was supplied with a bathing tub, there always had been a modest bathhouse in the village. During the years of the earl's absence, the baths had been bought by an enterprising woman who had added the attraction of comely filles de joie. Eager bathers came from as far as Warwick and Coventry. When young Henry and Simon repossessed the castle, they quickly learned of the facility's new offerings. Simon Fils, delighted, made it virtually his home, providing the proprietress with assurance that her filles would be untroubled in their trade. In return for this valuable protection he had free choice of her lasses. At first word that his father was arriving, he had made certain that no sign of anything but bathing would be seen.

Still, the earl marveled at the improvements to what had been a rather meager bathhouse a few years ago. Three cauldrons bubbled, steaming essences of rose, lily and lavender. Five new wooden tubs stood in satin-curtained booths furnished with tables well supplied with scented oils and old-style strigils for scraping the skin clean. Soap was an expensive innovation that had not reached general commerce in the Midlands. Large goose-down pillows lay on the tiled floor, with a remarkable supply of them heaped in a corner.

Simon raised his eyebrows at this prosperity. The matron hurried to explain, dipping a bow. "I have the best bath in the region, my lord. Ladies come from many miles away for my perfumes."

Not naive, but also not suspecting little Kenilworth to be a marketplace of vice, Simon accepted her answer and wished her venture well.

Bathed and refreshed, he met with his sons Henry and Simon.

"We are at full war," he told them plainly. "Don't doubt that what we propose with our elected government of the Provisions is an offense to every Crown. At some time Henry will be aided by armies from abroad. When that time comes, we will need Kenilworth for refuge. I'll send funds as I can. And, as I'm able, I'll return to oversee improvement of the defenses. In Palestine there are fortresses that a mere few men can hold against the Sultan's armies. As far as is practical, we'll replicate their walls and towers here."

Sobered by his warning, his sons nodded assent.

From Kenilworth, the Earl led his army on to Leicester where his own villeins, tenants, and the mayor and aldermen of the town greeted him with cheering, again mixed with sacerdotal awe. As in every city Simon entered, he caused the mayor and aldermen to swear to the Provisions, and to regard anyone who opposed them as mortal enemies. It was the vow that Simon required everywhere.

He and his knights rode on eastward, swearing Peterborough and Ely to the Provisions. Then he turned his army south to meet Richard de Gray at the Cinque Ports. The heart of England was encircled, the ports of her coast secured by the Provision's garrisons.

With the ports shut to armies from abroad, the whole of England might be won. As Simon toured the country with his forces, he was hailed as the people's champion, and revered as the sacred bringer of the Lord's New Age.

Yet beyond the cheering, chaos deepened.

With the royal sheriffs and their bailiffs driven out, and no means yet to appoint new men to keep the peace, all order was dissolving. Prisons were thrown open and hardened criminals set free in the surge of misguided jubilation. Murderers and thieves were glorified as victims of the corrupt era that was ebbing away. From attacks aimed at the Poitouvins, the folk now turned on any neighbor against whom they bore a grudge. And anyone accused of being weak in his support of the Provisions might be dragged into the streets and stoned, his house set ablaze.

Fields were left unreaped and fences unrepaired. Sheep and cattle wandered in the roads as mobs moved from village to village rooting out offenders who doubted the arrival of the Kingdom of the Lord. Violence was made virtue, the clearing of the way for the New Day.

In horror, Simon watched the mayhem heighten and spread. One night in his tent near Uxbridge, sitting at his camp-table, head in his hands, fingers pressed against his brow, he spoke his thoughts to Walter Cantaloup. "Father Grosseteste foresaw this. He told us, were we to renounce the crutch of kingship too soon, we'd fall into a disorder that would be the very turning out of Hell. I move among these people like a curse!"

Walter, far more than Simon, was a follower of Grosseteste, the prescient theoretician and Bishop of Lincoln who first proposed a parliament that would harness the erratic King Henry. Simon's struggling conscience was a danger to their cause. "Did Christ not say to his apostles, *For me you shall be made a curse,*" he offered gently. "The Lord's ways are not for us to understand."

Simon looked up at his friend. "Christ also said, *Know the tree by its fruit.* This fruit is poisonous. Jesus' followers were not violent men. Those people," his gesture in its arc included everyone outside his tent, "they are not acting as followers of Christ's words, but as men moved by Satan. Out there we see such mayhem as must cancel out the worth of any cause! There is the Devil's shadow over every victory we win."

# Chapter Seven

## THE QUEEN'S JEWELS
### 1263

As the Earl of Leicester began his campaign in the west country, the delegation sent from Oxford reached King Henry's Court. It was not well received.

At the Tower, in the narrow, brightly painted hall, beneath a canopy of crimson velvet salvaged from the fire at Westminster, the king sat with his brother Richard, the elected King of the Germans, on long absence from his dismayed subjects who were seriously reconsidering their choice of monarch.

The two kings listened to the Bishops of London and Chichester with stony expressions on their faces. Henry's palsy-drooping left eye and cheek sagged in such gray creases that he seemed the ruddy, burly Richard's grandfather.

Richard's twenty-year-old son Henry of Alemaine was with the delegation. His father studied him with a stern frown and detained him when the bishops were dismissed. "You stand with those who would impose themselves upon the power of the king," he warned the youth. "Their actions are treason."

"I stand with what I believe to be England's good, my lord," Henry bowed with respectful deference but answered firmly.

Richard's florid face grew purple with anger. "You answer me like this? Then I must have you put where you can give the issue deeper thought!"

Frightened, yet determined to adhere to what he saw as right after the long years of King Henry's misrule, Alemaine said mildly, "Father, it is thought that's brought me to where I stand."

"I'll hear no more from you! I'd rather see you chained in prison than listen to you speak yourself into a traitor's death!" The alarmed father ordered bailiffs to take his son away and lock him in a chamber of the tower.

When Alemaine was gone, Richard turned to his brother. "We must counter Leicester at once. His actions clearly aim at seizing the throne. Grant me an army and I'll ride to meet him."

"What army would you have me grant?" King Henry asked coolly.

"You must raise the barons!"

"Invite them here to London, so they may fully appreciate our weakness?"

"I doubt they'll take Leicester's part now."

"Who among them can we trust?"

"Then give me the mercenaries you have from France!"

"They've been recalled already for the Tower's garrison." Cocking his head at his brother's glare, Henry said with an odd smile, "Don't fret, Richard. There is no army large enough to quell the people when they're stirred up. But they tire. And the young lords are changeable. They follow Leicester now, but did they cleave to him at Southwark when I came back from France? Patience is all that's needed." With that observation, he would say no more.

Again and again in the next days Richard urged him to take armed action against the earl's march. Henry only withdrew into himself, wrapping his arms about his chest and rocking to and fro. Richard knew too well this symptom of his brother's fragile state of mind.

Reports continued of the general uprisings, murders and pillagings. Henry's Poitouvin sheriffs, the foreign supporters he had brought back from France and the newcomers he had welcomed swarmed to London, packing the Court schedule with their pleas. The king refused to hear them. Gradually attendance at Court dwindled as the petitioners fled on to the continent.

Word reached London of the fall of Dover and the Cinque Ports to de Gray in the name of the Provisions, and the closing of the London to Dover road by Gilbert de Clare. Then the taking of Hereford, Gloucester, Bridgenorth, Kenilworth, Peterborough and Ely. The Earl of Leicester's army was turning south to join Gray and Clare.

At last Henry relented, granting his brother the force of mercenaries.

"Now that Leicester holds all England you grant me a few hundred knights!" Richard raged in frustration. "Yet they may be enough. Cut the head from this leviathan that swallows up your land, and the body, I don't doubt, will crumple after it."

"Precisely what do you mean?" Henry asked.

"I mean that we must take the earl, any way we can."

"You have my leave." Henry gave a slight smile and a nod of his head. Then, "Would you bring Prince Edward with you on your campaign?"

Richard was thoughtful for a moment, the Crown's heir was well trained in warfare. But at Southwark, when Henry had returned from France to his long-delayed Parliament and the earl's armed followers stood ready to defend the Parliament against the king, Edward had taken the earl's part till the last moment. Only when battle was just hours from engaging, had he begged peace of his father and been reconciled. Henry had summoned the Parliament to meet with him and with the prince, averting war, confusing the earl's partisans, who fell away from him, and sending the earl to London Tower.

Since then Richard had pressed the idea with Edward that, if the power of the Crown was preserved intact, in his own rule he would be free to do as he felt best. Still he was uncertain of the prince's loyalty when the earl's life was at issue. Montfort had partly brought him up, had schooled him as a child. And too, when he was seized at the king's Parliament, Edward had protested mightily.

"No. I will not take the prince," Richard decided. "But I'll take my own son, so he sees the ruin that is done in the earl's name." He smiled at the clever plan he was conceiving. "It's clear Montfort thinks well of him."

Simon was leading his army through the Thames valley when Richard with his mercenaries moved to intercept him. The King of the Germans sent out his son to find the earl with a request for parley.

Alemaine returned to camp, reporting to his father in his tent. "Good my lord," he bowed, "the Earl of Leicester has given me no written answer. But he bade me wish you well, and asked me to convey his regret that he cannot pause at present. Though he will gladly meet and talk with you soon."

Richard looked in his son's kind, honest brown eyes and their innocence did nothing to ease his suspiciousness. His expression hardened. He raised his hand and struck his son, knocking him backward so he tripped and fell. "You warned him not to come!"

Sprawling on the tent floor, stunned, staring up at his father, Alemaine blurted, "O...o...of wh...what could I have warned him? You think I suspect you of t... treachery?"

Richard turned away from his son's bewildered eyes. "Oh God, help me!"

Alemaine was sent back to his not uncomfortable cell in London Tower. And Richard again tried to draw the earl to a meeting. But now his men searched everywhere and could not find him or his huge and ever-growing army.

As Richard's mercenaries combed Surrey, word came that Montfort had reached Kent, joining forces with Gilbert de Clare. Outmaneuvered, far outnumbered, Richard led his hired knights back to London to protect the Crown as best they could.

"What we must do," the King of the Germans told his brother, "is take all we have in the Treasury, flee to France and raise an army there."

"Noooo," Henry drew out the word, shaking his head solemnly. "Patience is our best weapon."

Queen Eleanor volunteered to try to move her husband. She found him in his chamber, studying a large drawing on several sheets of parchment stitched together. Edward sat on the window seat amusing himself with a toy ballista, aiming dried peas at the helmets of the guards below. The blond, tall and graceful prince stood and bowed as his mother came in. Henry glanced up, barely acknowledging her presence.

Crisply she asked him, "I interrupt your work?"

Henry looked to her and smiled. "I'm depriving my barons of their favorite hiding places."

"You're planning a campaign against the insurrection?" She raised her eyebrows hopefully.

"Look." Henry proudly turned the parchment around to show her. "Our new hall at Westminster will have no columns!" The drawing of the roof showed an intricate arrangement of hammer-beams and arches to span a broad floor.

The queen recoiled. "The land is risen in revolt, and you're busy with a drawing?"

"We'll have a palace finer than any other in the world."

"Soon we will have nothing! Not even our wits!" Queen Eleanor threw back.

Henry blandly ignored her, returning to his study of the plan.

"You're afraid even to look upon what's happening!" she cried in a frenzy of frustration. Then, tightening her mouth in a sharp line that gave her pretty face a cold, fierce look, she turned and left the room.

Henry gazed after her, but only for a moment before turning again to his plan.

Edward went to Henry's chair and laid his long-fingered, strong hand over the parchment. "Father, we must take action for our own safety," he urged.

Henry looked up into his face, so like his mother who had been the greatest beauty of her time. "The queen is out of sorts," he said, unconcerned. "She'll be better when we're back at Westminster."

"Give me what funds the Treasury holds. I'll cross to France and buy a force to bring against the rebels."

"We have mercenaries enough for our safety here in the Tower."

"Father, they're our warders! Not our protectors! There is no peace beyond the Tower's walls. We must take action!"

Henry blandly shook his graying head. "You're upset, Edward." Shrugging his thin shoulders, he muttered to regain his peace, "Do as you wish."

The High Clerk of the Wardrobe was summoned, the king's Treasurer. But when he heard what Edward wanted, his look turned bleak. "Good Prince, I've urged the king to hold back a reserve for emergencies, but he has never taken my advice."

"What do you mean?" Edward demanded.

"The Treasury is empty. Everything is spent for stone and workmen for the new palace at Westminster. I'm told that it will have a splendid roof over the hall..." The clerk held his breath in fear at Edward's look.

"We're building a splendid roof? Lord Treasurer, you've permitted our very substance to be squandered for a roof?" the prince roared.

The Treasurer looked meaningfully toward the king. "I've tried to counsel, but I cannot command."

"England will die of this new roof!"

Henry, roused by Edward's bellowing, took hold of his wrist and, looking in his blazing ice-blue eyes, said in a pacifying tone, "Calm yourself. I've had an augury. It says we will not cease to reign."

"The land's no longer ours, father! Will auguries put down this war?"

"You oughtn't to disturb yourself. It's not good for the blood," the king advised solemnly.

"Father, give me your leave to act as I see fit!"

Henry met the prince's raging glare pathetically, his store of patience drained. "Very well Edward. If you must, do what you will."

The prince left the chamber briskly. But in the anteroom the queen stopped him. Her delicate features were puffed and livid. "He's gone mad at last! A monarch of masons and decorators!" Her tone was full of hate.

"Did you hear what the Treasurer said?" the prince asked, heaving deep breaths of excitation.

She nodded. "He's drained the Treasury. As feeble a brain as body! I thank God you're none of him."

Edward flinched, but he had no time to question her remark as she took his arm and drew him toward her chamber, saying as she went, "We still have resources. My jewels are in the Templars' vaults. Sell them in France to raise your army."

Edward, halting her determined stride, hugged her. "Bless you, mother. I'll do it at once!"

Late that night Prince Edward, mounted on his Spanish destrier and accompanied by thirty of the royal mercenaries, left the Tower. All were armed with padded mail and short swords under long, plain robes. They rode out of the city to the Temple's compound in the suburb between London and Westminster.

As the prince roughly shook the clapper of the bell above the heavily fortified gate, the roused Templar on duty cried, alarmed, "Who rings at this hour?"

"It's the lord Edward, with a few friends," the prince called back, giving his speech the slur of drunkenness. "We have a wager about my mother's jewels and want to see them."

"My lord, the vaults are closed," the captain of the night guard said apologetically, coming out of the gate's small wicket door to pay proper respect. His long white robe, blazoned with the red cross of his Order, shone in the torchlight against the darkness of the Temple's massive stone bastion.

Edward dismounted and approached him, his blond curls bright, his smile as sweet as an angel's at prayer. "My captain, that would be a pity," he lisped. "Do you keep common hours even for me?"

The captain returned his smile placatingly but said, "These are troubled times, my prince. We have our orders."

Seeing sugared request had no effect, Edward turned even more amiable, intimately resting his arm across the captain's shoulders. "I told these fellows that the ruby in my mother's crown is a full two inches across," he murmured in the Templar's ear. "Have you seen it?" He seemed to lose his balance, gripping the captain's shoulder and laughing. "Good friend, have a drink with us!" He offered a flask that he held in his other hand.

"I'm not allowed," the captain demurred, flustered. Like many in his Order, he had a fondness for young men, and Edward's strong, warm arm embracing him rattled him considerably.

"Even when it's I who offer it to you?" The prince puckered his bow lips with the suggestion of a kiss and brought the flask up to the captain's mouth, running the tip of his tongue across his own lips in a lewd gesture. "Drink, my friend, to please me."

The captain opened his mouth and let the burningly strong wine flow down his throat.

"Very good," Edward drawled. "You would have your future king think kindly of you, wouldn't you."

"My lord…" the captain tried to protest, but only weakly.

"We'll drink together. All night if we please." Edward raised the flask and seemed to drink, but with his thumb thrust in the vessel's opening. He was utterly sober. Wiping his wetted mouth with the back of his hand, he resumed his grip upon the captain's shoulder. "We'll have your guards down here to drink with us. We're in a mood for… play." The shoulder hold bent to an embrace.

The insinuating tone that Edward gave his last word opened worlds of possibilities in the captain's heating brain. And truly, he dared not offend the prince who might at any time become his king. Who knew what chance of future royal favor might spring from such a moment? Would his superiors not laud him for securing so powerful a patron for the Order? They need not know how the friendship was sealed. He resisted no longer.

Trembling from the prince's touch and his own anticipations, he went back through the wicket door and opened the broad gates.

Edward and his thirty men led in their horses. Strung to their saddlebows were fat leather flasks of strong wine, tied and bunched like clusters of grapes. The mercenaries unhitched the flasks and brought them, following the captain as he led the way to the guardhouse just inside the gate.

Drawn by the unusual activity at such an hour, the whole night guard was gathered in the Temple's yard.

Edward, eyeing the assembled Templars, stopped the captain by the guardhouse door. "They must join us, too. I'd have it be a merry night for everyone." At the captain's pause he raised his silky golden brows, his blue stare wide. "No? But when I'm come into my own, it would be best I knew you all. "

The second in command looked at his captain, uncomfortable in the extreme. But one of Edward's men pressed a flask into his hand and muttered, "Sire, you wouldn't miss a night like this. A chance to be among the next king's friends."

Seeing his commander acquiesce, the man drank deeply from the offered flask, and motioned for the rest of the night guard to follow as their captain led.

"My prince, we must be back at our posts before the changing of the watch," the captain, his face flushed, told Edward. He took the prince's hand and pressed it in a gesture of presumed mutual cautions.

"When will that be?" Edward asked, putting his wine flask in the captain's hand.

Obediently the captain took the flask and drank. "Five hours from now," was his answer.

"Then we'll be gone in good time if our romp tonight is done before the angelus is rung?" The prince gave a slow smile.

The giddy captain gurglingly snickered and drank again.

By the warm light of a few oil lamps the men sat and lay about the floor of the guardroom, passing the wine flasks back and forth. When Edward and his mercenaries tipped the flasks up, they kept their lips well closed, feigning growing drunkenness. The Templars drank deep of the strong wine. The prince's mercenaries with drunken gesturing evaded the guards' inquiring touches. But Edward, curious, for he had never lain with a man, followed the captain to an inner room and permitted him liberties. When they returned, the captain's eyes were limpid with new passion, but Edward seemed displeased with the experiment.

From the uncommonly potent wine, the Templars were well besotted when the prince motioned for his men to stand and join him. He asked the captain, "Now where are my mother's jewels?"

"Oh... yes," the captain breathed vaguely. "That's why you came..." He was dazed, confounded by the effort to recall a time so long past, before his heart found rapture, though it was but a short while since. "I don't suppose there's any harm..."

Taking a heavy ring of keys from a small ironbound chest, he picked up one of the little pottery oil lamps to lead the way. While other Orders might have iron or even silver candlesticks, the Templars' affectation of poverty afforded them only the cheapest clay oil lamps for indoor use.

The mercenaries followed their tall prince as he followed the captain out of the guardroom. At the doorway Edward stopped, "They must come as well." He beckoned to the white robed men who sat and lay about the room, sodden amid the emptied, flattened leather flasks. "Else how am I to win my wager without witnesses?"

"A witness..." the captain agreed reluctantly.

"All of them. You, who on the morrow might be known as my... sweet friend, won't deny me this, will you?"

The captain, burning with that thought, nodded and gestured for the entire guard to follow him.

Stumbling to their feet, they obeyed his command. If any habit of precaution might have given them second thoughts, they were far too drunk to care. Taking the oil lamps with them, they all crossed the yard and entered the fortified building that held their treasury's vaults.

Bankers to the world, the knightly Order of the Temple stored wealth for everyone, issuing notes of credit that could be turned to gold at any Temple house from London to Acre and most major cities in between. The Temple's reputation for security had no rival. Founded to rebuild the temple of Solomon in Jerusalem, the Templars had long since discovered that lending money for crusades was lucrative, and lending money for its own sake was more lucrative still.

Like their brother Order, the Knights of the Hospital of Saint John, they were financiers now first, and fighting men only when circumstances in the East made it unavoidable. But the Templars' reputation was not as unsullied as the Hospitallers'. Common jest had it that their emblem, two knights on one horse, did not portray their vow of poverty carried to the excess of two knights sharing a single mount, but rather that their sexual tastes were such they were inseparable one from another even on horseback.

With many a glance over his shoulder at the exquisite prince grinning and stumbling along behind him, the captain led the way into corridors lined with heavy oak and iron doors.

"What's here?" Edward, his speech lispingly slurred, asked, pointing to a door at random. "Or there?"

"Everything," the captain beamed with pride, yearning to impress. "All the riches of England. The Wool Guild's yearly payment is arrived from Flanders. A great horde of gold."

"I want a look at that!" Edward stopped, wavering in his balance by the door.

The captain leaned unstably against the wall to brace himself and managed to bring out sensibly, "But dear prince, gold is merely gold and you must win your bet."

"Wish to see it!" Edward retorted like a pettish child. "Now I've just as much a mind to see the merchants' gold as Mother's jewels."

"No, no..." the captain resisted, a last fiber of caution still clinging. "My prince, come... this way. It isn't possible..."

Edward drew a short sword from under his nearest mercenary's robe. Suddenly quite sober, he presented the blade to the captain's throat. "I believe you'll find it very possible. Possibly imperative?"

The mercenaries, alert for the prince's move, all drew their weapons.

The wine fuddled Templars were surrounded at sword-point in the crowded stone passage. They reached for their swords but were pressed so close together, between the stone walls and the prince's men in front of and behind them, they could not quickly draw the long blades from their sheaths.

A Templar dropped his oil lamp in the confusion. The oil spilled in a streak of flame down his white robe, setting him on fire. He tried to turn and flee to the door, striking at the flames with his bare hand, but the oil and flame clung to his hand too. Shrieking as his hand burned like a torch, the Templar wielded his sword wildly, trying to escape. The completely sober mercenaries, blocking the rear of the passage, drove him backward, parrying his blows with their short, broad blades. Engulfed in fire, the Templar was forced in among his brother knights, catching their long, sweeping robes in his flames as they parried and struck at the prince's men blocking the way ahead. The loose and rippling fabric caught up the fire instantly.

Others of the drunken guards, trying to hold their clay lamps and fight at the same time, spilled more fiery oil upon themselves. Distracted, trying to crush out the flames, they took wounding blows and bludgeoning. The mercenaries drove them tight together, herded them like a crazed flock in upon each other till the oil-fed leaping fire wrapped them all. Then the mercenaries lunged and darted at the fiery confusion, prodding, piercing, slashing with their blades. The corridor was like a scene from Hell, men writhing in the whorl of orange fire, surrounded, stabbed and hacked by dancing, plunging shadow-shapes.

The captain fled up the corridor. Edward pursued him.

Thick smoke was gathering, enveloping the macabre slaughter in a lurid and obliterating haze that stank of burning cloth and hair and flesh. Shrieks, the crunch of blades against chain mail and the loud crackle of the oil and flesh fed fire, echoed with a din to deafen ears. Men bellowed in the agonies of death throes in the blazing yet still standing, battling pyre.

Gradually the uproar quieted, replaced by convulsive coughing and the sound of running feet receding down the passage. A door was opened. The choking, stinking smoke began to thin. Flames leapt brightly on the grisly heap of roasting flesh wrapped in blackened steel mail. Here and there a sooty sword protruded. The pyre gained new life, consuming its rich fuel merrily as the fresh night air came in. Edward's men stood by the door, gaining their breath as smoke billowed out past them. The passageway was hot as an oven.

When the flames subsided, a mercenary ventured in. "My lord are you safe?" he called.

"Here I am," Edward answered from a stairwell at the rear of the corridor. He held the captain pinned, his sword blade pressed against his throat. From the crease of a long, shallow wound the neckline of the captain's white robe was stained red. The mercenaries who had been nearest to the prince, at the fore, were further up the stairs.

Using their broad swords to bank the remains of their victims to one side of the passage like half-spent logs smoldering in a hearth, the mercenaries cleared a way through. Edward saw their dark shapes, silhouetted against the flagging fire, coming at a trot toward him at the stairs. Apart from singeing and a few minor cuts, none of his men were hurt.

"Now captain, tell me where my mother's jewels are kept – and the Wool Guild's gold," Edward said coolly, pushing his prisoner down the stairs and into the smoky, littered passage. The corridor was dimly lit by the guttering pyre and a shaft of unconcerned light from the early summer dawn that reached in at the open door.

The captain, shocked into sobriety, stumbling amid blackened remains of gashed and burnt bodies, leaned against the wall and vomited. When he could catch his breath he shook his head. "Kill me."

"Tell me first, then I'll kill you." Edward's teeth showed in a smile half vicious, half mockingly seductive.

The captain shook his head, the vomit rising in his mouth again.

Before the man could spatter his velvet riding robe, Edward dropped him. "We'll find them without you." As the captain retched up rancid wine, the prince roughly turned him, pinning him upon his back with his foot hard on his chest. "I'd be ashamed to leave here with my sword alone so little bloodied."

The captain, his bleached face filthy, stared up from beneath the velvet slippered foot.

"My dear," the prince studied him with a teacherly frown, "you lack what any woman knows – to know a man before you trust him, unless of course he's paying you."

He gestured for one of his mercenaries to raise the red crossed white robe of the Order and lift back the edges of the chain hauberk and pourpoint beneath. Into the exposed, soft, pale belly Edward thrust his blade and, hooking delicately, drew it slowly out again. He left the captain crying, soaked with blood and clutching at his drawn, pink entrails spewed across his groin onto the floor.

Regarding his victim as he wiped off his sword, the prince remarked, "You'll live awhile like that I think. Long enough to see us find the jewels and the gold." He had long since possessed himself of the captain's ring of keys.

The stinking fire was twinkling now with only a few red embers. Mid-summer's early morning sky shed rosy yellow light through the doorway at the corridor's far end.

"We must finish before the new watch comes," Edward said anxiously.

In the shadowed passage there were many doors. Though they had stopped by the Guild's vault and the assault had happened near it, which one it was seemed unclear now. Edward set to trying all the keys in the nearest door. As if luck were with him, the fourth key turned, he pushed the door open on utter darkness. A dry, musty odor met his face. Nothing met his touch but floor and walls. The room was empty. He went back to the passage and tried the next door. But here none of the keys seemed to fit. He went on to the next. A key turned and, entering, he stumbled over a low object.

The next man following steadied him and grasped the thing that had made him trip. "A cask," he said, feeling its curved sides.

"Open it," Edward commanded.

With the pommel of his sword the man stove in the lid. "Coins" he said, letting the disks run tinkling through his fingers.

In the dark Edward put down his hand and felt one of the disks. It was small but heavy for its size. Gold coins. His men were groping in the dark, finding casks stacked high.

"We've no time to look further. We'll take these," Edward ordered.

His thirty men busily hurried back and forth, carrying the heavy casks from the vault out to the yard where, in the early light, they lashed them to their horses' saddles, then returned for more. When the room was emptied and the last cask tied in place, they led their heavy-burdened horses out the gate. The suburb was quiet though summer dawn was well over the horizon; the first water-carriers were leaving to fill their wheeled tanks. At Saint Clement Dane the angelus rang out.

"To Windsor," Edward said softly. The smile he shed on his good mercenaries was warm, companionable, elated at their shared success.

At a quay on the Thames a river barge was tied, having unloaded its cargo the past evening. Edward waked its soundly sleeping owner, explaining his need to leave with his men and horses straightaway. Planks were set in place, the horses led aboard, and the vessel was loosed out into the morning's running tide.

# Chapter Eight

## LONDON BRIDGE
### 1263

The morning after Edward's nocturnal visit to the Temple, King Henry sat in his great, carved chair upon the dais in the Tower's royal hall. The queen, Richard and the clerk Walerant were ranged beside him for the holding of Court. Apart from the Court's staff of clerks and bailiffs, as it had been for the last week the hall was nearly empty, but for a small group of early-rising, urgent petitioners who stood at the dais' foot. The leader of the group, a burly man with a round and merry face, smooth-shaved chin and curling gray hair was Thomas FitzThomas, the Mayor of London. With him were the city's aldermen.

"The Earl of Leicester," FitzThomas was saying, "has written to us, good King Henry, asking what the disposition of the people of our city is." He handed to the royal clerk Walerant a strip of paper with the large seal of Montfort dangling from its edge. Several smaller seals, on a fringe of parchment tabs, kept the heavy wax disk company.

Walerant began to read aloud, "'To Thomas the honorable Mayor, the Alderman and People of London, Simon de Montfort, Earl of Leicester, John de Warenne, Earl of Surrey and Essex, Gilbert de Clare'... etcetera, etcetera," Walerant glanced down the list and then continued, "send greetings. By this messenger, we lords of England and upholders of the Provisions made at Oxford wish to ascertain..."

Henry, his head drooping, waved for the reading to cease.

Richard reached for the parchment and read it through as Henry, weary-seeming and without looking up, asked the mayor with a sigh, "What answer do you mean to give?"

FitzThomas bowed and in a clear and steady voice replied, "My lord King Henry, my lord Richard King of the Germans, my lady Queen, we wish to support the cause of the Provisions."

Henry raised his head, regarding the mayor as if only now was his attention fully roused. Tipping his head back and narrowing his eyes, as he did when he wished to bring his sagging eye to bear, he asked, "What is it that you truly want, Thomas? Have I not given London privileges above every other city?" As if hardening from his own words, he glared at the rosy, amiable face. "Well? Tell me. What more are you wanting from me!"

"Nothing my good king," the mayor bowed, flustered at this misunderstanding. "Nothing but the honest keeping of the Provisions to which the lords and you yourself have sworn."

Henry rose from his chair, his eyes so wide that even his drooping eyelid seemed fully open. "Can it be that even you are duped!" he shrieked. "Leicester is a usurper who wants nothing but my crown! The Provisions never have been anything other than his tool to lure men to his treason!"

The aldermen and mayor stared at Henry in amazement. Richard and Queen Eleanor stared at him too, but at this sudden rise from his passivity.

Henry sank back in his chair, motioning disgustedly for the petitioners to leave. As they bowed their way out of the hall, the king muttered under his breath, "They can take the earl's part and burn in Hell with him," and he began trembling as if chilled.

The queen, encouraged by his unexpected show of feeling, tried to take his hand. He drew it back pettishly. "You think, like they do," he hissed, "that he'll have my throne. But I tell you, he won't."

Before the aldermen and mayor reached the rear door, the Master of the Temple, Roscilyn de Foss, entered, passing them briskly. His long white robe flapped about his legs as, without waiting to be announced and with the steward running after him, he strode down the length of the hall.

Henry looked up from his dim musings to see Foss's face contorted with fury. "To what do we owe a visit from the Master of the Temple?" the king asked vaguely, barely rising from the abyss of his thoughts.

"My visit, my lord, is thanks to your son the lord Edward! If such a monster can be the true son of a king!"

Queen Eleanor's hands tightened on the arms of her chair, but she assumed a face of serenity and stood up. "It is the custom to bow when you address your king. Is this how you present yourself to us?"

"My lady queen," the Templar bowed, though he was shaking with anger, "my entire night guard has been massacred by your son!"

Henry frowned as if the Templar had said something in an unknown foreign tongue. Richard stared at Foss, the color deepening in his ruddy face. Queen Eleanor assumed even more haughty dignity.

In the brief, cross-challenging silence on all sides that followed the extraordinary accusation, recalling the prince's urgency the day before, Henry's frown sagged into drooping creases. In a voice very low, he asked the queen, "Where is Edward this morning?"

"Surely you don't give this crazed notion any credence!" Richard burst out at his brother.

"Some catastrophe apparently has happened that has made the Master of the Temple far from master of himself!" Eleanor said coolly, standing like a monument to outraged etiquette. "See how grossly he entered here. Send him away, if you would, my lord, until he regains his good sense."

"My lady, had you seen the burnt, butchered remains I've seen, you too would find courtesy difficult this morning!" Foss turned to Henry, "I demand justice!"

"What reason have you to accuse the prince!" Richard bellowed at him.

"My lord King of the Germans," Foss bowed low, truly struggling to regain self-control, "the captain of the night guard is still alive. He has borne witness that the lord Edward came, accompanied by knights, and overpowered his men with fire and with sword."

"The best trained knights in Christendom?" the queen asked tartly. "Surely our prince must be a wonder!"

"If that even could be so, to what possible purpose!" Richard thundered, enraged at this slander of his nephew.

"My captain said they claimed they wished to see your jewels, Madame. But they've stolen the Wool Guild's funds!"

Henry looked to the queen and pursed his lips.

"These are grave accusations!" Richard blustered, his face florid and his look furious. "I don't ask whether the Master of the Temple speaks truly of his witness's report. But in the dark of night the guard must have been deceived by thieves. No doubt there was conniving from within that made it possible." He turned to Eleanor. "Where is Edward? Let him put the Master of the Temple to right about his whereabouts last night, so we may begin searching for these thieves and murderers."

"Rather, brother, search for the culprits now, than offer insult to Prince Edward by asking him to account for himself!" Queen Eleanor retorted.

"I demand to question the prince!" Foss roared.

"You shall not see him!" Eleanor, still standing, shrieked at him.

"Good King!" Foss threw himself at Henry's feet, choking, hardly able to go on forming words, "I... require writ... against the Prince Edward... commanding him to face questioning..."

Henry, clutching himself tightly, looked down at the Templar. "I will not issue such a writ against my own son." He spoke hardly above a whisper. "Master Foss, leave our presence." Gesturing to the Court's bailiffs, he motioned for Foss to be escorted out.

Surrounded by armed men, Foss let himself be led away.

Henry arose, took the queen firmly by her wrist and left the hall with her. When he reached the privacy of his own chamber he shut the door and turned on her. "This is your doing! Yours and Richard's! You so stirred Edward with your fears that he's robbed the Temple!"

"My doing! Where are your courtiers! Where are your subjects! Even the people of London, whose peace you've bought by heaping them with favors, are rising now against you! And you still do nothing! You've wasted our treasury upon a palace you'll never see! Edward has done the only thing left him to do. If he's committed crimes, be they upon your head!"

Henry clutched himself as if a knife turned in his side. "It is not so!" The words squeezed out of him.

Eleanor looked at him in disgust. "You'll go mad again. If it weren't for Edward, I would welcome Montfort's rule!"

With great effort Henry forced himself to straighten and face her, raising his head upon his trembling neck. "Now you speak your true mind for once."

Eleanor turned toward the door.

"Where are you going?" Henry cried after her, sinking into a chair.

"To help my son!"

"You know where he is?"

"He is at Windsor. He sent word to me."

"I command you stay with me! Here at the Tower!" Henry put more force into his voice than would have seemed possible.

Eleanor gave a short, bitter laugh for answer and walked out the doorway.

That afternoon the queen's gaily painted, buntinged barge was drawn up to the Tower's water gate. Servants of the queen hurried across the yards between the buildings and the dock's steps carrying cases and barrels of foodstuffs and armaments onto the vessel. At the stern, among the packing cases, an elegant awning was set, its blue damask draperies fringed with golden bells and caught up with silk tassels. Within its shade, satin cushions were neatly arranged. The barge was of Henry's design for the ladies' summer outings. It had been a present to the queen in a past year peaceful and prosperous.

When the deck was fully loaded with the maximum the barge could bear, the queen and her waiting women went aboard, arranging themselves comfortably on the pavilion's cushions.

The barge pushed out from the steps. Its oarsmen dipped their oars twice, then raised them vertically. The vessel slid under the iron teeth of the portcullis at the water gate, and out into the Thames. The portcullis lowered behind it. The heavy barge's twenty oars fanned out and stroked the water, pulling the vessel against the afternoon current, toward Windsor.

Henry watched it from his chamber window in the Tower.

Within the barge's pavilion there was no cheery chattering as when the ladies' went on casual excursions. A tense silence prevailed. Heads bowed, shoulders stiff, the ladies busied themselves with their embroideries. Queen Eleanor sat in their midst, her dainty lips shut tight in a firm line.

The ancient dame Alice, the queen's principal companion since her youth, sat determinedly on a packing case out in the sun, like a fashionable cadaver, surveying the shore. What met her squint was a gathering crowd. Hoots and jeers chirped across the water.

"What are they saying, Alice?" the queen asked somberly.

"I don't hear the words but they're in a nasty humor," the hoarse, crisp voice croaked as the papery yellow face gathered its pleated creases in a frown.

"A mob. Well, let them shout." The queen smoothed her crimson silk robe across her knees with a hand that shook ever so slightly. "We will hold Windsor for our bastion, and Edward will gain such a force from France as will prostrate that mob at our feet."

"To be sure, my lady," Alice replied dutifully.

Along the quay at the river edge the crowd moved with the vessel, calling and gesticulating rudely.

Ahead loomed London Bridge with its double-file burden of buildings spanning the river, principally tanners' and butchers' shops, trades that needed water and a venting for disposal of waste to the tide's flow. One after another the shuttered windows on the bridge opened and faces peered to see the reason for the shouting. Seeing the queen's barge, they too began calling and heckling with the crowd on the quay.

The barge pulled steadily on toward the bridge. Slowly it passed into the swirling currents amid the bridge's massive pilings, and into the bridge's shadow. As the mid-ship slid into the dark, suddenly a stinking deluge gushed from somewhere up above. A latrine chute on the bridge had been opened, dumping its load of filth onto the vessel. Then another flood poured down, toppling the ladies' damask pavilion with a load of cattle-viscera and excrement. As a third latrine chute opened, the bargemen dropped their oars to shield their faces. The barge slipped back and sideways and wedged firm between the pilings.

Only the stern with its collapsed, filth-laden pavilion jutted into the daylight, the queen and her ladies scrambling indecorously out from its reeking folds. Lady Alice, nearest the fore, covered with blood and ordure, struggled among the cursing, latrine-drenched oarsmen, trying to reach the queen who stood, shrieking and trembling with rage, directly underneath the windows on the bridge.

"Queen of Leeches!" a housewife called down at her. "Here's my tax money for you!" and she pitched out the contents of her chamber pot, narrowly missing the queen's face.

The queen's ladies struggled to raise the pavilion for the little protection it could offer but they could not lift the sodden cloth. Failing, they ran among the packing cases forward to the shelter of the bridge. Alice's bony, gore-streaked hand grasped Eleanor's wrist and drew her along with them. Shielding her lady with her own scrawny body, she shook her free, bony fist at the windows above.

"Is this the way to treat a tart?" a male voice from the bridge laughed mockingly. "Treat her gently, she's the Earl's own leman!"

Another gruff voice answered him, "We got a bath'll make the whore smell sweet!"

A stinking blue liquid poured in a torrent onto the barge as a vat full of woad was pitched down a latrine. The foul dye soaked the queen, her ladies and all the mid-ship oarsmen in the bridge's shade.

The straining oarsmen had just worked the barge free, but in the new confusion it floated loose with the current, emerging stern-end first, still on the Tower's side of the bridge.

The assault from the windows on the bridge redoubled with a barrage of garbage, shouts and laughter as Queen Eleanor and her women passed from the bridge-shadow into full sunlight, filthy and with faces, wimples, veils and robes dyed with broad streaks of blue woad.

The captain of the barge haplessly looked to the queen for her order.

"Clearly we cannot pass," she said, her expression like stone. "We will return to the Tower."

"The Lord Edward will never sleep until he's avenged us!" Alice bawled up to the faces on the bridge.

Eleanor stood among the foul, stinking packing cases, staring at the bridge with eyes like points of steel.

From his window King Henry watched it all. As the barge approached the Tower he called down to the water gate, "Keep the portcullis shut! Don't' admit the queen, lest she bring down on us the anger of the Londoner." Then he withdrew, chuckling. "Let her go to Edward!"

The reeking barge with its bemired passengers rode the swells by the water gate for the remainder of the afternoon. At nightfall lights appeared on a quay just downstream.

"We've come to offer the queen shelter," a voice called out. It was Mayor Thomas FitzThomas, with a large tented cart and several mounted bailiffs.

The queen ordered her oarsmen to let the barge pass to the quay. She and her ladies landed and were taken as the mayor's prisoners.

# Chapter Nine

## MONTFORT TRIUMPHANT
### 1263

In Paris, Peter of Savoy paused at the entrance of an inn to watch a big dock cart unloading barrels of dried herring — far more dried herring than one would suppose an inn of this quality could use. He entered, went up the stairs to a private chamber and knocked on the door. William de Valence's squire answered. Beyond him, William was looking out the window. Beside him, on the window seat, sat John Mansel, King Henry's longtime favorite clerk.

"I think you'd better dine elsewhere," Savoy said lightly. "Your host here seems to be planning an off-season Lent."

"The herring?" William turned to face the gaily dressed Earl of Richmond, Queen Eleanor's uncle. "The delivery is for me."

"You're going into shop-keeping for the poor and destitute?" Savoy asked archly.

"I'm going to war."

"With dried herrings?"

"With money. Inside those casks of herring are smaller casks of coin. Enough to buy five-hundred Brabantines, the finest soldiers."

Savoy whistled through his teeth. "Very good!"

"We won't attempt the Cinque Ports, but in three weeks I land a force in the west of England, at Bristol, and join Edward."

"At last," Lord Peter breathed and showed his teeth in a wide smile.

"My lord of Richmond, I would not sing victory quite yet," John Mansel said grimly. "All England's held by Leicester, except

London Tower itself, and the castle at Windsor which Edward holds."

"What word do you have from King Louis?" Valence asked Savoy.

"He gives us his moral support, for whatever that's worth," Peter replied dryly. "But my niece Queen Margaret is warmer to our cause. She's quite stricken for her sister Eleanor. Boniface daily tells her tales of horror of the miseries of captivity. I believe she better bore her own travails in Egypt than she can her sister's enforced lodgment in the Bishop of London's manse."

"Will she raise an army for us?" Valence came to the point.

"Louis opposes it. But she has funds of her own that will be added to your herring."

"Well enough," Valence smirked.

In three weeks' time a fleet of ships approached Bristol. But as the vessel in the lead passed by the city wall to reach the quay a flight of arrows was discharged from the wall's towers. On the quay the town's militia stood armed with axes, ready to sever the ships' lines.

"Where is Edward!" Valence screamed at the railing of his flagship. "I can't land! We cannot land!" he cried at his captain. "Take us back to France."

At the other side of the city of Bristol, in the castle hall with the doors well guarded by halberdiers, Prince Edward met with the city's aldermen and the Bishop Walter Cantaloup, who happened to be present on his way to Worcester.

"I swear to you I favor the Provisions, as I always have!" the prince protested. "I'm merely passing by. You have no reason to hold me here."

"You've brought thirty mercenaries with you, into our city, my lord," an alderman said in a mild tone full of seeming deference. "And now there are strange ships seeking to land." His politeness did not impair in the least the coolness of his reasoning.

"I know nothing of that." Edward stared him down, then turned to Cantaloup. "Good bishop, you know well that I'm with your cause. Did I not work strenuously enough for the Ordinances? Have I not done everything I could, short of spilling my own father the king's blood?"

A man posted on the tower roof sent a messenger down. "The ships are turning back into the channel, my lords. They're not going to land."

Cantaloup watched Edward's expression. "Truly, by your most solemn oath, good prince, upon the Head of God, you do not know the mission of those ships?"

"Truly! I swear it!"

"Will you make public oath of your fealty to the Provisions, and your peace to the Earl Montfort and his cause?" the bishop pressed.

"Good bishop, I will," Edward answered with sober earnestness.

Cantaloup looked to the aldermen. "As the prince will swear us peace, I see no reason for you to detain him." He turned back to Edward and took both his hands in his. "I'm very glad you're reconciled to the lord Montfort," he said with a smile of considerable relief. "I know how highly he values your good will. May God keep you and him in unity."

In Bristol's square before the Hallows Cross, Edward, surrounded by aldermen, bailiffs and some hundred of the curious, knelt down before the bishop as his thirty mounted men waited for him with his Spanish destrier at ready at the far side of the crowd.

"I do swear to uphold the Provisions. And I grant my peace to all who do so with me," Edward said reverently, kissing the crossing of his sword's hilt which he held before him, the point toward the cobblestones.

"By the head of God you swear," the bishop prompted.

"By the Head of God, and by Saint Edward I swear."

The bishop made the sign of the Cross upon the prince's brow. Edward stood, sheathed his sword and walked toward his destrier as the crowd parted before him. Mounting, he touched spurs to the magnificent horse's sides and, with his men, galloped toward the city's eastern gate. As he passed a bailiff standing by the open gate, he drew his sword and struck the man a deft blow, slicing through his neck. "That's for your fellows taking me their prisoner!" he shouted as the man fell gushing blood and dying.

People came running, bailiffs, aldermen, all who had just witnessed the oath.

"Edward!" Walter Cantaloup shouted. "Before God..."

Over his shoulder as he dashed away, the prince threw back, "This is how I treat oaths wrung from me!"

At London, King Henry, wan, care-worn and no longer self-assured, listened dejectedly to the report of the failure at Bristol. Richard, beside him, was morose. The army raised in France had been their only hope.

"There's one good word from Bristol, my king," the messenger reported. "Prince Edward, by a ruse and valiant battling, escaped capture."

Henry nodded. His red-rimmed eyes were moist, his tears not forming droplets but following worn paths, seeping round the crevices at the corners of his eyes and into the long creases of his cheeks until they disappeared into his grizzled beard. When the messenger finished speaking, Henry brushed his face with the back of his hand, then rose from his chair as if to speak with some determination. His mouth opened, but his body turned. Bent over, he grasped the carving on the chair's high back and leaned his head against it.

Richard, rising, took hold of his brother's shoulders just as Henry's legs gave way. With his brother's help, the king sank back into his chair, hiding his face as he wept.

Richard dismissed the messenger and the royal clerks and bailiffs in attendance, the only people present in the hall. He sat in his own chair beside Henry, silent till his brother's shaking shoulders quieted. Then he said in a low, measured voice, "We have no choice but to offer Montfort peace. And place ourselves at his mercy."

Henry raised his head, turning toward his brother. "That's what is left?" he asked abjectly. Then he sank again, drawing his legs up onto the chair's seat, like a child nestling in its mother's lap. "I'm weary. Do whatever you think is best."

Putting his arm under his brother's shoulders and knees, Richard lifted him and carried him to his chamber.

The King of the Germans put his brother to bed himself. Then he summoned Walerant. "The king is issuing a letter to the Earl of Leicester … offering peace."

The clerk understood. While Henry lay silent, his hand pressed to his wet cheek, his eyes fixed on the blue painted wall of his chamber in the Tower, Richard dictated the letter of capitulation.

As Walerant left to have the letter copied and sealed at the Chancery, Henry reached for his brother's arm. His voice was small and strained. "If I must stay here as his prisoner, could I ask if I might have the walls repainted?"

Richard felt weak, nauseated, sick with rage and impotence. He would not answer him.

"I won't be here for long, a deposed king is an inconvenience…" Henry muttered with an odd smile, "…still, it would be a kindness…"

Richard pressed his brother's hand to make him stop speaking. "We'll beg nothing of Montfort," he said firmly.

After circling England from the southeast to the west, to the north and the southeast again, Simon approached London at last.

The sun itself seemed celebrating with a brilliant shine, giving all things vivid clarity. The sky was cloudless. Gentle, warm winds curled his army's flags and banners languidly.

While the arriving forces were still hours to the south, London's church bells began pealing in cascades of joyful sound as the city welcomed her champion. From the Cathedral of Saint Paul, Bishop Henry de Sandwich and his priests walked forth in procession chanting Glorias and Hallelujahs, bearing banners heavy with thread of gold and carrying a statue of the Virgin, held high on a garlanded platform. They solemnly walked a circuit of the city's churches, and from the churches more priests, monks and nuns joined their parade. Then they passed out of the city, crossing London Bridge to go to meet the earl beyond Southwark.

The dire time of wars and chaos, oppressions and tyrannies, the clergymen proclaimed, was at an end. The seed of God's Kingdom on Earth was safely planted and now would spread its peace triumphantly throughout the world.

Mayor FitzThomas had ordered Great Tower Street, from the Bridge to the Tower, to be arched with willow branches wrapped with flowers in the Earl's colors, red and white, a floral canopy above the whole length of the road. Roses and lilies perfumed the air. Breezes stirred the arch, casting a checkering of red and white petals onto the cobblestones beneath.

The passing of the singing clerics brought everyone out from his door: merchants, shopkeepers and craftsmen of all sorts with their wives, apprentices and servants. There were water carriers, peddlers, scholars, beggars, thieves, matrons, crones and children jamming the shaded, flower-dappled way, and far up every street that gave onto it.

The city's militia, both the day and night watch, manned the city walls facing south, not to defend, but to cheer. They blew gleefully upon their horns, their merriment beyond containing. Their jolly noise abruptly changed to trills of high-piping, excited calls that spread along the parapets answering each other, as the earl's line of march was sighted in the distance, led by the parade of clerics and the Virgin with her holy banners, her feet deep in blossoms.

Vintners had brought cart-mounted casks of their finest wines to offer the victorious knights. Bakers bore trays of sweetmeats: sugared almonds for prosperity; pastry balls filled with minced lark the herald of a new day; white cakes of marzipan each decorated with a dyed red lion rampant. The demoiselles of London of both high and low estate carried baskets heaped with flowers to scatter in the Earl's way. The entire capital was at giddy festival, a gaiety surpassing the open-air merriment of Eastertide, for this day was the Easter of the Lord's New Age.

Dominicans and Franciscans preached triumph and redemption on every street corner. Jongleurs in particolor satins juggled fruit and swords. Trouveres trilled on their pipes and danced, or beat their drums and sang the Earl's songs. Songs warbled from lilting pipes and were joined by the voices of the crowds.

*Il est apele de Montfort*
*Il est al mont*
*Et si est fort*
*Si ad grant chevalrie...*

Then a long, sustained blast of the horns upon the walls told London that the Earl was at the bridge.

A strange silence fell. Jongleurs caught their toys and let their arms hang at their sides. Trouveres lowered their pipes from their lips, placed silencing hands upon their drumheads, and stood still. Singing stopped. All faces turned toward the bridge.

There was a clattering of a thousand hooves upon cobbles and the jingle of chain mail and harness, sharply audible now in the sudden silence.

At the fore, the Bishop of London, with his priests bearing their statue of the Virgin, walked solemnly, followed by the banners of Saint Paul's and all of London's churches.

The crowd under the flower arches pushed back, oozed into side streets, making way.

Simon, black-bearded and bare-headed, dressed in black chain mail beneath a crusader's white surcoat blazed with the red cross, rode mastering his curveting war-horse to a collected walk. The great white destrier's eyes rolled at the masses of people, the noise and then the sudden silence of the staring crowds.

At Simon's side a large new banner, white with the fork-tailed red lion rampant, fluttered from a pole held by his son Guy.

As the priests strode on ahead, Simon and his bannerman passed into the shade of the canopy of flowers. Behind them the marching file extended, young lords with their flags, knights, foot soldiers, self-armed villein volunteers, the lesser priests and monks and nuns who had gone out to meet their hero, then a stream of ardent followers from every class and county. The long line flowed between the houses on the bridge and far back through Southwark, past the suburbs, into the countryside.

Simon, greeted by the London militia's ecstatic horn calls, led by the Virgin and all the city's priests, observed the dense and silent crowds, and was awed. Not by the astounding honor paid him. It was not an honor paid to him that he perceived at all, but a confirmation that his actions were indeed of God's will.

Passing along the shaded street, the red and white petals falling upon his dark hair and beard and white robed shoulders, he felt both justification and terror. For here truly was the Might of the Lord's Hand.

He knew himself to be unworthy in the extreme. No man was worthy of this, for who could be certain that his words and acts, in the moment that they must be done, *were* the Lord's will? For himself he had no hope of certain knowledge. For his cause he had more than hope, he had some growing confidence. Yet these breathless, adoring masses chilled him to his heart. He knew well this was the reverse side of the crazed mobs working Hades' ruin in the shires.

Simon kept his gaze ahead, at the statue of the Virgin swaying before him, and prayed.

Guy glanced toward his father, dumbfounded at the greeting, and too wise to feel pride. He saw the familiar, soft and inward focus toward the middle distance, unseeing, and he knew his father prayed. He did the same.

In the hall of the Tower, where the noise of the city had been deafening and maddening, the silence that followed was more frightening still.

King Henry, gray and hollow-eyed, sat upon his throne dressed in full state regalia, stiff, mute as a statue, his furred crimson cloak wrapped around him though the day was hot, and his cabochon-jeweled crown upon his head.

Richard, King of the Germans, also in his regal robes and crown, was seated by his brother's side. The secretary Walerant paced back and forth at the foot of the dais, the hem of his black robe flouncing round his feet, his hands clasped, pressed to his breast as if in prayer but really in utter anxiety. The Justiciar Philip Basset, black robed and festooned with gold chains, stood stiffly, arms pressed to his sides, beside Henry, but his hands were trembling so far past his control that the parchment statement of capitulation he held made a rustling noise. It was the only sound apart from Walerant's steady pacing.

Except for the four men at the dais and two bailiffs at the door, the hall was vacant. The mercenary force, seventy remaining at the Tower, had not been paid for months. They had stood down, considering their contract void. Many had fought for the Earl in the past and knew him as a preferable employer.

A double fanfare sounded as the Earl entered the Tower's gate.

Walerant halted in his pacing. The two kings remained motionless. After a few eternal-seeming moments there was the grating sound of many chain mail slippers on the stair, then at the door the earl's lieutenants appeared: Gilbert de Clare, John de Warenne and Guy de Montfort. They came in, then turned and bowed as the earl entered.

Simon, smiling broadly, with only a trace now of a limp, walked down the length of the hall. At the dais he bowed, then put out both his hands to Henry.

The King of England slowly stood, steadying himself with the arms of his chair. His voice came from his tight throat, small and tense. "I'm ready to go wherever you intend to put me."

Simon looked perplexed for a moment, then went down on one knee. "You are my king," he said with his head bowed. "I mean to see your people receive justice. My cause is the observing of the Provisions, not the seizing of your throne."

A shiver passed through Henry, quivering the long sweep of his cloak. "You wish me to live?" he asked in a whisper. "You mean me to go on... sitting here...?" Then he gave a bitter laugh, "... while you dictate to my secretaries in my name..." He lifted his crown from his head and held it out to Simon.

"Montfort, kill us and be done with it!" Richard, standing, burst out in furious challenge. "You have the power! You need play the hypocrite no longer!"

Simon rose to his feet and stood proudly, ignoring the crown Henry thrust toward him. "I've come to London to negotiate. If you have grievances against the government of the Provisions, we can deal with them through arbitration." He spoke in a calm tone. "I have no claim upon the Crown of England, nor do I mean to make any such claim."

Richard's eyes narrowed. "Why do you cling to this pretense, Simon? Take it while you can!"

The room was filling with the earl's followers. Simon stepped up on the first step of the dais and turned to face them. "We require," he addressed them in a loud, clear voice, "and King Henry has agreed, that all strategic castles of the land will be placed in the hands of loyal English castellans!"

The hall echoed with cheering voices.

"A Parliament shall be held six weeks from this day," Simon went on, "to elect and instate new ministers of the government, to reestablish justice. And to quiet the common uprising!"

Cheering resounded again. The young knights struck the flat of their swords against the walls, adding clangor to the din. The two kings on the dais sat still as stone, empty of expression, washed blank by the waves of cheers.

That afternoon Simon had a general summons sent out from the Chancery, calling all the barons, the clergy and the shire representatives to come to treat for the land's peace at London on September ninth.

Prince Edward was summoned to come from Windsor. His oldest friend, Henry de Montfort, delivered the summons himself.

Edward told Henry plainly, "Your father knows my views on the Provisions, and the Ordinances that would give the common people a voice. He knows how I put myself in jeopardy for them. But he uses force, and I will not be compelled!"

"Edward, let us have peace," Henry pled.

"My mother has been unspeakably ill-treated! The king and queen both are prisoners! The land is risen in revolt! And you speak to me of peace?"

"None of this is my father's doing," Henry urged. "He works for the peace of all. Join us, I beg you!"

"If I attend, it will be solely on my own terms, and when your father relinquishes his hold upon the Crown."

Henry took the prince's answer back to London. Simon, in a private chamber at his headquarters in the Tower, was writing instructions for Richard de Gray for the garrisoning of the ports.

When he heard how Edward replied, he bit his lip and looked down, ceasing to write.

Bishop Cantaloup, his brother Thomas and the Master of the Templars were conversing, sitting at Simon's table strewn with reports from the shires. Walter vividly had just described Edward's forsworn and lethal departure from Bristol, adding it to the Templar's details of the prince's robbery and slaughter at the Temple.

"Theft and murder at the Temple, Bristol, and now this! He's asking for beheading!" Thomas spoke up, all the more infuriated by Henry Montfort's message.

Simon turned away from them.

"You don't mean to let him dictate terms?" Walter pressed. "He has the conscience of a brigand and the ways of an assassin. And one day he'll be king!"

Simon looked at them, then nodded, his brow gathered tightly. "Yes. Edward must be curbed. That he's capable of these things... I believed we'd seen the end of his lawlessness. Clearly not." When he had rescued Edward from the Welsh at Ewloe, the intended death in battle King Henry had contrived for the prince's ruthless blinding of a child, Edward had been contrite and seemed reformed thereafter. He had pledged himself to Simon. The earl had hoped, even believed when the prince supported the Provisions, that he was changed, a man responsible and earnest, no longer a wild, dangerous child.

With Bishop Cantaloup and seventy mercenary knights, formerly the king's, now his, the Earl rode out to Windsor. The castle gates were surrounded by his forces, as at siege.

When tents were set and camp was made, Simon went and stood alone on the grassy slope before the wall, bareheaded and in easy bowshot from the parapet. "Edward, for the love we've borne each other since you were a child, come talk with me." His voice conveyed the sadness and the hurt he truly felt.

Looking down from the parapet, the prince stayed the bowshot of the thirty mercenaries he had brought from the Tower and the Temple. He agreed to parley. Accompanied by several of his soldiers, he went out the gate and to the Earl's tent, which was set up at a distance from the castle wall, well beyond the range of arrows.

"I've come to state my terms," the prince said curtly. He was dressed in a loose red velvet surcoat with his embroidered golden leopards en passant, and wore a full set of chain mail from Windsor's armory beneath it.

Simon, in his long, white, red-crossed robe and with no sword, stood in the tent's entrance. "Send your guards back, Edward, so we can speak alone." He spoke in a gentle, unchallenging tone.

"They go where I go." Edward raised his chin defiantly. But Simon's steady gaze, now as nearly always, kind when it was bent on him, was withering to his defenses. The Earl had brought him up, had taught him all he truly valued. As a child he wept because Henry, not Simon, was his father. In the depth of his heart he adored him.

" I give you my oath. You will be safe," Simon said earnestly. "Tell them to go back to the castle."

The prince still paused.

"Don't you trust me?" Simon asked, his tone sounding injured.

Edward nodded, abashed. "You're the only person I do trust." Turning to his mercenaries, with a jerk of his head toward the castle he said, "Go on back. It's all right."

They were unwilling to leave him, but he gave them such a hard look that they bowed and went back through the castle's gate.

Simon watched them go until the gate closed behind them, then he gestured for the prince to enter the tent. Edward, then Simon went in and the tent flap closed behind them.

Within were the Bishop Cantaloup and several heavily armed mercenary knights with swords and daggers drawn. Edward turned to bolt out. But behind him Simon now held a bare short-sword with its point toward him. "Put out your hands for binding," the earl said coolly.

"This is treachery!" Edward blurted.

"Yes, it is," Simon replied. "You see it's neither difficult, nor clever, to deceive. And those who practice treachery can expect no better for themselves."

The knights had roughly taken hold of the prince. They bound him with a stout rope to the tent's central pole, wrapping the rope several times around the prince's body, and binding his hands high on the pole so that his arms were stretched above his head.

Edward, muscular, athletic, slightly taller than Simon, his young beauty not coarsened yet, strained at his bindings. Never before had he felt the humiliation of bondage.

With the back of his hand Simon struck the prince hard across his face. As that cheek began to bleed, he struck the other cheek harder. "I've had faith in you, Edward!" His tone was cold with fury. "But there is in you a devil I detest! You take license only Satan would allow. I mean to see you broken, changed before you reach the throne!"

"You think the Lord sent you..." Edward, blood running to his chin, returned defiantly. Before he could finish he was struck hard again.

"I claim no such thing. I keep the vow that I, and you, and Henry – all of us took!" Simon cradled his raw knuckles in his left hand.

"My mother's been vilified..." Edward mumbled, his head drooping as he sagged against his ropes and blood dripped on the ground.

"God knows I repent my sins. Where's your repentance?" Simon glared at him.

"The London commons..." the prince lifted his head, trembling as his left eye swelled shut, but with a glint of rage in the wide, undamaged ice blue right eye.

Simon cut him off with a blow to his raised chin that made a cracking sound and sent his jaw askew.

He rubbed his reddened hand where Edward's blood mingled with his own. Then he grasped the prince by the hair, jerking his head back so that the one open eye met his sideways. "The Londoners, the folk of England, yes. The people raised in anger are a terrifying force. Are they not! I don't control them. Would that I could! It is my whole study to do just that and bring peace. *That* you may believe!"

He let go of the blond hair, knocking the prince's head down. The injured jaw hit the prince's chest and he cried out. Simon ignored his pain, adding, "The Londoners' actions do not excuse yours!" Standing back a few paces to signal that the beating was done, at least for the moment, he asked, "What can you say of the murder of the Templars, knights pledged to the Cross!"

Edward, tears making runnels through the blood that smeared his face to a red mask, raised his head, found Simon and focused blearily on him. He swallowed hard, trying to regain some manly dignity. His head felt like an apple crushed under somebody's heel. "We went to retrieve my mother's jewels," he muttered, moving his jaw carefully, finding it was dislocated but not broken. "We'd been drinking, and the Templars joined us in heavy drink." As if he lit upon an adequate excuse he added, raising his head higher, "I found the Order's... passions... were turning the Temple to a brothel of the most corrupt of lusts. By fire and sword I cleansed it." He tried to smile. Blood dribbled from his torn lip.

"And stole the hard-earned wealth of the Wool Guild as reward." Simon struck the prince's pulped face hard once again. "Until you learn, Edward, the conscience of a king, you will not be set free. And if you cannot learn, you'll find an early grave!"

The earl turned away from the prince who hung bloodied, fainted and sagging against the pole.

His white robe smeared and speckled red, Simon thrust the tent flap aside and strode out, ordering his men to take down the tent and display to the castle's defenders their commander, tied and beaten unconscious.

The thirty mercenaries hung out a white pennant. Gladly they joined their fellows already in the earl's service. Windsor surrendered.

All of England, and all of England's royal House of Plantagenet were in Simon's control.

# Chapter Ten

## A SUBTLE BALANCE
### 1263

Joy was heady throughout England. The great Earl and the forces of the Provisions had prevailed. The time of tribulations was ended and the New Age had begun.

In King Henry's name Simon called a general Parliament of the clergy, the shire knights elected by the commonality and of all the barons who were tenants-in-chief of the Crown. A new government was to be made and peace was to prevail.

"By every means we can, we must be sure our acts are right and have no taint of tyranny," Simon cautioned. He knew his ancient history well. The excitement of England's populace was all too like the mass up-wellings that raised tyrants in Rome. And spurred outrage in the Roman Senate. Since he was himself the focus of the current popular hysteria, he expected that his every action would be looked upon by cooler heads as the abuses of a Tiberius, a Caesar or a Sulla. He ordered scholarly writings searched, Grosseteste's, and Thomas Becket's, on the justified limiting of a king's power.

"Becket's amanuensis, John of Salisbury, took his master's thoughts to deeper study in his *Policraticus*," the scholarly Bishop Berkstead offered. "Kingship, in John's writings, loses the validity it draws from Christ if it fails to serve the good of the people."

Simon was aware of the cleric John's work but never had read it directly. He sent a messenger to Canterbury to find the manuscript in the monastery's library.

And he traveled to Hackington to visit his Aunt Loretta, as he had done when he was first befriended by King Henry. Loretta,

near a hundred years of age, was the last person still living who
recalled the workings of the Court of Henry II, before the decline
during the absent Richard's reign, the disorders of John's reign in
civil wars, and the disarray of the Court when Henry at age nine
received the Crown. During Henry's childhood the Court had
been run by his Poitouvin advisors who knew nothing of England's
traditions. As an adult, with information from Simon, who knew the
Court of France, the king had improvised according to his fancy.

The Earl consulted Loretta to reestablish what traditions
properly ought to surround England's king. And to determine
the exact powers of the Steward of England, the title that was his
inheritance with his earldom of Leicester.

Loretta, long ago the stately Lady Beaumont, Countess of
Leicester, was now a tiny, shriveled nun, her hands blue with the
branching of veins, and white as the bones that her thin skin barely
covered. But her eyes were large and dark, with the penetrating
sparkle of acute intelligence.

"The Steward," the fragile nun recalled quite vividly, "controlled
the door of the king's hall of audience. He determined who would,
and who would not, be heard by the king."

"As Steward I have rightful powers to bar from the king's
presence anyone who might harm the realm?" Simon pondered
for a moment. "It is enough. It's all I need."

"Indeed," Loretta observed wryly. "The Steward, in effect,
controls the realm."

Simon's whole effort was to remove himself as far as possible
from the functions of the government. At least so far as could be
done while maintaining the new government's security.

He was afraid of his popularity, the peculiar worship of him that
the friars' preaching had aroused. Everywhere he went, throngs
followed. The people wanted Christ Triumphant, invincible against
the enemies of Faith. King Forever of a Realm of Bliss. He wanted
merely a well-established means of harnessing an erratic king's
whims and his heir's violence.

If Simon was the Angel of the Coming Era, the archangel
Michael or perhaps the Risen Christ himself, the young knights

who had gained the miraculous success were, each and every one, the heroes of the people, the apostles of the New Millennium. They were cheered whenever they showed their faces. Like knights of old, their names were woven into songs. Those who had eked a meager credit before, fragilely secured by expected inheritances, now found merchants eager to heap massive credit on them. Their robes took on the summer garden hues of lush brocaded silks. They gave lavish feasts and drinking parties. For them it was a time of extravagance, of celebration without end.

All London was a festival. Except at the Tower and the mayor's manse. The queen was still in the keeping of the mayor and his aldermen. Simon visited her there.

Eleanor's glowing beauty had faded. Her blonde curls still nestled coyly on her shoulders but their coquetry, framing her puffed, aging face, was repugnant. Her large, sparkling and witty blue eyes now had a hard, sardonic glare.

Her chambers were well furnished. She and her ladies were treated with due deference, and enjoyed the finest wines and cookery the London Guilds could offer. But the ladies could not leave. Strong yeomen from the city's militia guarded them.

"You've come to release me?" she asked as Simon was shown into her chamber and the guard locked the door after him.

"I beg your patience, no. For the present you're safest here, but you'll be safer still when you're out of England. I'll arrange it as soon as I can."

"I am not a chess piece to be moved this way and that in this game you're playing!" Her slender neck was stiff but her eyes blinked with an uncertainty quite unknown to her before.

"What is happening in England is no work of mine." Simon spoke gently. He had loved her. Her circumstance, the evident breaking of the merry spirit he had known, he saw with pain. "Forgive me if you can. This," he gestured to the locked door, "is not of my ordering, nor is it my wish. But beyond it are people who might do you harm."

She looked down, her arms hanging dejectedly, but her fingers tightly laced. Tears were wanting to well in her eyes. In a small, childish voice she said, "Yes. I do believe you. But all you've done... everything has led to this! Could you not see?" she asked plaintively.

She had been the damning temptation of his life. He had turned away from her in jealousy when he realized he had a rival, and only that jealousy had cured him. Yet, broken, struggling to uphold her dignity, she was more poignant to him now than she had ever been before. He touched her trembling chin with his fingertips, and suddenly her tears poured down her cheeks.

"I'm trying to protect you. By God, my dear lady, this is not my doing."

She moved her head and pressed her lips against his hand. "It is. It *is* your doing!" she wept. "And I must not forgive you!"

If he had achieved one thing for his soul it was his break with his life's evil temptation, a lure of lust with the appeal of a strike at the royal master his heart despised. He had come to see his motive plainly, and loathed himself for it. It was the blemish he carried that brought his pride to its knees. He left Queen Eleanor quickly before the old, attracting twinge could take hold.

On September ninth the general Parliament was held in London, in the immensity of arched space that was the nave of the Cathedral of Saint Paul.

As the hour for the opening of Parliament approached, Simon, Walter Cantaloup, Richard de Gray, Robert Ferrers and Gilbert de Clare were in the vestry reviewing the agenda. Hugh Despensar joined them.

Gray looked to him and grinned, "This is the day we've waited for, my friend!"

Despensar was not smiling. "I pray it is," he said, but he seemed much disturbed.

The others looked at him questioningly. "Whatever's troubling you?" Walter asked.

Despensar gestured toward the nave where the meeting was gathered. "All's ready to begin, but most of the lords aren't here."

"Might the summonses not have reached them in time?" Gilbert worried.

"The churchmen from the furthest counties haven't failed to come," Hugh answered. "And from their numbers, it would seem that all the shire knights are here."

"You're suggesting that the lords refuse to come, as a gesture of their disapproval?" Simon asked.

"That's what I fear."

Just then the fanfare sounded giving notice that the king was entering. The Parliament was about to begin.

A throne had been placed at the crossing of the transept. Behind it, hung from a long silk-wound cord swung from the clerestory, was the royal crimson banner with the three strutting golden lions *guardant* of Plantagenet. Simon had made the arrangements himself. He wanted it to be very clear to all that King Henry still reigned.

Henry, wizened and gray, wrapped in his regal cloak and with a crown upon his head, was guided by Peter de Montfort as if he were an invalid, which he did seem to be. Prince Edward and Richard, King of the Germans, followed, surrounded by guards. Edward, his face scarred and blotched purple and yellow with bruises, was sullen. There was an audible gasp and murmur in the assembly at sight of the prince's evident brutal handling.

Richard, looking stern, did his best to maintain his dignity as if, as monarch of a foreign land, he had little reason to be here.

The crowd settled to silence, granting due respect. But when Simon walked to the dais steps the nave burst into cheers.

A clerk called the meeting to order.

New Provisions were offered, with a Council of only six members, to serve in pairs for four months successively, two to attend the king at all times. The shire knights and clergy unanimously approved, ready to grant anything the Earl seemed to wish. The assembly swore to uphold the new Provisions. King Henry arose, with help from Peter de Montfort, and in a voice nearly inaudible gave his own oath to the Provisions.

Then the new Council members were chosen. In a swell of eagerness the shire knights and clergy all voted for the men they knew the great Earl would approve: the Bishop Cantaloup, Peter de Montfort, Gilbert de Clare, Cantaloup's nephew Richard Mepham who was Archdeacon of Oxford, Bishop John Cheyham who had shown himself a sturdy advocate of the Provisions, and Simon himself.

Hugh Despensar and Nicholas the Bishop of Ely were to be Justiciar and Chancellor.

The few lords present abstained from voting, looked one to another and said nothing. The pool of councilors that held the king in check was smaller than before, and seemed to them to be all the earl's creatures. What Simon feared most was precisely what held their minds: the Earl of Leicester had England groveling at his feet. And they were not to be persuaded otherwise.

The Ordinances, requiring that the rights granted by King Henry to the barons, his tenants-in-chief, be extended to the lords' tenants, the common villeins, were affirmed. But, in the absence of so many of the lords for whom this legislation was most pertinent, the long-awaited vote could not be taken. So the Ordinances, which had caused the splitting off of most of the very barons who had won the Provisions, but who were unwilling to share their gains, remained still pending. Simon did not force the matter. He hoped the lords eventually would come to see the new system was to their benefit, and the breach would be healed.

The issue of the treaty with Llewellyn was presented. As the Earl Montfort wished, to bolster the security of England it was ratified.

So too the knights and clergy approved Simon's suggestions that prisoners taken during the campaign should be deported.

The few high lords eyed the mass of eager commoners filling the nave. They pursed their lips, exchanging tense glances and wished that they, like their friends, had ignored the summons to attend.

When the voting was done, the meeting was opened to the hearing of petitions.

The first petitioner to step forward was the Earl of Warwick, John de Plessis. He bowed to the king and to the new Councilors, Cheyham and Mepham, who were sworn in to serve the first term.

Then he looked to Simon, who was standing to one side below the dais steps, and he addressed the earl as if only his opinion mattered.

"I demand writ against Robert Ferrers!" he announced. "He seized Warwick Castle from me and holds it as if I were his enemy at war!" Warwick Castle and Kenilworth were neighbors, just five miles apart. If Kenilworth was the safe haven of the Provisions' cause, Warwick was strategic.

From where he stood near Simon, young Ferrers shouted back, "You hold lands of mine in Devonshire! And when I ordered you to open Warwick Castle in the name of the Provisions, you refused!"

"Robert," Simon put his hand on the young man's arm, "this matter is not for contention here, but for the judgment of the royal Councilors."

"My lord," Ferrers stared at him, "you approved that I make war on those who'd taken my lands, and that I see Plessis's castle was in friendly hands."

"By that I meant peace with the lord Plessis. I never ordered you to hold his castles from him. The Earl Plessis is no foreigner holding lands from the royal demesne. He is Warwick's rightful lord. We'll have no justice if we treat Englishmen like enemies, pursuing private grudges and taking each other's holdings. This was not a war for spoils, but a struggle to assert what's right."

Shire knights near the fore, overhearing Simon's words, passed them on to those behind. A wave of nodding heads in strong agreement rippled down the nave.

Ferrers glared, humiliated.

The case was submitted to the Councilors, who found in Warwick's favor.

Ferrers, in a fit of temper, turned to his friend Gilbert de Clare. "How could they find otherwise, when *he* said what he did! I only acted on his orders!"

Other petitions were presented. Petitions from outlying shires where crime and rioting were rife.

Simon stepped onto the dais, addressing the king and the Councilors. "This savagery that's fallen upon England must be ended! For the good of the government and of the people, severe measures must be taken now. I propose, for the land's security, that we establish Guardians of the Peace, and empower them with rights that will enable them to restore order swiftly.

Again the clergy and the knights cheered.

Guardians of the Peace were nominated. They would be supported by the shire's bailiffs and, if needed, would have armed forces of their own. They would have the power to punish crimes, even by hanging without trial if the evidence was sufficient: if the accused was caught in the act of a capital crime. Speed was essential to halt the violence. The slow process of the law courts was only extending the chaos.

The chosen Guardians were again all men the Earl would approve. They included his sons Henry and Simon, and his steward Nicholas Seagrave.

As the last session of the several days of Parliament came to a close, it was agreed that Parliament would reconvene on its previous regular date, the thirteenth of October, Saint Edward's day. There were to be reports on the initial effects of the Guardians.

With the Welsh treaty approved at last, Simon wrote to his wife in France. The time had come for her to bring their daughter Eleanor to England for the closing of the peace and her betrothal to Llewellyn, heir to the ancient princely title of North Wales.

Then Simon rode to Kenilworth with his son Guy and the hundred mercenaries he had acquired from the Crown. Many of them were men who had served him in Wales, and even in Gascony. All were pleased to have a sensible employer once again.

Simon rode silently, engrossed in thought. He was troubled by the Parliament. By the absence of so many of the lords. By the persistent deference to himself that seemed to make mockery of the very distribution of power that the system was intended to create. And he had word from France that the king's half-brothers of Lusignan, with other refugees, were trying to raise another foreign army. Their expulsion, while necessary, he knew bore this risk. War might not be ended.

At Kenilworth young Simon greeted his father and told him the engineer he sought to hire had come. Master William was waiting for him in the hall. After a brief rest, Simon toured the rim of the castle's island with the skilled builder. They studied the lake, the causeway, the knoll on which the tower sat. In the next days Master William, following Simon's advice, drew maps and plans and discussed with his new patron the fortress's points of strength and weakness.

A wall with multiple defensive towers was designed to circle the whole island, entered by a barbicaned gate. From the gate, high walls were to be raised down the length of the causeway that divided the Mere from the neighboring abbey's large pond. Fortified, the causeway's banks would form a strong, defended braye with a towered, massive second gate at its terminus to guard the swing bridge and the sluice that kept waters of the Mere from flowing off.

Additional kitchen gardens were laid out between the old tower and the wall beside the channel at the castle's rear. It could supply much of the food the garrison would need. No other fortress in England would compare to Kenilworth. It had been strong before, soon it would be unconquerable.

Simon had directed that the rents of lands seized from fleeing foreigners be used for the Provisions' defense. From this source there were abundant funds for building. He had given Kenilworth back to the Crown at the Oxford meeting in 1258. The castle no longer was his, it was one of the holdings of the government. As such, he saw no problem in using it to the utmost for the government's defense, financed by the recovered rents.

There were those who might think otherwise, who did not see the work at Kenilworth and might consider the monies spent as lavished upon his own home. Simon held military strategy of too much importance to trouble himself with such foolishness and risk losing time while armies were being raised abroad. Master William hired stonemasons. Work was begun at once.

The lords' refusal to attend the Parliament weighed heavily on Simon. He wrote to Roger Bigod, the Earl of Norfolk and Marshal of England, once strongly in favor of the Provisions.

The great bull of a man, who had held his weeping king in his arms but also always was the first to rebuke him, was not the man he once had been. The poisoning at Winchester had not destroyed him as it had Clare, but he was fragile and, for a man accustomed to being robust, his weakness made him fearful. He was afraid of Simon. Afraid of the role the commons assigned to the warrior he respected. For Roger, who had known Simon since he was a callow young petitioner at Henry's Court, that he might be the Angel of the Second Coming was ridiculous. More than ridiculous, it was dangerous to the very system they had worked hard to establish.

He wondered sometimes why Simon didn't simply kill Henry and assume the Crown himself. Dealing with him in that role would be far simpler than responding to the evasive posture he seemed to have adopted: the King of Heaven who had come to earth to make puppets of everyone else. To Simon's letter he responded with politeness. He was too sick to attend. Truthfully he was an old man now. But not so old that, if it came to somehow curbing Simon, he would not gladly join in.

While foundations for surrounding walls were being laid at Kenilworth, throughout England the Guardians of the Peace forcibly were putting down crime. Rioters by hundreds were being caught in the midst of pillaging, and were being hanged summarily. Bodies dangling from the village oak were now a common sight, the corpses left upon the trees by order of the Guardians as warning to any would-be wrongdoers.

Now villagers, instead of looting, were capturing the criminals they had set free from the jails. Surrendered to the Guardians, local miscreants filled the sheriffs' locked cells again and crammed the local courts' dockets.

Neighbors ceased attacks on one another and instead sought out the Guardians to lodge complaints. When grievances were major, the Guardians compiled petitions for the coming Parliament. Violence, in just a few weeks, was subsiding. Civil order, albeit by rough means, gradually was being restored.

At Westminster the reconstruction of the palace, which had bankrupted the royal treasury, was nearing completion. Although long makeshift wooden corridors still ran maze-like everywhere, the Chancery was finished and the king's apartments were receiving their last touches of bright paint. Henry, Edward, Richard and the Court of clerks and attendants were able to return, though still the two kings and the prince were under guard.

Queen Eleanor, freed from Mayor FitzThomas, had been placed on a ship and sent to shelter at the Court of her sister Margaret in Paris.

Henry gazed about at the walls of his new chambers, splendid with murals of hunting scenes and fables, just as he had designed. He smiled, a little gratified. But the bailiffs at his doors had faces new to him, and they took orders from the new Chancellor and Justiciar, not from him.

As the meeting of the October Parliament approached, Simon returned from Kenilworth. The night before the meeting was to convene, while he sat at supper in his chamber at an inn, his squire Peter announced an unexpected visitor. It was the Earl John de Warenne.

Simon rose from his table to greet the young man. Warenne had served very honorably in the recent campaigns. Though Simon had no clear idea of why he'd come, he was pleased to see him. "What brings you to me tonight?" he smiled encouragingly.

Warenne's lean face was fixed in a pinched frown. He stood like a troubled waterbird on his long, slender legs as if he searched beneath a pond's reflection for the fish that got away. "Good Earl," he said at last, "it's the matter of the distribution."

"Distribution?" Simon asked, perplexed.

"The distribution of the lands and rents we've taken from the lords who've fled. They'll be dealt with in this Parliament? I have increasing debts…"

"What lands and rents do you mean?"

Warenne met the earl's eyes, confused that his words seemed not to be understood. "Taken from Aigueblanche, from the Lusignan, Savoy, from the sheriffs and all the other Poitouvins who've gone. The lands you assigned to the care of your cousin lord Peter and to your sons until the distributions."

Simon was more puzzled than disturbed by Warenne's words. "There is to be no distribution. Those lands and funds are restored to the Crown for the land's defense."

"Lord Earl," Warenne blurted, "it's cost me all I have and more to fight this war for you!" He did not mention all that he'd spent since, lavishly on credit from the London merchants. Rents were due every Michaelmas, September twenty-ninth; he knew that the Exchequer was well funded now. "Surely my reimbursement can be made out of the rents that are collected? A trifle more might be fitting for my services, but I blush to ask!"

"Those rents, as I said, have been returned to the royal demesne," Simon repeated firmly, "and have been allocated for England's defense."

"Your cousin and your son are gathering the rents…"

"They remit every penny to the Treasury for use in the government's protection."

"Ferrers made a fortune in Derbyshire!"

"Ferrers will be made to give up anything he doesn't hold by clear right of inheritance."

"My lord, I protest! We served you in good faith!"

Simon's anger was rising. "And I came from France, and served *you* in good faith! Not to make you rich with spoils, but to see England's rightful government restored! You may leave now, Lord Warenne. I'll hear no more of your demands!"

# Chapter Eleven

## THE TIPWEIGHT
### 1263

The Parliament of Saint Edward's Day opened in the newly finished hall at Westminster. There were indeed no columns to obstruct King Henry's view. The gabled roof floated on a maze of hammer beams borne up, by all appearance, on the wings of angels. The oaken angelic host cast a benevolent regard upon the mortals below: knights and clerics assembling with their petitions from the shires.

The Guardians of the Peace had staunched the violence. Now claims for recompense came pouring in. Instead of raiding and pillaging, the abused were seeking satisfaction through the laws. It seemed the Guardians were meeting their task well.

King Henry sat in a new and deeply cushioned throne beneath a fine new canopy of crimson velvet fringed with gold. His hall was more regal than ever before, but Henry himself seemed withered, shriveled like a dried, impotent seed within its polished shell.

Prince Edward and King Richard of the Germans sat at either side of Henry in their own magnificently carved oak chairs with velvet cushions. The prince's face was scarred, but the bruises had faded. He and Richard were alert to the proceedings, yet remote as though retreating into their own thoughts. Henry was barely aware of anything. Sometimes his eyes were shut, his arms crossed and pressed tight against his chest.

Although the summoning had been sent out in September, requiring attendance by all of the great lords as well as the clergy and the elected knights of the shires, there were even fewer of the senior barony than had come to the last Parliament.

Simon stood to one side of the royal dais with Richard de Gray and Thomas Cantaloup, surveying the attendance.

Bishop Walter's brother Thomas, now Provost of Oxford and Provincial of the Order of Franciscans, was a scholar of theology and law. He too, though younger, had known Simon in their student days in Paris. Tall as his massive brother, but slender, he was more retiring and studious than Walter, who seemed made for knighthood. Now Thomas' office as Provost and Provincial, and his belief in the Provisions, was drawing him into the rush of worldly action.

"Are Hugh and Roger Bigod here?" Simon asked, squinting at the throng. The level-headed Hugh, Roger's brother, had been the Provisions' first Justiciar. He had opposed Simon at times, but his belief in their cause had been unquestioned. Simon had written again, urging both Roger and his brother to come.

De Gray, with good eyesight, told Simon gloomily, "No. Nor is Plessis. But de Vere and Lacey are here. They're the only ones of the elder earls. Most of these men I don't know. They seem to be local shire knights."

That both the Bigod brothers still were absent was bad news.

"Roger Mortimer? The lords of the Welsh borders?" Simon asked.

"None of them are here," de Gray answered.

Simon shook his head despairingly.

"It is very troubling that we lack the mandate of the senior lords." Thomas's tone was somber.

"As ever, they show themselves forsworn cowards." Simon's tone was resigned. He had hoped, but had expected no better from the lords who framed the Provisions, then balked at sharing their rights with the common folk.

But that was not the cause of why so many stayed away.

Simon's current fame he saw as an absurd aberration. One he tried to correct, with no success at all. It did not occur to him his commonly proclaimed holy mission was the core reason for the great barons' absence. Jealousy he tried to address by stepping away from any overt role in the government. But the lords' feelings now were far past simple jealousy. A prophet is not a prophet in his own land, as Jesus himself observed, and an angel is not an angel when you've shared the stench of battle sweat and peacetime kegs of wine with him for three decades. The lords were offended, appalled by Simon's hallowed fame and would condone nothing he sponsored.

In their absence the Parliament went on.

At the dais, claim after claim of losses suffered during the uprisings were read before the king and his Councilors. Supporters of the Provisions were demanding reparations from the royal purse, on legal grounds of Henry's breach of faith as cause of the disorders.

With a gesture of vague helplessness, King Henry turned the issue over to the Council. And the full Council of six met.

"What can we do?" Bishop Cheyham asked, totally dismayed. "If the Treasury was overflowing, I doubt we could meet a tenth part of these claims!"

"Although the current rents are in, the Treasury's empty except for the funds allocated for defense," Hugh Despensar, the Justiciar, informed them.

"There is a means of recompense at our disposal," Gilbert de Clare, spokesman for the young lords, offered. "That is, if we insist upon a fair division."

All looked to Clare, interested.

The heir of Gloucester argued coolly, "The Steward of England, on excuse of the land's defense, uses the rents taken from the king's foreigners. But what need is there for such costly defense as he claims? We have the Guardians, and hold the ports against invasion from abroad. The rents should be divided into shares to recompense all those who've given aid to us and suffered loss. Is this not in the Council's power to decide?"

"The rents have been collected for the Crown, as we swore at Oxford that all royal holdings given to the foreign born should be," Simon rehearsed for Clare, like a teacher catechizing a slow student. "The Lusignan in France raise armies against us. Access to England is not prevented by merely controlling the Cinque

Ports, as the attempt at Bristol showed. War still is a very real, impending threat."

"But the Treasury is empty! So we've just heard," Clare threw back insinuatingly. "Where *has* the money gone?"

The blatant accusation caught Simon off guard. He retorted, "The day of accounting was Michaelmas, barely two weeks past! The land has been in great disorder, yet you expect all rents to be remitted to the Treasury with more speed than in times of peace? Lord Gilbert, what is it you mean to imply!"

"I imply nothing. But I would remind the Council that all the holdings of the king's former secretary, John Mansel, have been given over to your son Simon. Neither Ferrers, nor any other of us who has fought, at loss of property and risk of our lives, may keep what we've seized. But your sons are given riches in abundance!"

"What was directed to my son Simon is in his keeping only as steward, Sire Gilbert. If you, or Warenne, or Ferrers, or anyone else does not like the dispositions I am making for the land's security, advise us as to better!" Simon's anger shot forth with singeing sarcasm at Clare's impudence.

"That is what I suggest. A better disposition," Gilbert returned with steadiness against the earl, astonishing even himself. "Divide the lands among those proven loyal to our cause."

Simon was livid. The insult, the insinuation that he had appropriated the spoils of the campaign to himself, was past his enduring.

Hugh Despensar brusquely intervened. "That would only perpetuate the Treasury's bankruptcy. We raised cry because the king had given out so many of his landed rents that he couldn't support himself without monstrous added taxes. As the Earl Montfort says, the rents must be returned to the Crown. The wrong is being remedied. What you suggest, Lord Clare, would be to disperse them again?"

Clare made a gesture of exasperation. "And so good Englishmen must suffer want..."

Simon, regaining his composure, said more calmly, "Lord Gilbert, when you and the Earl de Warenne and Robert Ferrers begged me to come from France, it was to reinstate the Provisions and drive out the foreign leeches. England is not yet secure."

"So we are told," Gilbert muttered.

"And so we must believe!" Bishop Walter broke in, placing a hand of benediction between Clare and Simon.

The Chancellor Bishop Nicholas of Ely added, "How can we decide who ought and who ought not to receive recompense? If we attempt such a division, we'll make enemies of all those we fail to satisfy. Better we plead the misfortunes of war and recompense no one, than attempt a dispersal that can only cause dissent, and will perpetuate the Crown's debility."

The bishop's argument carried the rest of the Council. They returned to the hall, reporting to the king that recompense would not be possible.

A rustle of dismay eddied among the young lords and petitioners. There was animated, angry talk.

Bishop Cantaloup stepped forward and explained the Council's reasoning.

Protest subsided but hard looks remained.

The meeting was dismissed.

Edward and Richard observed the flurry with interested attention. That evening Richard went to Edward's chamber. "Do you sense, as I do, the beginning of a shifting of the wind?"

The prince regarded his uncle with a cautious smile. "I see there's some displeasure with the Council."

"It is our chance, if we're bold enough to take it."

"I fear my father's in a poor way to make use of it."

"And yourself?" Richard raised his brush of red brows.

Edward gave him no response. The earl had set the Bishop Cantaloup to discourse with him on sin, in particular the horrors of a reign in which the king was impious and lawless, setting an example of violence for the entire realm. The prince was not unreached by Cantaloup's arguments. He hated above all the weakness and disorder of King Henry's reign and genuinely wanted to rule England better. Despite the beating, he still respected, even loved Simon. He was not incapable of seeing his own acts were sins, and if a public beating was his punishment, he accepted it. Even the great Henry II had accepted the lash for Becket's death. Living in restraint was what rankled him.

"Perhaps you favor Leicester's program after all?" Richard prodded. "And you mean to acquiesce? I remember you once heartily supported the Provisions."

Edward's blue eyes darkened. "What I think of the Provisions, and what I see in England now are very different things. There is a force at work that is remote from the Provisions, regardless of its claims. I see the king broken by that force and kingship itself made impotent. And my mother the queen has been insulted and defiled." His fair skin reddened, the muscles of his face tightened. His bruises from the beating were gone but scars still showed and whitened with the heightening of his color. "Yes, I noticed the dissatisfaction in the Court today. I'll use it if I can."

Richard studied him. "You still think well of Montfort, don't you. You'll fight the Bristolmen, the Londoners, the Welsh. But you won't fight him." He set his words out as a challenge.

Edward met his uncle's eyes, rising to the bait, but he answered only, "His alliance with the mob is wrong."

"He uses vicious hounds to down his game," Richard smiled cynically.

"A pretty choice of words, Uncle. But war is not the hunt. Nor is treating a queen, as my mother has been abused, a strategy the earl taught me. Yet he makes the Londoners his friends and his supporters. Not one of them has been brought to justice." Mastering his feelings, he got up to leave his chamber.

"Where are you going?" Richard asked.

"To sound out someone who seemed dissatisfied today. I saw my friend Leybourne scowling. I'll start there."

Roger Leybourne, formerly of the prince's Bachelry of followers, then outlawed for a time, had secured the London to Dover road for the Provisions. For his able service he had been rewarded, strangely, with the stewardship of the king's household. To him fell the task of seeing that the kitchen was supplied, that meals were served with proper decorum, that the functions of cleaning and serving operated smoothly. The office, with its slight spill of excess storehouse goods and moderate chance for graft, so far was his only reward. He had hoped for lands and rents and the idle life they afforded, not the busy attention to daily detail that the royal household stewardship required.

The prince found Roger in the kitchen studying the cooks' accounts.

"To what do we owe the distinction of a visit from Prince Edward?" Leybourne bowed with arch grace.

"My father has little interest in his food of late," Edward, leaning against the doorpost, said easily. "But he spoke today of lampreys. I've come to ask if you could obtain some for him."

"You seek me out yourself for that?" the steward asked, quite undeceived.

"No," Edward admitted, launching himself gently from the doorframe and, placing a hand on Leybourne's shoulder, steering him out of earshot of the servants. "Truth to tell, I was feeling rather dull and wished someone to talk to. You were good company when I still had my friends, in happier days."

"My lord," Leybourne made a slight bow, "you do me honor to remember me so. Come, it's quieter at this hour in the buttery." Taking a candle, he led the prince to the next room and shut the heavy door behind them, locking it for good measure.

Edward raised his eyebrows. "Am I not secure enough in this well-guarded palace?"

"We would have privacy, wouldn't we, my lord?" He held out the key to Edward. "You may have it if you wish."

Edward shrugged and didn't take it.

"Dull, my prince?" Leybourne asked. "Yours is not a spirit that knows dullness, if one who's served and lived with you may judge."

"Then perhaps I seek you for some other reason?" Edward smiled his always winning smile. "Perhaps dissatisfaction is the better word?"

"That might be."

"I doubt that I'm the only one who's suffering from it." Edward watched Leybourne's face in the shadowed candlelight.

"That also might be." Leybourne returned his smile.

"I remember that you were, in those days when we were companions, expecting an inheritance of lands in Kent. Have you received them?"

"Much is still unsettled," Leybourne said noncommittally. "I have my stewardship."

"That is to say, you've received nothing but hard work."

Leybourne's look acknowledged the tender point Edward had touched.

"You served me as a friend before," Edward said genially. He rested his strong sword-trained fingers gently on Leybourne's satin sleeve, idly bridging the space between them. "From what I've heard of your exploits on the Dover Road and in the forests, you're no stranger to high risk. In fact, if I've heard rightly, you thrive on it."

The corners of Leybourne's mouth pulled down in a smile at the prince's praise. He scratched his ear and looked at Edward sidelong. "What is it that you want of me, my prince?"

"Think how grateful I would be, as king, were you my friend now." Edward's voice was relaxed, innocent, as if the subject weren't conspiratorial. His golden hair was pretty as chick's fluff in the candlelight. Only the scars on his cheeks and brow detracted from his beauty.

Though Leybourne's quizzical expression was unchanged, he studied the prince carefully. Then, taking the prince's hand as it rested on his arm, he pressed the long, slender fingers. "Edward, you do tempt me."

"Shall I tempt you more exactly?" Edward returned the pressure of his hand.

"What can you promise?" Leybourne's eyes glittered in the soft light.

"I can promise your entitlement to your lands, that's merely your due. But, as my friend in need, I could offer you much more. A rich fief in Gascony perhaps? Would that suit you? That, I could bestow out of my own dukedom. But still more..." As Leybourne watched him intently, he settled himself comfortably on the shelf of the sideboard that held the royal serving bowls and ewers, at the outer edge of the candle's glow. His face was in shadow. "I could promise you the Stewardship of England, if you and I prevail." With the title Earl of Leicester, the stewardship was Simon de Montfort's inherited honour.

"My lord," Leybourne stepped toward him, then knelt before the sideboard, "give me your hand again in pledge of this, and I'm at your command."

Edward reached down and took Leybourne's offered right hand. "I give you my pledge. Seek out followers for us. We two alone cannot make good my promises."

"I'll find you partisans. There are others like myself, less than pleased with the Earl Montfort."

"Good. Let's meet here in three days at this same time. You'll give me word then of your progress." Edward brushed Leybourne's downy cheek with his cool fingers thoughtfully, then got up from the sideboard and put his hand out for the key.

Leybourne gave it to him. The prince unlocked the door and the two went out. The kitchen was dark and quiet now. Edward dropped the key back into Leybourne's palm, and with no further word went back to his own chamber.

When the prince next saw his uncle the King of the Germans, he said simply, "I've begun."

At the appointed time Leybourne and Edward met again. Leybourne had found several men to join them.

That evening at supper in the new dining chamber, the prince seemed lost in thought. Simon, the Bishop Cantaloup, Gilbert de Clare, the Earl of Oxford Robert de Vere and John de Warenne were all dining at the royal table with King Henry, Richard, Edward and Henry of Alemaine, who had been liberated when he was discovered in a chamber of the Tower.

Simon noticed Edward's abstracted mood. "You seem preoccupied, good prince?"

Edward looked up as if startled. "Yes," he answered with apparent embarrassment. "I've been thinking of my wife."

Simon tipped his head questioningly.

"I've neglected her. She was so pleased when I was with her at Windsor." He gave a brief laugh. "Now that I can't be there... I miss her." He shrugged with a boyish smile as if caught in a carnal dream.

Warenne looked up from his trencher, alert at his words.

But they bore such simplicity that Simon only nodded. The prince had not yet begotten a surviving heir. The peace of England depended, in part, on uncontested succession to the throne. There was good reason why the prince should not be parted from the Infanta Eleanor, his wife.

"What a wholesome wish!" Clare grinned cynically, knowing the prince avoided his tearful, adoring, devout wife like the devil confronted with holy water, preferring more spirited women with sophisticated, well paid skills. But he supposed that, since Edward's normally very active habits were curtailed, even his dull wife might seem alluring.

Alemaine, the shy and gentle member of the prince's friends known as the Bachelry, and party to the earliest of the prince's lewd rovings, stared down at the floor.

"Perhaps it could be arranged for Edward to go to Windsor?" Cantaloup asked, thinking of a secured Plantagenet succession.

"An escort can be arranged," Simon agreed. Anything that normalized the situation of the royal family ought to be tried. And Edward, of them all, was the most nearly to be trusted, the most favoring of the principals of the new government.

"You mean a guard for your prisoner, Steward?" Richard put in acerbically.

Simon darted a frown at the King of the Germans. "No one here is a prisoner. Disruptions we all know still plague England. Armed escort is necessary for the prince's safety."

Warenne spoke up. "I'll be happy to conduct Edward to Windsor. I can assemble a company for the prince's safe arrival."

Good." Simon did not cease glowering at Richard. "Let it be done."

Throughout the meal King Henry sat blank-eyed, barely picking at his food and saying not a word.

The next afternoon, Edward, mounted on his magnificent Spanish destrier and surrounded by his escort, took the road toward Windsor. He rode near the fore with Warenne, both their flags fluttering ahead of them. They had not gone far beyond the manor fields of Hyde when the prince turned to the young earl and said, with an amiable glitter in his sky blue eyes, "Leybourne tells me that you happily recall our times in Wales."

"I do, my lord," Warenne grinned back. "As do all the men with us, if you've noted who they are."

"I have. And I believe my fortunes have begun to rise. Am I not right?"

"We're all at your command, my prince," Warenne smiled broadly.

Edward pressed his spurs into his horse's sides and the powerful beast sprang forward. As he passed his flag-bearer, Edward leaned over and grasped the pole. Dashing ahead, his leopard banner streaming, he cried over his shoulder, "Come my friends! We have a country to win back from her usurpers!"

The company of his seeming guards let out a joyful yell, galloping after him.

Shortly after Parliament convened the next morning, at the far end of the hall there was a scuffling as a knight forced his way through the press of petitioners and Court clerks.

"My lord King Henry, and my lord King of the Germans," he bowed at the dais, quite out of breath. "I bring urgent news from Windsor!" He turned to the Earl Montfort who moved toward him from the lowest dais step. "Prince Edward's taken the castle and has slaughtered or imprisoned the garrison!"

Simon looked at the man in disbelief. "How did this happen?"

"The prince arrived last night, accompanied by the Earl de Warenne and guards with a royal writ of entry. In the middle of the night he and those with him overwhelmed the watch and slew most of the garrison as they slept."

Everyone in the hall was craning to listen. Then they were talking with a buzz that sounded like an infuriated hive.

A hard, grim expression strained Simon's bearded face. Richard, sitting bedside his brother, raised his eyebrows in delighted surprise. Even Henry roused from his lethargy.

Guy de Montfort, bursting with anger, came forward to the dais. "Father, let me take a force and march against him. Fine ways for a future king! He kills men while they sleep!"

"No, Guy," Simon said firmly. "Edward has no cause to arm himself and hold Windsor as if we were at war with him." He turned to the Bishop Cantaloup. "Walter, go to Windsor. Do what you can to persuade the prince we mean him peace if he'll return to Westminster."

"He's killed men by stealth, and not for the first time... I think you're very lenient," Walter growled.

There was shouting in the hall in agreement with the bishop's words.

"I don't want war with Edward!" Simon insisted. "And he won't be taken by a ruse a second time."

The Bishop of Worcester and the Bishop of Lincoln left for Windsor to negotiate a truce.

The next day Parliament convened again. The knights, the clerics, the Council members, the Justiciar, the Chancellor and the Steward of England were assembled. But no fanfare sounded announcing the arrival of the two kings.

The men in the hall waited, and waited, talking among themselves.

Simon sent a page to Henry's chambers to find the reason for the delay.

The page returned hurriedly to the earl and whispered, "My lord, the king's chambers are empty. His own servants are searching for him. The King of the Germans also has not been seen this morning."

"Bring me Leybourne, the household steward," Simon ordered. He intended to find out if the kings had been present at their breakfasts.

The page returned again, reporting in a low voice, "The kitchen staff haven't seen Lord Leybourne either all morning. There are people searching for the clerk Walerant as well."

The words came as a surprise. For all his foreseeing of worst possibilities, Simon had not prepared for this, beyond the guard of palace bailiffs he trusted completely. "God help us," he muttered under his breath.

With as much of an appearance of unconcern as his well-practiced years as a courtier afforded him, he walked over to Hugh Despensar, who was standing on the dais talking with Bishop Cheyham, and drew the Justiciar aside, murmuring in his ear, "You must have the palace thoroughly searched."

Despensar, reading Simon's dark but controlled expression, whispered back, "Could Henry be gone?"

"Be discrete in your search." Simon nodded toward the already annoyed and stirring assembly in the hall.

Despensar made his way out and summoned his chief bailiff. The maze of wooden corridors was searched as well as the rooms in all states of finish and partial construction. Every workman and servant was questioned. No one had seen the king, Richard, Leybourne or Walerant since the night before. Henry and Richard's body servants had been frantically but quietly pursuing their own searches for hours.

The chief of the bailiffs reported to the Justiciar. Despensar, approaching Simon with as calm a stride as he could manage, muttered his news in Simon's ear.

By now the Parliament's attendees were beginning to be alarmed. It was midday and the Parliament had not yet properly opened.

At the rear of the hall a very tired, road-dirtied youth stood arguing with a bailiff. Grudgingly the bailiff brought him forward to Simon at the dais. The boy flung himself into a clumsy, exhausted bow. "I come from Bishop Cantaloup at Windsor. My message is for your ears only, my lord."

Simon drew the youth up the steps and to the new private chapel behind the dais. "What is your message?" he asked when they were alone.

"The king and Richard of the Germans are at Windsor with Edward. All the great lords within a day's ride of London and Windsor – those who refuse to come to Parliament – are gathering to them in full arms with their knights. Every lord who is not at one with you is summoned by the prince. Windsor is become a battle camp."

Simon's expression grew as solemn as the statue of God the Father at the Last Judgment that stood nearby. "The worst I've feared has come, though not as I expected... Not Edward, and not so soon." With a wave of his hand he dismissed the young messenger and turned to the altar of the chapel. Kneeling, he prayed, "Father, can this endeavor truly be Your will? Let me leave these people who feverishly rail, but when a cure is near they betray it. Let me go to Palestine where I may do some good for Christ."

He remained kneeling on the tile floor, the tips of his fingers pressing his brow, his face buried in his hands. The only words that came to him were Father Grosseteste's *Feed my sheep.* Over and over with increasing urgency they echoed, the more he resisted them. Willfully he tried to silence the three words with the reasonable argument that he had tried and found the effort hopeless. He launched against the echo his yearning to return to the East. The plea seemed hurled back at him as selfish willfulness. Urgently he pled that this task in England, this confusing, thankless, wayward and disintegrating task, be lifted from him. His own words at Oxford answered him – *it is as well to die here among faithless Englishmen, fighting for Church and Christ, as to die in the Holy Land.*

At last he stood and turned to the door. Despensar was waiting for him, an alarmed, questioning, agitated stress stiffening his face and body, held in check by the earl's prayer. "My lord...?" His voice was hoarse with anxiety stifled with control.

Simon went to him and said simply, "The lords – the army of barons of England with their knights, are at war with the Provisions. They are at war with us."

Despensar already had forced the news from the messenger. "What should we do?" He eyed the milling, nerve-strung crowd in the hall, his fear conjuring as many facets of catastrophe as his imagination could produce. "Ought we to dismiss the Parliament?"

"That we must not do," Simon said steadily, "unless we mean to abandon our cause here and now."

From the doorway the earl's nearsighted gaze swept the hall. Not a face was recognizable from where he stood. The assembly was a multicolored mass, but he did not need to see the details to feel the tense strain that infected the room, as pervasive as a foul stench.

"We must tell them Henry's gone. We must prepare the country for the worst." Simon walked to the empty royal throne, turned and faced the hall, raising his hands for attention.

"Good men of England," he spoke in a dark, ringing tone, "as you already know, Prince Edward has gone from this Court to Windsor, where he holds the castle in a state of war against us. Now," his voice deepened in resonance, "King Henry and King Richard of the Germans are gone to join him. And the lords of England, forsworn from their oaths to defend your Provisions, are joining them, with their knights in full arms. War has come. If you wish to keep your rights – for yourselves, your children, and your children's children to the last generation that God grants to man – you must fight for them."

The crowd burst into explosive talk. Angry shouts pierced through the roar. The flats of swords were clashed against the stone walls like clanging bells of war.

Simon raised his hands again for silence. "Each man who can command armed forces, come to the dais and report the strength and kind of forces he is able to raise."

The shire knights swarmed toward the dais, jostling into a long line. The young lords formerly of Edward's company came as determinedly as the rest, angry at Edward for this latest betrayal of the cause they had discussed for months, for years, among themselves, and had agreed was best for England's ills.

One by one the lords and the knights of the shires came forward, knelt, swore again to defend the Provisions that granted Englishmen their rights and reported the number of men they could bring and with what arms.

Young Humphrey de Bohun pledged his own service with twenty armored knights and two hundred foot soldiers with crossbows. William Furnival, a new face at the Parliament, swore his neighbors of the shire would join him in a force five hundred strong, armed with short swords and axes. Heir to a rich double-earldom, Gilbert de Clare pledged three hundred mounted men with swords and chain mail. His comely face was abashed with the discredit he earned insisting there was no more danger of war.

So it went through the afternoon in Westminster's new royal hall, beneath the flock of oaken angels spread-winged under the roof's hammer-beams. The number of promised knights passed three thousand, the foot soldiers several thousand more.

But when it was the turn of Henry of Alemaine, Prince Richard's son came to the dais with a countenance bleached with concern. "Lord Steward, I beg pardon from this oath," his eyes met Simon's pleadingly. "I cannot pledge to oppose my father. Or my uncle the king, or my cousin Edward. But I swear, I never shall raise my hand against you or the Provisions."

"At Oxford he refused to swear," young Bohun, standing nearby, sneered. "Coward!" A long time companion of Alemaine, he spat on the floor.

The knight Roger Furnival, standing beside Alemaine, grabbed his arm roughly and turned him.

"I'm not a coward!" Alemaine faced Furnival as the man's hand struck across his cheek, leaving a broad red welt. He struggled to strike back but now his arms were pinned behind him. Rage was the feeling seething in every man in the crowd. Unwittingly he had made himself its ready target.

"Traitor!" Furnival struck him a second blow. The whole line of pledgers was converging, wrathful, breathing readiness to join in the beating.

"Leave him alone!" Simon commanded, stepping down from the dais and grabbing Furnival's arm raised to deliver a third blow.

"Anyone who won't support the Provisions is our enemy!" the young lord de Vere, pushing forward, yelled. "That is our oath!"

Someone behind the earl struck Henry and he toppled, kept from falling only by the raging crowd around him.

Simon grasped Alemaine by the shoulders and held him up protectively. "Are we so afraid of Henry Alemaine?" he bellowed, his tone rich with sarcasm.

Bailiffs had forced their way through the crowd. Simon handed the bruised, glaring-eyed young lord into their hands. To Alemaine's bleeding face and tearless, furious gaze, he said with disdain, "It's not the loss of your arms, Henry, that saddens me, but your inconstancy. Go! Return with all the forces you can muster against us. We have no fear of you."

Alemaine, regaining his balance, freed from the bailiffs' grip, stood a moment wiping blood from his split lip. The words, astonishing from the man he held in highest regard, left him confused, chagrined. Then the fury he felt at his attackers refocused. The glare he turned on the earl, so unlike his mild nature, was of utter hatred for this ultimate, uncalled-for insult. He turned. The crowd opened and let him pass, laughing, pointing and making rude gestures as he went, until he broke into a run out the door.

Returning up the dais steps, Simon met Despensar's eyes. "He is the most honorable of us all," he said in a low voice.

"I believe you saved his life. Was that why you mocked him?" the Justiciar asked.

Simon nodded, "He hates me now. So be it."

Turning to the crowd again, he said in loud, ringing challenge, "Are there any more of you who wish to leave? If so go now! We have no need of you!"

The room resounded with cries of oneness with the Earl and with the oath.

Steeling himself, Simon raised his hands again, and again the din in the hall sank to silence. "Even if you all fall away," he bellowed, his voice reverberating against the stone walls, "I, with my sons, will stand for the just cause we've sworn to uphold! Nor do we fear to go to war!"

There was a cheer outreaching all the others, searing in its noise, its battle-eagerness. The walls rang, and the angels above quivered with the cry.

"Return to your homes to arm!" the Steward of England commanded.

The Parliament was done.

# Chapter Twelve

## THE BRINK OF WAR
### 1263

With his sons Henry and Guy, his squire Peter, Nicholas Seagrave and his guard of mercenaries, Simon left Westminster and rode north to Kenilworth. From the moment the earl's company passed the village, construction work visibly had changed the landscape. Nothing was recognizable. A broad swath of the woodland on the knoll was now bare ground. Where the pleasant forest of great trees and mossy, root-girt ground had been was a smooth plateau of dirt encumbered with a lumberyard of cut and stacked green wood beams, and a stone yard to which great blocks were delivered on carts drawn by oxen. The lawn sloping to the Mere, at what had been the forest's edge, was inhabited by tired, grazing animals, resting before making the return trip for more stone.

On the cleared ground of the stone yard, where not a blade of grass was to be seen, more than a hundred muscular youths, apprentice masons, labored briskly and intently. From hair and face to jerkin, leggings and cross-garterings, they were all the same soft ruddy hue of stone dust, as was everything around them. The air itself was a mist of rust-red particles. Sweating rivulets down the fine grain of their powdered faces, the apprentices battered at raw chunks of stone, rough-shaping them to blocks, under the frequent glances of their masters who were finishing the blocks into smoothed masonry.

Unskilled laborers, four to a team – legs bare, feet wrapped with rags and with rag padding on the shoulders of their smirched jerkins – hefted the finished stones, slung on stout poles, and carried them to sledges deep-bedded with straw, to be drawn by oxen to the rising buildings.

Agog at the seething assembly of laborers, Seagrave, the pragmatic steward, gaped. "Whatever can pay for all of this!"

"King Henry, who's cried poverty so often, clearly has abundant funds, now that the Crown's domains are restored," Simon remarked sardonically. The Michelmas taxes collected by the Treasury were being sent to young Simon for the defense works here and paid to the engineer, Master William, who apparently was spending as quickly as the funds came in.

Ahead down the road, the familiar lake, the lawns, the bailey wall and red block of the castle's tower were hazed in the pervasive red dust of construction. Nothing seemed as it had been. A rosy veil hid from Simon's weak eyes almost all but what stood right in front of him.

Facing the road, at the near edge of the lake, was a towered gateway caged in scaffolding and nearly finished, with a heavy iron-bound portcullis already in place. Beams with block and tackle loomed toward the sky, each dangling a great stone in a sling as a mason, high in the scaffolding, with broad flat hands maneuvered the stone delicately into place.

Simon passed at slow pace under the raised portcullis, peering at the stonework of his braye with intense interest.

In the shade of the gate building, the hooves of the earl's and his companions' horses sounded with a loud, strangely hollow tread as they crossed the massive timber floor where the old sluice and swing-bridge had been. Beneath them was a new, stronger sluice keeping the waters of the Mere from receding. Were the dam and sluice to fail, nothing of the Mere would remain but a small stream at the bottom of a shallow little vale. The braye's massive double towered barbican protected the water-defense, and kept the Mere so broad that neither arrows nor any air-borne missiles were of use along a three- side sweep of the fortress' walls.

Beyond the gate's inner arch was a stone-walled aisle: what soon would be the parapeted defense works of the causeway that divided the Mere from the next-door abbey's pond and carried the road that was the only entrance to the castle's island.

Simon's palfrey, at the fore, shied, ears back and eyes rolling suspiciously at the noisy, people-ridden, narrow space. He held her steady with firm rein and quiet hands. In the confined passage, cramped by workmen and the partly finished walls that ran the length of the old causeway from towered gate to towered gate, the knock of stone hammers thudded like cracked chimes dampened in their pitch by the soft, deep bed of red dust.

As the riders held their mounts to a controlled walk through the teeming corridor, masons and workmen, deaf to the earl's trumpeter in the surrounding din, noticed the red lion flag and stopped working. The ear-battering noise fell silent. Workmen knelt on the uppermost stones. Those in the roadway pressed themselves to the walls and bent their heads, crossing themselves. Some reverently reached out to touch the Earl's horse's mantle. Many believed the Lord Montfort indeed was the Angel of the New Age and their own task was a holy one. Murmurs of the cheer *Montfort* sounded from everywhere and no particular direction, through the dulled clop and jangle of the horses.

A train of ox sledges was following the earl's men through the passage, bringing cut stones on sapling skids piled with a thick buffering of hay.

Emerging onto the castle's island, bounded by the Mere, the abbey pond and the channel, Simon and his entourage found the seethe of workers even more hectic here. Foundation trenching was completed and walls were rising all along the island's rim, though not so far advanced yet as the causeway's braye. Tall, triangular oak frames of counterweighted cranes marked off the sections of the outer wall, each part of the structure's length lying in easy reach of a crane's rotating radius. Raising and placing of wall stones was proceeding at a boiling pace. The site swarmed. The walls grew taller stone by stone even as Simon paused to watch.

Nearby he saw a number of his former villeins sitting on the ground, working busily, apparently quite happy at their tasks and so preoccupied they took no notice of the riders. Not skilled in stone cutting, they were trimming bark from logs and saplings. More of the local folk were hauling the rough-finished poles to the wall-works, binding them to form the next tier of rising scaffolding, assembling the tier, fitting it with flooring and with ramps. The noise of stone hammers was such a barrage of the senses, and the pressure for speedy work so great, that here no one took notice of the arriving of riders.

"The Crown will have a truly strong fortress," Simon remarked to Guy with some amazement at the speed and fineness of the work. "It is impressive, seeing what the Crown's purse of its own means is able to buy."

Guy was looking about, dumbfounded. Kenilworth had been the home of his childhood. What was it now? A formidable machine for war.

Advancing across the yard with a hundred armed men was no easy matter. Tents and wicker sheds for the laborers occupied the open ground like a makeshift, chaotic suburb to the inner castle. The abbey pond, downstream of the Mere, had come to have a stench like a latrine. A camp kitchen supplied the labor force from cauldrons hung on tripods of wood beams straddling small fires. The odors of pea soup and mutton mingled with the human scents of sweat and ordure to the brink of nausea for anyone not inured to the reek. Cities could be nosed from a distance, but Kenilworth's vile scent hung in a choking rose-hued dust cloud in the outer yard.

Pressing forward from the half-finished gate tower at the island end of the causeway, Simon, his companions and his mercenaries found the hammering confounding, near maddening. To their right, along the wall rising above the abbey water's edge, deep ditching marked the ground where towers would bulge outward. Ox carts were being unloaded of their burdens of rough, curving stones for the skilled masons. Neat heaps of blocks were carefully deposited to avoid avalanches. Men worked in the midst of their craft's thunder, cutting and shaping the massive, rounded sections of foundation stone selected from the seeming miscellany of each heap.

Simon led his company painstakingly across the yard, but paused at the inner bailey gate, motioning them to go ahead of him. Seagrave he kept by his side.

Squinting, he scanned the island's whole, broad outer yard. Engulfed by the workmen's camp, the trees in the orchard, planted for Eleanor twenty-five years ago, were in their prime but stood in files like poor beggars, their healthy green dulled rosy-brown with dust. The stables, newly enlarged, had a new paddock, but there were no horses. Young Simon, acting as steward, had written to his father that the work noise so alarmed the high-strung animals, he thought they should be taken up to Leicester until the building work was finished. The earl had agreed, and now appreciated the necessity quite vividly. At the barn, rail fencing enclosed several stolid cows grown used to the noise and busyness about them. Chickens were confined within tight willow wattle lest they scuttle under workmen's feet.

Surveying the frantic-seeming wreckage of construction, Simon wondered whether all the masons, and all the masons' helpers in England, were here. So it may have been, for their guild, like every other, had benefited by the Earl's work for the Provisions in 1258. And, unlike any other craft, the masons cherished mysteries of faith and of the Resurrection that paralleled the beliefs of the Joachites. Else such work as was proceeding at Kenilworth could not have been so vast and accomplished in so brief a time.

In a willow and thatch booth set up in the center of the yard, Master William bent over a rough-hewn table with his plans spread out as he conversed at a shout, mouth to ear, with a master mason.

In the confusion, no one had rung the castle's bell to announce the earl's arrival. Simon, on his big palfrey, at a walk rode over to the booth. From under the booth's low roof little more than the horse's legs and girth were visible, and the noise of hammers covered the arriving tread of hooves. It was the master mason who first noticed the horse and stepped outside.

Master William came out of the booth. Seeing who was looking down at him with a dark gaze of mixed approval and reproach, he bowed low.

"The progress of your work is highly cheering. But your security is non-existent," Simon said wryly.

"My lord, you urged speed, which entails a certain openness..." William bowed again, rebuked and sensibly contrite. "I've taken the liberty to commandeer some of your villeins and your servants for the work. I shall set some of them as watchmen."

"You've done miracles to accomplish so much so soon. But you must have better guards than local villeins. I'll see to providing them from the soldiers I've brought. ...Ah, also... do see to it none of your waste stone as large as a foot's diameter is discarded. Have such pieces cut as balls for mangonel shot." Simon, his praise and reprimand delivered, turned his horse back to the gate of the inner bailey wall.

In the inner yard, bounded by the old wall, the thunder of stone hammering was attenuated, the air somewhat shielded from the stench. Kenilworth was almost as it always had been: the chapel; beside it the countess's little rose garden, its blood-red rose hips drooping over the thyme-grown wattle seat. There was the same foyer housing the steps to the castle door, and beyond it the bake shed, brew shed, laundry – all the outbuildings were there, in repair and in full use. The vegetable garden was much larger, green with turnips and late carrots, and emitting a sulfurous exhalation from rows of cabbages. The newly cleared ground behind the sheds flaunted more rows of winter vegetables: parsnips, late bean and pea vines festooning trellises. On the sheds' thatch roofs, and on wicker stands set over every harvested row in the gardens, were baskets of drying apples, prunes and cherries. Before dust had coated it, the orchard had yielded a fine crop. More chickens trotted and pecked here, studiously nibbling the tattered rims of cabbage leaves.

It was home, here in the inner yard. Guy, holding his father's flag and waiting for his father and Seagrave, tilted his head toward the gate and rolled his eyes to his brother Henry. "All that out there is just a dream, thank God," he grinned.

"I'd call it a nightmare," Henry glowered.

The mercenaries had filed in, and Simon was come and giving orders for their camp. The outer yard was impossible. Housing would have to be built for the garrison along the bailey's inner wall. Until then the knights' own tents would have to serve. He sent Seagrave back to tell Master William to see to the work at once, to be completed before winter's cold made tenting a misery.

Now at last the tardy castle bell rang out in greeting.

Wiping her hands upon her linen smock, the Countess Eleanor ran out the foyer door. Her expression was a mix of joy and anxiety. Behind her came their daughter Eleanor and, at a run, their eleven year old son Richard.

Simon dismounted and met them, beaming, in high spirits. Richard threw his arms about his father's waist and could feel the hard, unyielding chain hauberk beneath his father's white wool robe.

"My children," Simon rumpled the boy's brown hair and hugged his daughter, now a tall and winsome sixteen with a playful smile. Then he folded his wife in his arms and held her for a moment, saying nothing. No apology could be enough for all of the decisions that had brought his family to this – to living in a hastily made bastion with war gathering against them.

Eleanor clung to him, shivering with stress just beneath her capable, controlled manner. She understood the implications of the frantic work in the outer yard and she was terrified. But she pulled away from him, sternly mastering her poise and brushing back a stray lock of hair that escaped from the thick loop of her brown braid. Although she usually railed at him, in this extremity she saw she must support in whatever way she could. At least in front of others. To her, the fortifying of Kenilworth told of closure of all other options for their lives.

"Ah," she sighed, "I've never been so busy in my life! I'm so glad you've come!" Her voice nearly achieved cheerfulness. Guy, Henry and the squire Peter were greeted by a smile of welcome that the countess strived to keep in place. Seeing her grown sons in armor, her true impulse was to burst to tears.

As she and her husband climbed the foyer steps together, Simon tried to match her effort at airy high spirits. "Master William seems to have powers of magic, raising so much so quickly. It's very telling – just how much the royal purse can buy from ordinary taxes."

"Many of those men are volunteers. Even master masons," Eleanor told him, walking with him into the hall. The countess was trembling again from the strain she was enduring. Her fingers fumbled nervously as she removed her work-smock to make herself more presentable. "The masons seem to think they're raising the New Jerusalem, or some such thing. Father Gregory insists the New Jerusalem is to be here in England. I don't know what to make of it," she laughed deprecatingly.

"If it brings us free labor I don't mean to question it." Simon looked down in her dark almond eyes. There was much he had to say to her, but he had no idea how to say it.

In the hall, where Eleanor had restored the great painted red lion rampant on the wall behind the dais, she ordered Slingaway, the kitchen boy, to fetch some wine and bring more chairs.

"Where is Simon?" the earl asked of his second son.

"He should be back from Leicester soon. He's been seeing to the care of your horses," the countess answered.

In a moment Garbage and Slingaway hurried in with goblets, and chairs from a corner storage room. Gobehasty emerged up the ladder from the corner tower's wine cellar with a ewer of wine.

Henry and Guy went off with their sister and Richard, who were eager to show them the changes to their old home. Simon and the countess sat at the table silently, neither wanting to speak. Seagrave had come back from the outer yard, but he and the squire politely left the earl and countess to themselves, and he motioned for the servants to leave as well.

When they were entirely alone, Eleanor asked, "How did matters go at Westminster?"

"Badly." Simon took a long drink of the wine, a Bordeaux he had brought back when he was viceroy of Gascony. He winced. It was turning to vinegar. Setting down the cup, he met her worried look and admitted, "Edward left. He holds Windsor armed against us. I believe Henry and Richard are with him. The lords who've broken their oaths to the Provisions are joining them in full arms. We are at war."

She said nothing, staring at him, her mind tallying the dread that must follow. Much of her married life, she felt from the start had been leading to exactly this, no matter how she railed and fought against it.

In the long silence he looked down at his hands, clasped, the fingers interlacing on the scrubbed surface of the table. Even so ordinary a sight as his own idle hands seemed strange, a false peace, a deceptive affront to what was pending. The stillness of the moment seemed almost obscene in its apparent calm, the hurly burly of the work outside a relief, as being nearer to the truth.

"Oh, dear God!" The countess finally turned away from him, covering her face with one hand. "Can't we leave? Just go?" she cried.

Simon stood up and took her free hand, drawing her to rise. Then he led her out of the hall, across the yard to the chapel.

Multicolored sunlight daubed the painted, flaking white walls with red, yellow and blue; all else was shadow. On the altar a candle burned for the consecrated sacrament, the presence of the Lord. Simon released his wife's hand and knelt, crossing himself upon the crusader's red cross sewn onto the breast of his white robe.

Eleanor knelt and crossed herself as well. "Let's go back to France while we still can!" she begged, tears filling her eyes.

"I cannot." Turning, he took both of her hands, pressing her cold fingers to his lips.

"What do you want with these people!" she demanded. "They've betrayed you again and again!"

"I gave my oath, and I mean to hold by it." What could he say of the conviction that prayer brought? The certainty that he should not leave and follow his own wishes, or even his good sense?

"We'll lose everything! Even our children's lives! For what?"

"For the chance that they will not have to live under tyranny."

"I don't believe it!" Crying choked her words.

He put his arms around her, kissing her brow as she bent her head and tried to twist away from him. "Forgive me! I beg you, forgive me."

"How? I can't understand!"

"There's nothing for us, or for our sons, in France. And nothing but oppression here if we don't prevail. I've prayed to leave, to go to the East. But what happens here is all that stands opposing a future of oppression... and not for England alone."

Slowly she nodded, not following his argument – for there was none offered that could convince her – but because his tone was vulnerable and pleading as she'd never heard from him before.

Her brown hair lay in short curls across the back of her pale neck between her looped braids. Simon kissed her bent neck. "Help me. Be of help. You have my whole heart and I need you."

She nodded again without lifting her head. "I will." She rubbed at her tear-wet cheeks with the back of her hand. "There's nothing else to be done..."

In the next weeks, as the walls and towers rose with astonishing speed, a stream of messengers reached Kenilworth reporting on the gathering of the Provision's army. Young Simon came from Leicester, and with him fifty of the Leicester knights, including Botevelyn and others who had served Simon in Palestine.

From Windsor, in King Henry's name, a denunciation of the Earl of Leicester's cause was sent to all of England. Orders were sent to the king's barons, calling them to meet in arms at Oxford, to put an end to the earl's treasonous rebellion.

"At Oxford!" Thomas Cantaloup himself brought the news to Simon. "It's against all custom for the king to enter Oxford, but he's ordered the university shut and the students sent home! It's as if he means to cancel the Provisions on the very spot that saw their birth!"

"It's a wise move on his part." Simon toyed with a writing stylus over a wax tablet where he was making notes for Master William. "By sending the students home, he disbands that faction of our followers. Or perhaps he'll find he's freed them to join our forces," he looked up and smiled. "Since the enemy occupies your home, father, you'll be our guest at Kenilworth, I hope? Until we triumph?"

"Thank you. I'll be glad of your protection."

In the inner yard, long barracks had been built against the inside of the wall to house the mercenary garrison. Now part of the outer yard was cleared, and more barracks were being built against the outside of the bailey to house the gathering army. The earl summoned to his hall one of his Leicester knights, Hugh Gebion.

"Go to Oxford for us. Take three mounted soldiers with you for your messengers. Watch what's happening there and send us word."

That evening Simon's cousin Peter de Montfort arrived. Exhausted from a fast ride from Gloucestershire with many changes of horses, he stumbled up the foyer steps, close behind the servant who ran to announce him.

"Cousin!" he shouted, "we're going to need those fortifications you're building! There's treachery…" He reached the hall and, seeing the Provost Thomas Cantaloup, stopped speaking. Bowing, he flushed with embarrassment and mumbled, "I beg pardon."

"Are you all right?" Simon went to his staggering cousin and helped him to his own chair.

Peter nodded. "I came as swiftly as six borrowed horses could carry me. Mortimer's attacked the border fiefs that King Henry awarded to the countess for releasing her holdings in France. Dylwyn, Lugwarden and Marden. Mortimer's captured a man of hers and holds him for a ransom of two hundred pounds. He's pledged himself to Edward. He says those fiefs are his by Edward's gift."

Simon's face darkened with grim resignation more than anger. He remarked with acid sarcasm, "Since I'm an accused traitor again, I suppose there's no cause for amazement. But Mortimer goes beyond the pale in demanding such a ransom."

It was Edward's clear breach with the earl and countess – this strike aimed to counter any appearance of lingering fondness for his aunt and uncle. Peter and Thomas were more dismayed than Simon. The prince's's attack upon the Templars, his vicious treachery at Bristol and his slaughter of the Windsor garrison, had done Simon all the hurt his heart could feel and he was hardened. If he had hoped the heir to England's Crown could be schooled, that hope died at Windsor.

"I came myself. I didn't want anybody else to tell you," Peter offered as if in apology.

Simon walked to one of the three tall arches in the south wall and looked out its long arrow-slit window to where the highest stones of the new wall could be seen, overtopping the roof of the chapel. He was silent for some time, then turned, facing his cousin and the Provost. "We'll pay Mortimer's ransom with our swords."

The earl sat at his table, writing for an hour, cutting the roll of parchment into narrow strips for each message. With his small seal of the fork-tailed lion rampant he impressed the warm wax dripped from a candle's flame onto each folded strip, sealing it shut. Then he called for several of his Leicestermen and handed each a letter, saying, "Take this to Lincoln to the Earl de Lacey; this to the Earl de Vere at Abingdon; Humphrey de Bohun Fils at Chelmsford," and so on until all the letters were given out. He instructed the knights, "Inform them we prepare at once to march west to the Welsh border." The letters set times and places for the joining of their armies on the march.

The next day, as the earl and countess, their sons and guests sat down to noon dinner, a horn call sounded from the braye. Hearing the high, shrill notes, Simon looked quizzically to his wife and sent his squire to the roof to see who was arriving.

As quickly as his legs could take him up the spiral stairs and back down again, Peter reported, "There's a lord arriving with an escort. They bear a flag charged with the fleurs de lis of France!"

Simon rose from the table and went down the foyer steps to the yard to meet the visitor. The bailey gate swung open and six riders in blue and gold tabards rode in with their lily-dappled flag. Surrounded by them was Piers Chamberlin, King Louis' counselor. The French escort was accompanied by two knights sent from de Gray at Dover.

As his servants hurried to take the arriving horses, Simon greeted Piers warmly. He knew him well from his years at Court in Paris. Piers was one of those who, as Louis' representative, had rescued him from London Tower in 1260.

Chamberlin dismounted, saying to Simon without preamble, "Lord Earl, we come with an offer from the King of France." Though he smiled, the smile was tight and far from warm.

Simon led him to the hall as Chamberlin explained, "Matters have reached such a point that Louis fears for Henry, and for you."

The earl's sons and Peter de Montfort had risen from their places at the table. The countess motioned for another chair to be brought. Cantaloup watched intently.

Chamberlin bowed to the countess and the Provost, then drew a letter from his robe and handed it to Simon. "Louis sends this to you privately. Even I don't know its contents."

The rolled letter was sealed with a lump of wax unmarked by any seal. Simon broke the blank wax and opened the parchment. The message was unmistakably in Louis' own handwriting.

*My friend,*

*In the name of England's Crown, Queen Eleanor, Savoy and the Lusignan are raising a large army. I have forbidden them the use of French ports for embarkation to make war on any Christian land. But Thomas, the Duke of Flanders, has offered them his port of Damme. The army already is gathered there. I urge you, without delay, agree to arbitration. It is the only help that I can give."*

Simon rolled the letter and tucked it into the blousing of his belted white robe. One of de Gray's knights had followed them up the stairs and waited in the doorway, clearly wishing to speak to the earl privately.

Simon turned to Chamberlin, his face, his voice showing the stern effect of what he had read. "A moment's grace, I must see to this man," he nodded toward the knight in the doorway.

Simon led Gray's messenger down the foyer steps and to the seclusion of the chapel. "How are matters at the ports?" he asked.

"Secure, my lord. John de la Haye is in command at Dover now with strength enough to fend off anyone. My lord de Gray tours all the other ports to put them in defense according to your orders. But I've brought a letter, confiscated from the Papal Legate's baggage." He fetched from the breast of his robe a rolled parchment bearing the golden papal seal.

Simon opened and read the document. It was a Bull ordering the friar Orders to cease preaching in support of the Provisions and the New Era – on pain of excommunication for heresy.

Simon's tense expression grew even more grim. He let the parchment snap back into its coil and thrust it down the front of his robe. Nodding to the knight, he said, "Take rest, there are barracks and dining quarters ranged in the outer yard. When you return to Dover, I'll give you a letter for the lord de Gray commending his confiscating this." He tapped the papal letter tucked within his robe.

Returning to the hall, where Chamberlin was seated now at the table, he rejoined his family and guests at their meal. Gobehasty was pouring wine into the Frenchman's cup, a decent wine Seagrave had found in the cellar. Simon sat at his place at the head of the table and raised his own cup for his servant to refill it. He drank the wine down, then sat some moments, silent in thought.

With his return, conversation at the table ceased. Chamberlin, the countess, all watched him with intense attention, held by his troubled, distant look. Noticing them, he smiled and his eyes regained their clarity and focus on the present. "All's well. A problem at Dover, but it's been resolved quite neatly for the present." Turning to Chamberlin, he said, "I'd have you tell King Louis that if King Henry will submit, we too agree to Louis' arbitration. I pray that this detestable war may be avoided."

Chamberlin did not linger, but left with his official escort that same day to find King Henry.

"I've had word that he's on his way to Oxford, where he's joining his armed barons and their knights," Simon told the French ambassador in a mild tone, as if the raising of all England's hardened armies against him was more a sad misunderstanding than catastrophe.

"You have your well placed spies…" Chamberlin's brows arched, expecting confirmation of an orderly secret government within the government, as the complaints of Simon's enemies in France led him to think.

"Common knowledge. Nothing to compare to Prince Richard's system, or Queen Blanche's," Simon grinned engagingly. "Tell Henry I'll be pleased to meet him in Paris again. Or, no… better not remind him of his previous, maudlin failure before France's Court."

"The issues are not as simple this time," the ambassador said soberly.

That afternoon the earl sat at his table drafting letters, ordering the suspension of the gathering of his army. The letters must go out at once if King Henry agreed to arbitrate.

Before half the letters were drafted, one of the men sent with Hugh Gebion to Oxford returned. He came in hastily, bowing to the earl. "My lord, Sire Gebion bade me inform you that King Henry has left Oxford already."

"His appointed meeting with the lords is not until the day after tomorrow…"

"My lord, there was word all over Oxford that the army raised by the queen was embarking. The king took all the armed men he could assemble and is marching on Dover."

Simon stared at the man, then began methodically tearing up the letters he had written. He summoned one of Gray's newly arrived knights to ride back to his master at once with the warning.

Two days later, Simon, in full armor, his shield and helmet hitched to the saddlebow of his strongest destrier, led out his knights of Leicester, his mercenaries, and every armed man, lord or commoner, raised in the midlands and gathered at Kenilworth. He left only a small garrison behind.

The cortege, with the red lion flag borne at the fore, was long, although far less of cavalry than commoners as foot soldiers armed with bows, axes and short swords. Assembling at the rear were new supply wagons built by Master William, filled with contributions freely given by the folk, and drawn by their oxen unhitched from their plows.

With his eldest sons, his cousin Peter, his stewards Seagrave and Thomas deMesnil at the fore, the Earl led his army out through the walled causeway and the barbicaned gate of the braye to the road east, toward Northampton where more young knights and foot soldiers waited to join them. If Henry agreed to arbitration, it would come when the armies were already in the field.

From the roof of the tower, Countess Eleanor, her daughter and son Richard watched the slow line wrap itself in clouds of red dust, sparkling here and there as sunlight glinted from a pike. Young Eleanor quietly took her mother's hand and pressed it. The countess's face was fixed, expressionless. Her feelings, smothered in her, she dared not let rise anywhere near thought.

Richard leaned over the parapet, watching gleefully for the long line of armed men on horseback was the grandest thing that he had ever seen. "All will be well, mother," he said with eleven-year-old confidence, kicking his feet against the wall and balancing on his chest upon the coping. "They'll kill King Henry, and then make Papah the king. Everything will be all right after that."

"King Henry is my brother and your uncle," his mother said quietly. "Whatever wrongs he's done, we must not wish him dead."

At Northampton, Robert Ferrers, heir to the earldom of Derby, and John de Lacey, the Earl of Lincoln, in perilous opposition to King Henry's summons, were ready to join Simon with their knights from the north. The growing army moved on.

As they marched, the Earl of Oxford John de Vere, young Humphrey de Bohun, Hugh Despensar, and hundreds of knights from the heartlands, the west and the south, joined them. The force grew to more than three thousand knights, and many thousand more armed men on foot. At Sevenoaks, south of London, they were met by Gilbert de Clare.

Dressed in full chain mail, with their long, slit riding robes in their bright heraldic colors, the earls and lords convened in Simon's red and white striped tent. Gilbert reported, "Henry's at Dover. Attacked so quickly, Haye had to surrender the port. William de Valence is said to be bringing five thousand mercenary knights."

"That leaves us quite outnumbered, and by men more trained than we are," de Vere fretted.

"Our knights of the Bachelry are not so green as you suppose," young Ferrers retorted, nettled by the older man.

"In addition to five thousand mercenaries, recall they also have the barons who have cleaved to Henry. We're outnumbered mightily," de Lacey shook his head, leveling his practical gaze at the junior lord.

Simon said nothing, engrossed in thought.

"Why not let the Londoners join us?" Clare proposed. "The whole city is clamoring to fight for our cause. They adore the Earl Montfort," he nodded toward Simon. Still stung by the earl's refusal to grant spoils, he added cynically, "I'm sure they'd fight to the death for you, my lord."

Simon emerged from his contemplations with a look at Clare like a tired swimmer in deep water who, rising to the surface, finds a shark.

"We're to rely on shopkeepers – in battle?" Hugh Despensar scoffed.

Despensar's deprecating tone brought him to reconsider. "With so large a mercenary force to face, what Clare says is true." Simon nodded amicably to Gilbert. "We can ill afford to overlook any ally. Let's raise what men we can from the Londoners."

The army turned north the next day, and a day later marched up High Street through Southwark to the foot of London Bridge. The earl made camp where he had camped before, at the time of the ill-fated Candlemas Parliament of 1260. As the army settled into inns and clusters of tents on vacant land, strung out from the foot of the bridge through the suburbs to the countryside, Simon, Clare and de Vere crossed the bridge and met with Mayor FitzThomas.

The mayor, flowery with smiles, his round face framed by its wreath of gray curls, assured Simon, "The citizens and militia of

London will be proud to take up arms under your command, my lord." He sent criers through the streets at once, ringing hand bells and calling out that all men who support the Earl Montfort and the Provisions should meet, armed and ready as soldiers for campaign, at Southwark market fairgrounds the next day at noon.

Simon, de Vere and Clare went back to their lodgings for the night. Although the enemy was still far to the south, the earl posted sentries on all of the approaching roads. His sons had taken a large chamber for him at Saint Thomas' Hospital's guesthouse, appropriately a hostel for pilgrims and those setting out on crusade. It was where he had stayed during the Candlemas Parliament and revolt of 1260. The abbot warmly welcomed him again.

It was November now. Darkness came early. By suppertime the crowded inns were glimmering with rush lights, candles and blazing hearths. The scent of roasting beef filled High Street. There was an air of excitement, of anticipation, almost of holiday as the army feasted and caroused. Drinking down their beer and wine, they rehearsed King Henry's grievous flaws and toasted their coming victory.

Carousing had gone on long into the night, the drinkers singing the earl's songs, battle songs and songs of heroes of the past, when a rider came dashing up High Street from the south, then turned and took Saint Thomas Street to the Hospital.

"Lord Earl!" he pounded on the guesthouse door. "Lord Earl!" he cried. A sleep-fuddled porter finally let him in and he was led to Simon's chambers. The squire Peter sleepily demanded what he wanted. "King Henry's coming!" the man panted. "The whole royal army is not an hour's march away!"

Simon, wakened, hearing what the man screamed, was up and dressing. So were his sons. "Cry the alarm!" he ordered his squire. "Shout in the streets! Have every man in arms and out on High Street at once!" He turned to Guy, who had been sharpening his sword and had not yet undressed for bed. "Go alert FitzThomas. We must retreat into the city. Have him raise the militia and prepare to close the city's gates!"

"I warned the encampments to the south as I passed," the gasping sentry told Simon. "They should be arming and joining you here."

Squire Peter, a cloak wrapped over his nightshift, went running barefoot to High Street crying the alarm. Guy, on his horse, made his way through the drunken crowds tumbling from the inn doors, and galloped across the bridge. In only a few moments he was back, working his way through the jostling press of men arming and mounting.

He found his father, already mounted on his great white destrier and just entering High Street. He pushed toward him. "The bridge gate's closed!" he cried above the noise of the crowd. "I couldn't convince the guards to open it!"

Down High Street Gilbert de Clare, who had followed not far behind Guy, was bellowing, "We're trapped! We've been betrayed! They've locked the city's gates!"

Panic was spreading through the mass of men jamming the street. Fright was sobering them.

"Find a boat and cross the river," Simon ordered Guy. "Rouse the mayor. Tell him what has happened."

Guy was wide-eyed. "And if he's done this for the king?"

"Do as I say!" Simon commanded.

Guy turned and forced his shying horse through the press of men again.

Simon, on his destrier, above the heads of men on foot, moved through the crowd along High Street, hoping his calm commands would bring order. Knights and foot soldiers milled in a churning, frightened mass of men that packed the roadway from the buildings on one side to the buildings on the other.

"Let's not stand here to be slaughtered like penned sheep!" Simon bellowed at them. "We'll surprise the surprisers!" He turned his horse and headed away from the bridge, southward, and the mass of men moved with him. He led them to the market field where High Street met the Dover Road in the broad, flat empty fairgrounds of Southwark. He ranged them in the darkness on each side of the road, commanding them to keep utter silence.

Well beyond the lights shed by inn windows, the field was black. The moon had set and mist obscured the starlight. The low hills to the south were invisible. Assembling foot soldiers and armed riders, stumbling into one another, appeared even at close range barely a darker mass in the darkness. Here and there a white surcoat showed a ghostly shape, paler than the surrounding black. Stripping off his own red-crossed white surcoat, Simon ordered that every white and light colored surcoat be shed.

Then all was still. Only an acute ear in the silence could hear the soft hiss of breathing of thousands of men and hundreds of horses. Now and then a harness shook, an animal snorted or chomped nervously on its steel bit.

Simon, in the dark, moved up the road and back, giving occasional whispered instructions to the men on each side. Their unseen faces all were turned toward the Dover Road, straining for a sound, a glimpse of the approaching enemy.

Then in the distance, on a rim where an invisible far hill must be, there was a spark of orange light, a torch. Another and another. Like golden droplets gliding on a thread they formed, descended and disappeared in the black void again, a short, moving necklace of light. The king's army was approaching down a slope at the horizon and into the bowl of a shallow valley.

The little chain of lights persisted. As the black air rose in a breeze from the south, the steady rumble of marching feet, the scrape of metal and the creak of turning wheels came delicately audible. Then, as if rising out of nothing, the torches showed much closer, clear and bright in the night air, lighting up the shapes of riders in shining steel helms and bright colored surcoats and mantlings.

The Earl rode at a walking pace quietly among his men, giving his last instructions for attack. His sobered troops' collected gaze was fixed upon the shapes in orange light steadily approaching.

Simon, at his son Henry's side, murmured the crusader's well-wishing, "God grant your right arm strength." To Henry's disconcerted nerves, a smile of battle joy sounded in his tone.

"God grant you strength as well, father." Henry muttered in return, his heart pounding with fear. He didn't share his parent's animal spirits for combat. His mind was ruthlessly casting up Grosseteste's prediction at his christening: *this child and his father shall die on the same day, and by the same hurt.*

The army coming nearer was also keeping silence save for the tread, creak and jingle of their advance. The Earl's forces waited, as still as threatened rabbits, tension high.

To the thousand straining ears, a new sound rose in the distance, not to the south but to the north. Opposite from the approaching army of the enemy. A roaring like sea waves, where there was no sea. Perhaps a sound of wind, but there was only a light breeze. A rushing like a flood, though the land was dry. The sound was growing louder every instant, and seemed to be coming from High Street. Simon peered toward the road down which his army had marched.

Southwark was filling with moving lights. Torches. Crowds of people, in the wavering flames' glow, were running in the street, shouting and calling. There seemed a river of light like a great conflagration.

One of the Earl's men furthest up the road to the north cried out, "London Bridge is open! The Londoners are come!"

"Retreat to the city!" Simon bellowed. His order passed instantly with unrestrained cries in the darkness through the waiting, frightened mass of men.

Simon rode up and down the road, herding his people away from the king's steady advance, and toward the sea of welcome light in Southwark. His forces, mounted men at gallop, foot soldiers running after them, moved swiftly into the engulfing, yelling, waving masses of Londoners. Torches danced and joyful shouts erupted. Townspeople, men and women, grasped the riders' stirrups, cheering, laughing, running with the horses. Foot soldiers, dashing as fast as their legs would carry them, mingled with the crowds and were raised up on shoulders, borne like heroes in the midst of the surging, screaming, laughing, whooping throng.

Simon and the Earl de Lacey, with the Leicestermen and knights of Lincoln, herded the army, then formed a rear guard between them and the royal force which, seeing what was happening, had doubled their oncoming speed.

As the king's army came on, the entire torch-lit mass of jubilant humanity, yelling as if a victory was won, rushed between the shops and houses on London Bridge and streamed in raucous deluge into the city.

As the last of the Provision's army ran across the bridge, Simon, his great horse turning, caracoling, was engulfed by Londoners.

Bellowing *Il est al mont, Et si est fort, Si ad grant chevalrie,* the crowd led him into the city as in triumph. Above, in the gate tower awash with flares, militiamen leaned far out of the windows, cheering as the Earl and the last soldiers of his army swept under the arch below.

Then, with the torches of the king's forces fast swarming along High Street, the great gates of London Bridge swung shut.

# Chapter Thirteen

## KING LOUIS ARBITRATES
### 1263-1264

King Henry stood with Richard and Edward on the bank of the Thames, regarding London. There was no vast army behind them, only the few lords who had arrived early at Oxford with their knights. The baggage train was far longer than the file of their troops. Dover had not surrendered. Valence's army, unable to land, had been forced to sail back to Damme.

Richard watched the thriving, busy city going about its day untroubled by the little siege at its bridge. All boats had been drawn to the city's side of the river.

"I'm minded what a short walk it is from London to Westminster every time I give thought to attack," the King of the Germans observed dryly. "When would the Court be safe if we make war on the city?"

"You favor King Louis' arbitration?" Edward asked.

"I don't see what else we can do." Richard turned from the city with a scowl.

"Are we so feeble!" the prince burst out. "The Londoners may use my mother's body for a sewer, but we must still have the grace – not to say cowardice – to arbitrate!"

"Remember, Edward," Richard met the prince's blazing blue eyes, "they're your future subjects, and your neighbors. It is their willing taxes that support the Crown."

"I'd rather every cursed churl in London felt my sword than offer them a cringing peace!"

Henry, who had stood silently gazing down at his own chilled hands, rubbing them together as if the action needed careful study, finally spoke. "Tell Chamberlin we accept King Louis' offer."

The royal secretary Walerant and the French ambassador, riding with a white flag of truce before them, crossed London Bridge. The massive gates were opened for them and they were led into the city and to the earl.

Reports already had reached Simon that the opposing army across the river was actually quite small. As the two men were shown into the Guildhall, he was sitting in session with his lieutenants, planning to attack by the river crossing upstream and take the royal forces from the rear.

Chamberlin and Walerant bowed. The German knight's big, blond, ostentatiously toothed face smiled as if he were offering alms among the poor. "Lord Earl Montfort, by his kind grace, the King of England will agree to arbitration by King Louis of France."

"Ah! So, now that he sees he's outnumbered, he will arbitrate!" Gilbert de Clare chirped like an angry sparrow. " How very wise of him! If he could have trapped us last night, we'd be dead!"

"You can tell him he'll have to agree to our terms now," Ferrers growled in his tenor voice, his head high, his eyes focused piercingly at the detested clerk.

But Simon stood up and motioned for the two young men to be quiet. "If this unfortunate war can be avoided, it would be best for all. What does King Henry offer?"

"He offers full truce," Chamberlin answered. "He agrees to have the barons who are still gathering at Oxford return to their homes. And he, his brother the King of the Germans and Prince Edward will withdraw to Windsor until the case is heard in France."

"That would be agreeable to us," Simon said firmly, and he offered Chamberlin his hand in pledge. "Tell King Louis we will meet with him and submit our cause to his Court's judgment."

"My lord Montfort!" Gilbert de Clare protested.

"We do not..." Ferrers burst out, but he was not allowed to finish.

With a stern look Simon waved both young lords to silence. "We have no wish to raise our swords against our king if he will only keep his oath, hearing and responding to his people's needs, as the Provisions grant."

After Walerant and Chamberlin left, Simon turned to Ferrers and Clare. In a tone that brooked no argument, he told them, "With Louis' decision in our favor, we will be able to put to rest our fears of Henry raising forces abroad. But, if we refuse to arbitrate and then defeat Henry, we will have a never-ending flood of foreign armies coming against us. Every king must see us as renegades and a challenge to the peace of every land. We must take this opportunity, which will not come our way again. If we lose, and I much doubt we will, how shall we be worse off than we are at present?"

He had not told them of the papal threat of excommunication, which would surely be sent again and again until the message reached the English clergy and was obeyed. An arbitration by King Louis could bridge the way to rapprochement with the Vatican as well.

Grudgingly the young lords acknowledged the Earl's right to have his way.

The royal army across the Thames was disbanded, its leaders withdrew to Windsor. Simon sent his partisans back to their homes.

With his Leicester knights, his mercenaries, his sons, his stewards and his cousin, the Earl returned to Kenilworth. Arbitration would take place at Amiens in two months, at the onset of the new year.

The weather was mild through November and most of December. Construction at Kenilworth progressed with its usual stupendous speed. And Simon prepared for Amiens.

With Thomas Cantaloup's advice on law and Church doctrine, he shaped his arguments. Gregory de Boscellis, years ago the tutor of Simon's sons, served as counselor as well, and compiled lists of properties confiscated from the Lusignan, Peter of Savoy, the Bishop Aigueblanche and the rest of Henry's foreign opportunists — properties dispensed with foolish generosity from the royal demesne, paupering the Crown. Peter de Montfort assembled the most telling cases of abuses by the royal sheriffs, while Seagrave chronicled the king's demands for excessive taxes. With letters to all the supporters of the Provisions, asking their contributions, more testimonies were gathered, detailing the brutal means Henry used to coerce money from the clergy and his tenants-in-chief.

Reading through the new lists of the intimidations, punitive appointments, forced marriages, and justice withheld till a monstrous price was paid, Simon remarked cheerfully to Thomas, "With such a tale of misgovernment as this, Louis must find in our favor."

Thomas was less sanguine. Rubbing his brow with his thumb and forefinger, he cautioned, "In the eyes of the Church our case is not so strong. The Legate who will join in the hearing of our case may consider this an instance of the Lesser dictating to the Greater, a reversal of the Divine Order. But, at worst, we certainly can argue that King Henry has been ignoble. That his own perversion of the royal dignity has bred perversion in his people, and only intervention in the form of the Provisions can halt the advance of perversion."

Simon viewed the Provost's reasoning, based on Aquinas, with extreme uneasiness. But any argument that cited Joachim's New Age, condemned by the Pope as heresy, was out of the question. "What of the *Policraticus* of John of Salisbury?" the earl offered as an alternative. "He argues cogently that a king only represents God's Will so long as he serves the good of the people. We have abundant proofs that Henry serves his own pathetically misguided interests, resulting in great damage to his people."

"The *Policraticus*, helpful as it might be, is not accepted doctrine in Rome. Aquinas predominates now."

"With his immutable hierarchies." Simon's glare pinned Thomas with a look of such distaste the Provost flinched, and answered meekly but persistently, "We must frame arguments in keeping with current theology, whatever we may think of Thomas and his theories' unwholesome implications."

Simon knew himself to be out of his depth. He must let Cantaloup blaze his own way through the forest of prevailing doctrine. He turned his focus to the cases of abuse and their evidence. From long knowledge of Louis' humanity and decency, and the French king's clear awareness of Henry's flaws, he was confident the Provisions would prevail.

Christmas was spent quietly at Kenilworth. Peter de Montfort and his son Peter were guests. But there was no dancing and merrymaking as the last time when the Montfort family were united for the holiday. The villiens were not invited to the hall for beer and beef, but were given their Christmas fare in the village. Kenilworth no longer was a home, but an armed fortress belonging to the Crown and readying for war.

To the mercenaries at the barracks inside the bailey wall and posted in the new towers spiking the walls and at the gates, roast meats, puddings and a generous amount of wine were sent. The sound of bibulous song filled the yards, now cleared of workmen's huts and the ordered chaos of construction. The strengthening of Kenilworth, surpassing every other castle in England, was complete.

Christmas dinner in the hall was solemn. Unsmiling, the countess cut the trencher loaves, young Henry carved, and Richard de Havering, the steward, served.

Simon's daughter Eleanor studied her cousin Peter whom she had danced with so joyously six Christmases ago. She was dark-haired and fine-featured like her father with deep eyes shaded by rich lashes, but she had a playfulness about her that was all her own. She watched her cousin critically. Once, in the high gaiety of the dance, she had told her father she would marry no one else. Now he seemed tame, callow compared to her own brothers – and Edward. "When shall I meet Llewellyn?" she asked her father, a touch of sadness entering her voice at thought of the betrothed she'd never seen, although she liked his poetic letters well enough.

"When the arbitration is concluded," Simon answered, a smile nestling in his dark beard, trimmed tidily and handsomely to fit beneath his chain mail coif and helmet. "It will be but a little while longer. You're impatient, my sweeting?"

Meeting his eyes, she blushed. It was the dazzling, impossible Edward who ranked highest in her thoughts.

Though the weather through December had been uncommonly warm, on Christmas Eve the cold at last set in with snow. Christmas Day brought a light thaw, but the next morning was bitter cold again, turning the thawed roads to ice that remained, solid as steel, for days with no sign of relief.

Simon, with his squire, his sons Henry, Simon and Guy, his cousin Peter, the clerk Bosecellis, Thomas Cantaloup and each man's several servants, mounted in the inner yard to begin the trip to Amiens. Dressed in heavy fur-lined cloaks with hoods, they rode out through the bailey gate. In the outer yard the trodden, muddy, red stained snow was frozen into peaks and hollows by the guards' boots and horses' hooves.

The riders made their way across to the walled causeway painfully slowly and cautiously, their horses sliding despite the caulk points in their iron shoes. But the road beyond was clearer. The travelers moved faster, achieving a normal brisk walk as their palfreys' hooves crushed through the thin coating of ice and found firm footing underneath.

After a few miles the road leveled, crossing broad, low-lying grasslands. A white slick spread everywhere, smooth upon the road, rippled into waves like a mackerel sky among the stubble of the fields. The horses' cleated shoes barely scratched the ice's waxy surface. Frightened, their feet sliding at every step, the beasts moved forward agonizingly slowly. A frigid wind came up. The palfreys were gummed with nervous sweat that froze upon their legs, their croups, wherever their furred bodies were not steaming.

The servants dismounted and, slipping on the ice themselves, pulled and urged the anxious animals along.

Fine pebble-grains of snow began to fall, stinging the men's faces. The horses blinked and shut their eyes, puffing clouds of steam from their flared nostrils. Thomas's horse impatiently tossed up its head. Its weight, thrown from tenuous balance, made it totter and skip sideways across the ice, unseating its rider. Thomas clung to the beast's broad neck. When at last it came to halt, its legs spread wide, its skin quivering in fright, he righted himself in his saddle and gave a nervous laugh.

"We've barely come six miles, Thomas. Don't be dismounting yet," Simon grinned, trying to make light of the mishap.

"I've never ridden such a long six miles before in my life!" the Provost retorted. "We should've waited till tomorrow."

"Perhaps, but tomorrow might bring worse weather," Simon said amiably.

"There is no worse than this, Cousin," Peter de Montfort's tone was flat, as he stroked his horse's darkly sweat-slick neck.

No village was nearby. There was no place of shelter in that broad frozen meadowland. The riders moved on at a creeping pace, skidding, sliding on the ice-sheened road. Snow ceased blowing in the wind, and the air cleared. The disk of the low winter sun leaned toward the white bed of the fields, glowing with barely the light of a candle flame in the yellowish gray sky. Deepening gray haze crept upward in the east.

"We'll spend the night at Catesby. It's a very few miles more," Simon offered encouragingly. His breath had frozen in his beard, giving him the hoary, whitened, icicle-adorned look of the North Wind himself. Guy smiled at the beauty of the effect and would have said something, but Thomas spoke up in his misery, "I'll praise God for a hot cider and a warm bed!"

Near Catesby the road forded a stream. Though it should have still been morning when they reached this point, darkness was closing around them. The riders paused at the stream bank. Snow here was trodden into slippery ruts where other riders had passed in the days before the hard freeze. The stream's surface was dark and mirror smooth.

Peter de Montfort leaned back, gently giving his mount rein and spur. Buckling its hind legs, the palfrey skidded down the bank and slid onto the sleek black ice.

Simon followed Peter, then came Thomas Cantaloup and Henry Montfort.

Peter's horse moved warily in the lead, ears flattened back, and rolling its eyes till the whites showed. In its terror the animal shed waves of stinking sweat, mist rising from its sides like a sheet of steam as it strained every muscle for balance, its spiked iron shoes skating outward at every step so that its legs spread wide. Then suddenly, halfway to the opposite bank, it refused its master's command, jerked at the loose rein and took the bit between its teeth, trying to turn around.

Simon's mount, too close behind to stop, shied out of the way and in the abrupt shift lost its balance totally. Its legs shooting out straight to one side, the big palfrey fell with a crunching thud into the ice. Simon was pinned and crushed beneath as the massive horse struggled and neighed, thrashing its neck to and fro, rolling, kicking its strong legs in the air as it tried helplessly to get up, grinding its saddle and rider into the sheared points and edges of burst ice.

Peter, Thomas and Henry, still crossing, had all they could do to control their own horses. Guy and young Simon, leaping from their mounts on the riverbank, were first to reach their father. Young Simon, running, sliding, reached the horse's head and grabbed its bridle at the bit, then lurched his arm over the horse's nose to stop its frantic swaying. Pulling the powerful neck forward, he forced the horse to lean its weight away from its pinned rider.

Guy, and now a servant, grasped Simon's arms and drew him out from under the animal. He screamed as his mangled hip and leg were dragged from beneath the massive weight grinding him against the broken saddle, jagged ice and the rocks of the shallow streambed.

Then Seagrave and the squire Peter were beside him. Simon's face was pale, waxy as the frost on his frozen beard. His breath came in long struggling gasps. His distraught eyes briefly met his squire's before he lost consciousness. Blood spread in a long red stain across the cracked and broken surface, into the dark, opened gap of chill running water.

"Bring him this way! It's only a little further to the inn," Henry Montfort shouted, reaching the far bank and dismounting. He fumbled in his saddle's leather traveling bag for a blanket to make into a litter. Guy, Seagrave and the squire Peter, sliding and struggling to keep their feet beneath them, carried Simon across the frozen stream to the far bank.

Henry was hacking with his sword at saplings growing by the waterside. "Take these for litter poles!"

The inn was among the few thatched cottages of Catesby a hundred yards or so up the road from the ford. Guy and Henry, Seagrave and the squire Peter trotted as quickly as they could on foot with the litter to the inn, followed by their entourage of mounted men and servants in the blue-gray darkening evening.

Simon, still unconscious, was laid in the innkeeper's own soft, straw-stuffed bed. A brazier warmed the room. The innkeeper's wife, a plump, solicitous woman who often had sold food and drink to the Great Earl as he passed by, was in a frantic flurry to be helpful.

"We need much more light," squire Peter told her. He had treated his master's wounds for more than thirty years. By the blazing light of every candle in the inn, he cut and folded back Simon's layered winter riding clothes, linen drawers and wool stockings, laying bare a wound. A long splinter of bone, accreted with calcified self-mending, broke through the skin of the thigh. As Simon lay on his back, his groin and hip showed badly bruised but the skin was unbroken. Heavy bleeding was coming from beneath.

With Guy holding the upper thigh, the gash flushed and drenched with the innkeeper's most potent wine, the barber-surgeon gently drew the broken bone back into place, praying that his master wouldn't wake and shift, feeling the pain. Using splints whittled from the inn's kindling wood, he bound a long strip of cloth tightly about the thigh.

With the break secured against further damage, and the innkeeper's stout wife holding the bound leg steadily, Peter and Guy gently turned Simon's unconscious body over. Carefully drawing away the bloodied, shredded remnants of his master's clothes, Peter exposed a large, open and ragged mass of blood and flesh. Simon's hip, ground between the thrashing horse, blades of ice and the sharp rocks of the streambed, was an oozing pulp of torn flesh, torn muscle and exposed, fractured bone.

Peter worked long into the night, flushing the wound with strong wine, probing, extracting bone splinters, gently forcing the already ill-knit bones back into place, packing the wound with healing unguents and boiled lint to staunch the bleeding, then wrapping his master's body in bindings of clean linen, praying all the while that God keep his master unaware until the gory and excruciating work was done.

It was past midnight when at last Simon lay quietly on his uninjured side, his broken thigh reset, his hip and lower torso swathed in bandages. In the morning he opened his eyes, his body throbbing in rolling, mind-engulfing waves of pain. Peter, hollow-eyed from sleeplessness, was by him with a flask of armagnac dosed with valerian and a small amount of an exotic caked-powder from the East. The substance was new to him, bought from a physician in London. A drug guaranteed to bring the patient to oblivion and, when wakeful again, some hours of suppression of pain. "Drink, my lord. This will ease you."

Simon tasted the liquid in the flask and gave a strained smile, "Arnaud's armagnac. You brought it..."

"This is our last. There is more in this than the wine only. Valerian, and I've put a touch of something new, said to be from Persia. I think it will make you sleep a while."

With great effort through his all engrossing hurt, Simon managed to say, "Let's use it sparingly."

"Drink it now, sire. Sleep will help you heal."

Simon drank deeply from the flask. As Peter gently wiped his lips and beard, he shut his eyes for a moment, resting. Then he opened them again and asked, with what seemed resignation, "What's my condition?"

"Your hip is broken badly, and your thigh bone's split where it was not well healed. It is reset. You've lost much blood. Probably a fever will set in. You won't be going to Amiens."

"I must. Even if I must be carried there!"

"Master," Peter looked into the glaring, bleared dark eyes and said firmly, "if you attempt it, my lord, you won't reach Amiens alive."

"I am going..." Simon said thickly as the pain for a moment took his breath away.

"For now, you're going to sleep."

Simon frowned but was too weak to counter his squire, and the liquor and drugs were beginning to have their effect. "You presume too much, Peter," was all that he could say before a heavy, dream-beset drugged sleep took him.

Thomas Cantaloup was waiting outside the chamber door when the squire emerged. "When can we go on to Amiens?" he asked anxiously.

Peter met the priest's anxious eyes unblinking. "My master won't be going."

"But he must!" Thomas protested, brows high in consternation. "What of the arbitration? He must present our case to Louis!"

"Father Thomas," Peter said in a quiet but firm tone, "it is not God's will."

Late that night Simon awoke, wet with sweat, in the throes of a high fever. Peter, sleeping on the floor beside his bed, woke at the sound of his changed breathing. He held the candle nightlight to his master's face. Simon lay on his chest, his cheek pressed against the pillow. "My lord?" Peter said softly. The dark eyes opened, cloudy, the whites red, the pupils reflecting the flame but unseeing.

Taking the leather pouch of medicaments from his belongings that he had thrown into a corner, Peter found a bag of a dried herbs and tossed a handful of its contents into the glowing coals of the brazier. Smoke rose, filling the room in a few moments with a pungent, penetrating, healing cloud. Simon moved his head, half conscious of the familiar medicinal odor. His mouth was dry, his lips cracking.

Peter left and roused the innkeeper's wife. From her he obtained hollow straws, used for blowing colored powders onto pastries, and for feeding invalids. He concocted a solution of wine and herbs to combat fever. Sucking it up into the straw, he placed his finger over the straw's upper end and put the lower end against his master's tongue so that the medicine would leak gradually into his dry mouth. All night, through a second night of sleeplessness, the squire fed his master drugs to counter the raging fever. And too he administered the drugged armagnac to quiet his master and ease his pain.

When dawn came, the fever had not yet broken. Simon, fighting to lucidness and the urgency of his reality from the remote distance of his strange, alluring dreams, whispered, his eyes focused and intent, "Thomas, and my son Henry... I must speak to them..."

The two came, standing sunk in worry at the bedside. Simon, lying on his chest, reached out his hand. Henry gave him his own hand and knelt near his father's face. Thomas knelt beside Henry so that the earl could see him also.

"You must go to Amiens without me," Simon said thickly, his tongue swollen and blistered, his fevered lips broken in thin lines of blood.

"I dare not argue our case without you!" Cantaloup pled.

Simon smiled feebly. "You are a doctor of law, Thomas. Louis..." he shut his eyes, but murmured a moment later, "is a man of reason." Incoherence, dreams, flickering visions played behind his closed eyelids, drawing him back to their painless, mindless region and he said no more.

As Thomas and Henry left the room, the Provost groaned, "God help us!"

Henry's eyes were wet with tears. "We must go, as my father says," he muttered. "Let us pray God gives us His words. Have hope, Father Thomas. Our cause is truly the Lord's."

Thomas, a priest, could not summon that much faith.

Leaving Simon at the inn with his squire and his son Guy, the rest of the party rode on to Amiens.

In two more days the earl's fever finally broke. The weather too had broken. The sun shown warmly and the roads were thawed. Guy rode back to Kenilworth to get a wagon, piled with cushioning hay, to bring Simon home.

The countess was waiting in the yard with young Eleanor when the wagon rattled through the inner gate. Simon, on a litter wrapped in blankets, was lifted out of the straw and carried up the foyer steps by Guy, Peter, Havering and Gobehasty. He was laid in the curtained bed that always traveled with the countess's furnishings. His face was haggard, gray from pain and loss of blood, but he lay quiet, sunk in drugs and dreams.

Days passed, then weeks. The squire ceased to medicate his patient so heavily and the earl rose to full consciousness. Slowly his body healed, as it had often before.

And now the house rang with his furious voice. He cursed and swore at his servants, at his squire, at his sons, his daughter and his wife. He was in a raging black temper, frustrated and helpless at the fate that kept him from the crucial arbitration. The only person who could speak with him with any hope of being spared insult was Master William, the fortress's engineer.

"His mind is so troubled about the meeting in France," the countess pled with the engineer. "Please, stay with him as much as you're able."

William sat on a bench by Simon's bed and delivered minute reports of every detail of the finishing touches to the fortifications.

Simon, prone on the deep feather mattress, listened with attention. Propping himself on one elbow, leaning over a wax tablet, he drew mangonels and trebuchets, ordering several built and installed on the towers.

"I fear," one day the earl began with uncharacteristic hesitation, "I may not ever sit a horse again. Can you build an armored cart that could be used in battle?"

William's narrow, intelligent face spread with his confident, thin-lipped smile. "My lord, I can build anything. If it's your wish, I'll build you a chariot as proof against battle's arrows, pikes and swords as a cook's pot against forks."

The engineer set to drawing on his own tablet.

Simon studied the sketches and gave an odd, bitter laugh. "I must be *the knight of the cart* after all." For the degradation of having once accepted a ride in a peasant's cart, Lancelot, the mythic paladin from France, the knight of devout faith overtopped by passion for his queens, mockingly was known as The Knight of the Cart.

Simon added softly, "Yes, build me this cart. The Hand of God crushes us to our fate – and then He laughs. Well He may."

An oak cart frame was erected in the outer yard, beside the smithy where Simon's horses were shod. With the engineer hovering at his side, the blacksmith hammered at his anvil for two days. Then the cart frame was wheeled into the dark back of the shop and there was more hammering and tapping.

After several more days, four of the earl's most massive horses, manteled in chain mail and clanking steel plates, were hitched as a team and backed to the rear of the shop. Then, as the hostler led the team forward, there emerged into the daylight a silvery object. A large steel box on wheels. Gleaming plates riveted together covered the whole body of the cart. Only the lower half of the wheels showed below the side-plates, and even there the spokes were covered with broad, shiny disks of steel. A small slot served as a window in the front. On one side was a steel door, its seams flush with the steel plates of the sides, with no hinges to be seen. The cart was an enormous strongbox, a vehicle of war as never seen before.

"I've built you a bright chariot worthy of Apollo," the engineer smiled proudly, "though it may be a trifle heavy to fly across the sky."

"May I not be like Phaeton," Simon grinned back as, in a soft sling-chair borne by his servants, he was carried to inspect it from each side.

Servants, hostlers, Simon's knights, everyone crowded to view Master William's invention.

Studying it, Simon's expression clouded.

"It meets your approval?" the engineer asked, with a pang of anxiety at his patron's look.

"I dare say it'll move as swiftly as a merchant ship on land."

William's smile faded.

But Simon added, "I suppose it is the best that can be done." He had himself carried back into the house, sullen and thoughtful.

Though Simon was disappointed, the onlookers in the yard were entranced by the bright, silvery machine. Word of the Earl's invincible steel cart spread out from Kenilworth. Soon, from York to Dover and the western hills of Wales, everyone knew that the Great Earl had been crippled by a fall and now rode in a silver chariot of war.

The cart itself stood in the barn, unused.

As February of 1264 dragged on, Simon slowly regained his strength. He sat in his sling-chair in the hall most of the day, dictating letters to his secretary, his fourth son, Amaury, who was returned from his priestly studies in Paris. In the long hours when there was no work to do, he had Amaury read to him from Augustine's *The City of God*. No one but Amaury, the squire Peter or the engineer dared to come near him for his temper grew even hotter with his returning health. At last, when he could tolerate his anxieties no longer, he sent his squire Peter to Amiens to report to him the progress of King Louis' arbitration.

Peter was back in just three days. "I met your sons, your cousin and Father Thomas at Saint Albans. I rode fast ahead to tell you they'll be here later today."

Simon grasped Peter's wrist and drew him close, studying his face. "The news is bad?"

"I beg you, let them tell you." Peter's look was bleak. Gently he tried to pull free.

Simon let go his wrist. He leaned from his chair, his elbows on the table, covering his face with his hands. "Oh, God," he muttered, "why did You keep me from being there?"

The squire looked at his master helplessly, then took advantage of the moment to slip away and tell the countess of the soon-arriving arbiters.

Simon, in a burst of anger and frustration, tried to rise, to walk. The pain was overwhelming and he fell back in his chair. His newly broken bones were, with the exception of the thigh, not where his legs were crushed before, but he had only just recovered from the torture's destruction, and now his hip and one leg were made useless again. He struck his fist against the oak table in rage, and struck it again and again. Amaury, hastily gathering up his leaping parchments, stylus and wax tablets, silently moved his lips in prayer.

In the afternoon, the horn sounded from the braye as the small company of riders neared the outermost gate. Eleanor had the tower bell rung in welcome, and she went down to the inner yard.

Thomas, Bosecellis, Peter de Montfort, young Henry and Simon rode in with their servants. There was no joy on any of their faces. Henry dismounted and hurried to his mother, taking her hands and kissing them.

"He knows already," she said softly.

Henry nodded. The rest dismounted and they all went, grimly mute, up the foyer steps.

They found the earl standing beside his chair in the hall. Though his body swayed with the pain and effort, his expression was stony and he eyed them with a piercing glare.

Tears broke from his son Henry's eyes. He knelt down at Simon's feet. "We failed you, father."

In a low voice, Thomas Cantaloup said, "Pope Urban upheld Pope Alexander's absolution of the vows to the Provisions. The King of France was forced to judge the Provisions untenable, impossibly opposed to Divine Order."

Simon's brow gathered in increasing anger as he eyed Cantaloup. "The Provisions themselves ought *never* to have been the issue of the arbitration! Only the king's submission to the Council of his people, and the keeping of his oaths! How could you let this happen!" Breathing heavily, he mastered himself and said in a growl between his teeth, "What does King Henry grant to his people?"

Cantaloup's eyes turned toward the floor, then sidelong. In a tone barely audible, he answered, "The king grants nothing. All castles and lands are to be restored to the castellans and lords of his choosing. He alone may select his counselors and his sheriffs, and they may be replaced only by his will. There is to be no law above the king, save that of the Pope."

Simon took a step forward, trembling with rage. "You showed the Court our complaints? The abuses of royal power? The incessant taxes? The worth of the lands Henry had given away?

Cantaloup nodded, cowering, his tonsured head half-buried in his cloak's rough woolen hood.

Henry Montfort, kneeling at his father's side, saw him wavering in pain, and stood at once, embracing him and helping him back to his chair.

Blanched with pain, Simon still could not take his eyes from Cantaloup. Hoarsely he demanded, "You showed Louis the records of Henry's grafts, the murders the Lusignan committed..."

"Good Earl, I did!" Thomas wailed, tears wetting his eyes. "Don't hold these things against King Louis. He, too, loses by this decision. All Christendom is put under Pope Urban's hand. Every king is made to bow to *him*! He means all men to be beneath the heels of kings, and all kings to be made the Pope's footstool!"

Peter de Montfort spoke up, his voice tight with emotion. "The Legate is bringing a Bull from the Vatican, declaring that if you refuse to obey King Henry, a crusade will be raised against you and your followers – against all men who won't submit themselves to their king's absolute rule, beneath the Pope and God."

Simon stared at his cousin, dumbfounded. "A crusade? Am I not a good Christian? What reason has the Pope to declare crusade against *me*?" He turned his eyes upward, his face twisted with agony. "My God, help me! Father Grosseteste, do you hear? You bade me lead your sheep!"

Bosecellis, who had been watching silently, standing by the earl, placed his hand on Simon's arm. "The Pope serves his own power. This is the day of mankind's suffocation." The scholar's tone was laden with cold anger. "A stone has been set upon the birthing New Era. But, my lord, these are the self-serving rulings of men. Though the whole world seems against us, with time and God's strength, we will prevail."

Simon was silent for a long while, one elbow on the table, his brow resting on his hand, his dark eyes unseeing, his thoughts turned inward. Then he raised his head and looked to Cantaloup. "Am I, and my followers, to be brought to trial for treason and heresy?"

"No, good earl," Cantaloup said, wiping his tears from his upper lip and cheeks. "King Louis required that King Henry swear to grant you peace, a general amnesty for all who accept this arbitration. No charter granting lands or titles issued prior to the Provisions may be rescinded. All former rights will remain as they were. So much as that King Louis could achieve, though the Legate much objected."

Simon looked at Thomas wearily. "King Louis once again would save my life." He sighed bitterly, and not resigned. "Does he imagine that he can return us to the bygone days of peace? He cannot wipe away the abuses that first brought us to Oxford. Must we let our children, and our children's children suffer what we find intolerable? Our afflictions will grow worse under this Pope's doctrines. I believe, when Christ said Our Heavenly Father has numbered each of us, and cares even when a sparrow falls, He did not intend that every man should treat those he considers more lowly than himself as if they were his slaves."

The countess stood beside her daughter near the hall's stairs. She turned to her daughter, burying her face on tall, young Eleanor's shoulder, and wept.

After a long pause, Simon spoke again, calmly. "Very well. We will return to the past. We will demand that Magna Carta be upheld. We will raise the land in arms against the king, until he satisfies the grievances of every Englishman!"

# Chapter fourteen

## THE LIONCELS AND THE PARD
### 1264

"While King Henry is still in France, go to the lands of Mortimer and pay our ransom for our steward there in steel and cinders," Simon told his sons Henry and Guy.

The brothers rode from Kenilworth at the head of the Leicester knights. England was at war again, and Simon led the battles from his cushioned chair at Kenilworth.

The Provisions were as dear as ever to most of the common people, despite King Louis' arbitration and Pope Urban's declared excommunication of its partisans. But there were also many who had second thoughts.

King Henry's support, as ever, was chiefly the senior barons. The uprisings of the folk, and pillaging in the name of the Provisions, had returned sporadically since the withdrawal of the Guardians of the Peace due to the arbitration. For Henry's lords, the king's denunciation of Montfort and his unruly followers was thoroughly justified. No angel of an absurd new era, the Earl of Leicester was the willful figurehead, if not the actual master, of the agents of Hell.

The City of Worcester rebelled in favor of the king. Hardly had Guy and Henry left for the Welsh border when Simon received a plea from Walter Cantaloup. The bishop dared not enter his own see. Simon sent word to Robert Ferrers to take his knights of Derbyshire to Cantaloups' relief.

Then in Gloucester, the same townsmen who eagerly had dug a tunnel for the Earl to undermine the sheriff's barbican now burned down Gilbert de Clare's house. Joan de Munchensey, the wife of King Henry's detested half-brother William de Valence and mother of Alice, the girl whom young Clare had been forced to marry, moved to Gloucester's castle, fortified in the center of the town. Announcing that she held the fortress for the king, and against her rebel son-in-law, she was recognized by the alderman of Gloucester officially as castellan. The garrison Simon had put in place surrendered to her. The city was Joan's, held for the king.

And from Dover, Richard de Gray wrote: *King Henry is returned from Amiens, with the Lord Edward, Richard of the Germans, Warenne, Leybourne and a multitude including all his Savoyards and Poitouvins he found infesting France, though Valence was not with them. Henry had the arbitration read to me and my garrison, and required our surrender. Begging your pardon, I never swore to accept this arbitration, and I refuse to surrender Dover on such an unjust outcome. This morning a troop of mercenary knights in the King's company left Dover with Lord Edward's banner in their lead.*

A courier returned from Henry and Guy with word that Mortimer's castle of Radnor was captured and the lands surrounding it despoiled. The earl's sons were moving to join Ferrers at Worcester. Then Ferrers' messenger arrived reporting Worcester had been taken and the houses of the royalists had been burnt to the ground.

Simon sent orders to his sons to cross the Severn River to the west bank again, meet a contingent of archers Llewellyn offered them, then retake Gloucester.

The brothers Montfort and their Leicester knights received the Welsh archers, and made their camp near the bridge that spanned the Severn at Gloucester.

On the opposite bank, the city's wooden palisade and stockade towers were manned for defense. The shut gate, the presence of the men upon the battlements, gave the city a far different aspect from when the Great Earl had come there only a few months before. The brothers pitched their tents and settled into siege.

Guy and Henry sat in Henry's tent at supper, arguing above their bowls of Lenten peas porridge, unable to agree on the best means to pierce the town's defense.

Henry's squire raised the tent flap and announced, "My lord, someone's here asking to see you."

Before Henry could demand who it was, John Giffard's pink-cheeked face looked in. Gilbert de Clare's friend, who had been with Clare and Ferrers when they begged the earl to come from France, beamed like sunshine at the brothers. "We're glad to see you here, my lords. May we come in?"

"Welcome, Giffard of Brimsford," Henry rose, holding out his hands in delighted greeting.

The tall, broad shouldered Gloucester knight came in, and after him another knight followed. "This is John Balun, a neighbor," Giffard made his introduction.

Henry sent his squire to unpack two more campstools from his supply wagon, and soon all four were seated with the modest Lenten meal before them.

Giffard, tearing off a crust from a round loaf and dipping it into his soup, asked outrightly, "How are you planning to take Gloucester?"

"We'll hold them shut till they surrender," Henry replied.

Guy made a sour face. "That could keep us sitting here till winter. Or longer. I can't see how we are to prevent them thoroughly enough from bringing in supplies."

Pressing his lips into a thin line of contempt, Henry added acerbically, "Guy's all for making a bonfire of that wall of sticks across the river."

"We cannot starve them, even if we hold the city gates tight shut," Guy protested. "They can restock from all along their riverfront, protected by their archers on the wall with a high trajectory that will outreach our Welsh bowmen."

"We'll build shielding screens," Henry retorted.

His mouth full, Giffard nodded. "Still Guy's right. Siege will take too long. As for burning the wall, yes, it's so much firewood, and so is the whole town. The Gloucestermen won't love our cause if we reduce them to ashes."

"So," Henry, peeved at this offhand rejection of both their plans, asked with an ironic gesture, "do you have a better idea?"

With his dining knife Giffard speared a piece of pickled herring from a dish Henry's squire had just brought to the table. "How many knights do you have here?"

"Fifty," Guy answered. "And a hundred archers."

"That'll be plenty to take the city, once we're inside." Giffard swallowed the herring and reached for another. "Balun and I have a plan..."

By the time he had devoured all the pickled herring, and completed his description of his plan, both Montfort brothers had broad grins.

"We'll try it," Henry said.

"We'll be ready for your signal," Guy added.

At Henry's order the siege was lifted. The Leicester knights folded their tents. All was packed into the wagons and the army left the Severn riverbank, retreating out of sight of Gloucester's wooden parapets.

Late that night two men on foot crossed Gloucester's bridge. They led a string of sumpter horses with empty woolsacks bound in bundles to their packsaddles. The men were muffled to the eyes in their cloaks and hoods. At the shut gate they pounded insistently and, in the French accent of Calais, one shouted to the tower, "Person? Up thair? Open!"

"Who are you?" a militiaman irritably called down. "What's your business, coming here at night!"

"*Nous*, ve..." the other man gestured to himself and his companion who had spoken first, "vool gaderers. *En passon par tout les villages, ici... a* Mooch Markle, no von bag *de* vool! *Mon Dieu*," he crossed himself, "dhe trouble ve see in dis lant!" He spoke in a mix of demotic French and Flemish-tainted English, and sounded weary, totally forlorn.

The other hooded figure urged, "You have thee wool? We pay thee beautifool price."

Like most people in the west country, the guard had his investment of a few sheep in the big flocks on the Cotswold hills and usually had wool to sell on speculation. "I'll let you in," he called down. "Wait a few moments."

The moments passed, then the wicket door in the great timber gate opened and the militiaman came out.

Annoyed, the Calais wool merchant insisted, "Open thees gate! We not leave horses outside to be steal!"

Reluctantly, the guard of Gloucester went back through the little door, unbolted and swung open a leaf of the great gate.

The wool gatherers went in with their string of horses.

Inside, another militiaman called down from the parapet, "How much are you offering?"

"Six pound silwer for dhee sack. Goot Flemish silwer. *Rien plus* dhis much silwer you take *en tout le monde!* 'ow much you hef?" the Fleming asked.

"One. Maybe two," the guard above replied, rubbing his chin. It was a *very* good price. The guard holding the gate open was counting up what the five bags stored in his loft were going to bring.

"*C'est necessaire* ve hef fifty bag. Doo hun'red, *c'est plus belle. Joyeuse!*"

The guard shouted down the length of the parapet, "Henny, how much wool you have to sell?"

By now the open gate had caught the attention of most of the guards on the river length of the wall. They were moving nearer to find out what was happening.

"What did you say?" a voice called down.

"These men want to buy wool. Six pounds silver the sack. You have some?"

"What are they paying?"

"You heard right! Six pounds a sack, Flemish silver."

Seven men climbed quickly down the tower's ladder, the whole of the gate and wall's night watch on that side of the city. They clustered in a group beside the open gate, eyeing the two wool gatherers with high interest.

"How many sacks you need?" one asked.

"Doo hun'red we mek purchus," the cloaked figure with the Flemish accent said.

The guards broke into animated, low-pitched talk among themselves. Forming a circle, their backs to the two merchants, they calculated the number of woolsacks that together they could supply.

As they were making up their count, the heavily cloaked wool gatherers drifted to a position between the militiamen and the street. Then they threw off their enveloping cloaks. John Giffard and John Balun stood in full chain mail with their swords drawn. Giffard lifted the horn he had slung at his belt and blew a long, loud blast.

The preoccupied militiamen turned, shocked, and recognized the young lord who was their city's neighbor.

"Good evening, Hobkins." Giffard grinned at a man he knew well, while presenting to him the point of his sword.

Hobkins had no time to answer. The beat of fifty horses' hooves, coming on at gallop, drummed in rhythmic thunder across the bridge. Armored knights poured in through the open gate.

The guardsmen standing nearby scattered in panic. But as the cavalry sortie entered, other militiamen, alerted by the horn, came running up the street, fumblingly nocking arrows to their crossbows. Guy, his brother's red lioncel flag streaming beside him, bore down on them, slashing with his sword.

The militia archers fled, their captain yelling with a deep cut in his shoulder. Gaining the relative shelter of a street corner, he turned and cried out, "Peace! Good lords! Peace! We surrender!"

Gloucester was taken.

As his Welsh archers marched in through the gate, Henry Montfort ordered them to man the walls in place of the militia.

The castle was still held by the Lady Joan, Madame de Valence. Henry posted knights beside its tumbled barbican, felled by his father months ago and not yet repaired, and Gloucester was secured, at least so far as could be done that night.

Giffard led the Montfort brothers to the Blackfriars' monastic house in Ladybellegate Street. The Dominicans, believers in the New Age, welcomed them to lodge there and use the house as headquarters.

Soon after dawn, Henry and Guy were both out touring their holding of the city walls and towers. Seeing all was secure, they returned to Ladybellegate Street to debate how to take the castle.

Shortly after noon, one of the Welshmen from the city's east gate came to them. "My lords, there's an army approaching from the southeast," he reported.

The brothers and Giffard went at a run with the archer to the gate tower.

In the distance a long, dark line, a flag flying at its fore, could be seen moving across the bright, clear spring countryside. Henry ordered the archers on the walls to prepare for attack and siege, and summoned the Leicester knights to be fully armed, ready to strike in sortie from the east gate. Then the brothers and Giffard waited, watching the slowly moving column drawing closer.

In an hour the flag at the fore could be discerned: red with three gold charges in the pose of *passant* leopards. They knew the blazon well.

"It's Edward," Henry, straining his eyes at the distance, said. "That's his Spanish horse beyond a doubt, and I can see his blond head."

There was tense silence. Then Guy broke the spell with a curt laugh. "Well, God's with us that he came today, not yesterday! We'd not have taken the city so easily, and he'd have trapped us from the behind."

Shaking off the fascination that held him staring at the troops' approach, Giffard announced, "I'd best go while I still can, and find us help. Ferrers can come down the river and attack Edward's flank if he sets siege. You stay and hold the city?"

"We certainly mean to." Henry's eyes were fixed on the advancing column.

In another hour, Edward's forces reached the broad, flat field before the bridge. They pitched their tents where Guy and Henry's tents had been.

On foot and unarmed, Henry of Alemaine walked out from the camp to the foot of the bridge. Atop the gate's tower, Henry Montfort's banner was flying, its three red lioncels rampant, curling and uncurling as the breeze gracefully folded the flag upon itself.

Alemaine squinted at it against the sun-bleached sky. Then he called out, "I have a message from Prince Edward for the holder of Gloucester." He knew exactly whose flag it was.

Henry leaned over the tower's battlement, far enough to let his cousin see him. "It's I who hold the city, Henry, as you see." He gestured to the flag languidly billowing not far above his head. "What is your message?"

"Prince Edward asks why you're holding the gate closed. He hasn't come here to attack you, but to assure you of his peace." Alemaine's voice seemed thin in the outdoors. He stood with his feet placed close together, his back very straight, with more the modest air of a page than the son of a king.

Henry Montfort called down, "If he hasn't come here to attack us, why has he brought an army?"

"The land's unsafe, Cousin," Alemaine answered. "You know that as well as he!"

"Tell him that we wish him peace also, Cousin," Henry shouted down. "But we wish, even more, to have the government of the Provisions. When he's willing to uphold the rule of law, we'll be at one with him, and with you also, as kindred ought. Else we're enemies."

Alemaine took the message back to the prince's camp.

Within moments Edward himself came to the bridge. Tall, elegant, powerful of build, and gleaming in a thread-of-gold tabard over his neatly fitted Spanish mail, his blond curls blew about his face in the quickening wind. He walked across the bridge to within easy bowshot of the tower. So close he was within range of a child's slingshot. There, addressing the tower without bellowing, he tipped his head far back, looking intently at Henry and speaking as in normal conversation. "Henry, this is not as it should be between us."

Alemaine had come with him and stood beside him, more than a head shorter than the prince. Edward turned and nodded, letting Alemaine speak for him.

"The Prince says, if you will be assured of his peace, he will swear to the Provisions here before you. You know he risked his life at Southwark in 1260. You know he believes in your cause. He asks you to greet him as the true friend he has always been."

Guy, coming up beside his brother, frowned.

Henry was thoughtful for some moments, moved by Edward's blue, beseeching stare. He called back, "I'll come down."

"Don't trust him!" Guy shouted, as his brother climbed down the tower's ladder.

Henry paused. "To refuse his offer is to force him to attack us. I'd rather try the truth of his words than deny him, if peace can be had," he said hopefully. "We know Edward favors the Provisions. He went so far as to call Parliament on his own, when King Henry stalled in France to raise an army against it. There could be good faith in his offer."

"I don't trust him! And neither does our father," Guy persisted.

Henry tried to think what their father would do, and decided to go talk with Edward. He completed his climb down the ladder, ordered the wicket door in the gate opened, and walked out onto the bridge to where Edward was waiting.

Guy leaned over the parapet. "If he favors the Provisions, why did he flee to Windsor! Ask him that!"

But Henry paid his brother no heed. He and the prince had been close friends since Edward was five and he was six. They had shared their coming of age, adventures of both battlefield and brothel. And Edward could instill great love in his friends' hearts. Henry had hope.

As he drew near, the prince put out his hand in welcome. "My friend. More than my friend, all but my brother." He deployed his radiant smile.

Henry maintained his aloofness as best he could, though his heart wanted to burst with relief, with happiness, with a reunion that could end the long nightmare of strife, if Edward could be won again to the Provisions. But he did no more than nod and smile in cool acknowledgement at first.

Edward put his arm around Henry's shoulder, hugging him to his golden, chain-mailed breast. "By God, let's have done with this warfare," he murmured earnestly, his breath warm on Henry's ear.

"I long to," Henry admitted, pulling out from his embrace. There was about Edward a certain enchantment. The closer one was to his person, the more weakened was one's power to resist him. It took all of Henry's self control to keep himself steady, aloof and critical. "Doesn't the judgment at Amiens separate us beyond hope?" he asked pointedly.

"The judgment!" Edward rolled his silvery blue eyes toward the heavens. He took Henry's arm, drawing him across the bridge and toward his tent, talking as they walked.

"If ever a Pope served his own ambitions beyond any trace of decency!" he crowed with cynical and bitter hilarity. "It's plain he means the Vatican to rule kings! You know that I'm committed to the Provisions. No one, save your father, has placed himself in greater jeopardy for them than I. The purpose of the arbitration was solely to bring us peace. Pope Urban has betrayed us all in his gross lunge for power."

"You'll acknowledge the Provisions then, and swear to their upholding?" Henry breathed. "Good God, Edward, if we could stop this now..."

Edward's limpid gaze held Henry's dark brown eyes. "You are my oldest and my dearest friend. You were my wise counselor when I was young, wild, sometimes out of my mind. I don't want ever to fight you, Henry." Truth sounded in his words, and they were true. Truer than almost any other words Edward ever had spoken.

Henry stiffened, uncertain what to make of this admittance, though he knew full well what wildness he meant.

At the entrance to his tent, the prince turned, in full view of his forces. He unsheathed with a steely hiss the beautiful bright sword Alphonse of Castile had given him when he was made a knight. Pointing the blade toward the ground, his two hands clasped below the pommel that contained a blessed relic, a fragment of Saint Edward the Confessor's true crown, he said loudly for all to hear, his eyes fixed on Henry's eyes, "By the crown of Holy Edward, I swear always to uphold the cause of government guided by the counsel of England's people."

With deft ease he slid the sword back in the sheath hung at his hip. "Will you believe me, Henry?" he asked, taking his cousin's hand and pressing it with his powerful swordsman's fingers. "I beg you, Henry, have faith in me," he said earnestly. "I shall be king one day. When that day comes, whatever's gone before, we will do well for England, you and I together. I pray, always believe these words of mine."

His eyes held by the prince's serious blue gaze, Henry returned the pressure of his hand. Joy leapt in him, the joy of faith, even of love restored, for in his heart he felt that Edward spoke the truth. And he believed his intentions, so far as any man may speak of the future.

"I do believe you, Edward. I place my faith, our friendship, my loyalty, into the balance, trusting you." He knelt down, his palms together, held out before him in the gesture of fealty, and said, "It is to you I pledged myself again. And to you I render the city of Gloucester, for you have been, and still are my lord."

The prince raised him up and embraced him with real warmth and relief. "Henry, we believe in the same things, you and I. Our day will come," Then he whispered again in Henry's ear. "Remember these words I've said. Remember them, and keep faith in me always." His tone was almost pleading, and he hugged Henry again. Then he stood back, calling his lieutenants.

Henry returned with the prince to the closed gate and called out, "Prince Edward has sworn to uphold the Provisions! He is at one with us! There is no need to hold the city shut against him. Open the gates!"

Reluctantly, Guy, on the parapet, nodded and the gates were opened. The prince's army peacefully filed into the city.

Joan de Valence surrendered the castle to the prince, her nephew-by-marriage, and all of Gloucester rejoiced at the peace.

The prince was told of Giffard's flight to Worcester to seek help from Ferrers. He had Henry send couriers to find Ferrers and Giffard, informing them of the peace and advising them to disband.

At the Dominicans' house that night Henry Montfort gave a feast, with Edward and Joan de Valence as his guests of honor.

"To reconciliation! To peace in England!" Henry offered as a toast.

"To reunion in our land." Edward raised his goblet and drank his wine down. Having it refilled, he added, "To you, Henry de Montfort, whom I've loved all the years I can remember. The first and best friend I've ever had!"

Guy drank, but not to the toasts. Sardonically he worked at getting drunk, and achieved his purpose. He was unsure if his misgivings sprang from jealousy, but his misgivings prodded him like devils with hot shafts. Few people were immune to Edward's charm, but Guy was one of them.

The merrymaking of the feast went long into the night. A trouvere in the prince's entourage sang the long tale of the prince's wars in Wales, and then the songs of the Provisions' partisans.

"There'll be good governance in England," Edward, deep into his wine, told Joan, as if imparting a sweet secret to the curve of her bare neck. She was deeply flushed, blushing, and when he let his fingers rest upon her breast she did not draw away.

But he turned then to Henry, saying in the same confiding tone, "My father's been wrong. Utterly wrong! Time and again."

Guy leaned from his place at the far side of Joan. "Last I heard, he was still king," he put in cuttingly.

Edward looked toward him, his smile fading. He was not fond of Guy. Then he found Joan's limpid eyes again and raised his cup, "To peace," he grinned, and he stood up. Holding his goblet aloft he cried, "To peace!"

"To Peace! And to Edward!" Alemaine chimed in. Everyone in the room, except Guy, echoed the toast and drank.

As he sat down again, Edward found his hand grasped, folded between Joan's hands and placed firmly in the valley of her warm lap. Her eyes were sparkling, and her perfume of lilies came ardently to him even through the fumes of his wine. He probed with his captured hand deeper between her thighs as her quickened breathing made him certain of his welcome. That night, in sheer delight, the prince cuckolded his own uncle. In future months the lady of Valence would show gravidly pregnant, rather too soon considering the long time of her husband's absence and his delayed return.

At breakfast the next day Edward, bathed, refreshed and happy, told Henry, "I want, above all, to be reconciled with your father. Go back to Kenilworth, you and your brother, and tell him I want peace."

"I'll do it very gladly." Henry could almost weep for joy.

That same afternoon the Montfort brothers, with their Leicester knights and Welsh archers, departed.

Behind them, the leopard standard of the prince curled over Gloucester's castle. Edward made his residence with his surprisingly amusing Aunt Joan, finding it strategic to stay in the west, enjoying her companionship for weeks.

At Kenilworth Simon had called a meeting of the leaders of his party. When his two sons arrived from Gloucester, the meeting was in progress in the hall. De Vere, the Earl of Oxford and de Lacey, the Earl of Lincoln; young Humphrey de Bohun; the bishops of Worcester, Lincoln and London, and the castellan of Dover Richard de Gray, were all assembled in a council of war. Simon presided from his cushioned chair.

Surprised, but glad to see his sons, he greeted them with, "You've come in good time! Tell us how matters are in Gloucester."

Young Henry smiled broadly. "We took the city easily, father. By means of a ruse." He told of the exploit of Giffard and Balun, the wool gatherers.

Simon interrupted him before he'd gotten further. Turning to de Vere, the earl said, "Then we can count the bridge at Gloucester ours," and he turned back to Henry. "Mortimer is taking his revenge for Radnor. He's burnt the bridges crossing the Severn, all except the Gloucester bridge. His intent is to divide us from our Welsh allies. He attacked Ferrers and Peter de Montfort. It is believed Prince Edward has sent a new royal force of mercenaries to his aid."

Both Henry and Guy stared at their father as if struck mute.

"Indeed, matters have moved that far toward full war," Simon nodded, misreading their shocked looks. "There are worse reports. The king is summoning the barons again to Oxford to meet him in arms. And in the south, our former friend Leybourne strives to secure the Cinque Ports to land the queen's hired army led by Valence. Leybourne's closed the road from London to Dover by taking Rochester." Simon shook his head, "We've had no good word, except your welcome news from Gloucester."

Henry felt faint, but he accepted the burden that his brother's glare placed on him. "Fa... father," he stammered, "my lords... bishops... I don't know what to say to these things... I'm sure I bring good news..." He gathered himself, reaching to believe again what had been so convincing on the field at Gloucester. "I was commissioned by Prince Edward himself to tell you of his vow to peace."

"Peace do you call this!" Bohun Fils laughed curtly, his eyes with a new sternness in his round, smooth face.

"Edward, before the gate of Gloucester," Henry insisted, "swore upon the holy relic of his sword to uphold the Provisions. He bade us bring you assurance of oneness with our cause."

Simon raised his dark eyebrows. "Edward swore?"

"He declared to me that his belief in the Provisions is still strong, that King Henry errs grievously. He asks peace with us... and in return I offered him my peace."

"He means that we gave Gloucester to him," Guy put in brutally.

"After you had taken it, you gave Gloucester to Edward..." Simon stared at Guy in disbelief.

"We're at peace with the prince," Henry urged. "In pledge of good faith, I left the city in his keeping."

"Better to admit you lost to him in battle our one remaining holding in the west!" Simon bellowed, rising from his chair. He was shaking with fury. "You know Edward's practices of lying and forswearing!"

"Father, upon my faith, he swore truly!" Henry begged. "He does not want to oppose you!"

Between his teeth Simon said slowly and deliberately, "Shame yourself no further, Henry. You've been made a fool."

Staring at his father, Henry's legs began to tremble. He never before had countered his father, but his whole being denied the accusation. "You're wrong, father! There is a faithful heart in him!" And he turned and ran from the hall.

The next day young Simon was dispatched with the royal mercenaries to aid Ferrers and Peter de Montfort.

Again, privately, Henry tried to convince his father that Edward truly did mean peace.

"The king's new summons to Oxford, how might Edward describe that?" Simon demanded. "And Leybourne at Rochester? Even if the prince wished peace, do you imagine he would oppose King Henry? He proved at Southwark how his vaunted courage fails him there!"

A few days later a guard from the braye announced that the knight John Giffard wished to be admitted. Henry was overjoyed and ran out to the yard to meet him.

"I thank God you're here!" His voice rose and he smiled for the first time in days. "You'll bear witness for me of the prince's peace!"

"Peace?" Giffard asked. "Edward has confiscated all my lands as punishment for having helped you. He fines your supporters to their total ruin. Gloucester is held under his garrison, and he sends troops north to join with Mortimer."

"Edward attacks us?" Henry stared, the slender prop he thought he had found was cut out from beneath him.

"He does! And he'll soon hold the west country entirely."

"He pledged to me his most solemn oath!"

"Oath or not, he gives us war."

"By Saint Edward's crown," Henry panted in shock, "may he be damned! May his lying tongue be *damned!*" The kindness, the good faith that was Henry Montfort's essence, was charred to ash in the blaze of his rage. His father was right. He had been manipulated and betrayed.

Embarrassed, Giffard looked away. He saw the earl, framed in the doorway, standing with the help of two canes at the top of the foyer steps. "Giffard, come here to me," Simon ordered.

At the sound of his father's voice, Henry turned around. He tried to speak but could not. He stood frozen as Giffard passed him and climbed the stairs to the door.

"Help me back to the hall," Simon said, as the Gloucester knight bowed low to him. "Tell me what has happened in the west."

Giffard, with the earl leaning heavily upon his strong shoulder, entered the hall and eased Simon back into his chair. He told of the events in Gloucestershire.

Silently Henry came into the hall, pausing by the entrance, struggling to gain some self-control. The gentleness of heart that was his shining quality since birth was shriveled by the flow of Giffard's words as, unaware of him, the Gloucesterman poured out his news. Henry wiped tears from his cheeks then, crossing the room suddenly and kneeling at his father's feet, he broke into the midst of Giffard's speaking. "Father, I dare not ask your pardon. But I swear to you before the Lord our Savior, I will avenge our betrayal! With Edward's death, or mine!"

# Chapter Fifteen

## LONDON AND ROCHESTER
### 1264

England was divided. The barons, even most of the young lords, swelled King Henry's army as it gathered at Oxford. The arbitration and the Pope's denunciation had shifted the balance heavily. Many of the clergy who had been loud for the Provisions renounced and denied the Earl's cause in the face of excommunication.

But the elected shire knights were firmly with the Earl, as were the Welsh. They gathered at Kenilworth with the lordlings of Edward's Bachelry, youths Simon had rescued at Ewloe, young men firm in their support of the Provisions. With them were Bishop Walter Cantaloup of Worcester and Bishop Henry de Sandwich of London.

In cities and country villages the emblem of Montfort sprouted like a rugged wildflower in springtime. Wooden boards painted with a red lion rampant hung over the doors of inns as sign of welcome to the Provisions' partisans. The common folk of England were with him. They yearned to believe in the coming of a New Era, the millennium that would bring equality to all mankind and the end of arbitrary privilege.

At Kenilworth the knight Hugh Gebion reported from Oxford. "Edward's come from the west with Roger Mortimer. They've joined their forces with the king's main army. Hugh Bigod and John Aldithley, as well as the Marcher lords, are there." He named the Justiciar and a Councilor who had been among the earliest elected under the Provisions. And he went on to tell the thoroughness of the opposition. "King Henry has the men-at-arms belonging to the earls of Hereford, Warwick, Surrey, Winchester, Cornwall, Devon,

Arundel, Pembroke, Richmond, Kent and Norfolk. Roger Bigod leads them, with the king's brother Richard." It was a recitation of nearly all of England's senior, battle-hardened army.

"Roger Bigod..." Simon mused with bitterness. "He claimed ill health and old age kept him from our last Parliament. But he is hearty enough to lead knights against us. No one was more loud in his complaints against King Henry. Yet this now... and Aldithley, a knight unheard of till his harangues against the king at Oxford, when the new government was first formed. I've lived in many lands, among Christians and heathens, but nowhere have I found a people so inconstant and deceitful as the English!"

Plump Humphrey de Bohun Fils, son of the Earl of Hereford, was livid. In fury he burst out, "I curse my father!"

Simon turned sharply on the earnest youth he had saved at Ewloe. "Humphrey, beg that God in His mercy wipes your words away," he said sternly. "We are not here to have sons cursing their fathers."

Exactly what they were there for was a nettling question. One Simon found far more filled with sorrow than he let his faithful, willing followers see. Sitting, elbows on his table, his forehead on the palms of his hands, his fingers in his dark hair, he said nothing for some time.

The shire knights and young lords, sitting on benches around the table in Kenilworth's hall, watched the earl silently. At last he raised his head and spoke. "It is a mighty army that opposes us. They far outnumber us, and in experience of war they outreach any forces we can muster. We are offered the terms of King Louis' arbitration. Or excommunication if we refuse – with defeat, and very likely death, to follow. Had we not best give new thought to what we are doing?" The hint of sarcasm, and his wry smile, brought no smiles in return.

"Have we come this far only to renege?" Walter Cantaloup scanned the faces around him, then settled on his friend. "If we fail now, we've failed forever. King Henry... No, *all* kings henceforth will know no law. We are at mankind's turning point."

"I think there is no better time to die than now," prickly Gilbert de Clare asserted, "before we see the tyranny we will be leaving to our heirs."

The old Bishop of London, sensitive as an open wound for his embraced, condemned theology of Joachim, stood up. "We must overturn this yoke of oppression that King Henry's fashioned, with King Louis' help, and which Pope Urban would lock on our necks! What we are battling is Satan's forces, working on the ambitions of unholy men!"

His outburst was extreme; wild condemnation of the man currently seated upon the throne of Saint Peter. Far beyond anything that Bishop Grosseteste, that arch-critic of Popes, would have dared to utter. But his words rang true for his listeners.

"I'm of the same mind as you, Reverend Father," Humphrey de Bohun Fils modestly stood up. Looking to the Earl he urged, "We beg you, lead us!"

Clare stood up beside him, "Lead us!"

"If the Lord Montfort leads," Humphrey added in a tone the more solemn for its softness, "I will follow him till my last drop of blood is shed."

Simon looked from face to face. "I ask you, you loyal men, and I advise you, let us make one last attempt. Let us send an embassy to beg another arbitration."

"You refuse to be our commander?" Clare asked, frowning.

"If war in no way may be avoided, I will be your leader. But let us try, this one more time, for reconciliation. If Magna Carta will be honored, we must be satisfied."

The Bishops of Worcester and London left the stronghold of Kenilworth for Oxford to beg King Henry for another arbitration. In a few days they returned. Walter bleakly told Simon, "Henry refuses. He demands your immediate surrender."

His dark eyes cast down, Simon merely nodded.

"Your son Simon, your cousin Peter and Ferrers followed Edward from the west," Walter told him. "They're camped just north of Oxford, waiting your commands."

Simon breathed a long sigh as if letting life itself pass from him. "Very well. That is how it must be." Looking to his knight Adam Newmarket, standing nearby, he ordered, "Go to Simon and tell him he must stay northward of the king and not engage in battle. We will go to London, gain what aid we can raise there, then march on King Henry. May the Lord defend us... if He truly favors our cause."

Word was sent ahead to Mayor FitzThomas, and to Hugh Despensar who still, as the Provisions' current Justiciar, held the Tower of London. Simon asked them to raise the Londoners to arms.

From Kenilworth a meager cavalcade of fifty Leicestermen, some four hundred young knights and novices, Welsh archers, squires, servants, common volunteers as foot soldiers, and wagons laden with supplies and armaments passed at ox-pace through the braye's high towered gate and toward the London road. Simon's red lion flag went at the fore between the tall gold crosses of the two bishops. Weaving among the horses of the ensigns, a trouvere cavorted, singing the Earl's songs and beating on his drum to the continuum of tread and creak and jingle of the march. The belled and parti-colored singer made an oddly merry leader for the somber parade. The banners of Clare, Bohun and Henry de Montfort fluttered behind him.

In the midst of the marchers, surrounded by a guard of Leicester knights, the Great Earl's shining steel-armored cart rattled over the stones and ruts. Closed inside it with his squire, Simon complained and cursed. Sun beating on the polished metal made the nearly windowless contraption an effective oven. And it climbed and dropped from rut to rut with tooth-rattling concussions.

"This is a machine of torture!" Simon bellowed. "I'd be better off on a foundered horse than in this box, basting in my sweat and shaking my bones like gamblers' dice! In the name of heaven, I've had enough! Get me my horse!" They had traveled two miles.

"Your hip's not healed, Master. You must not strain it in a saddle," his sweating, miserable squire-surgeon pled.

The cart lurched and dropped over a particularly bad bump. "To hell with your advice, Peter!" Simon roared. "My hip is being beaten to a pulp. I'll ride!" He picked up his sheathed sword, which lay on the bundled food and medicaments piled between their knees. With the sword-pommel he pounded on the cart's roof, near where the driver was perched.

The cart stopped, bringing the entire line of march behind it to a halt. In a moment the steel door opened. "Is my lord wanting something?" the infuriatingly sweat-free and helpful teamster asked.

"I'm cracking every bone I have in this cursed box! Help me out!"

Guy, riding beside the cart, assisted the carter in easing Simon to the ground and to where he could sit with his back against a tree. The squire Peter joined them.

"Bind my wounds so I can ride!" Simon glowered at him. "Guy, fetch my horses."

The march was stopped. Several of the lords dismounted and were gathered in a concerned group with glances toward the earl beneath the tree. Was he enough recovered?

While Guy returned to Kenilworth for his father's favored destrier and a comfortable and easy-paced palfrey, Peter bound the bandages more firmly about the brace he had fashioned for his master's hip and the splint for the still-weak thigh.

Clearly doubtful of his work, he said at last, "I can do no better, my lord. Ride if you must."

When Guy brought up the destrier, the squire's horse, and an undistinguished, gently-gaited, comfortably slab-sided mare from his father's stable, Simon looked askance at him, then laughed. "A pathetic mount for a maimed rider?" With aid, he stood, and with the help of several strong hands he was hoisted to his saddle. Sitting a horse for the first time in months, his whole demeanor seemed to calm as he settled to the saddle. He smiled, relieved, even happy. "Let's march on."

Guiding his mild palfrey forward, Simon went along the roadside, past his halted troops, till he came to his bannerman

Botevelyn at the head of the cavalcade. A mighty cheer went up as he took the lead. The trouvere danced around the placid mare's legs, gleefully singing, *Il est al mont, est si est fort, si ad grant chevalrie.*

From then on the armored car rumbled and bounced along in the midst of the army, unoccupied but for supplies.

Villeins in the fields stopped their spring sowing to watch the army pass. The earl, in full chain mail armor but without surcoat or mantling, and on his homely mare, passed them unrecognized. The common folk bowed their heads and blessed themselves as the two bishops with their crosiers passed, then knelt as the silvery cart went by, as if the sacrament were being shown in a holy procession. The Great Earl, not in his real person, but in his legend had become sanctified.

When the march reached London's Aldgate, horns blared from the city walls, answering each other from gate to gate. Church bells rang a tumultuous greeting. The Londoners poured from their doors into the streets. People shouted, climbed on rooftops, hung out of every window that might give view of the Earl's silvery chariot. If notice was taken of the meager number of armed men it was assumed this was only the Earl's private guard, the full army was camped elsewhere. The cause of the Provisions seemed, with the return of spring, to have miraculously quickened from the dead.

At London Tower Hugh Despensar waited in the yard with the Mayor Thomas FitzThomas. As Simon brought his mare to halt, the mayor bowed low, not in the least failing to recognize him. "Lord Earl, here is your new weapon." He made a sweeping gesture that embraced the city. "Within our walls there's not a man who hasn't armed himself and prayed for your return. We stand with you against the king, the Pope and the infernal arbitration!"

But later, in the privacy of the Justiciar's chamber in London Tower, Hugh Despensar's words were less encouraging. "Since the news came from Amiens, the city's been a hive buzzing with mischief. The Londoners are armed, it's true. But that they'll make an army I much doubt."

"We can ill afford to carp at our supporters," Simon smiled indulgently. "There are so few of them left."

"My lord, these men are likely to be as much a danger to us as to the enemy. I beg you, order them disarmed."

Simon leveled his dark, nearsighted eyes at Despensar. "The knights and foot soldiers you saw enter London with me, and your Londoners, are all the force we can muster against Henry, save the mercenaries who are with my son Simon, and the men of Ferrers and Peter de Montfort."

The Justiciar kept his severe, warning look.

"Very well," Simon agreed at the persistent scowl, taking the warning seriously. "Let's test them if you fear them so. Take them out to Prince Richard's fief at Isleworth and let them have their fill of mischief there, if that's their disposition. It will give us chance to see what arms they have and how they use them."

On the morning set by the Justiciar the city emptied. The open plain at Smithfield, just outside the city, swarmed with men of all sorts: young, old, merchants, workmen, peddlers, craftsmen, thieves and mountebanks. They came on foot or mounted on everything from handsomely caparisoned palfreys to swaybacked carthorses and asses so enfeebled they could scarcely stand.

The mob flaunted bright hues here and there, but chiefly dull colors predominated, cheap cloth of russet, perse or bleu de Nimes. Peddlers plied the crowd with stocks of amulets to ward off injury and, if that failed, bags of salve and lint. Whetstones for sharpening knives and swords were finding a brisk business, as were large and flopping leather saddlebags for booty. Pie men cried their crusted sausages and meat-filled pastries. A mood of festival prevailed. But it was sinister, a thrill, an expectation in the darker ranges of the spirit.

The Justiciar and Mayor, both in full chain mail, and safely guarded by heavily armed, mounted bailiffs, passed with blaring horns and beat of drums out of the city. Skirting Smithfield, they took the lead of the Londoners' march.

It was a walk of but a few miles to Isleworth. The Justiciar was back to his Tower by nightfall.

Exhausted, disgusted, Despensar made his report to the earl. "I led locusts to Isleworth. Nothing stands! Not a building, not a blade of grass. Even the ponds are destroyed. The Londoners are no fighting force to be turned loose anywhere! They slew the unarmed villeins with no mercy. But whenever a bailiff offered a little resistance, they turned and ran."

Simon's spy, Adam Newmarket, had arrived from Oxford. He too gave his report. "Henry marches upon Kenilworth. From there he means to attack Leicester and Lincoln. Your son Simon, the Lord Ferrers and your cousin Peter de Montfort are moving toward Northampton. They mean to block his advance, and they beg you to come quickly."

"They were told not to engage the king's forces!" Simon struck his worktable, then raised his head, his look heavy with the conclusion that waited but saying. "It seems, whether we wish it or not, the time has come when we must attempt to face our king in arms."

"The Londoners?" Despensar asked.

Simon shook his head. "Isleworth argues your point. They are worse than useless. See that they're disarmed."

That night Simon was sleepless. Alone in the Tower's chapel, he prayed till dawn. "Those who were our friends have fallen away, leaving a feeble remnant. In faith, if such is Your will, I'll lead these few. If Your new era is to be, Your strength must battle for us. By ourselves alone we cannot hope to overcome the armies ranged against us. I lead these men to dash themselves to death against a wall. " He was silent for some time, then he murmured, "God, help me. Show me Your will." But he heard only, *Feed my sheep.*

In the morning the Earl's army marched from the city, leaving the Londoners behind. Unruly crowds gathered along the way and threatened to block Aldgate. But the Earl's Leicestermen steadily bore down, their horses at an uncompromising trot, and the mob parted.

The army of the Provisions reached Saint Albans by late afternoon and pitched camp.

In the abbey's familiar guesthouse Simon prayed throughout another night. His squire, squatting beside his master's body stretched face down upon the chapel's stone floor, murmured, "My lord, you must sleep." And later, "Let me help you to your bed." But Simon, arms outstretched, cheek to the cold stone, would not answer him. His eyes were shut, but his lips moved continually in prayer.

Sometime after midnight there was insistent knocking at the church's rear door. Peter rose wearily to answer it.

The knight Philip Drieby burst in.

Simon raised his head, then turning carefully as his injury required, he raised himself, sitting painfully on the hard floor. "Philip, what are you doing here? You were with my son Simon."

"My lord, Northampton's taken by the king! He holds the city. Your son and cousin and your mercenary forces are his prisoners."

"I commanded them not to give battle!" Simon's temper exploded, as his squire helped him to stand. "The fools!" He shook off Peter's arm, the squire stepped back out of temper's range.

"My lord, I beg you, don't say so of your son. He is as brave a knight as one would wish to see!" Drieby insisted. "He held the city in good order to withstand assault. But some traitor showed Prince Richard a secret way in. King Henry's army coursed through the streets and Simon met them with unyielding courage. He led a charge so swift and full at them that at the clash his horse reared up and toppled backward, carrying him down."

Simon, making effort to calm himself, could have said this wasn't bravery but giddy horsemanship, but he knew the signs of battle nerves and would not dash the vision that gave Drieby comfort. The knight spoke with the passion of a man in recent battle who mistakes the wild and selfless gesture as a sort of victory. "Is my son hurt?" the earl asked only.

"No, my lord. But he's chained in Northampton's tower."

Simon put his hand up to his face, rubbing his sleepless eyes, then drew a weary breath and smiled to the loyal knight. "My son has more heart than I thought. God forgive me if I've misjudged him. Where are King Henry's forces now?"

"Marching to Kenilworth."

"The thirty mercenaries left as garrison and our new walls will give him pause." He recalled the king's own improvements to the castle: colored glass windows and a hearth in a bedchamber, draperies in the hall, a pretty painted boat on the Mere, manacles in the wine cellar. He wished he could see Henry's surprise at the impenetrable new fortifications. "We must go to Northampton to free my son."

At dawn Simon's army reassembled on the abbey's broad fallow field, ready to resume their march. Riding his gentle, ambling bay mare in review before them, the Earl told of his son's gallant charge, his capture and imprisonment at Northampton. "We go to my son Simon's rescue!" he shouted. A roar of readiness and a brandishing of eager swords gave him answer.

The little army marched from Saint Albans northward. They had been on the road less than an hour when a rider, coming at a gallop from the south, caught up. He wore the livery of the Tower of London and dashed past the troops in a last spurt of speed from his spent horse. Reaching the Earl he gasped, "My lord, the Justiciar begs that you return at once! All London has gone mad! Houses are on fire, and the Jews are being slaughtered!"

Simon stared at the messenger. "The Londoners were to have been disarmed! Can't the mayor deal with his own people?"

"They won't give up their weapons, Sire. And there won't be a Jew left alive if you don't come back at once!"

"My son is lying in chains in prison!" Simon bellowed. "You ask me to turn my back on him to save the London Jews from their own neighbors?"

Riding nearby, the old Bishop of London, Henry de Sandwich, overheard and brought his horse beside Simon. "Lord Earl, they are the children of Abraham who gave up his only son to God's will."

Simon returned the bishop's steady look icily. But the clergyman persisted. "They must not be touched until the Last Days see the conversion of the tribes of Israel. We cannot begin our campaign besmirched with their blood. For our souls, for our cause, turn back."

After several moments, his eyes locked on the wise stare of the bishop, Simon raised his hand, bringing the march to halt. He called to one of his knights. "Go at speed to London. Tell the Lord Justiciar he has an advocate with a tongue like the Lord's Own Judgment. Tell him we're returning."

Late that evening, as the army of the Earl re-entered the city, all was quiet. The Londoners were tired, sated in the aftermath of a bloody night and day. Whole streets stood fire-blackened. A veil of smoke hung in the motionless spring air. At the foot of Candlewick Street, outside a tavern was a great, quenched pyre heaped with human ash and bone. Women, bundled in black hoods, were picking through it, beating their faces and their heads, wailing with a cry as foreign and as ancient as Solomon.

Riding past them, Simon turned to Seagrave. "This is how the Londoners aid us! See these remains are buried decently with their own people's proper rites."

The steward, taking several Leicestermen, turned out from the line of march into the Jewry.

Like a drunkard waking to the ruin he wreaked in his stupor, the next morning the city came to life in hushed, repressed sobriety. All was subdued, with an edge of fear. Street hawkers moved silently past burnt house fronts that stood with bright sky and crazily angled, blackened wreckage showing through their gaping windows. Screes of charred and broken beams smoldered where blazing buildings had been hooked with long pikes and pulled down by teams of sappers to deflect the fire's spread.

Smithy's hammers did not clang this morning, but tinkled, making innocent ladles instead of the iron bludgeons they had fashioned yesterday. Traffic, even at Ludgate, was light. It was as if the city, like a wicked servant, had gone into hiding.

From the Jewish cemetery came loud, shrill moaning and the somber music of chanting in a foreign tongue.

Yet still the demands by the Earl and the Justiciar for disarmament had no result. And though the city was occupied by the Provision's forces, the meekness lasted only a few days, hardly longer than a tippler's malaise. There were spurts of looting, fighting in the streets. The Earl's modest army was like a bear cub with its foot caught in a trap, gripped and chained to the city merely to keep London's peace.

Days went by. Word came that King Henry attacked Kenilworth. With the mercenary garrison Simon had left, the fortress easily was held. The royal army, loath to waste time with so unpromising a siege, moved on, taking Leicester, Nottingham and Lincoln.

A man, anonymous in a green hood, who claimed to be bringing news of the king's advance, was admitted to Simon's council chamber at London Tower.

Tossing back the green cloth from his face, Robin knelt on one knee before the Earl and reported, "We've harried the king's army as it passed through our forest. He lost many good and well armed knights to our archers." His usual proud confidence gave him an irritating air, the more abrasive as he was both outlaw and pagan. Boldly he finished with, "I beg you, lord Earl, permit me and my followers to join you."

Simon turned distastefully away, but Clare caught his eye. "We need any aid that's offered." He spoke low, as if such counsel ashamed him.

"I am to lead an army of the city's mob and pagans?" Simon retorted acidly. "I hadn't thought I'd fallen quite so low as that."

"We must make one thorough try, with all the might that we can muster," Walter Cantaloup urged.

Simon stared at the priest in disbelief. "You would have these people with us? You know what they are."

"What the Lord brings, we ought not reject. He acts in strange ways. We must not presume to judge."

Simon looked down thoughtfully at the strange, outlawed youth kneeling before him, the detestable magic cord knotted quite visibly below his knee. Then, to the leaders of his army and his counselors he said, "It seems we've reached a point where we must either move against our king, with whatever forces, and in whatever way we can, or we must give ourselves up to his mercy."

"Let us attack!" Humphrey de Bohun stood and shouted in a burst of determination. The room was noisy instantly with Simon's counselors' agreement.

The Earl looked intently at each of the faces around him. "Then we must gather all our partisans, the Londoners included, for our strike. We shall go first to Rochester, where Roger Leybourne holds the city. If we succeed there, by some miracle, we may, with the Dover-London road again at our disposal, cut Henry off from help from abroad. Then, once we've tried these ill-assorted troops in march and combat, if you still insist, we'll move against our king, his lords and the royal army of England."

Rochester easily should be reached in two days' march. The strategy was as reasonable as a sane commander could devise. Bungling failure would risk no immediate reprisals against young Simon and the other prisoners.

Simon's lieutenants embraced the plan because it issued from his mouth, though what they wanted was to throw themselves at once against their king.

Again the army of the Provisions marched from London. But this time southward, and they were followed by a vast, straggling mob on horse and foot. Without adequate supplies of food or fodder, this crude second army moved in shifting parts, spreading across the landscape and raiding where it went. In two days time it gradually reassembled on the east bank of the River Medway.

Rochester, like a visage half-submerged in water, kept watch over the bridge that linked the Dover Road. Hovering above its rippling reflection, the city stood tall and bastioned, masses of wall-ringed slate roofs peaked at the top with the square towered keep of the castle and the cathedral's belfry.

After designating the grounds for his camp, Simon went to inspect Gilbert de Clare's siege position before the south gate of the city. The young earl had a force allotted from the four hundred knights and Welsh archers.

"Have it cried among our eager Londoners," Simon told Seagrave who rode with him, "that I want all boatmen skilled in river currents to come to my tent at dusk."

At the appointed time the men appeared, as rough and rude an assembly as one would expect from London's quays, but well-skilled in their knowledge of river flow. Lightermen, bargemen, harbor navigators, seamen stood, jostling and jesting among themselves in front of the Great Earl's tent, bloated with self-importance at being singled out for his battle plan.

Simon talked with them for some time. The camp was quite dark but for watch fires when they finally were dismissed. They left, sober and intent. Taking lighted torches and separating in small groups, they ran down along the riverbank. By the light of their flares, all night they combed the river margin for small boats, rowing their finds to a designated stretch of shore upstream.

The next morning was Good Friday. Nonetheless, Simon ordered his Welsh archers and his outlaw bowman to open heavy onslaught on the city's south and east walls, drawing Rochester's defenses to the landward gates.

Upstream, at the trill sounding of a horn, the horde of Londoners boarded the boats. Wallowing with their loads, the little vessels pushed off and passed on to the city with the river's flow, covering the surface of the Medway like spring petals carpeting a brook.

Riding the current well ahead of the flotilla went a single small ship with neither sail nor sailors. Her rudder lashed in place, she drifted by the river's flow alone, her trajectory carefully calculated. Fore of her mast a black column of smoke rose in bulging clouds into the yellow morning sky. She was laden with burning pitch, sulfur and fat. As the current carried her in a smooth arc toward the city's water gate, bright orange flames began to flutter on her deck.

Grappling hooks like spines bristled from the gate's lowest windows. But the current was too strong, the calculations of her drift too accurate. The ship came in, crashing and sliding along into the gate's portcullis, smearing her fatty cargo, and breaking up in blazing beams that lodged between the ribs of the iron barrier. Soon the wooden gate itself and the tower above it were burning.

As the smoky holocaust took hold, to save themselves the garrison jumped from the high windows into the river, just as the fleet of little boats bearing the Londoners came in, gliding among the swimmers. Knives plunged into the water right and left. The wash between the boats was stained red and littered with a flotsam of gashed and drowned corpses.

The first of the Londoners to reach the burning gate thrust their iron bludgeons and axes through the portcullis and prodded the fiery timbers. On the roof the great oak winch suspending the portcullis was engulfed in flame. Its stout ropes burning to frayed strings, the portcullis' weighty iron grill leaned outward. Soundless in the roaring fire, it swung down like a book's turning page, broke free and, taking down with it a clutch of unwary attackers in their boat, sank to the river bottom. One Londoner, his head bloodied, his arms frantically thrashing in the water, was hauled aboard the next boat sliding in.

Now the wooden gate, no longer with an iron grill before it, was fully vulnerable to blows. Struggling to keep their boats from moving in too closely to the heat, while keeping the arriving boats from crowding them, the attackers used pikes, swords and grappling hooks to pry at the weakened wood. Sparks scattering, charred slivers ripping loose, in minutes they had gouged a hole, widened it and, clambering from their pitching boats, risking the flames surrounding them, they forced their way through the breached gate and into the city. The boatmen behind them handed their vacated vessel back outward and brought in their own, jamming hull to hull. The Londoners clambered over the bobbing boats from one waling to the next to reach the gaping gate. Dodging through the fire, they ran out to the city's streets.

As the Londoners were landing, Rochester Cathedral's most deep-voiced bell began to toll the Lord's knell for Good Friday Mass. It was nine in the morning, the hour of the Crucifixion. The mob of Londoners moved up High Street, drawn by the sound of the dull tolling. As they went they broke into houses and raided shuttered shops, treating Rochester to the methods they had taught themselves in pillaging Isleworth and London's Jewry.

A cacophony of voices, panic spreading upward from the river, could be heard even at the city's eastern gate. Town militiamen on the east wall, returning the barrage of Clare's arrows, slackened their shot to listen. Cries of women, the high-pitched shriek of children, shrilled over the sullen ringing of the bell. Militiamen began deserting, dropping from the parapet into the street below and running to defend their homes. Leybourne and the Earl de Warenne on the parapet, commanded them to stay, then flailed with their swords at the deserters. The men only dodged and fled. Warenne, with his forces vanishing, called retreat from the wall. He and Leybourne and the men who stayed with them fled to the castle that overlooked the market square in the heart of the city.

The return of arrows at the east gate ceased. The wall, the gate, moments before so strongly defended, suddenly seemed void of life. Simon ordered his Welsh and outlaw archers to hold their shot.

The tumult in the city was barely audible outside the wall, above the penetrating deep knell of the bell. The Earl called for a ram that Bohun optimistically had brought with him. The gate was promptly staved, its battering meeting no challenge.

As Simon, mounted on his homely mare with his sons, Bohun, Seagrave, his young knights and Leicestermen beside him, was about to ride into the city, the sounding of the solemn bell came to a sudden, jangling halt. He glanced uneasily at Seagrave who rode by his side, then looked upward toward the bell-tower at the city's crest.

Just then Gilbert de Clare arrived at a gallop. His knights and archers were still embattled at the south gate. He came for reinforcements. Bound onto a horse he had in lead, a badly beaten man slumped, the badge of Rochester's militia on his bloodied pourpoint

Clare beamed with a fierce exhilaration that was repugnant on his pretty face. "Lord Earl, we caught this man and he's told us, after my persuading him a bit, that Leybourne and Warenne are withdrawn to the castle. Most of their soldiers were ordered to vacate by the city's south gate."

Simon commanded his trusted Leicestermen and Welsh archers to enter the city, make their way to the castle as best they could and hold it at siege. He divided his knights and foot soldiers and placed a contingent of them under Bohun and his son Henry's command to hold the east gate. The remainder of his knights, foot soldiers, and the forest bowman he led with his son Guy, Seagrave and Clare to the south gate, now the main focus of the battle.

It was late that evening when the fight at the contested gate was won. Carrying flares, Simon finally entered the city with his son Guy, Seagrave and a force of young knights.

High Street, lit by the Earl's flares, disclosed a shadowed view of pillage and half-hidden horrors. Two men carrying a cask of wine met friends with bundles of loot. An old man lay dying, wallowing in blood, his scrawny severed arm tossed a few feet away. As the darkness-bounded pool of the knights' torchlight moved on, a small boy, his head cracked open and blood trickling in his eye, appeared sitting mutely in an open doorway while, in the black room behind him, a woman whimpered in rape. Behind the next door, which was shut, a woman was shrieking.

Livid with rage, Simon pointed at the first house, ordering those who had proved themselves the least squeamish among his young knights, "Take whoever's there and cut his throat! And go there!" He pointed at the adjacent house noisy with high-pitched cries. "Spare no one who is harming these people! Take prisoners or kill them on the spot!"

Passing up the street as on a hideous tour of the precincts of Hell, Simon rode toward the cathedral. Guy, Seagrave and the youthful knights stared, sickened by what they saw.

Dimly visible shapes hurried everywhere lugging their spoils. As the Earl and his company turned their horses at Pump Lane, leading to the market square, a drunken party of revelers stumbled down the cobbles, greeting the cortege with a garbled cheer. One of the burly Londoners was dragging by the hair a girl not more than ten years old. Simon commanded that the terrified child be released. She ran, crying and screaming down an alley and vanished before he could send anyone to help her. Her captor and his friends were seized and tied. Simon ordered that every wrongdoer be caught, bound and taken to his camp outside the city.

The square had been readied for Easter with makeshift aisles of booths set up, needing only to be stocked and trimmed with flowers for the fair that would follow the joyous Sunday Mass. Sheltered behind sheds propped against the cathedral's north wall, Simon, Guy and Seagrave dismounted. The castle, across the market square, was within bowshot of the cathedral's broad, arched porch and was still under attack by the forest long-bowmen. The Earl's Leicestermen, as they had been ordered, stood ready, out of range, blocking the side streets lest the castle's holders try to escape. A few shafts still whirred from the high parapet through the torch-lit air. Screened by shuttered fair booths, the forest archers steadily returned the castle's shot.

Simon sent Guy to the Leicestermen, commanding them to join in the more urgent business of suppressing the busy Londoners. Then, leaning upon Seagrave's shoulder, and followed by his few knights not yet sent roving after murderers, rapists and thieves, he entered the cathedral by the north transept's door. Four of the knights carried flares. Behind them, an arrow, then another, dropped with a hissing rustle into the thatch of the sheds.

Within the vast cathedral another torch glowed straight ahead, beside the roodscreen where the transept met the nave. A man stood with two horses laden with bulging saddlebags. He held his light by the roodscreen's entry to the choir. Someone came through the opening carrying a silver candlestick and an armload of wax candles. He hurried to stuff his booty into a saddlebag and went back for more.

Catching sight of the light by the north door, the man with the horses shouted, dropped his flare and fled, dragging the horses to a shambling trot that echoed through the stone vaulting. His friend appeared a moment in the flare-light guttering on the floor, then fled after him out through construction debris by the south aisle.

Simon sent four of his knights in pursuit. Then, spent in body and spirit, his healing hip paining him to a degree nearing distraction, he walked toward the transept with Seagrave's help. The steward held a flare high.

On their pedestals, as the brightness moved past them, then left them in shadow again, the carved and painted statues of saints were muffled in black drapery, clothed in the mourning of Good Friday. Ominous, funereal beyond the obsequies for any mortal, the saints were mourning the descent to Hell of God Himself. Near the transept one pedestal was empty. Shards of its shattered statue nestled in the folds of its shroud on the floor. Its head had rolled until it came to rest in trodden dung by the roodscreen's entrance where, throughout the long day, other horses had waited as the looters worked.

Seagrave held his flare to the roodscreen's opening. The Earl took the light and entered the holy region by the altar, reserved for the bishop, his priests and monks. Three monks lay sprawled in the choir, their faces contorted, their white robes dark with dried blood. They had tried futilely, unarmed, to defend their sanctum. The great gold crucifix of the altar was gone, with all the altar's furnishings.

One of the Earl's knights, following him, picked up the looters' flare guttering on the stone floor, before it lost its flame entirely. With it he explored the nave. In moments he came motioning to Seagrave. The steward went, following him to the door of the old bell tower. Holding his flame high, the knight pointed where the rope rose up through the darkness. A corpse, the bell ringer, hung dangling, his stained white robe bristled with arrows as numerous as the spikes of a nettle. He had been used by archers for a target, as a tied goose on a pole might serve in a shooting contest. The plump face, bent downward, visible in the flare light, showed by its agony that he had lived far too long.

Seagrave brought the Earl and pointed to the impious, ghastly sight.

Simon vomited, a thing he never had done before, despite the battles he had seen.

Recovering himself, leaning against the tower wall, wiping his mouth and beard with an altar napkin a looter had dropped and the knight brought to him, he muttered, "This is the pit of Hell... harried and flung out at us. God save us!" Seagrave helped him from the bell tower and to a bench in the nave.

When he had rested, he commanded in a tone more of despair than rage, "Nicholas, take half the knights we have with us. Cry through every street that the Steward of England holds Rochester for the Crown, *and shall show no mercy to wrongdoers.* Any man caught in violent crime shall be seized and detained as our prisoner, to be punished as we see fit! And, if I find the men who made that holy man their mark, they'll pay for their sport at my own blade."

By dawn a herd of rope-bound prisoners was marched from a hastily constructed and well-guarded pen by the Earl's tent, and collected at the square's side farthest from the castle. During the night the marketplace had been cleared of all its Easter booths and much of its litter of arrows. A gaunt, stray dog, his long, pink tongue swinging, trotted across the abandoned no-man's-land.

At the center of the square a butcher's block of oak had been set out. Around it a few arrow shafts lay on the cobbles, testament to the risks taken in clearing the space. But now the tower's crossbowmen were withdrawn. Leybourne and Warenne, at the crenels, watched the guarded assembly of prisoners, perplexed. The people of Rochester clustered in the side streets, frightened after their day and night of horrors but curious to see what was happening.

Two knights untied and dragged the first of the arrested men out from the bedraggled clutch. Gripping him tightly at his armpits as he struggled and kicked, they bore him to the block and pressed him down onto his knees. A third knight, grabbing the man's hair, stretched his neck down firmly across the block and held it there.

Under the fascinated gaze of the men on the castle wall, and the citizens of Rochester who now were pressing closer into the square, Nicholas Seagrave came forward and, unrolling a parchment, read a name, then added, "A man of London, caught in the act of rape."

The most muscular of Simon's young knights stepped forward, twirling an axe in one hand to gain a sense of its heft. At the block he raised the axe and with a powerful down-stroke neatly cut off the man's head.

The act was so swift, so without pause for prayer or consolation, that a gasp went from the onlookers. It was the Earl's intention that the guilty have no chance to clear their souls with prayer. And too, speed was necessary. There were many prisoners.

The bound Londoners began yelling in protest. Shoved and pushed at sword point, they were roughly, temporarily silenced as the next man was taken to the block, pinned down, named, his crime announced and, despite his shrieking pleas, was neatly, briskly separated from his head.

The knights' squires and servants dragged the still twitching, jerking bodies across the pavement and pitched them into an oxcart standing by the cathedral's porch. One man gathered up the heads by the hair and took them to the cart as well. A boy, pilfering a head, kicked it along the cobbles as if it was a ball until his master, running after him, brought him back by his ear and made him toss it into the cart.

The terrified, jostling Londoners filled the square with bellowing protests again in mortal panic. The knights and their helpers went on with their grim work without a word. The onlookers were silent also. The only sound, apart from the bound men's screaming, was Seagrave's loud reading of names and crimes, and the dull, thudding strike of the axe.

One by one, each of the men caught in violence against the people of Rochester was forced to kneel. His name and his offenses were announced and, in full view of the castle and the growing audience of burghers, shopkeepers, wives and servants, he was mercilessly beheaded. There were so many that the strong and deft young headsman, tiring, began to make a crude mess of his job and had to be replaced. Soon his replacement was replaced as well. A system developed, each headsman retreating after three or four strokes to sharpen his axe and rest, while another man took up his task. The process lasted from morning into early afternoon.

By the time all the arrested Londoners had visited the block, there was a wide, glistening red pool around the hacked, drenched stump of oak and a smear like a marked road from the block to the cart in front of the cathedral.

For most of the morning Simon remained at prayer in his tent outside the city wall. But as the remaining prisoners grew few, he was, by his order, sent for. He stood leaning on the shoulder of his son Guy, watching the last blows of his crude, implacable justice.

When the grisly work ended, holding himself very erect despite the throbbing of his hip, Simon walked across the reeking square to the foot of the castle and looked up to the parapet. Well within shot of Leybourne's bowmen, he stood silently for several moments, looking toward the figures high above him, silhouetted against the bright spring sky. When no response came from them, he held out his arms in invitation of an arrow. Those on the battlement stared down at him, saying and doing nothing. At last he turned his back and walked steadily, painfully to the cathedral door. As the blood-oozing oxcart was lead away to a pit dug in the fields beyond the town, the army's servants set to work with water buckets, scrubbing the market's pavings.

Later that afternoon a solemn procession of the priests of Rochester's many churches, cloaked in the dark robes of Holy Saturday and Christ's descent to Hell, assembled in the square. A High Mass and funeral were said for the monks and townspeople of Rochester who had been slaughtered by the Londoners.

The Earl of Leicester knelt on the cobblestones despite his unhealed hip. He ignored the body's pain, his spirit's anguish was far greater. Dressed in a plain white woolen robe, the red crusader cross torn off, with no armor beneath, he held his arms out from his sides again as target for the crossbowmen. He remained kneeling throughout the long liturgy, waiting. But again no arrow came. On the castle's parapet Warenne had ordered his men to kneel also.

The Mass ended, the file of mourners passed beneath the castle wall, carrying their many biers down to the city's graveyard. On this Holy Saturday the city crept in a long line of black to the burial of its innocents.

Simon, rising from the cobbles with Seagrave's help, called truce of the siege of the castle until after Easter.

At the next dawn, in the street by the cathedral door, the Easter Mass was celebrated. The priest Laurence of Saint Martin performed the healing mystery of the Lord. Monks' voices rose in thin, sweet cadences, chanting the ritual of the day of Resurrection.

The Earl of Leicester, his sons, the lord of Gloucester, and Bohun Fils knelt on the square, their unarmed backs all within easy bowshot from the castle. And again Warenne kept the truce. The townspeople and the two warring armies joined in prayer together. The peace of Easter lay its quiet over ravaged Rochester.

Monday the siege was resumed. Richard de Gray brought reinforcements up from the Cinque Ports. The castle's gate was taken and the Earl's Leicestermen quickly took the tower's outer yard. But the inner bailey and the tower held. Sappers went to work to undermine the structures, but digging through the stony ground was slow.

Simon stayed in his tent outside of Rochester. His mood was morose, darker than his squire Peter ever had seen before. He remained in his tent near the river, and left the taking of the castle to his sons, Clare and Bohun.

A messenger from the Justiciar in London found Simon at prayer. "Lord Earl," he bowed when finally the dark, bearded head arose from the clasped hands, "my master has word that the king has taken the north shires and is marching upon London."

Simon met with his sons, Clare, young Bohun and de Gray. "We must withdraw to London," he told them quietly. "If you wish, leave enough force here to keep Leybourne and Warenne under siege."

His voice was hollow, his heart remote in darkness. Every word seemed to issue from him distantly, as if spoken by some other, unseen person who functioned for him in his absence. "Richard," he turned almost vaguely to de Gray, "take your men where you will. I release you from any bond that you may feel to me and to my leadership."

The next day the Provisions' army withdrew from Rochester. The banner of the fork-tailed red lion still fluttered at the fore with the flags of Bohun, Clare and Henry de Montfort, followed by mounted knights, some three thousand remaining Londoners assorted volunteers, the Welsh archers and their new companions, the forest outlaws with their impressive longbows.

Simon, lacerated in spirit, yearning for privacy, despite the jostling of his ill-healed wounds rode toward London in his armored cart.

# Chapter Sixteen

## LEWES
### 1264

Twelve miles west of London, in a broad field beyond the bridge at Kingston, the army of King Henry was encamped. Tents and banners in the colors of nearly every noble lineage of England surrounded the red and gold striped royal tent. The Welsh wars never had brought Henry such a following. But in the Welsh wars only those with lands on the west borders had suffered. Now everyone had losses from the general rioting and pillage. Pope Urban's verdict that the Provisions upset God's ordained channel of power seemed proven by the chaos all of England suffered. Even those who had composed the Provisions repented and had gone to the king's side. Especially those.

In the royal tent King Henry, his brother Richard, King of the Germans, and Prince Edward met with the Earl Marshall Roger Bigod, the Earls Humphrey de Bohun and Peter of Savoy, and the king's half brothers Guy de Lusignan and the recently arrived William de Valence.

Richard, his face florid, his burly shoulders hunched, was pacing angrily. "London is not burning, brother, because the men who were to set the fires have been found out by the mayor and arrested!"

"Then why do we stay here!" Valence burst out. "Montfort's at Rochester. Let's attack him and be done with it! We outnumber him so greatly there can be no doubt of the outcome." He cast a wilting glance at the King of the Germans.

"If we kill or take the earl, London will surrender," the senior Bohun urged.

"And Montfort must surrender if we hold London," Richard countered. His battle history was notorious for hesitation. Though few knew it, Richard never actually had fought in battle. Not in Palestine, where the Sultan's ambassador had granted all he asked without a blow. Even the recent march had been a harvesting of bloodless capitulations. Respected, wise, the elected King of the Germans' strength was in arguing – chiefly with his royal brother.

"One might almost think you were afraid to face him, brother." Guy de Lusignan pursed his lips in bitter insinuation.

Richard wheeled on him. But before he spoke, King Henry said quietly, "We march on Rochester."

The royal army passed peaceably by London and continued south. To the east of them, the army of the Provisions was marching with all the speed it could achieve to defend the capital. The forces passed with no knowledge of each other's movements.

At Rochester Leybourne and Warenne held out, besieged in the castle, and the besiegers, at sight of the immense royal army, surrendered. The two loyal captains rejoined the royal company.

"Montfort and most of his forces are gone," the hearty old Bigod, in consternation, reported to King Henry. "Gone back to London!"

"Then we follow him?" Guy de Lusignan raised his eyebrows as one proposing the obvious.

"Will you hear me, brother!" Richard bellowed at Henry. "Before we face Montfort, let us have every armed man that we can command! We have our mercenaries, paid for, sitting at Damme." He glared at Valence, who ought to have delivered them already.

Reminded of wasted money, spent on a thing so lacking in beauty as a troop of mercenaries, Henry looked much troubled. Seeing the king's drift, Peter of Savoy put in, "We could send ships for them from Dover."

"Why wait any longer? Are we cowards?" William de Valence urged defensively, as if the costly forces he had left at Damme were insignificant.

Richard saw through him and pressed his point. "When we were at Southwark and London Bridge was barred to us, you saw how easily the city was supplied from the river," he countered. "The fleet from Damme can close off the Thames. If the city is blockaded it will soon surrender!"

After some thought, Henry nodded. "Richard's plan is good. Let's have the soldiers and the fleet from Damme, since we've already paid for them."

Sleepless, gnawed and hollowed from within by a rage he had harbored for so long that, wormlike, it had worked the ruin of his spirit, Henry seemed a gray, leathery shell, his drooping, palsied cheek folded in hard-edged creases. His eyes were rheumy, his mouth slack in a flaccid line above his neatly barbered gray beard.

The royal army, with Warenne and Leybourne's men now joined to their vast number, marched south from Rochester to Dover. They found the harbor empty.

Word of King Henry's coming had passed among the ships' captains. Strong partisans of the Earl Montfort, they had all put out to sea, beyond the reach of royal command. No one seemed to know where they had gone or when they would return. There was no means at Dover to send word to Damme to retrieve the mercenary force and fleet.

In a fury of frustration Richard rode to the foot of castle, held now by de Gray on his own authority. The King of the Germans demanded, "In the name of King Henry, surrender!"

Gray, who had been watching the proceedings in the port from his vantage on the crenellated battlement, was hardly able to control his laughter. He leaned out and shouted down, "I'll give the castle up, and gladly, when a proper writ is issued by the king's Council and sealed by its chosen Chancellor, as you and all of us have sworn. But if you try to storm us, I've stones enough up here to crack your pates."

Achieving nothing but astounding insult, the King of the Germans went back to his brother's tent, livid, apoplectic.

That evening Richard sat at his brother's camp supper table, silent in anger, not eating but jabbing his dining knife into the table and gouging up splinters.

"Please... we don't want slivers in our hands," Henry said mildly. Then, with a teasing smile turning his lips, for he always enjoyed his much lauded brother's failures, he prodded, "This is your plan we're following. What should we do now?"

"How could I have known the ships would all be out!" Richard threw his knife and it stuck trembling in a wheel of cheese.

"Don't stab my cheese," Henry chided.

Richard jerked the knife out.

"Do you want a piece?" his royal brother goaded with a wry smile.

"No!" Richard was nearly at the point of real violence. "There are plenty of ships no doubt in other ports. We can tour the Cinque Ports and find all we need."

"Good. We'll do just that," Henry purred.

"Well? Have you any better plan?" Richard demanded.

"No. None," Henry returned blandly. "As you say, we'll tour the ports."

The royal army moved on. At Hythe and Romney the few ships' captains who could be found were made to swear their fealty to the king, but before receiving orders from the traveling royal chancery, they vanished out to sea.

The huge army of the king moved on toward Winchelsea, this time with the documents at ready.

The road from Romney passed inland through woods of oak and linden. Spring breezes by the southern coast were mild and moist. Tender leaves, glowing luminously in the penetrating sunlight, spread in an unbroken canopy, tinting the very air a misty green. Clumps of violets dotted with purple petals nestled among fat, snaking tree-roots. Sweet scents of flowers and young verdure gave off their perfume. The eye could penetrate this forest only a few yards, then view was lost in the mazy dappling of green light and greener shade.

Bigod felt uneasy, riding at the fore with Guy de Lusignan, Peter of Savoy and the king's two standard-bearers carrying aloft the strutting triple-lion flag of Plantagenet and Henry's dragon battle-flag with its drooping red silk tongue. "We might as well be blinkered for all we can see here," the old Marshall mumbled, glancing from one side of the road to the other.

Savoy, breathing in the fresh, pleasing scents, rode easily, enjoying the spring lushness of the place.

Guy, with a sly smile, replied to the not notably bright Marshall, "You're right to worry, Roger. I've heard the woods are full of lions in east Sussex."

Bigod threw back at him testily, "If you had any sense, there's one lion you wouldn't want to meet here."

"He is in London, Roger, and we should be too."

The immense line of barons, knights, foot soldiers, court clerks, servants, packhorses and wagons extended in slow-moving file far back through the forest. Their heraldry, in horse mantels, flags and robes, twinkled like beacons of foreign color amid the pervasive green.

King Henry, with his vanguard, reached Winchelsea by afternoon. There were no ships in the harbor. And the dark of night closed down with the last of the royal servants, packhorses and wagons still far in the woods.

Next morning, when Henry was intending to move on, they still had not arrived. A search party was sent to find them. Several miles into the forest they found the wagons, some ox-less and standing empty, others overturned, their beasts dead and butchered. The drivers' bodies lay scattered, spiny with arrows such as forest outlaws use. All the wagons' cargoes were gone.

The royal march moved on toward Hastings, stunned and more cautious.

But now outlaws harried the whole extended line of the march. At moments when least expected, long arrows skimming faster than the eye could see drove through knights' hauberks of chain mail. Screams of sudden pain and the panicked neighing of pricked horses punctured the steady mutter, tread and jangle of the march.

The clerks, the servants, even the foot soldiers, knights and barons were unnerved. Their mounts would shy at a fluttering leaf. The army moved forward at the greatest speed its men on foot could keep.

Leybourne, with his forest skills, was sent out with his own allotted force to counter the assault. But the length of the march and the denseness of the woods made it impossible to find the lone, free-moving attackers.

When the march at last reached open down-lands, the king's entourage breathed with relief. But the outlaws, creeping through the cover of scattered clumps of heather as distant from the march as their bows' long range would span, kept up their harrying. Nor even now could Leybourne find the assailants or prevent their random strikes. With more men lost, that night, camping at Hastings, King Henry held council.

"The march to Hove is long and as exposed to hazard as today's passage," Richard, his mood dampened from fury to cold, earnest strategy, told the lords. "The lord de Warenne has suggested we divide the distance into two days travel over safer ground, where we can keep our ranks closer, better defended. He offers the hospitality of his castle at Lewes for tomorrow night. There is also a large monastery where we can be refreshed."

"The tower's not commodious, but Saint Pancras priory will suit you well, my lord," Warenne bowed low to Henry. "I beg my lord will be my guest tomorrow evening." The young earl was eager to regain the king's good will after the part he played in bringing Montfort back from France.

In the morning, Warenne, Leybourne, Henry of Alemaine and Edward rode on ahead, with a guard of their knights, to give the prior of Saint Pancras warning of the coming royal guests and army. Riding fast, they reached Lewes by noon and settled their own lodging in Leybourne's little castle.

The building sat like an old chess piece, with neither wall nor outbuildings, beneath a steep slope that rose from a deep river valley to the level of the high downs. Their followers left at the tower, the four young lords went to the prior to give him the daunting news that the king and several thousand heavily armed and hungry guests would be arriving in a few hours.

Though there were a few cottages in a village, Lewes principally was a monastic community. Set in a vale bisected by the River Ouse, it was isolated on the east by a hill, and on the west by earthy cliffs that the stream had cut through the downs in thousands of years of gentle meandering. The high downs thrust into the valley three narrow peninsulas, and the river wallowed in a broad marsh, both features greatly limiting the valley's arable land. But Lewes was a perfect home for a contemplative Order in retreat from the world. The pending arrival of the royal army sent the monks into hysteria. The cellarer, the butler, the cooks were marshaled by the prior. Every type of food that could be found soon was being hurriedly prepared. And every monk, whether scribe or gardener or lector, was set to kitchen work.

When the main body of the royal army arrived, weary, nerve-shaken and hungry, a splendid meal was ready, with the prior's best wines decanted for the royal table, and a fine dish of fresh eels from the stream, for eels were well known to be King Henry's favorite food. Apart from Henry's eels, a copious feast was made of roasted beef, mutton and fowl. Every edible creature in the monastery's keeping, or in the little village nearby, had been slaughtered and cooked. But such a feast should earn royal gratitude, enough to buy replacement stock and more.

For the royal army, it was a very welcome rest and meal. Everyone drank deeply of the prior's wines, ate copiously of stuffed fowl, spiced fish, dripping loin of beef, and the delicate preserved fruits for which Saint Pancras Priory was famous.

Warenne, as host, served King Henry, and when the feast was done, the trestle tables borne away, he sat at Henry's feet. But as he perched, basking in royal favor, a monk entered, went to the prior, and the prior, who had known John de Warenne from baptism onward, went and drew the youth away to a little distance. He murmured in the young lord's ear.

Warenne returned to the king. "It appears we have visitors who have not been invited."

Lapped in the peace of Saint Pancras, Henry raised his eyebrows in mild astonishment. "Here?" His exhaustion, and the wine he had drunk, had loosened every nerve to an ease and amiability he had not known for weeks.

"It is the Bishop of Worcester, Walter Cantaloup, and the Bishop of London, Henry de Sandwich. They ask an audience with you."

"Well...," Henry's happy mood drooped. Reluctantly he nodded, "Let them come."

The monk went out and returned with the two rebel prelates. Both were dressed not in the splendid robes of their proper offices, but in the common brown wool cassocks of Franciscan friars.

Seeing them, Henry's demeanor chilled further. "You come looking modest, though you are not so modest when it comes to urging men to raise their hands against their king."

"We've come to beg your peace," the Bishop of London bowed meekly.

Cantaloup drew a letter from his robe and handed it to the royal clerk John Mansel. It bore Simon's own lion seal. "The Earl of Leicester asks only that you renounce your foreign advisors, and he will surrender and prostrate himself at your feet. We offer thirty thousand pounds in reparations for the damages that have been done. We admit that we are in the wrong, and beg your mercy."

Richard, who had drunk a goodly share of wine, took the letter from the clerk, read it aloud and threw it on the floor, crushing it with his mail-slippered foot. "Does Montfort imagine money will amend the damage he's inflicted throughout England! Thirty thousand pounds! Are we low merchants, to sell peace to treacherous usurpers and their vandal followers?"

"Mercy cannot be bought," the Bishop of London murmured, abashed. "The earl is trying to offer recompense, so far as possibly he can. He knows no gold can repair what has been done. He merely begs peace."

"He's terrified of our forces," Guy de Lusignan grinned.

A smile had settled on Henry's withered face as well. "You can tell him we would not grant him peace if he himself were here before us with his neck beneath our foot. He offends not only his king, but Our Lord on High, as Pope Urban has told the world."

With a sharp gesture Henry beckoned to Mansel and dictated his answer. To the royal refusal, Richard and Edward added their written challenges.

"Let him meet us on the field of battle," Richard said crisply. "Or, with all his followers, give himself up bodily to justice!" Having been offered what he took to be his opponent's soft underbelly of defeat, he was emboldened to meet him in arms at last.

Grimly taking the three letters of challenge, the bishops bowed and departed.

While the king's immense and lordly forces were reveling in Saint Pancras' wines, a much smaller army had been moving not far away, sifting through the dark woods. Led by the forest-wise outlaws, the Earl's followers traveled by moonlight along a narrow forest path and among the trees to each side: the Leicestermen and young knights on their destriers with white crosses sewn to the breasts of their surcoats, then twenty lordlings dressed in novice white. Behind them swarmed more than three thousand men, mounted on assorted beasts or trudging: Londoners and other volunteers in their common russet, perse and blu-de-nime, white linen crosses sewn on chest and back. With them too were Welsh archers, and outlaw folk from Sherwood, Sussex and the Weald with their leader they called Robin. In the soft moonglow of the night they moved among the shadows of the trees, the white crosses on their breasts dimly glowing like a flood of stars seeping across the forest floor.

At their fore on the narrow roadway four friars walked carrying a muffled lantern, a tall cross and the Bishop Walter's traveling altar cabinet on its shoulder-poles. After the holy men, John Botevelyn rode bearing the Earl's white flag with its rampant fork-tailed red lion. Beside him, Simon sat silent and thoughtful on his nodding, slab-sided mare. Then came three more flags blazoned with the unicorn of Clare, the argent bend of Bohun and the dotting of lioncels of Henry de Montfort, followed by the knights. In the midst of the cavalcade, flanked by the Earl's son Guy and the steward Seagrave, and drawn by its four chain-manteled horses, the Earl's steel-armored cart rattled and creaked, with the novices knights, archers and then the mob keeping up the slow but steady pace.

Near midnight this strange pilgrimage reached Fletching, a village of thatched cottages and a humble stone church only partly built, nested in a clearing of the forest. The friars, the lords and a few knights went into the half-finished church, Simon leaning on the shoulder of his squire Peter. The friar carrying the lantern set it on the simple wooden table of the altar. He and his brothers set out candles from the altar cabinet. Lighted, they cast a dim, warm glow over the sanctuary's makeshift partitions. A gold paten, a cruet of holy chrism, sanctified bread, and a thurible with incense were taken from the cabinet and arranged for the Mass as the Earl and his knights knelt and prayed. Within the hour two Franciscans, led by woodsmen, reached the village and went into the church.

Simon looked up from his prayer as Walter came and put his hand on his shoulder. "There is no hope," the bishop said in a low whisper. "Henry has refused all peace." He gave the Earl the three letters.

By the candlelight from the altar Simon read, then shut his eyes and nodded. "We accept the Lord's Judgment," he murmured. "For myself," he attempted a smile for Walter's benefit, "it will be a better death than being drawn and quartered. But we cannot save the young men who've come with us in good faith?"

Walter shook his head.

"The Lord's will be done." Simon crossed himself. "We must suppose their faith will carry them to heaven."

With Walter's help he got to his feet. There were dark hollows round his eyes, his face was thin above his full black beard. In his tent at ravaged Rochester, and ever since, he had not slept and had barely eaten, sunk in prayers of contrition and of doubt. To his friend he murmured, "Perhaps it's well it will be over now. I'm sick to death of leading evil men, and trusting faithless men. My regrets are only for the youths who've followed us so selflessly. Prepare us for tomorrow."

He went out to his followers. Cantaloup had his friars lift the altar table and carry it to the lawn outside the church. The army, fasting, gathered on the open ground before the church and down the road that ran between the cottages. The cotters, rush lights in hand, peered from their doorways at the thousands of men, most of them rough commoners, engulfing their tiny village. The moon had set. Apart from the cotters' cressets, there was deep darkness lit only by the broad spray of stars in the clear sky above and the candles flickering on the church's table.

The crowd knelt as Simon, standing by the altar, raised his hands. All was dark before him but for the pale rounds of faces and the white crosses sewn on every chest, and the white robes of the twenty novice knights kneeling nearest him.

In a voice loud and clear in the night air, Simon spoke to them. "May Heaven judge our cause, and have lenience to forgive us for our sins. Our intent, in faith, has been to do Our Lord's bidding. We give ourselves into His hands. We have asked King Henry's peace and grace, and it has been denied. We beg mercy now of Heaven for the keeping of our souls. Amen."

"Amen." The soft sound came from thousands of throats in the darkness.

Then Simon said to them, "Let those who have lived in hope of knighthood come forth and be knighted."

The white clothed figures arose and formed a half-circle: Guy de Montfort, Gilbert de Clare's younger brother Thomas, two sons of Hugh Despensar the Justiciar, the son of Nicholas Seagrave and fifteen more. They knelt again, and the Earl gave each the blessing and the ritual blow, the *colee*, with the flat of his sword on their shoulders. Then each youth stood as his squire formally fastened on his sword belt and his spurs.

When the knighting was done, the young men knelt with the whole company. As a friar clouded the air with incense from the swinging thurible, the brown-robed Bishops of London and Worcester passed through the assembly. Amid the crowd's low muttering confessions of sins they granted absolution, giving the bread of Communion, moistening their fingers with the holy oil and drawing the sign of the Cross on each man's brow, eyelids and lips. Last, Walter blessed Simon with the chrism, pouring out all that remained in the cruet over his bowed head.

When the army was blessed, the Bishop of London and the Bishop of Worcester said the Mass for the Dead.

The final hours of the night brought a curtain of fine mist as the men rose to their feet. The Earl of Leicester, in black mail with a white cross sewn upon the links, mounted his stolid bay mare and, with his flag carried beside him by his Leicesterman Botevelyn, he led out the march from Fletching.

The Earl and the red lion flag went in the fore, followed by the banners of the young lords. Then the silvery cart rumbled and bumped, attended by the Leicestermen, the four hundred and twenty knights, the Welsh archers and assorted volunteers. The bishops and their friars went back to the church and prayed.

Soon the outlaw woodsmen joined the march again as guides, and the company moved southward through the forest, then along the valley of the River Ouse for the remainder of the night. At the cool intense blue darkness before dawn their road, just beyond the village of Lewes, ended in a path running east and west. A tall scarp was before them. Turning west, Simon led his company to the top of its ridge for a view of the king's encampment at Lewes priory.

The ridge was a peninsula of the broad downs that spread westward, almost level but for a few hillocks, a ruffling sea of grass studded with bushes. Dew lay soaking the ground to hazy whiteness under the sky's spattering of starlight.

Simon brought his army up on the high, level ground and, with his sons Henry and Guy, Clare, Bohun Fils and Seagrave, rode southeast along the ridge to have a closer overview of Lewes. The downs' peninsula showed to be in the odd shape of an arm and wrist terminating in three fingers stabbing toward the Ouse's marshy valley, the priory and the village of Lewes below.

Guy was beside his father, describing all he saw from a little rise on the downs where the northern-most and middle fingers began their divide.

As Henry and Clare rode out to explore the two ridges to the south more closely, Guy rode to the end of the north tine that lay directly in front of them. He found himself facing the little castle, a candle nightlight visible within its shutterless window. He moved quietly, making his observations, his eyes dilated in the darkness, drawing in the shapes of the terrain under the starlight.

Informants had described Lewes valley, but it was far more intricate than their words had conveyed. The ridges were steeper, the valley narrower and more cramped by the river and its marsh than Simon had dared hope. Guy returned reporting that, from the vantage of the tip of the north ridge, the pitch-fork-like fingers appeared to pinch the valley to narrowed, canyoned ground between the sharp rise of the slopes up to the downs on one side, and the priory, the river, the village and the marsh on the other. On the far side of the river, to the east, was the mountain, and at its foot the road the king had taken from the coast.

The only exit to the northwest went past the little castle at the near end of the village. A short distance from its tower, the village's one road steeply climbed up the north scarp then down again, leading to the route along which Simon's army just had come. An armed force placed on this north finger of the downs would block the road and any escape to the northwest.

Report earlier had told there was a bridge across the Ouse, at the northeast end of the village. Simon had sent ahead his nimble foresters to break the bridge, cutting off the king's means of retreat back the way he had come.

Clare returned with his observations from the middle finger of the downs. The ridge was long, straight, and the drop to the valley very steep, yet passable for horses with good riders. The finger pointed directly at the priory. "I want that position," Clare announced. "There's not much distance between the priory, the marsh and the ridge's rise, and it is full of the lords' tents. We'll be attacking right into their camp. There's a road that passes westward by the foot of the escarpments. It goes toward Hove, I expect. We'll have to block it, but that shouldn't be difficult if we can bring in some men flanking from the west."

Simon smiled broadly. His many talks of strategy, with Clare attending, were showing their reward. "You take the middle ridge, Gilbert, and be the first to greet the king."

Henry Montfort came back with word from the furthest, southwestern finger of the downs. Indeed the western road passed just beneath it. But here the valley widened between the ridge and the marsh. The king's immense entourage had made use of the open land for a broad camp of wagons and non-combatant service tents. The western-most reaches of the valley were full of the royal march's grazing horses and oxen. And the Hove Road was blocked by string after string of the army's hobbled destriers, effectively forming a deep, living fence.

In time of peace such an arrangement might have been reasonable, with the army's slow-moving train of wagons passing late into the night along the road from Hastings, over the bridge and through the village, to the nearest camping place by the Hove Road, to be ready in position to leave in the morning, with the lords' horses nearest the lead. In time of war the placement of this service camp, like that of the lords' crowding the valley, was astounding foolishness, or utter arrogance. Or both.

The three means of escape from Lewes thus were all but closed. The Hastings Road by the destruction of the bridge during the night, after the king's wagons and rear guard had passed. The Hove Road by the royal force's own animals, servants and wagons. The one remaining roadway, toward Fletching, could be refused by an opponent placed on the northern ridge. And the knights of the vast royal army, those not housed in the priory, had littered the only available field of combat with their tents.

As the last report was heard from his son Henry, Simon threw back his head and laughed loud and long. When he stopped gasping from laughter, he managed to say, "Richard never was a decent commander in the field." Though the prince was respected for his wisdom, and the lords never questioned his leadership, at Sainte he had led his army to entrapment in a walled town. He seemed now to have done even worse, with a far bigger army.

Simon looked to the faces of his youthful lieutenants. "I think we are not lost yet."

The knights and foot soldiers, drifting across the downs, had come to halt near the rise where Simon sat upon his nodding mare, considering his strategy. The earl's sons Guy and Henry, young Humphrey de Bohun, Gilbert de Clare and Nicholas Seagrave were gathered around as he mulled the unexpectedly heartening news. He looked to the rim of the dark hulk of mountain in the east for the first hint of morning's lighter blue, then scanned the hue of the full horizon.

"What is that?" Simon pointed. From atop a small knoll on the furthest finger of the downs, a single form, a windmill, its frame of arms bare of their canvases, broke the meeting of sky and earth. Stripped of its sails for the night, it stood motionless as a Saint Andrew's cross against the star-strewn heavens. "Only a mill," his son Henry said.

"Henry," Simon beckoned him to come closer. "You and Guy, lead your men to descend the slope from that ridge, blocking the Hove Road as Clare suggests. Turn and come up by the road, flanking the lords' camp at the priory and keeping the river and the marsh at the king's back. You'll be crossing through the enemy's camp of wagons and horses. Put them in as much disorder as you can.

"Gilbert, you'll advance with Humphrey from the center, as you wish. You'll have the advantage of surprising men still sleeping in their tents. Run them down within their tents. Those who get out will still be at your mercy. You're mounted and they're not, and they cannot get to their horses, with Henry advancing from the west. Those housed in the priory may have horses stabled there. Before they can make a sortie, you'll have ample opportunity to turn the camp into a good deal more of an obstruction than they've arranged for themselves. But stay well clear of the priory gates. I mean to try our archers.

"Your Welshman? Or do you have in mind the outlaws, to pitch against the king's best lords?" Clare asked, prickling.

"They're so co-mingled now, is there much difference?" Simon caustically turned Gilbert's edged remark back upon him. "We're outnumbered so extremely that I mean to use every man we have. I've seen what rustics' simple bows can do. Yes, I mean to pitch the archers at the best targets. If they succeed, it's you, Gilbert, who will be given a fair chance to live."

Clare was silenced, and no one else dared object to the releasing of the lowly and outcast upon the greatest barons of England.

Simon went on with his battle orders. "Seagrave, take the Londoners and range them on the northern ridge, blocking the north road." He nodded toward the long peninsula that pointed to the castle tower. "Put my cart and lion banner there, behind the Londoners, as if I were observing the battle. Set my flag and a small guard by the cart. Array your people to the slope's very rim, in good view from the castle, then lead your vanguard down and attack the castle's door. And Nicholas, my friend, God be with you. I have little hope the Londoners will offer you much safety."

Simon turned back to his young lieutenants. "Behind you will be ranged the remainder of our foot soldiers. I will be to the rear of Clare's opening position, at the center fork, with the Leicestermen to bring support to whoever is hardest pressed. Our other knights will be shared equally between you, two hundred each with ten of the novices. There'll be no horn signal to announce your advance. Keep silence to preserve our advantage of surprise. Ready your men now. When the first true ray of dawn appears I'll raise my sword. Look to me for that sign to move forward."

The lieutenants went back to their men. The force was divided, the knights, in two groups, riding to the southwest and to the middle ridge, as the Leicestermen gathered by the Earl. As the rest of the forces on foot hurried after their knights, the crowd of Londoners followed Seagrave along the north fork, which was nearest, and which they could reach on foot in nearly the same time it took the knights at a canter to take up their positions. The cart, the flag and guard were set atop the hillock to the rear of Seagrave's men. Simon, on his inconspicuous bay mare, took his station with his loyal Leicestermen, behind Clare.

As the steward's shifting crowd of Londoners ambled toward their appointed place, a dark figure suddenly rose from the shelter of a bush and went quickly clambering down the slope.

"A sentinel! Stop him!" Seagrave cried. It was the only person set to watch whom anyone had found. The foremost of the mob dashed, tumbled, fell, rolled down the incline, closing on their enemy in a wild plunge of bodies, arms and legs. Then the heap of men sorted itself out. Climbing back up the slope, the first man to reach the steward grinned proudly, "We slit 'is froat." Another brought with him the steel cap and surcoat of the royal livery. Seagrave sent the surcoat and cap to the Earl with report of the killing of a sentinel.

The Londoners went on, reaching their allotted place with no further incident.

The common volunteers on foot, who had joined since the debacle at Rochester and had no part in it, Simon sent, half to his sons, and half ahead of his own reserve contingent of knights, backing Clare's position. The archers he placed behind these volunteers, ready to move forward as soon as they began their descent. "Aim for the priory gate. Your target is anyone who comes from there, with these exceptions. Should priests, monks, King Henry or King Richard come, you're not to aim for them. Everyone else who issues from that gate you are to kill if you can."

The insouciant outlaw leader swept a graceful bow, brushing Simon's horse's knee with his feathered cap. "You shall see, my lord, how able we are. And the two kings will be as safe as if they were at home in their own beds." Robin shouted to his men and cheerfully they bent their long, thin bows, strung them and took up their positions.

At the hillock a little distance in the rear, the pole of the Earl's flag was planted in the ground beside the big chain-manteled horses, and the driver climbed down from his seat to join the guard protecting the steel box on wheels.

The first of Seagrave's men to arrive at the north peninsula assembled along both edges, massing on the road that rose there from the valley, and crowding the tip of the escarpment. The castle was directly below them. They held their swords, knives, axes and iron bludgeons ready in their hands. Their fellows crowded onto the narrow finger of land, and those who couldn't fit straggled back as far as the steel cart's mound and beyond. Seagrave, on his horse, above the heads of his rude troops, looked back to his right, watching for the glint of Simon's sword in the dawn.

Further to the steward's right were Gilbert de Clare and Humphrey de Bohun with two hundred and ten knights at their command. They sat their horses at their ridge's brink, Clare watching over his shoulder for the signal. Still further out along the downs' triple prongs, Guy and Henry de Montfort waited with their share of knights, with Seagrave's newly knighted son posted to relay on to them the signal of their father's raised sword.

With his sharp-sighted squire Peter beside him, Simon sat upon his mare, watching the mountain to the east, its broad hunch filling the view beyond the priory and the River Ouse. The rounded hulk sheltered the valley from the early morning sky, filling the sunken land below with dark shadow even as the luminous deep blue of the night sky gave way to the first tint of rose. The shade the mountain cast on the three fingers of the downs was fast ebbing, and now dawn's pale light gleamed at the mountain's rim. Simon unsheathed his sword and held it high, its blade glinting in the first sunbeam.

The unicorn banner of Clare moved forward down the center slope. Henry de Montfort's banner of three lioncels dropped down, beginning its descent. And the men on the north peak began to trudge down their steep road toward the castle and the village, following Seagrave.

At the foot of the southwestern ridge, early foragers for the royal army's destriers were coming from their camp of animals to cut grass on the downs. They heard the jingling sound of harness and mail. Looking upward as they toiled, climbing the rough incline, they saw on the still deeply shadowed ground ahead the darker forms of knights in full arms skidding, plunging on their chargers down toward them. The blue-washed hill was dotted with moving forms.

The reapers began shouting. They ran, stumbling down the way they had come, shrieking alarm to the dense camp below. The noise of panic spread. In moments a trumpet blared, then another and another, each nearer to the priory.

Before the horn calls sounded, Clare and Bohun and their knights, descending from the center prong of the downs, had reached level ground. With the momentum of the cliff already hurling them forward, they spurred their horses to chaotic gallop in among the lords' tents, running down and trampling cloth and rope and poles, slashing to every side as sleepy, unarmed men struggled to emerge, entangled in their own shelters and bedding.

At the horn trills of alarm, half-naked, groggy from their night's carouse, the king's barons and knights beyond the first sweep of Clare's men scrambled from their tents, swords in hand. But the riders, with the advantage of mounted speed and height, turned, spread out and cut through them like reapers. The wounded pressed back against each other, obstructing their own defense with their bare bodies. More tents collapsed, covering the defenders like nets. Sword arms pinned by their own falling tents and ropes, without offering a blow the king's men were slashed, and trampled under the steel shod feet of the young knights' destriers.

Of those who, furthest from the center of the camp, stayed free of the collapsing tents, none had time for armor and all were on foot, soft prey for the young well-armored knights who rode fast at them and struck downward from the height of their saddles. The ragtag of volunteers on foot, following the knights down the scarp, swarmed, battering with iron bars, knives, swords and truncheons. The skills the high lords of England earned in decades of battles were nullified by the surprise, the crowding and mayhem of their camp, and the young energy and speed of their attackers. Clare and his two hundred and ten knights churned among the falling tents and struggling older men, trampling, wounding, killing in a frenzy of newly learned blood lust.

On the rim of the scarp that Clare, his knights and his men on foot had left, the Welsh and outlaw archers stood, their longbows ready, arrows nocked but pointed toward ground with the strings undrawn.

Minutes passed after the horn blasts. Then the priory's gate opened and the lords lodged with the king poured out on their destriers. They came dashing without surcoats or mantlings, some without armor in their hurry. In their midst, a gold crown on his helm, Richard King of the Germans rode, bellowing commands.

In unison, with a sweeping, swift and graceful gesture, the archers on the cliff raised their bows to arm's length, drew their bowstrings in wide angle to their ears, and let fly their arrows. Following the smooth movement, they plucked the next arrows from the quivers on their backs, nocked, aimed, drew and let fly again. And again. And again, with speed nearly faster than the eye could watch. Sheetings of arrows met the lords as they rode out from the priory's gate. Long, swift, sturdy arrows that drove through mail and pierced some steel helmets.

What few of the king's barons survived, spared behind the arrow-stuck bodies of their fellows, crashed into the confusion of the ruined camp, running down their own men fighting on foot, tangling themselves in the debris of tent-cloths, poles, camp furniture, and the bloodied bodies of the wounded and the dead.

Those who reached the battle from the priory made unintended and destructive rear attack upon their own wallowing knights, driving them under the hooves and into the blades of the young fighters maneuvering deftly on their horses through the havoc.

Richard, the gold crown on his helm marking him out, seemed spared the deadly arrows as if an invisible shield covered him. He spurred his horse to a gallop beside the priory wall, then vanished into the confusion at the wagon camp. The few barons who tried to follow him as escort were brought to chaotic halt by a swarm of blood-smeared commoners, white crosses sewn to the jerkins, wielding iron bludgeons at their horses' unprotected legs. Above the heads of the attackers on foot, arrows drove through the lords' armor. Trapped between the priory wall and the camp of collapsed tents spiked with broken poles at crazed angles, they fell to the grabbing hands of their lowly assailants who, hardly waiting to maim them, began hurriedly stripping them of everything including their smallclothes, seizing booty. The battleground before the priory, last night's bedchamber for England's greatest lords, was a mass of broken poles, heaped and trampled cloth, shattered camp furnishings, wounded and staggering naked men, terrified horses and dead bodies.

Clare brought his novice knights to retreat to the edge of the common folk's mayhem, engaging any lords who struggled out and taking them as prisoners for ransom.

Then from the priory's gate a second mounted rush came on, led by King Henry's own dragon battle banner. Henry himself, in his crowned helm, brave or suicidal, rode at the fore close by his flag. The sortie came to instant halt at the wrecked camp, and under a hissing deluge of arrows.

Untouched by the whirring shafts that were driving into everyone around him, Henry led away the few men who could follow in his charmed circle of safety. They went the same way Richard had gone beside the priory's wall, intent on escape past the baggage camp to the Hove Road. But they found the Montfort brothers and their knights in battle-frenzy there. They were forced back and surrounded. Behind the Montforts' knights, the encampment of the Chancery and the Royal Wardrobe was in flames. Clerks and servants were running, desperate to save chests of scrolls, barrels of pennies and cases of the royal tableware.

At the castle tower the horn calls had roused the prince's men. Edward woke to see the Londoners, white crosses sewn to their tunics, shambling down the steep road, not further than a hundred yards opposite the tower's window. Not as complacent as his father's lords, Edward and his men had slept in their pourpoint shirts and chain hauberks, and needed only a moment to buckle on their swords. Leaving Alemaine with a few men to defend the tower, the prince and his friends Leybourne and Warenne dashed out, soldiers following close behind their excited leader. The company's destriers stood ready-saddled, tied to staked lines beside the tower. Hastily tightening girths, freeing the horses from the lines and mounting, Edward and his men galloped up the road, swords unsheathed and eagerly waving.

At the sudden charge the Londoners tried to turn back, their disorderly advance doubling on itself in fright. The big destriers were upon them, the prince and his soldiers' blades working with no need for aim or parry, slashing necks, bare heads, shoulders, whatever was in reach.

Like sheep attacked by wolves the Londoners fled screaming. Seagrave shouted commands at his panicking flock, but they ran back up the road, or frantically clambered up the rocky scarp as the riders drove them along, slaughtering them, swords spattering blood like hailstones.

As Seagrave sat his mount, bellowing futilely, Edward and the first men with him passed him, intent on the Londoners. But after them a knight came up and struck Seagrave a hard blow that he failed to parry. Simon's steward, and friend since his first year in England, fell from his horse, a deep wound opening his side.

When Edward and his riders reached the crest, a number of the Londoners had reformed at a little distance, panting, their weapons dangling from their hands.

"Come to me, my foul-mouthed city neighbors," Edward, his blond hair bright in the dawn, grinned baring his teeth. "I have my mother's debt to pay."

The Londoners turned and ran again. The prince gave spur to his horse. He and his knights bore down on the dispersing mob at full volant. Running, falling, knocking each other down in their panic, the rabble spread all over the downs. With a roar of battle-joy Edward rode at them, his men scattering across the grass at high speed, chasing down the fugitives.

Following after the prince from the embattled camp in the valley, Roger Clifford saw the Earl's armored cart, all but deserted and glinting like a beacon in the morning light. Beside it the Earl's flag with the red lion rampant rippled lazily in a soft breeze. Chain mantled horses hitched to the cart cropped the grass around them as complacently as if they stood in their own meadow. Nearby, an anxious little group of Londoners was gathered with swords drawn.

"Look!" Clifford called to William de Valence who was coming up behind him from the hurly-burly of the battling. "There's where Montfort watches. We can make an instant end to this!"

"Let's take him!" Valence breathed heavily, his mouth drawn in a tight smile. He jabbed his spurs into his horse, forcing it to reach hard up the slope. Out of the nightmare behind him this moment came as utter joy. Since he was twelve he had dreamed of thrusting a sword into the Earl Montfort, the man he fancied tried to turn the king, his own brother, against him. Yelling for his men to follow him out of the battle, he led them up onto the grassy level of the downs.

When Valence reached the edge of the north ridge, Edward's knights no longer were in sight, but the tumbled bodies of men wearing the patch of the white cross littered the ground everywhere. A small, frightened clutch of Londoners stood around the shiny vehicle, timidly offering to defend it.

"Montfort is ours!" William de Valence cried fiercely, galloping toward the cart. The defenders turned and fled as fast as they could run. One better armed than the others stopped and turned back. The Mayor of London, FitzThomas, raised his sword against Valence. Before he struck a blow, William's sword crashed through his chain mail hood and he fell unconscious, blood gushing from his nose.

His tired horse stumbling, Valence dismounted, touched with his fingertip the burr the mayor's good steel mail had gouged in his blade, and strutted back to the cart yelling, "Montfort you're deserted! Surrender! You're a dead man!"

He tugged and pulled and drew the red lion banner's pole out of the ground and waved the flag toward the valley below, then threw it on the ground and trod on it with his chain-mailed feet. "Montfort is ours!" he cried to the valley again and again.

In the battle din nobody heard him.

Chuckling, giddy with his victory, his face dirty and smeared with blood from his bloody hands, he swaggered over to the cart.

Beside the cart, Clifford and the men who had followed Valence sat their horses, watching with amusement the unchivalrous performance. As Valence approached, they assumed sober expressions.

With a tight smile William yelled at the top of his voice to the steel door, "Come out and meet thy death, Sire Simon. Come, Sire Cripple! Have thy reward, long owed thee at Valence's hand!" His grin almost silly, he trembled with a thin, eager giggle. The huge horses hitched to the cart's shafts raised their heads from the grass, swiveled their ears and switched their tails nervously. The steel cart's door stayed shut.

Valence struck the metal plates with his sword's pommel. "Come out I say, thou traitor! Son of a devil and a whore!"

Clifford, dismounted now and sitting on the grass at a little distance, laughed, and not the nervous laugh of battle strain. To him, Valence seemed deliciously ridiculous in this moment that was so pregnant with success. He never had liked any of the Lusignan.

"Come out of there, thou coward!" William shrieked, losing any shred of patience in his sweaty eagerness. "Must I haul thee from thy casket, to thy worse shame?"

The blank steel cart showed no response. Valence let his sword fall to the ground. Gripping the door's handle, he jerked at it with all his might. The horses shied and bolted forward, he had to let go at once or be dragged.

Clifford got up and ran to the horses' heads, grabbing the lead horse by the bit.

As two of his knights unhitched the skittish team from their traces, William, teeth clenched and bared in a tight look of determination, picked up his sword and approached the cart again. He fitted the sword's point to the slim crack at the door's jamb, then drove it in up to the hilt. A muffled exclamation came from within.

An even wider smile spread William's lips as if his ears were yanking back the corners of his mouth. "I frighten thee, Earl Coward? Think on the moment, soon now, when my sword enters thy belly!" He threw his whole weight on the sword's pommel to lever the door open. The blade broke, leaving nothing but the grip and pommel in his hand.

The circle of his own men, watching him, audibly snickered. Clifford laughed loudly and outright.

Enraged, Valence turned on them, brandishing the sheared stub of his sword. "Choke on your laughing! Open the cursed cart yourselves if you can!"

Still smiling, Clifford and a few of the knights walked around the vehicle, inspecting its riveted plates carefully. They tried the door, then backed away.

"If we can't get him out, we can still be certain of his finish," Clifford suggested. "What do you say we roast him in his traveling box?"

Valence's scowl lifted. He cuffed Clifford's shoulder playfully. "We'll do it!"

Leaving Clifford and a few men to guard the steel cart, Valence and the rest of his knights remounted and set off along the north road that declined from the scarp and led to the forest and Fletching.

On the downs, littered with dying and dead Londoners, the crows already were settling. Occasionally startled by a groan or movement of the not-yet-dead, they rose up in a flurry, their black wings applauding this largesse that man in his madness provided them.

At the cart Clifford and Valence's men idled. Lying on the dew-damp grass, comfortable and dry on cloaks they had untied from their saddles, they watched the crows, the clouds, and listened to the battle sounds below, confident that though they weren't fighting, they were playing the most essential part in the coming victory.

When their waiting extended well past an hour, from their saddlebags they fetched bread, cheese, sausages, and Clifford provided a prettily painted goatskin flask of fine wine. They had a pleasant meal, then napped. Two stayed awake on guard, playing a friendly game of dice and sipping the last of what remained in the flask.

It was well into the afternoon when Valence and those with him returned to the cart. Tied on their horses' cruppers, behind their high-cantled saddles, were bundles of branches from the forest floor. Dismounting, they unloaded their kindling, carefully arranging it beneath the cart's steel-covered wheels.

While they were gone, Clifford had sent two men through the battling in the valley to the priory for fire. The men, to their master's gratification, returned safely, carrying a precious firebox stocked with glowing coals. Several of the royal knights trailed them from the battlefield to watch the fun.

It took a long time for the heaped, damp branches to catch, but finally a blaze was dancing around the silver wheels. The bright steel multiplied the flames with eddying reflections. As more wood was tossed beneath the wheels, the fire grew more lively. The underside of the cart blackened with streaks of soot, like broad bars, across its mirror of the flames stroking it. Loud thumps and muffled shouting could be heard from inside the armored box.

The cart's assailants had withdrawn a little distance from the heat and smoke. William tipped his ear toward the cries, just audible above the crackle of the flames. "Montfort's feeling warm," he snickered.

But Clifford frowned. "I hear two voices. ...Neither sounds much like the earl. Are we certain Montfort's in there?" He looked to Valence.

"Why do you look at me!" William exploded. "You're the one who brought us here!"

"I think maybe it's not the earl..." Clifford moved closer to the cart, tipping his ear toward the blaze till the ends of his dark locks recoiled, singed by the heat. He stepped back. "We must find out."

The noise from in the cart had increased to shrieking panic, quite audible now even above the fire's roar.

"That's not Montfort!" Clifford exclaimed. "Were all the devils in Hell pinching his entrails, he wouldn't yell like that."

He picked up a stout branch from the collected kindling and dove toward the fire, scattering its flaming sticks out from beneath the blackened steel wheel-covers and the charred wooden wheels. Others joined him, heaving the fire apart and away, pulling up damp grass and sod and flinging it on burning kindling until the fire was scattered everywhere but underneath the cart and every trace of flame was quenched with smoking mats of grass.

The cart, its steel plates hot enough to loosen the rivets in its oaken walls, now succumbed to sword points driven into its door's seam. Several of the knights set to work, prying at the door, and broke away a fire-blackened corner. "Mercy! Have mercy!" someone cried within.

"Who are you!" Valence bellowed at the unfamiliar voice.

"Loyal men of London!" a voice rasped. Head pressed to the hot floor, a face peered through the opening and recognized the red martlets of Valence's surcoat. "My lord of Lusignan!" the voice managed between choking coughs, "We're friends. Spare us! We're servants of the King of the Germans!"

After much strenuous work, the door was wedged apart enough for the sweat-soaked, fainting prisoners inside to squeeze out. Two nearly roasted London aldermen, agents of Prince Richard commissioned to set London ablaze, staggered and lay down on the grass, exhausted, cooling under the afternoon's blue, sunny sky.

Valence, Clifford and their knights, energy and spirit spent, sat down as well to gather their wits and think what to do next. Clifford fetched from his saddlebag another leather wine flask he kept in reserve. William, weeping in fury and frustration, seized it from him and drank deeply with long gulps.

They were still sitting by the charred, wrecked cart, the unconscious Mayor of London lying nearby, the cart's team of horses blandly cropping grass at a little distance in peaceful equine company with the knights' destriers, when Prince Edward, Leybourne, Warenne and their men returned, riding across the downs, tired from their killing spree, their swords, their horses and themselves soaked with the blood of Londoners. Exhausted by their glut of vengeance, they ambled slowly across the wide sweep of grassland, their destriers' heads nodding wearily. Edward rode up to the men lying by the fire-blackened armored cart.

"Where's my father the king?" he asked, wiping his blood-smeared face with the even bloodier back of his hand. Blood hung clotted and dangling in the curls of his pale hair.

William looked up, fuddled and still seething with self-centered rage. Not for a moment since he left the valley had he given any thought to where King Henry was. With more of Clifford's wine in him than was wise under the circumstances, he stumbled groggily to his feet and scanned the valley below.

The ruined camp of toppled and crushed tents lay in late afternoon shadow, a broad and silent wreckage strewn before the priory, the castle tower, and reaching to the thatched village beyond. To the south, from the bank of the Ouse to the sodden marsh, to the Hove Road, the open ground was blackened with the leavings of a fire, but no one fought there now. Some wagons of the royal entourage were still smoking, and among them a few figures moved. But the dragon battle banner of King Henry was nowhere to be seen.

# Chapter Seventeen

## THE BATTLE'S AFTERMATH
### 1264

Edward, Valence, Leybourne, Warenne and their knights on the hilltop descended the escarpment to the castle. The few men the prince had left with Henry of Alemaine as guard were still there. They had watched the battle from the roof. Being admonished to keep the castle, they had taken no part in the mayhem but sheltered any of the lords who managed to reach them. Regarding King Henry's whereabouts, Alemaine said he thought the king was in the priory.

Edward took off his blood-soaked chain mail and pourpoint, and ordered his squire to brush the links of his hauberk and leggings clean. The pourpoint was filthy beyond restoring. Washed, dressed in a fine short velvet robe and stockings, suitable for supper at the prior's table, he walked, with a small bodyguard, over to the priory.

He had entered the tower by its door that opened to the road up to the downs, without inspecting the valley. In the lowering blue of late afternoon shadow as the sun declined behind the downs, the village's shuttered windows, closed doors and utter silence did not much surprise him. But the sight around the corner did. Alemaine had told him of the battling, yet nothing prepared him for what he now saw at close range.

Naked dead and dying men were everywhere amid sharp, shattered tent poles, broken campstools, cots and overturned, emptied traveling chests. Trodden, shredded, blood-sodden tent fabric was heaped and flattened over and under everything, with its tripping, cumbering folds.

269

A magnificent destrier thrashed lying on its side, its legs caught up and ripping holes through the sturdy cloth as it bound itself in the twisted shreds like a sheep hobbled for sheering. Beneath the animal its crushed rider lay bleached in death, the cloth around him red with the blood his struggling mount pressed from him. The dead man was Walerant, the German knight and royal clerk. Nearby, half-wrapped in torn canvas, John Darlington lay clutching his side with bloody fingers, still alive and groaning piteously. By him was the clerk Henry Wengham, an arrow through his neck, his head smashed by a horse's hoof.

Raising Darlington, more in anger than tenderness Edward demanded, "What's happened? Where's the king?" The royal clerk tried to speak but blood gushed from his mouth and he gagged. Edward set him down again lest the bleeding man soil his fresh robe. The king's clerk and legal counselor was no soldier but was dying like one. The prince ordered his guards, "Take him to the castle. And whatever wounded men you find who may be helped. Give them what care you can."

The clerks, except for Walerant, were not trained warriors. And Walerant's death plainly was an accident.

In the shadows Edward did not pause to see who else was dead or dying. His pressing need was to see that his father was unharmed and safe. Paying no more attention to the welter of bloody battle mixed with the jumbled wreckage of the camp, alone he clambered through the rubble to the gate of the priory. Two young knights he didn't know, in dirtied, bloodied white surcoats, stood guard. They looked at the prince oddly but forwarded his command that the entrance be opened for him.

Within, the forecourt of Saint Pancras was full of unfamiliar young men. In a moment Edward was surrounded, his arms pinned and his sword taken from him. Guy de Montfort, as the steward Seagrave was severely wounded, was in charge, and serving as keeper of the door as well. "Prince Edward," he bowed, his eyebrows arched in some astonishment, "how have you come here?"

"I walked in peaceably by the gate. Obviously." Edward said curtly, standing straight, unstruggling in the overwhelming restraint crowding upon him. "I was seeking the whereabouts of my father. But I see I've blundered into the wrong camp."

A smile spread across Guy's bemused face. "On the contrary. I'm sure King Henry will be glad to see you." With several of the red-stained young knights in white accompanying him, he led the prince to the priory's chapel.

King Henry lay prone on the steps before the altar, still dressed in his hauberk of gilded chain mail. His head was buried in the crook of his arm.

Edward went and knelt beside him. At the prince's touch on his shoulder, Henry looked up with a frightened jolt. "Edward!" he gasped, astonished. "You're alive? Oh," he moaned, white spittle showing at the corners of his mouth, his face wet with crying. "I thank God you're safe!"

The prince did not know what to say, uncertain what their condition was except that, unthinkably, they both seemed to be prisoners of a gaggle of knight novices and Guy de Montfort. He wrapped his arms around the trembling old man.

Henry, tear-smeared, his face yellowish gray and deep-creased from exhaustion, pressed his sagging cheek to Edward's chest.

Embarrassed, the prince gently pushed away the king's shoulder. "You've been taken prisoner by Leicester?"

Henry looked in the ice blue eyes that never lost their haughty self-assertion. "They fought like devils, with a strength past normal men. And people came out of the town, I think, and stabbed our horses' bellies. Some say they saw angels in their midst."

"They say that? Really?" the prince remarked coolly with a smirk. "Crossing the battleground, I saw not a feather other than the fletchings of arrows. Perhaps angels don't shed. You're not injured?"

Henry shook his head. "Where were you in the battle?"

"Paying my respects to the Londoners. I'd have thought all England's barony could take care of themselves. Where's Richard?"

"No one knows."

"Where is Montfort now?"

"He's gone with the main body of his force to take the castle. He thinks you and Richard are there."

"At the castle?" Edward gave a short laugh. "We must have passed each other. I've just come from there." He turned and sat on the steps. For a few moments he looked carefully at the young men guarding him. "So... that's how it is," he muttered. "These pups have squashed your lords... Who'd have thought it possible." Rising, he pressed Henry's hand. "Alemaine and the mercenaries hold the castle strongly. We're not beaten by these children, or even by the Hand of God, quite yet."

The prince stood and strolled down the altar steps to where Guy stood waiting. "I have to piss. As I see I'm your prisoner, will you give me conduct to the privy?"

With three well-armed new-made knights for escort, Edward crossed the yard of the priory to the reredorter.

It was his habit to familiarize himself with every place he stayed; he knew the abbey's compound well, though he had never been there until yesterday. An elaborate reredorter stood at the far end of the enclosure, behind the monks' dormitory and against the priory's south wall. A branch of the river that skirted the marsh was channeled to provided a flow of fresh water through stone washbasins, then through an open conduit that ran behind the long seat-ledge of the privy and out by a small arch in the wall that opened to the marsh. The prince had been much impressed by this tidy arrangement.

Going through the door to the privy, Edward turned suddenly, thrusting the nearest of his guards against the stone doorjamb and knocking the second off balance with his foot. Instantly he had the sword of the first in his own hand, jabbing the youth with his elbow an injuring blow in the stomach, as he kicked the second man, knocking him to the floor and giving him one more kick in the face for good measure. As the third youth raised his sword, Edward jabbed his elbow again into the struggling man pinned behind him, bringing a squirt of blood to the youth's mouth and doubling him over in pain. Reaching smartly past the uncertain blade the third member of his guard presented, Edward sliced a blow to the neck that instantly killed him. The one he had knocked down tried to rise. Face bloodied, the lad lifted his sword, but Edward landed a heavy stroke that cut through his skull and sent him sprawling, paralyzed and dying. Dripping sword in hand, the prince jumped the privy ledge, ran splashing along its flowing drain and squeezed his broad shoulders through the drain's arch that opened outside the priory's wall.

When the prince and his escort didn't return within what seemed a reasonable time for use of the privy, Guy went himself with several men to the reredorter and found the two slaughtered knights and the third clutching his stomach, spitting blood. Between retching gory gobbets, the youth motioned toward the drain arch. Cursing, Guy ordered the marsh searched for the prince.

A mile from Lewes, above the Hove Road where the ridge of the southern finger of the downs rose slightly higher, the windmill stood, the wooden framework of its arms spreading their dark grill over the pink-golden sky of evening. The valley and the ridge's slope already were obscure in deep lavender shadow. Four shapes climbed up the cliff, three in the white surcoats of new-made knights, their horses straining on the steep embankment, the fourth, in the drab jerkin and cross-gartered leggings of a peasant drover, clambering up agilely beside them. The mounted youths, their helms and shields hooked to their saddlebows, rocking and clanking against their chain mailed thighs, talked as their tired horses worked.

"The old lords fought as if they hadn't held a sword in years," one dark-haired youth with impish eyes laughed softly, too tired for a heartier peal of derision.

"They had too much to drink last night," another, red haired and freckle faced, offered with the wisdom of his eighteen years. "When was the last time most of them had fought? In Wales? Gascony? I don't recall hearing of their glory then either. If Edward's force had been here, it'd been a different matter. They're real mercenaries."

"There were hard fighters enough here, de Baer. What of the March lords?" a tall, thin youth, the third rider, put in.

The freckled one's look became distant, remembering some moment earlier in the day. "They fought hard... But when the king turned back, the Marchers turned and kept on going toward the village. The must've forded the river somewhere. Cowards!"

They said nothing more while their mounts lurched up the last and steepest part of the slope, then they were on the downs. Seeing the sun already gone below the horizon, the thin youth, whose name was Vernon, asked wearily, "Beavis, look, it's getting late. Shouldn't we go back?"

The impish knight, addressed as Beavis, asked the man on foot, "Are you sure you saw him come this way?"

"Sire, I swear it! And he was alone."

"If the churl's wrong, we'll be the very laughingstock for this," the thin knight remarked petulantly.

Grinning, Beavis turned to his other companion, de Baer. "Vernon's afraid they'll say we're so green that we can't tell a castle from a windmill." He poked his tired horse's ribs and it broke to a reluctant canter.

"I'd rather be laughed at for challenging a windmill than shamed for letting the prince escape, if he's in there," the red-haired knight replied, jabbing his horse hard and galloping past his friend. "You both can go back to the priory if you like."

"What? And leave you to face such peril alone?" Beavis spurred to a gallop, catching up. Even Vernon set his horse into a brisk, shambling pace.

Arrived at the foot of the little knoll, the three gazed up at the mill. The wind-polished frames of its arms reached into the dimming sky, the highest edge rimmed with brilliant red reflection of the sun, already set from all but the arm's high vantage.

Beavis stood in his stirrups and in his broadest bardic imitation declaimed, "Behold how the fearsome giant doth stretch forth his arm, reddened with gore, whilst with his other three he beckons us to our doom!"

De Baer leaned over from his saddle and punched Beavis's shoulder. "Poet! When we're mocked for this silly deed, you can write our song."

"And I'll sing it, cheered or mocked," the imp-eyed youth grinned back.

By the door of the mill they dismounted, giving their horses' reins to the drover who, running and panting after them, had just caught up. The new-made knights each drew his sword.

Beavis tried the mill's door. It was bolted from within. He looked to his companions with raised eyebrows. "So, this is a fool's errand? If the door is barred, there must be *somebody* inside." He stepped back a pace. There were no windows in the structure, only the opening at the top where the wind shaft entered the mill's cap.

"Come out, thou prince-turned-miller!" Beavis shouted. "Come out, or we'll come in and drag thee out!"

"Oh, prince-turned-miller," de Baer cried, struggling to suppress his laughing, "come bless us with the flour of thy realm!"

Slowly the mill's door opened. Within the dark doorway, the dim light still in the eastern sky dully glinting on his fine armor and the golden crown upon his helm, stood Richard, the King of the Germans.

Smiles faded from the three youths' lips. De Baer, closely face to face with Richard, wavered for a moment as if he might bow, but raised his sword's point instead.

With the dignity of the ruler of an empire, Richard met the astonished eyes of the novice knight. "I am unarmed. You mean to strike me?"

"D ...do you surrender to us peacefully, my lord?" de Baer stammered.

Without another word, Richard unbuckled his sword belt and gave sword and scabbard to Beavis. Then he removed and gave over his crowned helm to Vernon. Bare headed and surrounded by his three astounded captors, he walked down the hill, the drover trailing after them with the spent horses.

By the time the three lads and their captive reached Saint Pancras it was dark. The Earl of Leicester had returned from the castle, leaving a siege force camped at its door. Simon sat at supper in the priory's refectory with his two sons, young Humphrey de Bohun, Gilbert de Clare, and the knights John Giffard and John de Burgh. A young knight, Roger SaintJohn, stood reading aloud the list of prisoners taken.

"...the Earl of Norfolk, Marshal of England Roger Bigod; the Earl of Arundel, John FitzAllen; the Earl of Kent, Godwin de Burgh; the Earl of Warwick, John de Plessis; the Earl of Hereford, Humphrey de Bohun; the Steward of Scotland, John Balliol, and with him the Scots lords Robert de Bruise and John Comyn; the lords of England Henry Percy, Philip Basset, William Bardolf..."

De Baer, Beavis and Vernon delivered their prisoner, who stood between them with as haughty a stance as if in his own Court.

Simon looked from the King of the Germans to the three youths in white. Struggling to suppress outright laughter and keep as much solemnity as he could manage for Richard's sake, he welcomed his captive. "My lord, how glad I am to see you at our supper. I shall have a place set." Then to the captors, "My knights, how did you come by this singular victory?"

Richard stood erect and silent. Shame, or rage, if there was either in him, were hidden by his rigid, regal bearing, as Beavis and de Baer told the story of the mill.

Simon studied the three, a wide, proud smile turning the corners of his lips, framed by his neat beard. "Knights for just one day, and you make conquest of an emperor? Truly," he began laughing uncontrollably at last, bringing out the words as best he could, "what a precedent you set for novices!"

Beckoning to a serving monk, the Earl, regaining some semblance of decorum, ordered, "Provide a place at our table for the King of the Germans. He's surely not eaten since yesterday."

The King of the Germans was offered a well guarded seat, a trencher slice and roasted meat, fare far simpler than the priory had served the night before.

A little later the Bishops of London and Worcester arrived from Fletching. They had come expecting to attend at their friends' burials, but had been met in the forest by a messenger with the amazing good news.

"The Lord has shown His will!" Walter exclaimed in awe, then turned and repeated the words, even louder, to everyone in the refectory. All that he believed, of Grosseteste's teachings and his faith in the Earl, and of the coming New Age, was here this day justified.

Simon's dark eyes met his friend's, then looked down. "So it would seem." And he broke a piece of sauce-soaked bread and ate it. The battle's outcome was indeed miraculous, but he was not certain yet what he should think of it. The future, for him, gaped with unknowns. He had expected to die. Now not only were he and most of his army still alive, but they held a great part of England's barony and two kings as their captives. If any peace was to be found from this extraordinary position, it would take much thought and care in the achieving.

"Saint George and angels were seen fighting on our side!" young Bohun eagerly reported to the bishops.

"Where is the king?" the Bishop of London asked. "We've heard he is unhurt."

"He's dining alone in the chapel," Simon answered, swallowing. He dabbed his napkin to his mouth and got up from the table. "Now that you're here, we can set our terms with him."

"Now? This evening?" Gilbert de Clare looked up at the earl, surprised.

"Now. It would be unduly cruel to leave Henry wondering if he's about to be beheaded. But if you're tired you need not come."

"I'm coming." Reluctantly Gilbert got up and followed the Earl and bishops, and the army's new-appointed secretary, the young knight Roger SaintJohn, who gathered up and took with him the wax writing tablet and stylus that lay by his trencher on the tablecloth.

Beneath the light shed by two fat white candles in an iron candlestand, King Henry sat on the altar steps, his thin elbows on his chain-mailed knees, his gray, haggard face propped and masked by his two hands. The supper that had been brought to him lay on a tray on the top step, untouched. The king dropped his hands forlornly and looked up as Simon and the others came in. His body tensed. "You've come for me already?"

"We've come to settle our terms," the Earl, stopping in front of him, ignored his tone of terror. "We must have the prisoners you took at Northampton and elsewhere released at once. The Earl of Derby, my son Simon, my cousin Peter de Montfort and his sons, Hugh Gebion, Adam Newmarket, Baudwin Wake,..."

SaintJohn, standing beside the Earl, checked off the names written on his wax tablet, then offered the names of the rest, held from the Northampton debacle and Henry's northern march of conquest.

His eyes fixed on Simon, his lips tight shut, King Henry nodded his assent when the list was completed.

"We have the matrix of the royal seal, retrieved from the body of your clerk Wengham," the Earl said. SaintJohn brought out the heavy seal from the blousing of his surcoat and presented it. "With your permission," Simon bowed to Henry, "the order to release the prisoners will be sent over your seal."

"Why do you want my seal?" Henry muttered bitterly. "You can make your own, 'Regis Simonis, Primi.'"

"I don't bear that title," Simon said quietly. "England's peace is all I wish, under the good guidance of the Provisions. Beyond that, I want to have no part here among your people." He turned to SaintJohn, "Copy the order for the prisoners' release, seal it, and see it's taken this very night to Windsor where the prisoners are kept." To the king, he added, "We also require your writ commanding the royal castellans, bailiffs and sheriffs to cease any resistance on your behalf against us."

"Do what you will." Henry waved his hand with pettish weariness. "Let me sleep. Whatever sleep you mean for me."

"You don't wish to have your freedom tonight?" Simon smiled patiently.

"My freedom? You mean it's time already for the axe?" Henry gave a cackling little laugh, then looked up into the dark eyes he had known so well for so long. "I heard that at Rochester your men had a great deal of practice. One was quite skillful. Might I beg his service?"

"I mean your freedom. We will accept your sons Edward and Edmund as hostages in your place, as ongoing guarantee of your good will." He included Edward's only brother, the hunchback child for whom King Henry desperately had sought the Crown of Sicily.

"Edward is free?" Even the sagging, creased eye opened at the unexpected news.

"Edward is free. But I would have him as our hostage in your place."

Henry smiled to himself and said in a low voice, "Why should I order him into your hands?"

"Because he'll probably be safe in prison, and you might not survive it. Though I wouldn't touch a hair of your head, I can't vouch for the scrupulousness of my followers."

"King Henry, please agree to the exchange," the Bishop of London urged. Until now the bishops and the others had witnessed the proceedings silently.

Henry looked to the bishop, then to Simon. "Otherwise I am to live, but you cannot guarantee my safety?"

"Exactly," Simon replied.

Henry nodded. "I give you Edward. And Edmund." He shifted his position on the step. "I'm tired. May I go to bed? What has the prior done with my traveling bed?"

"One more matter. Then you'll be escorted to your chamber, which is furnished as you left it this morning. We must have the government of the Provisions reconfirmed. Or amended by some council elected for that purpose by the people as well as the lords."

"Leave me to rest!" Henry twisted about on the step like a spoilt child annoyed by his nurse. "Don't you ever tire, Simon? Or does a day of killing men make you afraid to sleep?"

"Our terms of peace must be agreed upon tonight," the Earl said firmly. "Only after that may you, and I, sleep."

"Then have it as you will!" Henry cried pettishly. "I confirm your Provisions!"

Simon turned to SaintJohn, who nodded when he finished writing. The Earl looked to the two bishops and Clare, "I'm satisfied. We have the foundations for our peace." He bowed low to the king. The others bowed also and left the chapel with him. In a few moments four guards came to take Henry to the same elegant guest chamber he had occupied the night before. Everyone except the Earl's posted sentinels retired for the night.

Shortly before dawn, where the Earl's young knights huddled in the dark under their shields for arrow-screens facing the castle tower's door, the quiet suddenly was broken. Edward, with the men he had found, attacked the besiegers from behind, forcing his way to the door. Alemaine and the wakened mercenaries within quickly unbolted and opened the door for him.

That same dawn, riders were seen fording the Ouse then galloping toward Hastings.

Simon was wakened at the priory. He ordered his son Guy and Gilbert de Clare to go in pursuit. "Take twenty of our mounted men and ride after them at once, whoever they are."

After breakfast, Simon interviewed his fellow earls who were his prisoners, beginning with Roger Bigod. "You know as well as I how much King Henry lacks in kingly competence. Why would you not come, and solve our differences at the Parliament we've labored to create?"

The burly old lord, never fully recovered in strength since the poisoning at Winchester, narrowed his eyes and looked askance at the Earl of Leicester. "Because, from the start, you made the Provisions your own tool!"

"I! I did what was necessary after Richard led you all off before our work at Oxford was finished! There was no strategic need to pursue the Lusignan to Winchester, and the health and lives of how many, including yourself, was the price!"

Bigod looked sullen. "It served you well enough."

Simon lifted his head, his beard rising in resistant gesture at the implication. "Richard de Clare accused me for his own reasons. I swear to you, I poisoned no one! The Lusignan fouled the drinking water in Winchester castle's well, just as they'd poisoned Louis' army at Frontenaye."

"Maybe. But you took advantage," the Marshal glowered stubbornly.

"What would you have had me do? Stand by when all the lords were sick and dying? Ought I to have been paralyzed by amazement, rather than put into effect the good programs we had devised?"

"You might have waited till we recovered."

"We had our chance at that moment! We'd persuaded Henry to replace the sheriffs, the bailiffs and the royal castellans. But it was clear our opportunity was brief! As soon as he was able, he would bring an army from abroad, and undo any chance of an elected Council with meaningful powers over him. All the clergy on the Council were with me. Action was needed at once, or all we'd done would have been lost!"

"You turned everything to your own interests." The broad, unshaven, puffy face was dogged with resentment.

Simon's nails dug in his palms as he controlled his temper with the old earl who never had been very bright. "Were I to follow my own interests, I would not be in England, but in Palestine. And done with all of you! But I gave my oath to support the Provisions of Oxford. If you recall, we all swore to regard anyone who opposed the Provisions as our enemies, whether it cost us the loss of our wealth, our lands, or even our lives. I've kept my oath! But, as soon as the common folk asked that rights be granted them as well, our oath seemed to dissolve for most of you!"

"Why don't you just kill Henry and take the Crown? You could kill all us prisoners, and have earldoms and baronies to give to every one of your low followers."

"It has been suggested. There are many who'd be very pleased. That I don't, should be the strongest argument that I do nothing more than keep my oath. And that I truly want no part of England!"

Simon had Bigod returned to the locked buttery, and had several other of his lordly prisoners singly brought to talk. He received from them the same rebukes. Rather than anger himself further, he summoned no more of them.

In mid afternoon Guy returned. "We chased the riders to the coast. They've shut themselves up in the castle at Pevensey. Clare holds them at siege. We believe they're William and Guy de Lusignan, Peter of Savoy and John de Warenne, with some of their men."

"If so, it is essential that they not escape abroad to raise forces against us." Simon sent more knights to strengthen the siege.

The guard at Lewes' tower was substantially strengthened. The Bishop Cantaloup and the Prior of Saint Pancras went to the little castle.

"Lord Edward!" the prior called up to an arrow-loop window. "The king has made his peace with the Lord Montfort and his followers. King Henry and King Richard of the Germans only await the restoration of their freedom. King Henry and the lord Richard grant yourself, Edward, and prince Edmund and Henry of Alemaine in exchange for themselves as hostages!"

Edward stood by the side of the window in the tower's upper room and shouted down, "Tell Montfort he won't have me except he comes and takes me!"

"For the peace of the land, for your honor, Edward, redeem your father the king's freedom!" the prior shouted back.

"Edward! Expect no aid from those who fled!" Walter Cantaloup cried out. "They are held fast at Pevensey!"

That anyone had fled was happy news to Edward. Taking up the brimming bucket that served as night-privy for the men in the tower, the prince trotted up the steps to the roof, showed himself briefly at a crenel and tossed the contents of the bucket on the bishop and the prior. "There's my answer!"

At Saint Pancras', as the Walter and the prior made thorough use of the reredorter's bathing facilities, the day was spent by Simon in reviewing the prisoners, selecting which men safely could be set free and setting their ransoms.

"I won't have the accusation this time that I take wealth to myself," Simon said caustically to the washed and laundered Bishop

Walter, as he noted each prisoner's captor and the ransom to be paid him. Amounts in weight of coin were set for each, but no lands were to be confiscated. SaintJohn made record of all the arrangements under the heading Mise of Lewes.

For the sake of England's security, Simon retained a number of the prisoners himself: Prince Richard, the Marshal Roger Bigod and most of the earls who commanded large numbers of knights' services.

The next day, the sixteenth of May, was busy with the notes of ransom and the freeing of prisoners. Prince Edward remained in the tower, though the two bishops and the prior again, from a safe distance, urged his surrender.

On the morning of the seventeenth, a scrap of white cloth was hung out the tower window as sign of capitulation. Edward gave himself up to a substantial guard of young knights. After him, out the door came Henry of Alemaine, Clifford, Leybourne and some hundred and thirty men, several of them deep in fever from infected wounds. Those who needed nursing were given to the priory's care. Mercenaries among the force were ordered to the king's service, under the command of the Earl Montfort. The remainder was sent to Saint Pancras' large, secure and now emptied buttery, to be kept there behind locked doors and under heavy guard.

Simon Fils, Peter de Montfort, Robert Ferrers and the rest of the king's prisoners, released from Windsor by orders carried by the first messengers sent out, arrived at Lewes. When they entered the refectory they found King Henry seated in somewhat makeshift state in the prior's oak chair upon a platform that raised the prior's table and the lector's podium a step above the level of the rest of the hall's floor. Simon stood by Henry's side, as Steward of England. Except for the surroundings' monkish spareness, time seemed to have leapt backward to 1258.

Astonished, the returning men bowed to the decrepit king who seemed, as usual, to be taking little notice of anything around him. He nodded toward them absently.

Beaming with happiness, the Earl came down the platform's step and embraced his son warmly, then draped his arm familiarly across his cousin's shoulder. "You're both well?" he asked, studying his son's face with more kindness than Simon Fils recalled ever seeing before.

"Yes, Father," the hero of Northampton glanced down, uncomfortable beneath the unaccustomed, warm gaze. But his heart swelled. He drank in the praise as a sponge absorbs its life-element through every gaping pore. Simon embraced him again and, though he said nothing further, his gesture, his fond look, were noted by everyone. Henceforth Simon Fils was to be treated as a hero.

The business of the day was the allotting of control of the chief points of power. SaintJohn read the royal writs, sealed with King Henry's seal. What freedom the king now had would be very circumscribed, and closely overseen by his Steward of England. In fact he would be allowed no freedom at all.

"The lord Henry de Montfort shall go to Dover to hold the castle and serve as castellan for it and all of the Cinque Ports. He shall let no person without royal writ, recently sealed, enter or leave the land. No goods shall pass without careful inspection. The lord Simon de Montfort, son of the Earl of Leicester, Steward of England, shall administer the holdings of the Earl of Norfolk, Marshal Roger Bigod, and the holdings of the Earl of Warwick John de Plessis and of the Earl of Kent Godwin de Burgh, until order is deemed fully restored to the land. The lord Guy de Montfort shall perform like services for Richard the Earl of Cornwall known as the King of the Germans, and he shall guard at Wallingford, said Richard's strong castle, all prisoners remanded to his care for the security of the land. And Sire Simon, son of the Earl Montfort, shall go to Pevensey at once, there to relieve Gilbert de Clare and diligently prosecute the siege of the castle there."

Humphrey de Bohun Fils and several of the young knights remarked glumly on the placing of the prisoners of greatest value, and Dover and Pevensey, the two posts of most urgent concern, into the hands exclusively of the Earl's sons. Later they talked heatedly among themselves, but said nothing openly to the Earl.

The next morning, before they left on their commissions, Simon met with his three sons. "I'm placing my trust in you." He looked on them confidingly, as equals, as he had never done before. "Your appointments are temporary. My greatest hope is to leave England as soon as possible. But to leave the land at peace and in good order. There is no one that I trust other than you. We have not won a war so much as we've been burdened with the curing of England's ills. And England is like the sickly emperor of the tale who when he was not cured at once, had his physician hanged."

He pressed each of them to his chest, holding them a moment to his heart. Then he said softly and gravely to them all, "Take no monies for yourselves. Live modestly on what is allotted to you from the royal taxes. Be certain no one has cause for complaint due to your actions. You've been given the most honorable commissions. Undoubtedly there will be jealousy. You will be closely watched, your actions subject to attack. Do not fail me."

He walked with them out to the priory's courtyard and waited while they mounted their destriers, then left with their armed escorts of white-surcoated young knights.

Prince Edward and King Richard, their arms bound to their sides with chains, heavy swags of chain binding their ankles underneath their horses' bellies, waited with the other prisoners, amid a heavy guard, to be taken to Richard's surrendered stronghold at Wallingford.

Leaving at the same time were the two bishops. Simon crossed the yard to them and, reaching up, pressed Walter's hand as it rested on his woolen-robed thigh, holding his palfrey's reins. "The Lord be with you." Simon's dark eyes, wide in a hopeful smile, met his friend's gaze. "It will be only with the aid of King Louis in France, and the Pope, that can we hope for a lasting peace, free from threat of invasion."

Walter, in the blousing of his robe, bore Simon's letter to Louis asking for a new arbitration in light of the miraculous victory at Lewes.

# Chapter Eighteen

## YOUNG SIMON
### 1264

"I must see King Henry!" Richard de Gray shouted at the door of Saint Pancras' refectory.

Callow and officious young guards barred his way. "No one sees the king except by permission of the Steward of England."

"I mean to lodge complaint!" shouted the burly red-haired, newly supplanted castellan of Dover and the Cinque Ports. He had served as Governor of Gascony and advised Simon before the Earl had taken up his own viceroyship there. He had been loyal to Simon at great risk when nearly every lord in England had turned against him. He was a faithful friend to Simon for a quarter of a century. Simon had released him, and did not know he had returned to Dover, still commanding the main harbor and the Cinque Ports.

At the noise, the son of Simon's injured steward, young Nicholas Seagrave, came to the door, his white robe billowing in his hasty stride. "Good my lord, the Steward's permission must be obtained before you may gain entry."

"Since when does Montfort determine who may and who may not enter the Court!" Gray exploded.

"It is old custom, my lord. The Steward of England has the regulation of the door."

"I must crawl on bended knee to Montfort?" the livid castellan erupted. It was he who, at his own risk, had hindered the king from gaining his mercenary force through Dover or any of the Cinque Ports. That there was victory at Lewes was in large part to his credit.

The youth only pursed his lips in cool disapproval of his impolite expression.

In fury, Gray strode away, his chain hauberk flapping about his knees, rustling like the spitting of a threatened snake.

On the twenty-eighth of May, 1264, two weeks after the battle at Lewes, the Court of King Henry III at last left the Priory of Saint Pancras and passed in stately progress to London.

By June the Guardians of the Peace were reestablished, now with powers to arrest any commoner who bore arms without a royal permit. The Guardians again could hang without trial anyone caught rioting, looting or causing serious threat to the peace. A stern blanket of quiet was laid over England. And a new Parliament, including newly elected knights from each shire, was summoned to come to London on June twenty-fourth.

There were a few for whom the new order was not the least oppressive. Young Simon de Montfort, the hero of Northampton, breathed, opened his eyes, and for the first time in his life felt strong, capable, felt the glory of his daydreams turned into reality. He held power. He was honored. He was magnificent.

Simon Fils had grown to be a young man pleasing in appearance, with the soft brown hair, the prominent nose and chin of his mother, and her large, inquisitive almond-shaped brown eyes. His body, well trained for combat, was tall and powerful, slender and not lacking in grace. He discovered, from the flatteries of many, that he was handsome. From a lonely, shy and cynical boy never in step with the world around him, he was risen to popularity and glory.

To the common folk of Pevensey he was their own champion of the New Age. Village girls brought him offerings of sweet cakes and meat pies, and there grew in Simon a lively interest in the village girls. He spent the spring less with his soldiers at the siege around the castle than in the privacy of haylofts and woods, thanking his admirers with carnal and tender attentions. No hummingbird was busier among the grateful flowers than the young lord Simon de Montfort.

One afternoon in the warm languid days of late June, there passed by Pevensey a startlingly elegant cortege. Scarlet-liveried outriders conducted a tented litter borne by two huge, perfectly matched black palfreys, their headstalls decked with plumes, their harness fringed and embroidered in bright red. From the corners of the crimson palanquin's roof, long, supple sabers of pheasant feathers bobbed, frilled with arching cock feathers like avian bouquets. The litter's floor stirred the air with long gold fringes thickly strung with bells; their tinkling music gave a sweet, incessant lilt to the tread of the horses. Behind the floating tented glory was a troop of servants, all well mounted and in scarlet livery, even to the maids mounted on white mules. After them, surrounded by a well armed guard, a tall-sided and brightly painted wagon lumbered, drawn by four cream colored oxen, and even they were decked with fringe and bells.

Simon watched as if he saw a vision out of fairyland. "Who is that!" he asked, barely above a whisper.

"Isabella Fortinbras, the Countess of Devon and Aumale," John de la Warre, his second-in-command, who knew the district, answered.

"Some silly and fastidious old crone?"

"Actually, the young widow of an old lord killed at Lewes. I believe she's twenty-two, and probably the richest heiress in England," de la Warre grinned knowingly.

"A plain wench whom no one would want but for her money?"

"Why don't you go see for yourself?" De la Warre's eyes twinkled mischievously. "You have the power to stop her train and inspect it, since it passes near our siege and her lord was, beyond question, our enemy."

Simon's broad lips spread in a smile. "Come with me, John." He called several knights from the camp to make a daunting escort and they cantered up the road after the parade, intercepting the leader of the countess' elegant outriders. "Halt! We must see what passes here!" Simon sternly commanded.

"My lord, it is only a lady and her household en route to her manse," the outrider bowed, cautious and obedient. "We beg that she not be disturbed. She is in deep mourning."

"In mourning indeed. With her attendants all so gay in scarlet?" Simon observed archly. He turned his horse and rode back to the litter.

Its crimson curtains were drawn tightly shut, but even at this standstill the tinkle of bells livened the breeze. The silken draperies charged the air with the costly, musky perfume of the civet cat.

"A wealthy old man's little plaything," Simon smiled to himself, impressed. He reached over from his horse and yanked the curtain aside.

Within, deep among red velvet cushions, a young woman, a little book of poetry lying open in her hand, glared back at him. Her dress was of black velvet, her veil of black silk worked with silver thread. Her skin was milky fair, touched rose upon her flushing, angry cheeks. Her eyes were large and dark, furnished with dense black lashes beneath the delicate line of her frown. But Simon's gaze rested upon her mouth, full-lipped and smooth as ripe summer fruit, and so he missed the fury of her glare.

He held the curtain parted, staring at her, hardly hearing her demand, "You'll let me pass, Sire!" The tone was not that of a hapless, shy young widow but of a woman accustomed to command. Isabella Fortinbras early had left docile childhood behind.

Simon gazed, unhearing her order.

As he made no move but only held the curtain, peering in, she called to her steward, who had ridden up protectively and sat his horse beside Simon. She told him to resume their walking pace. As Simon's knights received no order to stop and search the wagon, the parade went slowly on.

Still holding the curtain open, Simon nudged his mount along, keeping abreast of the gently swaying palanquin.

"You stay near Pevensey?" he asked.

"I do not," came the crisp answer as the countess attempted to resume her reading.

"Where do you go, then?"

"That is not your concern."

"Where will you stop tonight?" His interest grew moment by moment, knowing he was teasing her. He was the more inflamed by every chilly answer.

"That's even less of your concern," she snapped.

"I'll ride with you…"

"You will not!"

"No. Please," his voice was soft, tender. The adoration of Pevensey's lasses had convinced him that to be near him was to succumb to his charm. He began the precarious maneuver of climbing from his saddle to the swaying litter. The palfreys shied at the strange shifting of their bearing-shafts. The tent rocked wildly, nearly upsetting. The countess shrieked.

As the countess's steward fretted in confusion, John de la Warre, turning from where he rode ahead, pulled his horse up close and grabbed Simon's horse's bit as the animal balked, its half-dismounted rider stretched over the widening space. Giving Simon a hand back to his saddle, he remarked with cooling intent, "My lord Montfort, we've gone past Pevensey…"

Simon, precarious between his halted horse and the forward-moving palanquin, let de la Warre help him back to his seat. But before he turned his horse's head away from the firmly re-shut drape, he apologized, after his fashion. "I must go my lady. But I give you my promise that you'll see me soon again." He reached down and pulled a bell, for keepsake, off the palanquin, then he spurred his horse and rode back to his siege with de la Warre.

On June the twenty-fourth, Parliament met in London at Saint Paul's Cathedral. Four newly elected knights from each shire attended, with England's prelates and a few, although not many, of the lords. No word had come from France to answer the request for a new arbitration. Simon had written again, begging that new arbiters be appointed quickly. But in the interim some government had to be formed.

Vague, distracted, gray as a cadaver of a few weeks ripening, King Henry in his crown and robes of state, sat on a magnificent chair set in the center of the platform at the transept's crossing. A huge new crimson flag with the three gold lions *en passant guardant* of Plantagenet hung behind him. The Steward of the Realm, in his customary robe of plain black wool, stood at his side, one step down. And below him stood his clerk.

Roger SaintJohn, as interim high clerk, announced the lords, the clerics, the knights of the shires, and then intoned in his young but pleasingly full voice, "From the King of France there is being sought a granting of fresh arbitration to heal the breach of England's community. Until such arbitration achieves an accepted solution, the business of the realm must be met. For this purpose, Henry, King of England, the third of that name, grants to his faithful subjects, as represented by the persons of those gathered here, the right to elect three Nominators, who will in turn choose and be responsible for nine Councilors, three of whom shall at all times be in the king's attendance, to advise and make determination on all issues of England's governance."

The shire knights cut off the speaker with a roar, "We want Montfort! Montfort! Montfort!"

"No. No," Simon frowned at the blurred mass he saw before him as it swelled with excitement and its unwanted demand. "Choose others for the Nominators and Councilors! I'm not to be chosen! Not as councilor, nor any other office!" His voice, bellowing refusal, was small in the roar that echoed off the groined ceiling and the high stone walls. He knew he must absent himself completely from the government before the great lords would be satisfied, and the Provisions' government restored to proper balance.

At the front of the crowd the Bishop of Durham, hearing Simon, cried back at him, "Who but you, good Earl! Our Lord on High has placed you as our leader, to bring us forth from these evil times!"

"I've done all I can!" Simon shouted at the bishop through the unceasing din. "Let other men lead you now!'

The bishop had come to the foot of the steps, and with him the Bishop of London Henry de Sandwich who, reaching up and laying a cool, thin hand on Simon's arm, begged, "Lord Earl, we

are as wandering sheep without a shepherd if you don't lead us."
He truly believed the angels fought on the Earl's side at Lewes.

Walter Cantaloup joined them, dressed like all the bishops: in
his See's best cope of cloth of gold, his crook capped with a thick,
curled tendril of gold, his high miter glittering with broad bands of
golden thread. He preferred his rough Franciscan robe, but here
it was the Church, and not himself, he spoke for. His broad face
was tight with a stern look. He had not expected Simon to retreat
like this. Here in public, in what he saw as crisis, he meant to use
every weapon in the arsenal that their long and close friendship
provided him to bring Simon to reason.

"My friend, you left a land once before when it was in mortal
need of you. That land, the home of our Savior Jesus Christ, was
divided and destroyed by an invader. Good Earl – my friend –
for your soul's sake, do not make that error again, abandoning
England in her need!"

Simon looked from London's bishop sharply to Walter, cut to
the heart by the perfectly aimed strike. "Bishop Cantaloup, my
leaving England will help heal England's wounds."

"You thought that, too, when you left Palestine," the bishop
bludgeoned him. "As your leaving brought on ruin there, such
an act of irresponsibility now, however well intended, will bring
ruin here."

"Walter…" Simon attempted to protest, but his friend, ruthless
for the cause he believed to be God's work, would not let him
speak. "The Lord's Own Hand gave you your victory at Lewes.
How dare you turn from Him again?"

The blows struck at the weakest, most tender, fearful crevice
of Simon's soul. He looked at the bishops ringed around him,
and at the yelling, demanding crowd. "Very well. I will accept your
naming me one of the three Nominators. But no more!"

Gilbert de Clare and Stephen Berkstead, the Bishop of
Chichester, were chosen as the Earl's co-Nominators.

"We shall make a list of names of all those whom the community
proposes for the Council. We, as Nominators, will choose the nine
to be the king's Council from among those named, selecting

the best and wisest men, not merely those who share our views," Simon proposed resignedly.

Clerks passed through the crowd in the nave, writing the names offered. Chiefly they were names of men with the Earl's army at Lewes or the released prisoners from Windsor, and in all cases strong partisans of the Earl. They were heroes now, well known to the upholders of the Provisions. Not one name of a great lord who fought on the king's behalf was volunteered, save that it met with hoots and derisive comment and was not added to the list.

The next day, from the clerks' tablets of names, Simon, Gilbert de Clare and Bishop Berkstead selected nine Councilors. The chosen were the Bishop of London Henry de Sandwich; the Bishop of Worcester Walter Cantaloup; his brother Thomas Cantaloup the Provost of Oxford; and his nephew Richard Mepham also of the university; the Earl of Oxford Robert de Vere; young Humphrey de Bohun whose father the earl was still imprisoned; Peter de Montfort, Simon's cousin; and the knights Adam Newmarket and Roger SaintJohn. With Berkstead as a second voice to his, Simon, time and again, had refused to agree when he considered the candidate supported by Clare to be inadequate. The list of Councilors was entirely Simon's choice.

The appointed Council members were announced to the assembled Parliament. Simon did not go to the platform, but stood far to one side by one of the broad columns where the transept met the south aisle. From most of the nave he was out of sight, which was what he wanted.

The ravaging of Rochester had loosed the last string of his hopes for the English. He had expected to die at Lewes and, with his followers, face ultimate Judgment. But the Judgment had been to live, in a victory of fewer than five hundred knights and novices against the combined strength of all of England's armies. Apart from securing the government of the Provisions, he had no idea what he was to be doing now, except he felt it as a certainty that the vanquished lords should be appeased – if there was some way he could accomplish that. This meeting of the shire knights was not helping.

Whatever the miraculous victory meant, he was utterly spent with weariness; any spur of rage, of indignation, blunted. The lords of England were self-serving cowards, the common people worse than beasts. He wanted a new arbitration that would recognize the astounding display of the Lord's Hand at Lewes: that would lift the onus of the Provisions' strike against the revered hierarchies of Aquinas and let England subside into the furrow of a system, new to the larger world but repeatedly well-plowed here – a government by elected representatives that would advise and harness a wayward king.

But most of all, he wanted to be gone, to have nothing more to do with England or the English.

Bishop Berkstead's voice reverberated against the soaring stone of Saint Paul's as he read off the names of the nine Councilors.

At first there seemed a shimmer of disturbance. Then loud outbursts, shouts rang, a clamoring roar that gradually took form in the cadence, "Montfort! Montfort! Montfort! Montfort for King!"

Simon remained where he was by the column, weariness fighting with rising anger.

The noise grew louder, gaining in pitch and urgency. Even King Henry drifted from his stupor to alertness.

The Bishop of Chichester looked about, helpless, the resounding protest focused at him. He knew where Simon was standing and finally darted from the platform to the side aisle, taking the Earl by the arm and trying to draw him to where the crowd could see him. Against his efforts Simon was immovable. "In Heaven's name, Lord Earl, you must answer them!" Berkstead urged, terrified by the uproar.

Reluctantly, Simon walked with an angry, contemptuous stride to the platform and up the steps.

The nave burst into cheers of "Montfort!" which gave way to even louder bellowing, "England's king!"

Simon raised his hands. A moment, and the massive cheering died away, the great nave fell silent, obedient to him. The Earl's voice carried clearly, sharply through the long building, "Your Council has been chosen! I will accept no office beyond what I have already filled as Nominator!"

There was agitation in the pool of humanity filling the cathedral to its walls, like the ripple at the rise of a leviathan. Too stymied in confusion to erupt and be truly threatening, the demanding spirit of the moment shimmered, then broke to its insistent noise again. The assembly had become a mob, driving itself onward, higher and higher in its pitch. Whatever orderliness the Parliament of commons might achieve was at the brink of shattering.

Simon raised his hands high once more. "I will agree," he conceded in the charged moment, "that, with my fellow Nominators, I will oversee the Council's work until a new and permanent government is formed by arbitration! Until that day, I agree to continue in my ancestral office of Steward of England!"

It was necessary. The assembly cried "Montfort!" time and again, but the tone of danger, of imminent dissolution, no longer had its thrilling tang of revolt.

The June Parliament of 1264 was dismissed. In small, civilized meetings of the nine Councilors, the *Ordinatio*, the constitution of the interim government, was shaped and polished.

When next the Parliament would meet, the issue of the rights of commoners would be the chief work on the agenda. Not only must the people have their share in rights that limited the powers of those above them, the poor should be secured from want, so far as possible. The *Ordinatio* would establish the right of every man to live free from oppression, and free from the sufferings of poverty. It was an astonishing proposal, but filled with hope for all that the New Age was to bring.

Simon smiled at the optimism of the Councilors. Since Lewes, he had ceased to suppose that reason was any accurate predictor of the future. But he was displeased with the general assembly's outcome. He acquiesced as temporary leader of the government. Peace was so fragile, and horror so recently close at hand, that, until the new arbitration, he felt he had no choice. He wrote to Louis a third time, urging the arbiters be named at once.

Young Simon, in London for the Parliament, enjoyed his visit, as he now was enjoying himself everywhere. He was an easy target for flatterers. Fresh clutches of opportunists already were spawning. He had been lauded as the hero of Northampton, but as a son – the namesake son of the Great Earl – he now had the appeal of a mayfly before hungry trout. Everyone who'd be a swimmer to the source of success sought to be immersed in this new river of power. They made Simon Fils their darling, entertaining him lavishly whichever way his tastes might turn. Including hours spent with wealthy London merchants' sumptuous courtesans. When the Parliament ended and he was constrained to return to his tedious siege at Pevensey, Simon Fils did so with a dismal heart.

Through the early summer he tried to amuse himself with the plump breasts and yielding thighs of his devoted coterie of wenches. But his thoughts drifted more and more to his entrancing vision of that undoubted goddess of delights in her perfumed palanquin.

Young Simon was gone, nowhere to be found, in some woodland bower fancying the mouth that pressed his was the swelling, smooth lips of the Countess Isabella, when the men he held at siege broke out. He wandered into his encampment at evening to find utter confusion. The Lusignan brothers, Peter of Savoy and Hugh Bigod, whom they hadn't known was there, had escaped, smuggled from the port in a fishing boat.

Simon sighed with relief. With only John de Warenne apparently still in the castle, he saw no need to stay there any longer. In a report to his father he told of what had happened. Then, with his friend de la Warre, he set out to find the lady of his passion, Isabella, the Countess of Devon and Aumale.

His father did not take the news of the escape at all calmly. The missive came on the same day that he at last received an answer from France. The letter was from Piers Chamberlin. No date was set for a new arbitration and no arbiters had been appointed. Piers wrote only:

*The Queen of England, here in Paris, is gathering more aid for her army and intends to invade England in the second week of August. She has at her command twenty-thousand men-at-arms in Flanders and is seeking from King Louis a fleet of ships for their transport.*

The escape from Pevensey would provide the queen with her two favored battle commanders.

In King Henry's name, Simon had a general summoning to arms proclaimed, set over his own lion seal. He did not send summons to most of the lords. New sheriffs, castellans and bailiffs had replaced the king's men, as had been done in 1258 under the Provisions. The new sheriffs read the call to arms in every shire's village. The commonality, not the lords, was being called to arms, to assemble in early August along England's southern and eastern coasts.

While the Great Earl prepared for yet more war, his son Simon, following the Countess Isabella's route, which was not difficult as everyone recalled her splendid equipage, arrived at Guildford, in Surrey. He learned of a manor of the Fortinbras a little further on, at Farnham.

But now, viewing the great manse, Simon bethought himself of wooing earnestly. So, with his friend John de la Warre, he continued on up to London to find a proper courting gift.

The goldsmith that his rich, new friends in the city recommended was a jeweler of the finest skills. The master craftsman brought forth a silver goblet in the shape of a rose, its stem the flower's leafy sprig. Then another goblet, of glass as clear as green ice with sharp bosses over its entire surface, cased in a netting of gold basketry. Another goblet was of heavy gold, with champleve depicting a forest inhabited by tiny birds and deer. "Think of yourself sharing your wine with her, your lips pressing the same spot on the rim where she has sipped." The sleek goldsmith licked his lips deliciously. He was thinking not of wine or love but of his profits.

Young Simon shook his head. He had something more personal, even more intimate in mind. Something he would take pleasure in handling, something destined to rest upon her breast.

From a gold repousse casket deeply ornamented with a scene of battling knights, the jeweler brought forth a necklace of rubies like gobbets of heart's blood. Simon fingered it, then shook his head again.

From the casket next came a rather plain fibula, the whole of it, except the gold tendrils of its setting and its pin, was a large uncut stone as blue as the sky at its deepest evening tinge. Isabella's eyes were dark, a dark blue much like this, Simon thought he remembered. His breath caught at the beauty of the stone in its simple setting. "What is this?" he asked, taking it in his hand almost reverently.

"The stone of wisdom and good fortune. You choose well, my lord. It is a rare sapphire," the jeweler smiled.

"I must have it." Simon's voice, in the first passion he had ever felt for an object, came as a whisper. "What is the price?"

De la Warre rolled his eyes in dismay at the figure quoted. With no attempt at bargaining, Simon fished from his robe's blousing a bag heavy with the tax coins meant to fund the siege.

In the room he took at the inn at Guildford, and shared with de la Warre, Simon Fils studiously composed a letter; wrapped the astounding gem into its vellum folds and dispatched it, by his friend, to Farnham. It was customary to make serious offer of betrothal by way of an agent. He did not consult his father. Why should he? He was nearly twenty-five. Anxious, more at the waste of time before she would be his than from any doubt what her amazed answer must be, he paced his small chamber, waiting de la Warre's return.

De la Warre came back with the letter not even unwrapped. "The lady will not see it," he reported, with a look that betrayed his skepticism of the whole endeavor.

"She knows who I am?" Simon Fils asked, confounded. His name alone should have flung open her doors.

"She knows very well who you are," his agent said, meaning to eradicate all hope and send the costly fibula back to the jeweler.

But Simon would not hear discouragement. He went back to Pevensey and gathered his servants, a few knights and baggage, intent on laying chivalrous siege to the manor of Farnham. At sight of the approaching military convoy, Isabella's villeins went fleeing to her manse.

The steward, with several stout men armed with truncheons, came out onto the road, but when they saw the armed advance they circumspectly went back to the house. A letter went out to the knights, carried by an inoffensive, gaudy little page in velvet tabard and peacock plumes, and addressed to the commander of the investing force.

Simon received the missive as his men began to pitch their tents amid the browsing, mildly perplexed cows and sheep on the manor's fallow field. The countess' letter called for the immediate withdrawal of troops.

Simon gave the plumed and velvet child his answer in one carefully rehearsed sentence. "Tell her I cannot leave for she holds my heart captive."

When time enough had passed for his answer to have been received and contemplated, Simon went himself, alone, to Isabella's door. The scarlet robed, gilt-trimmed major domo met him with a curt, "The Countess Fortinbras will not see you, my lord."

"Then tell her I'll remain here like her sentry till she will." Dreamily, he sat down on the step, un-sentry-like but well content to be in her vicinity until she relented. Which no doubt must be soon.

When, some hours later, the major domo returned, the young lord Montfort was allowed to enter. Political expedience had argued his case. Simon found the countess in her shadowy, cool hall, surrounded by her women, her every serving maid and member of her staff, including sturdy stable and kitchen men armed with their whips and cleavers.

Modestly, the besieger knelt as close to his beloved's feet as the crowd around her would permit. He tried to reach the hem of her black silk gown to kiss it in a humble gesture of his passionate devotion.

Her feet drew back, and two of her waiting women moved with the precision of chess pieces to obstruct his reach.

Isabella, on her draped oak chair, glared at him frigidly. "Sire, I wish no more from you than that I and my people might be untroubled by you. Your importunity only the further disinclines me to your suit. I am in mourning for my lord. Bear that in mind, if you are able," she added tartly, bringing titters from her women-in-waiting.

"I am a fire that must be quenched," Simon Fils answered, having read the phrase in a little book he bought in London, in imitation of the one she had held in her hand in her palanquin. Over and again he had read its verses, soothing and enflaming his spirits during his sleepless, fantasy-filled nights. Languidly he let his gaze rest on the full red lips that memory had kept fresh in his mind's eyes. For the moment his whole desire was to stay right where he was, doubting his trembling legs would hold him even should she offer to lead him to her bed.

Returning his gaze with deep distaste, Isabella said crisply, "Use no such language with me, Sire! You have no right."

"I have the most right," her would-be husband insisted, "under the compulsion of my sovereign heart which rules my every breath." He blessed his reading. The inspired words came right to his mouth, amazing even him.

Becoming somewhat fearful of him as he seemed out of his mind, Isabella turned sideways in her chair, averting her eyes. "You will take your men and go from here?"

"No, my lady. I cannot until you render me satisfaction." He used the term of challenge of one-to-one combat. "Honorably," he added lest the term, offered a lady, might seem too bluntly laden with sexual demand.

Insulted beyond bearing, the countess rose from her chair, her attendants moving like a defensive cordon around their champion. With a well-aimed foot she stamped upon the hand that propped Simon's submissive kneeling bow. "Get out! Get out of my house!" she screamed and aimed a kick that, had her supplicant not moved quickly, would have caught him in the face.

Shaken, scrambling to his feet, then bowing low to her from a safe, standing position, her confused suitor withdrew. The major domo, smirking at his mistress' boldness, escorted him out to the door.

Simon and his several knights and servants remained camped in the fallow field. In an adjacent field wheat was being reaped, the villeins moving with a steady swing of scythe, glancing at the idle knights and their string of horses beneficially, if unintendedly, manuring the land for next year's crop. They were not displeased with the visitors who made no hostile moves, and who were finding entertainment among the local wenches. Next year's bastards, like the fields, would have a fresh, wholesome infusion from the knightly class. The countess was in mourning. They did not think ill of her resistance to the comely youth who could be a wise marriage asset, given the drift of the realm. A year and, perhaps if he was patient, he would win her hand.

John de la Warre took his commander's frequent, heated and poetic letters to the countess, but brought back no replies.

The ardent lover seemed not at all disappointed. He spent the warm July days sprawled on the Fortinbras lawn before the manse's iron-bound oak door, composing his love notes, reading in his little book the song of Bertrand of Borne to the stately, tall and slender Lady Audiart who loved him not. Or inscribing into memory the venerated venery of Ulrich von Lichtenstein. He fancied himself bound, stripped naked as Saint Sebastian on a pageant cart, his lady, bow in hand, with flaming shaft after shaft piercing his burning flesh.

When Simon Fils had been at Farnham for six days, engrossed in this self-stimulating, self-sustaining, so sweet torture, a courier from his father brought him an irate command to return at once to Pevensey.

With the highest pique, he had his camp packed up, and he left Isabella's door. But he sent as a last gesture an ardent promise that he would not leave her for long.

As August arrived and moved into its second week, the entire southeast coast of England became densely populated. A single, endless-seeming throng stretched along the beaches and cluttered the cliff-tops. Common Englishmen encamped, armed and waiting for invasion. The farsighted among them scanned the Channel. Small boats and merchant ships from the Cinque Ports patrolled its waters. Storm clouds were seen, but no enemy vessels were sighted.

The Steward of England had ordered a punitive suspension of trade with Flanders, and the mercantile Flemings had withdrawn their support from Queen Eleanor's campaign. With her sources of supply cut, her army made unwelcome, and every inch of landing-spot on England's nearest shores teeming with hostile villeins and yeomen, the queen was forced to order her costly army to disband.

By the end of August it was clear the planned invasion had collapsed. The Steward of England issued orders from the king that everyone should return to his home and reap the autumn harvest.

With de la Warre and six of his knights for guard, Simon Fils left Pevensey and galloped back to Farnham. To his astonishment, the countess no longer was there. He followed her to Dorset, but she got word of his pursuit and moved on to Devonshire.

Imagining herself safe, Isabella Fortinbras was out on a Devon moor with her ladies and her ornamental little page, enjoying the sport of flying a hawk at a heron that was chained to a large stone.

As Simon Fils neared the countess' manor house, he saw the hawk circling high in the sky. He turned from the road to watch it, leaving his escort behind. The bird suddenly dropped like a feather-fringed missile, talons stretched out for its prey. Simon followed the bird's stoop downward, and saw the countess standing at no great distance with her people in the field.

Isabella, dressed no longer in deep mourning but in a light silk gown of blue that fit her body with the closeness of the membrane of an egg, stood with her back toward her manor and the road. She wore no veil or wimple, her black hair was coiled into a braid that circled the top of her head like a coronet, leaving the slender nape of her white neck bare.

Overcome with desire, young Simon jabbed his heels into his horse, springing forward at a gallop toward her.

The ladies were shrieking in delight at the mayhem of wing and claw as the hooked beak tore at the gray, already bloody fluff on the heron's back. The tall bird, huge wings beating, leapt on its stilt-like legs, clacking its long, overreaching bill in hapless self-defense. No one saw the horse and rider coming on. The countess was laughing, wringing her hands and shouting encouragement to the little brown hawk that without doubt would be the mortal victor.

Riding swiftly toward her from behind, on irresistible impulse Simon reached down and hooked his arm under Isabella's shoulder. His horse still coursing at a gallop, he dragged her up toward his saddle. The countess's laughter choked in a gasp of surprise. Clutched by his strong arm, only half-hauled to his lap with the ground skimming beneath her feet, she shrieked, she yelled, she kicked wildly. Simon held her firm, careening down the field. Isabella's thrashing feet struck his horse's belly with such frantic force the confused animal turned, wheeled and, finding itself still mercilessly kicked, bucked out of control of Simon's one hand on its reins.

The maids and page were running after them, shouting, leaving the hawk and heron to their fate.

Trying to master his frantic mount, and at the same time improve his grip on Isabella, Simon pulled the countess to his chest, the back of her neck just before his face. Giddy with a thrill part passion and part battle-joy, he pressed his feverish lips to the white skin. The tightly coiffured head jerked back, smashing and bloodying his nose.

Beyond words, beyond thinking, Isabella fought, clawing at the air, at the horse's neck, at the arm gripping her, protected from her nails by the thick canvas quilting of a pourpoint. Her feet, striking out, now only thrashed the air.

The horse regained direction from Simon's hand on its reins and sped toward the road, dashing over the dry moor-grass far ahead of the runners on foot. Straining to keep his hold on the furious, struggling, writhing lady, Simon Fils clutched her bosom, her waist, her hips as she pitched over, head down, on the other side of his saddle.

Seeing the ground streaming past not far below her head, Isabella's shrieks rose by an octave, from rage to real terror. Grabbing what she could, she clung, bracing herself, head down, her hands tight on Simon's ankle and spur. Stumbling over rough ground, the destrier careened in fright at this monstrous, noisy burden; a forefoot struck the hollow of a badger sett and the big horse pitched forward. At the same instant the countess twisted and Simon changed his grip, trying to raise her. She fell, hitting the ground, still clinging to Simon's spur and ankle. Dragged over the rough grass, Isabella's thin robe shredded; her legs, bared, were scratched and cut. Simon himself managed to pry her hysterical, clutching fingers loose, and she collapsed, gasping and crying on the turf.

Seeing what was happening, de la Warre had left the road and followed his commander, dashing through the crowd that pursued on foot, then circling back. When Isabella fell, he was only a few yards behind. He came up, leaping from his horse. The lady lying on the ground was sobbing in hysterics. Her legs were bloody. Dark, bloody smears blotched her torn gown where the silk adhered to her scraped skin. De la Warre knelt down and gently gathered her up. Gratefully she put her arms around his neck and sobbed.

Recovering control of his horse, Simon rode up as his second-in-command carried Isabella to her arriving, breathless people. Glaring up at him, de la Warre said through clenched teeth, "You fool! She could have been killed!"

The maids took their mistress from his arms, clustering around her solicitously and darting furious looks at her clumsy abductor.

Simon's heart, full near to bursting with joy only moments before, suddenly was empty, hollow, drained and chilled. He felt barely able to move his hand on his horse's reins to guide his mount back to the road, where his six knights stood watching, reshaping their sardonic grins to stiffened sober looks.

That night Simon Fils camped out on the moors.

De la Warre had gone to the manse with the countess's people, and remained there as the countess's guest. That very night Simon Fils' second-in-command wrote to London, asking that he be assigned to other service. A servant of the countess left hastily, carrying the message to the Earl Montfort.

His heart shattered, young Simon led his knights back to Pevensey.

# Chapter Nineteen

## THE INTERIM ORDER
### 1264

While the young lord Simon was pursuing love, England's fragile peace was being wrought and hammered by his father.

Invasion by the queen's army no longer seemed imminent. It was time for the Earl and Council again to press King Louis for arbitration. The Court of England moved to Canterbury to speed communication through Dover. Louis, willing to help, took his Court to Boulogne. The Bishops of London and Worcester traveled back and forth. Gentle Henry of Alemaine was freed from imprisonment in his own family's castle at Wallingford and sent to join the bishops as England's ambassador. Alemaine's support of the Provisions, his innate decency and intellect, his close kinship to the two kings offended by the Lewes victory, made him the ideal agent to plead for reconsideration of the issues. Though he was earnest and honest in his appeal in France, he returned with the bishops with nothing achieved.

After Alemaine's report to the Council, Simon questioned him. In the quiet of the sumptuously draped, cushioned and oak-paneled chamber of the absent queen's absent Uncle Boniface of Savoy, the Archbishop of Canterbury, Simon asked young Henry confidentially, "Tell me, what is it in France that so blocks our negotiations?"

"You ask that in the very home of the archbishop who is in exile?" Alemaine replied. "It is the Church that is opposing you, good Earl. And your bishops are of little help. They refuse to receive Boniface back on English soil, and they make their own inflexible demands upon Rome. They've thoroughly outraged Guy Folques, who's now the Cardinal Legate."

Simon's gaze dropped to the floor. "So that is what it is." He sighed, folding his arms across his chest as if to contain his annoyance. "I should have guessed that, tasting victory, Bishop Cantaloup would take on more. But could he not have worked for our peace first?" he mused painfully. "Folques, for years, was Louis' own confessor. Antagonize him, and of course Louis won't act."

"Folques considers you in rebellion against the Church, refusing two Popes' dicta regarding the Provisions, and expelling bishops confirmed in their Sees by Rome. Even though he knows their own monks reject them. Folques argues that you rely on the theology of heretics. That you defy God's clear Will."

Simon was standing by Archbishop Boniface's polished marble table. His gaze settled upon the ivory crucifix that stood on it. He picked it up, then set it down again. Nervous, tense, he walked to the broad oriel window and looked out at a small tree twisted by the shade of the towering cathedral. After a few moments he sighed and walked back to the table, resting his fingers on the ivory cross thoughtfully. "Louis will do nothing that is opposed by the Church." Looking to the young man patiently awaiting a decision, or to be allowed to leave, he asked, "What would you recommend we do?"

"My lord?"

"What do you think should be done?"

"Truly, my lord…" Alemaine was thoroughly flustered, realizing he was seriously being asked for policy. "Truly, much as I believe the best means for avoiding monarchy's flaws are to be found in the Provisions, I see no hope for their acceptance by the Church, even in some modified form."

Observing the youth whose innocence and intelligence, he considered, made him as nearly beyond reproach as any living man could be, Simon asked, gently yet more pointedly, "What would you do, were you in my position?"

"My lord, I thank God I'm not. I fear I'd have no recourse. King Henry, as we all know, and if we're honest will admit, has proven time and again that he's unfit to rule. Yet the whole world seems set against our imposing upon him the sensible recourse of an elected council. I think I would be sorely tempted, were I you, to decide matters simply. To lock King Henry in a chamber somewhere, forgotten like the Maid of Brittany, and declare myself the king."

At the young man's words, Simon burst out laughing. He threw back his head, his neat, dark beard lifting, and laughed long and loud and with a bitter edge. When the spell of his odd mirth died, his eyes moist, he leveled his look at Henry Alemaine. "Do you really think the English lords would accept me? A foreigner? A Frenchman by birth?"

"Didn't the Norman William supplant the weak King Harold?"

"What of King Henry's heir, Edward?"

"In a just world, ought not strength combined with foresight be a better claim than birth? Truly, though I love him as a friend and cousin, I fear Edward as a king."

Simon was thoughtful for some time, then he said to the young man, "No. I would not take from Edward what is his – if he can mend. But I would see him reign under the constraint of a wise, elected council. We must find arbitration for our cause, for the sake of England's future as well as the present reign. There is no other choice. Go back to France and try again."

Alemaine, on sudden impulse, knelt at the Earl's feet, lifted the hem of the plain black woolen robe and kissed it. "My lord, you once disparaged and shamed me, but you were right. And I know you now to be a truly righteous man. Were my homage not paid to my father, I would give you my liege. May God preserve you."

Simon put his hand on Alemaine's arm, raising him up. His smile was sweetly astonished, "And were you free, I would be honored to accept your liege. I know of no one else of such constancy and goodness. Go back to France, Henry, and seek that one solution that will save our land, our honor and our lives."

Alemaine returned to King Louis' Court at Boulogne. But Cardinal Folques opposed any negotiations. He demanded first the release of the noble and royal hostages and that he either be permitted to go to England, or all the English bishops must come to him.

The bishops Walter Cantaloup, Stephen Berkstead and Henry de Sandwich met with Simon upon their return from France.

"Folques means to demand the English bishops' withdrawal of support of the Provisions. If we refuse," the gaunt old Bishop of London said angrily, "he means to strip English churchmen of their benefices and give over all our resources to foreigners, whom he considers the more faithful sons of the Church!"

"The time has come for that severance from Rome that Father Grosseteste foresaw!" Walter sputtered in rage. The implications of his words burned in everyone's thoughts.

Simon, his eyes tight shut, hands clenched and gripped behind his back in utter frustration, spoke as if the words were wrung from him. "The peace of England falls away from us the more we reach for it!" He looked sternly at the three bishops, "The Church, the whole world comes against us. If we are doing the Lord's Will, God help us."

"Lord Earl, this breach with Rome was inevitable," Stephen Berkstead's sad, placating tone spoke louder than his words. "Our churches' funds have been bled off by Rome's legates since King John's time. The churches themselves stand empty of priests, while foreigners who won't set foot on English land collect rich incomes from them. If the break with Mother Church comes now, we can at least say politics, England's insecurity, hinders all clergymen, except us three ambassadors, from traveling to the continent to answer Folques' summons. And that it's far too unsafe for him, or any legate, to consider coming here. We can make our severance as gradual and gentle as possible, as if it were merely the outcome of war."

Cantaloup nodded, and added the point, "When true peace comes, and Rome again tries to assert her power over us, we'll have our episcopacy strong and independent, accustomed to self-rule and unified."

"You'd deny the quieting the Guardians of the Peace achieve? Would it not be more tidy to tell Cardinal Folques that *I* will not permit our bishops to leave?" Simon asked tartly, seeing quite clearly onto whose shoulders they meant to shift the blame. "I'm said to hold the King of England in thrall. Now you'd have me be the tyrant of England's Church as well?"

"Simon," Walter bridled at his friend's biting tone, "it is essential for England's good that we sever from Rome."

"Perhaps that may be. But I still hope for a gentler solution through arbitration. Can Louis find in favor of the oppressor of bishops? No, Walter! I'll not be made the scapegoat for your hopes to break with Rome!"

At the Earl's insistence, the three bishops traveled yet again to France to try to appease Folques. This time they took with them a program that asked only for the French king's consent. Their *Compromissio Pacis* promised reform of the English Church and the naming of three new Nominators, by whose choice the king's Council, bailiffs, castellans, sheriffs and all royal officials would be appointed anew.

Louis was asked to form a committee of five men: any two Frenchmen, any two Englishmen *and* the Legate Guy Folques. The five would select the three Nominators. The *Pacis* only stipulated that the Nominators be Englishmen. All further that was asked was that free passage and residence be granted aliens in England, the charters of liberties already granted to towns would stay intact and, finally, that King Henry, Edward, the barons, sheriffs and royal bailiffs would grant peace and set aside all rancor against the Earl Montfort and his followers, and that no retribution would be sought.

It was Simon's declaration of resignation.

Folques refused to permit the *Compromissio Pacis* to be read to the French Court.

"The Legate demands that the hostages be set free first. And that he come to England himself at the beginning of September," Stephen Berkstead reported to the Earl.

"Does Folques quite understand," Simon's voice was strained to the outer borders of self-control, "that the five may be *anyone*, provided he himself is *included*? And by their choice, Henry may have any Council so long as they are Englishmen?"

"Simon," Walter's tone was as gentle and placating as his pastoral training taught him, "to us, your offer seems all but complete capitulation. But in their eyes, we are demanding that a government by Council be accepted. Its membership is beside the point. We are dictating to three kings and the Pope."

When the bishops left for France again, Simon sent Ambelard, the Master of the Templars for all of England, to Cardinal Folques. The Templar would offer his Order's strong and ghastly evidence of the attack upon the Temple's bank to argue against the wisdom of King Henry's and the future King Edward's untrammeled rule.

The Legate met Ambelard's forceful words with rage. "You tell me of the slaughter of your knights! And I tell *you*, Montfort and his people flout the commands of two Popes! The issue is not England's peace and form of rule, but who shall dictate to the world! Simon de Montfort? Or the Vicar of Saint Peter and Our Lord's anointed kings?"

Chagrined, more than chagrined, infuriated, the Templar reported to the Earl.

And still Simon would not give up. He saw no alternative. "If in no way we can appease Folques, we must make one last attempt to reach Louis himself." He drew up a new version of the *Pacis*, proposing, for the Committee of Five, the Bishop of London, the Provisions' Justiciar Hugh Despensar, the Abbot of Bec whom he knew Louis admired, Louis' own brother Charles of Anjou and the Archbishop of France, the now quite elderly Odo Rigaud. Majority decision would be in Louis' hands. Folques was bypassed.

"I ask only that Louis permit these men to work a healing peace, whatever it may be. I will leave England. I want *nothing* here. Let them make whatever government they will."

The three bishops, this time accompanied by Peter de Montfort, carried the offer to the King of France.

Louis had their document read aloud to his Court. He looked to Folques, "The Earl Montfort is trying, by every conceivable means, to make peace. What more would you have of him?"

"I ask his *obedience!*" Folques weighted his words with venom. "And the submission of the bishops of England to the Mother Church! Montfort answers my commands in name of Holy Church by removing my name from his petition. He places himself on high, beneath only Our Lord. He leaves us no recourse but to cast out his name from those of the faithful."

"Cardinal Folques!" Bishop Cantaloup's eyes blazed with indignation, "It is not Mother Church you defend! It is your own reach for power! And, for your own sake, you would excommunicate a righteous man!"

Folques turned on the Bishop of Worcester. "You and your fellow bishops are in rebellion. The Church has suffered your ill-counseled attacks with well-reasoned requirements, mildly seeking to bring the wayward back into the fold. But she does not forget who her abusers are!"

Henry de Sandwich, his whole gaunt frame shivering with anger, shook his boney fist. "It's men like you who claim to be the ministers of Christ, but who know nothing of His mercy! And filch His Name for their own ends!"

"What you speak is blasphemy, old man!" Folques bellowed at the frail bishop, his unctuous mask cracking.

"It is too late." Walter put his hand gently on the Bishop of London's thin shoulder. "The breach is come and it cannot be mended."

The next morning, in the Cathedral of Boulogne, the Cardinal Legate Folques performed the ritual of excommunication of Simon de Montfort and all his followers, lay and clerical alike. Intoning the curses of eternal damnation, he overturned a tall, thick white candle, stamping its flame out upon the stone floor as if the light of godly hope and faith were snuffed.

As he finished, turning from the altar, he found a courier kneeling at the foot of the altar steps. "Your Eminence," the courier said in Italian, in the dialect of Rome, "I bring urgent news. Pope Urban is dead. You are recalled to the Vatican at once for the choosing of the new Pope."

When Folques met with the English bishops, delivering to them the bulls of excommunication and of interdict against the Earl Montfort, those who sustained his cause and those English churchmen who refused obedience to Mother Church, the three bishops already had heard the news. Hands at their sides, they refused to take the velum rolls. "You excommunicate as Legate of a Pope who is no more. Your power is invalid," Bishop Henry de Sandwich said staunchly.

"A new Pope, when he is elected, may see matters differently," Bishop Stephen Berkstead smiled, returning Folques' unctuousness. "He may see that, obstructing our generous offers, you are driving from the Church her loyal sons who have been abused for two generations, but who ask only for justice and can yet be at one with Mother Church."

Bristling at the insouciant imitation of his manner, Folques blustered, "You're blinded by your arrogance! You still attempt to dictate to Rome when you should prostrate yourselves before God's manifest Will!"

At Dover, Henry de Montfort, as his office required, came aboard the bishops' ship as soon as it tied to the quay, before anyone debarked or anything could be unloaded. The Earl's eldest son was in high spirits as Master of the Ports. He had confiscated all the Flemings' goods in warehouses in Dover, and through their sale had made a fortune for the new government's treasury. He had the glow of a prosperous man of business, lightly intoxicated with his own energy and success.

"Welcome, dearest bishop," he greeted Cantaloup affectionately. "But you look like you're suffering the headache. Was your crossing so rough? The sea looks calm from here."

"It is my traveling bag that gives me acute pain," Walter replied with a dim smile. "Would I could be bled of it, before the poison that it carries spreads."

"Your luggage bears contamination? I am under firm instructions to let no tainted thing enter the port. Beg pardon, but you must submit your bag to surgery."

With a conspiratorial grin, the burly bishop dug from his travel-stained leather sack a large gilded scroll case. "Take care, Henry, there are important papers here. Excise only those that have a rotting stench."

Tapping out several scrolls, Henry extracted two with large gold seals and looked at their stamping. Then, dandling the two scrolls by their seals, he affected a stern frown. "Good bishop, you bring gold into this country without proper license? I fear these items cannot enter our port." He pitched the documents of excommunication and of interdict over the ship's rail into the sea.

"Remarkable," Cantaloup sighed, "I feel already cured."

The bishops went directly to Oxford, where Parliament was to convene on October twenty-ninth. The entire high clergy of England, all abbots, priors, bishops, Masters of the Knightly Orders, and the Provincials of the friar Orders were attending. Though the lost bulls could not be read, Bishop Henry de Sandwich felt honor-bound to tell the meeting about the excommunication and the interdict attempted by Folques.

"Folques' intentions are utterly irreconcilable with our needs!" The Bishop of London argued for final severance of the English Church from Rome.

But the elderly Bishop of Bath did not agree at all. "There soon will be a new Pope. Is it not the work of evil to be hasty? Parting ourselves willfully from the Rock of Saint Peter? If we are contrite and loyal, the new Pope may look on us more leniently. While stiff-necked rebellion will surely make him our enemy." He argued cogently, then he added, his small blue eyes blazing beneath his bushy gray eyebrows, "If you will not be obedient churchmen, nonetheless I will!"

Consensus to sever from Rome had been nearly complete, but the Bishop of Bath set spinning a new round of confusion. There seemed no clear, evident path of what was right. The prelates' meeting ended only with agreement they would meet and debate again in two months time, at their next meeting at Reading.

As the clerics disbursed, the elected knights from the shires met with the nine members of the Council to present their petitions.

Hearing what peace was achieved in the land was most urgent. Voting on the new, wide-reaching reforms of the *Ordinatio* was postponed until the shire knights had been heard.

The principal complaint from the shires was that the sheriffs' courts were still in disarray. The legal system had been sundered by the upheaval of the commons after decades of corruption and abuse. The Councilors concluded that the king and Council should make a Great Eyre of all the shire courts of England and set each court functioning aright.

To attempt the reforms prescribed by the *Ordinatio* was premature, even dangerous, until law and order fully were restored. The far-seeing system that would give the commons parity with the nobility in rights, and even might end poverty, was set aside.

The project to reform the legal courts was immense enough, requiring that the royal Court, complete with Chancery, Treasury and all the sovereign functions, travel throughout England: a Progress that would take many months, possibly years.

King Henry and his predecessors customarily had traveled from one royal fief to another with no greater motive than good hunting. As the cycle of the customary eyre was repeated with only slight variance each year, it had been possible for anyone seeking the Court to have some notion of the royal schedule. But this proposed excursion, while of far more merit than past wanderings of the Crown, would require a new system of scheduling, lest the Court be utterly cut off from necessary messengers. A committee would be needed to address the complexities of such a tour.

After all the petitions of the shire knights had been heard, changes in appointments of castellans and Guardians of the Peace were read.

King Henry, his palsied eye drooping till it was almost shut, listlessly observed the doings of his Council without taking part. Since Lewes he had grown even more feeble. The constraints he felt sapped the last reserves of his cynical resistance, his one strength. His mind drifted. He slept much of the time, his soft snoring giving undertone to the meeting's speakers. His slack mouth gaped and puffed and gently gurgled now and then but did not interrupt the Parliament.

Letters to England's sheriffs were written in his name. His seal was used. The Council appointed Ralph de Sandwich, the Bishop of London's younger brother, to be Minister of the Wardrobe, the controller of the Royal Treasury. Peter de Montfort was made the Keeper of the Royal Seals. Thomas Cantaloup, the Provost of Oxford, was chosen Chancellor, and Hugh Despensar was returned to his office of Justiciar. The Parliament was functioning smoothly as the king slept. Henry withdrew from all effort with the struggles that had cramped and demeaned his life for too long.

As the meeting drew toward its close, Gilbert de Clare stepped to the fore. "I have a complaint to submit," he said curtly, with a sharp glance shot at the Steward of England who was standing far to the side of the dais. "I fought at Lewes, and my arms did their part for the victory. I took more than a few high noble prisoners. In good faith I remanded them to the Earl of Leicester's steward's keeping at Saint Pancras' Priory. But when the ransoms were distributed, my captives' ransoms were credited to the Earl Montfort. I was sent to Pevensey, keeping me from speaking for my claims. To this day I have received nothing!"

Simon came forward from his place of carefully assumed obscurity. Facing the assembly, he explained calmly, refusing to take offense at the young man's implied accusation, "The captives the Earl of Gloucester speaks of, to the honor of his bravery and military skill, are great men whom it has been necessary to retain for the safety of England. Ransoming would, of course, require they be set free, which could impair the general peace of your land. Hence no ransoms have been set as yet. The lord de Clare must have patience for a while."

Clare, frowning like a hawk, threw back, "Someone collects their rents!"

"My son collects the rents. They are in safekeeping for each prisoner. When the prisoners can be released, and pay their ransoms, those funds will be remitted, each to his proper captor. Lord Clare, you'll have your share then, but not before. Nor were you sent to Pevensey so that you could be cheated. But because I, at the time, deemed you the most able man."

A stirring of discomfort eddied through the assembly, and a buzz of angry comment at the audacity of the lord of Gloucester. Glances ranging from annoyance to outrage were cast toward Clare.

Humphrey de Bohun Fils, who had been first to question the withholding of the ransoms, was dismayed. Though he had complained, he owed his life to the Earl Montfort and felt for him the adoration of a young man for his hero.

Clare turned to Bohun but saw he would find no support. The rising heat of the meeting nettled Gilbert to recklessness. "Remitting of my ransoms to me must be at your sole discretion, good Earl?" He made an insolent bow. "Was I not a Nominator with equal rank to yours?"

Steadily Simon controlled his temper. He was seeing in the young man the stamp of his father's haughtiness. "The defense of England is a burden that has been placed in my hands. Further, the Council has approved my keeping of the men I hold imprisoned. But," he added with wilting condescension, "if you feel more competent than I in these matters, submit your opinions to the Council. I will gladly relinquish my responsibilities to one who is more wise."

His last words were met with a roar of derisive laughter that unstrung the tension in the hall.

Gilbert, crimson to the roots of his auburn hair, subsided to his place near the forepart of the crowd, among the few earls present. To Robert Ferrers, who stood by him, he muttered, "Who is Montfort to dictate what is to be done and what is not? What is the Council that we fought for? Nothing but his voice multiplied!"

After the Parliament, the king and his Council returned from Oxford to Westminster. The new Court was deliberately lively and splendid with great show of state. A pair of magnificently liveried heralds in tabards of gold baudekin added dignity to the royal dais, and halberdiers in quilted scarlet pourpoints garnished with gold trim flanked the doors. Some of the tax monies clearly were spent to restore and improve upon the regal grandeur. Under Simon's hand the Court, in display of State, took on a similarity to the Court of the Emperor Frederic. So far as appearances would serve, the Earl wanted no one to have cause to say the King of England was demeaned by the existence of his Council and the trammels on his power due to the Provisions.

Trouveres performed for the amusement of the king, whether he was awake or not. Beneath the spread wings of the wooden angels in the hammerbeams, the court was astir with clerks to serve and lawyers, scholars, theologians to advise the Council. All manner of petitioners and visitors were granted entry, for the Steward of the Realm wanted no one to complain that his way to the king was obstructed.

Families driven from their homes by the disorders came begging writs for resettlement.

Friars came. Here, and nowhere else, could they freely preach the millennial theology of Joachim del Flor. Thomists came as well. A spirit of free discourse was nurtured.

Drawn by word of a new, inquiring atmosphere in England's Royal Court, Roger Bacon came and found a stimulating world of open-mindedness for the sciences, for any subject that the reasoning intellect found apt. King Louis indulged scholarly discourse in his private chambers. But here, in the reconstituted Court of King Henry III, everyone mingled openly. Not since the time of the liberal-minded Frederic had there been a royal center so welcoming to matters of the mind. And in England, unlike in the empire, there was no fear of the whims of an autocrat.

Trade began to flourish. Italian merchants came petitioning for the reopening of the ports. And Flemings came demanding return of their confiscated goods. Though there was only an interim government, the daily operation of the system was forming working channels effective in meeting the land's needs, except in the still troubled outlying shires. And the absence of the great lords gave the Court a unique leaning toward the bourgeoisie and scholars.

Young knights who had fought at Lewes lingered at the Court and were made much of as heroes. Inns in London and Westminster were full to their capacities with visitors, and the streets were loud with friars proclaiming that the Lord's New Age was achieved. In London the New Jerusalem was made real. God's Kingdom had come at last, and it was England.

That autumn of the year 1264, in the royal hall at Westminster, at the opening of Court two Councilors were in attendance each morning: usually the knights Roger SaintJohn and Adam Newmarket. The Chancellor Thomas Cantaloup and the Justiciar Hugh Despensar also often were present. King Henry would be ushered in, walking with the helping arm of Peter de Montfort, Councilor and Keeper of the Seal. Last, the Steward of England would arrive, hurriedly with several vellum rolls in hand or with a burdened clerk following him at a trot. The hearing of petitions would begin.

On the morning that the Flemish merchants were to bring their claims in protest of the confiscation of their cloth, Simon appeared even later than usual. As he entered, briskly striding to his accustomed place at the side of the dais, a reaction of astonishment brought the mumbling room to attention. All eyes turned toward the Steward. For Simon was not dressed in his usual plain black woolen robe. He wore an even plainer cloth, if such were possible. Un-fulled, undyed white wool that hung thinly, almost like sackcloth upon his tall frame. Not even peasants' jerkins were made of such raw fabric that had only reached a midpoint in its manufacture.

At first, with a performer's presence, the Earl seemed oblivious to the amazed stares. Then, as if he became suddenly aware of some oversight, he bowed low to the king. "My lord, I beg your pardon and indulgence," his voice rang clearly through the hall. "If my robe seems improper, it is because I haven't had the time to send my cloth to Flanders for finishing, I've been so preoccupied with the task of averting war with armies from abroad."

As the meaning of his words sank to his hearers' understanding, the crowd in the royal hall burst out laughing, then cheering.

English woolen cloth in its raw state, such as the Earl was wearing, was shipped abroad to Flanders for finishing. By wearing the unfinished fabric, and linking it to England's defense, the Steward brought to every mind the recollection of the recent willingness of Flanders to rent ships and offer billeting for troops to invade England. He was striking a blow at the Flemings' case. Simon was not a member of the Council. By his own insistence he had no part in Court debate, but his gesture made his position brilliantly apparent to everyone.

And set the season's fashion.

First, the young knights at the Court appeared in undyed white wool. Then, from those gallants flaunting their love of country, the costume spread everywhere. Knights, merchants, workmen, villeins, wives and children dressed in the dull raw white wool. A wave of whiteness took hold in London, then in every market town and village of the realm. Parishioners appeared not in their best on Sundays, but in raw homespun. Simon's popularity saw measure in the rapid spread of the wearing of coarse white wool. Unfinished wool became the badge of England's independence from the world. A home economy, loyalty, England for the English. And for love of the Great Earl.

The bright heraldic colors of the barons who opposed the Earl stood out boldly and were seen by the commons as a mark of infamy. Political division showed itself in white versus vivid hues.

Most of the great lords who had taken King Henry's part and fought at Lewes had escaped or, by the autumn, had paid their ransoms and been set at liberty. There were some who had taken neither side in the conflicts. And a few, like Richard de Gray, who had fought on the side of the Provisions. But almost none of the great lords now took part in the government.

Loudest among the disaffected were the March lords and their leader Roger Mortimer. The Marchers had fled Lewes in full arms, taking their prisoners with them. Three times, through June, they had been summoned to the king's Court to discuss the ransoms of their captives. They ignored the summonses. In mid-July Simon had gone west and, in a swift assault on the lands of Mortimer, had taken hostages for the Crown. Finally Mortimer agreed to come to London to negotiate.

But the appointed day passed and he did not appear. Instead, to keep any more surprise attacks from being launched against him, he burnt the reconstructed bridges spanning the Severn. And, despite the treaty, he resumed war upon the Welsh.

In November, as the king and Council began a preliminary eyre of the shire courts to restore order in the land, Simon with a hundred knights rode with the royal company as far as Worcester. Then he and his troops crossed the Severn in boats and joined forces with Llewellyn.

"I had not thought I'd live to see the day when English knights would come to our defense against Englishmen," the Welsh prince beamed, his broad face framed by his curly hair, a picture of happiness. "Lord Earl, you keep your promises."

"It was with much thanks to your archers that we won our government," Simon replied with graciousness, and truth.

"No," Llewellyn shook his head. "At Lewes you won by the Hand of God." When a passage of quiet seemed to give him opportunity, he broached another subject. "I pray for another promise to be kept. I've been told that you have brought your daughter from France. Might we look to a confirmed betrothal?"

Simon smiled. The Welsh leader had proved himself, and though a link with one of Henry's daughters would be preferable politically, he liked Llewellyn and was pleased he wished this joining with his own family. "It's time that you and Eleanor met. Yet there is time enough, when our peace is secure, for a wedding to seal our peace. Will you be my guest at Kenilworth at Christmastide?"

With the aid of Welsh scouts, Mortimer and his forces were found and pursued into hiding in the rough lands of the west. Then, at Montgomery, the March lords intercepted the Earl's forces and gave battle. Badly beaten, they surrendered. As punishment, more to convince them of the wisdom of obedience than do them any long-term hurt, Mortimer and his allies were banished to Ireland for a year.

Then the Steward of the Realm, worker of peace, retired from both Court and field and took Llewellyn to Kenilworth as his guest for Christmas and his first meeting with Eleanor la demoiselle Montfort, his betrothed.

# Chapter Twenty

## THE BETROTHED
### 1264

Simon looked upon the peculiar circumstance of his life in England with deeply divided feelings. Pragmatic in his religious beliefs, he held to Christ's injunction, *Know the tree by its fruit.* Would a God of infinite wisdom use rapine to bring about an age in which the governance was put into the hands of common men? What stronger argument against their worthiness to govern themselves, than the behavior the folk were showing, given their freedom?

Yet the victory at Lewes seemed inexplicable. Simon's knowledge of military craft forced him to accept that while his strategy had been well-thought, the conquest by his few young knights so massively outnumbered and out-skilled was a true miracle. And now every means he tried to free himself of England was obstructed, seemingly as Walter argued, by the Hand of God. The hand was actually the Legate Folques'.

Of his popularity – the better word was worship though he blocked it from his mind – wherever he went the villeins knelt by the roadside, crossing themselves and reaching out to touch his horse's mantle. He was profoundly displeased. Yet it made possible his influencing the government without directly taking part in it.

So he faced his life in a spirit of resignation, touched with some bitter humor. Mankind was treacherous. And God, for whatever reason, had made him His plaything.

At Kenilworth the Countess Eleanor presided, with two recently arrived royal guests, Prince Edward and Richard the King of the Germans. A troop of young March lords had launched a surprise attack on their prison at Wallingford and succeeded so far as to break through to the courtyard. Guy de Montfort, in charge of the castle, had brought Edward, shackled, to the battlement. His sword blade at the prince's bared throat, he demanded the attackers leave, drawing the blade across the pale skin till those below could see the prince bleed. The Marchers retreated. Edward and Richard were transferred under heavy guard to Kenilworth where their keeping was more secure. Edward had never taken much interest in Guy; now he hated him, but otherwise he was happy with his change of lodgment.

The hall at Kenilworth was bedecked with greens for Christmas. On facing walls, ropes of holly swagged the draperies of the three soaring arches. The tiled floor was deep in rushes scented with mint. A suitable feast was planned for Christmas Day, and the servants and cooks were busy preparing.

Richard, the King of the Germans, sat in Simon's great oak chair at the head of the table on the dais, reading. He had been given free use of the earl's chest of books. Having rummaged through Cato's speeches, Caesar's Gallic Wars and pious saintly commentaries, dipped briefly into Grosseteste's work *On Tyranny* and abandoned it with distaste, he was idling through the romance *Curial and Guelfa*. Imprisonment brought license to spend his time enjoyably. Truly, without responsibilities for the first time in his life, he sensibly intended to enjoy himself. His nephew, his namesake Richard, tousle-headed and sweet tempered, played by his feet with bits of wood carved in rough shapes as mounted knights.

On the dais step young Eleanor and Edward sat playing chess. Neither was playing with much skill or attention. As he moved a pawn, Edward's hand brushed hers; the atmosphere between them fairly shimmered. The prince had been at Kenilworth only a day, and that spent settling his living arrangements in the mid-most of the large upstairs chambers where the narrow passage in the south wall made guarding him easy. This was his first hour of idleness.

He had been present, at age seven, when his pretty cousin was born, and he was charmed by the infant then. As she grew to a boisterous hoyden of thirteen, during the Parliament of

1258 when the earl's family was in London and he had visited them often, he had been more than charmed by her. They had indulged in coy flirtation. Now she was a demure young woman of nineteen. The woolen robe beneath her fur-lined pellise curved over a high, neatly rounded bosom and narrowed to a waist that he might half-encircle with his hand.

With a gesture so slow it could not be mistaken for an accident, he brushed her hand that held her bishop. She looked up and saw his lips, equally slowly, assume a smile, his eyes, shaded by his thick fringe of blond eyelashes, regarding her. She blushed, torn between an impulse to draw back her hand or leave it where it was, pretending to ignore his touch.

Paying poor attention, Edward moved his queen and found his king in checkmate by her bishop. "Well, well, my heart, you win," he laughed, his eyes meeting hers, and holding hers locked in his blue stare.

Eleanor's face flushed rosy pink, bordered by her neatly combed and plaited brown hair. She picked up the chess pieces and put them back into their box. "You let me win that." Shyly, she lowered her eyes from the gaze that didn't leave her. "I won't play with you unless you treat me like a grown person. I'm not a child you have to coddle with easy wins."

Edward glanced away, resettling himself upon the step, his fingers clasped comfortably about his folded, long, well-muscled, crimson-stockinged legs. "I made a mistake. I wasn't at all intending to treat you as a child, cousin. Quite the contrary. Have you no other games to pass the time?"

Alarmed by her response to him, her agitation, Eleanor breathed steadily and deeply, trying to suppress the heat that kept rising to her cheeks. "I think not," she said untruthfully, she wasn't certain why. "I could play my lute for you. I'm not very good…"

"I am."

"Then you'll criticize me."

"I'll teach you. Fetch your lute."

In a few moments Eleanor returned with a fine Parisian lute, its belly formed in elegant stripes of light and dark woods.

Edward was sitting on the top step of the dais, his length of crimson legs spread wide below his short velvet riding robe. "Come, I'll show you the manner of fingering I learned from the troubadour Elie Rudel. My dukedom of Gascony's infested with good musicians." He motioned her to sit on the step below him, in the angle of his legs.

She hesitated, then sat, his long limbs extending on each side of her. He bent over her, taking her hands, and his breath was very warm against her neck. A straying blond curl brushed her cheek. With her hands in his, he carefully arranged each finger on the strings. "Now, try the stroke," he murmured in her ear. Her hands, held firmly in his, brought a lovely chord from the instrument. "Easy, isn't it," he whispered. Then, still holding both her hands, he played a slow, melodic phrase.

"It's beautiful," she breathed, barely able to speak as he deftly moved her fingers over the strings.

"And this…" He pressed her finger to a string and moved it, sliding while it sounded, letting the tone rise with a sob like a startled bird.

"Oh… yes," she murmured, encircled by his arms, warm in the hold of the beautiful, gallant, taunting, dangerous cousin who had teased her dreams ever since his visits years ago. In those days she had nurtured a sly bond between them, a bond naughtily alluring. Now, in his embrace, she felt unstrung, her fingers limp and not of her controlling even had she wanted to move them other than how he guided. She felt possessed of him, the lute firm to her bosom and her furred pelisse, his warm thighs pressing against her sides where the pelisse opened to the body-clinging woolen robe beneath.

Ought she to escape? To get up, flee to her room? Insult him – and escape from what? Her mind replied to the clutch of anxiety with a spark of the old impishness. He was merely teaching her the secrets of the lute.

She relinquished herself to his tutoring. Between his holding thighs, her breath came quicker as she let herself sink to a honeyed, heated languidness that floated in the music's flow, her only motion guided by his hands enclosing hers. The cutting strings, pressed much firmer than she would do, hurt and sent pain through her arms. But it was another sensation, elsewhere, in a part of her she had not known existed, but was drawing her mind with a fascination that was empty of all thought, and was pure sweetness. The mind-luring sensation began to make the quickening music seem distant as her new focus grew more intense – until its strain held her whole body taut, rigid between his legs, straining – toward what? Her fingers clutched hard in his grip as the breath-stopping high edge of the sensation drew all her being to itself, holding her tight to the brink of its suspense. For some time their joined hands had been moving faster over the strings, gaining tempo from the first languidly stroked melody, to reach now a crescendo of long, loud plunging strokes of chords that, gasping, took her beyond the edge and left her quivering and pulsing, panting with sweet, insistent throbs that she had never felt before.

She leaned her head on Edward's arm, her breath in long, slow sighs of contentment like full wakefulness in the depths of dreamless sleep. Her face was flushed, and the quivering still leapt within her. She thought she should be alarmed but the sensation was too sweet.

Into her ear Edward murmured, "What music can do to us, cousin! Am I not a good teacher?" She felt something firm and moist slip across her neck where her long braids parted, and she realized it was his tongue.

As the melody had grown wilder, Richard glanced up from his reading but saw nothing more than Edward giving young Eleanor an impressive lesson on the lute.

The prince lifted the relaxed slim-fingered hand he held and pressed it to his lips. "We must study together often while I'm here. Until you're quite proficient? Shall we try another tune, or do you need a rest?"

Just then, from the barbican at the far gate came a horn call. The earl and his expected guests were arriving at the braye. In moments the countess' steward Trubody dashed from the foyer door and crossed the hall to the stairs, hurrying to the bell tower.

Edward stood up and brushed his velvet tunic smooth. Eleanor stood, quite flushed, feeling confused but with enough presence of mind to try to hide it. She glanced at him, a little frightened, but his expression was as unconcerned as if she were not in the room.

Richard went on reading.

The countess came down from the floor above, took her young son by the hand, drawing him from his concentrated play beneath the table, and motioned to her daughter to join her outside. Above, the bell in the tower began ringing in loud welcome. The earl was arriving with his one daughter's betrothed.

The cortege, the red fork-tailed lion flag and Llewellyn's wyvern banner fluttering at the fore, emerged from the high walls of the causeway and crossed the outer yard, where the arriving company of knights and mounted soldiers broke rank to settle into camp while the earl and his guest rode on.

The inner gate was held open by Gobehasty, with the countess's servants Garbage and Slingaway ready to take the horses. Simon and Llewellyn rode to the foyer steps where Countess Eleanor, her daughter and youngest son stood waiting, smiling in the bright December sunlight.

Simon's trim beard bracketed a smile full of open happiness at being home.

Llewellyn pulled his stare from the blushing young woman standing at her mother's side and bowed from his saddle to the countess, then dismounted and bowed again, deeply and formally, to the lady who was to be his mother-in-law. Only then did he permit himself to scan his bride-to-be from head to hem of robe.

At his look, though it was gentle and appreciative, young Eleanor became so hot with blushing that she thought she might faint. She had exchanged letters with this man when she was thirteen and had pictured him quite differently: tall, a darker version of her cousin, and dressed in rags. Here was a man stocky of stature, dressed as any lord might be, with ears that protruded like wings from his curling, short and dull brown hair. She could perceive all this with her mind, though her body was protesting with a flurry of new throbs. The fainting sensation rose again, stronger, making her totter. Her mother quickly grasped her arm.

"The lord, Prince of northern Wales, Llewellyn, my lady the Countess Eleanor, my daughter Eleanor, and my son Richard," Simon introduced them, looking at his wavering daughter, perplexed. He moved to his wife to embrace her but found his limp daughter thrust in his arms. With a laugh the countess muttered, "I think she's overcome by meeting her betrothed."

In her father's strong hold, young Eleanor recovered herself and stood on her feet, blushing deeply in the midst of her father and mother's kiss of greeting. The three separated, Simon stepping back to present again the Prince of North Wales.

"Welcome, Prince Llewellyn," the countess smiled to the lord whose grandfather, as term of an earlier treaty, was husband to her eldest sister Joan. Marriage links between the Plantagenets and the princes of Wales had been formed before. But Llewellyn was not that sister's grandson and no relation that would bar a joining due to consanguinity.

She held out her hand to Llewellyn, who took it, kneeling on one knee gallantly. "My lady, I am your servant. I hope to deserve the happiness you and your husband grant me."

Pleased with his unimaginative but gracious response, the countess raised him up, handing him to young Eleanor, whom she hoped was enough restored to behave with proper cheer. "This is my daughter…"

The earl and countess, with young Richard by the hand, went up the foyer steps, leaving the betrothed pair together to follow them.

Eleanor stared at the man dressed in dusty velvet, his thick legs in purple stockings that ill matched his tunic and red woolen cloak. They had been betrothed for six years, with varying commitment in the twists of politics, but now it seemed they would indeed be wed. Her brain reeled at the thought, though this morning she had been looking forward to this meeting. She tried to force her mind back to her calm and happy disposition a few hours ago.

Of the letters they had exchanged when she was still a child, his were in verse, translated from the Welsh of his own poetry, hers the usual scribblings of a girl's inconsequential news. She had grown fond of him, delighted with his pretty, amorous songs. He, revering her father and bound by the necessary treaty, had nurtured a mild imaginary pleasure to a warmth he could conceive as passionate desire for the bride that must be his.

He reached to take her hand. She noticed he was hardly taller than she was, and her gaze kept drifting to the ears that stuck out through his hair. She felt his warm, fleshy hand press hers. The sensation seemed perverse after Edward's strong, slender-fingered grasp. Her breath caught at the recollection. Her blush rose fast again.

Llewellyn wondered at this extreme modesty, and let her hand go.

Music sounded as the door of the hall opened and the earl, the countess and child Richard went in.

Edward was perched with one hip resting on the table on the dais, playing a loud and fast *estampe* on the lute, as King Richard tried to read. The prince set the lute on the table and Richard laid aside his book, but neither stood – their remaining seated a deliberate expression of their superior rank above their jailer and his ally.

The earl and Llewellyn, coming in, gave bows in the direction of the king and prince in recognition of the deference that was their due.

Edward was glorious as usual with his brilliant corona of blond curls, his face acclaimed for angelic beauty, his very short, expensive crimson tunic making impressive display of his long muscular legs. His slender, pale hand rested, relaxed and idly innocent at his groin. His eyes met his deeply blushing young cousin's eyes and he gave a slight smile, then he turned his blue stare coldly to the man who was his rival as lord of Wales.

Llewellyn felt the very hairs on the back of his neck raise like hackles. He had met Edward's forces in battle and sometimes defeated them. But here in the refinement of a high noble home he felt outmatched in ways obvious, and in ways only his instincts seemed to fathom, for to doubt the purity of his bride was to question the earl's decency.

The countess, the earl, everyone but the three young people, seemed oblivious to the exchange that was no more than a motionless posture and meeting of eyes. The countess directed the betrothed pair to where a cushion made a soft seat of the lowest step of the embrasure of a window arch.

Servants came to the table with chairs, goblets and a ewer. Richard, with no intention of giving up the great, carved seat of the master of the house, was unchallenged and everything was arranged around him.

Edward, unhitching his supple leg from the table, taking the lute with him, sat on the top step, where he had sat before, strumming a tune softly to himself. He let his fingers delicately play over the strings, his golden eyelashes screening his eyes. He seemed to ignore all but his music.

The tune, for young Eleanor, was a light variation on what she had just been taught, and moved her as if she breathed in fire. Her color still very high, she tried to pay attention to the man beside her, who seemed rather distracted by the music as well.

Llewellyn spoke in a low voice meant only for her ear. "Your cousin, you understand, is my enemy?"

Slowly she nodded. She knew that of course. But her heart gripped, wondering what he meant in saying the obvious just then.

"He may do what he can to hurt me," the Welshman murmured, seeking to draw her gaze. There was in his tone the same tenderness and vulnerability that she remembered in his letters. "You do understand my meaning?" he asked uncertainly.

She took a long breath and managed to sound almost righteously offended. "I am to be your wife," she said, as if that ended further discussion along that vein. She was not practiced at dissembling, but she was learning.

The evening brought a feast, then everyone retired, Edward, Richard and her parents to the large rooms above, she and her little brother each to their own small rooms on the same floor but in the corner towers; Llewellyn to guest accommodations built into the barracks in the outer yard.

By the next morning Guy and Simon Fils had arrived to spend the holiday. The Montfort family was assembled, except for Amaury, now treasurer for the Archbishop of York, and Henry at Dover.

Greeting was strained between Guy and Edward who still bore the long red welt across his neck from Guy's blade. "Good morning, cousin," Guy said with a sharp light in his eyes. The prince coldly returned his look and silently resumed reading the little volume of Julius Caesar that his uncle Richard had discarded in search of lighter matter.

The earl, his Welsh guest and his sons Guy and Simon left soon afterward to run the countess' allaunts at deer in what remained of Kenilworth's forest after the builders' predations.

When they were gone, and the countess was fully occupied elsewhere with Trubody, planning the next several days' meals, Edward idly laid down his book and rose from his perch on the table. He strolled up the winding staircase, looking for his cousin. Four years of his childhood largely had been spent at Kenilworth. He knew the castle's every room, but it was not until he reached the roof, with its three small chambers in the corner towers, that he found her in the old schoolroom, reading a crumpled packet of letters. They were Llewellyn's verses and she conned them with a student's determination.

Edward quietly sat down beside her on the bench. She braced herself and attempted to keep on reading while trying to think of how to fend him off. Refusing to acknowledge him, she sat staring at the creased piece of parchment in her hand, but any actual reading had halted.

With his swordsman's strong fingers he gently stroked the little coiling tendrils of brown hair where her braids parted at the back of her neck, then he drew her thick maiden braids back over her shoulders, arranging them with delicacy till he seemed satisfied.

She stayed very still with her eyes fixed on a letter that had begun shaking in her hand.

He did no more than let her feel his warm breathing on her neck for some time, until he was very certain she had ceased reading, and all of her attention was on that warmth, tense and waiting for what he would do next. Then he let her wait a little longer before pressing her neck lightly with his lips.

A short intake of breath escaped her. Like a stalked rabbit, her heart beating hard and every muscle tight, she made no move. She dared not.

He drew back, then bent to look over her shoulder. The letter was in Welsh, with French translation. "Trash!' he said with nerve-quaking abruptness, shattering the charged quiet he so deliberately had fashioned. He snatched the parchment from her hand.

She turned toward him, freed, mobile again, startled and angry, and tried to grab the letter back. But he was far too strong and his long arm easily held the letter past her reach. At her attempts it get it back, he laughed, his white teeth showing, his eyes merry arcs watching her, excitement rising in them with the roughening play. Both hands over his head, he tore off a piece of the letter and, with a lewd gesture, placed it in his mouth, chewed it to a wet ball and spat it across the room.

"Edward... please..." Eleanor begged, starting to cry in sheer frustration and fear. "Please... give it back! Don't tease me!"

"But I will. You can't think I mean to let *him* have any happiness of you?"

"Oh, God help me!" She started to rise from the bench but he caught her arm and pulled her down beside him again.

"It isn't the little runt of Wales you want in any case, is it my dear cousin." He held her, forcing her close against him. He laid his arm around her shoulders, almost as he would with any friend. "Come. Let us tell truths. You love me, don't you."

His request for truth brought it. "Yes," she admitted, turning her gaze away from him and trying to turn her face as well. His hand, grasping her chin, would not permit it. "But all you want from me is to hurt ... Llewellyn," she blurted, finding it difficult to speak her betrothed's name.

"You're making this complicated, sweeting." He pressed a soft kiss to her neck, letting her chin go. "First, as we are being honest, that's certainly not all I want from you. And second, yes I do, but I can hurt him other ways as well."

She tried to force his arm off of her shoulder. "It isn't that you care for me."

"You know better than that." He let her draw back, but held her large dark eyes with his intent blue gaze. "I do care for you. And it hurts me unspeakably that you're to go to him. I've done everything I can to stop it."

"You've blocked the treaty because you claim Wales as your own."

"True," he smiled broadly and winningly. "But that doesn't mean that your betrothal isn't part of the treaty's offensiveness." He let his hand rest on her thigh as easily as if touching a thing he owned. "Cousin, we have known each other..." his words took on weight, "since we were far too young to act as our hearts wanted. You know this is the truth. Llewellyn's but a recent, ridiculous addition to the obstacles."

"Your wife for one."

"Definitely, my wife for one. Actually, I give her only so much of my attention as will keep her busy with her nursery. Her prayerfulness rather puts me off, like the too sweet stench of certain incense. But even if I divorced her on grounds of consanguinity, which I can do, I couldn't marry you for the selfsame reason, and we're so much closer kin. You know, gossip says we're not cousins, but brother and sister."

"How could that be! You're just saying that because you like to shock people. King Henry... with my mother... his sister?"

Edward broke to laughter. Subsiding from his mirth, he picked up her hand and half consciously toyed with her fingers. "That's not the pairing that's implied. Why does your father dress like a penitent?"

"Because he's very devout." Eleanor's brown eyes looked incredulous and offended.

"Devout men aren't necessarily penitents. Has it not occurred to you that, while I have my mother's fairness, in body I look far more like your father than like my mother's family or the king? For years, until I was a hero after Ewloe, Henry never called me 'son.' And have you never questioned why he hates your father, though your father's served him well?"

Eleanor lowered her head. "He couldn't do what you're saying."

"Couldn't he?"

"The king doesn't favor my father because, please pardon my saying it, he is mad."

"That's fairly obvious," the prince smiled, setting her hand down in her lap. "My mother once said to me, seemingly for that reason I suppose, 'Thank God you're none of him.'"

"She said that?" Eleanor looked in his eyes to see if he was teasing her again.

His expression was unusually serious. "So," he concluded, "there's nothing for it, but for us to have joy of each other as we can. We have no other hope, have we?"

She tried to remove her hand from his. Instead of withdrawing, his fingers burrowed deeper in her lap while his other hand brought her chin up close to his. She opened her mouth to object and met his kiss, gentle, not to frighten her.

Edward's breathing had quickened and he drew back. "Such music lessons lie ahead of us, cousin."

"I've given up the lute," she said in self-defense.

"No you haven't. You're just starting to be good at it. You're going to improve, and startle everyone with your musicianship. Really, you don't want to give it up, I think." He kissed her again, this time letting her feel the well-practiced seduction of his sensuality.

The schoolroom became their trysting place, as once, before it was a schoolroom, the little chamber was the clandestine refuge of another pair of lovers. But the prince, experienced, made certain there were no problematic results.

At noon dinner after that first morning in the old schoolroom, Countess Eleanor sat with her brother King Richard at her right,

Llewellyn at her left. The King of the Germans and Edward flanked the earl. The countess talked with the Prince of Wales of the peace treaty, then of wedding plans for the coming summer.

Edward leaned upon the table rudely, idling over his food and watching his cousin, seated down the board, to the left of her betrothed with a shared wine goblet between them. Under his fixed blue gaze her hands shook.

Llewellyn noticed. "Are you not feeling well?" he asked solicitously.

"Oh... yes. Quite well." She turned to him and smiled, lest he think her sickly.

Edward, relieving her of the burden of his gaze, his purpose achieved, sat back properly and turned to young Simon, at his right. "What's this I've heard of your wooing Isabella Fortinbras?" Smiling blandly, he placed a morsel of gravy-soaked bread into his mouth. "You attempted something like the rape of the Sabines, then dumped her on a moor?" His pale eyebrows rose in query as he went on chewing.

Young Simon colored to the roots of his dark hair and his hand tightened on his dining knife.

"You're better off without her." The prince prodded his victim. "She has habits vicious as a cat. She scratches. I still have the marks. Where, it would not be polite to show."

Young Simon stood, bleached with anger. "Don't you speak of her!"

The earl glanced up from his pleasant reminiscence of the Holy Land with Richard. "Sit down, Simon!" he said sharply. He too knew of his son's embarrassing wooing.

Simon Fils sat, burning with rage and humiliation.

Edward leaned across the table again, glancing toward Llewellyn. The Welshman was staring back at him with undisguised hatred. His betrothed sat with her head bent, her brown braids dangling forlornly over her neat pelisse. Suddenly she got up and ran from the room to the stairs.

Her mother, bewildered, excused herself, rising from the table and following her.

King Richard raised his eyebrows, looking to the earl.

"She wasn't feeling well," Llewellyn offered in a kind attempt to cover for her. He was increasingly perplexed, and uneasy to the point of having a strong urge to throttle Edward, though he wasn't certain why.

"A bit flighty? Or sickly, do you think?" Edward smiled, breaking off another piece from the edge of his bread-trencher. "You don't have to marry her, you know." He chewed thoughtfully, his eyes not moving from Llewellyn.

"I will," Llewellyn answered, clearly and precisely. "Just as, one day, I'll dance on your grave." The pleasant sociability of the meal palled.

Late that night, as the earl and countess undressed for bed, Simon asked with concern, "What's wrong with Eleanor?"

"Your squire Peter has seen her and given her a dose of chamomile. He says she isn't sick, just fretful. She told him she doesn't want to see Edward ever again." The countess laughed, half mockingly. "That's hardly possible. What does she imagine? That she must be such a partisan of the Welsh cause?"

"If she said that, keep her away from him."

"Oh, come now!"

"He is not to be trusted."

"He can be obnoxious, I grant that. But they've known each other since the day she was born."

The next day, though she had intended to avoid Edward, young Eleanor went up to the schoolroom at the same time as the day before. She was going to tell him she would never speak to him again.

He was there, waiting for her, playing a lilting tune on the lute.

She took a deep breath, stood straight, and began, "I am betrothed..."

He cut her off, "Yes, I know that. You've come to me only for your daily lesson on the lute. Which will give us both so much pleasure. I've arranged it with your mother, you're to have a private lesson with me here each day at this time, so long as I'm a prisoner. I have the key to the door from Trubody." He fetched the key from where it hung on a cord around his neck and placed it in her hand. "We needn't fear being interrupted by anyone."

Intent upon refusing him, instead she sat down on the bench and began to weep. Tears of helplessness, of guilt, of shame that there was in her heart something that leapt with joy. For as long as she could recall, she had known that it was Edward, and only he, she ever would desire.

He sat on the bench beside her, touching the tears running down her cheeks with the tips of his fingers. "*My love…*," he murmured. "I'm called a liar, but you must believe those two words are the truth. This is no the time for tears, this may be our only time with each other."

# Chapter Twenty-One

## THE KING'S COUNCIL
### 1264 – 1265

Since late autumn it has been clear that an arbitration by King Louis was not going to be granted. While the Earl Montfort was in Wales subduing the Marcher lords, and then at Kenilworth, the Council had turned its attention to England's final healing. The Councilors for the winter sessions were the London Bishop Henry de Sandwich, the Oxford Provost Thomas Cantaloup and the knight Adam Newmarket. Hugh Despensar the Justiciar met with them. Arrangements for the remaining prisoners, the extent of the general amnesty and the ultimate form the government would take all had yet to be decided.

Embracing their responsibilities with caution, though no amount of care could be sufficient to avert inevitable and perilous complaint from one faction or another, the three Councilors took up their tasks in a chamber set aside for them in the palace at Westminster. First they addressed the issue of the royalist exiles in France. Here was a lever that might dislodge the threat of foreign invasion.

Thomas Cantaloup pointed out, "We cannot truly face the world and claim the country is in good order when the Archbishop of Canterbury cannot come to his own See." That the queen's young uncle had never learned his Latin properly, could not make his way through the liturgy without constant prompting, and beat the monks of Canterbury as if they were galley slaves – and they emphatically did not want him back – was not the issue. In the eyes of Rome, his forced absence was proof of rebellion and possibly of Joachite heresy.

"Granted. But if Boniface is allowed back, what of his brother Peter of Savoy?" the gaunt Bishop of London raised his wiry gray brows.

"Along with the whole clutch of Lusignan bastards?" Newmarket added, as if *their* return must be out of the question.

"If King Henry swears to peace with us, as he must do, must we not grant even his nasty half-brothers peace also?" Thomas Cantaloup asked with tepid hesitation.

"I would say yes," the Justiciar responded, sitting among them with the gravity of the Castellan of the Tower of London and chief power of the courts of law. He consistently had upheld the king's legal rights, which were everything not granted specifically elsewhere by charters. "We can expect no peace while there are high-born exiles in France using their condition to wring pity and anxiety, and raising funds for their cause. The Lusignan, the Savoy, will come without armed forces and will have to live under the restraints of law," he argued reasonably. "Unlike when Henry was able to pardon them, no matter what graft, what thefts, assaults and murders they committed."

The bishops de Sandwich and Cantaloup were swayed, over Newmarket's strenuous objection. It was decided the king's grant of amnesty, initially intended to exonerate the Earl and his followers from taint of treason, must apply to everyone impartially and from all directions.

With similar application of this newly embraced principle, the Council concluded that all men still held prisoner should be released: Prince Edward, Richard King of the Germans, the earls of Warwick, Arundel and Kent, and a number of lesser lords still held at Wallingford.

When he returned to Westminster from Kenilworth, Simon read the Council's proposals with dismay. "And if the Lusignan should use their freedom to bring an army?" he asked caustically.

"That can be prevented easily enough," Hugh Despensar replied with comfortable assurance. For years he had resisted what he felt were the Earl of Leicester's overreaching demands. "Didn't we discourage the queen's huge army that was to sail from

Damme? Were it needful, we could raise the commons any time, as we did last August."

"You're too certain of the populace, my lord Justiciar. They've shown themselves a force I hope never to see loosed again. Rather call upon the minions of Hell, than raise the sort of commoners who eagerly take up arms." Simon, the military strategist, put Hugh firmly in his place. "I like this freeing of the prisoners no better. For the land's security, this is perilously premature."

"But if these matters aren't settled soon, the King of France, the Pope, all Christendom will have good cause to censure us." Thomas Cantaloup was rattled by his fear that the Vatican might excommunicate and shut his university on the very proper grounds that they still taught the Joachite millennium.

"So we should release the wolves upon the hens and import more wolves to help them?" With the history of the failure to achieve new arbitration, at this point Simon could not comprehend such abject reasoning and saw it as arch foolishness. He leaned upon the parchment-littered table, regarding the Councilors one after another like students who had got their lessons wrong.

The toughened old Bishop of London bridled at the earl's display of power and superiority. He was commencing to feel Montfort might have more of arrogance than wisdom in his ways. "England's safety ultimately does not lie in armaments and tactics, but in a government that is God's Own work. It is He who keeps us safe, though we lie down in the valley of the shadow of death."

Into the charged, angry silence that followed Sandwich's little speech, Newmarket offered Simon the diverting information: "My lord, we've summoned to the next Parliament not only the representatives of the commons, but spokesmen chosen by the chartered cities as well. They're to take part in our work, shaping what we do with a wider consensus. With special care for the *Ordinatio.*"

Simon was still glaring at Henry de Sandwich. "Good Bishop, we are at the birth of your New Age, not its fulfillment. What you imagine already is done will take a thousand years to reach the safety you presume we enjoy now."

"God's hand was with us at Lewes..." Newmarket said hopefully.

"Adam, unlike you, there are plenty in England and abroad who were not there and see only outrageous revolt in our victories. By undoing what we've achieved by the Lord's help, do we not make ourselves unworthy of His miracles?"

What certainty the Councilors had felt was set into confusion by Simon's arguments. He added as a final thrust, "If you would have me stay and risk my honor and my body for your cause, I shall continue to retain the prisoners I deem dangerous to England's security."

Leaving the meeting, profoundly irritated, Simon went searching for his fellow Nominators, Clare and the Bishop Berkstead. He found the young Earl of Gloucester first. "We must remove these Councilors! They're drunk with what success we've had and are wanting to bring back the exiles and release our prisoners."

"That would be inconvenient, wouldn't it." Clare, lounging, reading in a cushioned oriel of his family's London manse, deliberately ignored the courtesy of rising at the earl's entrance. "You had assumed that you could keep the incomes of the prisoners, their taxes *and* their rents, for at least another year or two?"

"Their taxes, as you well know, are spent for the general defense. But, out of personal interest, I thought you might care for the loss of their ransoms."

"I've gotten what was due me for the men freed so far. I've given up hope of anything further, since you've drawn every source of wealth and power into your own hands. And now you want to disband the Council?"

"Gilbert, I left the life I chose – in Paris with plans to return to the East – at your own insistence." Simon stood stiffly, regarding the insolent puppy with the controlled anger of a parent toward a spoilt child. "I'm beginning to find your judgment is as perverse as your father's was, and you haven't his excuse of disease."

While he could still restrain himself, Simon left to find Berkstead. Only two of the three Nominators' votes were needed.

Berkstead already knew the Council's plans. "Yes, they do hurry to set men free and bring them home," he nodded placidly.

"They're putting everything we've won at hazard!"

Berkstead drew a deep breath and assumed a professionally beatific smile. "You've served the Lord long and well, good Earl. But, like any man of war, you magnify the risks. It's time for reconciliation now. For mercy."

"Must I remind you, most of the lords of England remain hostile to our cause. Their refusal to attend our Parliaments is a clear statement." Simon was mystified that no one but he seemed to grasp the obvious. "In their eyes, all we've done is illegitimate. And I am the one who is blamed!"

"Might not the freeing of the prisoners and the return of the exiles be the very thing to persuade them? I wouldn't have the current Councilors removed. It could suggest tyranny, the cancellation of the very government we're trying to establish. My lord Montfort, forgive me, I believe the Council's plan is best."

Simon considered leaving England then and there. But where could he go? For him, at present, the Christian world, except in England, was barred by his excommunication. He and his family would face isolation at the least, with high risk he would be tried again for treason, now with most of Christendom against him.

Only in England, and only if the new system succeeded, could he foresee any future for his family and any safety for himself. Once the elected government proved able to guide the monarchy in wholesome paths, and peace was truly achieved, he might hope the ire of the Vatican, and the world under its sway, would be appeased. But there was no guarantee even then. He was bound to England and its fate as surely as if he were a prisoner himself. He was trapped, very nearly as straitly as his hostages at Wallingford and Kenilworth.

Parliament opened with the new, expanded attendance of the commoners, with merchant and craft guildsmen and men to speak for every town, added to each shire's four elected knights. But only five of England's earls attended: Leicester, Gloucester, Lincoln, Oxford and Norfolk. The only addition since the battle of

Lewes was the outspoken but aged Roger Bigod, Earl of Norfolk, Marshal of England, ransomed from his prison. There were just twenty of the lesser barony, all partisans of the New Order. Among the great lords, apart from Bigod and the few still devoted to the Provisions and Montfort, the shunning of the Parliament was complete.

Westminster's hall was a jostling, gossiping mass of Englishmen nonetheless. In addition to the commons, all the high clergy were there, each with his own urgent petition.

The unforeseen worst had happened. A new Pope was elected, to be known as Clement IV. He was none other than Guy Folques.

No clemency could be expected from this Clement. His attacks upon the teachings of Joachim, on the English, in particular on their bishops with their new notions of governance, and his absolute support of Aquinas' hierarchies, were what had earned him his elevation to the supreme power of the Christian Church. The College of Cardinals that elected him well understood the bolstering of the Church's powers.

The English prelates, on receiving the news, met at Reading and voted for final severance from Rome. They went on to the Parliament with their agenda ready.

"Now that England's enemy is on the Papal throne, we can expect no leniency or fair consideration," Bishop Walter Cantaloup pled before the king, his Council and the commons-packed assembly.

The Councilors agreed to support the break with Rome. If, for Simon, there was any good to be found, it was that his warnings, in large part, were vindicated.

"Down with the legates and all the foreign leeches!" someone in the hall cried out. The fast rising noise of agitated voices confirmed the staunch stance. "We will defend our land!" "Down with Pope Clement!" Like horn calls, rallying cries rose above the din, whipping angry sentiments. The men who were the peoples' voice were drinking in again the long distilled and heady essence of rebellion, and were again intoxicated.

Into this atmosphere of rage, the king's terms of general amnesty were read. The decision at once was that Prince Edward, King Richard of the Germans and three of the earls must stay in the Earl Montfort's safekeeping. The March lords, whom he had defeated in Wales, must remain banished to Ireland, and Edward's own fiefs in Chester, Staffordshire and Derby were given to the Earl, the better to see that the Marchers stayed abroad.

It was a stunning and quite unexpected victory for Simon.

And Gilbert de Clare was far from pleased. Standing in the forepart of the hall, striking a posture of languid insolence that suited his entrancing auburn beauty, he listened to the hubbub, and the rich gift to the Earl, then stepped forward to the dais, bowing low to the king and Councilors. "More lands for the Montforts?" Stepping onto the dais so that he could be seen by everyone, he turned and addressed the assembly. "Did we fight our fellow Englishmen to make the Montforts rich? They bleed the rents that were meant to fund our country's safety. They grasp at every rich donation doting Fortune tosses in their way!"

His words so astonished his hearers that there was a rustling of confusion through the hall, each man asking his neighbor if he had heard rightly, and what was meant?

""You doubt me, fellow Englishmen?" Clare shouted. His face was lovely as a girl's, the sword scar down his cheek adding the tang of bravery to his glamor. Experience had marked him. He was no mere ornamental presence. As a commander of armies he had learned well how to move men. Like a mirror of his father's youthful comeliness and power, he also had grown into his father's eloquence.

"You look upon this man," he pointed to Simon, who stood below the dais in undifferentiated company with the other earls, "as if he were an emperor, Caesar himself! As if he were a god begot of gods. Are men to be set free? Caesar says 'thumbs up,' the men go free. Caesar says 'thumbs down,' they languish in prison till he's done with them. He claims to be caring only for England's safety. The truth is, he gets richer every day! From the King of the Germans, who holds the richest rents in all of

England! From Prince Edward, the Earls Arundel, Warwick and Kent! What do you suppose they all are worth? Until lately, he held the Earl Marshal. Norfolk's fiefs were returned to him well sheared of rents! My lord, Earl Roger, will you swear here, before this meeting, to what you told me?"

Bigod, standing next to Simon, gave a sideways glance at the bearded, bleached face and locked jaw of fury, and shrank from answering Clare. He had known Simon for thirty-five years. Though he thought him arrogant, and was perplexed that he didn't simply seize the Crown, not for a moment did he suspect him of graft. What he had muttered to Clare, in a fit of pique, was true. But he suspected that the Montfort sons who managed the funds were incompetent and that the earl knew nothing of it.

Clare looked down at the burly, aging Marshal with disgust at his silence. "I need no one to swear how the earl's son Henry sells Flemish goods at Dover, as if he were trading his own merchandise! Good men, we've handed England to the greatest foreign leech of all! This Frenchman…" At last he was interrupted.

Simon, his face rigid with restraint, had made no move nor spoken so much as a word of reproach, for fear that if he gave way for an instant he would kill Clare where he stood. It was mild spirited Henry Montfort who pushed his way onto the dais before Gilbert had finished. With one blow to the face he struck the young earl down and was upon him, straddling him, his knees pinning the thrashing arms spread-eagle, hands around the elegant white throat as he bashed the auburn curls to matted blood on the dais' thin-carpeted stone floor. "That's for my honor," his felling blow announced. As he battered the head, the blue eyes glaring up at him, he shrieked, "Damn you, Gilbert! Watch me well as I kill you for your insults to my family!"

It was Simon himself who took hold of his son to wrench him off. Henry struggled against the unseen hold, bellowing, "No one tramples on my family's honor!"

"Stop! Henry!" The voice and its command froze Henry and loosened his hands enough that his father was able to pull him to his feet without his strangling and dragging Clare along with him.

Old Bishop Henry de Sandwich knelt, raising Gilbert's head from the bloodied carpet. Royal bailiffs appeared, lifting the Earl of Gloucester to stand on his unsteady legs. Though he reeled in their support, he had not lost consciousness. As they led him from the dais, he made them pause a moment and he looked at Henry, still being restrained by his father's hands. 'Meet me in the field, Montfort, if you truly have any honor left!"

Young Simon had reached the foot of the dais. "We'll meet you anywhere!" he tossed back the challenge.

"Henry! Simon!" the earl bellowed at both of his enraged sons. "We have courts, and the Council for dealing with such accusations." He looked to the three Councilors, and at King Henry who was smiling, comfortable in the deep cushions of his regal chair. Even the king's sagging eye seemed to have gained sparkle from the comedy so perfectly performed for his amusement.

Turning from the king in disgust, Simon looked piercingly at the three fretting, bewildered Councilors. "If the Council has concerns as to the holdings of the lands and rents in trust with members of my family, we will be glad to submit full records for inspection."

"We require no proofs of your honesty, good Earl," Bishop Sandwich hastened to assure. Cantaloup and Adam Newmarket nodded in agreement, not wanting to seem to take Clare seriously.

Clare, leaning heavily on the two bailiffs, raised his blood-dribbling head and looked back toward the dais. "See from whose mouths Montfort speaks... They're so accustomed to doing his bidding, they have no minds of their own."

Not many heard him as he was helped from the hall. But at the door he stopped again, shaking off the men who supported him and trying to stand on his own. Turning back to the hall, he shouted with more voice than it would seem he could command. "Montforts! If you still claim your honor, I'll see you at Dunstable Fair for a trial between us. A *tourney a outrance!*"

Then he was gone, leaving a flurry of commotion behind him. His friends, John Giffard among them, separated from the throng and followed after him.

After they had left, the disturbance did not quiet but increased. Cantaloup called for attention. He was ignored. King Henry, doubled in his chair, seemed stricken with a spasm: it was laughter. The meeting grew more and more heated, with struggles forming knots that became fights. The uproar moved far beyond control. The Justiciar hurried to the king and, bundling up his mirth-convulsed frame from his chair, led him from the hall to his chamber at the rear of the dais. Thomas Cantaloup stood waving his arms, shouting inaudibly that Parliament was dismissed.

The three shocked Councilors, meeting that evening, decided the remaining issues would be settled among themselves, rather than risk another convening of so volatile a Parliament. The king's and Prince Edward's oaths were still to be taken. And, most crucially, the form the government would have to be resolved, at least for the foreseeable future, which did not stretch very far ahead.

Gloucester's behavior stunned them. All nine members of the Council met and decided to keep the present government, including its officers, intact in its current form indefinitely. It would be this government to which King Henry swore his peace and his support. The grand project of participation of the towns and guilds was in abeyance. No one was happy with the outcome, but plans went forward for the taking of the royal oaths of peace, and a limited amnesty.

In the next weeks, while Westminster readied for the great state occasion with pomp sufficient to impress the world that the Plantagenets still reigned in majesty, at Dunstable very different preparations were begun.

The whole of England knew of Gloucester's challenge to the Montfort brothers for a tourney *a outrance*: to the utmost limit. Such a meet might be fought in single combat between two champions, or might be fought by opposing companies of knights. In either case the challenge was to the death. Although the tourney opened on marked ground, pursuit was neither limited to place nor time. When not single individuals, but companies of men took part, it could be the opening of true battle. The onset of a private war.

Henry and young Simon returned to Kenilworth. Their father remained in London in discussions with the Council. A contest between one of his sons and Clare for the family honor was not a thing he would oppose. Either of them outweighed and outreached Clare and was schooled beyond Clare's skills. He had been fond of Gilbert. Yet the boy's growing reflection of his father's worst traits made his removal unfortunate, but wise, before his eloquent persuasiveness could cause more havoc.

At Kenilworth there were many young knights who had fought at Lewes, and who kept the fashion of undyed white woolen robes. When they heard of Clare's insults they were eager to strike at him themselves. But the Earl had stipulated that only single combat would be tolerated.

Word of the challenge reached even to Ireland, to the ears of the exiled Marcher lords. The young Earl of Gloucester, despite headaches and dizziness from the battering, had gone directly to Dunstable. As he lay on his pillowed cot in his tent, his squire announced visitors: Roger Mortimer of Ludlow, with several border lords and William Maltraverse.

"The good Earl, Steward of England, writes to me that I must not receive you," Clare, lying supine and unmoving, a wet cloth pressed to his head, looked up at his guests. He fumbled among some papers scattered on the tent floor, beside his bed, and retrieved one. Holding it out, he asked, "Lord Mortimer, as you're a true Englishman, what should we do with this?"

Mortimer took the letter with the Montfort seal, dropped it on the floor and broke the wax seal into pieces with his heel.

Clare smiled, removed the compress on his brow and sat up, feeling better already.

After the arrival of the Marchers, Gloucester's camp at Dunstable grew rapidly. Every able lord and knight offended with the governance of England since the victory at Lewes came to join him. Among them were many with great noble family names: Burghs, Plessises, Beaumonts, Fitzallans and Longspees. From Scotland came Bruces and Balliols; and from the king's scattered service came d'Urbervilles, Bassets, Spencers, even the son of Nicholas de Meulles. And lesser knights, from everywhere in England, came until the camp at Dunstable comprised a formidable army. The elder lords, disaffected ever more since the first schism at the Parliament of 1258, aloof from the new government, and finally parted from the partisans of the Earl by the defeat at Lewes, with focused bloody-mindedness sent their sons and nephews to join Clare.

Roger Leybourne and Roger Clifford, among those freed from Simon's keeping by the king's amnesty and order of the Council, went at once to join Clare's gathering force. With John Giffard, who had helped the Montfort brothers take the city of Gloucester, then watched them lose it, they were made captains of an anti-Montfort field. A royal summons could not more effectively have raised armed forces for the king.

With such a response across England, it was not long before Simon learned the contest would not be fought one-to-one, but that an army was opposing his sons. And they too had their answering forces, assembling at Kenilworth.

At Westminster, Simon had the Council ban the tourney by order of the king. From a royal herald, liveried in the red and gold bars of Plantagenet, Clare received the order to disband. In the middle of the tourney ground he held the parchment high, its heavy gold seal dangling for all his followers to see, then he threw it onto the wet grass and trod it under his mail-slippered foot. "When King Henry commands me, in his own right and of his own free will," he shouted to the wide circle of watching faces, "then I will listen and obey! But I owe no allegiance to the minions of Montfort!"

Like Clare's camp, Kenilworth too had become a magnet – for the Montfort partisans. Young knights and would-be knights came to join the brothers. Practice with sword and jousting lance was held in the outer yards. There was an air of festival, almost of pageantry, a repeat of the great tourneys in France, though of a plainer and more rural style.

From the battlement Prince Edward watched with the child Richard, as in his own childhood with young Henry and Simon he had watched from that same vantage when the earl and Peter de Montfort practiced their skills. Richard, at nine, was overcome with glee, picking favorites among the bright heraldry of surcoats, and howling with dismay when a favorite was knocked from his horse.

Edward watched, measuring the untutored skills on display before him, and he smiled to himself. "When I am king," he repeated his own words of long ago, "there shall be jousts again in England." And he added, "Such novices as these will either improve, or not be allowed."

A messenger, sent by the earl to his sons to stop them, failed to arrive. The Montfort brothers moved with their followers to Dunstable.

The fair ground was on a gentle slope that faced the south, a windswept surface where the moist grass, frozen by a burst of chilly February wind, had turned straw beige under the white haze of a sun that glowed soft as a daisy puff in a gray sky.

To the north, at the crest of the slope, was Dunstable's old city wall. Viewing space along its battlements already was roped by speculators and rented at high price. Daily the field below the wall saw practice jousts, though limited to knights training against members of their own sides. Hoots and jeers from opponents were answered not in the field, but by small sorties on foot at night between the camps. Drunken scuffles, the consequence of rousing personal hatreds, added fresh animosities to the official challenge. In each camp there were self-appointed wardens who would rush to break up fights and retrieve their men before they suffered harm. Neither camp wished to see their combatants injured and retired before the tourney's opening day.

The gathering at Dunstable had grown into a major popular event, an event that claimed the attention of all classes: knightly, mercantile, or poor.

To the west of the marked tourney field was Gloucester's camp, spreading far behind the banner of the rampant unicorn of Clare, set at the field's west edge. Ringing the distant rim of bright colored tents were wagons, strings of horses, then a small city of temporary sheds for farriers, armorers, cook shops, and sellers of every sort of merchandise from cups and dining knives to belts and scarves as wooing gifts.

At the east side of the field, in mirror image of the west though not so colorful in heraldry, behind the triple lioncel flag of Henry de Montfort stretched more tents, more wagons and more tradesmen's sheds. Campfires blazed like orange flares dotting both wintry encampments. But to the south, skirted by the road to London, the broad, grassy incline lay grimly uninhabited, a no-man's land. Here, it was intended, on Tourney Day the combat would spread freely to whatever distance might be reached when the pursuers finally killed or captured all of the pursued.

The arrival of so many wellborn, unwed young men provided great occasion for the hopeful maidens of Dunstable and its region. And brothels in the town kept open night and day. The enterprising houses of pleasure, like the inns, and even private homes, hung painted signs above their doors with the red lion rampant or the unicorn of Clare to announce which side they favored. Partisan street brawls were common, not only between tourney participants, but bands of apprentices, urchins and even solid burghers. Emotions were high-strung. The mayor was forced to keep the city's watch on constant call. Though the very air was charged with violence, no one in Dunstable could remember a time when life held so much thrill.

On the afternoon of February twelfth, two days before the tourney was to start, two flags, followed by a large company of knights and bowmen on foot, were sighted from the city's highest tower, approaching on the London Road. The flags were the red and gold bars of the king's service and the white flag with the red fork-tailed lion of the Earl Montfort. Simon, fairly healed now, at the head of the royal mercenary force and a large troop of archers, left the road and, at the walking pace of his great, manteled destrier, advanced to the center of the tourney field.

The busy camps quieted but for the noise of the wind crackling the flags. Spectators on the city wall fell silent. At the midpoint between the flags of Henry de Montfort and

Gilbert de Clare, the Earl halted. Wintry sunlight glinted off the helms and pikes of the professional soldiers following him. The pennants and flags before all the tents on the wide slope flapped loudly against their poles, but there was no other sound as the arriving force deployed in rank and file across the south end of the field, the archers setting their wicker shields behind the cavalry and readying their bows.

Simon, in his black chain mail and white surcoat with his red lion on the breast, remained unmoving on his white-mantled horse. He waited.

Slowly, reluctantly, Henry de Montfort and his brother Simon emerged from their camp and walked across the long stretch of dry grass to their father. Gilbert de Clare, rather more slowly, came also.

The four met at the field's center, the three young men on foot, the Earl regarding them from his high saddle. His horse shook its head, rattling its bit, adding its metallic jingle to the dull thunder of the flapping flags.

The Earl looked down first at Clare. "Lord of Gloucester, King Henry has forbidden this meeting for tourney. You are commanded to disband your followers." Each word fell like a stone dropped onto stone, ringing with finality.

A sneer of irony drew back the corners of Clare's lips. "The king's commands must be observed by me? While you flout every law of the land? Sire Simon, it is against the laws of our land to travel with a private army." He gestured toward the ready ranks of mercenaries blocking the foot of the field. "And you, a foreigner here." He shook his head reprovingly. "I'd call that a severe breach of the law, perhaps not short of usurpation."

Though he remained still as a statue, but for the flutter of his horse's mantling, Simon narrowed his eyes on the youth he had rescued in Wales. Whose father, from being a rare close friend, had become his bitterest enemy. He said calmly, "These men keep England's peace, Gilbert, which you would destroy."

"There is no peace, lord Steward!" Clare spat back. "Look at the men who take my part, if you believe there's peace!"

"It's you who undoes all we fought together for!" Henry Montfort shrieked, held still only by the utter stillness of his father's presence.

Simon turned toward his son. "You imagine yourself to be better? You've given cause for the Provisions' enemies to unite in arms! If you and your brother don't disband your friends and quit this place at once, I've come to take you forcibly, and put you where you'll have the benefit of neither sun nor moon!"

The earl jerked round his horse's head, pressed spurs to its flanks and galloped to the north side of the field. Half his force of stern-faced mercenaries broke to a crisp gallop following him, and formed again in rank beneath the city wall. The archers held their bows with arrows nocked, ready to draw and send their first volley in among the camps at each side.

The two Montfort sons, at the center of the field, watched the clean professional maneuvers. Their haughty postures shrank like breath exhaled, to a slumped walk back to Henry's flag. Jeers and whistles of derision followed them, from Clare first, then from his whole camp.

With the young knight Baudwin Wake beside him, blowing a blast upon a horn for attention, Henry Fils ordered his followers to disband. The Earl's mercenary knights and archers remained motionless, alert, at ready. Gradually the many tents on the east side of the field came down, were tied onto pack horses with all their owners' equipage, and the camp dwindled to a disheartened long line moving toward the London Road, led by Henry Montfort's lioncel flag. The mercenaries blocking the south side of the field parted to let them pass.

The men of Gloucester's camp cried every insult they knew, then became inventive with more colorful slurs until the exercise became a game, a contest of lewd hilarity. But under the scrutiny of the Earl and mercenary force, no one ventured across the field. The retreating Montfort partisans, in the high wind, heard little of the shouting, and nothing clear enough to give them an appreciation of the vivid ridicule hurled at their backs.

The tourney's threat was stifled, for the present. But it had served to provide the anti-Montfort faction with a standing army, and an encouraging idea of their strength.

On the fourteenth of February, King Henry knelt in his magnificent, part-finished abbey church of Westminster, before his Council and the high clergy of his realm. In the gloom of a dim wintry day that gave only a dull illumination through tall, still unglazed windows, the king, ringed by his Counselors and nine bishops, bent over the abbey's large, jewel-encrusted Bible. His cloak of cloth-of-gold stood like a range of mountain peaks about him, as if the rich fabric itself disdained his hunched, decrepit back. His Crown of State, seemingly grown too large, tipped forward perilously on his brow. In a small, weak voice he repeated his oath like an oppressed schoolboy, as his current Chancellor, Thomas Cantaloup, slowly, patiently read the words to him.

He swore that he would keep and honor the new government. And he took solemn oath that should he or his heirs fail to keep this pact, the lords and men of England, in accord with the rights granted by his father King John in the Magna Carta, should rise and arm themselves against him. It was a repetition of the clause that had dissolved King John's reign in civil war. But it was all that the supporters of the Provisions had remaining in undisputed rights.

The solution the Council had embraced was to reinstate the Magna Carta, adapted to the needs of the present government.

When the oath was completed, Chancellor Thomas Cantaloup and current Councilor Richard Mepham, one at each shoulder, helped raise the king to his feet and guide him to his pillowed throne. When he was well settled, Henry wrapped his arms around his chest and began slowly, rhythmically swaying to and fro, as nine bishops pronounced excommunication upon anyone who broke the king's oath.

In March, Edward was conducted under heavy guard from Kenilworth, and swore at Westminster the same oath that the king had taken. The amnesty was made royal writ. Messengers were sent to France to bring the exiles word of their freedom to return.

The Council hopefully summoned a general Parliament at Winchester for the second day of June. The barons, and especially the exiles, were called to attend. It was to be the final reconciliation.

But the Earl of Leicester kept his royal prisoners, Richard at Kenilworth, Edward under the surveillance of Henry de Montfort with a large party of the Leicestermen. Gilbert de Clare had called for a new tourney, at Northampton after Easter. As long as the Earl of Gloucester retained his large company of noble knights and men-at-arms, however much the amnesty was cried by the king's heralds, the threat of war was real.

Gradually, through March and early April, the exiles returned to England: Peter of Savoy the Earl of Richmond to London, his brother Boniface to his See of Canterbury, the Lusignan brothers to Pembrokeshire, where William was not pleased to discover his wife pregnant.

Also returning were the Poitouvins: sheriffs, clerks and bailiffs who had made their living corruptly in the Crown's service and had been driven from the land by the commoners they routinely cheated and abused. In England, but not in office, they found livings as armed guards for hire, or as scribes.

Queen Eleanor, however, stayed in France. From her sister Margaret's Court she continued to raise aid against the powers she claimed nullified the rule of the Plantagenets.

# Chapter Twenty-Two

## ODIHAM
### 1265

After the oaths had been sworn and the business of the Court completed, Prince Edward was taken south amid Henry de Montfort's quite adequate armed guard, to Odiham.

Though Richard the King of the Germans remained at Kenilworth, the Countess Eleanor, at her husband's advising, had moved most of her household and some of the knights billeted with her to her own castle of Odiham. Kenilworth's yards needed to be cleared of a dismaying amount of horse filth; the Mere and, most urgently, the abbey pond downstream next door, needed time to recover from the runoff and the pitching of so many urinals. And too, the bastion's stocks of food and fodder needed replenishing.

Wooden palisades had been newly built at the edge of the man-made island where the rotund single tower of Odiham stood in gold-hued stone upon its little hump of land. Since the time of King John, the castle's only gate was guarded by a small stone barbican and drawbridge which, when lowered, spanned the stream that served as one side of the moat. An assortment of new sheds were scattered through the enclosed yard: a much enlarged cook shed, smithy, servants' quarters and a warehouse. An ample guard of knights was kept within the wall, but most of the men set their tents on the fallow field, their horses grazing with the manor's cows and oxen.

To guard a single prisoner, Odiham was very safe. Edward was granted freedom of the castle's knoll within the wall, and even beyond if well accompanied. The general peace, while not affording him his freedom, had loosened the straitness of his confinement to a degree.

The day after his arrival brought a clear spring afternoon. In company with Henry de Montfort, the prince walked outside the wall, along the grassy verge of the stream. Yellow primroses were underfoot. Frogs splashed away from the strolling feet in panic, eddying the water's slow-moving surface. Dragonflies hovered and a white butterfly flicked past the prince's face, drawing his blue gaze after it. It was a day warm and tender for the opening of hearts.

"Such lowly things have more freedom that we ever know," the prince mused, following the butterfly's erratic path.

"Some lose their freedom from their own duplicity," Henry replied caustically.

Edward turned toward him. "I hold no grudge against you. I've acted as I must, and with intent never to harm you."

"Is that how you forgive your vows to me at Gloucester?"

"Truly." Edward sought to meet Henry's eyes but failed, his cousin keeping his look averted and himself defended. Edward pressed, "I took the city from you without raising a hand against you. Isn't that worth something? And every word I said to you, I meant. Why do you refuse to understand me?"

"You taught me well that nothing you say is to be trusted."

"That... I find painful. What can I do?"

"At this point you're in such discredit, I have no idea."

The conversation had become strained. With no more words, they idled for a few paces, then went back across the bridge, Henry motioning to the tower for the planks to be raised and the gate closed securely behind them. He parted from the prince, letting him wander where he would within the confines of the island.

Young Eleanor had been watching for their return. She and the prince behaved coolly toward each other in public, almost never speaking or letting their gaze meet. Only the continued lute lessons in the old schoolroom at Kenilworth suggested they were anything other than enemies. The move to Odiham had brought an end to the lessons.

As Edward, head bent in thought, laxly paced the yard, she joined him.

"Have you found a substitute for our schoolroom yet?" he asked. She shook her head.

"Let's at least find somewhere we can talk," he said with no smile and no hint of teasing.

They found, behind the warehouse, a quiet spot, although securely overlooked by the guard-platform of the palisade. There was no one within hearing. Edward sat, stretching his crimson-stockinged legs out on the grass. Eleanor sat at a little distance, plucking violets from the ground around her skirt and making a tiny nosegay.

"I miss our lessons." He smiled saucily, "You're very dear to me you know, though not as skillful with the lute as might be." He pulled up a few blades of grass and let them sift through his fingers. She turned her head away. The passion that she felt for him warred with every other feeling. She had been in a state of misery for months. Often she cried, even when they were together. But his presence and her love were too strong.

"Tears again? You know I don't like that. Have I not been as good as my word? You're still a virgin. Are you a wise or foolish one?" he asked with mockery tempered by genuine tenderness. "Our sweet times can't continue..."

She looked up, stricken with the complexity of feelings that divided her heart in several aching pieces.

"What I have to say to you is in earnest." Though he wanted to take her hand, he dared not make any move toward her. They were being watched from the parapet. "If I were to escape, would you come with me?"

"If I did, what would I be? Your concubine?" she asked with a bitter pursing of her lips.

"My mistress. Almost every king has had them. Except Richard, who preferred boys. And Henry I suppose."

"King Henry prefers boys?" she asked, amazed.

"That wasn't what I meant, but there's a thought," he laughed, then mused a moment. "I don't see what they see in it." She looked at him, confused. He answered her look. "Men with men."

"You've done that?"

"My sweeting, I've done everything, especially when there was strategy in it."

"And I? Am I strategy?"

"You, my darling, are a serious departure from any sensible strategy. If your father ever finds out, which I suppose he must of course if you leave with me, he won't stop till he has my head on a pike. Or I have his."

"Then you have my answer."

"You won't come with me. I thought not. It was an error, asking you. You'll no doubt tell your brother my intentions and make it more difficult. It's completely in your interest to keep me here. But don't try me too far. You'll find my restraint may have limits. "

"You mean… you once said if I married Llewellyn, you'd see he knew that he was cuckolded?"

"No, I don't mean that." He lay back, one hand beneath his golden head. Between the long fingers of his other hand he twirled a blade of grass, holding its spinning thread up against the blue sky. "From what I hear of the news of the world, I much doubt there'll be a wedding. Not between you and Llewellyn. This summer or anytime."

"What have you heard?" Eleanor did not know whether to be happy, sad or frightened.

"Nothing I'd tell you, my dear. Except what your brother knows full well, that Gilbert has an army. It was your brother helped him get it." His lips spread in a wide, amused, voluptuous smile. Then he blew the grass blade from between his fingers and turned, lying prone with his head propped on his hand. "That's why I ask you now. Come with me. Soon I may have some place to go, a refuge. A happy one with you there."

"What of my father?" she asked curtly.

"I wish to heaven, as I'm sure he does too, that he would just leave England. Go to Jerusalem. Spend his skills on Saracens. And leave England to me." He sat up, brushing bits of last winter's dead grass from his velvet sleeves, and said crisply, "I'll want your answer soon. Think well on it."

Gobehasty appeared around the corner of the warehouse. "My demoiselle, here you are! Beg pardon, but my lady wants you." He bowed low to Edward, who idly picked a last blade of grass from his tunic and blew it at Eleanor. "Go. You're summoned. Trot off with your mind full of the possibilities."

Frowning at him, Eleanor got up and, without another word, followed the servant away.

Edward lay a long time, seeming to study the clouds that drifted from the rim of the palisade to disappear beyond the warehouse eve, then he stood up, brushed smooth his elegant tunic and stockings, and went in search of his cousin who was his keeper. He was dissatisfied with how his conversation with Henry had been left.

He promptly found him coming from the door on the other side of the warehouse, a wax tablet in his hand.

"Let us speak, Cousin. I've more to say to you than was said when we parted."

"I have only this to say to you, I saw you talking with my sister. Leave her alone."

"I do, apart from lessons on the lute – with your mother's encouragement."

"I mean to see what progress she's made before those lessons continue."

"Oh, she has made great advances with her fingering," the prince replied lewdly, teasing.

Henry stopped in his stride toward the tower, turned and stared at Edward.

"She's quite mastered the *Vestiunt silve*." The prince's look had shifted to pure innocence. "Leafy woods, bird song... you can't object to that."

"I'll hear it," was Henry's clipped reply.

"If you're in a mood for nothing but suspiciousness, I can't speak to you. Though what I have to say is serious."

"Then say it."

"Very well. You and I both know Clare has an army. The issues between us have not yet been decided past all change. And risk of war. What I ask of you, Henry de Montfort, my cousin and my oldest, best loved friend, though now you don't believe it, is a mutual pledge of peace."

"Ha! My dear, lying cousin who will swear to anything if it serves him!"

"Henry, I will never fight you. Not if there is any means to stop it. That is what I'm trying to say."

"Keep your lies for those who don't know you."

Edward's fine lips bent in a forlorn smile. "You itch to kill me, don't you. I can see it. Unarmed, I suppose I'm spared only by the trouble you'd face if you did it here and now. I dare say, in the future, you may want to even more. But what I'm telling you is this, regardless of what you feel, you have my love and peace."

That afternoon, when dinner ended in the broad, circular solar of the tower, Henry required that his sister play the *Vestiunt silve* on her lute, and sing it to entertain their mother.

She did it well, as Edward knew she could, for they had not entirely neglected her music. The countess, her waiting women, even Henry, all who heard her were impressed.

When the song was done the shy musician, a strand of her brown hair escaping from a braid and straying across her cheek, handed the lute to Edward. Modestly, she sat down on a cushion by her mother's chair.

"Now, Edward," Henry, leaning against the solar's wide stone mantle, smiled sardonically. "Let's hear what the teacher can do. I don't believe I've heard you play before."

"Ah, but we've played together so often, cousin," the prince gave an insouciant, sly grin. Taking the lute, he let his skilled fingers strike a chord, then play lightly over the strings, adjusting their pitch a little. Standing before the maw of the great hearth, where only a small fire burned to warm the spring night air, he rested one foot on a stool and set the lute comfortably to his hold. "What shall I sing…"

The countess smiled radiantly. "Give us that same sweet song Eleanor sang."

"Ah, no, it would invite comparison. I know..." He struck the strings and played a tune, trying its form for the words he had chosen, then sang,

> *Si linguis angelicis*
> *Loquar et humanis*
> *Non valeret exprimi*
> *Palma nec inanis*
> *Per quam recte preferor*
> *Cunctis Christianis*
> *Tamen invidentibus*
> *...Emulis prophanis*

The prince ended the verse and played a coda before beginning the next.

Henry remarked, "My lady mother, how well he chooses, don't you think? The singer says he's raised above everybody, but excluded by his sins from salvation."

"Abelard." Edward struck the lute and it gave out a crying chord of emphasis. "Who should know better the 'wages of sin?' Would you have me sing more of it?"

"Yes," the countess nodded, but her son said "No" at the same time. He saw that his sister apparently knew the other verses and was deeply blushing.

Edward grinned, "Probably you're right, Henry. The poor man's in a quandary. Should he cast his seed upon the ground, or pursue the tender, hidden target of his venery?"

The countess straightened in her chair. Her daughter turned her burning face away, and Henry crowed, "You see, our prince is too uncivilized for the company of ladies."

And so the afternoon of music on the lute ended.

That evening the earl arrived with his son Guy and a combined force of two hundred of his young knights, mercenaries and Leicestermen. A horn announced him, and he crossed the lowered drawbridge with Guy and several lieutenants while the remainder of his men circled to the fallow field to pitch their camp.

At the fine but hasty supper the countess ordered prepared, Edward sat to his hostess' left, Simon to her right. The earl observed the prince with interest. He seemed affable, courtly in his manner to his aunt, though reserved toward the earl himself.

With no effort to conceal the grim news, Simon told his wife, "Clare has renewed his challenge of a tourney, now to be held at Northampton. I mean to be here for two weeks, then join with the king and Court to go to Northampton and see that these meets are stopped permanently." Leaning toward the prince he said," You'll be coming with us, Edward."

"Ah. I'm not quite used to being told so bluntly where I'm going, though I should be by now. But *whither thou goest*... I shall be content to go." He smiled with wry amusement. "I'm rather like the prize hawk. If there's a contest at Northampton, whoever wins may keep me."

When the meal was over, the table was cleared and the hall was arranged for the night with palettes of straw on the floor for the newly arrived knights. The Montfort sons' camp beds stood to one side, near the prince's bed and far from the door. Simon and Eleanor withdrew to their chamber above, in the solar. Young Eleanor's cot was with them, at the wall's curve by the hearth with screening for her privacy and theirs.

In the center of the room stood the great paneled and canopied oak bed where the earl and countess had spent their newly wedded, happiest hours. The countess had brought from Kenilworth her fine fur coverlets and damask curtains, heavy white draperies dotted with her own embroideries of double-tailed red lions.

"We haven't been here together for so many years... I can't think when last," Eleanor pondered, undressing within the tented privacy of the vast bed.

Simon stretched out naked on the coverlet, tired, relaxed in the rare happiness of being home. Released, for the moment, from the troubled world beyond the sheltering bed curtains. He let his eyes rest on his wife's body, a trifle plump. She was fifty now and had borne seven children. He was content. With her, there was peace. There was safety, rest, and pleasure without sin.

Feeling the same preciousness of their moment of seclusion, her dark gaze passed over him like a caress. She touched one and then another of the many scars that marked his body like signatures of the hazards of his life. "So many wounds. My God, so many..."

He took her hand, folded it in his and held it for a long moment to his lips. Then, grinning, "Do you remember the time you counted them?"

"We were young... and there weren't near so many then." She was pensive. But the severity of their crisis, coming at last as she had always known it would come, had strengthened her, and made her cherish these rare visits of her husband. Fate, having arrived at last, she found herself not unprepared for it. Shivering off the weakening moment of regrets, she smiled saucily, "We had been wicked and they were penance strokes for me." The thought flew through her mind that some of the scars there now might be from lashings for someone else, but she flung the idea quickly on its way. She would not let it spoil this night.

Simon sighed. "Scourging, I found, doesn't help much." His mood darkened, but he was determined, as she was, to let no gloominess spoil his return, and he kissed her hand again.

Touching a gaping whitened mark where the grain of lint packing made the flesh rough, she murmured, "But the battle wounds are worst." She ran her finger along a mark near his neck, then gently pressed it with her lips. Lying down beside him, the warm skin of his arm against her breast, she risked the question that was troubling her mind. "Why do you have so many knights with you?" Anxiety colored her whispered voice.

He was about to turn and take her in his arms, but he was tired and her question put him off. He lay back, his head on her white linen-covered pillow and said simply, "I need them at Northampton."

She pursued, "But if there's danger there, why are the king and Court going?

"The Council feels their presence..." He broke off, irritated. "They're fools, and I can neither guide them nor stop them. Perhaps, when they see for themselves the men Clare has amassed, they'll understand their prayers for peace have not accomplished peace. And that I don't keep hostages for my pleasure in their company."

"Then there may be more war?" Eleanor's voice dropped. She was so very weary of the years of fear.

"If it comes, this is the last." Simon turned to face her. "Gloucester, Mortimer, all the lords who oppose us will be at Northampton. If matters can be settled there, contention should be ended. Then the Parliament in June will make a final peace."

Satisfied with his answer, Eleanor smiled and stretched herself languidly against his muscular body. "Then we're nearly done here. We'll go to France after the Parliament, then to the Holy Land?"

"That I don't yet know. If England is at peace, will the rest of Christendom grant peace to Simon de Montfort?" He smiled into her large, almond eyes a little creased now at the corners. "You know Pope Clement has declared me excommunicate and under interdict, along with every other member of our cause. Whether that will change with peace here, who can tell?" He ran his fingers through her graying hair, loosed from its braids and spread over their pillows. "But staying in England could be a fine thing, seeing a new way for men to live. Don't you think?" He was lying, but he hoped she would accept fiction, at least for the two weeks that they could spend together.

"You trust the English now?"

Drawing her face to his, he kissed her lips. "I have no other choice." He kissed her again, and stroked her hair, not playfully as when they first lay in that bed, but with love worn by years to deep tenderness. "Think no more of the future, my heart, it is all nearly done."

# Chapter Twenty-Three

## WEST OF THE SEVERN
### 1265

After Easter, Simon with his squire, his knights, his sons Henry and Guy, and Prince Edward, left Odiham. At London they joined the king, the Councilors and the Court for the trip to Northampton and then the long-planned eyre of England's courts of justice.

The king's kitchen, the Wardrobe – which included not only his clothes, but also his furniture, from beds, bedding, linens and draperies to table service, tables and chairs, and his private money as well, along with the entire functioning office of the Chancery with all its clerks and baggage of ink, pens, wax, styluses, parchment, maps and lists; and the Officers of the Chancery, the Wardrobe and the Court, with their servants and traveling possessions: money, food, clothing, horse harness; the workers of all the services that might be needed on the way, from farriers should a horse lose a shoe, to wheelwrights should a wheel break a spoke; and the hostlers, kennelmen and falconers for the animals the travelers would have with them – all would be traveling with the Earl, under the collective term: the Court. And the royal Treasury would be coming as well, for the tour of local courts would impose fines and that would require the Clerks of Accounts and their servants and wagons loaded with past records and the ongoing records of fines. And, of course, a large wagon with the Treasury's barrels of gold and silver coins.

Though the king regularly toured his land, he seldom if ever brought with him so many of the functions of the government. But, with the anticipated lengthy touring of local courts, the presence of the massive record-keeping and tax-collecting apparatus was deemed necessary.

Thus the royal entourage that left London for Northampton, while far from the grandeur of King Henry's Progress through France eleven years before, was immense, unwieldy and slow moving.

Simon's steward, the senior Nicholas Seagrave, recovered from the wound he took at Lewes, rode beside the Earl in the vanguard of the ambling march. The Earl had set his cavalry of assorted Leicestermen, mercenaries and young knights from Lewes to guard the Treasury, the person of the king, and to sweep the long line constantly to discourage casual brigandry along the way. Thomas de Clare, the younger brother of Gilbert, pledged his service, saying he was ashamed of his brother's disruptive challenges. Young Humphrey de Bohun, ever staunch, was there, as were the sons of Ralph Basset and John Beauchamp, though their fathers were with Clare. Peter de Montfort and his son Peter rode beside Henry and Guy de Montfort. None had been summoned, but they feared the dangerous possibilities the tourney presented and had come to Simon of their own accord.

"Why aren't we accompanied by a proper army?" Peter asked his cousin, utterly perplexed at this uncharacteristic lapse of caution.

"I act under the command of the Council." Simon's look spoke weariness and resignation, and bemusement as if he watched the playing out of forces that were beyond any man's hand. "They imagine, if we go in peace, without armed assistance, conflict will be avoided."

"What do they suppose Gilbert has gathered? They'd parry steel blades with an olive branch? If every clerk here could wield a sword, we might have an army adequate to face Clare," Peter eyed the march behind them with distaste. "Must you do as those fools on the Council tell you!"

"What would you have me do?" Simon's dark eyes met his cousin's consternation. "This is the government of a Council of freely chosen men. What we fought for. I myself was the Nominator of these Councilors."

Peter was silenced, but he was more troubled than ever.

It took much of the first day merely for the parade to pass through Aldgate. There was no hope they would reach Saint Albans before nightfall, the usual first night's resting place in travel from the city to the north. The itinerary was to go from Northampton through all the shires between there and Winchester, where the convocation of the Parliament with the elected knights was to be held in early June. It was hoped the senior barony would be persuaded to attend, that a settlement at Northampton would bring reconciliation between the new government and the lords. The June Parliament was being called the Peace Parliament.

With so many clerks in black upon their mules and jennets, the flow had a meager, somber look, though at the fore the great triple lion flag of Plantagenet flapped, flanked by a handsome set of royal heralds in red and gold barred liveries. Trumpet and drum announced the coming of the massive march that would delay commerce and cause traffic to halt. Fanfares served to warn travelers ahead onto byways. Traffic scattered into cross-country detours that trampled young wheat, peas and beans in the fields.

After his heralds and a guard of the Leicestermen, England's monarch rode like a nodding crone, enveloped in all the glory gold and crimson damask could provide. His splendid, arch-necked horse lent living majesty to his presence, though the king himself, like a shrunken bean, had none.

Beside him rode Prince Edward, yellow-headed and superb on one of Simon's handsomest, but safely slow-paced palfreys. Next in the line of march came the Justiciar Hugh Despensar and the Earl Steward Simon de Montfort, the bishops Walter Cantaloup of Worcester and Stephen Berkstead of Chichester, the Councilors, the great wagon of the Treasury and any knights who were not on current duty of patrol. After them trundled the endless black-robed stretch of clerks, and the russet, dun and *bleu de Nime* of servants, then the high-walled freight wagons, sides pitched outward, so massive that only two could pass on a road where fourteen horsemen could ride abreast.

The tread, the creak, the jangle, the incessant chattering of voices, spiked with occasional shouts, the constant blare and rumble of horn and drumbeat at the fore, filled the spring air with unpleasant din, a sound that shook a body's inner cavities like fear.

But it was not fear that the dull Progress inspired, rather an appalling sense of inconvenience for everyone participating and for anyone in its vicinity. Inconvenience, annoyance, and an awareness of strategic error on a very grand scale.

However, the long, slow cavalcade made a fine marketplace for itinerant peddlers and mountebanks. Beer and cheap wine were plentiful from casks strapped to their hawkers' chests. Pies, sweet or savory, gave off their herbed and honeyed scents from trays suspended from their bakers' necks. Jugglers, compounders of remedies and, it seemed, the whole fraternity of trouveres in England, cluttered the roadside, making good profit, as too did the defter pickpockets and thieves. Thanks to the roadside abundance, much of the clerkly and servant section of the march shuffled forward well-fed and drunk.

On the fifth day of travel, as the vanguard approached Northampton, the fair ground came into view, its tall poles flicking the long streamers of pennants, its high awninged pavilion in place. But there were few bright tents of knightly heraldry.

Edward, drawing in his palfrey's rein till he was beside Simon, had a sardonic smile. "This is a sorry meet you've brought me to, Uncle. It seems no one has come."

A rider left the tourney ground and was approaching the head of the Progress at speed. As he neared, a banner-man at the fore shouted back, "The badge of Prince Llewellyn!"

"Let him pass to us!" the Earl called out.

The rider swerved onto the margin of the roadside, passing the heralds and the blasting horns, then reining to a halt and guiding his horse in among the guard and toward the Earl Montfort. Passing King Henry, the knight swept his cap from his head and bowed low in his saddle, "Good king, greeting."

The regal cadaver barely took note of him.

As he came up to Simon, the Welshman offered no more than a nod of his head to acknowledge Prince Edward.

"Welcome," Simon smiled warmly. "Llewellyn's knights are among the few I had not expected to see here."

"My lord I've been sent to warn you. The lord Clare and those with him will not be coming. Gloucester and his army wage war against us in the west. He, with the English barons and the Marchers, who ought still to be banished in Ireland, are burning our lands and those of your supporters and slaying everyone who tries to oppose them. William de Valence's mercenary force from France has been brought to land and joined with him."

"Where is this fighting?" Simon's expression showed surprise and, chiefly, resignation. He had expected this. If not today, then soon.

"When I left, my lord held Clare at siege in Gloucester. Valence was marching from Pembrokeshire to his relief."

The two bishops and the Councilors had brought their horses up within hearing.

"Let's go to Gloucester then!" Walter Cantaloup said heartily, as if the Hand of God was all he intended to rely upon. As indeed it was.

"It is not a tourney, but an army in the field, that you would hurry to engage, Walter." Simon spoke in a stern tone that his friend had never heard addressed to himself before. "I've tolerated the hopefulness of this Progress, but it would be insanity to move any further with this horde of drunken clerks in place of knights!"

"My friend," the bishop countered in a peremptory voice as equally unknown to Simon, "it is England's monarch and his Court who go to Gloucester. Not as challengers, but as peacemakers, to unite the subjects of his realm. And to demonstrate to them the king is free, is safe, and reigns by his own will with the guidance of his Councilors."

"They'll see there's no cause for strife," Bishop Stephen Berkstead pressed. "It will be apparent that nothing but Clare's hurt pride has raised this violence. Those who support him will certainly abandon him for peace."

"Simon, we must make our peace with the lords now. While they're gathered as they are. This is our chance!" Walter insisted.

"With Clare capably whipping up the lords' already unappeasable stance against us, you'll have no peace now!" Simon answered him as if speaking to one who had missed the last seven years of duplicity, resistance and war. "Our only hope is in armed victory and their submission. These are not men waiting to parley, but men sharpening their blades for your death and mine!"

"We go with the government in our train," the Councilor Richard Mepham insisted. "No one can interpret that as hostility. To meet them with an army would give the lords, indeed the whole world, the appearance that the King of England is a captive and his Council rules by force."

Berkstead urged the point further. "Our Progress so clearly manifests the king and government at one, bringing peace and good order to the people through their courts, that in itself it is the best witness to calm concerns of those who think the king is oppressed and that the land is ruled against his will."

"I believe, lord Earl, your views are overridden by the Councilors," the Justiciar Despensar observed coolly.

Simon drew a long, quiet sigh. "Then, like Heaven's Fool, I must place everything, myself included, into Our Lord's hands. For if we go forward, as you would have us do now, nothing else can save us."

"It is the Lord's Hand that has brought us here," Walter said with utter confidence. "What is His Will, will be done no matter what we do."

"It's also said," Simon replied acidly, "*Thou shalt not tempt thy God.*"

"We've followed your advice of armed strategies," Berkstead countered, though trying to be gentle. "They haven't brought us peace. Let us embrace this chance to go to England's high barons, in good faith and open vulnerability, and see whether that persuades where resistance has failed."

The Progress gathered on the empty tourney field that night, making a brief settlement of tents, wagons and campfires. Then, early the next morning, the endless-seeming, dark and plodding file took shape once more and turned west.

Guy rode up beside his father. Simon's beard-framed face was grim. "I beg to ask!" he blurted, "Father, why do you risk yourself by going any further with these fools?"

Simon did not answer for some moments, then he said, "I pledged my life, before God, to our common enterprise. If I leave, the cause of curbing kings to serve their peoples' needs will certainly be lost."

"But this is madness!" Guy insisted.

"The Councilors need time to learn the burdens of their office. What I pray for is sufficient time. And too, I pray I'm wrong, and our unchallenging condition *will* argue for peace."

"Father, you don't believe that!"

Simon bent a deeply serious look on his son. "You must return to Odiham, you and your brother Henry. Take your mother, your sister, all our people to Dover. Hold them ready to embark for France."

"And leave you?" Guy's every sense revolted at the implication of the order. "I'd rather be pitched headlong to Hell than not be with you when you face our enemies!"

Simon studied his broad-shouldered, earnest, favorite son. "God help us, then," he muttered.

"God help us," the Welsh knight, riding near them, said also. An outsider and not of rank, he restrained himself from speaking. But he thought the earl and his followers were marching to their ruin. It would be the ruin of peace between England and Wales as well. He stared at Edward, who rode relaxed and swaying in his saddle with uncaring grace. If looks were daggers he would have made the prince a target as stuck with blades as at a throwing match.

Tears were in Guy's eyes. But his father was dry-eyed and smiling calmly. He reached over and pressed his son's hand where it rested on the high ridge of the saddle. The gesture brought Guy to say sharply, "I'll find it hard to believe in God if He lets you be betrayed."

"We none of us know His intent. Believe in Him, Guy. Our own understanding is no more than an ant's that looks up from the grass presuming to predict the movement of the stars."

When the creeping Progress finally reached Gloucester, Clare had withdrawn. The city opened its gates to its king, and the alderman gave a feast in the castle hall.

Travel weary, life weary, King Henry sat on the finest chair the city could provide, at the center of the long table set on a high makeshift dais. But he only toyed with the dish of Severn River eels so obsequiously prepared for him. He had grown very thin.

"Your favorite dish," Peter de Montfort coaxed, hovering over the king like a nurse with a cranky infant.

A short distance down the board, Prince Llewellyn who, at Simon's insistence had been admitted to the city and invited to the feast, sat talking with the Earl. "My scouts report that Clare and the army of the barons are camped in the Forest of Dean. The Marchers have gone with Mortimer to Ludlow, and Valence still waits in Pembrokeshire." His lively dark eyes looked penetratingly at the Earl's steady gaze. "My father, if I didn't know you better, I would think the pallid faces in your train were convent-bred and knew no handling of the sword." His words were heavy with irony.

A laugh squeezed uncontrollably from Simon's chest. When he ceased laughing, he said soberly, "They are no more than what they seem. Convent-bred. Useless to fight so much as a worm. You may be certain this is not my wish. The king's Council refused absolutely to counter the lords and Clare with arms. It is their belief peace will more quickly be secured this way."

"If you lack men…"

"I have many supporters in England. I can raise an army if need be."

"Lord Earl, if your son may speak without more impudence than he's already dared: an army takes time to raise. You yourself are in immediate danger. Clare, and the lords with him, hold you as the sole cause of dissension. And Mortimer and the March lords are your enemies in proportion to how much you have befriended me."

"Then, if the danger is to me alone," Simon said gently, "there is no danger. I am merely Steward to the king. And the weakness of my influence is plain in that we are so undefended."

"You take a daunting risk."

"Undoubtedly." Simon's lips turned in a weary smile within the border of his dark and graying beard. "But how better can I prove I'm not the dictator they say I am?"

"I have my best company of archers with me. They are yours. Keep them about your person. I ask this not for your safety alone, but for the peace and the welfare of my people."

Simon nodded. "I accept them. And I thank you for your care."

"I myself will come with you, if you permit."

Simon studied the Welshman whom he held in deep respect, whom he deemed worthy of his daughter. Lowering his head, he said softly, "I will be pleased to have you with me. On one condition. If I tell you to leave me, you will, no matter what the danger to myself and those with me."

"You force a promise from me that I'm loath to make. But, if you will not have me stay otherwise, so be it. For your love and faith, I submit, even if it brings the shame of being called a coward."

The conversation had been in undertones, below the hearing of the others. Simon pressed Llewellyn's arm in a gesture of thanks, and of a comradeship he felt for no one else except his son Guy.

The next morning John Giffard and Roger Clifford sat upon their horses outside the western gate of the city, holding on a pike a white flag of truce from Clare. They were conducted to the king and Council and negotiations began. The Councilors were much gratified by this confirmation of their policy of traveling unarmed.

For two weeks the negotiators went back and forth, Clifford and Giffard to Gloucester; Bishop Cantaloup, the Justiciar Despensar and Thomas de Clare to the camp in the Forest of Dean. Cantaloup urged Gilbert to come to Gloucester for greater ease in making peace, but the leader of the army of the barons only moved his forces slightly closer, to a castle of Mortimer's at Wigmore.

"He's fearful for his safety," Cantaloup explained to the Court in Gloucester.

Simon exploded. "He's biding his time! Stalling while this absurdly large assembly we have with us depletes the stores of food in Gloucester's vicinity! He toys with you, before moving in for siege."

Walter answered steadily and firmly, "I believe he is negotiating in good faith."

"Coming here unarmed," Simon lost his grip on his patience, "was coming to a feast with neither knife nor teeth! If you would have Clare feel your earnestness, show him your strength first!"

"I'd have feared treachery more if he stayed camped in Dean," the Councilor Adam Newmarket said with gravity, as if he were a battle-wise marshal of the field.

"Our supplies indeed *are* running low," the Justiciar nodded in a rare show of agreement with the Earl. "Hereford is closer to Wigmore. Let us move there, where fresh supplies can be had if the negotiations are prolonged."

Hereford was far west of the Severn River, with few river crossings to the east where most of the supporters of the Provisions lived. Where an army, were it needed, could be raised.

"To move to Hereford could cut us off from any help from friends." Simon let his words drop like iron weights into the soft, resisting sand of the Council's argument.

"Our coming, friendly and unarmed, has brought an end to hostility," Bishop Berkstead reasoned. "Valence and all the forces he's brought from abroad are camping peacefully. The Marchers have made none of their customary raids against the Welsh. And Clare has promised to meet with us directly, once he is assured of his safety among us. The lords, when they see how the prodigal son is welcomed home, will make their peace with us. Good Earl, your thoughts are those of a soldier, and you've served us well. But now is the time for milder policies."

"It is remarkable how obscure the common tactics of military conquest are to a doctor of divinity," Simon observed caustically.

"And how blind to the power of mercy a man of war can be," the doctor of divinity retorted.

The royal entourage moved deeper into the Marchers' territory, Llewellyn and a hundred of his best archers with them.

The Progress, though thinned by leaving in Gloucester the clerks and servants deemed unnecessary for ongoing peace talks, nonetheless moved with the slowness of a cripple, cumbered as it was by the great wagons of the royal household, the Chancery and Treasury. It took three days to cross a distance normally traveled in less than one. And time was pressing. The Parliament in early June was not far away.

Eagerness increased among the Councilors to have their business with Clare done so they could move on to Winchester and the assembly with the knights. The chance had now been lost for demonstrating the capacity of the king's tour to solve disorders and resuscitate courts of law before the meeting convened. But the Councilors happily supposed they would be bringing the lords gathered at Wigmore to a parliamentary union of all England at peace.

Instead of the quickened negotiations the Council expected, ready to embrace the prodigal Clare's return, the talks at Hereford proceeded no more swiftly than before. Tension rose.

"We fought to free ourselves from foreigners who held the king's richest lands!" Roger Clifford, as Clare's spokesman, threw out hotly in the placid faces of the Councilors. "But the lord Montfort still holds the strongest castles! Not till he surrenders them will we believe he is not usurping royal powers!"

"This is a mad excuse!" Simon wide-eyed with anger, retorted. "Were it not that your lord, his friends the Marchers, and William de Valence break England's treaty with the Welsh, call for disruptive tourneys, have raised an army of the barony, and bring foreign soldiers onto England's soil, there'd be no need for fortified castles!"

"You are a wall, a stone mountain, lord Earl!" Clifford hurled back. "Do you deny that England lies prostrate in your hands? The king and prince your prisoners?"

"Yes, I deny it!" Simon bellowed, clenching his fists in a searing effort of restraint. "Where do you see men-at-arms enforcing my will? You've spoken with the prince. Were he my prisoner, I assure you, that would not be allowed!"

"If Edward's condition may be called freedom, then no one is enslaved who is not actually bound down with chains! You need no men-at-arms! You're surrounded by men so entranced they have no will but to do your bidding!"

Simon's face darkened, his grip upon himself broke, and from his whole body came the convulsion of a long, loud, bitter roar of laughter.

There was silence as he quieted and steadied his breathing. Then the Earl said calmly and clearly, "Were anything done as *I* would have it, I'd not be here with you in Court, but with good soldiers facing you on the battlefield."

Clifford looked at him for several moments, then turned on his heel and left the hall.

Talks of peace and reconciliation were ended.

In drizzling rain the next day, outside the gates of Hereford stood an army. Beside the unicorn banner of Clare, in long, brilliant array were the flags of the Earls of Norfolk, Lincoln, Surrey, Hertford, Derby, Salisbury, Winchester and even Oxford. Virtually every senior baron capable of raising arms was with de Clare.

Simon's squire Peter peered from the city rampart and reported what his good eyes saw to his nearsighted master standing beside him. "The lord Roger Bigod, Richard de Gray, Roger Leybourne, the Earls de Lacey, de Bohun and de Vere. John Aldithley who was so loud with us at the first Parliament, William Bardolf..."

Simon gestured for him to cease the unbearable list of their former friends. Leaning with his back against the wall of the parapet, he stood looking toward the middle air, at nothing but the void, with his hand over his mouth. Past vows, past assurances, pleas that he come from France, ruffled like the dry pages of a chronicle through his thoughts. Deceit and perfidy seemed written over all by some sardonic hand, some influence that went beyond naming. After a while the words came slowly from him, "Louis led a crusade in full faith and lost nearly forty thousand men. I've done what the Lord seemed to guide me to do. And look where my fellows in our shared enterprise are now. What are we to understand...?"

Peter, pursing his lips, glancing down at the besiegers, then at his master leaning wearily against the wall, could only offer helplessly, "The Lord's Will is hard to know."

Heaving himself from the wall to stand straight, Simon replied with an odd smile. "Perhaps not. Surviving mankind's jealousy and treachery, our Father always leaves to us. He didn't spare His own Son, did He. I recall Henry once saying, 'Why should we expect any better?'"

Gathering the folds of his worn spirit, he added, "It's time to see what Llewellyn's archers can do, before Clare digs a mine and saps our wall, or sunshine dries the city's roofs and he sets us on fire." He clapped his hand to his squire's shoulder and went down to the street to give the orders for attack.

With a sheeting of arrows from the walls, and a swift sortie of the Leicestermen and young knights from the gate, Clare's army was thrown back from the field to the shelter of the forest, more than a mile away.

The besiegers did not return. But the disastrously slow-moving train of clerks, the king's household and Court and the cumbersome wagon of the Treasury made escape improbable. Anchored by the Royal Court's amenities, Simon and those he led were no freer to leave Hereford than if Clare stood at the gate.

"Now will you measure the wisdom of bringing clerks instead of soldiers to the west?" Simon acidly rebuked the Councilors.

The Justiciar Hugh Despensar was the first to admit, "It would seem you've been right."

"I have a letter here, to my son Simon," the Earl held the piece of parchment high for all to see. "Ordering him to raise our army to defend the Provisions and its government. And to come to our relief as soon as may be done. With the permission of the king's Council, I will have it sent."

"Send it," Roger SaintJohn nodded.

"Could it be that so many of the lords – lords who were with our cause for so long – meant only a show of oneness?" Walter Cantaloup asked feebly, confounded at betrayal by so many friends. "I dare not believe that our own partisans, our friends for years and through so many trials, truly stand against us now."

"You saw them, Walter. Lapdogs, all of them," Simon said with an airy smile. He was, after all, being vindicated. Yet again. However painful and perilous the vindication was, it had a certain recompense. "They yipped until they gained attention and were offered what they wanted. But they've turned snappish at the hand that offers it to them."

Grief was in the bishop's eyes, and fear was in the eyes of the other Councilors.

The Justiciar spoke up firmly. "Send for your army, Lord Montfort."

The urgent letter was sent, carried by de Baer to young Simon, who was presumed to be at Pevensey.

The army of the lords and the Marchers remained out of sight. But the roads from Hereford were held closed. Daily Simon sent out a few of the Leicestermen. And every day, at a different point along the roads, the sortie met with flights of arrows or large companies of armed men. The Court was trapped.

May came to its end. There was no chance that the king and his Council could meet the shire knights in Parliament at Winchester on the second of June. The meeting with the lords, which had so hopefully been planned as the great achievement of the Parliament of Peace, had come not as reconciliation, but as war.

One dreary spring day followed the next as rain soaked the fields outside the walls of besieged Hereford.

One evening, after riding out with his knights of Leicester on a sortie, Simon went to the cathedral to pray. At the high altar where Bishop Aigueblanche, amid his monks' resounding chants of *Gloria*, had surrendered to him just two years before, Simon knelt. "Father, I beg... take this burden from me. I can do no more. Show me what you would have me do." He lay face down on the steps, his arms spread wide.

He lay there for some time before rising to his knees. Then, with head bowed, he spoke the *Pater noster*, no more comforted than had he prayed to nothingness.

He had not yet risen when he heard footsteps in the nave, approaching him. Remaining as he was for several minutes more, eyes shut, hands clasped before him, at last he raised his head to see who knelt by him.

It was Edward, his blond hair a yellow shimmer in the altar's candlelight. "We seem to be of one mind, Uncle," the prince smiled.

Simon raised his eyebrows doubtingly. "How is that so, my prince?"

"To ask the Lord when we may leave this tiresome place."

Simon nodded, amused. "But I pray for one thing more. That the Provisions will survive, once we have left."

The prince turned and sat on the step, leaning back and resting his elbows on the topmost step. "Though you doubt me, I too pray for that," he said in quiet seriousness.

Simon stood, then sat on the top step, the prince's head near his shoulder. "Were you king, Edward, you would keep this, or some better elected Council?"

"This Council..." Edward laughed shortly. "Surely you won't contend that their judgment is better than yours – or even mine. You were their Nominator! You chose these fools because you thought them safe. It was a grave error to let your creatures have their freedom and dictate back to you. Perhaps that's God's mistake as well. Giving us our freedom to run about haphazard as we do."

"You are impious..." Simon remarked without rancor. His own thoughts were not so very different at the moment.

"Am I? I don't think so. And I don't mean to repeat your mistakes."

"I'm sorry that I hadn't more of your education in my care. He paused, "If not an elected Council, what would you have?"

"I pray you'll see, some day."

"Do you pray that? And will it please me?"

"If aught that I can do will please you. But what I'll fashion for England's governance will be of my own making, not yours." He looked to Simon's shadowed eyes, smiling boyishly. "And I'll wrestle you for that chance, until I've won."

Simon laid his hand on Edward's shoulder. "We two, of all, should not be enemies."

Edward turned his head to better face Simon. "When I was a child, I wished I was your son." He paused a long moment, then went on boldly. "Some say that I am."

Simon drew a long breath, staring down the nave toward the cathedral's far west wall and its glowing, starry blossom window. For a moment his mind thrust out an odd memory of when he was in Gascony and briefly changed his shield's device to a lily, for Job's lily among the tares. The window was no more than a blur of colored light, but he found it comforting. Then he became aware again that Edward was watching him.

"If it is true, then little crippled Edmund shall be king." Edward's lips smirked, but his eyes were serious. "He'll easily be hamstrung by your Council. There is still that way you can win. By public confession."

Simon rested his head in his hand, covering his eyes, his elbow on his knee. "What is it that you want, Edward?"

"The truth."

"Truth? I'm uncertain of all truths now."

"The truth I ask should be simple enough."

Simon brought his hand down and looked at the bright, beautiful face regarding him, its blue eyes wide as a questioning child's. "You are presenting me with the choice of you or Edmund as England's king? If you want honesty, Edward, let's begin with what we both understand. A confession on my part would not guarantee belief. Furthermore, if there were any chance of Edmund's rising to the throne, you'd kill him."

"Oh my." Edward shifted on the stair. "Am I so wicked as that?"

Simon's eyes were sad beyond fathoming. "Don't give credence to the gossips, Edward. No son of mine would slaughter Templars, would break his solemn oaths as you have done. Would blind a child."

The prince drew back, then composed his face to the controlled insouciance that he adopted long ago to cover every feeling. He stood up. "My lord, you're not a man, like I am, who tells lies. I shall guide my actions as if I believed you honest. And may God judge us both."

Stretching languidly, his mood suddenly brightened. "Uncle, I grow melancholic, being idle all day long. What I'm in need of is exercise." He looked down at Simon who remained sitting on the stair. "We've seen nothing of our besiegers now for weeks. Give me leave to ride out in the field, with all your Leicester knights to guard me if you wish, and I will trouble you with no more foolish questions."

Though a stab of uneasiness touched him, Simon said, "I see no reason why you mightn't exercise outside the wall." He stood, relieved that their talk was over, and wondered what it might have had to do with his prayer.

An escort was selected for the prince: Henry and Guy de Montfort, Thomas de Clare, young Humphrey de Bohun and the steward's son Nicholas Seagrave, to be accompanied by servants, hostlers and armed attendants on foot.

The next morning Edward arose in an unusually merry mood, which was noted by everyone who saw him. With his companions he rode out to the field. The unceasing rains, that had made every day dreary, paused for this one morning, letting the sun shine in a sumptuous display of warmth and light.

The prince was ebullient, his primrose colored curls shining in the brilliance of the fresh daylight. His grin was wilder and merrier than it had been for many weeks. "I feel as though I could fly," he laughed to Thomas de Clare. "Let's have a race!"

Start and finish points were set to mark a course along the city wall. The prince and his five guardians formed a line at the start, waiting for the signal. The Welsh archers guarding the wall gathered along the parapet to watch.

"*A volant!*" the prince cried, and the line broke from a standstill to full gallop and the stretching stride beyond. The horses flung forth their legs, nostrils flaring, ears laid flat. They ran headlong. The line of powerful destriers held abreast, then wavered, curved, stretched out, and spun into a straggling skein as it careened over the ground. The archers cheered and shouted. Townspeople waved from the high gabled windows that peeped above the wall.

The first to reach the course's finish was young Seagrave on a fresh-broke horse from Simon's Leicester stud of destriers.

When the riders gathered again, walking their tense, excited horses in circles at the starting point, Edward eyed Seagrave's colt. "Impressive animal. May I try him?" the prince asked.

A second race was run with Edward riding Seagrave's young, raw mount. But the colt had spent his eager strength in the first dash and could not win again. Guy de Montfort's unprepossessing nag surprisingly paced it, then passed it with ease.

"Let me try that beast of yours," the prince amiably asked Guy at the finish.

"What? You'd ride my long-legged rat?" Guy tossed back, much pleased with his old destrier's performance.

"There's more than beauty in who wins the race. Come, let me see what this ugly thing is made of."

Like the crow flattered by the fox, Guy let Edward ride his horse.

A third and fourth heat were run, each time the prince exchanging his destrier for the winner, till all the animals stood with their sides heaving, creamed with thick, white foaming sweat.

But Edward's eye was caught now by another horse, a handsome black colt held by a groom. "Whose creature is that?" he asked.

"He's mine. I just bought him here in Hereford," Thomas de Clare answered. "I thought to bring him out to try his gaits."

Edward studied the horse with an appreciative eye. Its chest was deep, its legs sturdy, long and cleanly muscled, and with full, round haunches set a little high. Nervously the animal swiveled its ears and rolled its eyes till the whites showed, watching him as he moved around it and ran his hand along its belly. Its black skin by the saddle's girth quivered like beating butterfly wings at his touch.

"Fine animal," Edward announced with a connoisseur's laconic brevity. "Let me try him."

"You're welcome to him, my lord," Thomas easily agreed.

The prince jumped in the saddle. The startled colt tensed every muscle to resist. Edward gripped firmly. Easing forward with a sensitive hand upon the reins, and with controlling steady pressure of leg and balance, he took the spirited animal for a well-collected walk once round the racecourse by the city wall.

On the rampart the archers lounged, alertness mellowed by the entertainment of the races and the fine picture the sunny-headed prince made on the glorious black charger. Someone called down, "Edward, go on! Show us his paces!"

"I've a mind to do just that," the prince grinned saucily up to the parapet. He opened his hold a little, and the horse moved forward at a graceful amble. It threw its legs forward with a brisk, extended stride that covered the ground swiftly even at this easy pace.

Edward, smiling broadly, returned to his companions. "You've gotten a fine animal for me, Thomas. Come, I'll race you all again."

"Our horses are tired," Henry de Montfort answered. "You can race him another day."

"We'll race today, Cousin." Edward drew his mount's head around to face the course once more and jabbed his spurs into the high-strung colt's ribs. At the hurting prod and sudden freedom in its bit, the animal vaulted forward. Gathering its superb haunches, it sprang, thrusting the earth back beneath its feet, trying with all its mighty strength to escape from the spur, escape from the rider. Escape.

The wind of his speed in his face, Edward glanced back and shouted over his shoulder, "Henry! See if you can catch me before I reach Wigmore!"

The archers on the parapet and the onlookers on housetops cheered as the horse swooped like a swallow beside the city wall, then curved away to dart across the field toward the road north.

Henry, Guy, Seagrave and Bohun leapt back into their saddles, jerked their horses' heads around toward the rider far ahead of them, and kicked hard with their spurs. Their spent beasts tried to run again, but the rider on the fine fresh horse had too much of a lead and was gaining distance with each stride. The gap only grew wider as the four rode after him though the pursuers spurred and lashed their mounts, urging them past their strength.

The prince reached the road at the far end of the broad field. The ground beneath his mount was flung away now even faster on the firmer footing. Soon, for the riders trying to pursue, the prince was out of sight. Edward was gone.

# Chapter Twenty-four

## ESCAPE
### 1265

Edward reached the castle of Wigmore and there, before Gilbert de Clare, the senior barons of England and the Marcher lords, he swore to reinstate and to uphold the Provisions. And he swore to let no person foreign-born hold lands or castles, or advise the king. Thus the lords and Marchers, most of whom had refused to extend any rights to England's common men, gave the appearance of having no complaint except against the Earl Montfort.

From Hereford Simon sent out messengers from the Chancery with urgent calls for aid. The Guardians of the Peace were summoned to bring men-at-arms against the rebels at Wigmore. To the Countess Eleanor at Dover he wrote advising her to hold the castle in readiness for war. She must have the Masters of the Cinque Ports swear their loyalty again to the king and the Provisions, and pledge to resist the rising civil war fomented by the lords and Prince Edward.

Most of the messengers were waylaid – or suborned.

Royal writ went out raising the knights of the shires and all partisans of the Provisions to assemble in arms at Winchester and place themselves under the command of Simon de Montfort Fils. And to young Simon, the Earl sent the knight Baudwin Wake with another urgent message ordering him, as soon as his forces were assembled, to bring them at once by way of Worcester to Hereford.

Three weeks passed as Simon waited, pacing the walls at Hereford, counting the days it could reasonably take for a relieving army to be raised.

Edward and his forces moved through the March counties, taking Bridgenorth, Shrewsbury and Gloucester. The few Guardians of the Peace who received commands from Hereford dared not oppose the prince.

No word came back to Simon confirming that his orders reached his son. Wake had not returned. But the return trip was hazardous, and Wake could be useful in raising the army. Calculating the time needed, the Earl planned to leave Hereford and meet Simon Fils on the march. Hereford's diminishing supplies required that the Court move soon. So large a company of visitors as the royal entourage was a burden at this time of year, when winter stores of food were low and could not be replenished until the first harvests.

When adequate days had elapsed for the shire knights to arrive in arms at Winchester, Simon had the Court, with its Chancery and Treasury and its necessary clerks, servants and baggage, assemble for the move. Scouts reported that the roads from Hereford were still patrolled. This was to be no Progress but an escape by stealth.

In the darkness of the brief mid-summer night of June the twentieth, before the moon had risen, a procession came out of Hereford's east gate: the royal ministers and Councilors, the decrepit king, dressed in borrowed armor, the Earl's sons Guy and Henry, Llewellyn, the two hundred young knights and Leicestermen and the hundred Welsh archers, the knights' squires, the royal clerks and servants and the great, cumbersome wagon laden with the coin barrels of the Treasury. Clerks of the Chancery, the wagons of record-keeping, supply and furniture were left behind.

The march went without flares and nearly silently, harness and chain wrapped with sound-muffling rags. Even the horses' and oxen's tread was quieted with rag wadding tied to hooves. A boy with a bucket of tarry pitch ran by the Treasury wagon, applying thick lubricant to the axles to keep them from squeaking. Packings of straw between the barrels of coin and against the wagon's high walls minimized shifting and creaking.

As quickly as the wagon of the Treasury could be dragged along by a team of twelve oxen, the parade crossed the field, not visible even as a line of shadow in the blackness of the night. Teamsters urged the oxen to their quickest shambling pace by pulling at their halters. The Welsh archers, with their willow-screen shields and as many arrow-filled quivers as they could carry on their backs, trotted after the wagon.

When they reached the forest, the steward Seagrave, in the lead, opened one side of a lantern. By its soft glow he found the narrow, pebbly dirt track that led off among the trees. Not the eastern highway, but an obscure detour. He kept the forward movement to a quick pace. The big wagon scraped under branches. A teamster, perched on the wagon's hooped canvas hood, hacked away the boughs, clearing the way. The crack and rustle of his cutting was the only sound, as if a night-bound woodsman blazed his way homeward in the dark.

As the march traveled, the young knights, wherever the track was wide enough, rode back and forth urging the men on foot and the long ox team to keep up the pace.

While they still had some of night's concealment to protect them, the train emerged from the forest at the north branch of the River Wye where the road sloped down to a fording place. Without pausing the men and animals splashed through the flowing water. Above, the open sky showed the broad glitter of the Milky Way, and a thin crescent moon rising as sharp and clear as if it had been carved of wax. The long file made an undulating path of blackness through the shimmering, starlit surface of the rushing river. Several Leicestermen dismounted to help push the wagon's wheels over the rocky streambed, keeping it moving steadily lest it sink into the mud.

"Where do you calculate we will meet your son's army?" Hugh Despensar asked Simon, riding beside him, their destriers cloaked in black mantling from heads down to hocks.

"We may meet him at any time. He is to bring his army by way of this route."

"I pray he comes soon." Walter, on the other side of the Earl, muttered. "The runners and your oxen can't keep this pace much longer."

The runners had been sweating heavily in the warm night air and panting audibly; the cool river was welcome. The ox team lapped the water that coursed nearly to their broad black muzzles, but they kept moving forward as their drovers, immersed to their chests, pulled hard at their halters and nose rings.

Climbing up the steep bank on the east shore of the river, the men on foot were soaked but refreshed. Horses shook themselves, rattling their riders' teeth and scattering droplets everywhere. Water poured out at the bottom of the rear wall of the wagon as if it were a sunken boat raised from the deep. The oxen strained against their oaken yokes, but the added weight of water retained by the straw packing made dragging the wagon up the bank a painfully slow process.

Reaching the summit, the march was sheltered in woods again. Near complete darkness closed over them under a dense canopy of summer leaves. The air was warm. Lindens were in bloom. Invisibly their yellow flowers seeped a soothing honey scent into the night. The teamsters' and archers' lungs ached from long, heavy breathing as they pulled at the oxen and tried to keep up with the horses' amble. They inhaled the soothing perfume and wished the lushness of the spring could be enjoyed in less desperate fashion.

Only Seagrave's one-sided lantern showed the pale earth track ahead. Everyone followed him in utter blindness, close-packed, guided by slight sounds and the smell and warmth of those near them.

Their way became more hilly. The woods thinned and the star-washed sky emerged in patchwork. Then a broad swath of stars, stapled by the slim moon, showed over them again. Bushes lined the path's way, festooned with earthbound stars of wild clematis as dense and glowing as the sky.

Panting, heaving, the men on foot were beginning to straggle. The oxen, eyes rolling and long tongues dangling from their black, drooling lips, were plodding ever slower.

King Henry, feeble always and weighted with armor, was complaining in a querulous voice that was getting louder despite constant hushing.

Councilor Bishop Walter, riding with the king, nudged his mount forward till he reached Simon again. "We must stop and rest, my friend. We can't keep on like this."

The Earl glanced at the massively built bishop dressed in chain mail. "Walter, we are all but undefended. We must meet Simon's forces, then we can safely make our camp. He oughtn't to be much farther ahead."

"The road's getting steeper. Henry can't withstand this. He's as weak as an invalid."

Simon sent scouts ahead with another one-sided lantern, and kept on moving forward at the best pace his tiring progress could keep.

The scouts, an hour later, brought no word of young Simon's army. But neither had they sighted the enemy. Simon allowed a pause for a brief rest.

The archers and teamsters lay down under the bushes. King Henry made a move as if he wished to be helped to dismount, but Peter de Montfort stopped him. "My lord, we're only pausing a few minutes to give the oxen and the men on foot a respite."

"You care for the welfare of oxen, but your king you would run to death." Henry let his head roll limply to one side but spoke with a clarity that had become unusual for him. He seemed to find grim humor in his own remark.

"There's no place to camp here, no open ground," Peter pointed out with practicality. "Come my lord, we've given you the most comfortable mount and we're moving at no great speed."

Simon rode up, joining them. "My king," he nodded respectfully from his saddle, "the rebels disrupting your peace may be nearby. We must join my son's forces, or find some defendable place before dawn, which will come all too soon now." His tone was firm but not without some pity for the feeble man slouching in his heavy armor.

Henry's utter collapse of body and spirit was alarming. Simon was fully aware that, however little Henry ever had been able to fulfill what was required of a king, he could have no relief from his fate until he died. As long as he breathed, he was king, the necessary pivot of whatever government there was.

The Earl rode back into the lead and ordered the march to move forward again. His archers, still panting heavily, got to their feet and followed. Teamsters scrambled to their oxen and with whip and tug at halters, dragged the massive wagon forward again.

As dawn came, the Malvern Hills rose ahead, shading the early morning light to purple duskiness. Larks sang in the gorse bushes amid spiny leaves and brilliant yellow blossoms. Moist, cool air lapped the hot faces of the marching men. Horses flared their nostrils, taking in the new day's aromas, gratified by scents of grass. They chomped their steel bits, swiveled their ears and shook their manes, hopeful of breakfast. The oxen snorted ropes of wet drool, slavering and lolling their pendulous pink tongues.

The cavalcade moved very slowly, pushing upward along steep sheep tracks where dainty-footed flocks had migrated, time-out-of-mind, from winter lowlands to high summer pastures, but where no other traffic broadened the ways. Scouts, ahead on hilltops, scanned for sight of Edward's or Simon Fil's army. There was no sign of either.

Nor were there any villages among the mountains, only the rough, high summer meadows of the great flocks of Herefordshire and Gloucestershire, flocks composed of the impersonal shares of distant lords and townsmen, their invested wealth. White, woolly backs freckled the green slopes as far as the best eyes could see.

Shepherds, lounging in the dewy grass with their dogs, watched the strange parade that broached their idyllic privacy and went so oddly bundled with muffling. Amid the armed and chain mailed men they saw one, bent and nodding, with a gold circlet crown over his mail hood, and they stared in sullen awe, watching their king go by. Their hearts, like nearly all commoners, belonged to the Earl of Leicester. But neither his flag nor the king's, nor any flag at all led this mysterious company.

All morning the march climbed laboriously up hills, gathering a little speed on the down slopes. At noon they reached the River Teme, and still young Simon's army was not seen. The Earl stopped for a rest at last.

Some shepherds came. "We bring cheeses for the king, and the Great Earl if he's here," they said in humble English. A dirty-faced youth proffered a skin sack bulging with wads of sheep cheeses wrapped in soft, moist leaves.

"Simon, reclining on one elbow on the grass, smiled to them and answered in their own language, "I am the Earl of Leicester."

The youth flung himself onto the ground and kissed the hem of Simon's black surcoat, then crossed himself. "May the Lord be with you, my lord. And may He protect you always!"

"I thank you." Simon's dark lashes gave his sleepless eyes solemn shadowing. "It is indeed the Lord's help and protection that we lean upon."

The other shepherds also knelt, crossing themselves in the presence of the man the friars taught them was the Lord's own angel of the coming Age of Grace for all mankind. They kissed their fingers and reached out to touch his clothes, then pressed their fingers to their chapped, dirty lips again as if receiving magic from the touch.

Simon was too tired, and too moved by their simplicity, to chide them. He accepted the cheeses and had them distributed among the archers and the teamsters, who had been laboring the hardest and were hungriest. One cheese, neatly wrapped in mint, he sent to King Henry.

Helped from his horse, the king lay in thick damp grass, his back propped against a tree. A shepherd's dog, waving its plumy tail, trotted to him at a moment when he was alone and tried to lick his face. Fending it off, but smiling on the deeply creased but mobile side of his face, Henry chuckled, "I had a picture of a dog like you, fetching a lost crown. I lost the picture when my palace burned."

The dog panted and waved his tail eagerly as if the man, sitting so graciously at his own height, might toss something for him to fetch. Henry patted the willing head.

In a few moments Peter de Montfort came back. "It's not much further from here to Worcester. The Earl is going to move on now."

Still stroking the happy dog, feeling himself a little strengthened by its adoring spirit, Henry looked up. His drooping eye sagged almost shut, but his other eye focused clearly on Peter. "Does the Devil drive Montfort? He seems to need no rest like mortal men."

"We don't know how closely the rebels may be following us. Until we meet with the Provisions' army, our only defense is our speed."

After a few minutes respite the men were again on their feet or mounted on their horses. The nearly silent cortege went on in full daylight, perilously in full sight of anyone from hill to hill.

Early in the afternoon the road at last crested the Malverns. From their high vantage the scouts looked down across the Severn Valley below. There was no sign of dust, of flags, of any large shape that could be an army.

At the scouts' reports, Simon, riding beside Seagrave, grimly ordered, "We must cross the river and seek safety at Kenilworth." It was evident that, for whatever reason, young Simon's army wasn't coming to their rescue soon enough.

"My lord, that's another thirty miles from the far side of the river," Seagrave hesitantly pointed out.

"There is no nearer place that we can stop with any safety," Simon answered heavily, as tired as the rest, and aware that Edward probably was waiting on the river's farther side.

The march moved quicker downhill, the oxen at a shambling trot that was a brake to the heavy, coin-laden wagon's free rolling. Now flat, cultivated fields spread below them from the hills' margin. There were fiefs with manor houses, and clustered villages each pinned with the square block of a church belfry. In the far distance the shaft of Worcester Cathedral's tower now and then could be seen until it stood before them.

Riding ahead with his son Guy and several of his Leicester knights, Simon came to Worcester's bridge. The bridge, he knew already, was destroyed by Clare. But the boats that normally lay drawn up on the shore had all been taken to the far side. The river was deep, fast flowing, engorged with upstream seepage from the rains that had been falling so frequently for weeks. There could be no fording here, and no ferrying until the boats were brought back.

The city wall came to the river's edge and, like the face of an ocean cliff, in the high flow was dangerously coursed by swift, foaming water. But beyond the wall, downstream there were cottages huddled in the city's suburb. People had begun to gather there, staring at the strange, dark assemblage of travelers on the far shore. They motioned, arms waving, pointing to the shattered bridge and to the boats drawn up on the sloping, flooded grass. But nothing they shouted could be heard above the river's roar.

Turning to his strong, capable son Guy, Simon asked, "Can you swim across?"

Looking at the river's fast glide as it spun a broken branch away with an arrow's speed, Guy hesitated pensively, then nodded. "Someone must. We need the boats." Not many men knew how to swim, but Guy and his brothers as children had spent many a hot summer day swimming laps across the wide Mere at Kenilworth.

"Gather as many boatmen as you can to bring boats here," Simon told him. "Row them to this side. If need be I'll send knights to cross back with you for the rest of the boats. By the time all the boats are brought across, our whole company should have reached here." The Earl spoke as if the roiling river was no more than a quiet pond to be easily navigated, but he knew otherwise. He had faith in Guy: that if the crossing was impossible his sensible son would turn back, and he would have to form some other plan.

Guy unlaced his hauberk, the mail on his arms and legs, his chain slippers, his thick pourpoint and padded leggings: all his clothes but his linen drawers and shirt. Upstream of the city wall, watermill wheels churned. Below the wall an open conduit channeled filth into the river's flow. Guy dove into the water at an angle facing upstream, in hope of avoiding the vile outflow of the conduit and to give himself every advantage of the tide. But before he could right himself to swim, the water swept him along, his head bobbing downstream rapidly, not much distant from the near shore. With a mighty stroke his arm lifted and pulled, and he spun a little further out, whirling in the eddies of the flood.

Spinning, pulling with all his considerable strength, his head emerging at moments with a shaking of droplets from his dark, flattened locks of hair, Guy kept the east shore sighted, and edged gradually toward it in a long diagonal that swept him far downstream, but decently away from the spewing conduit.

Behind the cottages of the suburb, on the river bank a crowd was gathering, cheering the swimmer as if they watched a sport.

Simon, with his faithful Leicester bannerman Botevelyn beside him reporting what his better eyes could see, stayed motionless on his black-mantled horse. At last Botevelyn, tersely but with much relief, announced, "He's reached the other side."

The Earl could see a moving shape that was the villagers converging at the water's edge, and then a pale dot that was his white-clothed son rising among them.

His energies spent with stress since they left Hereford, concern for Guy having taken all of his remaining reserves, Simon said quietly to Seagrave, "Prepare our knights to help with the ferrying." Dismounting, he lay down on the embankment to rest, but with his head propped on his hand so he could watch the other shore.

As Simon's nearsighted eyes followed the pale detail-less shape that was what he could see of Guy attended by a dark mass that was people moving with him, he thought they went too quickly from one smudge he knew to be a boat to the next, and next. There was much agitation, gesturing he could detect. Odd. And not encouraging. Then Guy's whitish shape vanished among the villagers and, though Botevelyn peered for him, there was nothing to be seen for what seemed a long time, but was perhaps at most a quarter of an hour.

Then Guy appeared again, accompanied by more followers, at the upstream end of the city's high wall.

Leaving the cheerful, encouraging mob of townsmen who accompanied him as, soaked, half-naked and barefoot, he crossed through Worcester's streets from the city's south to north gates, Guy broke into a run along the water-stroked grass upstream of the churning mills. Far up from where his father and the company on the western bank were waiting.

He dove into the river, shook his head clear and, judging the fast current better this time, used it to carry him diagonally back to the west bank. Stumbling, he caught his balance and ran, dripping and spraying water with each stride until a squire, riding fast, brought a horse in lead to him. He flung himself onto the saddle and came galloping until he reached where his father stood waiting for him.

Bracing himself with a hand against the horse's broad neck, he gasped, trying to catch his breath. His wet hair clinging to his face and dripping down his chin, he blurted, "Boats are all broken! Their bottoms' staved. The townspeople say Clare's and Mortimer's men did it. Everyone in Worcester's cursing them and offering us what help they can. But they can't find sound boats for themselves. Everything along the river's smashed. Bishop Cantaloup's monks have been at constant prayer vigil for him and for us."

Simon straightened, his eyes scanning the dark shapes that were the wrecked boats littering the opposite shore. "Truly. May God help us."

Across the rushing river, above and below the city wall, crowds were still gathered, watching.

The main body of the march was grouped at a little distance from the undermined and fallen bridgehead where the river plunged in whitened waves over the broken stones. Guy, drying himself as best he could with a horse mantle, put on his clothes and suit of mail and mounted his own old, favorite destrier. His wet hair still clung round his head and neck in tangles.

Bishop Walter, who knew the region well, his own neighborhood for thirty-five years, nudged his horse to Simon. "There is a ferry raft the shepherds use, upstream above the city. Or, even with the river high, I've never known a time we couldn't ford at Kempsey."

The knights remounted. Oxen, nibbling to stubs all the grass they could reach from their yokes, were dragged back to the line of march. Archers shouldered their burdens of quivers and wicker shields. King Henry, who had been napping on the ground, was placed, protesting, back on his high saddle. The sorry progress moved four miles upstream.

Evening had come. The vernal sky was luminous with lingering rose-yellow light from the low sun. Blue shadows were merging one with another at a stately pace across the landscape.

At Kempsey the first riders, knights of Leicester, urged their tired mounts into the gently sloping ford. Dark, purplish silhouettes, they broke the silver-pink reflection into bubbling waves as the water streamed around their horses' legs. The Leicestermen moved cautiously, managing their destriers in the strong current. With a sudden splash the horse and rider in the lead plunged down. Neighing in panic, the animal was swept along, kicking, striking its legs against submerged rocks, unable to get a foothold. Its rider, cumbered in chain mail, struggled to stay with his mount. Engulfed in the strong current of deep water downstream of the ford, the destrier sank until just its head and neck was seen, swaying, straining through the bright surface. The rider was gone. An arm broke the sky-bright flow for an instant. A moment more and both horse and rider were lost beneath the pink glaring, seething surface.

The other Leicestermen, halting when they saw their leader fall, turned back upon each other. Milling, slipping, clambering, they made their way back onto shore.

Simon had been watching at a few yards distance with his cousin Peter and the Bishop Cantaloup. He did not speak of the drowned man, or of the ford that clearly was dug out to make crossing impossible. He merely said, "We must find what cover we can, make camp for tonight, and try again tomorrow to find usable boats." His tone was of grim resignation.

The Bishop rode down the riverbank some distance, dismounted and knelt, praying that God welcome the soul of the man who was lost. Then he remounted and caught up with the slow moving parade that plodded back into the hills to find concealment.

Through the night, Henry Montfort and several of the Leicestermen kept watch over the makeshift camp hidden in a clearing cut by shepherds in the dense growth of bushes. On a stone outcropping with good view of the valley on both sides of the river, the Earl's eldest son sat, wakeful and cursing at the slowness of his brother for not having brought up his army long since.

Before dawn, when the first tints of light made shapes visible in shades of blue, his father climbed up and joined him. "I'm here so you can sleep, Sire," Henry smiled gently.

"Do you see anything on the far side of the water?"

"No sign at all of an army."

Neither spoke for some time, then Henry said, "I've been wondering all night why Simon hasn't come. I suppose he's had as much trouble as we in crossing. Or," he didn't want to speak his worst fear, "perhaps we haven't seen Edward's and Clare's forces because the battle's being fought somewhere else."

"If there was a battle, I'd think the Worcester folk would have heard of it. Guy says that, apart from the summons of the knights in arms to Winchester, they've heard nothing at all of our partisans."

"God! What's Simon doing!" Henry burst out.

"Whatever keeps him, we must fend for ourselves," his father answered bleakly.

Climbing down from the rock, Simon's ill-healed bones made him conscious he was asking too much from them. Ceaseless riding brought his hip to agony. But pain from wounds was a long-accepted part of his life. Refusing his son's helping hand, he limped to the camp to give the first orders of the day.

Several young knights were sent down to Great Malvern Priory, in the valley below their camp, to ask for food and drink. Leicestermen were sent north and south along the river to search for Simon Fils, and any boats that could be had or fords that might be safe. The youths sent to the priory came back with an abundance of bread and cheese, wine and smoked fish. The royal entourage, fasting since leaving Hereford, except for the cheeses given by the shepherds, ate gratefully.

It was evening before the knights sent to find Simon Fils, or some means of crossing the Severn, returned. Beavis, their leader, reported to Simon. "People up and down the river say the boats are all destroyed and the fords dug out. They say Mortimer had his own men do it."

"Mortimer is thorough," Bishop Walter said dismally. "May he be cursed!"

Through the summer evening's long and leisurely twilight, Simon sat on a high rock overlooking Great Malvern, gazing at the dark speckling that was its cluster of buildings around its old chapel. An ardent wish that he had spent his lifetime as a monk welled up, and he heard his own bitter laughter at himself. Nearly at the outset of his time in England he had begged Grosseteste to let him leave the Court and join the Franciscan friars. The bishop, his mentor in everything he knew of England, had refused and threatened to oppose him if he tried. The old theologian and rebel, whose extraordinary mind had first imagined an elective government, insisted that his place was by the king. There he would do great things. It was Grosseteste who commanded, *Feed my sheep.*

"Well, here I am, Father," Simon mumured sardonically to the oblivious, empty air. "A shepherd among shepherds in the hills of Malvern, leading an unlikely flock. But I am, as you commanded, *at my king's side.*"

If Bishop Grosseteste's spirit hovered near him, he had no sense of it. Lonely since the first day he came to England, he felt isolation now that made all past sensations of it seem high conviviality in comparison. Staring at the specks that were the priory, he muttered, "How glad I'd be to change my life for any one of yours."

Bereft of strategy, maneuvered into an absurd condition that he would never have allowed had he insisted upon dominating the Council, wandering fecklessly with England's monarch whose complaining was incessant and well justified, Simon had no idea what to do next. The future was reduced to one step, one breath, following upon another... until movement and breath stopped. Relief from his burdens would be welcome when it came.

The valley below and the sky above had lost all light except the thin, hazed moon when his son Henry came looking for him with a muffled lantern to guide him back to the camp.

By morning he had determined what to do.

The Earl called the young knights Eastley, Pelvedon, Beavis and Wake to him. To Eastley he said, "I've chosen you because I hear you're a strong swimmer."

"I am, my lord," the youth answered, pleased at being singled out from among his friends.

"Cross the Severn and follow it south to Bristol, where John de la Warre is holding the city for our cause. Tell him to gather ships to ferry us across the river at its mouth. Tell him we will be at Caerleon seven days from today. Even at our slow pace, we should be able to do that."

Of Wake he asked, "You too swim strongly, as I'm told."

"Yes, my lord Earl."

"Then go and find my son Simon. Tell him to have his army, a week from today, at Bristol, ready to meet and protect us when we land."

To Pelvedon and Beavis he said, "Find Prince Edward and Clare's armies and let me know where they are. Return to me at Tintern Abbey in five days.

The young knights left to fulfill their orders. The camp in the Malvern Hills remained where it was hidden for another day of rest, generously fed by the monks of the priory. Because of land disputes, the clerics of Malvern were no friends of Bishop Walter Cantaloup. But they were of Westminster's See, and their bishop, Henry de Sandwich, was as earnest an ally of Montfort's cause as any man could be.

At the full light of dawn, on their second day above the priory, the worn and shabby cavalcade moved out, southward toward Caerleon. They traveled along rough mountain ways, led by shepherds.

Simon recalled the shepherds he had seen in Palestine. Not driving their flocks along with dog and crook, they strode ahead of their willing sheep. He pondered what the Church might be if the Vatican led in the manner of the shepherds Jesus knew, instead of wielding threatening dog and rod.

The roads they climbed were mere trails etched into cliffs by flocks moving from winter shelter in the valleys to the high, sweet grasses of summer mountaintops. The huge Treasury wagon leaned and teetered crazily, two wheels on the outer edge of the track, two bumping along the steep rocky incline. Men at the oxen's heads dragged at the halters, urging the terrified team on, while other men, archers and teamsters, pushed and strained to keep the heavy, gold and silver laden wagon from toppling.

The company camped on a high plateau at evening, and again shepherds appeared with gifts of food. A campfire was made and lambs were roasted for a feast for everyone. Even King Henry ate heartily of the savory, wild-garlic-rubbed meat.

Cheeks bristled with four days' growth of beard, the knights gulped milk from sheep-bladder flasks. Without the shepherds' skill, streams of sheep milk squirted over their sweated, dust-grimed faces and their dirty black surcoats.

Adam Newmarket found a patch of wild strawberries, tiny red dots demure amid their ruffled and pinked leaves nestled in the grass. He plucked the patch clean, offering his cupped handful to Simon and King Henry.

At dawn of the fifth day since they left Hereford, the company trudged on, the archers driving along a little flock of sheep bought with coins from the Treasury.

On the narrow, treacherously slanted path, everyone but the king led his mount. Steel horseshoes gave poor footing on the stony ground. Horses' eyes rolled in terror at the airy abyss that dropped away from the ledge. Effort to move forward was perilous, far worse than it had been before. Such tracks were commonplace for agile shepherds and their cloven-footed mountain-dwelling charges, but for horses' unyielding broad hooves shod in slick metal, they were nearly impassable.

At a place where a scree of broken stone sloped down on one side of the way, a rock-jutting wall of unstable dirt and boulders rose on the other, a work crew had to be set to hack at the mountainside, widening the path so that the wagon could be drawn forward at all.

Then one of the wagon's rear wheels slipped off the track entirely. The heavy-laden, massive cart leaned dangerously over the precipice, but the wheel caught, braced on a boulder just below the path. Instantly a crowd of men were running to help. They pushed and tried to lever the wheel back on the narrow ledge. As they struggled, beneath the iron-rimmed wheel the supporting rock cracked, broke and fell tumbling away. The wagon lurched, tipping out toward the empty air, and began sliding backward. The oxen, sensing catastrophe, stopped pulling and lowed with pathetic moans, ignoring the teamsters' lashings. Shifting, bumping against each other in their panic, straining to part themselves from their spans of wooden yokes, they bellowed like the day of doom was come.

Simon came round to the head of the team. The men at the wagon's rear were straining with all their might, but the ground under their feet was crumbling and sifting away, erupting in little avalanche that scurried down the cliff.

"Unload the treasury's casks!" the Earl commanded.

Young knights, at peril of their lives, climbed up into the wagon, dug the casks from their hay nests and handed them out. But only a few were salvaged before the wagon lurched badly again, the path under a front wheel starting to fall away.

"For your lives' sakes, let it go! Cut the team loose!" the Earl bellowed.

The young knights jumped out. The teamsters and archers used their strength to hold steady the wheels on the side of the rising wall of cliff until everyone was safe. Then a teamster hacked the ropes that bound the oxen to the wagon's massive whiffletree. As the last rope frayed and broke, the oxen, feeling their freedom, ambled forward. The teamsters and the knights at the wagon's rear scrambled fast backward against the cliff.

Leaning far over, like a ship caught by a wave, the wagon tipped further and further, then crashed. Rolling over and over, crushing the wooden arches of its hood, smashing one side, the wheels, then the other side, it broke into boards and beams, arced wheel fragments, spokes and hoops, spilled hay and barrels down the precipice. The jettisoned barrels went rolling, bouncing gaily, leaping down the steep slope, flagrantly distributing a rain of gold and silver coins, the wealth of England's Royal Treasury.

The mountainside, disturbed to rivulets of flowing earth and stones, threatened major avalanche. The slope was too fragile, too treacherous for even the boldest of the shepherd guides to climb down and fetch back the coins. But they took note of the spot and foresaw their futures as rich men.

Simon stood at the brink of the still sifting, crumbling path and looked down at the havoc below. Behind him, teamsters were trying to catch and restore order among their quivering, still yoked but liberated animals.

The Justiciar joined the Earl. "What can we do?"

"We will carry as many of the saved coin barrels as we can on our horses."

The casks were bound onto the destriers' high saddles. And the march, with England's government far poorer, moved on.

That night, guided by their shepherds, they camped in a pleasant little dell where a stream ran, bordered by tall, ancient oaks. The men found wood for fires and slaughtered half of their flock of sheep, butchered and spitted them. Mutton and water from the stream made up their rustic meal. The decrepit king ate with his Councilors, sitting on the grass, then slept as everyone but the posted sentries did, on the soft turf, wrapped in his horse's sweated, dirty black mantel.

The next morning at dawn the march moved south again. Without the wagon, it moved far more easily and quickly, but the way was still so difficult the horses had to be led. By now, even with cloth wrappings, the chain mail slippers of the knights had cut through their soft riding-shoe leather and into their feet. With their armored slippers, hauberks and chain leggings bundled onto their horses, the Leicestermen and young knights marched in their underwear, their robes shredded for foot-wrappings. Squire Peter was generous with his unguent for sores, but his supply soon was spent.

While Simon remained dressed in his black suit of mail, even he went with no slippers, his feet bound with rags. Only the king, who rode, was still decently clad.

That night when they camped, Bishop Walter, peeling away his foot-wrappings, studied his swollen, livid bruises and blood-caked cuts.

A Welsh archer genially plumped himself down on the ground beside His Grace, observing in rough French, "They're nothing like mine." He untied his cross garters and unwrapped his filthy, shredded leggings. The foot he proudly showed to Walter was black and horny, hard with broken calluses split and oozing putridly.

The bishop looked at the archer, humbled by his cheerful, uncomplaining spirit, then he bent over, kissing the filthy, reeking foot.

The Welshman jerked back, stunned.

"Brother, you make me ashamed," the Franciscan Bishop of Worcester confessed to the archer's beard-bristled, shocked face. "When we can ride again, you must take my horse."

The shepherds still led the royal company on south along obscure sheep trails lest Edward's or Clare's scouts find them. They reached Tintern Abbey. Though the monks were Cistercians, and under the patronage of the family of Clare, they gave the Earl a friendly refuge. Like all the clergy of England they were at war, after their fashion, with the Vatican and looked on the success of the Great Earl's cause as their best hope.

Washed, their beards shaved, their wearied muscles and their wounded, swollen feet well soaked, the king and his obligatory company rested.

Beavis and Pelvedon, whom Simon had sent out as spies, had not yet reached Tintern. Through the night, scouts the Earl posted watched for the youths who should have been at the meeting place already.

The next morning Simon could wait for them no longer. But, as horses were being saddled for the continued march, Pelvedon came riding in. He came up to the abbey gate at full gallop. Slipping from his horse while his mount was still moving, he stumbled to the Earl's feet. His face was flushed, his eyes white-hazed. "Edward!" he gasped, his voice thick from between cracked lips. "He knows that you meet ships at Caerleon!"

Bishop Walter, standing by the Earl and about to mount, reached down to try to lift the youth up from the ground. Pelvedon shrieked in pain. His arm was bloated, his left hand crushed at the wrist and at the joint of each finger. "He's been tortured!" Walter met Simon's horrified frown.

"I... escaped..." Pelvedon whispered in explanation. "Beavis is dead."

Simon sent for his surgeon squire.

Peter, cutting away the youth's pourpoint to bare the arm, revealed the reddened bulge, shiny as if the bloated skin would burst, with a long streak of crimson from the arm to the boy's chest. "It's too late." He looked to Simon helplessly. "His blood is tainted from the wounds. There's nothing I can do."

"Edward is at Monmouth," the lad whispered.

Monmouth was just five miles away.

Simon had Pelvedon carried to the abbey's infirmary where, in raving fever, in a few days he would die.

King Henry, sitting his horse at a short distance from the youth's collapse, observed blandly, "I was born at Monmouth. Did you know?"

Simon had the cortege move on at once. They left the abbey. Now, free of the wagon, they cut out cross-country toward Cearleon, fifteen miles to the southeast.

At noon, with no sighting of Edward, they reached the wooded hill above the town. The Earl kept his people hidden in the forest. He posted sentinels to watch for the prince's advance, and for his ships coming upstream from Bristol. To a cliff that afforded the best view of the estuary down below, Simon went with his squire Peter and the far-sighted Seagrave.

Caerleon, famed as King Arthur's ancient city, perched over the River Usk, which joined the Severn in a channel five miles distant. From the hilltop, Bristol's harbor could be seen across the widening waters to the southeast. Northeastward, the Severn disgorged from between the walls of a chasm. Directly south was Bridgewater Bay. To the north of the spot where Simon stood was the plane of Caerleon, and the Monmouth road to Edward.

The water of the channel showed deep indigo. The sky above was clear, cloudless, a brilliant blue, infinite in volume and penetrable as the sea. Eyes gazing at it pulsed with spots and sought relief in the cool prospect of the bay. The water now and then glinted with white crested waves. It was a perfect day for sailing.

A steady breeze ruffled the grass on the hilltop, bringing with it scents of sea salt and of wild roses blooming on the slopes below.

As their horses grazed behind them, the three sat on the turf, Seagrave and the squire squinting toward Bristol, where they could just discern the harbor and the bulky shapes of several merchant galleys. One after another, in the morning brilliance, the ships appeared to move out under oars, then unfurled their white sails and began tacking up the bay against the rivers' flow.

Simon could see bits of white against the blue of the water. "They come for us. Thank God," he murmured.

Turning toward the Earl, grinning at the happy sight, Peter's glance swept northward. His smile suddenly dropped, and he said under his breath, "Oh God, please, no..."

Seagrave and Simon turned to see what held Peter's eyes.

There were boats, hundreds of them, flowing out from the cliff-walled mouth of the Severn. Under oar and with the river's spate carrying them, they were making rapid headway toward the merchantmen.

The merchant galleys, small-seeming in the distance as a child's toy fleet of woodchips, with oar and sail were tacking slowly and laboriously northwest, then northeast, then northwest, against the heavy current. The boats from the Severn moved as quickly as seed husks on a flood, sweeping toward the ships, then in among them. For a long held-breath the merchantmen forged on forward.

The boarding, the battling on their decks and amid their oar-benches, was as invisible from the cliff as if it occurred in another world. The ships would not have carried much in armaments. Simon, Seagrave and Peter stared, transfixed as a hare before a nodding snake. They could do nothing, though the ruin that they watched was as much theirs as the far ships'.

The white sails seemed to shake, the merchant vessels losing headway, turning, drifting, erratic, then succumbing to the river flow. An orange brightness flickered on a dab of white as a sail was eaten with flame. Spinning, with no power of oars to sustain against the south-surging current, the merchantmen drifted among the tiny husks besetting them. Then, like orange beacons on the water, the flaming ships, one after another, broke away and floated erratically downriver. Had their crews abandoned them, diving from their fired decks? Or had they all been killed? The last ship of the rescue fleet, not yet far out from Bristol, turned south and arced back to its port.

Simon, saying nothing, stood up, brushing the grass from his black surcoat. He fetched his horse and mounted. The other two, stunned and silent, followed him.

The Earl summoned a meeting of everyone at his encampment. The young knights, Leicestermen, Welsh archers and Councilors were all eager to embark and leave Wales behind.

Simon spoke directly, clearly and loudly so all would hear with no mistake. "There will be no ships coming for us. We must retreat from here as best we can. We will try to reach Hereford."

Simon sent his Leicesterman Philip Dreiby to find what had become of his son Simon, and – if he lived and still had an army – to tell him to bring barges of his own to cross the river. To come as promptly as he could to Hereford.

From Caerleon to Hereford was a distance of some thirty miles. The hazard-beset travels of the royal entourage were reaching full circle.

Simon took the march along the main road for the greatest speed, the horses at a canter, the Welshmen running to keep up as best they could. The slow oxen and their teamsters long since had been left behind.

Edward's army, very near, was never seen. Pushing on through evening, the riders reached the safety of the walls of Hereford. Welsh archers straggled into the city all through the night.

# Chapter Twenty-five

## THE RESCUERS
### 1265

John de Baer, the first of the earl's messengers to reach young Simon, found an intact boat on the bank of the Severn, crossed the river and reached Pevensey with no difficulty. But the young lord Montfort was not there. From the captain of the castle's garrison he learned Simon Fils had gone to Sutton, a manor formerly of the Montfort holdings but returned to the Crown's keeping. The fief was near a manor of the Fortinbras, the captain told Baer with a sly smile. The messenger rode on east to Kent.

The gray stone house at Sutton had been taken over by young Simon and his friends. They lounged in the oak-paneled hall and out in the garden, where red roses spangled bushes Eleanor had planted during the tense summer of 1252, when the earl was standing trial at Westminster for treason. Pregnant and unable to bear the stress, the countess had retreated to their nearest country holding.

Very drunk, though it was early afternoon, Simon Fils gloomily gazed at a rose drooping above his head, as he lay sprawled on a turf and wicker garden seat. "I could eat this rose." He broke the blossom off where the flower met the stem and measured the tender fan of petals with his teeth. Shifting his supine position, he emerged from his reverie and addressed the unkempt head of a young man sitting on the ground with his arms outspread, shoulders resting on the wicker-walled seat at his back. His dark hair, threaded with bits of grass, nodded in stupor a few inches from Simon's eyes. "She's going to *marry* de la Warre?" Simon asked for the hundredth time since morning.

"I told you... that's what her steward said." John Evyile, the son of the Royal Forester and Simon's closest friend since the defection of de la Warre, rolled, steadying himself with one hand on the ground, till he sat facing his commander. "Is there no more of your father's Bordeaux?"

"Go down to the cellar and see for yourself." The Earl's son waved airily toward the house, where a few of the casks of wine Simon had brought when he was Viceroy of Gascony had found their final lodgment and had not been discovered and confiscated for the Crown. The servants of the manor, partisans of the Earl, and knowing his son since he was a small child, had welcomed Simon Fils' unauthorized settling at the house.

As Evylie attempted to rise to his feet, wavered, and failed, there was a clattering of hooves on the paving of the manse's cobbled entry. A rider hurriedly dismounted. Leading his horse by the rein, he strode across the lawn to where he saw the young master lying at ease.

"My lord Montfort!" Baer addressed the figure draped over the garden seat.

"What is it?" Simon asked, both his eyes shut, his wrist resting across them to shield them from the red glare of the sun through his eyelids. Thinking it was a messenger from his own men at Pevensey, he pettishly threw back, "Can't you leave me alone!"

"My lord, what I have to say is urgent!" Baer pressed, appalled by what he saw, and the reek of wine he smelled.

Recognizing the voice now, and pricked by the pressing tone, Simon uncovered his eyes, raised his head, then sat around properly on the seat. "John Baer, the capturer of emperors. What are you doing here? I thought you were with my father."

Tears marked the young master's face, wet streaks from the corners of his eyes back to his hair. Baer saw he must have arrived at some painful moment, he couched his tone more mildly. "I bring an urgent message from your father. Edward has escaped." His words were carefully measured, seeing he must impress them past the distraction of whatever was upsetting Simon. "A great many of the barons, with their knights, are gathered in arms with Clare, and now are under the prince's command. The Earl your father must have all the forces you can raise. He commanded me to tell you to go to Winchester at once and gather all our partisans and the shire knights who will be meeting there for the Parliament. Summonses already have gone to the sheriffs, ordering that the shire knights are to come in arms. You're to lead the army from Winchester, by way of Worcester, to the Earl at Hereford."

Simon gazed at the messenger as if he peered up from the bottom of a well, with the world above only a rippling reflection of himself. The words reached him with no more weight than plashing water-music. Wavering, he struggled to clear his mind. What had been told him was important, that much he understood. Breathing deeply, he began to feel a little less vague. He had Baer repeat his commission. "A pox upon this war," he mumbled at last, when he had grasped the words with some understanding.

With the crush of his sorrow over Isabella's perfidy clinging to him like dead weight, Simon Fils slowly gathered his belongings and, in a couple of days, left with his companions for Winchester. It was not war, but Isabella Fortinbras that filled his mind in cycle after cycle of obsession. He wanted to go nowhere, but to howl out his heart in a shut room.

Word already had spread over England that the Great Earl was in need of aid. The army of shire knights assembling at Winchester came from every part of the land. They were joined by other knights, sheriffs, townsfolk, even outlaws from the Weald and Sherwood, villeins, Englishmen of every sort and class. They crowded into Winchester. The knights' tents made a second city in the fields. But most men came less well equipped. Those with money jammed the inns, sleeping on benches and the floors of common rooms. Those without money slept in doorways, or crushed the young crops by sleeping on the planted fields. The monks and townsmen of Winchester, strong partisans of the Earl, welcomed all they could into their homes and gave food to those they couldn't shelter. But days passed and the young lord Simon, their commander, did not come.

Simon Fils ambled west in leisurely fashion, by way of Tunbridge, spitefully sacking Gilbert de Clare's manse there and supplying himself with stolen wine. Near Crawley he was so sick from drinking that he slept for a day. Then he moved on, stopping at Odiham. His mother, sister and little brother already had left with the knights of the garrison. The caretaker who stayed behind greeted him with wringing hands and panicked voice, but Simon only collapsed on the great bed in the solar and slept. It was two days before he moved on with his friends to what, before its return to the Crown, had been the Monfort hunting lodge at Chawton.

"My curse upon wars," the young master laughed, rolling on the sloping lawn with Evyile looking down at him.

"Don't you think it best that we keep going?" his friend, not drinking near so heavily any longer, prodded. "Your father, we've been warned, is in immediate need of your help."

Simon turned and lay flat, his cheek pressed to the grass. "Why would he need my help?" The idea seemed ludicrous that the father, who commanded everything except perhaps the stars and clouds, should need *his* help. "He has Henry, he has Guy, and the king and all his Councilors to do his bidding. Why can't he leave me alone?"

"You're drinking too much," Evyile observed in extreme and tactful understatement, but it was all he dared venture.

Simon Fils lay, arms and legs spread on the grass as if the whole weight of the sky pressed like a monstrous column on his back. He tried to keep his mind shut to Evyile's annoying prodding. Shut to everything. But, like a door hopelessly closed against a flood, through the sill's crack black melancholy kept seeping, and the melancholy's name was not war, but Isabella.

At Winchester the days of waiting dragged by, anxious hour after hour. The townsfolk, wearying of their guests and running low on ready supplies of food, served and donated less generously than they at first had done, when it seemed the army would assemble and move swiftly to the Earl's support.

Hunger does not take long to operate, bringing on disorder. The bridges and the riverbanks soon were crowded with men deploying makeshift fishing lines. Those less honest stole to feed themselves. Shops were looted by armed men. At the inns, as men's belongings vanished, arguments, accusations, then fights broke out. Fighting spilled into High Street, turning into riot. Swords, pikes, knives, the weapons brought for the Great Earl's sake, were used in brawls that wrecked common rooms, overturned carts and peddlers' booths and left men, would-be soldiers and the peaceful folk of Winchester, indiscriminately wounded. Women were spared only because they dared not leave their homes. Bailiffs began by locking brawlers in the castle's tower, then by expelling them from the town.

When at last Simon Fils and his companions reached Winchester, much of his army already was dispersed, and he was assailed with complaints. As a Guardian of the Peace, he was formally responsible for curing riot. Overwhelmed, he raised his hands, shouting, "We'll make good your loses! I promise, I shall make amends to you! You will see justice done!"

Simon Fils knew that in Winchester's castle were kept the royal rents collected from the southern shires. He ordered the treasury opened and the funds distributed: reparations to silence the complainers. But the setting of proper sums required hearings. He announced he would hold a court, and the people of Winchester entered their names, creating a long list for the hearings. While John Evyile wrote down the name of each petitioner and his claim, Simon toured the town.

The city was full of armed men, dirty and unshaven from days of sleeping in the streets. They shouted after the young lord as he went pacing by on his white destrier. "Long live Montfort!" Grinning, they shook their fists in eagerness, glad that their commander had appeared at last.

Treading out along the riverbank, Simon recognized someone he had seen before. Dressed in woodland green, the man known as Robin was sitting with a number of his companions, benignly and patiently twitching whittled tree limbs strung with cords that sank into the stream. Seeing the young lord, the outlaw handed his makeshift fishing pole to the man nearest him and stood up, smiling in recognition. "We'll be going soon, my lord Montfort?"

"First we must make reparations," Simon replied, pausing his horse, his arm akimbo with his hand upon his thigh. "It's good you have your men fishing. We'll be hanging those caught stealing."

Robin ignored the jibe, and said in a tone that sought an earnest reply, "From what I hear, we're badly needed in Hereford, my lord. Might it not be best to let justice in Winchester wait?"

"An outlaw urges justice be delayed? What an amazing thing! Whenever I need judicial advice, I know now where I can find it." Simon smiled caustically, turned his horse and cantered back to High Street.

The sylvan outlaw looked after him, very far from pleased.

The next several days Simon Fils spent in court, hearing complaints of thefts, assaults and rioting. With a liberal hand he dispensed the royal rents. Innkeepers left his court happy, with more than enough to make repairs. Shopkeepers left with funds to replenish their ransacked shelves.

In the castle's yard a gallows was set up, the tower's prisoners were brought in file, one roped to the next, and hanged like a market of duck carcasses, with unceremonious speed. Their bodies were tossed into a common grave. The Guardian of the Peace created spectacle enough to bring instant quiet to the town.

Simon allotted funds from the royal rents to pay for food needed by the many who still lingered, eager to fight for the Earl. But still the army did not take form and march.

The young knight Baudwin Wake, sent by the Earl, found Simon Fils at Winchester, still holding court and hearing pleas. He delivered his extremely urgent message.

"I'm to go to *Bristol*?" the Guardian of Winchester's peace asked in a high, strained voice. His own sources of information had told him that was where John de la Warre was, the person he least wanted to see again, much less command.

"You must bring your army there to meet your father in three days! We thought you'd be much nearer by now!" Wake's face was turning crimson with fury. It was past his skills to keep a messenger's courteous control.

"Well I can't leave here just like that!" Simon retorted with a scowl at what he regarded as Wake's impudence.

Wake stared, confounded. "My lord, the Earl your father is in a most desperate way! He has no arms but the Leicestermen, a few of us, and some Welsh archers. And the king is with him! If you had any idea what our travels have been..."

Had the young knight been speaking privately to Simon, his words would have borne little weight, but he was shouting in the court. All Winchester would know. Reluctantly, Simon Fils called a postponement of the remaining hearings. In his enveloping mist of melancholy he could feel no sense of urgency. And he did not relish facing de la Warre at Bristol.

The enormous mass of armed volunteers, unused to marching in a body, left Winchester at last, spreading out behind the lion-dotted flag of Simon Fils and wandering over the countryside. They were hard to keep moving, and impossible to keep in any rank and file. Simon lacked the ability to drill them, or even the spirit to spur them on to more speed.

On the third day since Wake had reached him, Simon was less than half way to his appointed goal. At Bradford, late on the fifth day, a traveler brought word that de la Warre's flotilla of merchant ships had been sunk by Clare.

Feeling some relief that there was no more need to meet his rival, Simon turned his unwieldy forces around and marched back to Winchester, to resume his abbreviated court hearings.

The Earl's third messenger, the Leicesterman Philip Drieby, eventually found him there. He brought the latest news, gathered in his hazardous passage. "Prince Edward holds Shrewsbury, Bridgenorth, Gloucester, and now Worcester and Caerleon. Your father requires that, as the Severn's bridges are destroyed, the fords gouged out and there are no boats, you must build boats or rafts at once. The Earl is trapped and must be brought relief! You're to bring your vessels to cross at Kempsey. There's a large stockaded farm building there if you need shelter, but don't attempt the ford. The Earl is waiting for you at Hereford."

The urgency of Drieby's tone at last roused Simon Fils. "Return and tell my father that we come. And tell him that I bring an army of ten thousand men. He has no cause to fear Edward and Clare." The count of his forces might not have been exact, but their passage through the countryside was like the locusts of Egypt. For all he knew they might be more than ten thousand. "Tell my father that all England is in arms for him."

"Bring them up, my lord!" Drieby looked at him piercingly.

"I shall, Sire Philip, but I must build some boats it seems. That will take a little while." Simon Fils glanced upward as if competently calculating. "Collecting timber, and craftsmen, doing the work… about three weeks, I suppose. Master William at Kenilworth no doubt will help. My father can't expect that we come with new-made boats from here. Tell him I move to Kenilworth."

Doubtful, chilled, but knowing young Montfort well enough to avoid riling him to pettish resistance, Drieby pressed no further than to add, "God grant you speed, my lord."

Simon Fils led his swath of locusts north, gathering donations of food, money and timber as he went. To maximize his collections, he passed through Oxford, Northampton and Coventry, all without meeting resistance, or anything but cheers for the Earl's cause. That there was peril anywhere seemed to have more the character of fretful fantasy than military reality. The whole of England it appeared supported, cheered, even worshiped his father. Any sense of urgent need faded from young Simon's mind.

The shifting mass of armed men, and the wagons laden with timber and supplies, did not reach Kenilworth until July was well advanced. Master William was commanded to build boats. Not for the entire army, that would be impossible, but for a force sufficient to relieve and bring forth the Earl and royal company from Hereford.

Again the outer yard of Kenilworth was loud with hammer and saw. With the family gone to Dover, the spectators this time were the stronghold's small mercenary garrison, Simon Fils and his appointed captains: young friends from Lewes and London; and Robert de Vere, the Earl of Oxford, who, sensing emergency when

Parliament failed to meet properly, brought fifty of his knights. Robert Ferrers, alarmed as well, arrived with additional archers from Sherwood and twenty knights from Derbyshire.

Kenilworth's manor fields were trampled by a vast camp of lesser men-at-arms and amateur foot soldiers while the captains lodged in the castle, where the King of the Germans, under guard, was still perusing the Earl's library, and playing chess with the steward Thomas Demesnil. The youths, with their excessive drinking, were a distasteful addition to Richard's limited society, but he was glad for de Vere's company.

By the morning of the second day of August, Master William announced that the boats were completed and ready-mounted on new carts, with teams of oxen requisitioned to drag them from Kenilworth to the Severn at Kempsey.

Drinking heavily, in dull spirits while he waited for the vessels to be built, young Simon felt a distinct lift of his energies now that he was actually ready to go at last. His subordinates had busied themselves on Kenilworth's fallow field, drilling their enormous following to march properly and respond reasonably to orders. As reasonably as could be expected in two weeks with such rabble.

For their hard work and their impending departure, Simon deemed a celebration would be fitting for his friends. "Let us bathe ourselves, eat, drink and rejoice as knights in ancient times!" he proclaimed. "Tonight we will make merry! At dawn tomorrow we march to Hereford."

"I thought warriors of old spent the night before battle at prayer," King Richard skeptically remarked to de Vere, who also was frowning. "Has he no thought of the soul?"

"Once we're dead we'll be entirely soul, probably in torment," Evyile, overhearing his elders, retorted with an impious grin. "Prayer hardly will avert it. I mean to enjoy my flesh, especially while I can take my pleasures at the cost of the Crown's Winchester rents."

Richard's cold stare at Evyile made even Simon Fils uneasy. For privacy and the greater delight of his companions, he arranged to hold his feast in the bathhouse in Kenilworth's village.

The bathhouse once had been an innocent establishment purveying nothing more than scented cleanliness. But long since, in the absence of the manor's lord, it had become a brothel of widespread notoriety in the Midlands. Its corpulent and cheery madam, to protect her business, thoughtfully had groomed young Simon's favor during his time as castellan. Now, with his army's presence, she had reaped the benefits, enlarging her staff of willing wenches to serve the knights and any foot soldiers who had the means to pay. Most of Simon's captains had favorites among her girls. Some felt quite tender links, despite the monetary nature of their intimacies. With the army's departure the next morning, it would be an occasion of farewells.

Simon sent casks of wine from his father's cellar and had Ralph, the castle's baker, make dozens of meat pastries, commanding him to have them brought on the Countess Eleanor's best silver trays that had been left for the service of the King of the Germans.

The army, strewn all over the manor fields beyond the fortified walls of the braye, was mostly without tents, but comfortable enough in the fine July weather. Everyone was notified to be ready to leave at dawn. For their night's cheer, with no thought for their condition in the morning, Simon provided beer in plenteous amounts from the stores for the castle's garrison.

Out beyond the castle's wall, along the roadside stood the boats, each mounted on its cart with whiffletrees and traces at ready. Great high-sided wagons of supply also were there, loaded not only with quantities of cured meat, flour, wine and beer, but with the flags, shields, chain mail arms and helms, the harness, horse-trappings, and even the clothes, tents and camp furnishings of the young captains and their commander. They would have no need of them tonight. Simon Fils believed his celebration until dawn actually would add to his subordinates' efficiency: all that need be done in the morning was hitch up the oxen, and the march was ready to move on without a moment lost. Young Simon, his energy surging at last, was much pleased with his arrangements.

It was thirty miles from Kenilworth to Kempsey. Fast riders could make the distance in half a day, though a horse spurred to such sustained speed would go no further without risk. A march with ox-drawn wagons, going quickly as could be, might take three days but no more.

By evening on August second, the festivities had begun. In the bathhouse foyer were heaped the cloaks and robes, the swords, poniards, even the stockings, drawers and shirts of the captains and their merry commander, for in a bathhouse the accepted mode of dress was nudity.

Within the bathing hall three great cauldrons heated, misting their perfumes of lavender and rose. And, for this special occasion, Mistress Maggie provided expensive, musky civet oil. Five wooden tubs stood in a row. Frames hung with red satin curtains drawn around them served as freestanding screens for privacy. But here were so many youths and *filles de joie* that the privacy of a mere five tubs was nullified.

Most of the young knights neither minded being seen nor seeing. For those who must have privacy, their host had ordered his mother's second-best bed draperies brought from the castle to close off a corner of the room. Maggie's own furnishings consisted of a multitude of large, down-filled and scarlet-covered cushions scattered and piled everywhere on the tiled floor.

Though it was still bright summer twilight outside, the windowless room was dark, lit only by a pair of candle-stands that shed a dim and shadow-patched illumination. Only at the far end of the hall, where fire burned in the cauldrons' cave-like hearth, was there much light.

Trays of meat pies were on tables by each tub and generously distributed over the floor. Casks of the best of the earl's remaining Bordeaux, hoisted from the castle's cellar, were propped on trestles along one wall, and spigoted so that each guest liberally could help himself to the vintage of his choice. The guests were doing so, unabashed.

The air was steamy, rank with perfumes, with odors of food and wine and human flesh warmed by summer's heat, the hearth's hot waters and Mistress Maggie's entertainments.

Boisterous early in the evening, the bathhouse had quieted now. Pairs had long since settled on the cushions, murmuring, fondling in leisurely fashion, getting to the business of their farewell couplings, and coupling again.

Ferrers, the heir of the earldom of Derby, sprawled across the cushions with two happy girls.

Simon Fils, in a warm tub with a dark eyed whore he fancied looked like Isabella, sipped his wine, his eyes half-closed, sweetly dreaming as she washed him and caressed him with attar of rose. Maggie hovered discretely, making certain that he was well pleased.

Still later in the night the revel roused to noisy, drunken gamesomeness in salute to the ending of the summer's languid irresponsibilities. Crumbs of meat pastries littered the trays and were scattered over the floor and the wine-stained cushions.

Totally drunk, some of the lordlings with the stamina of their young years were hotly at renewed pleasures with their partners, while others, more devoted to wine than to women, vomited and drank more. They would have headaches in the morning, but never before had they tasted wine so fine. They meant to claim as much of it as their gullets could encompass even temporarily.

A few hours later still, everyone lay sleeping on the floor, bodies male and female intertwined as they had been when consciousness deserted them. The stench of wine, of vomit and perfumes, and every human fluid, permeated the thick air.

Maggie, who never touched drink stronger than milk, was counting her billing and her costs and figuring her profits in the little room beside the hearth where she securely stored her money, her ledgers and her jars of scents. She glanced out at the bath hall. Its vista of young bodies sated with love and wine brought a broad smile to her painted, liberal lips. She had never been one to believe the priests' warnings of Hell. Her business was lucrative, gave delight, and at worst brought the breeding of a better class into the villein population.

As she was pondering her happy trade, she thought she heard a sound coming from the foyer where her customers' clothing and weapons were left. From the tiny window of her office she could see it still was dark outside, though in mid-summer dawn came very early. The sky must have become cloudy, she thought. Maggie had clientele who were likely to arrive at any time of night and even into morning. She rose to intercept whomever it might be and tell them that the bath was taken for a private celebration.

At the same moment young Simon, sleeping lightly on cushions on the floor with his girl's head resting on his belly, opened his eyes and looked toward the sound at the foyer.

Silhouetted against the foyer's single candle's light, a tall figure was standing in the hall's doorway.

"Father!" Simon gasped.

The man gave a soft laugh and shifted his position, leaning nonchalantly against the doorjamb. With the movement of his arm Simon saw the sheen of a sword-blade, then caught a glint of gold embroidery on his chest.

"Edward…"

"I regret disturbing your revel." The prince waved his sword idly toward the room, where bodies were beginning to stir, reaching toward wakefulness. "It looks to have been a splendid night, and you didn't think to invite me! An unpardonable oversight. I would have enjoyed it. Maggie is my friend as well you know."

Maggie's white face had shown briefly at her office door, then vanished with a cautious clicking of door bolts.

Roger Leybourne and Gilbert de Clare appeared at Edward's side. Gilbert, with a down-turned smirk, scanned the room where naked youths were gathering enough wit into their bleared heads to sit up and receive their first clear understanding of who had wakened them.

Simon Fils burned with embarrassment and rage. He roughly thrust the girl away from him. She let out a cry as she hit the tile floor and he stood up.

Edward pointed the sword blade toward his bare, vulnerable chest. "Cousin, you're not dressed for fighting. Do sit down again."

The young captains all were awake now, but none dared move. The room was filling to the crowding point with well-armed men with their swords drawn. Behind the prince, more men were gathering up the clothing and the weapons from the foyer.

"You're going to slaughter us like chickens?" Simon challenged, summoning his considerable but seldom used bravery. "I didn't think you so low, Cousin, as to murder naked, unarmed knights."

"Ah, well... no, I'm not," Edward laughed lightly, sheathing his blade. "It would make a disgusting mess and appall Maggie's wenches." He glanced behind him and saw the foyer was well stripped of every garment and weapon. Outside the door, one of Simon Fils' great wagons stood, being loaded with the last of the bathhouse pilferings.

Withdrawing from the doorway as he was signaled by Clare, who was in charge of the loading, Edward motioned for his men in the hall to follow him. To Simon Fils he swept a parting bow, ornamented with exaggerated courtesy. "I'm sorry to leave, but I must go. I have an engagement to keep soon with your father."

The prince disappeared. In a moment there was the clattering of a large cavalry's hooves.

When the nearby din subsided, from the open doorway came the distant sound of creaking as the wagons, stocked with Simon's and his captains' armor, flags, weapons, tents, clothing and supplies, moved off down the road. Edward and his escort galloped to overtake them. Distant too was the low thunder of a herd being driven away, as Roger Mortimer's men stole all of the army's horses.

Naked, young Simon, Ferrers and their friends burst from the bathhouse door as the riders receded up the road with shouts and hoots of ribald victory.

In panic, the sobered, stripped youths dashed up the road to the fortress. The drawbridge at the new north gatehouse was up, at least that much was well done. Simon dove into the channel that moated the north wall. His companions who were swimmers followed him. Shouting the current password to the night watch, he led his friends to the boat landing and from there to the inner yard and the main hall.

The steward Thomas Desmesnil was sleeping on a straw pallet plumped upon a bench, with a cresset nightlight near him on the table. He woke, startled, to see in the dimness a number of fair bodies running through the hall.

"Get us clothing!" young Simon shrieked as he dashed up the winding, lightless staircase to the bell-tower to ring the alarm.

The bell still clanging, swinging of its own, he ran down to the chamber floor, where Desmesnil stood fretting, afraid to open his master the earl's chests.

Simon rushed from room to room, throwing open every chest that the countess had left behind in her move to Odiham. She had not left much, and only the earl's books, left as a kindness to the King of the Germans, were stored in his chests. Simon Fils' own clothing, and some of this brothers', thoughtfully had been packed in the now stolen wagons.

He broke into the room where Richard was sleeping, woke the King of the Germans and grabbed all of Richard's clothing from his clothespress, which had been sent from Wallingford.

"What are you doing!" Richard cried.

But Simon didn't stop to answer, as Evyile joined him. He ran down the stairs with an armload of robes, stockings, shirts and drawers as Evyile collected all of Richard's boots and shoes.

Hastily Simon distributed the sumptuous clothes of a king among his captains.

By now the castle's servants, roused by the ringing of the bell, were gathered in the hall, each holding a cresset lamp, lighting a scene of frantic confusion.

"We must find arms!" Simon was yelling, as he and his friends hurriedly covered their nude bodies with the King of the Germans' finery.

Simon grasped Evyile's arm. "I'm going to Warwick to get what I can there. You go to Northampton. Come back with clothes, with arms, with horses as fast as you can! Edward's marching on Hereford!"

With a horse stolen from the village tavern's stable, Simon rode fast to Warwick, five miles away. At the great castle, occupied by the Earl's castellan, there were arms and clothes and horses to be gotten, but not enough for everyone stripped by the prince's theft.

Bringing back what he could, Simon took his re-clothed, re-armed and re-mounted men to Coventry. All day August third, Simon Fils and his captains scoured the region to re-equip their army.

Early on the morning of August fourth the force was ready to march again. The re-arming was a stunning accomplishment of speed and ingenuity, all the more amazing in its contrast to the time young Simon took to arm initially. But even burdened with the wagons, Edward had the lead of a full day and night.

Traveling swiftly and lightly, young Simon hoped to catch the prince before he reached the Severn.

# Chapter Twenty-Six

## EVESHAM
### 1265

At Hereford there was no word at all of young Simon. Drieby never returned. It seemed apparent that whatever forces had been raised had met the armies of the prince and Clare and been defeated or, even more likely as the hapless Court at Hereford remained undisturbed, Simon Fils' army was engaged in the maneuvers of a campaign.

Before siege closed their gates, before the already depleted stocks of food were gone entirely and starvation set in, the Court and its few defenders must move again. Must try to reach the safety of Kenilworth's massive new walls.

Simon ordered men out into the now unguarded forest to cut wood. In Hereford's market-square makeshift rafts were built and mounted on wheels. They were small, and with a single axle each so they could be handled easily and pulled swiftly by a horse. But a raft could ferry no more than ten men, or two or three blindfolded horses.

After dark on the night of August second the rafts were hauled out through the city's eastern gate. King Henry and his Justiciar and Councilors, with the Earl Montfort, his sons Henry and Guy, his cousin Peter and his son, his steward Seagrave and squire Peter, young Bohun, the Welsh prince Llewellyn and his archers, the guard of Leicestermen and a few young knights made up the modest cavalcade. The Welsh archers rode clinging to the bobbing, jogging, bone-bruising rafts. Quickly they crossed the open fields and went at a canter through the forest.

As the sky was lifting to the dull light of a gray dawn, hazed pink in the east where the sun still crouched behind the hills, they reached the banks of the Severn. They had done in hours what before, with the great wagon of the Treasury, had cost a night and a full day. Their horses were foamed with sweat and the riders on the rafts badly hurting from the rough trip. White fog lay on the river, clothing the smooth, swift waters with a fairy cloak of void. Spring flooding had subsided. Though the current was still strong, if the fords had not been gouged no rafts would have been needed.

Simon deployed timbers, rope and poles he had brought on one of the rafts. Leicestermen drove a sturdy piling of the timbers into the river's embankment. The first raft was rolled to the water's edge with a long rope aboard secured at one end to the piling. As the primitive little vessel, its wheels and axle removed, was launched, tied closely to the piling, six men boarded, with more timbers and with poles for guiding the raft. Bishop Cantaloup accompanied them to help them find a shallow landing place in the fog.

Dark figures half submerged in whiteness, they moved smoothly outward, paying out the rope as they poled the ferry across the river. Reaching a gentle embankment on the eastern side, they clambered ashore. Four men unloaded the timbers as two held the raft steady. The knights drove the heavy wooden beams into the ground to make another piling, then bound the rope securely so the remaining rafts could cross, guided by it against the river's flow.

As the other wheeled rafts arrived amid the waiting riders at the riverside, the archers, cursing the bruising, bone-jarring trip, set to work removing their rafts' wheels and axles. The plan was to bring the wheels and axles across, reattach them and carry the archers onward at the horses' rapid pace. But the men begged the Earl that they never again be put to such a ride, promising they would gladly run the remaining way to Kenilworth, some thirty miles.

The delicate process of persuading blindfolded, nervous destriers onto the rocking rafts was a slow business. Simon crossed with two horses and two men on the second raft, ordering his sons to be the last to cross, staying to command the west bank if they were attacked. He sent two of the men from the first raft on ahead with the horses as scouts, to report immediately if they found the enemy. And he ordered a man from each arriving raft to pole the lightened vessel back across the river to ferry over more men and horses.

As the white bank of fog thinned to a veil, then vanished and the river turned blue under the morning sky, raft after raft was launched, crossed, and cycled back. More Leicestermen crossed with their horses, gathering a small protective cavalry on the east shore. Then Peter de Montfort carried the feeble king aboard with his Councilors Newmarket and SaintJohn, and the Justiciar Hugh Despensar. The next rafts brought their horses. King Henry again was dressed in a borrowed suit of mail, but with no crown upon his hood.

Bohun Fils, crossing with the son of the steward Seagrave and young Peter de Montfort, knelt on the embankment and kissed the ground. "We've done it! I don't want to spend a day ever again in those wretched hills." But his broad, triumphant grin failed to raise his friends' spirits.

"Pray God we don't meet Edward in a moment," young Seagrave muttered soberly.

The Welsh archers, with Henry and Guy Montfort, crossed in the last cycles of the rafts. It was past noon and a brilliant summer day when the whole company at last was assembled on the eastern bank of the Severn. August third was warm, radiant with glaring sunshine, the sort of day to gladden hearts that had nothing to fear. A day that made everything seem clearer, sharp of outline and detail – and visible for many miles. A day innocent of any chance of concealment.

The crossing took longer than Simon had hoped and he was not pleased. With the enemy probably near, silence was kept. Harness had been muffled again before they left Hereford.

Through soft murmurs the Earl's orders were spread. One of the scouts returned with report: Edward's headquarters were at Worcester, only three miles distant. But he and his forces were not there at present. Where they had gone no one seemed to know. Simon decided the only hope of safety was to try to reach Kempsey, not far up river from their landing, and lie hidden until they could move under the cover of night.

The Cotswold Hills were luxurious with wildflowers celebrating the abundance of the rains and now the sunshine. Wild thyme carpeted the soil and blanketed boulders; honeysuckle rambled, spangled with blooms that sugared the air; yarrow and campion pennanted the wayside and heather bushes stood bedizened with tiny flower bells as copious as bubbles in foam. The earth smelled lush, soothing, vital.

Simon breathed in the aromas and remarked to Walter, who was riding by his side, "I read once of an ancient land where flowers bloomed so generously and their perfume was so heady that hounds could not follow the scent of their prey. Would that we were in that land."

"*Homo homini lupus.* That land was Sicily," Walter, who knew his classics even better than Simon did, replied with irony. "Recall, it was Sicily's attractions that brought us to this pass. Were Henry less determined to have Sicily for Edmund, he'd never have risked England to the Pope, and we probably would still be yielding up our taxes bit by bit."

Simon gave a curt, bitter laugh, thinking of the clergy's claims for the New Era. "If this is how Our Lord moves man to fulfill His intent, it surely argues the mystery of His ways, and that human planning has no part in it."

They had traveled only a few miles from where they landed when Walter pointed out above the green mass of trees the saw-tooth outline of a battlemented roof against the sky: his Kempsey manse. "I fortified my house when Worcester turned treacherous," he told Simon with a touch of pride.

The Earl regarded the theologian's tower. It was less a structure of defense than a chivalrous whimsy. But he held his tongue from saying that, if they were found here, he prayed his son's army would come quickly.

The thought pained him like a stab. He was lying to himself again. If his son could have come, he would have come long since. Their only hope was in reaching Kenilworth. From that sturdy defense, perhaps spurred by the inconvenient popularity he and his cause had among the commons, he could negotiate surrender with an amnesty that would spare the lives of his sons and followers. He doubted there could be amnesty for him.

Walter watched his face, the eyes dark, long-lashed and darker still in the shadowed hollows of long sleeplessness, the mouth fine but stern, nested in the beard gray-streaked and trimmed neatly for the helm, the ever-tousled black hair, much grayed too. But the face was still the handsomest he knew, except perhaps for Edward's, and despite the many battle scars the body bore, the visage was unscarred but for the creases of grief and disillusionment.

The little royal company with its defenders stayed concealed at Kempsey, resting for the remainder of the day. Lookouts were posted along what the bishop pleased to call his battlements, but no enemy was seen.

The August afternoon grew very hot. Though everyone was tired, they could rest but ill in their heavy-padded, sweated pourpoints and chain mail. King Henry complained and demanded a bath, but none was to be had.

Worse than the lack of a tub, but for beer and baskets of last year's dried fruit the bishop's larder was empty. The king's entourage chewed leathery slices of apple and pear and tough prunes, washing them down with stale beer. With the bishop always at Court, there had been no need to stock Kempsey.

As evening and a skim of clouds dimmed the brilliant day, Simon himself roused everyone. They remounted their destriers in Walter's courtyard and moved on. The moon was nearly full, but a thickening hood of rainclouds scudding rapidly in from the west was drawing a mercifully obscuring screen of darkness underneath its glow. Soon the landscape, except where flickering white light shuddered from cloud to cloud, was black, moonless and starless. No rain fell yet.

The little royal cavalcade moved on by touch and the soft thud of its horses' hooves. At the fore an archer trotted as quickly as his legs would carry him, a lantern in his hand with one of its four sides open to show the way immediately ahead. The entourage moved at a trot up hill and down.

But the sheep paths were confusing. The march went astray several times, lost in the dark, each time having to double back to find the route northeastward. Their progress was slow, though at least their wandering was as confounding as a wily fox's trail that would leave hounds whimpering, running in circles. Had they not been lost, they should have reached Kenilworth by dawn. The day was August fourth.

At last they did reach Pershore's bridge and crossed the River Avon, entering the green valley called Evesham. From both sides of the road plum trees hung their swelling, unripe burden at hand-height for the riders and brushed the heads of those running on foot. Every croft was planted with an orchard. Seagrave Fils, in the vanguard, picked a plum. Biting into the unripe fruit, he spat the piece out. "Bitter as gall," he whispered to Humphrey riding at his side.

In the dark, moist breeze the orchards' leaves rustled like unfolding silks, their luscious growth mellowing the air. Walter remarked to Simon, "This valley is well named *Eve's hame*, the home of life. Alcinous' garden for plenty if you will, except they do have seasons other than an endless summer here."

As his horse ambled, Simon drew a sigh of frustration mixed with resignation. He was weary of fighting the fate that thrust up every form of barrier, however well he planned. The maze of the night's travel had brought him past anxiety and rage. He replied, "I ask only that we cross this pleasant place quickly. We're utterly exposed from here through the Midlands until we reach Kenilworth. And we have little time left before full daylight."

"You think the enemy is following us?"

"If Edward isn't, he's a fool, and nothing that he's ever done suggests that." Simon was thinking much of Edward, and of Edmund. If Edmund were made king, the Council very likely could rule him.

But if Edward were king... The prince had shown himself unteachable, ungovernable, and unguided by anything but his own violent impulses. As king, his untrammeled ways would have the authority of the Papacy and Aquinas' hierarchy to put them past any hindering. Simon grimly pondered whether he ought to have killed Edward. To murder a prisoner was not within his scope. If the Lord granted him the chance to challenge him... If they reached Kenilworth, the prince undoubtedly would put them under siege very soon. That could be the opportunity. Edward would not resist the lure of a challenge.

Simon bleakly made his new plan. He once had loved Edward, more dearly even than his son Guy whom he loved best. But bastards were thought to be perverse, and Edward displayed every perversity. The army Simon Fils raised must certainly be lost. A challenge was the only hope remaining to keep Edward from the Crown.

The Earl pondered: amnesty for his followers, and a personal challenge to Prince Edward. It was all that remained that he could do for the cause he was coming to hold sacred, even if no one else but benighted commoners and hopeful clergymen believed in it as he now did.

Gradually, since the miracle at Lewes, the knotty thread of events had brought him nearly to feel certain that what had been begun at Oxford, though its end would not be reached yet for a thousand years, was indeed the *Novus Ordo Seclorum*, the New Order of the Ages. If God willed, he would keep Edward from stifling it.

But what God's will might be, in the living here and now, had shown itself to be beyond his fathoming.

He prayed they would reach Kenilworth before the prince found them. And if they did not? If Edward caught them? For himself there would be no mercy. Drawing and quartering, the punishment for treason, would be his death in a short time. He felt a recoiling twinge at the humiliation and horror of a traitor's public execution. But battle held no fear for him. If conflict came it would be welcome, his only guarantee of death with honor and in the muted pain of battle joy. But for the faithful knights with him... he must bring them to safety, if God granted.

A peculiar calm settled upon him. Perhaps it was only that he was so very tired. But a deepened resignation came over him, with the decision to destroy Edward, if the Lord permitted. And if not, he was content with the Lord's will. He vaguely mused that on this day, perhaps, he at last had reached the mild plateau of old age and obedience to fate. He was fifty-two.

His face, to his friend's gaze, showed the somber, mortal depth of his thoughts, but also apparent peace.

Simon turned to Peter de Montfort Fils, riding behind him, "Carry back word that we will not stop, but keep as fast a pace as possible till we reach Kenilworth. If we lose the men on foot, so be it. They must do as they can for their own safety."

Guy, riding beside his brother Henry, ground his teeth. "What has become of Simon and the army!"

"Isn't it quite clear?" his brother answered darkly. "He's met Edward and lies dead on a field somewhere with all his forces in a lake of blood around him."

"You think the battle is already lost?" Guy asked, more cynical of his middle brother's competence and so still moved by hope.

"I'm certain father believes it. You saw his face when he turned to give the order. He's in mourning."

"He's been wearing black again since Rochester," Guy shrugged, never very open to his brother's perceptions.

"I'm not speaking of his clothes, but what I saw in his eyes just now."

As dawn grew to full light on August fourth, they were passing along the bank of the Avon River as it meandered around the abbey town of Evesham. The way to Kenilworth lay over Evesham's bridge, through the town then northward up a broad, gentle, sloping pasture known as Green Hill. It was only twenty miles to the safety of the walls of Kenilworth. But it was the twenty most open and vulnerable miles of the journey. Now in hours of daylight.

"When do we rest?" King Henry peevishly whined to his Councilor Peter de Montfort, riding by him. A small suit of chain mail had been found for the king, he seemed to have shrunk to no more than a brittle, stooping frame of bones. There was a small helmet for him too, plain, with narrow eye-slits. It dangled on a chain attached to Peter de Montfort's saddle.

Henry's gray face hung in draping pleats of palsy on one side, the eye all but shut; the other side was gouged with creases of old age too withered for his fifty-seven years. Peter recalled his antique cousin Loretta looking heartier at a hundred. "We're not to stop until we reach Kenilworth, my lord," Peter informed him.

"I can't go any further!" Henry squealed, dry white mucous crusting at the corners of his thin lips. "You mean to drive me till I die! May God curse you!"

With his tone the squeak of an idiot and his face, framed by his chain mail hood, as gray as a corpse neglectfully left unburied, his complaint seemed to Peter to carry some conviction. He rode forward to his cousin the Earl.

Simon's response was a terse, "We cannot pause."

Peter rode back to the king, but came forward to Simon soon again. "My lord, my friend, I really think he's past his strength. If he dies, I needn't say what we'll have gained with Edward to be crowned."

"You believe Henry's that fragile?"

"I do, or I wouldn't trouble you. I know how urgent it is we move quickly."

They were entering the abbey's town. People, going about their morning business, hurried out of their way: the water carrier with his barrel on a barrow; the egg seller with her basket of eggs; a servant on a errand with a message; monks; housewives; an apprentice delivering a repaired saddle completed in the night on hurried order. Evesham was a world of mankind in miniature, busy on an ordinary morning, oblivious that there could be fellow beings anywhere fleeing and in danger of their lives. Startled, astounded, shaken from their norm, the folk of Evesham darted from the way of the oncoming destriers and the exhausted, trotting archers, as if invasion unaccountably was flooding through High Street. Doors slammed shut, shutters closed, the thoroughfare briskly was emptied but for the crowding stream of knights, the king's small entourage and the tired archers.

Peter pressed forward yet again to warn Simon of King Henry's failing condition.

With a strained breath of submission, against his better judgment Simon curbed his horse and raised his hand to bring the march to halt at Evesham Abbey's broad, arched gate. "We'll pause and breakfast here, if the good monks will serve us," he sent the order back. "The king is very tired. We must give him rest."

The Earl sent scouts on up the road, and back the way they had come, to watch for Edward and, as if there still was hope, for young Simon's army.

In the abbey, Simon sent watchers to the roof of the tall bell tower as well.

The abbot came from morning prayer to greet his unexpected guests. He, like most of England's clergy, favored severance from Rome and looked upon the Earl's cause as one with his own. Bishop Cantaloup was a close friend.

"Good morning, father," Simon greeted the abbot. "May we impose upon your hospitality for breakfast? The king, and all of us, are in need of refreshment. But we have very little time to spare."

"Edward may be near," Walter pressed further. "Can you feed us quickly? We're a few more than two hundred, and we have our hundred archers."

The abbey customarily fed far more than three hundred of its own community, its pantries were well stocked. The monks prepared a generous meal, accomplishing the cooking in short time, with eggs, flour and salted and smoked fish from their own stores. As breakfast was being prepared, the abbot and Bishop Cantaloup said Mass for the soldiers.

While day-old bread, cheese and milk was provided for the archers out in the abbey yard, the king, his Councilors, the Earl, and the young lords and Leicester knights were seated at long tables in the refectory and served a hearty meal, with new-baked, unleavened bread and the plum preserves for which Evesham was famous.

Benignly, Walter smiled to the abbot, "We eat unleavened bread like the Israelites fleeing Pharaoh."

Simon, hearing him, remarked caustically, strained at last to rising rage by the delay, "Pray the Lord ignites a pillar of fire for us, as he did for them."

The men at the long tables ate silently, tense and aware this pause was perilous. Their wandering in the hills during the night was a catastrophe. Only one third of their journey was completed, the rest lay in full daylight and through open land.

The night's threat of storminess, however, had developed. Dark clouds were rolling their gray knuckles overhead. Sunbeams still sheeted golden light beneath, giving a luminous clarity for the far-sighted and rendering the landscape in a warm, unnatural hue, vivid as an unsettling dream. Nerves already strung to hissing pitch, the watchers on the roof of the bell tower found the strange light and the close, warm summer air ominous, peculiarly frightening, beneath the hovering, racing sky of bulging clouds.

Within the crowded refectory there was tense silence, but for the sounds of eating and the droning voice of the lector reading the morning's Psalms. *The Lord is thy keeper. The Lord is thy shade upon thy right hand. The sun shall not smite thee by day, nor the moon by night. The Lord shall preserve thee from all evil. He shall preserve thy soul. The Lord shall preserve thy going out and thy coming in from this time forth, and even evermore."* Some, who had finished eating or had little appetite despite the fasting of the march, muttered the devout words with him.

Then on the tower roof, dust and what might be flags were sighted in the distant northeast. One of the watchers dashed down the stone stairs and across the yard to report to the Earl. The northeast. Kenilworth's direction. The man was bursting with hope though no scouts had come back.

At the exciting report, Simon touched his napkin to his mouth and left the table, beckoning to his squire Peter to come with him. The news astonished him. He had expected any movement sighted would be coming from the south or the southwest, in pursuit.

With his squire he climbed the tower stairs two at a time and reached the tower roof just as the other watcher was turning to come down. "My lord!" the man, breathless with joy, shouted, "The flags! They're your son Simon's! And many, many more! Young lord Simon joins us with his army!"

Almost not daring to believe the news, a cry, nearly a laugh, escaped Simon's lips. Leaning on the parapet, he demanded of his squire, "Peter... what other flags?" Tears moistened the corners of his eyes. He brusquely wiped them off with the back of his hand.

"Lord be praised!" Peter, squinting, gleefully reported. "The flags of the Earl de Vere, Ferrers... Oh Master, so many! It's an immense army he brings!"

Simon leaned back against the wall, his body trembling as if every muscle, tensed for so long, had forgotten how to relax. A wide smile was on his lips. "Oh, God! Praise God, my son is here at last."

The grim thoughts he had been harboring lifted. There would be a battle. No doubt Edward would know by now of their day spent at Kempsey. Battle would come soon, but with a good chance of victory for the huge army his son led. He felt a pang of shame for having doubted Simon.

Others were coming to the roof and peering to the northeast. Young Humphrey de Bohun let out a cheer and it was taken up by everyone. Gray-headed Nicholas Seagrave bellowed, "Vivat Simon Fils!"

Bishop Walter raised his hands, facing the northeast, and gave his blessing to the oncoming soldiers.

Word was sent down to the hall and the whole room broke to cheers and ribald singing in relief from the strain. Only the king sat silent, staring at his food, nodding in imbecilic irony.

Except for him, relief rocked everyone, lofted, buoyed, raised the company on a flood tide of anticipated victory. The monks pressed their guests' hands in congratulations and murmured words of thanks to God for the rescue of the men whose cause they cherished too.

A scout, riding fast from the south, galloped through the town, dismounted in the abbey's yard and burst into the refectory. He looked about, amazed at the cheery faces. The abbot, going to meet him, sent him hurrying on to the Earl in the bell tower. Reaching Simon on the parapet, the scout blurted, "I bring good news! I see I'm not the first. Coming from the south is a great army! In their fore is a flag I know: John Evyile's! They're friends!"

Simon bent over and began to laugh convulsively, a laugh of painful, cramping relief as the last fiber of doubt was sundered. He laughed loud and long, finally bringing out the heart-raising words, "My son brings *two* armies!"

Wiping his eyes, he asked his squire, "Peter, tell me more of what you see."

Young Bohun, leaning out over the parapet, cried, "There's dust to the southeast as well! I see a third army coming! If it's Edward, he'll find a damnable surprise!" His tone was shrill with glee.

The scout sent northward had not come back, but no matter. He no doubt was with Simon Fils, giving him report of the Earl and king at Evesham.

Squire Peter, peering to the south, was so much in the throes of hilarity that he could hardly speak the words, "Flying at the fore... they've even got that torn rag from Hinkley! ...Your ensign in Palestine!"

Simon clutched his side, aching in a spasm of laughter and relief. "Tell Boteveyln... in the refectory...that Simon brings his precious old banner."

From the north, where the ridge of Green Hill was crossed by the road, a rider came on at volant. Reaching the level ground at the hill's foot, he disappeared among the buildings at the outskirts of the town. In a few moments his horse clattered into the abbey yard. Dismounting, he followed a servant's gesture and dashed up the tower's stairs. "My lord," he threw himself down before Simon, "a huge army comes against you! Flee for your life!" Looking up, he saw everyone was laughing at him. "My lord, believe me!" he panted, wondering if he had fallen among madmen.

With a broad, assuring grin, Simon placed his hand on the youth's shoulder. "It's my son Simon's army that approaches. We are saved."

"My lord, no! I nearly joined them! I know who they are!"

Just then the Squire Peter, squinting at the march approaching from the northeast, cried out. "They're lowering their flags! My God... Oh, God, no... Your son's flag at the fore is going down. Edward's flag with the gold charges is rising!"

At the same moment Bohun yelled, "The flags to the southeast are lowering! Rising in the lead is blue and silver! Clare!"

Simon stared at his squire. Then squinted to the northeast. The endless, broad dark line in that direction had at its fore a speck of red, blown out to its full length by the wind. A multitude of colored specks were rising behind it. "Who are they?" he asked his squire, his voice so low that it was barely audible.

Peter strained his vision at the far bits of color. "My lord... the flags flown now are the king's barons'. Near the prince's flag I see Roger Mortimer's ensign."

"So... They've met my son and defeated him." Simon turned to stare at the army in the south, approaching toward Evesham's bridge.

Churning thunderclouds overhead, scudding from the west, were narrowing the band of gold daylight, casting a running shadow that drained the distant orchards to dull gray. The first fattened raindrops began falling, dimming view of the southern army though their triumphant flags still caught a glimmer from the low beams of the sun. Then a veil of rain obscured the marchers, vanishing their force as if they had been nothing but a frightening mirage. To the northeast, the vanguard of that vast army was disappearing too, behind the broad hunch of Green Hill. From the southeast the moving swath of oncoming forces was maneuvering with speed, closing off in a well-executed sweep any chance of escape.

The river in its deep curve embraced the town. The bridge was the one passage to the south. Green Hill rose in the terrain's only other route for leaving Evesham, its grassy, sheep-nibbled slopes descending to the Avon at both west and east. To flee, there were no choices but the bridge or the road over Green Hill's crest.

Simon looked southward. The rain, soaking the tower rooftop now, was settling to a steady downpour, a gray gauze filtering the view to simplified masses. The army nearing from the south efficiently was moving toward the bridge, yet still was some distance off.

He looked to the east. Nearsighted as he was, he could see the large, flowing mass curving in precise alignment with the rear guard of the army to the northeast, their approaches perfect in a well-thought strategy, using the terrain as a trap.

The dark, resigned, determined look that had been in Simon's eyes much of the morning, returned. As he watched the elegant and deft maneuvering of the encircling forces he gave way to a curt laugh in a momentary prick of pride. "Edward comes on well. Nor is it surprising. It was I myself who taught him this."

Turning to Walter he said softly, "Give me the Last Rites." Drawing his friend away from the others in the downpour of rain, Simon knelt on the wet roof at Walter's feet.

"Oughtn't I to give the rites to all of us?" the bishop asked, his voice caught in his throat as if his heart choked him with fear, with unstrung amazement, with sheer rage.

"I have hope they will escape, if they go quickly," Simon said with a calm that confounded his friend. "For myself there is no hope. *Confiteor Deo omnipotente, et tibi pater quia peccavi nimis in cogitatione...* I deplore and repent my sins as deeply as my soul can reach. I beg the Lord may grant me mercy. And I confess my intent to rid England of Edward, if Our Lord permits. Father, if you can, knowing that I hold this intent, bless me."

"I beg the Lord's mercy be upon you." Walter could barely speak the words, tears seeping down his cheeks in the wash of falling rain. "Would to God I had not made you stay and that you'd gone to Palestine."

"Too late, too late for such regrets," Simon said gently. "We waste time. Give me the Last Rites." His friend did as he asked, drawing the cross upon his eyelids, lips and forehead through the raindrops, then embracing him and crying in despair he could withstand no more.

Simon stood up, freeing himself from the burly bishop's grip. He turned and walked down the stairs, and all those on the parapet followed him.

The entire company, already told the news, was assembled in the rain-streaming courtyard. Peter de Montfort sat upon his destrier beside King Henry, who was mounted and covered by his plain, ill-fitting helm. The heavy steel bent his neck forward, encasing England's monarch in anonymity.

The Justiciar Hugh Despensar, the Councilors Roger SaintJohn and Adam Newmarket, the Earl's sons Henry and Guy, the steward Seagrave and his son, young Humphrey de Bohun, Peter de Montfort Fils, youths who had been knighted in the woods of Fletching and followed the Earl since, the Leicestermen and the hundred Welsh archers all stood, mounted and on foot, under the barrage of water from the lowering, windy sky.

Silently they watched the Earl come from the tower's doorway. His horse was held by his squire Peter, ready for him by the abbey's shut gate. The black mantle was gone. Fetched by the squire from his master's leather traveling bags, the white mantle with its blazon of the red fork-tailed lion rampant of Montfort draped the big destrier. Laid on the high saddle, as a good valet would set out his master's clothes, was Simon's lion-blazoned white surcoat. Beside it, his helmet and red lion shield hung on a chain.

From those concealing bags that he had borne behind his saddle, Peter also had brought forth the red lion flag of Montfort and King Henry's red and gold banner, the strutting lions of Plantagenet. Near the gate, Nicholas Seagrave bore the Montfort ensign high on a pike given him by the monks. Roger SaintJohn held a matching pike with the royal flag.

Simon did not mount. He stood, surveying the men who for so long and at such danger had followed his leadership.

"We are outnumbered," he said in a loud voice, "to a degree that makes resistance foolhardy in the extreme! The enemy approaches from all sides. *I release you! Go!* While you still can escape! Cross the bridge at once! Flee straight west from the riverbank. You can reach safety if you leave now. Before the army to the south can deny you the bridge!"

"What will you do, my lord?" young Bohun cried back, his dark hair soaked, adhering to his chubby cheeks.

"I go to meet those who are coming for me."

"Then we go with you!" Roger SaintJohn shouted. Turning his mount and the royal flag to face the crowd in the abbey's yard, he yelled, "Do I speak for us all? Do we go with the Earl?"

The response rumbled, echoing off the stone walls of the buildings that enclosed the yard. Wordless as thunder but clear in meaning, the blaring, melded voice said *Aye!*

Simon raised his hands. When the din silenced, he shouted with all the command that he could put into his voice, "I cannot save you! Save yourselves! Go now!"

"We won't leave you!" his son Guy threw back in his one moment of defiance of his father.

"Flee! Save the cause of the Provisions!" Simon bellowed, darting a furious glare at Guy. "Live! You are the last chance for our cause to survive!"

"We go where you go!" his cousin Peter de Montfort called back at him. "There is no cause! Nothing to fight for without you!"

Simon went to his son Henry, mounted on a horse near him, and gripped his chain mailed arm. "For God's sake leave! *Take them!* They've got very little time to cross the bridge!"

"No, my lord." Henry met his father's blazing eyes calmly. "Peter is right. There is no cause without you. I go where you go. You know it must be so."

"Walter!" Simon bellowed, searching for the bishop in the group behind him, sheltered from the rain by the tower doorway. Cantaloup came to him, his long robe flapping over the wet cobbles.

"In the name of Heaven, help me, Walter!" Simon pled.

"They will go nowhere but with you."

"Give me your cross!"

From under his copious chain hauberk, the bishop drew the large gold cross he always wore, pulled its cord over his head and handed it to his friend. Simon said angrily, "If they must go with me, you'll have much work by noon. I doubt resistance can be held so long as that!"

The squire Peter, leading his master's destrier by the bit, brought him to Simon. "Master, I beg you, give me a sword and let me go with you."

"You never go with me to battle. Stay here, Peter. If I return with wounds, I'll need you." Simon managed a smile for the servant who had been devoted to him since he first came to England. The link between them was closer in many ways than any other bond in either of their lives. But they both knew, if he returned with wounds they would be past helping. Tears were running from Peter's reddened eyes. He grabbed his master's hand and pressed it to his lips.

Reaching to his horse's saddle, Simon took the lion-blazoned surcoat and drew it on over his black chain hauberk. Then he looked at the faces around him in the falling rain. Some, nearby, were clear and familiar, those further off were blank to his weak eyes.

"The Benediction and the Absolution. Say them for us all, Walter." The Earl's voice was as cool as an order, and he knelt down on the abbey's puddled paving.

Those on their horses dismounted with a loud rustling of chain mail that mimicked the sound of the rain. The archers knelt behind the knights. All bowed their heads. But Peter de Montfort left the king mounted, like a statue of a forlorn knight, bent and drooping in the storm above a pool of soaked, bowed heads.

Walter, his voice fragmenting with feeling, recited the Benediction and the Absolution. The abbot sent two of his monks running to the church. They came back swinging a smoking censer and bringing the vessel of holy oil. Taking the chrism, the abbot moved among the kneeling men, touching each man with the blessed oil of the Last Rites as the Bishop of Worcester, his broad face washed with tears and rain, recited the words for the dying.

When the bishop stopped speaking, Simon held up Walter's gold cross to the crowd of men kneeling and blessed with the holy oil. "The enemy comes to meet us," he said in a loud yet strangely mild voice. "We commend our souls to God, for our bodies are theirs."

The Earl, white in his blazoned surcoat, mounted his white-draped destrier.

The company crossed their chests, and stood. The knights remounted. The archers adjusted the quivers on their backs and strung their bows, holding them at ready in their left hands. Their wicker shields they long since had discarded on the all-night run.

"We march up the north road. God willing, we may cross the ridge and have the height's advantage before Edward's and Clare's forces can join," Simon told them in a ringing shout. "When the enemy comes to meet us, we form a wedge, its point toward Prince Edward. Fight for Edmund to be king! Through him the Provisions may prevail! May God be with our cause!"

Turning, he set his destrier to a smooth trot out the gate. The storm had lessened to a lax drizzle, as if pausing to take breath.

In the lead, to the Earl's left, Nicholas Seagrave bore the Montfort flag, and to his right Roger SaintJohn carried the gilded banner of Plantagenet. It was the King, his royal Councilors and the Steward of England who marched to meet their foes.

After the flags and the Earl, King Henry, with his Councilors by his side, rode out the abbey's gate, Llewellyn, Bohun Fils, the Earl's sons and cousins, the young knights, the Leicestermen and the hundred Welsh archers following in file. Passing the abbey's almonry, they moved up High Street at a steady trot.

Along the way, people came out of the shops and houses. They stood solemnly by the building walls or knelt in the space afforded by doorways, and they crossed themselves in prayer. The only sound in the rain-sodden August morning was the tread of the march.

A blind woman beggar in rags broke the quiet, suddenly darting out toward Simon's horse. "Lord Earl, bless me!" she cried, holding her bare, gaunt arm up to him while her free hand felt for and dragged at his horse's mantle.

He looked down at her as his destrier drew her along; her sightless, pale and dirty face shone with undoubting faith. "The Lord's blessing be upon you," he heard himself saying, "...I beg you, pray for me." She released his horse's mantle and crossed herself, moving back to the building wall as the march passed.

As Simon and his company left the outskirts of the town and started up the sloping road, only the broad hill with its few drenched sheep cropping the wet grass could be seen. A dog barked frantically at the approaching horsemen, winding its tail in excitement as a shepherd, with whistle and shout and brandishing of his crook, drove his little flock down the slope and away toward the west.

The wind was rising again. With it, the laden clouds freely let down their rain in diagonal sweeps that ruffled the grass upon the hill like surf. The patter of raindrops on the knights' helmets was deafening.

Simon's hand rested on his sword's pommel at his hip. For the first time in recent memory, except those brief, deluded moments on the tower roof when it seemed his son had come, he felt at ease, almost happy. Whatever life required of him, it would soon be done. Within the privacy of his helm his lips moved in prayer.

Edward's army, advancing from the north, and Clare uniting with it from the east, were still unseen beyond the ridge. Simon sent for Llewellyn. His daughter's betrothed promptly rode up to him.

"How are your archers' spirits, my prince?" one helmet asked the other.

"They don't much like this hill, they'll be on lower ground than Edward," the Welshman answered honestly.

Simon laughed, sounding nearly merry. "Well, by the arm of Saint James, do any of us like it? If they can launch one volley, over our heads and into Edward's advance, that is enough. Then let them break and run as fast as their feet will carry them. Westward. Tell those who can swim to swim the river and go home. And, my son, go with them. Now is the time to keep your promise. See that our cause survives."

"My lord, if I escape this day," Llewellyn said, his broad, tanned face open and earnest, "I give you my word, I will not let Edward live!" Without waiting for reply, he turned his horse and cantered back to the archers with their orders.

Lowering, mud-colored clouds heaved and rolled above. In sweeping sheaves and veils the rain now plummeted. Gobbets large as pebbles ricocheted off the road as if Heaven meant to stone the earth below. Flickers of lightning darted in the west, followed by low mutterings and grumblings in the air. Wind carried the two flags out in shivering sheets eastward, flapping and recoiling in the raindrops' battering.

It was a long, gradual slope to the summit of Green Hill. On each side of the wide field the hillside fell more steeply, creasing in a little valley to the west, where the ridge extended in a shoulder toward the river. The turf was flooding in the downpour with a flow like running glass. On the roadway, water drew streaming miniature rivers that scurried dirt and rocks along in washouts and pooled in every slight depression, gathering debris.

The advance moved slowly against the storm. Buffeting gusts with heavy sprays of rain beat and puffed the horses' mantles like sails against their pacing legs. A toiling, brain-assailing thunder, crashing down the sky, was pinned nearby with glaring strokes of lightening.

At the brown-tinged dim horizon on the hill's summit riders appeared. First in the east. Then the west. Pennants fluttered, more and more each moment. Two silhouetted armies moved laterally across the ridge to form a long unbroken line ahead, spanning east to west. A red banner with gold charges and, beside it, a helmetless blond head arose among the mounted figures westward of the center.

Simon motioned his son Henry to him. Shouting through the rain's pounding din upon their helms, he commanded, "Array our knights in close phalanx behind me, the archers spread across the wedge's base. The phalanx broad and shallow, to keep our men well clear of our own arrows."

Henry moved back. The advancing formation took shape across the hill's wide field, spreading outward from the road. Simon guided his mount to the left, and the broad wedge shifted, angled slightly westward, aligning with the red and gold banner and the blond head without a helm.

Behind the Earl, near the apex of the wedge, the royal flag and the flag of Montfort beat against their poles like hysteric clapping hands. The Councilors, and Peter de Montfort with the king, were ordered further back and flanked by Leicestermen. Shields were adjusted, swords drawn but held low.

Simon, his sword still sheathed, turned and raised both hands as if holding a bow, as signal to his archers. The archers nocked their arrows, waiting for the Earl's gesture for them to take aim at the riders on the crest, draw and let fly.

They waited, as the heavy brown clouds sighed, pouring a cataract of rain that for the moment cloaked all view.

In the roar of falling water, a cry came from the ridge above. "Earl Montfort! We require your surrender!"

The voice was Edward's. The prince, on his great Spanish destrier, silvery bare-headed with water streaming down his face, rode out ahead of his line. He saw the hundred archers in the nearing formation, but gave no indication of his danger.

Simon drew his sword, drops pattering off the smooth steel blade.

With a crack like breaking sky and a brilliant flicker that turned the landscape black and white, the sudden downpour eased as quickly as it had begun. In resigned mumbling, the storm drew its obscuring skirts down the hill's east slope. The air brightened a little as the rain thinned to a soft diagonal shimmer.

Edward came nearer, his horse side-stepping across the slick wet slope. The line of men behind him began their descent. Flags in an endless-seeming row spread out behind him, ruffling in the strong breeze with a beating like the wings of a flock of migrating birds.

"Lord Montfort!" the prince shouted again. "You are surrounded. You're outnumbered! I grant quarter if you surrender *now!*"

The broad, pointed phalanx continued at a steady pace up the water-streaming hill, leaning against the wind that penetrated chain mail, chilling the soaked padded pourpoints beneath. The space was narrowing between the advancing triangle of riders with their archers on foot, and the descending knights moving slowly in long line down from above. Behind the first rank of flags another and another appeared at the hilltop and began to descend.

"Surrender!" Edward cried again, his voice a high-pitched scream. "*Surrender now! You won't break through!*"

Simon continued on. Through the slit of his helm he watched the dot of bright hair, the blond head in the haze of rain. When he was some two hundred yards below, he raised his sword high as the signal to his archers. They pulled their bows taut. The Earl's sword swept forward, and the whirr of a hundred arrows sang as the shafts flew over the phalanx, arching westward of the hilltop. As the well-aimed shafts climbed and peaked against the wind, and bent their way east to their targets, Simon pressed his spurs to his mount's flanks. With a leap the horse sprang forward, galloping, sliding on the soaked grass, laboring toward the dot that was a blond head.

A hundred arrows plunged in the advancing line. It faltered and broke as the barbs probed scattered marks.

An instant of chaos, then those uninjured in the baulked, disrupted vanguard, and those intact behind it, dove forward. They charged without waiting for their leader's permission. On the hilltop, riders and horses struck by arrows were shunted aside in their own army's headlong careen.

Behind Simon, his knights were moving faster, trying to gain momentum, laboring up the hill. The archers, as ordered, flung down their encumbering bows and quivers and ran westward.

Among them a single rider galloped. Llewellyn, cursing that he was fleeing like a coward, was faithful to the Earl's command. He would live and fight Edward another day. Looking back, he saw the endless ranks at the hilltop break formation and charge down upon the small phalanx of knights,

"*In God's Name, surrender!*" Edward yelled, spurring after his own men, his sword waving. "*Halt! Halt!*" he cried to the riders around and now ahead of him.

The army plunging from the ridge, barons of England, strategy abandoned in their rage at Montfort – their rage checked only while the enemy was out of sight and their small number unknown – took no notice of the prince's commands. They came on at volant made breakneck by the flooded slope and slippery footing. Those on the west swept in fastest, flying down the steep terrain, driving the Earl's phalanx eastward, nearer to the road again.

Simon, at the point of his advance, was brought to halt amid a buffeting of horses colliding with his mount. He met sword blows. Parrying, wheeling his staggering destrier, he countered strikes with shield and blade. His assailants' blows were hard and close but without aim at the impact. Horses tangled, jostling against each other in unbalanced confusion of legs, stirrups and flapping mantles till the riders regained some control. Behind Simon his phalanx backed and spread, battling the stream of oncoming fighters. Simon backed, withdrew, then tried to push forward toward the blond head on the rise above.

Lightning flashed, blindingly white, letting blows land without parry. And the rain fell hard again. Thunder broke as if the sky itself were cracking into shards. Startled destriers bucked wildly, eyes rolling in terror, though swords clashing about their ears only made their trained responses keener to their rider's will.

Nicholas Seagrave went down, his mount rearing and overturning onto him. In the press of men and horses, as he tried to free himself and rise, he was knocked down again and trampled in the mayhem of steel-shod hooves.

In the dark after the nearby lightning's glare cries were everywhere. The eye-confounding, bright instant let blades arc unstopped by parries. Men drooped with wounds. At the pause of resistance as they took their injuries, their enemies thrust in deadly strokes.

Blades swung, landed, crushing and breaking through mail, battering until defense faltered and the deathblow was inserted. Men beaten from their horses scrambled to their feet, staggering, shields high to meet strokes from above. Roger SaintJohn clambered from his dying horse, still gripping the royal flag. A rider charged at him and he fell, cleanly severed through the neck where his helm and hauberk met. His killer seized the flag out of his hand as he toppled away.

As the downward rush of attackers forced them, Simon's knights gave ground, spread outward, each man taking clusters of assailants backward with him until Green Hill's whole slope was scattered with clots of fighters, each congealed around a single struggling man.

Surrounded, Adam Newmarket fought like a beast, slashing wildly with his sword till someone circling at his back struck hard, driving a blade through his spine. He tottered, looking frantic for an instant and, in the pause, a blow struck at his neck, another cracked his helm, smashing his head within the steel and he fell face down on the wet ground. Before the victors could strip their prize, young Humphrey de Bohun rode up yelling, "Montfort!" and struck one man dead. The others promptly stabbed Humphrey's horse, bringing him down. As the heir to a double earldom fell and lay winded for a moment, his attackers pinned him, pulled away his helm, deftly cut the lacings of his chain mail hood and held a blade at his throat, demanding his surrender.

One slumping knight, his companion separated from him, was pierced in the leg by a lance. Crying out, he tried to pull his mount away from the fighting, but slid off of his saddle. The attacker, tossing aside his lance, dismounted and drew his sword. He raised his blade to give the death stroke to his victim who was wallowing in the grass, blubbering, with both hands gripping his injured thigh. The glint of the rising steel, just visible through his helm's eye-slit, sent the fallen knight to shrieking, "Don't kill me! I'm Henry of Monmouth!"

His assailant was perplexed by the name, but he knew the voice. He knelt, lifting away the injured knight's helmet. In the dim brown light and beating rain, King Henry's sagging, withered face appeared. "My lord!" Hugh Bigod gasped. "I'll get you from the field!" And he carried Henry in his arms out of the battle.

The storm that had retreated eastward and was drenching Offenham had brought an even wilder sister in her train. Wind driven, opaque sheets of rain were sweeping Green Hill like ruffling pages, hiding then revealing the fight, then obscuring it again. Peter de Montfort met blows with Roger Leybourne. Then Roger Clifford joined, striking Peter with a battle-axe between the shoulder blades. Peter's right arm rose up as he fell. Leybourne, with no parry blocking him, using all his might, drove his point through the grating chain mail into Peter's chest. Peter's son maneuvered his horse protectively over his father's dead body. Clifford buffeted the youth's helm with an axe, denting it and bowling him off of his mount. Before he could get to his feet, Clifford seized him, and Leybourne pinned his arms behind his back. Young Peter was dragged from the field as their prisoner.

Though the battling was fierce, many of the prince's and Clare's men held back on the fringes, waiting for their chance to move in on the target of their choice. Edward, with John de Warenne, watched from high ground by the roadside. The prince's face was pale, set in rage. "Why wouldn't he surrender?" he muttered through his teeth.

Guy de Montfort, fighting with unmatched fury, climbed nearly to the hill's summit. But he was far from the rest of his father's forces and surrounded by Gloucester's men, who took turns several at a time, striking, prodding, teasing as though playing a deadly game of blind man's bluff. They hit at him and at his horse with long pikes, well past the reach of his sword. Tiring of their sport, one thrust his pike through the old, uncomely destrier's belly and the trusty animal went down on its knees. Climbing free of his dying horse, Guy turned and turned, his shield meeting blows from all directions, his sword flailing, spoiling his opponents' aim. But more men crowded around, cheering and taking turns, until one with a long lance jabbed its point past the parrying blade and into Guy's side. As he doubled on the lance, his taunters moved in, driving their swords through his hauberk until he crumpled, helpless, soaked with his own blood in the wash of rain.

Some hundred feet west of the road, not far above Simon, his son Henry was fighting. A sword cut through Henry's horse's neck and the animal pitched head-foremost to the ground. As Henry sank with his mount, his assailants quickened their strokes but were blocked by his shield.

Edward, on the road not far away, saw Henry go down. Near the prince a riderless horse, blood smeared down its neck and in its matted mane, was darting aimlessly in panic. The prince spurred toward the destrier and caught it by the bridle. "John!" he cried to Warenne. "Take this to Henry Montfort!"

"Henry Montfort?" Warenne asked in amazement.

"Do as I say! *Now!*" Edward bellowed at him, handing him the bridle.

Confused, and not particularly willing, Warenne, with the horse in lead, approached the writhing knot of men. "Tell him that I sent it!" Edward called after him.

The fight around Henry was slipping downhill, away from the cautious Warenne. A big horse in a badly slashed white mantle was moving toward Henry as well, dragging a thick cluster of mounted fighters as it went. Glancing up, Warenne saw its rider wore the white surcoat with the fork-tailed red lion rampant.

Simon reached his son. "Get up behind my saddle!" he bellowed, covering Henry with his shield and meeting clanging, ringing sword strokes with his blade.

Henry thrust his sword into the chest of the horse of the attacker nearest him, and horse and man fell back. With room to fit his foot into his father's stirrup, he swung up, sweeping away a sword thrust as he did. But as he settled on the destrier's broad crupper, a shuddering went through the big animal. A pike was driving through its breast, emerging just behind the Earl's stirrup.

The destrier heaved sideways as if trying to dislodge the shaft, then fell grunting, blood spurting and spreading down the wet mantle and coursing from its open mouth and gagging tongue.

William de Valence dropped the pike he had embedded in the horse. Simon and Henry slid down, reaching the ground standing as their mount heeled to its side and collapsed. They stood back-to-back, carefully maneuvering free of the horse's thrashing legs. Together they gave ground down the slope. Simon deftly canted his hacked shield, returning the blows of a knight with a black shield marked with diagonal gold bars.

Wind-driven rain was falling in cascade with distracting, ceaseless clatter upon helms. The sky, the hill pulsed brilliant white with shattering thunderclaps overhead. On the ridge-top a group of knights stood silhouetted in the flickering bright glare. The Marcher lords, fresh, watching the battle from the crest, now spurred their horses down the slope, led by Roger Mortimer.

At Simon's back, Henry now was fighting the mounted knight of black and gold who was battering from above. A shield Simon knew well, Leybourne's, was nearest him. Mortimer spurred his horse into the press, raised his sword to strike Simon, but caught Henry turning instead.

Too heavy, the blow bent Henry's arm, pining his sword close by his side for an instant. The black and gold knight, seeing opportunity, struck fast, a slash deep into Henry's shoulder. He recoiled, badly wounded, his arm hanging loose. Staggering, he lurched into his father's back. Beyond resisting, he was struck again and sank to his knees. A blow from Mortimer drove into his chest and his sword fell from his hand. As he crouched behind his father, Mortimer's next stroke plunged down his neck. Henry rose an instant as the blade was drawn out, then he fell back dead against his father.

Thrust forward by Henry's fall, Simon missed his parry. A blade bit through his chain mail sleeve into his arm. Now his opponent Leybourne was joined by William de Valence, his helmet cast aside, his lips in a tight smile. Mortimer and the knight in black and gold were advancing over Henry's body. All four bore down on

Simon in the instant he flinched from the wound. He gave ground further down the slope, his right arm weakening as the deep cut spouted blood. He struck with all of his remaining strength, his blade chattering as it met Mortimer's and then Valence's swords in a single sweep. He turned and turned, avoiding the bodies of the fallen, slipping and sliding downward on the rain-drenched, blood smeared grass.

Few on the broad field of Green Hill were still fighting. Around the Earl men gathered, his enemies, watching, whistling, mocking. The end was clear so nobody was betting. Surrounded, encircled, Simon kept on meeting blows from Valence, Mortimer, and now Gilbert de Clare joined them, fresh for he had taken no part in the fighting until now.

From the road Edward cantered over. "*Stop*! Take him prisoner!" he shouted. But no one paid attention. They were intent on the kill.

Simon parried the blows without thought or method, it was what his body knew how to do. And he would not surrender. The blow he took into an artery when Henry fell was weakening him. More strokes succeeded and the loss of blood was dulling his brain. Of all the men opposing the prince's armies on Green Hill, he fought last and alone.

Guy de Lusignan rode up to take his tiring brother William's place. Simon still fought well enough to weary his combatants. The cheering and jesting had ceased. The blows aimed at him were delivered with silent concentration. The crowd around him was quiet now, watching, as if the spectacle of gallant death were holding them mute.

The rain had slackened and the sky's dark, ominous brown shade had lifted to a pale and fragile blue. A distant flash of lightning seemed to idle for eternity before its thunder's rumble whispered from the east. Green Hill was quiet but for the single ringing sound of sword on sword and thud of sword on broken shield. Simon was turning more slowly, meeting blows more weakly. But his attackers were tiring as well. Blood from his wounds stained his chest and back and sprayed from his arm with each sweep of his sword. Mortimer drew away, leaving the last strokes to fresher men.

Edward rode closer on his great destrier. "For God's sake, spare him! Seize him!"

As if in protest, Simon struck, slashing Guy de Lusignan across the hand.

"No!" Guy bellowed at the prince defiantly. "He's ours!"

His eyes fierce, furious at the refusal of his order, Edward jabbed his spurs into his horse and galloped up the hill to where his flag's pole was stuck in the ground, the flag's embroidered satin wetly clinging to the shaft. From there he turned briefly to watch the slow-moving, deliberate cluster of men below, then he rode out of sight down the far side of the slope.

Within his helm, Simon bared his teeth in a smile at Guy de Lusignan and struck him again, but tottered from the force of his own blow that failed to be lethal. Mortimer, engaging at the instant of imbalance, aimed a strike to Simon's side that crushed the chain mail, bit deep through the soaked wadding of his pourpoint and into flesh and bone. Simon gasped, pitching forward, but straightened to meet a strike from Leybourne, as the knight in black and gold thrust a blade deep in his back.

The Earl's sword fell and he raised his empty hand. Stumbling, he staggered among his assailants as they freely struck at him, until he fell at their feet. He raised his bleeding arm as if to ward away a blow, and Leybourne leaned upon his sword, driving it through Simon's chest in the *coup de grace*.

A trailing gust of the storm, fleeing eastward beyond Evesham, darted one last lightning bolt. It struck with shimmering brilliance, fingering the abbey's bell tower. The heavy bell swung, tolling. It tolled and tolled until its swinging ceased of its own accord.

The battle was ended. For three hours it had been sustained, though its outcome from the first had been undoubted.

Edward and Clare withdrew with most of their knights, with Valence and Guy de Lusignan following. Across the field the lesser knights, the looters, moved, stripping the dying and the dead.

A few of the Earl's assailants stayed by him: Mortimer and Leybourne and the knight in black and gold who, taking off his helm, revealed the impish face of William Maltraverse. The three set to work unfastening the ruined armor and torn, bloody clothes, removing them from the gashed body.

It was noon when lightning struck Evesham Abbey's bell. By that afternoon summer heat and flies had settled on the quiet of Green Hill. The grass had dried, the sun shone hot and cheerful in a sky of cloudless blue.

A group of brown-robed monks walked up the road, followed by several carts, each pulled by a pair of oxen. In the lead of the small procession was the Bishop Walter Cantaloup, carrying the abbot's gold cross on its staff. The men in the procession sang as they walked, they chanted the dirge for the dead.

Unloading makeshift litters from the carts, the monks moved across the slope, searching for anyone still living among stripped bodies. They found Guy de Montfort, riddled with wounds but breathing. His hand moved and he groaned in near unconsciousness, as two strong monks lifted him onto their litter and carried him to their cart.

Far down the field, three monks climbed the slope toward the bishop, who waited by the oxcarts on the road. They led him some hundred feet westward to a shallow hollow. There a man lay prone, crying in the bloodied grass. Beside him was a naked torso, gaping with fresh wounds and lined and blotched with scars, the palimpsest of a long history of injuries. Clinging in the sticky blood of the new cuts were bits and shreds of a hair shirt. The head and limbs were nowhere to be seen.

Walter stared in shock. Forcing himself to some control, he knelt by the man who lay prostrate crying.

The man raised his head, his face red, crumpled with grief. "Why did they do this?" he asked without hope of an answer. It was Simon's squire Peter, who knew the body's signature of scars as well as if they were his master's name written into his flesh.

Walter prayed, moving his fingertips from fresh wound to fresh wound and where the limbs, the head and manhood were missing. He prayed for Simon's soul's peace. Looking to Peter, who knelt now in prayer with his contorted, tear-streaked face concealed by his hands, he murmured, "The abuses he suffered, in every way that a man can sustain, are now ended. God surely has welcomed his soul."

Pressing his hands beneath, to gather the ghastly torso into his arms, Walter's fingers touched motion, cold and agitated, chilling. Startled, frightened for an instant, he jerked his hands back. Then taking courage, he embraced his friend's body again, and lifted it.

A spring of fresh water spurted from the ground, bubbling, splashing, washing the death-pale, bloodied, wound-gaping skin. The new spring flowed with force, filling the little hollow, then running in spate through the grass and down the slope, uprooting the turf as it carved a runnel that obviously had never flowed before.

Monks, standing by with a litter, stared, confounded at the stream. The bishop too, clutching the ruined body in his strong arms, watched the astounding flood.

At a murmur from the monks, Walter laid Simon's body on the litter, but could not take his eyes from the surging new spring. As the monks took up the litter to carry it to their cart, the bishop told them, "Return with flasks and take this water to your church. We are witnessing a miracle of Our Lord's Grace."

Salve, Symon Montis-Fortis
totius flos militiae,
Duras poenas pasus mortis,
Protector gentis Angliae.

Sunt de sanctis inaudita
Cunctis passis in hac vita
Quemquam passum talia;
Manus, pedes amputari,
Caput, corpus vulnerary,
Abscidi virilia.
Sis pro nobis intercessor
Apud Deum, qui defensor
In terris exterritas.

# Author's Note

Simon's spring of miraculous, healing waters still persists. It was noted especially for curing blindness. The blind, the sickly, came to it in devout faith and were healed, until taking water from the spring was declared a capital crime, an act of treason.

I traveled to Evesham in 1978 to see the battlefield and look for what had been called, with typical anonymity, The Baron's Well. I got off the train in Evesham's station and, intent on asking directions, I caught up with three people who were walking ahead of me. As they turned toward me, I saw all three were blind.

Nearly no one, that day in Evesham, knew of The Baron's Well. Someone directed me to an estate on the summit of Green Hill where there turned out to be a decorative stone fishpond. Green Hill was, and still is as I write, an open, uncultivated field except for a row of houses bordering the road – the same road Simon marched up to his last battle.

From the estate at the hilltop, I clambered down the field searching for any sign of a spring or rivulet. Eventually, in the midst of a few small bushes, I found a spring with watercress sprouts raising their greenery over a little reflection of the sky. Visitors find it, as I did, and take samples of its water without mortal threat or hindrance.

After Simon's death the miracles attributed to him were so many that they literally fill a book: The Chronicle of William Rishanger. Few saints can claim so many miraculous good works.

Thirteenth century theologians cited the several ways the battle at Evesham paralleled Christ's death on the Cross. Both events took place between nine in the morning and noon. Both were accompanied by a thunderstorm. At Jesus's *giving up the ghost,* lightening struck the Temple in Jerusalem, tearing the veil of the

Covenant. At Simon's death, lightening struck the bell tower of Evesham, causing the bell to ring a knell all on its own.

Tradition has it that Simon's mangled torso was given sacred burial within Evesham Abbey's church. The abbey was destroyed in the Dissolution of Catholic institutions by King Henry VIII. What remains at Evesham is the magnificent bell tower. The rest is in ruins open to the sky, with a lawn marking the nave of the church. Beneath where the altar steps had been, the skeletal remains of a torso have been found.

Simon's severed head purportedly arrived at Mortimer's castle at Ludlow, where Dame Maude *foully shent* it, in the words of Robert of Gloucester.

Simon Fils, bringing up his forces with remarkable speed, considering he had to dress, re-arm and re-mount his captains, arrived in time to see the knights of Roger Mortimer marching northward bearing the Earl's head upon a pike. Young Simon fled back to Kenilworth where he held off Edward's siege, the longest siege in England's recorded history, and eventually negotiated a truce that let him leave England for a life in exile on the continent.

At Dover, the Countess Eleanor, her daughter Eleanor and son Richard heard of the debacle at Evesham and the countess went into mourning for three days: secluded, eating nothing and seeing no one. From her still extant accounts roll we know much of the countess' doings from the time before Simon's last visit at Odiham with his knights to her flight from England and eventual sheltering in the convent at Montargis.

The convent was founded by Simon's sister Amicia, whom he probably knew only slightly as she was older, married, and spent many of her years in retreat with the holy community she founded. When the convent was destroyed during the French Revolution, Countess Eleanor's account roll, a long strip of vellum, each sheet sewn end to end, was found wedged into a crevice in the convent's stone wall.

Ten years after the debacle at Evesham, Simon's daughter Eleanor, thanks to the efforts of her brother Amaury who remained a respected clergyman and officer of the Church, was allowed to sail from France to wed the Welsh Prince Llewellyn. At sea her ship was boarded, she and Amaury were seized. Her brother was taken to imprisonment in Corfe castle, but Eleanor was brought to Edward's Court where she remained for three years. It was not until 1278 that Edward permitted her to wed Llewellyn, and then he arranged the wedding celebration himself, at Worcester on his own saint's day.

In Wales Eleanor gave birth to a baby girl, probably too soon after the wedding. The child was named Gwencillian and was removed to a convent, where she spent her life very obscurely for what should have been a Welsh princess. In 1282, giving birth to a second daughter, Katherine, Eleanor de Montfort died. This second child was heiress of northern Wales and was wedded to the prince of southern Wales, uniting the two realms.

Henry Tudor claimed descent from this princely Welsh line, and Henry VIII, in the genealogical tree he had painted on the wall of the hall at Winchester, proudly claimed through his Tudor lineage his ancestor Simon de Montfort.

During the reigns of Henry VIII and Elizabeth I, the Chronicle of Matthew Paris, which so assiduously records the Vatican's ill use of England, was made available in print. It offered an argument ready-to-hand to justify, with its history of papal abuses, England's parting from the Church of Rome.

Amaury, Simon's scholarly son, thanks to his sister's pleas to Edward, was released from prison in 1282, two months before Eleanor's death. Like his brothers he was forced into exile, though he brought suit against the prince, by then King Edward I, to regain the Montfort lands and titles. Purportedly he renounced his priesthood and sought to be made a knight to avenge his father's death.

The youngest son, Richard, after being supplied with socks, the cost of which is carefully recorded in the Countess Eleanor's accounts, was sent to Bigorre, the *comte* in the Pyrenees that Simon had acquired by temporary purchase, and the holding of which was contested by Gaston de Bearne whose wife was the Countess Pironelle's youngest child. Nothing more was ever heard of Richard, age twelve at the time. It is probable he was in the company of Philip de Montfort, Simon's Outremerine cousin Philip's son, who was a member of the Court in Paris and whom Simon apparently had named as his steward for Bigorre.

Guy de Montfort survived the battle of Evesham, nursed by the monks of the abbey. He, like his brother Simon, fled into exile in Europe. There he became a renowned military leader affiliated with King Louis' brother Charles of Anjou. His fame and honor were so great that he wedded Margherita da Aldobrandesca, Countess of Savona, in the church at Viterbo, and received the title Count of Nola. The noble family of Orsini de Balzo trace their lineage from him and quarter the fork-tailed rampant lion of Montfort in their heraldry. I am grateful to Valentia Baciu for an extensive genealogy of Guy's descendants.

Guy's life might have rested in good fortune, but his brother Simon, who appears to have gone mad, not without cause, found him and persuaded him to join in an attempt to avenge their father's death. At it happened, the first target available to them was the kind, innocuous Henry of Alemaine, who paused in Italy on his way home from Prince Edward's crusade in the Holy Land. The brothers came upon Henry praying in the church at Viterbo, and slew him in the midst of his prayers at the church's altar. The crime was so shocking that Dante awarded the Montfort brothers a special place in his Inferno.

With all Europe seeking the scandalous murderers, Simon Fils vanished, but Guy, betrayed, was caught and imprisoned. Most accounts say that he died in prison, but one scholar believes he escaped, thanks to the political influence of friends and relatives, and that the story of Guido de Monteforti inspired Alexander Dumas to write *The Count of Monte Cristo*. Guido appears as a character in the opera *Les Vêpre Siciliennes* by Verdi, which Dumas saw shortly before he began to write *Monte Cristo*.

Prince Edward went on to reign as Edward I, the conqueror of Wales and the *Hammer of the Scots*. The Provisions of Oxford, with its Parliament meeting at regularly appointed times – deciding issues of England's governance, requiring the king to uphold its decisions, and including elected representatives of the common people – was suppressed. King Henry, in the few years of life remaining to him, summoned the lords but seldom, the elected representatives of the commons never.

Edward, seeing the value of reports from the hinterlands, summoned representatives of specific classes and groups for consultation, but it was not until Edward had been reigning for twenty-three years, in 1295, that commoners and representatives of towns, elected for the purpose, were summoned to the king in a parliament at all similar to those Simon held. And the king was not bound to follow their advice.

Nonetheless, the founding of Parliament is dated – by historians who think ill of a man who captures but does not kill his king – from Edward's meeting of 1295, rather than from Simon's parliaments or those immediately following the Provisions of 1258. Hundreds of years would pass, and Oliver Cromwell would seize England, before an elected Parliament again would meet regularly, decide issues and have full powers to enforce those decisions. The model of government that Simon de Montfort made a reality survived as template, and ultimately prevailed.

Though, in an effort to stifle a rebellion of his followers, it was made a hanging crime to utter the name Simon de Montfort, in the twentieth century the suppression of his name finally was eased. Montfort University at Leicester now commemorates him. A few biographies have been written, some generously seeking what his motives may have been, some critical and caustic, built upon the writings of his enemies.

Queen Elizabeth II sponsored the signal of Simon de Montfort's return to acceptability by having a commemorative exhibit of the Battle of Evesham at its seven-hundredth anniversary, in 1965. In that same year a simple stone memorial for Simon was dedicated at the site of the altar of Evesham Abbey's church by the Speaker of the House of Commons and the Archbishop of Canterbury. Simon would have been pleased with the honor.

# HISTORICAL CONTEXT

The Earl of Leicester's whereabouts between August of 1260 and August of 1262 are a matter of differing opinions. Some historians, assuming the trial notes still in existence pertain to a trial in England in1260, maintain he was in England until 1262 while his cause of extending the Provisions' rights to the commons was waning. Even though the Earl Montfort was notably among those not invited, assertion is made that he attended the King's meeting with the lords in November of 1261, at Kingston-on-Thames, where Henry successfully suborned the barons by a qualified apparent agreement to much of the Provisions.

I hold that the extant trial notes are from an actual trial before Queen Margaret in France in 1262, not a mere arbitration. The notes are in the *Bibliotheque Nationale,* not The Public Record Office as they ought to be if they recorded an official legal action in England. Nor would the recorded defense that Simon provided for himself have succeeded in exonerating him in any English court.

I believe there was an aborted action in England by King Henry against Simon in 1260, ending with the arrival of Archbishop Riguad, King Louis' Minister of State (which is on record), and the earl was in France for two years after that. (See Labarge, *Simon de Montfort,* p. 199.) His being haplessly in England while his movement disintegrated is inconsistent with the well-documented rise of the mystical view of him at that time among the populace. The only instance that could seem to indicate his participation during then: the ineffectual summoning of shire representatives in his name and the names of others, only demonstrates the importance of his name, and does not prove his presence, or even his knowledge of the attempt. Negotiations with the Welsh, attributed to Simon in October of 1260, arise from an error of date in Bemont's *Montfort*, 1930, and belong properly to October 1259, as I've pointed out in Volume III.

If the issues King Henry held against the earl were unresolved in 1260, as the legal action in fact heard by Queen Margaret in 1262 would argue, Simon's presence in England in the intervening time would have been exceedingly perilous.

*King Henry has given us leave to attend the tournaments.*

The French tournaments at this time, and Edward's attendance with his companions, are historical. The passage in this volume dealing with those tournaments is fictional.

*to curb the king's abuses*

The kings of England were free to tax their direct liegemen however they pleased. The Norman lords who had come with William the Conqueror, and their descendants, possessed their holdings in England solely by the king's grant. Magna Carta had provided, since 1215, that the king must obtain the lords' agreement to any taxes, with a few exceptions, beyond the knights' services they owed in time of war, or the monetary equivalent.

King Henry III had become exceedingly adept at forcing their consent through coercion. It was in rebellion against these coercive tactics that the lords had succeeded, in 1258, in obtaining the Provisions of Oxford, creating a Parliament that met regularly three times a year and had the power to select a Council, the head of the royal courts of law (Justiciar), and the keeper of the royal seals (Chancellor) without which no document issued by the king was valid. Through these officials and this Council, constantly present with the king, the Parliament was able to constrain the king to act according to the wishes of the people's representatives. Composed of the king's barons and four knights elected by the (male) commoners of each shire, the Parliament provided a channel of control of the government by the people of England.

During Simon's time of dominance, elected representatives of the towns and guilds were added. These Parliaments of 1264-65 were true models of England's later Parliament composed of the House of Lords and the House of Commons: the prototype for all governments that have followed this bi-cameral form, including the Congress of the United States with its Senate and Congress.

Regarding the offensive taxes that spurred the rise of this innovative form of government: the excessive taxes Henry was accustomed to extracting usually were a percentage of all the lords' movable property. The confiscations would be gathered by the sheriff local to each of the lords' holdings. Some of the property collected would be of gold or silver that could be melted down and struck as coin by the royal mint. But most of it would be in livestock and personal possessions. To convert this property into funds, the sheriff would have to sell the goods and livestock, most likely through the markets and fairs of the towns. A sudden dumping of any commodity on a market normally would lower the value of the commodity, but a relationship existed between the king and the towns enabling the leading burghers to force the king into granting the towns and guilds special rights in exchange for their maintaining an orderly market. Similarly, the king could influence the burghers by threatening to rescind those rights.

By this means, among others, capital worth, beginning as the rents of agriculture, passed from the lords to the towns with a resulting gradual growth in wealth and power for the towns, and a gradual depletion of the wealth and capacities of the lords.

The capital accumulated by kings was spent chiefly in hiring mercenary soldiers and other costs of war, and in architecture, though some of course was spent on the costumes and jewels deemed necessary to present a regal appearance, and much was spent on gifts to courtiers. In the towns, architecture and, above all, the growth of trade tended to absorb the increase in capital, compounding the increase in wealth and capacity of the burgher class.

*Jean de Joinville*

The Steward of France was one of the few to survive the debacle of Louis' 1240 crusade and go with him to Acre. His record of the crusade and biography of Louis are among the most important documents of the thirteenth century that are readily available to the modern reader. Joinville tells of Louis' favoring him, and there is no doubt of it since Louis named him Steward of France despite Montfort having been promised the office. The characterization of Joinville here is fictional.

*put your last will into writing*
For Simon's will, which he had already composed on January first, 1259, see Bemont, *Montfort,* 1930: pp. 276- 279, with a facsimile insert between pages 278 and 279. The neat chancery style handwriting is that of Simon's son Henry, not because of any inability on Simon's part, but because a will, in the handwriting of the principal and trusted heir, should be unquestionably understood and accepted by that heir.

A note regarding medieval spelling: Henry who, according to their letters preserved in the *Monumenta Franciscana,* was considered by Bishop Robert Grosseteste and Gregory de Boscellis a fine scholar, spells his own name, Henry, five different ways in writing the single page of the will. It would seem that spelling then was more a challenge to the imagination than a matter of conformity. T.E. Lawrence's correspondence with his editor regarding irregular spelling, published in the opening pages of *Revolt in the Desert,* is one of the particular delights of Lawrence's work, and is apt for anyone dealing with medieval writings. Readers of 12th and 13th century manuscripts had best have a liberal and phonetic approach. The modern practice that discredits content on the basis of nonconformist spellings would have been thought irrelevant and small minded.

*Ah, yes, the revered Aquinas*
Thomist theology was to hold sway until the Reformation and the Enlightenment, and indeed is still regarded highly by The Society of Jesus and many other Orders.
*"We hold these truths to be self evident, that all men are created equal, that they are endowed by their Creator with certain inalienable Rights…"*

the words of the Declaration of Independence directly counter Thomist hierarchical theology and evolve from the ideas promoted by Joachim del Flor, John of Salisbury, Robert Grosseteste and Simon de Montfort, though the thirteenth century movement had been suppressed and largely forgotten, except in essence, long before the eighteenth century.

*I've been sent to put a letter in your own hands from my superior in Rome."*

See Labarge, *Simon de Montfort*, p. 201, for Simon's extraordinary appearance before the October Parliament held during King Henry's absence, and of his reading the papal letter to that meeting. The circuitous route of the pro-Provisions letter before reaching Simon's hand is my own conjecture, based on the recent death and replacement of the Pope.

*The morning of the trial,*
Simon's trial, as offered here, is essentially an edited version of the actual notes of the trial. I studied the original documents in the Montfort Archive in the *Bibliotheque Nationale*. The humor is Simon's. For part of the surviving transcript of Simon's trial before Queen Margaret, see Bemont, *Simon de Montfort*, 1884 (reprinted 1976), article XXXVII, pp. 343-53.

*"I seldom go without horses and arms. It is the way I usually travel."*
From the trial transcript: *"Le roi dit que le conte i vint adonc a chevaus et a armes." "Le conte dit qu'il n'i vint n'a chevaus n'a armes, fors en la manere qu'il est costumiers d'aler aval le pais."* I was so stunned by the insouciance of this answer that I found it hard to believe Bemont's translation until I had the actual, original record of the trial in my hands at the *Bibliotheque Nationale*.

*"I am called Robin,"*
*who lived by thievery and went by the names of Weyland or Robin and practiced their old rites*

Faery, deriving from *fay*, meaning 'faith' and the old French ending 'ery' meaning 'pertaining to' as in bak-*ery* is the collective term for these peoples. See OED, *fay*. See also *Robin Hood*, Holt, J.C., Thames and Hudson, 1982.

The survival of communities of the pre-Christian Celtic cults was interestingly documented in the 1920's by the archeologist and anthropologist Margaret Murray in *The God of the Witches*, *The Witch Cult in Western Europe* and *The Divine King in England*. Eminent historians, in defense of the reputation of the Crown, attacked Murray's work and, for a time, made the citing of her books highly problematic. That the ancient cults did survive certainly well past the thirteenth century, identified with the practices of witchcraft, is beyond most cavil.

The association of *faery* with tiny incorporeal sprites appears to begin with Shakespeare's *A Midsummer Night's Dream*. That Shakespeare knew fairies to be quite substantial human beings of normal or only slightly diminished size is evident in *The Merry Wives of Windsor*, when the witty and vindictive wives terrorize Falstaff by deluding him into thinking he has fallen into the hands of fairies – who are none other than the merry wives and their grown daughters.

Falstaff's fear was not without foundation if Murray is correct, for she cites numerous instances of human sacrifice. The Old Faith, as she describes it, was built upon a ritual of human sacrifice repeated every seven or nine years on one or another of the cults' high holy days: Candlemas, February 2; Beltane, May 1, Lammas, August 2; All Hallows, November 1. Modern *neopagans*, using the term Wicca to describe their culture, will dispute this, but Murray's findings are supported by Matthew Paris's *Chronica Majora*, and earlier writers whom she cites.

Brother Matthew reports an incident when King Henry was visiting his manor at Woodstock. As the king slept, a man broke into his room and attempted to murder him. Henry, in his nightshirt, managed to flee and call his guards, who captured the intruder. The man claimed he was the "rightful king" and that he had "the mark of the king" on his shoulder. (Murray refers to this scarification on the shoulder.) Far from merely dealing with the man as a dangerous lunatic, Henry had him not only drawn and quartered as if he were a usurping traitor, but had the four pieces of his body dragged behind horses through the streets of the four ancient holy cities: London, Coventry, Winchester and Canterbury.

*Simon prepared to leave for Palestine.*

With agreement to the treaty (April 30, 1250) Queen Margaret made in Damietta with Turansha, King Louis, his queen and principal lords were set free and sailed for Acre, which, with Tyre, Sidon and Caesarea, was held again by the Christian lords and communes of Outremere, though Jerusalem was in Moslem keeping. But most of the Christian prisoners were retained, pending the payment of the ransom.

Two days after the signing of the treaty (May 2) Turansha was murdered by his own Mameluk soldiers at a feast celebrating his victory. The murder was led by Baibars Rukn ad-Din who had rallied the Moslem forces after Louis' surprise attack had nearly won Mansuorah for the Christians. Though the gift of the elephant may have been promised by Turansha, its delivery much later apparently was by Izz ad-Din Aibek's gracious order. (See Runciman, p. 272, Vol. III.)

Izz ad-Din Aibek was chosen by the Mameluks to rule Egypt in Turansha's place, but his ascendancy was immediately challenged by an-Nasir Yusuf, who occupied Damascus. Thus the split of the Moslem forces between Egypt and Damascus, which had worked to the crusaders' advantage at the time of Prince Richard's 1240 crusade, was renewed.

King Louis, remaining in Outremere for four years, 1250-54, spent his time taking full advantage of the situation, at one point even succeeding in making treaty with the Mameluks in Egypt which, if the Mameluks prevailed, would have returned all of Palestine, including Jerusalem, to the Outremerine kingdom. He did succeed in obtaining from Aibek an exchange of prisoners, including Christians still languishing in prisons since their defeat in 1244 by the Khoresines, and 3,000 Christian prisoners taken since then – all these in exchange for just 300 Arab prisoners held by the Outremerines. (The gift elephant actually showed up in company with the released Christians. See p. 276, Runciman, Vol. III.)

Louis also had treaties with the Assassins, and was able to use the threat of Mongol invasion to secure alliances among the Islamic factions. Though militarily his crusade was a disaster, Louis himself, in his devoutness, forthrightness and wisdom, so impressed the Muslim leaders that there was talk that if he would convert to Islam, he would be their choice for sultan.

Louis' departure (April 1254) for France resulted in Christian Palestine returning to factional chaos. The division now chiefly was due to a split between Venetian and Genoese mercantile interests, and involved the knightly Orders and Outremerine lords who were their factional allies. But the lucrativeness of Arab-Outremerine commerce with Europe was sufficient for the Islamic leadership, engaged in their own quarrels and fearing the Mongols, to leave Outremere undisturbed apart from its own internal turmoil.

The Outremerines' split of their loyalties resulted in extreme consequences nonetheless. Conradin, the son and heir of the Emperor Frederic's son Conrad, who was himself the son borne by little Yolanda, Queen of Jerusalem, was the titular King of Jerusalem through the Holy Roman Empire's claim to the Crown. In the past, opposition to the Empire's claim had been the one issue the Outremerine lords could agree upon.

In the separate question of the Sicilian Crown, the infant Conradin had been displaced by his uncle Manfred, Frederic's belatedly legitimized third son. But Manfred had not been accepted as emperor by the German princes, who chose King Henry's brother Richard in his stead.

For the Crown of Jerusalem, as an alternative to the Empire's candidates Conradin or Manfred, the Ibelin Queen of Cyrpus, Plaisance had been named regent. The Ibelin claim was derived from a lineage springing prior to Yolanda. Plaisance's son, Hugh, an infant, was recognized by the Pope, the Hospitallers, the Genoese and their Outremerine Ibelin allies as the rightful king.

But the split between Genoa and Venice, by 1260, was so emphatic that the Templars and the Outremerines, led by Simon's pro-Venice cousin Philip de Montfort, supported the child Conradin regardless of his being of the hated Emperor Frederic's line. They defeated a Genoese fleet and sacked the Genoese quarter at Acre. (p. 285-6, Runciman, Vol III.)

A truce was achieved in January of 1261 assigning Tyre as the Genoese city in Palestine, Acre as the Venetian and Pisan port. Queen Plaisance, for her wisdom and good character, was accepted as regent for the Crown of Jerusalem, to which her son Hugh was, for the moment, the agreed heir. But Plaisance died in September of 1261 and new contention broke out, challenging Hugh's rights and reigniting the issue of the rightful heir and regent. (See p. 289, Runciman, Vol. III.)

Curbed in Palestine, Genoan activity shifted to Constantinople where the Greek Emperor of Nicaea, with Genoese support, replaced the Roman Christian dynasty that had held the Byzantine throne since the Fourth Crusade. The dominant Christian power in the Levant was returned to the Greek Church. From this victory the Genoese prospered greatly, for it gave them control of trade in the Black and Caspian Seas where alum, essential in fabric dying and used in medicine, was mined, and where increasing caravan trade from the distant Orient and Russias arrived for embarkation.

In Outremere, the Montforts and their allies the Templars continued to be hostile to the Ibelins and the Hospitallers, while the Teutonic order of knights, with the deaths of Frederic and Conrad, shifted their focus to the Baltic, where they had extensive holdings since 1226 that were intended to encourage the spread of Christianity in that region.

Simon, in France, undoubtedly knew what was happening in Palestine. His cousin Philip de Montfort's son Philip was at the Court in Paris, associated with Louis' brother Charles of Anjou, and Simon's son Guy had become a favorite in Charles' household.

During his time in Palestine, 1240-42, Simon had shown himself singularly able to unify the quarreling factions, but the issues were more complex and far reaching now. The latest news he could have received in 1263 would have been that Queen Plaisance was dead, the Crown of Jerusalem had several claimants, and the hostilities between the Genoese and the Venetians was dwindling to brawls among sailors. Jerusalem was still in the keeping of Islam.

*for the reaper who is like unto the Son of Man*
See Revelations 14 -20.

*the palace at Westminster has been struck by lightening and burned to the ground.*
*The Thames at Westminster froze solidly from bank to bank,*
See *De Antiquis Legibus Liber,* p.51. Heaven seemed to be punishing King Henry with both fire and ice. In addition to the destruction of the palace by lightning, the Thames froze over as far upstream as Westminster, a thing unknown then in living memory. It was popularly said among the commons that the Channel would freeze to make a convenient bridge for the Earl Montfort to invade England. The event now is looked upon as a record of the beginning of what has come to be called Europe's Little Ice Age.

*four young lords arrived begging to speak with him. First among them was elegant young Gilbert de Clare*
Gilbert de Clare, and his companions who went to Paris and urged Simon to return to lead their cause, are cited in the *Annales of Dunstable,* p.222.

*"But I'll as willingly die fighting bad Christians here for the freedom of the Holy Church… and England!"*
This is what Simon is reported by his contemporaries to have said. "Bad Christians" can be taken to refer to both the lords' failure to keep their solemn vows to the Provisions, and their

refusal to extend mercy and charity to the common people. Simon's concern for the position of the English Church I feel reflects anxieties about the rise of Thomism which, by justifying the supremacy of kings, and of Popes above them, would return the English Church to its abject state prior to the arguments of Becket, John of Salisbury and Grosseteste that aimed to curb royal and papal powers and strengthen local self-determination. See the *Chronica Johannis Oxenedes*, p. 226.

Simon's return to England is also recorded in the *Annales of Dunstable*, p. 221 and *Flores Historiarum*, Vol. II, p. 431.

*At Hereford the army found no besiegers camped before the city's walls*
*At Bridgenorth, unlike the other towns they passed*

For the seizing of Bishop Aigueblanche and taking of Hereford, Gloucester, Bridgenorth, and the western campaign, see Rishangers's *Chronicle*, p. 11, and Robert of Gloucester, *Metrical Chronicles*, Vol II, pp. 736-39.

*Late that night Prince Edward, with thirty of the royal mercenaries, left the Tower fully armed under plain robes. They rode out of the city to the Temple's compound*

That Edward robbed the Templars of the wool guild's fortune, stored in their vaults, is a matter of recorded history: June 26, 1263. How he accomplished this amazing feat is left to speculation. The Templars, ranked as the foremost men of combat in their time, as guardians of their banking operations were not likely to permit theft without offering resistance. Basing this fictional passage on the Templars' purported homosexuality, and Edward's well-recorded profligate and ruthless behavior in the years before 1265, I offer this as a possible answer.

Edward's theft is recorded by the Dunstable *Annals Monastici*, Vol. III, p. 222 and by Gervais of Canterbury, Vol. III, p. 222-23. Michael Prestwich, in the footnote on p. 39 of his *Edward I*, gives an interesting view of the efforts of some historians to exonerate Edward for this remarkable instance of criminality.

*As the mid-ship slid into the dark, suddenly a stinking deluge gushed from somewhere above. A latrine chute on the bridge had been opened, dumping its load of filth onto the vessel*

Knowing what was available to the residents on London Bridge, I have enlarged upon the statements in the *Annals of Dunstable*, Vol. III, pp. 223-24; and the *Flores Historiarum* Vol II, pp. 481-2 regarding what exactly was dumped upon the queen when her barge was stuck beneath the bridge. Woad was certainly available. The malodorous blue dye was used by cloth manufacturing businesses located on the bridge specifically so that they could dump the vile substance directly into the river and not pollute the streets. There were also butcheries, again so that their refuse could be dropped into the river and washed away. And there were household latrines.

The chroniclers, writing from hearsay, specify vile insults and rock throwing, but I believe it far less likely that there was a stash of rocks on the bridge than that there were latrines and vats of woad. See also Wykes, p. 136. Rishanger's exact words (Chronicle, p. 12) for what was pitched at the queen: *intercepta est a Londoniensibus, et ab eis enormiter blasphemata, atque exclamata turpiter quod non licet recitare, jactuque lapidis et luti subtus pontem vilissime repulsa.*

*The King of the Germans sent out his son to find the earl with a request for parley.*

June 29. See Rishanger, *Chronicle*, p. 18, also Labarge, *Montfort*, p. 211.

That Simon thought it was a trap is suggested by his avoidance of the meeting. Some historians hold that he deliberately refused a genuine opportunity for peace negotiations. With the commons as roused as they were, I think it doubtful there would have been peace even if Richard's attempts were honest.

*Simon approached London at last.*

Simon's heroic greeting upon his entry into London, the agreements King Henry signed and the Parliament of September 9, can be found in the *Flores Historiarum*, Vol. II pp. 456-7.

*"We require,"* he addressed them in a loud, clear voice, *"and King Henry has agreed, that all strategic castles of the land will be placed in the hands of loyal English castellans!"*

The *Annales of Dunstable*, p. 224 and the *Flores Historiarum*, Vol. II, p.457 provide detailed record of King Henry's capitulation.

*Simon rode out to Windsor. The castle gates were surrounded as at siege.*

The *Close Roll*, 47, Henry III: citation of this event curiously refers to the troops being sent to besiege the *aliens* (a pejorative term used for Henry's half-brothers the Lusignan and for the queen's relations of Savoy, among others) though it is quite clear that it was Edward who fled to Windsor and held the castle after robbing the Templars. However, it was not long before various Poitouvin knights and royal appointees joined him there. Official records, chronicles and all other documents of the period must be read with an understanding that they contain what in modern parlance is called "spin" either in favor of or against Montfort and his partisans.

*The earl, aware of the cleric John's work but never having read it directly, sent a messenger to Canterbury to find the manuscript in the monastery's library.*

Simon did send to Canterbury for the *Policraticus* of John of Salisbury at this time. Presumably, he previously was guided chiefly by Grosseteste's treatise *On Kingship and Tyranny* and his private conversations with his mentor.

Grosseteste almost certainly was familiar with the *Policraticus*, which may have been the seminal theory for the founding of Parliament and the curbing of kingly powers. Becket, whom John of Salisbury served as secretary, was considered first in the line of saintly protectors of the rights of man against the claims of kings. Again we have the spectacle of the far greater liberality of the

12th and 13th centuries, prior to the ascendancy of the teachings of Thomas Aquinas.

Regarding the government as it had been run in keeping with the Provision of Oxford and Westminster, see Knappen, *Constitutional and Legal history of England*, pp. 128-129; and Chrimes, *An Introduction to the Administrative History of Medieval England*, pp. 123-28, and especially p. 127, for the *Forma Regiminis* devised at this time (1263).

*In King Henry's name Simon called a general Parliament*
The Parliament of September 9, 1263 confirmed the Provisions of Oxford as embodied in the Provisions of Westminster, but the meeting lasted only three days. *Annales of Dunstable*, p. 224; Rishanger *Chronicle*, p.15.

*Beyond the gate's arch was a narrow, stone-walled aisle: what soon would be the parapeted defense works of the causeway that separated the Mere and the next-door abbey's pond, and carried the road that was the only entrance to the castle's island.*
The defense works at Kenilworth, ordered and probably designed by Simon, were so extensive that later the castle, used as refuge by the earl's supporters, could not be taken, and the longest siege in England's history ended with a negotiated free passage for the defenders to depart. For payments to the engineer William, which continued to be made into August, 1265, see Labarge, *Montfort*, p. 242.

Entrance to the castle grounds now principally is from the ditch side, where Dudley, Earl of Leicester in the 16th century, built an elaborate gate. There was an earlier gate at that location as well. John of Gaunt, in the 1360's added palatial residential structures within the tower's bailey, and his son Henry Bolingbroke, as King Henry IV, used Kenilworth often as his residence, as did Richard III. Elizabeth I gave the elegant residential property to Dudley, her favorite, upon whom she also bestowed the title Earl of Leicester. Dudley built a magnificent banquet hall, other outbuildings and gardens to receive the queen on her grand Progress in 1575. Gaunt's and Dudley's buildings are now crumbled, helped in their decay by Victorians with a taste for picturesque ruins. The castle tower that was Simon's home was packed with explosives and the arched wall facing the ditch was obliterated by Cromwell's forces in 1649.

### The Parliament of Saint Edward's Day

Often the Parliaments of September 9th and October 13th are confounded into one by historians, and even by the chroniclers. Gilbert de Clare's attack upon Simon for not distributing the booty and prisoners probably took place at this meeting, not the earlier one.

### I saw my friend Leybourne scowling. I'll start there."

For Edward's escape with Leybourne, see Prestwich, *Edward I*, p. 41. Roger Leybourne, John de Vaux, Ralph Basset, Hamo Lestrange and, oddly, John Giffard, are listed as being with Edward at this time. Giffard seems to have migrated back and forth between the royalists and the Montfortians. Since he appears on Montfort's side at Lewes, might he have been a spy? While saying these men reaffirmed their vows to the Provisions, Prestwich suggests they were suborned from the earl by promises of land and monetary reward.

### "Prince Edward's taken the castle and has slaughtered or imprisoned the garrison!"

Edward's two shelterings at Windsor are sometimes confounded into one. On the other hand, Bemont records that after the October Parliament, "Edward retired to Windsor with his father and his partisans." *Simon de Montfort,* 1930, p. 203. It seems hardly likely that the prince, recently having been seized from Windsor, and Henry having capitulated to Simon at the Tower, were free to merely "retire" with their partisans to Windsor, which they then held it in defense against Montfort.

*"Even if you all fall away,"* Simon bellowed, his voice reverberating against the stone walls, *"I, with my sons, will stand for the just cause we've sworn to uphold! Nor will we fear to go to war!"*

Henry of Alemaine's refusal to take the oath, and this reaction from Simon, are factual. It is my belief that Simon made this famously rousing statement as a means of diverting danger from Alemaine. Here is how Bemont (*Montfort*, 1930, p. 204) translates the exchange with Henry of Alemaine: 'I can no longer fight against my father, my uncle, against all my relations. That is why, sir earl, I shall leave you, if you will allow me, but I shall never bear arms against you.' —'Messer Henry,' replied the earl, 'it is not the loss of your arms which I deplore, but your inconstancy. Go then. Return against me with your arms. I fear them not.' For Simon's "I with my sons" speech see the *Chronicon de Bellis,* p. 17. There, also, is another quote from Simon: "I have seen many peoples and countries, Christian and pagan, but never have I seen a nation so fickle and forsworn as the people of England." The exact occasion of these two quotes is not specified in the chronicles.

*"There's a lord arriving with an escort. They bear a flag charged with the fleurs de lis of France!"*

Several accounts have Simon with his partisans, and King Henry with his entourage, traveling to Boulogne on August 16, and September 15th and 16th. Undoubtedly King Louis attempted to arbitrate at this point. And Queen Eleanor was in France, agitating. *Annals of Tewkesbury,* p. 179, records the widespread fear in England of invasion from France. For Queen Eleanor's attempts to involve Prince Alphonse in an invasion of England, see Boutaric, *Saint Louis et Alphonse de Poitiers,* pp. 104-5.

Simon's massive efforts to defend England's coasts from invasion were never without cause. Nor was his persisting sense of England's military peril motivated by an over-ambitious reach for personal power, as his opponents and some historians would have it, but by his accurate understanding of the offense that England's elective government presented in a monarchical world and his strategic response to that danger.

*"We're trapped! We've been betrayed! They've locked the gates!"*
The incident when Simon's army was caught at Southwark by King Henry's advance, with the gates of London closed by "traitors," then opened by the populace, is recorded in Rishanger, *Chronicle*, p. 22.

*Near Catesby the road forded a stream.*
The incident of Simon suffering a broken leg and hip while crossing the stream at Catesby, on the way to negotiations at Amiens, is recorded in the *Annales Monastici,* Vol III, page 227. See also Labarge, *Montfort*, p. 221.

*"May I not prove a Phaeton in my use of it,"*
Simon's armored cart was actually referred to in its Old French equivalent as his "armored car," the association with "cars," chariots of antiquity, being intentional. For the modern reader this term would conjure a far too recent piece of military equipment. The vehicle seems to have been a box-like cart heavily protected with plate armor.

The twelfth century Arthurian tale of the Knight of the Cart, by Chretien de Troyes, conveys the idea that for a knight to be seen riding in a cart, like a peasant, meant indelible shame. The words *chevalier* and *knight* are terms specifically for horseman. The French Revolution brought the ancient shame of a cart forward again, as the rude farm carts called tumbrels were used to display the long-imprisoned, dirty, bedraggled nobles as they were taken to their deaths at the guillotine.

Simon and William here refer to the Greek and Roman myth of the god Apollo who was believed to drive his chariot, which was the sun, across the sky each day. In an amour with a mortal, Clymene, Apollo begat a child named Phaeton. Growing to manhood, Phaeton disbelieved his mother's claim that Apollo was his true father. He insisted on proof: the right to drive his father's chariot across the sky for one day. His wish was granted by his father, but Phaeton so failed to control the chariot's horses that the sun dipped toward the earth, endangering the whole world with annihilation by fire. To save mankind, Zeus cast a thunderbolt and Phaeton was felled, but the earth was saved.

*"Pope Urban upheld Pope Alexander's absolution of the vows to the Provisions.*

Bemont explains Louis' arbitration decision, and the entire catastrophe at Amiens, as resulting from the pressures of the two queens and the Vatican upon the King of France, and Guy Folques's movement against the Church in England. See Bemont, *Montfort,* 1930, p. 206 -8.

*"While King Henry is still in France, go to the lands of Mortimer and pay our ransom for our steward there in steel and cinders,"*

For Simon's military movements, see Bemont, Montfort, 1930, p. 209, and the footnote on that page for a list of studies of Simon's strategies.

*Late that night two men on foot crossed Gloucester's bridge. They led a string of packhorses with empty woolsacks*

For the taking of Gloucester by Giffard's wool-gathering ruse, and Henry de Montfort's ignominious retreat, see: *Annales of Dunstable,* p. 228; *Annales prioratus de Wigornia (Worcester)* p. 448; and Robert of Gloucester, Vol. II pp 740-1.

*the lady of Valence would show gravidly pregnant, rather soon considering the long period of her husband's absence.* Joan de Lusignan, nee Joan de Munchensey, was wed when very young to William de Valence, bringing the king's half brother the fortune of her dowry. It was their daughter Alice de Lusignan whom King Henry forced Richard de Clare to allow to marry his fourteen-year-old son Gilbert (see Montfort Volume III.) Evidence regarding Alice includes later documents related to her divorce from Gilbert. By the time of Guy and Henry's taking of the city of Gloucester, Richard de Clare had died, and Gilbert, though not yet recognized as Earl of Gloucester and Hertford, was the proper lord of Gloucester. Reasonably, his child bride would have been living in the castle, attended by her mother.

Joan, evicted from Windsor Castle the following June by Simon's orders, pleaded advanced pregnancy as reason why she could not be moved. She was transferred from the fortress anyway. See Labarge, *Simon de Montfort*, p. 238, and her citations from the *Calendar of Patent Rolls.*

Labarge does not remark on this curiously early date for so advanced a pregnancy that it could provide reason not to travel, even in a litter. William failed repeatedly to land with the armies he had raised with the encouragement of Queens Eleanor and Margaret. Only late in the spring of 1265 did he succeed in reaching England. Either Joan was in the earliest stages of pregnancy, or someone other than William was the child's father. Or possibly her claim of pregnancy was a lie, but would have been an embarrassing one in view of her husband's absence. That Prince Edward had remained with Joan for several weeks at Gloucester, while sending out his troops to secure the western cities and shires, is factual.

Interestingly, years later Alice de Lusignan, in connection with her divorce from Gilbert, claimed a relationship of her own with Edward with some hope of marriage. Had he wished, Edward might have gotten a divorce on grounds of consanguinity with the Infanta Eleanor. But he was even more closely related to Alice, sharing Isabel of Angouleme, Dowager Queen of England, as paternal grandmother.

*Many of the clergy who had been loud for the Provisions renounced and denied the Earl's cause in the face of excommunication.*

The excommunications of the supporters of the Provisions are recorded in the *Registres d'Urban IV,* nos. 768, 770 and 776. And also by Thomas Rymer in the *Foedera,* regarding the bulls March, 16, 17, 21, 23 and 24.

*Your son Simon, the Lord Ferrers and your cousin Peter de Montfort are moving toward Northampton.*

For the interesting action at Northampton, see Thomas Wykes, pp. 144-45. Apparently the prior of Saint Andrews guided young Simon's troops over the priory wall and into the city.

*"Within our walls there's not a man who hasn't armed himself and prayed for your return. We stand with you against the king, the Pope and the infernal arbitration!"*

The Londoners refused to accept the arbitration at Amiens. Bypassing the city's aldermen, Mayor FitzThomas instituted a "commune" of the people, and had them arm themselves for the Provisions' cause, which for them was synonymous with Montfort.

*Take them out to Prince Richard's fief at Isleworth and let them have their fill of mischief.*

Simon did, at Richard's fief of Isleworth, deliberately try out the Londoners as a potential military asset. He appears to have been appalled by the result. It is factual that he subsequently refused to include them in his army, and when he left for Northampton, they sacked the Jewish neighborhood. Realizing the roused and armed populace could not be left in the city, he took them with him to the attack on Rochester – with more disastrous results. After decapitating those caught in the act of crime, eventually he set up the remainder of the blood-lusting amateurs for slaughter by Prince Edward at Lewes. See *Royal Letters*, Vol. II, p. 247 for the Londoners' attack on Isleworth. See also Wykes *Annales*, Vol. IV, pp. 140-1.

*"You ask me to turn my back on him to save the London Jews from their own neighbors?"*

What incited the attack upon the Jews was a rumor that they had made copies of the keys for the city gates, had knowledge of underground tunnels, and were planning to set fire to the city.

In fact four London *aldermen*, allying themselves with Prince Richard, under his orders attempted to set the city on fire. Though the aldermen were seized in the act, nevertheless the people of London attacked and destroyed the Jewry. A cynical element of individual self-interest may have been involved. With the destruction of records, and of lives, many debts held by Jews ceased to be collectable.

Mayor FitzThomas, in creating a 'commune' of the people of London, bypassed the usual channel of the city's governing through the aldermen. This may be why those four aldermen were so enraged as to seek contact with Richard and to plot to burn the city. See *Annales of Dunstable*, Vol. III, p. 230.

In times of great stress the creating of scapegoats and finding of dark plots is an all too familiar occurrence. The fire of London in 1666 was believed to have been started, and reignited repeatedly, by foreign agents though the fire's innocent and unfortunate cause by accident, and spread by flaming cinders in high wind, was well known.

Simon has been accused of slaughtering Jews. He most certainly never did, though he did drive out the Jews from Leicester when he was young and his mentor, the Bishop of Lincoln (at that time Dean) Robert Grosseteste, had just opened a residence for homeless Jews in London, hoping to convert them. On the occasion of the London attack, Simon saved the lives of Jews at the expense of leaving his own son and captains imprisoned and vulnerable to reprisals.

Wykes records that a man named John FitzJohn killed a Jew named Cok, and that Simon forced John to give over his resulting spoils. In the heat of mob violence, it may have been impossible to execute John for the murder without igniting more violence. Depriving John of his gains may have been the most that could be dared in the volatile moment. Wykes, a royalist, in seeing Simon as the sole cause of the uprisings, with greed and personal ambition as his motives, puts the most sinister interpretations on his actions, and modern historians often have followed his lead.

*Alone in the Tower's chapel, he prayed till dawn.*

Why Simon remained in England, leading the opposition to the king, when he could have accepted the amnesty Louis provided for him and gone to Palestine at last, is a problematic question. The fact is that he did stay. To account for his motivation I've turned to descriptions of his character provided by those who knew him best: that he was given to periods of severe depression, and was deeply religious. It seems plausible that he remained in England, acting on the guidance of prayer. To most modern historians who do not take religion seriously as a factor, such a motive would not be conceivable. To a religious mind in the midst of a conundrum such as Simon faced, turning to prayer would be obvious.

Wykes, and other of Simon's detractors, would have his motive personal ambition, which fits well with modern materialism. But no one, least of all an experienced military strategist as Simon was, would have seen the situation at that moment – with virtually all of England's battle-tried army of lords and knights, and with foreign mercenaries also, ranged with the king – as an enticing opportunity for personal success.

*Henry attacked Kenilworth. With the garrison Simon had left, John Giffard easily held the fortress. The royal army, loath to waste time with a siege, moved on, taking Leicester, Nottingham and Lincoln.*

For Giffard's energetic custody of Kenilworth, see Labarge, *Montfort*, p. 230. Though there is no indication that it was done under Simon's orders, Giffard also took the castle of Warwick, destroyed it and retained the Earl and Countess of Warwick as prisoners. With whatever was left at Warwick in Montfort hands, it is understandable that later young Simon went there first to supply himself with armaments.

*Fore of her mast a black column of smoke rose bulging in cloud-gasps into the yellow morning sky.*

*A corpse, the bell ringer, hung dangling*

For Simon's Good Friday attack upon Rochester, his use of a fire ship, the London mob in boats, and the atrocities committed by his forces, see *Flores Historiarum,* p. 490; Rishanger, *Chronicon De Bellis,* p. 25; and Wykes, p. 146. Rishanger credits Simon with introducing to the English the use of fireboats in warfare. He had the advantage of having in his company Thames boatmen knowledgeable in river currents.

Regarding the use of the bell ringer as an archery target: a common event at fairs was a contest to shoot and kill a bird tied to the top of a tall pole. In *The Game of Kings,* Dorothy Dunnett describes the sport in sixteenth century Scotland.

*The drivers' bodies lay scattered in the roadway, spiny with arrows such as forest outlaws use.*

Labarge, *Montfort,* p. 232 says, "the baronial army was aided by the archers of the Weald, that wooded country between the north and south downs. These bowmen served as valuable auxiliaries and guerrilla fighter, emerging unexpectedly from their woods to harass the king's baggage train and pick off the stragglers." Charles Osman, in his study of the battle of Lewes, refers to archers. (See below.)

Who were these bowmen of the Weald? They appear to be of the same class of woodsmen whose fame survives in the tales of Robin Hood. After the battle of Evesham in 1265, for two years John Eyvlie maintained Simon's cause with a force of similar woodland bowmen in Sherwood Forest, near Lincoln. After the battle of Lewes, and the rise of belief in the Earl as a worker of miracles, mention of the name Simon de Montfort was made a capital crime punishable by hanging.

Under that repression, the Robin Hood tales may have furnished the safest means of keeping the memory of Simon's cause alive. With his name banned, it is understandable why other names would have been substituted, notably that of Richard the Lion Heart. Anyone who knew King Richard's history well, would have known the king who caused England to be disastrously taxed to raise his ransom from Austria on a frivolous charge of stealing a hawk, and who afterward waged costly, losing wars in France, would not be the longed-for hero of the common man, even if he was preferable to his brother John. In any case, the era of the greedy and repressive sheriffs was during Henry III's reign and the predominance of the Poitouvins in the Crown's service, following the reigns of King Richard I and King John. The Robin Hood tales fit the era of King Henry III and Simon de Montfort's ascendancy better than any other period.

*"The Earl of Leicester asks only that you renounce your foreign advisors, and he will prostrate himself at your feet. We offer thirty thousand pounds in reparation for the damages that have been done. We admit that we are wrong, and beg only your mercy."* For Simon's offer of these abject terms of peace, see Rishanger *Chronicon De Bellis*, p.29, and *Annales Monastici*, Vol. II, Waverly, p. 357.

*The crowd of men knelt as Simon, by the altar, raised his hands*
See Rishanger, *Chronicon de Bellis*, p.30, and Kingsford, *The Song of Lewes*.

*Even the Welsh contingent now bore the slim six-foot span across their backs.* The Welsh are credited with introducing the longbow into England's armies. It was the longbow that brought victories to the three King Edwards, in Ireland, Scotland and on the continent, until at last it was understood by England's enemies that chain mail could not withstand the force of this very simple, inexpensive weapon.

We know that Simon had both Welsh archers and forest outlaws among his following, and that the king's army's march to the Cinque Ports was harried by bowmen from the Weald. (See Charles Oman, *History of the Art of War in the Middle Ages*, Volume I. AD 378 to 1278, pp. 424-30.) Oman, in his classic study of the Battle of Lewes, puzzles over the failure of the various chronicles to mention the bowmen in the actual battle of Lewes. But none of the chroniclers were eye-witnesses. Neither do the chronicles mention where the king's extensive encampment was. And Oman treats the battle as if the royalists had time to arm, mount and form up in proper battle array.

If the royalists' first knowledge that they were under attack came from the foragers, which is agreed upon in every contemporary report, then the speed of a mounted advance down the slopes, the smallness of the valley and the need for the king's camp to be somewhere near the priory, argue that there was no time or space for the royalists to arm, mount and form in proper "battles." Oman quotes the number of fully armored knights as 1,500 for the king and 600 for the earl. In his view, that is excessive.

I believe it is high for the earl's army of young knightly partisans and of Leicestermen (of whom he had a maximum of sixty, and at any given time some were not available for combat.) For the king's army, I believe that count is low, considering he had almost all of the principal barons, and they each commanded between forty and one-hundred-and-twenty knights (also not all available or willing at a given time.) I estimate the king's mounted forces as at least three thousand. This campaign was far more popular, due to the upheavals all over England and blamed on Montfort, than any campaign Henry waged at any other time.

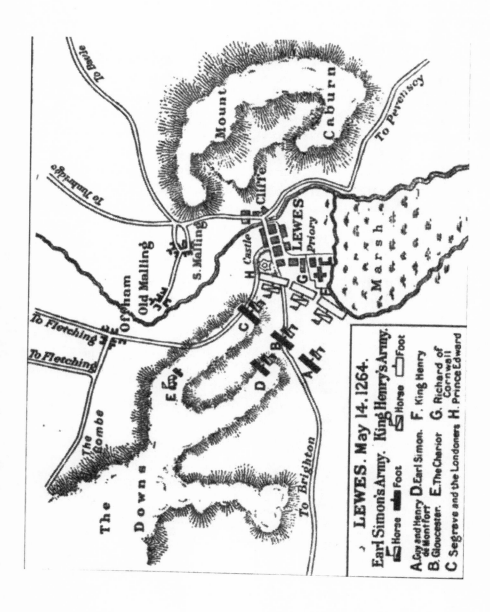

From Charles Oman, *A History of the Art of War in the Middle Ages*, Volume I, 378 – 1278 AD. Courtesy of Wikipedia.

*Simon sat upon his nodding mare,*
There is no record of what horse Simon was riding at Lewes. Since he was doing a great deal of riding though his hip was probably not yet fully healed, I have given him an undistinguished slab-sided palfrey mare for optimal comfort, though he undoubtedly did have at least one destrier of his own somewhere with his march. Certain it is that if he were riding one of his familiar breed of destriers, he would have been recognized, and Valence and Clifford would not have wasted their time and effort attacking the armored cart in the belief that he was there.

*Slowly the mill's door opened. Within the dark doorway, the last light of the day dully glinting on his fine armor and the golden crown upon his helm, stood Richard, the King of the Germans.*
The remarkable capture of King Richard in a mill by three novice knights is factual. (See Labarge, p. 235.) The similarity of Cervantes' aged novice Quixote's challenge to a windmill at the opening of his career suggests the Spanish author may have known *The Song of Lewes,* and the chivalrous deed of the new-made knights that gained them everlasting fame – of a humorous sort.

*"I give you Edward. And Edmund."*
For the terms of the *Mise of Lewes* see Rishanger, *Chronicon de Bellis,* p. 37; *Flores Historiarum,* Vol II, p. 49; and Wykes, p. 152. Some historians, in an effort to minimize Simon's victory, refer to King Henry's "escape from the field." If he had done so, why would he have traded his own freedom for that of Edward and Edmund?

*"...the Earl of Norfolk, Marshal of England Roger Bigod; the Earl of Arundel, John FitzAllen; the Earl of Kent, Godwin de Burgh; the Earl of Warwick, John de Plessis; the Earl of Hereford, Humphrey de Bohun; the Steward of Scotland, John Balliol, and with him the Scots lords Robert*

*de Bruise and John Comyn; the lords of England Henry Percy, Philip Basset, William Bardolf..."*

Excerpted from the list of Simon's prisoners taken at Lewes. That Simon interviewed any of them is conjecture, but it would be strange if he did not take the opportunity to try to bring some of them around to his point of view.

*By June the Guardians of the Peace were reestablished,*
See *Calendar of Patent Rolls,* 1258-66, p. 318, regarding the Guardians. Complaints against them argue that they far exceeded their official authorization.

*"Isabella Fortinbras, the Countess of Devon and Aumale,"*
For the comic and pathetic wooing of Isabella Fortinbras by Simon Fils see Labarge, *Simon de Montfort,* p. 248.

*with no bargaining, Simon fished from his robe's blousing a bag bulging with the coins to fund siege.*
Simon Fils was accused of buying a wooing present for the Countess of Aumale with monies entrusted him from the royal taxes. For Pevensey, Simon Fils received feudal knights' service and various payments, including 700 marks as late as November.

While I spend much more time on this episode than is found in histories of the Earl Simon, my reasons are not purely romantic. These incidents with Isabella are the best example historical records give us of Simon Fils' character, and come as near as can be to explaining his later erratic behavior.

Young Simon's brother Henry's "turning wool merchant" by confiscating and selling the Flemish traders' wool is remarked on caustically by Wykes, p. 159.

*Simon was not dressed in his usual plain black woolen robes. He wore an even plainer cloth, if such was possible. Unfulled, undyed white wool*
This episode, and its impact on fashion, are recorded by Rishanger, *Chronicon de Bellis,* p. 29.

*On June the twenty-fourth, Parliament met in London at Saint Paul's Cathedral.* The significance of this Parliament is considered by many historians to be seminal in the evolution of modern democracy. The elected representatives of the commons were summoned not only to report on the condition of the land, as in 1258 and since, but to take active part in shaping the new government in a more formal way than ever before – recognizing a rightful place for the representatives of the commons in the very structuring of the government and legislation. See Bemont, *Montfort,* 1930, pp. 215 to 221.

Some historians credit the Parliament summoned for January 20, 1265 as more significant than the June 24, 1264 meeting in the development of democracy. The January 1265 Parliament did result in far more participation of the commons by default, in the absence of the lords. And yes, almost all of those who attended were there by election of the commons. But the June 1264 Parliament was a clearer attempt at a bicameral government as in modern times, and better adhered to the template of the Provisions of Oxford.

*"We want Montfort! Montfort! Montfort!"*
For the offering of the Crown of England to Simon de Montfort at the June Parliament of 1264 see *Flores Historiarum,* Vol. III, p. 362 and *Documents of the Baronial Movement of Reform and Rebellion,1258 -67,* pp. 298 – 9.

*The Queen of England, here in Paris, is gathering more aid for her army and intends to invade England in the second week of August.*
See Bemont, *Montfort,* 1930, pp. 220- 21 for a discussion of the gravity of the threat of invasion from France as instigated by Queen Eleanor, and of Simon's many letters to France in his efforts to bring about the queen's army's disbanding.

*He wrote to Louis a third time, urging that the arbiters be named at once.*

Simon's state of mind must be supposed from his actions. That he wrote to Louis, repeatedly begging for another arbitration, is history.

*Compromissio Pacis*

For the desperately persistent negotiations with Louis, see: *Calendar of Patent Rolls,* 1258 to 1266, p. 347; Shirley, *Royal Letters,* Vol. II, p. 257 and 264. For Simon's arming of England against the expected invasion, see *Calendar of Patent Rolls* 1258-66, p. 360. Bemont argues that, in agreeing to reopen arbitration, Louis admitted to the cancellation of the Amiens decisions. See Bemont, *Montfort,* 1930, pp. 222 -23 and footnotes 1 and 2.

Though Louis moved to Boulogne, and Henry's Court, under the control of his Council, moved to Dover, agreement was not achieved. Through agents the discussions continued into August 1265 without a satisfactory result, although, usefully, in November, 1264, Queen Eleanor, as a result of the negotiations, was stopped from selling rights of the English Crown in Gascony in exchange for funds to raise an army for the invasion of England.

*"The Legate demands that the hostages be set free first. And that he come to England himself at the beginning of September,"*

For Folques' (sometimes spelled Fourcad, Foucod or Foulquois, and in more recent times Fawkes) conflict with the English Church and excommunication of Simon, see Wykes, p. 156 – 57: and Rishanger, *Chronicon de Bellis,* pp. 38-39.

*A troop of young March lords had launched a surprise attack on their prison at Wallingford and succeeded so far as to break through to the courtyard.*

See *Robert of Gloucester,* Vol. II, pp. 751-52, and *Flores Historiarum,* Vol. II, p. 503. Some versions have the defenders threatening to put Edward in a mangonel and shoot him over the wall if the attackers won't retreat. This tactic is more believable in regard of the infant William Marshall (his father's famous response was to invite his adversaries to go right ahead as he had *hammer and anvils enough to make more and better sons*.) It would have been clumsy indeed to seat a large and resisting adult into the bucket of a mangonel.

*On the dais step young Eleanor and Edward sat playing chess.*
Edward's behavior during his retention at Kenilworth and Odiham, as described here, is fictional. That he was ribald, dissolute, charming and devious in his youth is not questioned.

That Eleanor la Demoiselle was a likely target of seduction is speculation, largely suggested by Edward's granting permission for her, years later, to travel from France to Wales to marry Llewellyn, then having her kidnapped at sea and detained at his court for three years. It appears that when he finally did permit her wedding to the Welsh prince, at Worcester on his own saint's day, he attended and paid for the celebration himself. The bride appears to have been already pregnant, and to have given birth to the daughter Gwencillian too soon after the wedding, with the resultant life-long seclusion of the child in a convent. A daughter Katherine, born later, was treated with the honors of a princess of Wales, and eventually wedded the prince of southern Wales, bringing the unification of the country.

*"That's for my honor," his first, felling blow was announced."*
For Clare's accusations and Henry de Montfort's violent reprisals in front of the Parliament of January 1265, see Rishanger, *Chronicon de Bellis*. p. 32. For the conflict between Simon and Gilbert de Clare, and for another view of the entire period 1258 – 65, see the interesting fragment Bemont reprints in his 1884 *Simon de Montfort*, pp. 373 – 80: *Fragment d'une chronique redigee a l'abbaye Battle, sur la guerre des Barons*, Oxford, Bodl., Rawlinson, B, 150. Curiously, this source elsewhere claims King Henry was "captured" in bed and asleep at Lewes. He was no doubt caught unprepared, in bed and asleep, though he eventually seems to have sallied from the priory in arms and with troops. It is well to remember

that even the most respected chronicler of all, Matthew Paris, was writing for the most part from hearsay, though he seems to have been present at the Churching of the Queen in 1239.

*"I've come to take you from here forcibly, and put you in a place where you'll have benefit of neither sun nor moon!"*

Simon's picturesque threat to his sons at his breaking up of the tourney *a outrance* at Dunstable is one of the direct quotes we have of him. Undoubtedly he had in mind the tower cellar at Kenilworth which King Henry, when he renovated the castle during Simon's first exile (1240 – 1242), had fitted with manacles. The Montfort sons would have been very familiar with that damp, grim pit. See Rishanger, *Chronicon de Bellis*, p. 32. Another of Simon's more colorful statements is in a letter to King Henry when, as Viceroy of Gascony, he warns of impending revolt by the Gascon lords, and that *ni poet ni chavalier* will stop them.

*Prince Edward was taken south amid Henry de Montfort's quite adequate armed guard*

Henry Montfort's custodianship of Edward is remarked in *Robert of Gloucester*, Vol. II, p. 755.

*Pange lingua igitur*

From the *Si linguis angelicis*, probably by Peter Abelard. Though the Countess Eleanor's account role survives from this period of her stay at Odiham, and we know what was purchased and how large the household was at any given time, we do not know exactly how they entertained themselves. The scenes here are fiction.

The playing of a musical instrument was an essential part of a noble education, along with knowledge of chess and some proficiency at drawing. The poetry of Abelard, and particularly the *Si linguis angelicis*, would very likely have been known to Edward and have appealed to him. The first two verses are, in my own translation:

| | |
|---|---|
| *Si linguis angelicis* | *Neither angels' tongues* |
| *Loquar et humanis* | *nor man's common elocution* |
| *Non valeret exprimi* | *Serve to tell, in pander's praise* |
| *Palma nec inanis* | *Or fool's reprobation,* |
| *Per quam recte preferor* | *How, though I'm raised* |
| *Cunctis Christianis* | *Over decent Christians,* |
| *Tamen invidentibus* | *Envy's favorite villain,* |
| *Emulis prophanis* | *I stray from salvation.* |
| | |
| *Pange lingua igitur* | *So let my tongue confess* |
| *Causas et causatum* | *The cause and circumstance,* |
| *Nomen tamen domine* | *Without uttering my lady's name –* |
| *Serva palliatum* | *Let her seem a mere convention,* |
| *Ut non sit in populo* | *To the ears of all but her,* |
| *Illud divulgatum* | *No plaything of the common,* |
| *Quod secretum gentibus* | *Safe, unknown to all mankind,* |
| *Extat et celatum* | *Forbidden and well hidden.* |

The song goes on to be quite blunt about the practicality of masturbation versus the desire for illicit coition.

*At London they joined the king, his Councilors and Court for the trip to Northampton and then the long-planned eyre of the land's courts of justice*
Some historians have Simon's travels to the west being purely military. Had that been the case, surely he would have sent one of his sons with an army, rather than risk the king, the Royal Treasury and Chancery with only the most minimal of guard, as he did. A royal eyre to restore justice had been discussed in Parliament and, it would appear from the composition of this entourage, that this was this venture's purpose.

*"They imagine if we go in peace, without armed assistance, conflict will be avoided."*
The Council's persistent impression that if they proclaimed peace, there was peace, is attested by numerous entries in the

*Calendar of Patent Rolls,* (1258 - 66), for the spring of 1265. Also see the *Royal Letters* of that period.

*the king's household and Court were no freer to leave Hereford than if Clare still stood by the gate.*
For the unwieldy Progress of the Court, the aborted tourney at Northampton, and the entrapment of the Court at Gloucester and Hereford, see: *Waverly, Annales Monastici,* Vol. II, pp. 361-62; and *Calendar of Patent Rolls,* 1258 – 1266, pp. 423-24.

*"See if you can catch me before I reach Wigmore!"*
See Annals of Dunstable, *Annales Monastici,* Vol. III, p. 239; Rishanger, *Chronicon de Bellis,* p. 43; *Flores Historiarum,* Vol. III, p. 2. The escape occurred on May 28 and is described by Wykes as having happened while Edward and Thomas de Clare were out hunting. The Battle Abbey fragment describes the event not as hunting but as a race. See Bemont, *Simon de Montfort,* 1884, p. 378.

*From Hereford Simon sent out messengers of the Chancery with urgent calls for aid... Royal writ went out raising the knights of the shires, and all partisans of the Provisions, to assemble in arms at Winchester and place themselves under the command of Simon de Montfort Fils.*
See *Calendar of Patent Rolls,*1258 - 66, pp. 428 – 29, 434.

*the night of June the twentieth, before the moon had risen, a procession came out of Hereford's east gate*
See *Rishanger, Chronicon de Bellis,* p. 43; *Robert of Gloucester,* Vol. II, p. 758-9. There would have been seven hours from sunset to sunrise on this mid-summer night.

*"I had a picture of a dog like you, fetching a lost crown.*
See *Close Rolls,* 1254 -56, p. 326. See also *English Medieval Wall Painting,* Tristram, E.W., 1990, reprint (of 1944 edition.)

*The bridge, he knew already, was destroyed by Clare. But now the boats that normally lay drawn up on the shore had all been taken over to the far side.*

See Rishanger, *Chronicon de Bellis*, p. 43.

*At Kempsey the first riders, knights of Leicester, urged their tired mounts into the gently sloping ford.*

See Wykes, p. 168.

*"Cross the Severn and follow it south to Bristol, where John de la Warre is holding the city for our cause.*

For Simon's attempted strategy at Bristol and its failure, see Wykes, p. 168.

*Simon Fils ambled west in leisurely fashion, by way of Tunbridge, spitefully sacking Gilbert de Clare's manse there and supplying himself with stolen wine.*

*When at last Simon Fils and his companions reached Winchester, much of his army already was dispersed, and he was assailed with complaints*

For Simon Fils' itinerary, see Rishanger, *Chronicon de Bellis*, p.44,

*Simon deemed a celebration would be fitting. "Let us bathe ourselves, eat, drink and rejoice*

For Simon Fils' bathhouse festivity and Edward's strategic use of it, see: Rishanger, *Chronicon de Bellis*, p. 44. In *Edward I*, p. 50, Michael Prestwich claims that it was a female transvestite spy named Margoth who led Edward to his surprise of Simon Fils "in his bed in the town." Undoubtedly Edward had plenty of informants and knew exactly what Simon Fils was doing, as he probably also had a very good idea of the Earl's movements, to be able to bring up his forces as he did at Evesham. See *Annales Monastici*, Vol. II; Waverly, pp. 363-4; Vol IV, Osney, pp.164-8; Vol. IV, Wykes, pp. 169-71; and *Guisborough*, pp. 199-200.

*After dark on the night of August second,*
For Simon's escape from Hereford, crossing of the Severn and attempt to reach Kenilworth with the royal party, see Wykes, p. 168.

*Simon decided the only chance of safety was to try to reach Kempsey,*
See Rishanger, *Chronicon de Bellis*, p. 44. Also Labarge, *Montfort*, pp. 254-55.

*"Homo homini lupus"*
"Man is a wolf to man." Plautus, *Asinaria*

*Novus Ordo Seclorum*
The term for Joachim's New Age. Taken up by the Masons, particularly the 18th century members who founded the United States of America, the term appears on the one-dollar bill beneath the Masonic pyramid and all-seeing eye, a striking demonstration of how Joachim del Flor is still with us.

*"When do we rest?" King Henry peevishly whined*
Undoubtedly King Henry knew that Edward's army was nearby and he was doing all he could to delay Simon's reaching Kenilworth. He was familiar with the improved defense works from his own fruitless attempt to take the castle the year before. For the pause for breakfast at Evesham, see Rishanger, *Chronicon de Bellis*, p. 45,

*The Lord is thy keeper;*
In Benedictine practice, on this Tuesday, August 4th, 1265, the psalms read at this hour would have been the 119th, 120th and 121st. My thanks to the Camaldolie Benedictine Sister of Transfiguration Monastery for this research, and especially Sister Shielah.

*The flags! They're your son Simon's!*
See *Guisborough*, p. 200. This chronicler has Squire Peter shouting, when the deception is revealed, "We're dead men! It's not your son's flags! The king's son comes from one direction, the earl of Gloucester from another, and Mortimer from a third!"

*"He comes on well.*

Rishanger, *Chronicon de Bellis,* p. 45. The chronicler records Simon's words as, *"Per brachium Sancti Jacobi sapienter accedunt: nec a se ipsis sed a me modum istum didicerunt."* 'By the arm of Saint James, he comes on well: nor is it surprising since he learned this strategy from me." As there were abundant witnesses on the rooftop who later were available to Rishanger, this may be exactly what Simon said, though of course in French, not the Latin in which the chronicle is written.

*"Then we go with you!"* For Simon's effort to have his followers leave him as he went to face the arriving army, see Rishanger, *Chronicon de Bellis,* p. 45.

*"The enemy comes on to meet us. We commend our souls to God, for our bodies are theirs."*

Simon de Montfort's last known words. Rishanger, p. 45, quotes Simon. *Nunc commmendemus Deo animus nostras, quia corpora nostra sunt (sic!)* (the *(sic!)* is in the Camden Society text.)

*The night's threatening storminess, however, had developed...*
*The storm, retreating eastward past Evesham, cast one last lightning bolt that struck the abbey's bell tower.*

For the battle of Evesham see Rishanger, *Chronicon de Bellis,* pp. 45-7; *The Chronicle of Walter of Guisborough,* pp. 200- 202; *Robert of Gloucester,* pp. 762-66; *Annales Monastici,* Vol, II, Waverly, 364-5; Vol. IV, Osney, pp. 168-9; Vol. IV, Wykes, pp. 171- 75; *Johannis de Oxenedes,* pp. 228 – 30; and *De Antiquis Legibus Liber,* pp. 75-6.

*"Earl Montfort! We demand that you surrender!"* The voice was Edward's.

For Edward's efforts to halt the battle, even to his sending a horse to rescue Henry de Montfort, see *Annales Monastici,* Osney, pp.176-7.

*"Don't kill me! I'm Henry of Monmouth!"*
See *Guisborough*, p. 201. The chronicler explains this by saying that the king was a simple man. Senile or frightened out of his wits might better explain it, for Henry was never "simple."

*And the knight in black and gold who, taking off his helm, revealed the impish face of William Maltraverse. The three set to their work stripping the corpse.*
See Rishanger, *Chronicon de Bellis*, p. 46: *"Comes Leyc., capitaneus eorum, capite truncatus, pedibus et manbus amputates, cujus capud uxori Rogeri de Mortuo Mari, in castro Wigorniae praesentatur ..."*
Robert of Gloucester specifically accuses William Maltraverse of dismembering Simon's body.

It perhaps should be considered that Simon was venerated by much of the populous at this time and the dismemberment of saints was commonplace, providing churches with relics for which they paid dearly. Though Simon's body was mutilated by his enemies, it is not impossible that some of his attackers may have had an idea of profit, now that the politically dangerous earl was out of the way. However, the head, the chroniclers agree, was taken to Ludlow castle, to Roger Mortimer's wife, who reportedly was a witch, and she abused it.

Rishanger lists among the dead (pp. 46-47) Peter de Montfort, Hugh Despensar, Ralph Basset, William Maundeville and John Beauchamp, and among the wounded Guy de Montfort, Humphrey de Bohun Fils, John Vesey and Peter de Montfort Fils.

The worship of Simon de Montfort was quickly made illegal, so the disappearance of the severed parts is understandable, whether they were merely discarded by the men who hated the earl, or were sold off to his worshippers as relics and encased in silver and gold casks.

*A spring of fresh water bubbled up from the ground*
That a spring of healing waters came up when Simon's body was lifted from the ground is well documented, not only by William Rishanger and Robert of Gloucester, who were strongly biased

in Simon's favor, but by subsequent edicts that made it illegal to take water from the spring and caused the spring to be guarded by armed men.

Rishanger, *Chronicon de Bellis,* pp. 67-8, identifies the man who was entrusted with Simon's severed hands, and whose life was changed as he carried them. Like Saul, knocked from his horse by the voice of the crucified Jesus, this man was converted by seeing Simon's hands clasped in prayer before him in the air. He was Richard Bagard of Evesham; his witnesses were William Beacham and Peter of Salisbury.

Alice of New Burton was paralyzed on her left side for thirty years but was cured by water from Simon's spring (Rishanger, p.69.) Henry of Stodeley, blind from birth, received full vision after application of the spring's waters. That neither Simon's gallantry nor humor failed him after death, is suggested by this witness (Rishanger, pp. 68-9): The Countess of Pembroke (William de Valence's wife Joan) had an asthmatic palfrey that had been sick for two years. When it drank at Simon's spring, getting its whole face and head wet, it was cured of its wheezing. The countess gave alms to Evesham Abbey in thanks and confirmation of the miracle.

Rishanger's list of recipients and witnesses of Simon's miracles, commoners and men and women of power and consequence alike, extends to forty pages.

Salve, Symon Montis-fortis
Rishanger, *Chronica de Bellis,* p. 110.

# LIST OF CHARACTERS

Adam Newmarket, knight, strong supporter of the Provisions at Oxford in 1258, repeatedly elected to the king's Council.

Aigueblanche, Peter, Bishop of Hereford, advisor to King Henry

Aimery de Lusignan, half brother to King Henry, son of Isabel of Angouleme and Count Hugh of La Marche, bishop-elect of Winchester, enemy of Earl Simon

Alexander IV, Pope 1254 to 1261

Alice, principal waiting woman to Queen Eleanor (fictional)

Alice, daughter of Joan and William de Valence, wife of Gilbert de Clare

Alphonse, brother of King Louis, made Count of Poitou after Henry's defeat by Louis.

Amanieu d'Albret, Gascon lord in rebellion against England, leader of a conspiracy against Simon

Amaury de Montfort, Earl Simon's elder brother, Count of Montfort l'Amaury in Normandy, Marshal of France

Amaury de Montfort, fourth son of Earl Simon and Countess Eleanor, later a cleric

Ambrose, Dominican scholar, supporter of the millennial teachings of Joachim del Flor

Blanche, Queen of France, mother of King Louis

Beatrice of Savoy, mother of Queen Eleanor of England and Queen Margaret of France; countess of Provence, sister of Peter of Savoy, Boniface Archbishop of Canterbury, Thomas of Flanders and Garsende of Bearne

Boniface, Archbishop of Canterbury, uncle of Queen Eleanor, younger brother of Peter of Savoy

Clement IV, Pope from February 5, 1265 to1268. Formerly Guy Folques, jurist and confessor to King Louis, opponent of England's Parliament and reforms of royal power

Conrad, Frederic's legitimate son, heir to the Hoy Roman Empire after his older brother Henry's death. Child of Queen Yolanda of Jerusalem and claimant to the lordship of Outremere

Conradin, son of Conrad, legitimate heir of the Holy Roman Empire, including Outremere and Sicily

Edmund, "Crouchback," King Henry and Queen Eleanor's son, born hunch-backed

Edward, heir to England's throne as Edward I, Duke of Gascony, claiming Duke of Wales, son of Queen Eleanor

Eleanor, Queen of England, also called Eleanor of Provence, daughter of Beatrice of Savoy, sister of Queen Margaret of France

Eleanor, Countess Eleanor de Montfort, sister of King Henry III, wife of Earl Simon de Montfort, Countess of Leicester, formerly known as Eleanor of Pembroke from her childhood marriage to William Marshal, Earl of Pembroke

Eleanor, daughter of Earl Simon de Montfort and Countess Eleanor, also known as Eleanor la Demoiselle

Eleanor, Infanta of Castile, wife of Prince Edward, very much younger sister of King Alphonse the Wise

FitzNicholas, steward of the royal household

Frederic II, *Stupor Mundi:* the "Wonder of the World" for his science, and his disregard for Christianity and attacks upon the papal power. Holy Roman Emperor, King of the Germans, and of Sicily and Palestine, overlord of most of Italy. Deceased before the opening of Volume III. His heirs are Conrad, his son by Yolanda, Queen of Jerusalem, Manfred, a legitimized bastard, and Conrad's son Conradin. His marriage to King Henry's sister Isabel made him brother-in-law to both Henry and Simon.

Furnival, a knight, supporter of Montfort

Garbag, kitchen boy in the Montfort household.

Garsende de Bearne, Countess of Bearne, mother of Gaston, sister of Beatrice of Savoy the mother of Queen Eleanor.

Gaston de Bearne, Count of the province of Bearne in the Pyrenees, leader of the rebellion of the Gascon lords against England: cousin of Queen Eleanor, conniver against Simon. Claimant to Bigorre through his marriage to the Countess Pironelle's youngest daughter.

Gilbert de Clare, son of Richard de Clare, the principal leader in the creating of the Provisions of Oxford; member of Prince Edward's knights bachelry

Gilbert Marshal, Earl of Pembroke, son of William Marshal, first husband of Countess Eleanor. He has refused to return Eleanor's dowry.

Gobehasty, servant in the Montfort household

Gregory IX, Pope from 1227 to 1249

Grosseteste, Robert, Bishop of Lincoln, Provincial of the Franciscan Order in England and Provost of Oxford, creator of the concept of an elected parliament, Earl Simon's spiritual guide and confessor.

Guillaume de Rion, Gascon lord in rebellion against England. Simon as viceroy delivered a legal decision against him, making him a personal enemy

Guy de Lusignan, half-brother of King Henry, son of Henry's mother Isabelle of Angouleme and Count Hugh of La Marche, enemy of Earl Simon

Guy de Montfort, third son of Earl Simon de Montfort and Countess Eleanor

Henry III, King of England, Henry Plantagenet, also called Henry of Monmouth, son of King John, nephew of King Richard

Henry of Alemaine, also known as Henry of Wallingford, son of Prince Richard later King of the Germans, nephew of King Henry III, early and steadfast companion of Edward

Henry de Bracton, judge of the King's Bench, author of the seminal work, *De Legibus et Consuetudinibus Angliae* (On the Laws and Customs of England.) With Granville, one of the two founders of modern English law.

Henry Montfort, eldest son of the Earl Simon de Montfort and Countess Eleanor

Henry Wengham, secretary to King Henry

Hugh Bigod, younger brother of Roger Bigod, chosen Justiciar for the Provisions

Hugh le Brun, half brother of King Henry, eldest brother of Guy, William and Aimery de Lusignan, died on King Louis' crusade

Hugh Despenser, supporter of Simon, last Justiciar under the provisions, ancestor of Spencer family

Hugh Despenser, son of Hugh, follower of Edward

Hugh of Dive, Marshal of the King's Household

Humphrey de Bohun, Earl of Hereford and Essex

Humphrey de Bohun, son and heir of the earl, follower of Edward

Innocent IV, Pope from 1243 to 1254

Isabel, of Angouleme, Queen Mother of England, mother of King Henry, Prince Richard and Countess Eleanor by her first marriage to King John; mother of Hugh le Brun, Guy de Lusignan, William de Valence and Aimery de Lusignan by her second husband, Count Hugh of La Marche, head of the Lusignan family in Poitou in southwestern France.

Joachim del Flor, 12th century monk, proposed three ages of mankind's history: the tribal Age of the Father, the Age of the Son with the rise of nations and the Church, and the Age of the Holy Ghost, in which nations would dissolve into a single world order governed by elected representatives of the common man. He held that central authority, including the Church, would wither away as the Holy Spirit communed directly with each soul. Though Joachim's books were burned in the 13th century, his ideas formed the theoretical foundation for many of Simon's followers, for peasant revolts in the Renaissance, and contributed inspiration to Robert Grosseteste, Oliver Cromwell, Adolph Hitler and Karl Marx.

**Joan, Countess of Pembroke,** nee de Munchensey, wife of William de Valence

**Johanna of Flanders,** Princess of Flanders, hostage in Court of France as a child, betrothed to Simon but rejected by him, married to Thomas, Count of Savoy, Queen Eleanor's uncle.

**John Darlington,** royal clerk

**John, King of England,** father of King Henry III, Prince Richard and Countess Eleanor, brother of Richard the Lion Hearted, son of Henry II and Eleanor of Aquitaine, also known as John Plantagenet and John Lackland. Died when his son Henry was nine years old.

**John FitzGeoffrey,** Justiciar of Ireland, a framer of the Provisions of Oxford

**John Mansel,** principal secretary to King Henry

**John de la Warre,** lieutenant of Montfort

**John de Warrenne,** Earl of Sussex

**John de Warrenne,** son and heir of the earl, follower of Edward

**Joinville, Jean de,** Steward of France, one of the few survivors of Louis' crusade: later, author of a memoir of Louis' crusade and life

**Llewellyn, Llewellyn ap Gryffid,** Prince of Northern Wales, in rebellion against King Henry and English rule.

**Louis IX,** King of France, Saint Louis, Earl Simon was brought up as the child-king's companion

Manfred, illegitimate son of the Emperor Frederic II, claimant as Frederic's heir after the death of Conrad

Margaret, Queen of France, wife of King Louis, sister of Queen Eleanor of England

Mary, Countess Eleanor's elderly waiting woman (fictional)

Neville, Ralph, follower of Edward

Octavian, commander of Pope Alexander IV's mercenary armies.

Odo Rigaud, Archbishop and chief Minister of State for France

Othon de Grandison, protégé of Peter of Savoy attached to Edward's and the Infanta Eleanor's household

Peter, squire to Earl Simon, also known as Peter the Barber

Peter de Montfort, knight, cousin of Earl Simon, firm supporter of the Provisions of Oxford

Peter of Savoy, uncle of Queen Eleanor, favorite of King Henry, granted by Henry the title of Earl of Richmond, elder brother of Boniface the Archbishop of Canterbury

Philip Drieby, young knight, follower of Simon

Piis, brothers, burgesses and castellans of La Reole in Gascony

Ralph Basset, knight of Drayton, follower of Edward

Raymond de Fronzac, vicomte of Fronzac, Gascon lord in rebellion against England, conspirator against Simon

Raymond, Count of Toulouse, sometime ally and sometime rebel against his overlord King Henry, supporter of the Albigensians and enemy of Simon's father.

Richard de Clare, Earl of Gloucester, principal framer of the Provisions of Oxford, father of Gilbert de Clare

Richard Croxley, abbot of Westminster

Richard de Grey, former Governor of Gascony, supporter of Simon

Richard de Montfichet, knight, by 1258 he was the last survivor of the barons who won Magna Carta, supporter of the Provisions of Oxford

Richard de Montfort, fifth and youngest son of Earl Simon and Countess Eleanor

Robert Ferrers, heir to earldom of Derby

Roger Bigod, Earl of Norfolk, Marshal of England, brother of Hugh Bigod

Roscylin de Foss, Master of the Templars in London

Sanchia, sister of Queen Eleanor of England and Queen Margaret of France, second wife of Prince Richard (not Henry of Alemaine's mother.)

Seagrave, Nicholas, steward-general for Earl Simon and Countess Eleanor

Simon de Montfort, Earl of Leicester, former Viceroy of Gascony, husband of Countess Eleanor, brother-in-law to King Henry and Prince Richard.

Simon de Montfort Fils, second son of the earl, also known as Simon fils

Simon de Montfort, father of Earl Simon, Count of Montfort l'Amaury in Normandy, hero of the Third Crusade, leader of the Albigensian Crusade, died in battle at Toulouse when Earl Simon was a child.

Slingaway, kitchen boy in the Montfort household

Thibaut de Champagne, Count of Champagne and King of Navarre, in the Pyrenees bordering Gascony. An instigator of the Gascons' revolt against England.

Thomas DeMesnil, Simon's steward for Kenilworth

Thomas FitzThomas, Mayor of London

Thomas of Savoy, Count of Savoy, eldest brother of Beatrice of Savoy and uncle to Queen Eleanor. Married to Johanna, Princess of Flanders, Simon's childhood friend and disappointed betrothed.

Urban IV, Pope from 1261 to 1264

Walter Cantaloup, Bishop of Worcester, follower of Bishop Grosseteste, firm supporter of the revolutionary Provisions of Oxford.

William Ferrers, Earl of Derby, supporter of the Montfort cause

William Maltraverse, knight, companion of Edward, his father a knight of Kent

William Maundeville, follower of Edward

# LIST OF CHARACTERS

William de Valence, half brother of King Henry, brother of Guy and Aimery de Lusignan, son of Isabel of Angouleme and Count Hugh of La Marche

# BIBLIOGRAPHY

**Primary Sources:**

Montfort Archive, *Bibliotheque Nationale*, Paris. There is preserved, in this boxed archive of original documents, the trial notes and a brief autobiography by Simon written in 1260 in preparation for his trial before King Louis for treason against King Henry. (In the event, the trial was actually heard by Queen Margaret of France.)

Publications:

*Annales Monastici*, ed. Luard, H.R., 1864-69:
    Vol. I, Annals of Burton
    Vol. II, Annals of Winchester and Waverly
    Vol. III, Annals of Dunstable
    Vol. IV, Annals of Osney; Chronicle of Thomas Wykes; Annals of Worcester

*Calendar of Charter Rolls,*Vol. I, 1226-1307, Public Record Office. Kraus Reprint, Neldeln/Liechtenstein, 1972. (Note: Kraus reprints are not complete.)

*Calendar of the Liberate Rolls*, Volumes I and II, Public Record Office, 1916.

*Calendar of Patent Rolls, 1232-1272*, Henry III. Public Record Office. Kraus Reprint, Nendeln/Liechtenstein, 1971. (Note: Kraus reprints are not complete.)

*Chronica Johannis Oxenedes,* John of Oxford, ed. H. Ellis, Rolls Series, 1859.

---

# BIBLIOGRAPHY

*De Antiquis Legibus Liber: Cronica Maiorum et Vicecomitum Londoinarium,* Stapleton, T. Camden Series, 1846.

*Documents of the Baronial Movement of reform and Rebellion, 1258 – 1267,* ed. R. F. Treharne and I. J. Sanders, Oxford, 1973.

Eccleston, Thomas of, *The Coming of the Friars Minor to England, XIIIth Century Chronicles,* translated by Placid Herman, O.F.M., Franciscan Herald Press, Chicago, 1961.

*Excerpta e Rotulis Finium in Turri Londdinensi Asservatis Henry III, 1216-72,* ed. by C. Roberts, Public Record Office. 1835-36.

*Exchequer: The History and Antiquities of the Exchequer,* Madox, Greenwood, 1769-1969, Volumes I and II.

Gervais of Canterbury, *Historical Works of Gervais of Canterbury,* ed. W. Stubbs, Vols. I and II, Rolls Series, 1880.

Goldin, Frederick, *The Lyrics of the Troubadours and Trouveres,* Original texts with Translations and Introductions, Anchor Books, New York, 1973.

*Grosseteste, Roberti, Episcopi quondam Lincolniensis Epistolae,* ed. by H.R. Luard. Rolls Series, 1861.

*Dicta Lincolniensis,* ed. and trans.: Gordon Jackson, Grosseteste Press, Lincoln, 1972.

*R. Grosseteste Carmina Anglo-Normannica: Robert Grosseteste's Casteau d'Amour and La Vie de Sainte Marie Egyptienne,* Burt Franklin Research and Resource Works, Series No. 154, New York, 1967.

Guisborough, *The Chronicle of Walter of Guisborough,* ed. H. Rothwell, Camden Society, third series, LXXXIX, 1957.

---

John of Oxford: *Chronica Johannis de Oxenedes*, ed., H. Ellis, Rolls Series, 1859.

Joinville, Jean de: *Chronicles of the Crusades by Jean de Joinville and Geoffrey de Villhardouin*, translated by Sir Frank Marzials, Digireads.com Publishing, 2010.

Laffan, R.G.D. *Select Documents of European History, 800-1492*, Volume I, Henry Holt and Company, New York.

**A note on the Chronica Majora**: I have used several editions of the chronicle of Matthew Paris as they happened to be available to me. For readers' reference I principally use the Bohn 1854 edition as it is most likely to be available in universities or other good libraries. The 1684 edition, in Latin, I possess and use for checking the translations but, as I cannot expect my readers to have that edition available to them, I have not cited it in the Historical Context. While the Paris chronicle proceeds to the year 1273, after 1259 it is by another hand.

*Matthew Paris's English History, from the year* 1235 to 1273, volumes I to V, translated by the Rev. J. A. Giles, Henry Bohn, London, 1852. See also the Bohn 1854 edition in three volumes. Kessinger Publishing's Rare Reprints. (incomplete) www.kessinger.net.

*Rerum Britannicarum Medi: Aevi Scriptores*, or *Chronicles and Memorials of Great Britain and Ireland During the Middle Ages*, Kraus reprint 1964. (Note: Kraus reprints are not complete.)

*Matthaei Paris, Monachi Albanensis, Historia Major, Juxta Exemplar Londinense* 1640, *verbatim recusa*, ed. Willielmo Wats, STD. Imprensis A. Mearne, T. Dring, B. Tooke, T. Sawbridge & G. Wells, MDCLXXXIV (1684)

*Matthaei Parisiense, Chronica Majora*, Kraus reprint, 1964. (Note: Kraus reprints are not complete.)

# BIBLIOGRAPHY

*The Political Songs of England from the reign of John to that of Edward II*, ed. and trans. T. Wright, Camden series, 1839.

Rishanger, William, *The Chronicle of William de Rishanger, of the Barons' War: The Miracles of Simon de Montfort*. ed. J.O. Halliwell, Camden Society, 1840. Also known as the *Chronicon de Bellis*

Robert of Gloucester, *Metrical Chronicles of Robert of Gloucester*, Wright, W.A., Rolls Series, 1887.

*Royal Letters, Henry III*, ed. W.W. Shirley, Rolls Series, 1862.

## Secondary Sources:

Baker, Timothy. *Medieval London*, Praeger Publishers, New York, 1970.

Bemont, Charles, *Simon de Montfort, Earl of Leicester*, translated by E. F. Jacob, Oxford, Clarendon Press, 1930

*Simon de Montfort, Comte de Leicester, Sa Vie (120?-1265)*, Slatkine-Megariotis Reprints, Geneve, 1976. *Reimpression de l'edition de Paris 1884.*

*Roles Gascon, 1242-1254*, 3 volumes, pub. Francisque Michel, 1885; and Supplement 1254-1255, 1896.

Boutaric, Edgar. *Saint Louis et Alphonse de Poitiers*, 1870.

Chancellor, John, *The Life and Times of Edward I*, Weidenfeld and Nicholson, London, 1981.

Chrimes, S.B. *An Introduction to the Administrative History of Medieval England*, Basil Blackwell, Oxford, 1959.

# BIBLIOGRAPHY

Cosman, Madeleine Pelner. *Fabulous Feasts: Medieval Cookery and Ceremony*, George Braziller, New York, 1976.

Furnival. *The Babees' Book: Medieval Manners for the Young*, ed. Edith Rickert, Cooper Square Publishers, Inc., New York, 1966.

Green, John Richard. *Green's History of the English People*, Lovell, Coryell & Company, New York, Volume II, 1878-80.

Green, Mary Anne Everett, *Lives of the Princesses of England*, London, 1849.

Holt, J.C., *Robin Hood*, Thames and Hudson, 1982.

Homans, George Caspar. *English Villagers of the Thirteenth Century*, Russell & Russell, New York, 1960.

Howell, Margaret. *Eleanor of Provence, Queenship in Thirteenth Century England*, Blackwell Publishers Inc., Malden, Mass., 2001.

Johnson, Mrs. T. Fielding. *Glimpses of Ancient Leicester in Six Periods*, Simpkin, Marshall. Hamilton, Kent & Co., London, and John and Thomas Spencer, Leicester, 1891.

King, Edmund. *England, 1175-1425*, Charles Scribner's Sons, New York, 1979.

Knappen, M. M., *Constitutional and Legal History of England*, Harcourt, Brace and Company, 1942.

Labarge, Margaret Wade. *Simon de Montfort*, Eyre & Spottiswoode, London, 1962.

*A Baronial Household of the Thirteenth Century*, Eyre & Spottiswoode, London, 1965.

# BIBLIOGRAPHY

*Saint Louis, Louis IX, Most Christian King of France*, Little, Brown and Company, Boston, 1968.

*Gascony, England's First Colony, 1204-1453*, Hamish Hamilton, Ltd., London, 1980.

Maddicott, J.R. *Simon de Montfort*, Cambridge University Press, 1994.

Murray, Margaret, *The God of the Witches*, Sampson Low, Marston & Co., London *The Witch Cult in Western Europe, A Study on Anthropology*, Oxford, The Clarendon Press, 1921 *The Divine King in England*, reprint, Faber and Faber, 1954

Nagler, A.M. *The Medieval Religious Stage*, Yale University Press, New Haven, 1976.

Nicol, Allardyce, *Masks, Mimes and Miracles: Studies in the Popular Theatre*, George A. Harrap & Company, Ltd., London, 1931.

Prestwich, Michael, *Edward I*, Yale University Press, 1988.

Power, Eileen. *The Wool Trade in English Medieval History*, Oxford University Press, London, 1965.

Powicke, Maurice. *Medieval England: 1066-1485*, Oxford University Press, London, 1931.

Pye, N., ed. *Leicester and its Region*, Leicester University Press, Leicester, 1972.

Renn, Derek. *Norman Castles in Britain*, John Baker: Humanities Press, New York, 1968.

Runciman, Steven. *A History of the Crusades, The Kingdom of Acre*, Volume III, The University Press, Cambridge, 1955.

Salisbury-Jones, G.T., *Street Life in Medieval England*, The Harvester Press: Rowan and Littlefield, Sussex, England, 1975.

Slaughter, Gertrude. *The Amazing Frederic: Stupor Mundi et Immutator Mirabilis*, The Macmillan Company, New York, 1937.

Turner, Ralph V. *The King and His Courts, The Role of King John and Henry III in the Administration of Justice, 1199- 1240*, Cornell University Press, Ithaca, N.Y., 1968.

Waddell, Helen. *The Wandering Scholars*, Henry Holt and Company, New York, 1927.

Made in the USA
Charleston, SC
14 April 2012